Love Is PATIENT

ROMANCE COLLECTION

Love Is PATIENT ROMANCE COLLECTION

True Love Takes Time in Nine Historical Novellas

Erica Vetsch, Vickie McDonough
Janet Lee Barton, Frances Devine, Lena Nelson Dooley,
Darlene Franklin, Jill Stengl, Connie Stevens

BARBOUR BOOKS
An Imprint of Barbour Publishing, Inc.

Print ISBN 978-1-63409-661-4

eBook Editions:
Adobe Digital Edition (.epub) 978-1-63409-736-9
Kindle and MobiPocket Edition (.prc) 978-1-63409-737-6

All scripture quotations are taken from the King James Version of the Bible.

Published by Barbour Books, an imprint of Barbour Publishing, Inc., P.O. Box 719, Uhrichsville, OH 44683, www.barbourbooks.com

Our mission is to publish and distribute inspirational products offering exceptional value and biblical encouragement to the masses.

Printed in Canada.

Contents

The Spinster's Beau

by Jill Stengl

O Lord, thou art my God; I will exalt thee,
I will praise thy name; for thou hast done wonderful things;
thy counsels of old are faithfulness and truth.

For thou hast been a strength to the poor,
a strength to the needy in his distress, a refuge from the storm.

Isaiah 25:1, 4

Chapter 1

Mackinac Island, July 1823

Thump-thump-thump! The insistent noise roused Jane from her sleep. Blinking in darkness, she sat up. Someone pounded at the front door. Her brother stirred in the next room, grumbling to himself as his feet hit the floorboards.

As her mind cleared, she remembered—Mrs. Pennyfeather must be in labor! Jane flung on a wrap and poked her head into the hall just in time to hear Jordan say, "At this hour, Sergeant? The good doctor must be losing his sanity. Miss Douglas certainly will not—"

"Jordan, I told you about this days ago," Jane interrupted from her doorway. "I promised Mrs. Pennyfeather and Dr. Beaumont that I would assist with her delivery."

Candlelight flickered on Jordan's frowning features as he turned, but before he could speak, Jane called, "I'll be out in a moment!"

A voice answered faintly. "Doc says to bring bandages."

Jane agreed and closed her door. In the square of moonlight on her bedroom floor, she changed into an old work gown. *Bandages?* She wound her hair into a tight knot and secured it with five perfectly placed pins. *Why bandages?* An old sheet from the linen press could be torn into strips when needed. She added it to her basket of supplies.

Jordan waited in the entry, lips tight and eyes cool. Even in his nightshirt and bed shoes, Lieutenant Jordan Douglas was an imposing figure.

"Jane, I strongly disapprove. Midwifery is a job for old women, not young ladies, and you have no need of employment—"

"Dr. Beaumont says I'm an excellent midwife. Granny trained me well, and I want to use my skills to help people."

"Dr. Beaumont." He snorted.

She hitched her chin higher. "You shouldn't snort. It's undignified."

He growled something incoherent. "At least make an attempt to observe proprieties, Jane."

"Always I observe proprieties, little brother. In this line of work, I seldom even speak with men. Please don't worry. I imagine I'll return home tomorrow."

The moon cast black shadows across Fort Mackinac's parade grounds, but its light glowed on the mane and rump of the doctor's sturdy gelding. Jane climbed up to the carriage seat without help. Sergeant Fallon, Dr. Beaumont's orderly, snapped the horse into a trot, and the little trap's wheels crunched on gravel. After a wave from a guard, they rolled on through the fort's north sally port and down the winding road to the village.

A breeze carried the pleasant humidity of summer across the Straits of Mackinac, picking up a hint of pine and cedar in its passage and sweeping away less-inspiring smells. A magical moonlit pathway sparkled across the lake's rippling surface. *Thank You for this little glimpse of heaven's beauty, God. Had I stayed in bed, I would have missed it.*

"Is Mrs. Pennyfeather's labor far along?" She broke the silence.

"Uh, I w–wouldn't know."

She turned on the seat, trying to study the young man's features. Even by moonlight, he looked guilty. "Sergeant, what are you hiding?"

"Doc told me to get you there one way or another. It isn't Mrs. Pennyfeather. There's been a f–fight in town, and Doc n–needs your help."

"My help? Sergeant Fallon, I am a midwife!"

"He knows that, but he says he needs you. One of the men got cut up bad—" Fallon gulped. "And the other's got a broken jaw and a smashed nose. I c–c–can't manage them. Doc says a w–woman might do the trick, and he knows you can endure"—he took a deep breath—"blood."

Jane jerked on the seat to face forward and stare blankly ahead. Should she order the sergeant to take her back home? Part of her mind insisted "yes," but an unexpectedly adventurous *thump* of her heart cried "no!" Dr. Beaumont thought she might be useful!

Dr. Beaumont lived in the officers' stone quarters across the parade grounds from Jordan's wooden quarters. Jane had made his acquaintance soon after her arrival at the fort. Although she thought the fort's military surgeon somewhat eccentric, she greatly admired his medical skills. The knowledge that he valued her skills in return added starch to her spine.

"Very well, I shall endeavor to help. Who are the injured men, and where are we going?"

Fallon's slim shoulders straightened. "They took 'em to the Northern Hotel." He sounded more cheerful. "It's McNaughton and D–D–Durant."

He sounded as if she should know the men by name, but Jane knew few people on the island besides pregnant women and new mothers. Since Granny's sudden death last autumn brought her to live with her army officer brother, she had lived a quiet life. Not that her life with Granny had been social either. Young men had never sought Jane's company and probably never would.

"Doc can save 'em if anyone can," Fallon said with solid confidence. "He saved St. Martin's life, and that was impossible."

Nearly a year earlier, a young man on the island by the name of Alexis St. Martin had taken a shotgun blast in his stomach from close range. Jane had not yet met St.

Martin, but she had heard many renditions of his story. In all of them, Dr. Beaumont ranked as a heroic healer.

"I've heard that his stomach wound has not yet entirely closed."

"No, but he's alive. That's a miracle in itself."

"Dr. Beaumont is an excellent physician, yet life is in the Lord's hands."

"If you say so, ma'am."

Fallon reined in the horse in front of the Northern Hotel. Unearthly shrieks and shouts seemed to descend from the dark sky above.

Fallon gazed upward, wide-eyed. "You'd b–b–best hurry."

Picking up her basket, Jane climbed from the carriage.

The hotel's owner met them in the entry. "Please try to quiet him," he whimpered. "My guests are threatening to leave!"

"I'll see what I can do." Jane hung her bonnet and cloak on a hook and peeled off her gloves. A pleasant sense of importance swept over her. "Do we have hot water?" She always requested hot water for deliveries, but it should prove useful in any case.

"I took a kettle up minutes ago."

"Good. Please boil more."

The man bowed respectfully.

They climbed steep, dark stairs; then Fallon knocked on a chamber door.

"Enter." Dr. Beaumont's invitation pierced the uproar from within.

Fallon opened the door for Jane but remained out in the hall. "Good luck," he said.

She straightened her shoulders and stepped inside. Despite an open gable window, the small chamber was stifling. Several men clustered around a table upon which something thrashed. Shouting numbed her ears. A lamp hung crookedly from a hook on the slanted ceiling; two others hung on the walls. A pile of bloody garments lay on the floor. Jane's nostrils cringed at the stench of whiskey, tobacco, and unwashed bodies, along with the reek of blood.

Dr. Beaumont looked up from his bag of surgical instruments, his face flushed and sweaty. "Ah, you're here. I need to begin immediately. Multiple lacerations and profuse bleeding, though no apparent harm to major blood vessels. Muscle sutures are needed, however. If the patient lives that long."

Jane pretended complete comprehension, nodded, and rolled up her sleeves.

Another barrage of swearing and execrations rebounded off the crowded chamber's walls. Steeling herself, Jane slowly turned. Four sweating men strained to pin down a man spread-eagled on the table, his torso draped in blood-soaked rags, his lower half clad in equally bloody deerskin breeches.

Jane blinked and swallowed hard. *Durant*—she remembered now. *Mad Durant, he was called. Who could forget such a man?*

Dr. Beaumont removed a blood-soaked rag from the patient's abdomen. Jane focused on the patient's injuries. Cuts and gashes marred his chest, arms, and shoulders. A fifteen-inch gash laid open his upper belly from one side of his rib cage to the other, a shallow wound, but ugly. White sinew and bone gleamed in the exposed flesh. A few inches lower and deeper and Mr. Durant would be dead. . .and perhaps the world would have been better off.

She removed towels and an old quilt from her basket, filled a basin with hot water and placed it near the doctor's bag, then donned a serviceable apron. Her strong fingers ripped the sheet into long strips and rolled them neatly. Exactly what else the doctor expected her to do remained to be seen.

Dr. Beaumont brandished a needle threaded with gut and prepared to stitch. One of the assistants held a bottle to the patient's lips. Durant took several swallows before spewing the liquor from his mouth. The bottle fell on his chest, and whiskey gushed out, soaking him and one of the helpers. Durant shrieked and swore again as the liquid burned in his wounds.

Jane's knees quaked. The heat and the horrid smells made her head swim. If she fainted now, the doctor would never respect her again. She gave her head a shake and tightened every muscle in her body.

Nothing seemed to rattle Dr. Beaumont. Jane watched his lips in order to understand his orders through the cacophony of profanity. "See if you can calm the patient, Miss Douglas. Whatever it takes. He'll die for certain if he doesn't stop fighting me."

Chapter 2

Jane circled the table, sliding along the wall behind two of the trappers to stand near the patient's head. "Mr. Durant, please try to calm yourself."

He met her gaze and spewed more blasphemy. Pity for his obvious torment blended with Jane's fear and disgust. Such wounds would test the fortitude of the strongest man. Durant might be a wicked sinner, but he was God's creation, formed in God's image, and as such, he deserved her kindness and sympathy.

Dr. Beaumont began to stitch a partially severed muscle in the patient's abdomen.

The man holding Durant's left arm let go, staggered back, and crumpled. The other three trappers watched in surprise as their burly companion melted to the floor, his face gray. One of them looked at Jane and chuckled, though his eyes were frightened. "Fainted dead away, he did."

Jane grabbed Durant's arm before he could interfere with Dr. Beaumont and further injure himself. As soon as she caught hold of his massive forearm, she realized that, weakened though he was, she would never be able to restrain him should he thrust her aside. His skin was cold and damp to her touch, and he shivered. Blood trickled down his biceps from a shallow slash and dripped off the side of his shoulder from another cut below his collarbone.

His hand grasped at the air until she caught it with hers and held it firmly. Dirt encrusted his short fingernails and outlined every knuckle. He turned his face toward her, and she looked into his bleary, tortured eyes. Tears had traced pale streaks down his temples and cheeks. Despite the reek of whiskey on his breath, he appeared to be rational. Perhaps if she got him talking. . . "What happened?" she asked.

"He pulled a knife on me," he gasped. "I didn't have one. I would have beat him but. . .for one lucky swipe."

"You're lucky you ain't fat," one of the leg holders commented. "He'd have spilled your guts."

Durant addressed more profanity at the trapper, addressing him as "Gerard." Jane met Mr. Gerard's gaze and received a nearly toothless grin.

Dr. Beaumont tugged at a stitch to secure it. Durant howled and jerked Jane's hand down to press against his mouth. For the first time, he was quiet, his eyes squeezed shut, his jaw muscles bunching.

"Give him something to bite on," Gerard said. The yellow-haired man holding Durant's other arm offered a plug of tobacco. Meeting Jane's blank stare, he flushed and put it away. He then offered a dirty leather glove, but Durant refused it with a curse, pressing Jane's hand close to his lips. Disturbed, she tried to ease her hand away, but he held it firmly in place. Reasoning that he was now quiet, she made an effort to endure.

Dr. Beaumont worked quickly, pausing only to rethread his needle. Jane watched his nimble fingers and studied the neat row of stitches across Durant's hairy belly. Then her face heated at the realization that she was actually viewing a man's bare torso! If Jordan ever discovered the details of this adventure, he would never allow her to leave his house again.

Why must her brother be so controlling? She was a grown woman, responsible for her own behavior whether wise or foolish. One of her few clear memories of her father, who had died when she was eight, was his blunt observation that "Jane was born for work, since God did not see fit to bless her with beauty." Granny had tacitly agreed with him, preparing Jane to support herself as a midwife.

Now that Jordan planned to marry, Jane's need for independence loomed large. Lucretia had her virtues, but Jane dreaded the prospect of sharing a house with her. The dainty beauty had a way of making Jane feel more plain, awkward, and undesirable than ever.

Feeling another tremor shake the table, she asked Mr. Gerard to pass her quilt, the old quilt usually reserved for wrapping up newborn infants. Gerard gave her a questioning look but obeyed. She wrapped its soft folds over Durant's shoulders, careful to keep it away from Dr. Beaumont's work.

"You'll get it all bloody," one of the trappers protested.

"It will wash." With her free hand, she tucked a fold around Durant's head, ignoring possible lice. His ragged breathing filled a silence.

Giving a shuddering gasp, the trapper holding Durant's left leg suddenly let go and rushed from the room, bracing himself on the door frame with a white-knuckled hand as he went. "Two down, two to go," Dr. Beaumont muttered. "Miss Douglas, uncover the next wound for stitching. Is he unconscious?"

"I'm not sure." She touched Durant's temple and pushed shaggy blondish-brown hair away from his face. His eyes opened. "No, he is awake."

"Keep doing whatever you're doing."

Durant's usually squinty eyes were wide and staring, their pupils tiny. His grip on Jane's hand tightened and loosened repeatedly. "Mr. Durant, look at me." Fear tightened her heart. "Mr. Durant!" She squeezed his hand and stroked his face. Was he dying?

Dr. Beaumont doggedly stitched up another wound and snipped off the gut thread. His clinical detachment suddenly irritated Jane. "Doctor, he is still cold and shivering. What shall I do?"

"Whatever you can think of. You're keeping him still, which is most important at this point. All I can do is repair the damage. If his brute strength can't keep him alive, nothing can. You might pray, since you're a religious woman." Needle in hand, he glanced up at her. "You need to move over, however."

Jane shifted position to stand directly above Durant's head. He would not release her hand, so her arm bent at an awkward angle, wrapped beneath his chin. When the doctor started stitching the gash below his collarbone, Durant winced and looked around.

"I am here," she said. His frightened eyes focused on her, and some of the tension left his body.

Softly she began to sing the first song that came to mind, one she sometimes used to calm a screaming infant. "Oh, where have you been, Billy boy, Billy boy? Oh, where have you been, charming Billy?" After the last verse, she looked up to see the other two trappers staring at her as if spellbound. Heat rushed into her face.

"Sing 'Over the Hills and Far Away,' if you please," Gerard requested, gripping both of the patient's moccasin-clad feet.

Durant's eyelids fluttered. "More," he requested in a hoarse whisper.

She licked her lips and began to sing, her voice sounding thin and weak. When she reached the chorus—

I would love you all the day.
Ev'ry night would kiss and play,
If with me you'd fondly stray
Over the hills and far away.
Over the hills and far away.

—the inappropriateness of the lyrics struck her. Yet she kept singing and smoothing Durant's tangled hair and beard. Had anyone else ever treated him tenderly? Was his mother perhaps still living and praying for her prodigal son? Or had he grown up wild because he received no loving-kindness as a child?

Durant had to release her hand while Dr. Beaumont closed the cut in his upper arm. The doctor then moved to the patient's right side to repair a deeper slash across his chest. Jane shifted her quilt to cover Durant's left side and leave the open wounds free. But his big hand lifted in search of hers, disturbing the cover. She laid her left hand in his, and he pressed it to his cheek.

His grasp was weaker now. Silently she prayed, her lips moving as she gazed at his pale, dirty face. His prominent nose was crooked, as if it had been broken more than once. His cheeks were tanned like leather and creased, yet his skin was soft to touch. *Lord, this man's life is in Thy hands. If it be Thy will, let him recover. If not, please touch his soul with Thy love and carry him to paradise this day. Let him repent like the thief on the cross.*

Jane wiped her tears on her sleeve. She mourned deeply every time a delivery ended in a stillbirth or a mother's death, but this patient was different.

He needed to know the Lord. How could she tell him?

"Love divine, all loves excelling, Joy of heav'n,
to earth come down—"

His limp fingers relaxed, barely holding her hand. Jane's voice broke into a sob.

"More," the trapper Gerard begged. "Please, ma'am."

She took a deep breath and tried again.

"Fix in us Thy humble dwelling,
all Thy faithful mercies crown!
Jesus, Thou art all compassion,
pure unbounded love Thou art;
Visit us with Thy salvation;
enter ev'ry trembling heart."

Her palms framed Durant's face, her thumbs caressing his temples. His great chest rose and fell rapidly, shuddering with each breath.

He stopped breathing.

Jane lifted her head in dismay. But then he exhaled quickly, drew in another deep breath, and held it. The doctor had just inserted his needle in the final wound, a shallow cut over the patient's hip bone.

Jane bent over and spoke into his ear. "Mr. Durant, I know the pain is terrible, but Dr. Beaumont is almost finished. Please try to live. God has wonderful plans for your life. He loves you. Your life has a purpose."

His quiet whimper started her tears flowing again. "Don't give up, Mr. Durant."

"Gus," the blond trapper said. "August is his given name."

She murmured into his ear. "August. Please, August. Try to live."

At last, Dr. Beaumont stepped back and brushed off his hands. "Finished. You may bandage him later, if necessary. Now, Miss Douglas, if you'll step this way, our other patient waits across the hall. I packed his broken nose with rags in order to stop the bleeding before you arrived, but now we must set his jaw, which is badly broken. I believe he will be eating nothing but liquids for many weeks to come, if he isn't hanged for murder before he fully recovers."

The trapper who had fainted dragged himself up from the floor and joined his companions. All three looked drawn and pale. "Do you need our help with McNaughton, Doc?" the yellow-haired trapper asked.

"I'll probably need you to hold him still while I set the bones, Mr. Armbruster. Bring that whiskey along, if there's any left." The doctor picked up his instruments and replaced them in his bag, then gave Jane an inquisitive glance. "Miss Douglas?"

"Shouldn't someone stay with Mr. Durant?"

The doctor lifted a brow as if surprised that she would question his judgment. "I'll return to check his condition after we care for McNaughton. I'd be grateful if you would remain and clean up afterward. Sergeant Fallon will send for the undertaker if necessary. Come along and sing to McNaughton for me." A smile softened his face for an instant. "As I had anticipated, your presence provides exactly the distraction we require."

"But we cannot leave Mr. Durant alone. . ." *To die.*

Dr. Beaumont frowned at his patient, then looked up at Jane. "Do as you like. The men will assist me with McNaughton. I'll find someone to take you home later." He picked up his bag and left the room. "Gerard, Nutt, Armbruster, bring some of those lanterns and come with me."

Mr. Armbruster plucked Jane's sleeve. She met his gaze and blinked in surprise at the rapt admiration in the young man's blue eyes. "If ever I'm dying, I pray you'll be with me, too, Miss Douglas."

Chapter 3

Dr. Beaumont left soon after he finished setting McNaughton's jaw. Jane caught Gerard and Armbruster in the hallway and begged them to help her bandage Durant. They then moved him from the blood-soaked table to a feather tick that lay on the floor of the cluttered chamber, which was apparently the hotel's storage area. The men tried to be gentle, but the movement wrenched agonized moans from Durant.

Jane tucked the quilt over her patient. His feet stuck out at the bottom. The man was six feet tall, maybe more. "You can rest now," she murmured, smoothing stringy hair away from his forehead.

How could Dr. Beaumont leave her alone with a dying patient? Well, not exactly alone, since Fallon was staying, but she had no great opinion of the stuttering sergeant's medical skills. "I'm a midwife, not a physician," she muttered.

"You done a mighty good job for a midwife, ma'am," said a hoarse voice.

"Thank you, Mr. Armbruster." Jane rose and turned around to see the two trappers hovering near the door. One lantern still hung from the ceiling, its dim glow casting more gloom than illumination over their sober faces.

"If Durant don't live, 'twill be none of your fault, ma'am," Mr. Gerard said, scratching his grizzled chin. "No man could ask for better care than you gived 'im."

"I'd stay and help more, ma'am, but you got Fallon here, and I ain't good at nursing," Armbruster said.

"Sergeant Fallon and I will care for both your friends for the rest of the night." Relaxing her habitual reserve, she smiled. "Thank you for all you did tonight."

The trappers exchanged glances, and Mr. Gerard grinned at her. "Reckon the pleasure was ours. Doc called you 'Miss,' so's I reckon you ain't married."

Jane felt her spine tighten. "I am not."

"Cain't for the life of me guess why, but I'm powerful glad of it. Reckon I'll be calling on ya soon, Miss Douglas." Gerard gave her a gap-toothed grin and a wink, donned his fur cap, and headed out the door.

Lamplight glowed on Armbruster's pale, lank hair and fuzzy chin. He turned his red stocking cap between his huge hands. "Gerard's too old for you, Miss Douglas. I got a place down on shore and good prospects for the future. If you'd have me, I'd settle here on the island. If you'll think on it, ma'am, I'd be mightily grateful." His voice cracked on every other word. "My mother named me William Henry Armbruster, and you can sing 'Billy Boy' to me anytime you like, ma'am."

"Thank you, Mr. Armbruster. I am honored." Jane hoped she sounded gracious. Armbruster beamed and bowed, then ducked through the doorway.

After the door closed behind him, she blinked. " 'Billy Boy,' indeed!"

Mr. Gerard was near fifty if he was a day and Jane towered over him. Armbruster was probably five years her junior and looked younger still. These trappers were the type of men she most despised—dirty, uncouth, illiterate, irreligious—the type who ogled anything wearing skirts. She must look truly desperate indeed if such men thought she would welcome their attentions.

Durant moaned. Instantly she knelt at his side, felt his throat for a pulse, and laid her cheek on his forehead, as she would do with a baby. He felt slightly warm. She rose and unhooked the lantern, bringing it close to his bedside. With a damp rag, she gently washed grime, sweat, and blood from his face. Pain creased his forehead. She tried trickling clean water into his mouth, but it dripped from his cracked lips.

Lips that spewed blasphemy and made lewd remarks to virtuous women. . .

The door squeaked on its hinges. Still kneeling, Jane turned. "Sergeant Fallon. How is the other patient?"

"Surly but quiet. He can't insult me with his jaw bound up, and the bandages cover most of his ugly face." A smile tipped Sergeant Fallon's trim little mustache upward at the corners. "How's Mad Durant? The doc doesn't think he'll l–l–live through the night."

"I know. He's in terrible pain."

Fallon talked on, casually referring to Durant in terms that raised Jane's brows. She had been exposed to more profanity and vulgarity this one night than in the sum total of her prior existence.

"Sergeant Fallon, if you don't mind—"

"Sorry I left you with the w–w–worst job," he interrupted. "Doc didn't think Mad Durant would throw a l–l–lady around, and it l–looks like he was right—unless maybe Durant was too weak to throw you by the time you arrived. You're bigger than I am anyway."

Jane frowned. "If you have nothing better to do, Sergeant, would you please assist me by hauling hot water from the kitchen? I need to clean this room, and I imagine Mr. McNaughton's is equally soiled."

The pink-cheeked sergeant grumbled but obeyed her request. Jane took soap from her basket and set to work scrubbing rags, dirty towels, and Durant's bloodstained shirt. Diligently though she scrubbed, the stains would only fade to a pale yellow. She fingered the gaping rent across the shirtfront. The garment required extensive repair. Upon examining his fringed buckskin jacket, she determined it unfit for salvaging.

She loaded Fallon's arms with dripping laundry and instructed him to hang it up on the lines behind the hotel.

"What lines?"

"There must be laundry lines. Go find them."

Again he grumbled but obeyed. Jane savored the power of command. Always before, she had been the laborer and her grandmother or her brother had given the orders.

Fallon returned, brushing off his damp sleeves. "Looks b–b–better in here. S–smells better, too. I'll clean up Durant while you straighten the other room. Unless you w–want to do the job. Big cuss, ain't he? Even taller'n you."

Jane drew herself up. "Sergeant Fallon, must I remind you that I am a lady and the sister of an officer? Your unguarded language is an insult."

His face turned red. "I b–b–beg pardon, ma'am. F–forgot myself."

Jane crossed the hall to McNaughton's tiny closet of a room. The stench nearly choked her. From the rope bed, beady eyes regarded her from either side of a bulky bandage that covered most of the man's face.

"I've come to clean your room, Mr. McNaughton."

The man reminded her of a bear, thick-limbed and covered with coarse black hair. Despite his evident pain and weakness, something about the way he watched her work set off warning chimes in her head. But then, if Durant were conscious, he would stare in just such a rude way.

When Jane returned to Durant's chamber, dawn lightened the window and dimmed the lantern. A snoring Fallon sprawled on the floor, resembling a swimming frog.

Jane knelt beside Durant's pallet and felt for his pulse, finding it weak and rapid. She laid her hand on his chest to feel his shallow breathing. Her own breathing went shallow. Angry with herself, she inspected his largest wound. Blood stained the bandage over his left ribs where the knife had cut deepest. The few uncovered cuts looked puffy but clear of discharge. Sergeant Fallon had done his job well. The patient smelled much better and looked clean except for his mop of hair.

Gazing at Durant's face, she touched his forehead. Was it hot? She laid her cheek against his. A bit warm but not dangerously so. She trickled water between his lips. This time he swallowed, his Adam's apple bobbing beneath his scraggly beard.

"Are you awake? Will you try to drink from a cup?"

His chin jerked down and up, and his eyelids moved.

Jane slid her arm behind his neck, lifted his head gently, and held the cup to his lips. He took three gulps, then grimaced and stiffened.

"More?" she urged.

He took a few more sips. She saw a quick glimmer of his pale eyes before he turned his face and hid it against her. Warmth flooded Jane's entire body. She set down the cup and took his head and as much of his shoulders as she could hold into her arms, cradling him close, feeling the heat of his breath.

Such a pity to behold this powerful man reduced to this state, yet her heart reveled in his need of her. She smoothed his hair away from his face and kissed his forehead. Her fingers trailed over his features as she studied his face in detail. He sighed deeply and nestled against her; the pain lines on his countenance relaxed into blissful peace.

Jane gently laid him down and backed away on her hands and knees, then sat back on her heels and covered her burning cheeks with her hands. *You fool!*

A nurse cared only about the recovery of her patient. If by some miracle Durant recovered from these injuries, he would undoubtedly kill himself another time: capsize a canoe in a drunken stupor, pick a fight with a touchy Ottawa, or simply drink himself to death.

Shaking her head slowly, she closed her eyes, remembering. . .

This year, as every year, as soon as the ice melted off the lake in spring, Mackinac Island's population had exploded from a few hundreds to a few thousands. Trappers and Indians alike brought their winter's catch to the American Fur Company's headquarters, and most remained on the island for the summer. Tepees dotted the shores, and men crowded the streets. Obeying her brother's warnings, Jane avoided the town whenever possible.

But one late morning after assisting at a delivery, she had walked unescorted along Market Street. Hearing footsteps behind her, she turned around and looked up, way up, into the leering face of Mad Durant. "Hello, beautiful."

Jane wrinkled her nose, recalling the stench of him, the frank admiration glinting in his eyes, the sweaty expanse of his tanned chest, and his dirty beard and filthy buckskins. Her current weakness must be due to the fact that this revolting creature was the only male ever to call her beautiful. He probably said such things to every female he met, but her susceptible female heart ignored that obvious fact even now.

She studied her patient's inert features and sighed. *Dear Lord God, please guard my heart against unwise affections.*

Chapter 4

Durant drifted in and out of consciousness. Sometimes he awoke to see one of his trapper friends or Dr. Beaumont or a pale young orderly named Fallon, who attended with obvious reluctance to Durant's personal needs.

He kept hoping, but *she* was never there. Had he dreamed her? If so, he wanted to sleep forever. Dim but delightful memories teased him whenever he drifted in that mist between waking and sleeping. Gentle hands stroking his face, a sweet voice singing of love and kisses. The clean, fresh scent of her when she bent near. For the first time in his life, pleasant daydreams of marriage and family filled his waking thoughts. Maybe love was real after all, not just a word invented to torment mankind with the impossible.

She had prayed for him, and strangely enough, he had liked it. When she talked to God, he could almost imagine that Someone out there listened. But where was the lady now?

One afternoon, Dr. Beaumont came to check on him. "You've got the constitution of an ox, Durant, to lose that much blood and come out alive. I almost sent Sergeant Fallon for the undertaker that night."

Durant winced as the doctor probed his uncovered wound. "There was a woman."

"Hmm. Healing well. No significant inflammation. Good scar tissue forming here. You'll have almost full use of these muscles. Amazing." While rewrapping the injury, he went off on a spiel of Latin names and medical procedures that meant nothing to Durant.

"Who was she?"

Dr. Beaumont met his gaze and frowned. "A midwife I called in to assist me. She's married with five grown children. Fat. Ugly. Kind soul, though."

"You lie."

A smile twitched the doctor's lips before he rose. "I'm sending you home, Durant. Your friends will come for you. Eat hearty and build your strength before you attempt anything rash."

"Tell me her name," he begged.

"Good day." The doctor picked up his bag and disappeared into the hallway.

Had he been delirious, imagining an old woman to be young and fresh? He carefully scratched at the bandage around his ribs. Some of the cuts had already healed enough to have their stitches removed, but the doctor wanted to give this one another few days. It itched.

Heavy steps ran up the hotel stairs, and Armbruster burst into the room. "Gus! The doc says you can go home today. I borrowed a wagon."

Durant struggled to sit upright. Pain ripped across his belly. Clenching his teeth, he stretched one hand up to request Armbruster's aid in rising.

He dressed himself in wool trousers that sagged around the waist.

"Gerard brung your clothes." Armbruster helped him ease his shoulders into his clean shirt. "Your buckskins were stained and ripped past saving. Betcha that jacket kept McNaughton from spilling your guts on the ground."

"I've got hides. I'll tan new ones." He noticed faint stains and multiple criss-crossings of tiny stitches on his shirtfront. "My shirt. Who mended it?"

"Miss Douglas. She brung it back a few days ago." Armbruster helped him slide his feet into his moccasins. "Next time, don't get into a fight less'n you've got a weapon besides your thick head."

"Miss Douglas?"

"The woman what helped Doc sew you up."

Durant wrapped his arm over the younger man's big shoulders and shuffled toward the door. *"Miss.* She's unmarried? What's she look like?"

"Scrawny little thing. Big nose. Squinty eyes like yours. Nasty temper. Good midwife, though, the doc says."

"Dr. Beaumont told me she's big and fat and kind and has five grown children."

Armbruster chuckled. "Reckon I forgot."

Durant gave his full attention to the stairs until they reached the landing. "Why hide her from me? I'm no monster."

"Her brother is an officer at the fort, and he don't know she stayed with you all night. Sergeant Fallon was here, too, and McNaughton, but Lieutenant Douglas wouldn't care about that. His spinster sister, alone with all us men?" He shook his head.

"What is she truly like?"

"Guess it don't matter if you know. We likely won't never see her much. She mostly only leaves the fort for a birthing or for church." Armbruster sounded sad. "I asked her to marry me when I drove her home. Gerard asked her, too, but she turned us both down. Kind she was about it, though. I figure the lieutenant wouldn't let his sister marry a no-account trapper. Word around town is that some official from the Company has his eye on Miss Douglas."

Armbruster settled him down in the bed of the wagon, and Durant stared up at a blue summer sky. Miss Douglas—out of reach? *No.* The rich official didn't own her yet!

"She touched me and sang to me," he said.

"I was there. I wanna die like that, like you did, with Miss Douglas crying and touching her sweet face to yours." Armbruster sounded beatific. "Praying plenty, too. She's real religious."

"God listened."

"If I was God, I'd listen to her."

"Armbruster?"

"Yeah?"

"I didn't die."

"I know that!"

Durant nodded. "Just making sure you knew."

Armbruster climbed to the wagon seat and clucked up the horses. Every jolt, every pothole was painful. Durant sang to himself, "I would love you all the day. Ev'ry night would kiss and play."

Armbruster spoke to him from the wagon seat. "She sung that to you while the doctor was stitching."

"I remember." He would become a man she could admire. Plans spun through his mind.

By the following day, Durant had thought of a way to locate and meet Miss Douglas. Billy Armbruster asked around the island about expectant mothers and proudly spouted off a short list. "Mrs. St. Francis is next, they say. She lives on lower Main Street. Miss Douglas visited her only yesterday." He sat in Durant's one good chair, tilting it back on two legs.

"Doesn't Dr. Beaumont deliver babies for townspeople?"

"Only if they's expected troublesome. He's army surgeon. You was lucky he come to save you." Armbruster tipped his head back, lifted a bottle, and guzzled whiskey, then choked and spat a mouthful across the room.

Durant watched the liquid soak into the sand floor. Would Miss Douglas want to live in a shack? If he could remember her face, he might have a better idea what she would expect of a husband.

"The doctor expected me to die. God saved me."

"I expect you're right. But God didn't make no stitches in your skin." Armbruster threw back his head to laugh, and the chair fell over. He lay on the floor and stared soberly at the ceiling. "D'ye think He done that? Flung me off for being disrespectful-like, I mean?"

Durant rubbed his forehead, suddenly tired to death of Billy Armbruster's company. Tired to death of himself.

Chapter 5

At last the mother's howls ended, and a baby's thin wail brought a tight smile to Durant's lips. All night he had waited and prowled Main Street; ever since his lookout, a Métis boy of seven, brought him news that the St. Francis family had sent for the midwife. Just before dark, Miss Douglas had entered the log home, but Durant's fleeting glimpse of her told him only that she was tall.

He rose and began to pace, aware of his pounding heartbeat. Never before had he worried about what to say. Words had always come easily; in English, French, or Ottawa he could ingratiate himself with almost anyone.

But this expected encounter was different. It mattered. It mattered terribly.

For hours, he had stewed and worried, and now he felt light-headed from lack of sleep. What if he said the wrong thing and alienated her forever? Possible scenarios had haunted him throughout the night. One minute he imagined her slipping into his arms and promising him eternal devotion. The next, he envisioned her screaming and running from him in horror.

He leaned on a fence post and rubbed his eyes. Dawn brightened the eastern sky. How much longer must he wait? The little house was now peacefully silent. Durant knew the St. Francis family only by reputation. Devout Catholics, they would scorn to associate with reprobate trappers. He suddenly wished he had lived a different sort of life.

Dangerous thoughts.

He cast them away.

"She will be well?" the nervous father asked, gazing down at his sleeping wife and child.

"Oh yes, Mr. St. Francis. Mother and daughter are both doing very well indeed." Jane pulled on her gloves and picked up her basket. Her eyes burned from lack of sleep, but a sense of accomplishment warmed her heart. "Keep Mrs. St. Francis in her bed today and be certain she drinks a lot of water."

"I should walk you back to the fort."

Jane opened the door and smiled at him over her shoulder. "It is light outside; please don't trouble yourself. What harm could come to me between here and the fort? Congratulations again, sir, and God bless you."

She stepped into the quiet street and soaked in fresh air and silence. A little flock of ducks whistled overhead, quacking as they braked for a landing on the lake. A sliver of sun appeared above the horizon; a rosy glow filled the eastern sky and reflected in the water. Could any place in the world be more beautiful?

"Miss Douglas."

Jane jumped and dropped her basket. She could see nothing in the shadows, her eyes still dazzled by the sunrise.

Mr. Durant stepped into view. "Don't be afraid, Miss Douglas. All night I've waited, hoping to speak to you. I. . . I. . ." He twisted his cap between his hands.

If anything, he looked more disheveled than ever. Gray trousers sagged around his hips—of course, braces would have rubbed his healing wounds. The shirt she had washed and mended with such care hung unbuttoned halfway down his chest, revealing black stitches and puckered scars, and from there down, the buttons were in the wrong holes. His black-and-white-striped waistcoat wasn't buttoned at all. Moccasins and a red stocking cap completed his odd ensemble.

However, she noticed one positive difference. He was clean.

When his eyes caught the first rays of sunlight, she read in them genuine hope and admiration. "Mr. Durant, how good to see you standing up and looking well!" She extended her hand to him, and he clutched it with both his large hands, stepping close.

"Thanks to you and your God. I've seen you before around town. I didn't know it was you. I mean, I didn't know. . ." He seemed tense and excited. "May I. . . May I walk you home?"

His reaction to her touch startled her; she had intended no more than a polite greeting. Perhaps his quick breathing was due to exhaustion, her own caused by surprise.

"It has been only a fortnight. Are you certain you have the strength?" At first glance, he appeared hearty, but his ill-fitting clothing proclaimed lost weight. The skin around his eyes was taut, and she sensed a frailty at odds with his apparent brawn.

"I have the strength." His pale green-gray eyes studied her face. "If you pick up your basket, I'll carry it. I. . .I can't bend."

"Thank you, but it isn't heavy. You shouldn't carry things yet." She carefully extracted her hand from his warm grasp and scooped up her basket. Thoughts and worries whirled through her head in confusing disorder. "Are your wounds healing well?"

"Yes." With utter lack of self-consciousness, he slid his hand inside his open shirt to touch the black stitches. Jane didn't know where to look and felt her face grow hot. He was like a child in a man's body.

"Dr. Beaumont will remove these stitches tomorr—uh, today. I'm healed, just weak still," Durant said. "He says I need to eat and build my blood."

Jane started walking, and he fell into step. Conflicting reactions unnerved her. The rational part of her recoiled from a man so completely lacking in initiative and moral strength. Why did her flesh react to him so strongly? Common sense warned her to give him an icy set down. But she had prayed for an opportunity to share the message of Christ's redemption with him, and God had provided this time.

"I'm glad you came to speak to me, Mr. Durant. I cannot help but believe that God spared your life for a reason."

She glanced up to gauge his reaction. His smile set her heart pounding. Quickly she looked down, clutching her basket's handle with both hands.

"You spoke of Him as my God, not as yours," she continued. "This troubles me. Do you know the story of Jesus Christ, Mr. Durant?"

"The baby in the manger. I know the story."

"His birth is only the beginning of His story. Can you read?"

"A little." He sounded less cheerful.

"Then please read either the book of Luke or the book of John in the Bible. Do you own a Bible?"

"No."

"Then I shall get one for you. Actually, I always carry a spare Bible." She stopped partway up the bluff, dug through the basket, and pulled out her Bible. "I sometimes read it to my patients. If you wish, you may keep it. Here, I will lay the ribbon marker at the book of John. If you have questions about anything you read, you might ask the new missionary, Reverend Ferry."

He accepted the Bible. "I promise to read this John book if you let me see you again. I *must* see you. May I come to call?" He tipped his head to peer beneath her bonnet's brim.

Jane's throat felt tight. "If you come to meeting this Sunday, I will gladly speak with you. Reverend Ferry will be preaching."

His narrow eyes widened. "I'm not a religious man."

"I know. As I said before, I believe God saved your life for a reason. Your duty is to discover that reason. Perhaps there is more purpose to life than you realize."

"You nursed me to life to convert me?" His voice held an edge.

"I prayed and begged God to spare your life so that you might come to know Him." Her voice quivered. Embarrassed, she turned her face away and braced herself for a barrage of blasphemy.

"Thank you, Miss Douglas." He walked slowly down the hill, head bowed, her Bible tucked beneath his arm.

Chapter 6

Durant wormed his fingers down into warm sand. Lying flat on his back near the lakeshore after a swim, he felt the heat of midday sun on his bare skin like a healing touch. Only pink scars and tenderness remained of his lesser wounds. The gash across his ribs still broke open if he twisted or moved quickly, but soon it, too, would leave behind only a scar and memories of pain.

Scars and pain. Bitterness and emptiness. Four words that summed up the life of August Durant. At twenty-nine, he had nothing to show for his life. The rickety shack behind him on the shore was his best claim to a home. Each winter, he worked hard at trapping; each summer, he sold his rich harvest of furs; and each fall, he had to work odd jobs to provide himself with enough food and supplies to last the following winter. His work supported people like the clerks at the American Fur Company headquarters—people who invested their money wisely instead of drinking and gambling it away.

If he had died of his recent injuries, no one would have mourned. His fellow trappers might have volunteered to dig his grave, and they might have paused five minutes to consider their own mortality when the preacher mentioned "dust to dust," but then their lives would have continued on without noticeable loss.

Miss Douglas had cried for him. She had wept and prayed and. . . Her caresses had been given only in charitable kindness to a dying patient. He desperately wanted to believe otherwise, but in his heart, he knew. A woman like Miss Douglas, so lovely, innocent, softhearted—in short, everything a woman should be—would never, *could* never view Mad August Durant as a man to admire and love.

He wanted to change. But aside from bathing more frequently and dumping out his whiskey, he didn't know how.

Tomorrow was Sunday. He could attend church meeting and see her again. Perhaps she would greet him and offer her hand. She would introduce her brother . . . He grimaced. Lieutenant Douglas would forbid his sister even to acknowledge a shiftless trapper who panted after her like a homeless dog. Her brother would encourage her to marry a man of good standing in the community—a man deserving of such a wife as Miss Douglas.

Durant rolled over on his belly to look for the book he'd been reading. A ghost knife stabbed him in the ribs, and he jerked up on his hands and knees. Teeth clenched, head hanging, he waited for the pain to abate. His trousers, coated with sand, clung to his legs.

Carefully he reached out one arm and picked up Miss Douglas's Bible. It couldn't hurt to try again, although the sections he had read so far left him puzzled. Too many of the words came from some strange culture and meant nothing to him. "Messiah," for instance, and "Levites." Some of the stories were interesting, even fantastic, but he had no idea why Miss Douglas thought he might find in them some hidden purpose for his life.

Perhaps he was not as good at reading as he had thought. Seated Indian-style, he lowered his head and ran his fingers through his drying hair. Sand dropped onto the open book in his lap.

He glanced to his left, then to his right. No one in sight. He prayed softly: "God, if You're real, help me understand this book. Miss Douglas says my life has a purpose. If it does, I want to know."

"Come, Thou Fount of every blessing, tune my heart to sing Thy grace." Jane felt as if she sang alone, although she saw other mouths moving. Rev. William Ferry stood upon a rock and waved his arm, but she could barely hear his voice.

Many visitors swelled their numbers today. Many of the Indians who had camped on the shores for the summer came to hear the new missionary preach. Lacking a building, the people had set out logs as pews. Foul weather sometimes forced the church into homes or shop buildings, but today the skies were clear. No stained glass window could be more inspiring than the view from this point near the Indian agency. The lake sparkled like a blue jewel, and the plaintive mew of gulls accompanied every hymn.

Rev. Ferry preached about God's love, mankind's sin and need of salvation, Christ's sacrificial death on a cross, and His bodily resurrection. Jane prayed as she listened that the message of salvation would touch hearts among the listeners. Several enlisted men from the fort had come with their families. Jane knew of some who had recently been thinking deeply about their relationship with the Creator.

Jane sat with Jordan and his fiancée, Lucretia, the daughter of an American Fur Company official. The lovely girl seemed enthralled with Jordan despite his rather severe manner and inhibited emotions, and he was obviously smitten with her. Yet, while pleased for her brother, Jane reserved judgment about her future sister-in-law. Perhaps the coolness she felt toward Lucretia was unmerited. She hoped so.

Lucretia's father, the widower Mr. Henderson, was seated on the aisle and gazed so fixedly at Jane that she felt heat rise to her face. He was an educated gentleman, dignified, handsome—a pillar of church and community. To be noticed by such a man was an honor. . .yet Jane wished he had never noticed her. He was more than twenty years her senior and had the unappealing habit of clacking his false teeth.

At the end of the sermon, Rev. Ferry gave an invitation that any desiring to pray and receive salvation might come forward. One of the military wives rose and stepped forward, closely followed by her husband. Jane rejoiced. Then a trapper wearing a buckskin vest and breeches but no shirt walked up to join them. A gray-haired Indian man rose with sober dignity and walked between logs to approach the rock.

The sound of a man's sobbing reached Jane's ear. A drunk, no doubt, making a commotion. Her stomach tightened. She glanced up at her brother, but his eyes were closed.

The noise grew louder as the weeper approached. That gruff voice sounded familiar. A dreadful suspicion struck Jane. Her suspicion was verified as a tall figure shuffled past and approached the rock. *Durant!* He fell to his knees and covered his head with his arms, still sobbing and wailing something incoherent. Her stomach knotted. Was he drunk or truly repentant?

"Disgraceful," she heard Jordan mutter to Lucretia. Mr. Henderson slipped into the aisle and went forward to support Rev. Ferry.

The others at the improvised altar knelt beside Durant and bowed their heads. Mr. Henderson laid his right hand on Durant's shoulder, his left hand on the other trapper's bowed head. He and the missionary consulted each of the people quietly while Mrs. Ferry led the congregation in singing a hymn.

Rev. Ferry looked up, smiling. "Brethren, let us rejoice. Today our Lord has brought five sinners to repentance. Join us now in prayer." Bowing his head, he led a simple prayer. Jane heard muffled voices repeating the words after him.

She tried to breathe but sucked in a sob. Tears burned her eyes. Her heart gave praise to God for His grace in reaching out to these five people.

A thought sneaked in while her guard was down. Would Mr. Durant become strong in faith, or would the cares of this world choke him and drag him back into darkness? *Dear Lord, please provide the encouragement and instruction he needs in order to become firmly grounded in Thee.*

Rev. Ferry ended his prayer and encouraged the new believers to take the step of baptism. The Indian man nodded and pointed at the lake. Apparently he saw no reason for delay. Rev. Ferry looked taken aback, but when the other four agreed, he nodded his assent and led the way to the shore.

Mr. Henderson returned to watch the proceedings with his daughter. Jane knew he tried to catch her eye, but she avoided looking at him.

One after another, the new believers proclaimed their faith, and Rev. Ferry cupped his hands to pour water on their heads. But when Rev. Ferry turned to Durant, the big trapper caught him by the arm and waded out into the lake, dragging the missionary behind.

"What is he doing?" Lucretia Henderson asked her father.

They could not hear the animated discussion between the trapper and the missionary, but Jane suspected what he wanted. Trust Durant to make a scene even at his baptism. "He wants to be immersed."

"But why? This is appalling!" Lucretia's voice carried, and Jane saw heads turn in their direction.

"There is nothing wrong with it. He is the sort of person who does everything in a big way," Jane said, feeling strangely defensive.

"You know that man?" Lucretia asked.

"I know of him."

"Nearly everyone in the territory knows of Mad Durant," Jordan said in a dry tone. "If his conversion is genuine, it will be a true miracle."

"He seemed sincere," Mr. Henderson said. "God's Spirit can reach even the foulest sinner. Let us hope and pray for the best."

Standing hip-deep in the lake, Rev. Ferry reached up to lay his hands on Durant's shoulders. He asked a quiet question, but Durant's reply boomed out clearly. "I believe that Jesus Christ died to pay for my sins. He was buried, rose from the dead, and now lives in heaven. My purpose in life is to proclaim His salvation to everyone I meet and to follow in His steps. I ask the missionary to baptize me as a sign so all may know that my life belongs to God now and always."

Jane blinked back sudden tears.

The missionary baptized August Durant "in the name of the Father and of the Son and of the Holy Ghost." Durant emerged from the water dripping and grinning from ear to ear. Splashing to shore with huge steps, he let out a whoop that echoed from the bluff. Jane's heart drummed so hard that she feared her brother would overhear.

The big trapper's features appeared illuminated, and he hugged his fellow believers, even the Indian, drenching them with unrestrained enthusiasm. "Praise God! He's real! I believe, and now I know He's real!" He thrust his fist high over his head.

Jane gave a little cry, seeing a shock of pain on his face, and she bit her lip as he reeled and nearly doubled over. The other trapper caught and supported him.

Jordan gripped Jane's arm. "Where are you going?"

"I'm afraid he's reopened his wound," she said weakly.

"What wound? If he is wounded, he had better see the doctor." Jordan frowned down at her, then glanced from side to side to make sure no one overheard him. "The man is a worthless trapper, Jane. He amounts to nothing, owns nothing. This religious fervor will quickly pass, and he'll be drunk on the streets again. I've seen it happen time and again. Have nothing to do with him."

She said nothing, but her joy faded. Jordan was probably right.

"Come." Jordan offered her his arm. "Let's go home."

Chapter 7

Weeks passed. A summer storm struck the island and churned the lake waters. Lightning blazed and forked overhead. Durant had always loved thunderstorms, and now that he knew their Maker, his appreciation for the power and splendor of each storm had magnified tenfold.

"Durant? Is that you?"

He turned around, then rose quickly and wiped water from his face and chest. "Good evening." A lightning flash revealed his visitor, a man wearing an oilcloth coat and a broad-brimmed hat. "Mr. Henderson, come inside. I'll build a fire."

The coals on his hearth required coaxing before they decided to lap up the birch bark he offered. Slowly he encouraged the little blaze into a crackling fire, feeding it with chunks of oak and maple. Water dripped from every crease of his trousers. Suddenly he felt cold and foolish.

"Why were you sitting outside?" his visitor asked, shaking the rain from his coat and hat. At Durant's invitation, he sat in the best chair.

"I was swimming when the storm hit. Since I was already wet, I stayed outside and talked to God while I watched His display of power."

Henderson lifted his brows and stared. "Ahh."

"If you're thinking I'm drunk, you're mistaken." Durant grinned. "Crazy, yes; drunk, no. I dumped out all my whiskey and haven't drunk a drop in weeks. I got depressed and went back to it once, but I couldn't swallow. I don't know how He did it, but God took away my taste for the stuff."

"Amazing. News of your changed life has spread throughout the island, Mr. Durant. Your interest in things of the spirit is most commendable. In fact, I came today at Rev. Ferry's behest to offer you instruction in the Word of God. We have spoken of this with four other new converts—Armbruster, Dowdy, McNaughton, and Gerard."

Durant nodded. "I know them well." He had talked all four trappers into attending Sunday meeting. McNaughton had come to the service, still in shock after Durant apologized for breaking his jaw, and he had gone forward at Rev. Ferry's invitation along with Dowdy and Gerard. Only three days ago, out on the lakeshore, Durant had led Billy Armbruster in a prayer of repentance and commitment to Christ.

He poked at the fire with a long stick and watched sparks fly. "I accept the offer, Mr. Henderson. I need a deeper knowledge of my Lord God, and I hunger after a committed human relationship."

"We honor your enthusiasm for God, Mr. Durant. But I think it best that you become well grounded in the scriptures before you attempt to evangelize."

Durant turned to face the older man, watching firelight play on his dignified features. "I want to learn, Mr. Henderson, but I can't stop talking about God while I wait to become 'grounded,' as you say. I tell people that He's real, He loves them, and they can know Him the way I do because of Jesus Christ. That much I know. If someone asks a question I can't answer, I'll send him straight to Rev. Ferry. How's that?"

After a moment, Mr. Henderson nodded. "I suppose that will do. Our study group will meet Wednesday evenings at my house."

"Thank you. Are you a married man, Mr. Henderson?"

"I am a widower. My wife passed on to glory four years ago."

"You were happily married?"

"So much so that I contemplate remarriage. Why these questions, Mr. Durant?"

"How do I make a woman love me enough to want to marry me?"

Henderson glanced around. "You wish to bring a wife into this hovel?"

"I live here only in summer. In winter, I share a cabin near my trapline."

Mr. Henderson made an odd clicking noise. "A woman deserves a house she can make into a home. She also wants a man she can respect and admire. Have you any aptitude for numbers? You might apply for a position as a clerk at the Company. We prefer to hire married men; they tend to be more dependable. With a steady income, you might build a cottage on the island and raise a family."

Durant reached inside his shirt to scratch at his itchy scar and nodded. He could work figures both on paper and in his head. The position of clerk held little appeal, but if the sacrifice might win him a wife. . .

"You have a particular woman in mind?"

He pictured Miss Douglas's round face, her clear eyes. "Oh yes, I do."

"A note of warning, Durant. If you marry a nonbeliever, she might draw you back to the world. Does she love strong drink?"

"No, she loves God and knows Him well," Durant said with confidence. "She saved my life by praying, and she gave me a Bible. I read the book called John, but it confused me, so I came to meeting like she asked. The missionary preached about Jesus coming to earth to die in my place, and all at once, it made sense."

"This woman invited you to meeting?" Henderson's brows knit in thought.

"She told me it was the only way I could see her again. I went to meeting for her sake, I confess, but I stayed and listened for Jesus' sake. A fire lit inside my soul that day, and it will never die. Now I live for Jesus Christ." His voice rang with conviction. "I believe God planned for me to marry my angel, but even if she'll never have me, nothing can take away the peace and purpose I've found."

Henderson shook his head and clicked again. Was it his teeth? "I confess I cannot guess the identity of your chosen woman. Attendance has gone up since the missionary's arrival, and there are many new faces in the congregation." He rose, donning his coat and hat. "I shall see you at Bible study Wednesday evenings, Durant. Good evening."

Chapter 8

The following week, after Sunday meeting, Lucretia pinched Jane's arm. "Who is that man? The big one with the crooked nose. I don't think I've seen him before."

"I'll tell Jordan you're looking at other men," Jane teased. She turned her head and looked, then turned her entire body. "Oh!"

"What? Do you know him?"

"It is—it is—August Durant."

Lucretia tilted her parasol back and studied him, squinting against brilliant sunlight. "Why do I know that name? I don't recognize the man."

I scarcely recognize him myself. Durant's laugh boomed across the open area. Clad in plain but neat garments, his hair and beard trimmed short, he talked with Mr. Gerard, Billy Armbruster, and two men Jane did not know.

"Durant," Lucretia repeated. "Papa has invited several new converts to meet at our house for Bible study, and I believe he mentioned that name. I intend to be elsewhere when our house fills with trappers. They stink."

"For Bible study?" Jane repeated. Her mouth opened again, but no sensible conversation came to mind, so she closed it and met Lucretia's quizzical gaze.

"Are you feeling well, Jane?"

Jane fanned her face with her hand. "Perhaps we should move under the trees."

Lucretia glanced past Jane, and her expression brightened. "Ah, here come our men." She rose on tiptoe and waved.

Thankful for the interruption, Jane turned to see her brother and Mr. Henderson approaching. Henderson met Jane's gaze, and his expression softened. "Miss Douglas, how well you look."

"Thank you, sir." She curtsied slightly.

"I have invited the Hendersons to dine with us today," Jordan announced.

"Very well. We have plenty," Jane said.

"Jane always prepares enough Sunday dinner to feed a crowd," her brother added.

"In that case," Mr. Henderson said, "might we ask two of the Bible study students? I am certain they would enjoy Miss Douglas's cooking, and I hope that after speaking with some of these trappers you might find yourself called to join my charitable project, Lieutenant Douglas. These men require solid doctrinal instruction."

Lucretia let out a peep of disapproval, but Jordan looked flattered. "Me, a Bible teacher? Although the notion intrigues me, the invitation for supper must come from my sister. Jane?"

Lucretia's elbow jabbed Jane in the ribs. Startled, she achieved a smile. "I do not object." Hearing Lucretia's frustrated sigh, she continued. "Lucretia has been telling me of your plan to instruct these new believers into scriptural truth, Mr. Henderson. I find it most commendable, and I hope my brother agrees to assist you."

Mr. Henderson looked gratified. "Then if you will excuse me, I'll extend your gracious invitation." He bowed and moved to intercept the trappers.

"Oh, Jordan," Lucretia sighed. "I wish you had discouraged him. Why must he encourage those savages to mix in civilized society? If he wants to lower himself to their level, I won't object, but when he forces us to endure their foul stench and backwoods manners. . ."

Behind a bland smile, Jane imagined pinching Lucretia, then repented of the unchristian thought as she realized she'd had similar thoughts about the trappers herself.

"Your father feels called to extend God's grace to the unfortunates in this land, my dear. You should honor him for his magnanimous sacrifices." Jordan turned to Jane. "Thank you for supporting him in this, Jane. Your encouragement means more to him than you know."

Henderson brought Durant and Armbruster forward and made introductions all around. Jane nodded acknowledgment with silent dignity, catching an amused gleam in Billy's blue eyes and an ironic note in August's voice: "Miss Douglas, the pleasure is all mine."

Unlike Lucretia, she offered her hand to each man. Durant pressed her fingers and released them only when she gave a little tug. No one else seemed to notice.

"Lucretia, you ride in the Douglas carriage. I'll drive the men up to the fort." Mr. Henderson nudged his daughter toward Jordan, who offered his arm.

Jane glanced up in time to catch August's quick wink before she hurried after her brother and Lucretia. Crammed on the end of the narrow carriage seat while Lucretia snuggled up to Jordan, Jane stared into the distance.

Lake Huron seemed a deeper blue today, and after recent rainstorms, the island was like a glowing green jewel. A fresh breeze rustled the treetops, and Jordan's horse whinnied. From behind, Henderson's horse neighed in reply. Jane could hear the three men talking in the other carriage, their voices distinct, their words unintelligible.

Delight and frustration wrestled within her heart. So few men had ever paid her any notice that August Durant's attentions sent her spirits soaring. Yet he had nothing to offer except romance. Why did she find him so appealing? Weather-beaten and craggy, he could never be termed handsome, yet one glance from his squinty eyes made Jane weak in the knees. *Ridiculous!* She tried to breathe deeply, but her breath caught in her throat.

"Don't worry, sister; you needn't speak to the trappers. You and Lucretia might excuse yourselves early if you wish." Jordan's tone held sympathy.

She gave him a weak smile.

Conversation at the dinner table was lively. The trappers downed a tremendous amount of roast beef, vegetables, bread and butter, and cherry cobbler with cream. Jane observed that Durant and Armbruster watched and copied the way her brother cut and ate his meat. They looked ill at ease but made few social gaffes. More than once, August's gaze intercepted Jane's across the table. She picked at her meal and drank a lot of water.

Methods of evangelism, denominational differences, and the primary importance of Christ's deity comprised the afternoon's conversation. Durant debated theology with Mr. Henderson and Jordan. Armbruster just ate and listened.

Mr. Henderson followed each of Durant's questions with a click of his false teeth, a quirk of one brow, and an amused glance toward Jane or Jordan. *Why?* In Jane's opinion, Durant's questions indicated careful thought. He had obviously been studying his Bible.

"Rev. Ferry says I might help him at the Indian mission come next summer," Durant said.

"I imagine your knowledge of native languages could prove useful. Maybe you could help the reverend learn them," said Jordan.

Durant nodded. "And I wish to preach the Word myself."

Mr. Henderson and Jordan exchanged startled looks. Mr. Henderson cleared his throat. "An admirable ambition, though entirely impractical. As I told you once before, a preacher requires years of training and seminary."

"Peter and John were unschooled fishermen, yet Christ chose them to preach His gospel. I do need Bible training, and I'm working to get it; but for now, I can tell everyone what God has done for me and let the Holy Ghost do His work in men's hearts. And women's," he added with a nod at Jane and Lucretia.

Jane wanted to applaud. " 'Go ye into all the world, and preach the gospel to every creature,' " she quoted. "I would like to help at the mission myself. With the children."

Durant met her gaze and smiled.

"God already uses Gus Durant." Armbruster spoke up in his deep, hoarse voice. "He used him to tell me and McNaughton and the rest about Jesus. God uses him just like he is." He smiled at Mr. Henderson, showing all his large white teeth. "All he needs is to know a little more about Christ than the people what he's teaching know and to keep on preaching the pure Word."

"Yes. . .well." Mr. Henderson cleared his throat again.

Surely Durant and Armbruster must notice Henderson's condescending attitude, yet both trappers remained polite and respectful. After the meal, Jordan invited the men into his sitting room. Lucretia joined them, preferring even the company of trappers to helping Jane wash dishes. If that girl was ever going to run her own household, she had a lot of growing up to do.

Jane tried to pray while clearing away the meal, but rising anger muddled her thoughts. *So superior, we Douglases and Hendersons, with our fine manners and our spiritual maturity. How gracious we are, deigning to feed and enlighten these poor ignorant boors!*

The kitchen door opened a crack, and August Durant peered through. Placing a finger over his lips, he hushed her exclamation. "Meet me on the shore past the cow pastures?" he asked softly. "I must speak with you alone."

"Meet a man alone? Jordan will never allow it. What could you possibly have to say to me, Mr. Durant?"

"I must ask you something of importance. Please come."

She wiped her wet hands on her apron. "Absolutely not."

"On the shore." The door closed.

Chapter 9

Jane checked the mantel clock. Jordan snored on the settee. If she slipped out now, he might never notice her absence. Her discussion with Mr. Durant must be brief and final. The man must understand once and for all that she would never care for him as more than a distant acquaintance.

Checking her reflection in the hall mirror, she tied her bonnet beneath her chin. Hectic color filled her cheeks.

She fretted while descending from the fort. What if she were seen alone with Mr. Durant and word got back to Jordan? What if Durant misread her presence? She must be decisive and convince him of her complete lack of interest.

It would help if she could first convince herself.

Her heart drummed in her ears. What question did he plan to ask?

Evening sunlight danced on the lake's surface. A boat skimmed across the waves, its sails shining white against the deep blue. Gulls wheeled overhead, and a loon warbled in the distance. Already the air held a hint of autumn.

When Jane reached the shore, she shaded her eyes against the sunset and scanned the beach. August sat on a rock, his face lifted to the sky, his lips moving. Her steps crunched on gravel and pebbles. Hearing her approach, he rose and removed his cap. His face was full of glory. "Miss Douglas, you came."

She clutched her shawl. He stepped toward her. Anxiety gripped her throat as her body responded to his proximity. What would she do if he attempted to kiss her? But what nonsense! Why would he want to kiss a plain spinster?

"Today I heard Miss Henderson call you Jane. That is your given name?"

Wind whipped his straight brown hair and tugged at her bonnet.

"Yes. Jane Cornelia Upshaw Douglas," she squeaked.

"Jane." He purred the name, and her heart turned over. He stepped closer and gently grasped her elbows. "Please marry me, Jane."

His eyes—they glowed from within, speaking volumes.

"Dear God, help me!" She covered her face with her hands.

He released her arms instantly. "Jane, what's wrong?"

She rocked physically, battered by conflicting emotions. Anger prevailed. "How dare you?" she wailed. "I scarcely know you. How dare you presume that I—" A sob caught in her voice. "Why would I want to marry a man who lives in a shack?"

"I'm different now, Jane—you know it's true. If you'll marry me, I promise to provide for you—a house, food, anything you need. All I want is a home with you as my wife. I never wanted anything so much." His voice sounded as rough and choked as hers did.

Touched in spite of herself, Jane looked up at him. His quivering lips were nearly her undoing. "But you have no employment." Irritation at her own weakness sharpened her tone.

He prowled back and forth on the shore, then picked up a rock and heaved it at the lake. Far out in the water, it landed with a loud *plunk* and a splash.

He spun to face her. "I don't care if your brother and the others look down on me, but I thought you were different."

She winced. "I see how you've changed, Mr. Durant, and I'm so very pleased and. . .and proud! But. . ." She flapped her hands in frustration.

His eyes narrowed intently. "If I owned a house and earned a steady income, would you marry me?"

Her mouth opened and closed twice before she thought of anything to say. "I would at least reconsider your proposal, Mr. Durant."

A glimmer of light returned to his face. "You'll wait?"

"Wait?"

"Wait for me to make good."

As if she had a lineup of beaus waiting to sweep her away! "How long?"

"One year?"

"Yes. I—I promise to wait."

Durant lingered after Bible study. "Mr. Henderson, may I speak with you a moment?"

"Certainly. What can I do for you?"

"Sir, you once suggested that I try for a job as clerk at the Company."

Henderson nodded. "I did indeed. We have no openings at present, but next spring, I expect that situation to change. You would be an asset to the Company, I've no doubt."

Durant nodded shortly, turning his new flat-brimmed hat in his hands. "I plan to spend one last winter trapping to earn enough to build a nice house. Spring is when I'll need that job. I can do figures, I know furs better than most, and I'll have the Lord watching over my shoulder to keep me as honest as the day."

"I'm sure you will." Henderson smiled a fatherly smile. "Young man, whatever has become of the woman you wished to marry? I never see you in female company at church. Has she left the island, or did she refuse you?"

A knot tightened in his chest. "She is waiting to see what I can make of myself, sir."

"I see. Well, perhaps she is wise. Come see me next spring, and we'll get you that clerk position." Henderson gave Durant's shoulder a thump and turned away.

Chapter 10

May 1824

The ice was out.

The trappers were back.

Had August made good his promises?

Jordan and Lucretia had married just before Christmas. Although their happiness pleased Jane, being constantly around the cooing lovers grated on her nerves. She felt like a servant in her brother's home, sleeping in the loft, trying to make herself small and scarce. And now, Lucretia was in the family way.

Even if August never returned, Jane knew she must find another place to live.

Mr. Henderson pushed away from the table and sighed. "The man who marries you, Miss Douglas, will never need to hire a cook," he said, wiping his mustache with a napkin. "An excellent meal, as always."

She smiled briefly. "Thank you, sir."

He cleared his throat. "And now, I should like a word with you alone, my dear, if your brother will allow it?" He lifted his brows toward Jordan.

"Certainly, sir." Jordan sounded eager. "You may take the sitting room." He smiled at Jane and lifted one brow.

Henderson rose and bowed, indicating that Jane should lead the way. As the sitting room door closed behind them, a dreadful certainty entered her heart. She wanted to spare Mr. Henderson the humiliation of her refusal but could not think how to prevent his declaration in a way that wouldn't seem presumptuous.

He claimed her hands. "Miss Douglas—Jane, I believe you must know what I wish to say." His blue eyes glimmered. "When my wife died, I thought my heart died with her. But your Christlike spirit and generous heart caught my attention as soon as we met. Please accept my proposal of marriage and make me the happiest of men."

Jane studied his handsome face and his dark hair frosted with gray at the temples. "I cannot accept, sir, although I deeply appreciate the honor of your proposal."

Startled hurt flickered across his eyes. "Why ever not?"

"You must know that I think of Lucretia as my sister; we are nearly of the same age." This seemed kinder than telling him he was old enough to be her father. She slipped her hands from his grasp. "I do not care for you as a prospective husband, Mr. Henderson, although you hold my respect as a man of God."

He smiled in apparent relief. "My dear Jane, respect is the basis for most happy marriages. The difference in our ages is not insurmountable. I am just turned fifty, and I am in excellent health. I hope you do not find me hideous?" His expression revealed confidence in his own appeal.

"Certainly not, sir, but neither do I wish to marry you."

The first Mrs. Henderson had been short and exceedingly plump, judging by her portrait displayed in the Henderson parlor, but Jane knew that if she were to accept Mr. Henderson's proposal she would never escape the woman's long shadow. Why would any woman wish to succeed the perfect wife?

Worse yet, she would become Lucretia's stepmother, and her children would be Lucretia's brothers and sisters.

Mr. Henderson assumed a patient tone. "I know that your brother would never consider you a burden; nevertheless, his house is not large, and when the children begin to arrive. . ."

"Actually, I have received another proposal of marriage."

He blinked in surprise. "Indeed? Might I ask the identity of my rival? I have never seen you in the company of another man. Is your brother aware of this?"

She flushed. "My brother is unaware. Circumstances. . .uh, compelled us to wait before. . .um, finalizing. . .things."

"Circumstances?"

"Yes. Finances and. . .and such."

"Yet he has declared himself to you."

"He has."

"A Christian man?"

"I would never consider the proposal if he were not."

Mr. Henderson paced across the room and gazed out the window at the lake's silvery surface. "And you prefer this man to me?"

Jane stood mute.

"I suppose he is young, handsome, exciting. Jane, consider your future."

"I do consider my future, sir, which is why he has gone away for a time."

Turning, he lifted his aristocratic chin and studied her for an interminable moment. "Is this man mature enough to appreciate your gentle spirit, or does he focus on your aptitude for hard work?"

Jane concealed her indignation. "I believe he loves me for myself, not for my abilities."

Henderson's eyes narrowed. "Is the man a new believer?"

"Relatively new, but he is maturing quickly in the faith. Already he is doing the Lord's work."

"Did you encourage him to attend church before he accepted the faith?"

"I did."

Mr. Henderson's jaw clenched. A strange expression flashed across his usually serene countenance. "Durant."

"Yes, sir." A feeling of pride welled up in her heart. "Please don't tell Jordan or anyone else."

Mr. Henderson's eyes studied the floor as if reading a message there. "Assuredly, I will tell no one."

Chapter 11

Durant, you're back!" Quick footsteps descended the wooden stairs of the American Fur Company's island headquarters. Henderson approached between stacks of pelts—mink, otter, fox, bobcat, ermine, fisher, beaver, marten, skunk. The older man's hearty handshake lifted Durant's spirits. "Good to see you, young man. Such stories I've heard about your exploits! I confess I'm surprised to see you here this spring."

The clerk on the other side of the counter from Durant observed this greeting wide-eyed.

"It's good to see you, too, sir," Durant answered. *Surprised?* Something rang false here. "I was just telling your clerk here that I've come about the position with the Company."

Mr. Henderson lifted his brows.

"We discussed it last fall," Durant prompted.

Mr. Henderson still looked politely blank. "What position?"

Durant inhaled the familiar, musky scent of furs and rested one hand on the rough-hewn countertop. "You advised me to apply for a position upon my return to the island this spring, so I've come."

Concern and regret filled the older man's face. "My dear fellow, when you failed to apply last autumn, I assumed you had changed your mind. We've already hired Orford here to the position." He clicked his teeth.

"I tried to tell him that, sir," the rabbit-faced clerk said hastily, "but he insisted you had a job for him."

"I'm terribly sorry, Durant. I'm sure you'll find something else. The Lord will provide for His own." Henderson placed a consoling hand on Durant's arm. "I should think you could eke out a living with your trapping."

The bottom slowly dropped out of Durant's world. "You have nothing else, sir? In the storerooms? Supply? Transportation? I'd do anything."

"Nothing on the island. You might try one of the mainland posts."

"I see." Pride sustained his calm front. "Reckon I'd best be looking elsewhere. I won't take up your time." He backed up a step. "You're well, sir? And your family?"

"Healthy as a horse myself, and Lucretia will make me a grandfather next winter." Henderson's voice held an unusual edge. "But then I plan to start a new family of my own. You may already have heard. I've proposed marriage to a worthy woman, a Miss Douglas."

Durant concealed his reaction. "Miss Douglas?"

"Yes, the sister of an officer at the fort. You might remember her from church. Fine figure of a woman. Intelligent. Hardworking. Silken hair with auburn highlights, soft brown eyes. I never thought I could love again, but I confess myself a lost man." Henderson chuckled softly.

"And she has accepted?" Durant's voice cracked. Dread crawled through his bones.

"An autumn wedding, I believe. We'll be certain to invite you and all the other trappers and natives who still attend church. My bride shares my compassion for the heathen."

"She promised to marry you?"

His teeth clicked again. "Am I not blessed by the Lord? Until Sunday, Durant. And again, my deepest apologies for the misunderstanding."

On the open shore, Durant perched on a rock, carefully set his fancy beaver hat in a safe place, and stared out at the lake, which was gray beneath cloudy skies. A moist breeze ruffled his hair.

Empty dreams crashed around his feet. Raging jealousy licked at his heart. In his imagination, he wrung Henderson's scrawny neck until that gloating smile disappeared. "He knew it, God," he roared, shaking his fist at the sky. "He knew I hoped to marry Jane. That old man stole her from me and rubbed my face in it. Him and his stinking money."

A flock of Canada geese took flight from the shore in a thunder of wings, then settled out on the lake, still honking their outrage.

Durant wanted to break something, smash something. He wanted to get roaring drunk and forget. But then he would wake up sober and remember worse than ever. That cycle ended nowhere; he knew it well.

"All my hard work over the winter, Lord, was it for nothing? If I sell my pelts, I'll have cash enough to build a house, but without Jane, it means nothing."

That fatal conversation spun through his mind once more. Tears scalded his cheeks. *Silken hair. Soft brown eyes.* His fists pounded his thighs. Once or twice, he had glimpsed a softness in Jane's eyes when he unexpectedly met her gaze, but usually her expression was mildly disapproving. Would he ever be man enough to please her? Would he have an opportunity to try?

"And she has accepted?"

Henderson had avoided answering a direct question not once, but twice.

Durant's head popped up. Certainty filled him. *She hasn't accepted him yet. She hasn't accepted either of us yet. She promised to wait a year, and she won't break her promise. Not Jane.*

Inspired with fresh hope, he gave a shout that rumbled out across the waters. Three months he had to reach his goal, to gain her respect. "Whatever You will, Lord, I'll do it. But. . .the only thing I know is furs."

Hearing a step on the gravel, he turned. A burly trapper and a middle-aged Métis man gazed at him. "Uh, you all right, Durant?"

"Hello, McNaughton."

"We trailed you out of town."

"It's good to see you again." Durant shook his former enemy's hand. "I don't know your friend."

"This is John Wildcat. He's a fisherman."

Durant greeted the stranger respectfully.

McNaughton's ugly face glistened with sweat. "We followed because word has got around that you had a good year on the trapline, and I—we—was hoping you might want to invest in a business proposition. I know you and me ain't been friendly in the past, but God changed that. I can't think of a man I'd rather do business with besides you, and Wildcat agrees with me. He ain't a believer yet, but he listens. I figure you can convince him about Jesus Christ if anyone can."

A smile tugged at Durant's lips. "Go on."

Jane added flour to the dough and kneaded it vigorously, rolling it over and over on the board. *Why hasn't he come to see me? Has he forgotten me entirely?* She punched her fist into the soft mass.

"Jane, are you listening to me at all?"

Lucretia's voice penetrated her mental fog. "I'm sorry. What were you saying?"

"I asked you how long I should boil the beef before I add the vegetables."

"I believe it has boiled long enough. Have you washed the new potatoes yet? We could add the carrots we thinned yesterday, though they are small. Add as many vegetables as you like. It is so good to have fresh produce again after that long winter." She and Lucretia had spent the morning working in the fort's produce garden at the base of the bluff.

Jane set the dough to rise and covered it with a cloth. The muscles of her neck and shoulders felt like taut wires, and a permanent knot weighted her chest.

"Father will be here soon for dinner," Lucretia remarked. "Jane, I don't mean to pry, but has he mentioned anything to you yet about. . .about marriage?"

Jane's hands stilled. "About marriage?"

"Yes." Lucretia's voice sharpened. "He asked Jordan months ago for permission to court you. More than once, he has spoken with you alone, yet no announcement has been made. Father says nothing, but he seems unhappy. Jordan and I don't know what to think."

Jane tried to smile. "Wouldn't it trouble you to think of your father marrying again, Lucretia? I am scarce five years your senior, hardly of an age to be your stepmother."

Lucretia set down her knife, caught Jane by the arms, and stared into her face. Two vertical lines appeared between her brows. "Jane, I must be honest with you. Jordan and I wish you would marry my father and make him happy again. He is lonely, and you are lonely; despite the difference in your ages, I believe your union would be felicitous. Do you want to stay here forever? Much as Jordan and I care for you, these quarters will become crowded once we begin having children."

Jane lowered her gaze and felt Lucretia's grasp tighten. "I do not wish to stay here forever, but I have other options."

"Other options? You cannot live alone, Jane. You are too young, and rumors would abound."

"I might marry—"

"Yes, you might marry my father. He is easily the most eligible man on the island. Your options are limited. An army private? A trapper or an Indian? I hardly think so. Jordan would never allow it. You are incredibly blessed that my father even noticed you."

Jane lifted her chin but kept silent. Until and unless August approached her again, she could say nothing. But what if he never returned? Would it be so terrible to marry Mr. Henderson and move into his fine home? Better than living and dying a pitiful spinster.

Lucretia gave her a little shake. "Jane, you begin to anger me. What is wrong with my father that you refuse to consider marrying him?"

"I don't love him, Lucretia."

"You would come to love him in time. He is a good man and fine looking."

Tears pricked Jane's eyes. She wanted to tell Lucretia about her dilemma, but would the other girl understand?

A commotion at the front door announced the arrival of Jordan and Mr. Henderson. Jane encouraged Lucretia to entertain the men while she finished preparing the food.

Lucretia's mood turned shrewish, and Jordan spoke too loudly. Only Mr. Henderson seemed calm during the meal. As usual, he praised Jane's cooking. Jane handed the praise on to Lucretia, who merely glared at her.

"I spoke with McNaughton and Armbruster today in town," Jordan said. "The believing trappers wish to resume Bible study this summer. Have you the time and interest?" he asked Mr. Henderson.

With a loud *clack*, Mr. Henderson appeared to chew on the idea. "I might have time to teach a few of them."

"McNaughton and Durant surprised everyone by purchasing a boat a few weeks back. It seems they have taken up fishing. Like the apostles Peter and Andrew, I suppose." Jordan laughed. "McNaughton tells me they have a ready market for their catch, both here and in Mackinaw City. A half-breed guides them to the best fishing spots, and Durant preaches to the savage while he works. They say Durant preaches the gospel everywhere he goes. Can you imagine?"

"More of his mad ventures," Mr. Henderson said with a humorless chuckle. "One must wonder what distorted version of the gospel such a man preaches. Despite these rumors we hear of Durant's supposed evangelistic fervor, he seems as foolish as ever regarding business. I had offered him a steady job as a clerk at our headquarters, but he chooses instead to buy a boat. He has also set up shop as an independent fur dealer."

Lucretia gasped. "An independent—? After all you've done for him, Papa! How could he do such a thing?"

"It is legal for him to do so, though some might consider it unethical," Mr. Henderson remarked. "I fear the man lacks a conscience as well as any semblance of business acumen. Truly, one can expect little better. Much though I respect Rev. Ferry, he and other such zealous missionaries blind themselves to the fact that the lower strata of society are born lacking what we would consider a basic moral code. The trappings of religion are like whitewash on a sepulcher, to borrow our Lord's apt simile."

"If this is your opinion, why bother teaching them the holy scriptures? You cannot deny that the Lord has transformed Mr. Durant and Mr. Armbruster and the other saved trappers from the inside out. It is common knowledge," Jane protested, no longer able to hold her tongue. "And Rev. Ferry supports Mr. Durant's evangelistic efforts, so he must be preaching the true gospel of Jesus Christ."

"Nevertheless, I fear the transformation is incomplete. Not long ago, I met a trapper named St. Pierre who claimed Durant as his brother-in-law."

"Durant has a wife?" Jordan asked.

"We can only assume so."

"Unless that man married Mr. Durant's sister," Lucretia suggested.

"That's my daughter—always believing the best of people," Mr. Henderson said in a pitying tone.

Jane caught his meaningful gaze. A wave of loathing swept over her. Even spinsterhood was preferable to life with a man like that.

Chapter 12

As the summer dragged on, hope withered in Jane's heart. News of August Durant occasionally reached her through Jordan or through one of the other trappers, but she saw her former beau only at church. He sometimes caught her eye, but she always looked away quickly and hid her feelings.

Had he completely forgotten his marriage proposal? Had all memory of Jane slipped from his inadequate brain during the long, icy winter? Or maybe he truly did have a wife somewhere, a poor abandoned woman, and maybe some children.

Jane's emotions ranged from hot fury to cold hatred, from fiery resentment to icy disdain. She cried herself to sleep, beat her fists into her feather tick, and screamed into her pillow. Night after night, she prayed for God to help her forget that unworthy, faithless excuse for a man. Some days, she thought her heart had healed, but one glimpse of August in town or at church was enough to reopen gaping wounds of hurt and resentment.

Why had Durant entered her life only to destroy her meager happiness? Could she ever return to a state of fulfillment in the role of spinster midwife? He had awakened longings and sparked fires that she could never again ignore or suppress.

One morning, Lucretia felt peaked and remained abed. Housework kept Jane's hands busy, but her mind was free to brood and analyze and fret. Outside, the sun shone brightly, yet strong wind gusts howled around the house.

Last evening, while walking home on a side street after assisting at a birthing, Jane had passed Durant's new cottage. Smoke trickled from the chimney, betraying his presence. A shingle before the door advertised his fur-trading business.

So, he had moved in and established himself as a prosperous citizen. *Her* little dream house was now the headquarters of his upstart company. She tried not to stare at the cottage or admire its simple charm, but her lips quivered and a tear escaped down her cheek. Turning away, she had rushed up the bluff and hidden away in her tiny attic bedchamber, unable even to wail out her fury for fear of being overheard.

Chop. Chop. Chop. Slices of potato fell away from her knife. Between chops, she heard an echo. Pausing, she listened. The knocking continued. Someone was at the front door.

Wiping one sleeve across her brow to remove sweat and clinging hair, she dried her hands on her apron and hurried to the door. A broad back met her startled gaze, and her heart skipped a beat. August turned around. "Jane."

She stared. Shiny boots on his big feet, woolen trousers, his shirt and waistcoat buttoned, his coat neatly fitted and clean. A beaver hat, which he removed. And, biggest change of all, clean-shaven! His eyes studied her with an apprehensive yet hopeful gleam. "May I come in?"

"My brother is out, and Mrs. Douglas is indisposed."

"It's you I came to see."

Jane stepped back, almost too numb to speak. He was so very grand. She felt shabby in her old work gown. "Come into the sitting room, please."

In the sitting room, he turned to face her. Rubbing the brim of his hat with both thumbs, he tried to smile but failed. "You don't seem pleased to see me."

The mantel clock ticked off long seconds. "Why have you come?" Her voice wavered.

A muscle twitched in his cheek. "You must know why. It's been nearly a year, and I've come to—to repeat my offer of marriage. I've built you a house, and my income is steady with the prospect of growth in the future."

A wave of emotion slammed into her heart—relief tumbled and blended with anger and fear until she could think of nothing reasonable to say. "I hear you've become a fisherman and that you've set up a fur-trade business. Mr. Durant, do you consider me a mercenary woman? I asked only a house and some evidence of responsibility and commitment. I require neither wealth nor consequence."

He blinked. "I know that."

"Then why did you turn down the position Mr. Henderson offered at the Company only to set up a questionable rival fur trade, and then purchase a fishing boat when you knew nothing about fishing? Am I to view these wild speculations as evidence of steadiness and careful planning for the future?"

He took a step toward her, but she raised her hand to warn him away. "I await a convincing explanation, Mr. Durant."

What she really wanted was assurance of his passionate devotion! Why didn't he see that? Why didn't he ignore her stupid objections and sweep her into his arms? He was so big and fine and wonderful!

A puzzled look flickered across his face. "I plan to give you one. I fully intended to take a job as clerk at the Company when I returned to the island, but there were no available positions. The only business I know is furs, so I started my own trade. McNaughton and John Wildcat asked me to join them in purchasing a fishing boat. From Wildcat, I'm learning the skills of it, learning how to read the lake and find fish, and I get a good return on my investment. I wanted to have something solid to show before I came back to offer for you again. I'm far from rich, but God has blessed my efforts."

She compared his story to Mr. Henderson's version and recognized contradictions. "Mr. Henderson says you turned down a job at the Company to join this wild venture and then set up a competing trading firm. How could you be so ungrateful?"

August's chin and brows lowered. "There was no job waiting for me."

She flung up her hands and huffed. "Why would he lie?" *Of course he lied!*

"He's my rival for your hand, Jane. He told me himself when I returned in May, and he tried to make me believe that you were already planning the wedding. But when I thought it over, I knew you would keep your word and give me my year to make good. So I fixed my sights and forged ahead. As far as my setting up a rival fur trade, there's no law on the books or anywhere else giving the Company a monopoly. I'm not the only independent dealer on the island. A few trappers prefer working one-on-one with an equal, a man they know will give them a fair deal."

"You're saying the Company cheats trappers?"

He sighed. "I'm explaining my business, not accusing his. Jane, I'm no catch as a husband, and I can see you're set against me." He rubbed one hand down his face. "I knew the odds were against me but figured you were worth the risk."

Her heart pounded in response, yet doubts remained. "Mr. Henderson told me he met your brother-in-law, a Mr. St. Pierre."

A thread of anger sharpened his voice. "Mr. Henderson says a lot of things, and you seem to believe them all. I married young, but my wife died. I'm hiding no secrets or vices from you. You are the only woman I've asked to marry me since Harriet died." A rueful expression crossed his face. "In fact, you're the only woman I've ever really *asked* to marry me."

Jealousy surged and bubbled around her ears. He *had* been married before!

"You loved your wife?"

He hesitated. "We grew up as neighbors, and I guess I loved her in a way. A poor way. I didn't really want to be married; it was all her idea. I was only nineteen, weak and irresponsible and stupid. She was a year older and bossed me, but once we were married, I hated being tied down. Then she died." He bowed his head and grimaced. "She needed a midwife, but none was near. The baby came too soon, and it was dead. Harriet just kept bleeding, and I couldn't stop it. I nearly went crazy with guilt."

Jane laid her hand on his forearm. "It wasn't your fault, August. Things like that happen sometimes. I doubt even Dr. Beaumont could have saved her."

He covered her hand with his and pressed it. His keen eyes searched hers, probing, questioning; then his gaze lowered to her lips. Heat swept through Jane's body. She wanted to touch his face and sing sweet songs and surrender herself as his woman. She wanted him to hold her and kiss her and claim her.

But he hesitated.

She jerked away and took refuge in resentment. "Why would you want to marry me? You scarcely know me, and today is the first time you've spoken to me this year. I have difficulty believing that you care for me at all. We're virtual strangers and entirely unsuited to each other."

He closed his eyes and took a deep breath, then caught and held her gaze. "I love you, Jane. I love everything I know about you, and I long to know you better. You're cold to me now, but I've seen the beauty inside you, and I crave more. A year has passed since you prayed me back to life, yet still I dream of your singing and your touch. I believe God brought us together, and through you, He returned love and purpose to my life."

Jane's knees quaked beneath her. "You simply felt gratitude toward your nurse, nothing more. I cannot be the purpose for your life, or all these changes you've made mean nothing."

"I'll admit that I began to change with you as my goal, but somewhere along the line, God swapped goals on me. If you won't marry me, I'll probably sell the house and my share of the boat and move off the island, but I'll never return to my old life, Jane. If God wants me to continue as an evangelist, then that's what I'll do. If He wants me to serve Him as a fur trader, that's what I'll do. My only certain goal is pleasing and serving Jesus Christ. I can do that with you at my side, or I can do it alone."

Jane stared at him in awe. She didn't deserve the love of a man like this.

"I built your house, Jane. Please come see it," he pleaded.

"Go away and. . .and just go away!" Her face crumpled.

He paused for a long minute. "Forever?"

"Yes! No. . .I don't know." She began to cry.

When he spoke, his voice was husky. "I will go away for a few days, as you ask. We'll be taking the boat up north to look for whitefish. Please pray while I'm gone, Jane. If you haven't changed your mind by the time I return, I promise I'll never bother you again."

He paused just outside the front door. "I'll be praying, too." He donned his hat and strode away with his shoulders and head bowed.

Jane shut the door, leaned her back against it, and slid down to the floor. Her hands shook, her body shook, and tears gushed from a bottomless wellspring behind her eyes. "Lord Jesus, please help me!"

Chapter 13

Jane stood on the overlook near the fort's cannons and shaded her eyes. Wind whipped at her shawl and tried to rip off her bonnet. Out on the lake, it puffed the white sails of a Mackinac boat and sent it skimming over the lake's choppy surface. Three dark figures were aboard. Jane waved, but none of them looked back.

"I've seen the beauty inside you, and I crave more."

What beauty had August Durant seen in her? The beauty of God's love, yes—but he now carried that love inside himself. Why did he still pursue Jane as his wife?

She slowly turned back to the fort and returned to her brother's house. Work always awaited her there. While working, she felt important, useful.

But August had said nothing about valuing her work skills, her cooking, her physical strength. He craved her beauty.

Tears welled up and spilled over. What beauty? Standing before Lucretia's fine walnut sideboard, she inspected her appearance in its mirror. Sad brown eyes met her gaze. Shining hair capped her head, pulled straight back into a thick knot in back. A severe gray wool gown skimmed her figure. Her complexion was clear, her features relatively even; her body curved everywhere a woman's body should curve. Studied feature by feature, or even as a whole, her appearance presented nothing objectionable. She was nothing particularly special to look at, perhaps, but neither was she disagreeable.

For the first time in her life, a man found her worth pursuing—and she had rejected him. Not because she found him unworthy, but because she felt herself unworthy of his love. Too plain. Too ordinary.

All afternoon, while working around the house, she prayed and thought and examined her heart.

When August had been a drunken, dying, filthy, hopeless wreck of a man, she had felt herself superior in every sense and therefore had been willing to offer loving words and tender caresses as a kind of balm to his spirit. But after he recovered, after the Lord repaired his broken spirit and transformed him into a spiritual giant, she feared that her paltry beauty could never satisfy him.

"I am afraid of love," she whispered to an armful of firewood before stuffing it into the stove. Mr. Henderson offered a loveless marriage and an escape from any need to be beautiful. Yet in her heart, Jane knew she still craved romance and love enough that Mr. Henderson's proposal had never tempted her.

"I want to be beautiful, God." Her tears dripped amid the carrot peelings.

August had recognized and loved her beauty while he lay wounded and weak. The allure of her womanly spirit, not her appearance, had won his heart.

She dumped the peelings into a slop pail and started chopping vegetables for stew. Suddenly she sat down on a kitchen stool and pulled her apron over her head.

"Dearest merciful God, I have looked down on everyone else, trying to make myself feel superior. I wanted to be pursued and sought after, yet I spurned the man who valued me most! I expected August to ignore everything I said and only read my heart. Nothing he said or did would have satisfied me because I have hated myself all these years. Oh, dear Lord, how blind and foolish I am!"

Tears washed her face, and repentance dissolved the knot in her chest. "Forgive me, Lord. Teach me to love freely! Make me beautiful for dear August. Make me beautiful for Thee."

Evening sunbeams touched the lake and islands, reaching between thick black clouds like long, glowing fingers. Frowning, Jane watched the approaching storm through her attic window. Surely August and his partners would return to a safe harbor when bad weather threatened.

Two days had passed since they sailed away. Two days Jane had spent reading her Bible, bathing her heart in repentance, worship, and blossoming joy. The Lord had assured her of His love and adoration. In His eyes, she was perfectly beautiful.

Now she longed for August's return.

Hearing Lucretia's plaintive call, she climbed down the attic ladder. Thunder rumbled, or had that been the ladder's vibrations?

"Jane, I'm craving fried onions," Lucretia said from amid a mound of pillows.

"Are you certain you could keep them down?" Jane asked. The poor girl had been dreadfully ill these past few weeks. Her stomach rejected almost everything.

"I don't know, but I'm so very hungry, and fried onions is the only thing I want. Please make some for me."

"Yes, dear."

"Jane, you look different. What happened?"

Pausing in the doorway, Jane asked, "In what way do I look different?"

"I don't know. You look almost. . .pretty, somehow. Glowing. Are you in love?"

A smile tugged at Jane's lips. "I believe I am." Before Lucretia could respond, she slipped away.

Onions crackled on the stove, filling the kitchen with their pungent aroma. Jane gazed out the kitchen window just in time to see lightning rip across the sky. An immediate crash of thunder shook the house. Rain pelted the roof and the windows, blown by strong gusts of wind. Jane pictured that little fishing boat being tossed by furious waves.

Dear Lord, please protect him!

Durant, McNaughton, and Wildcat crouched beneath a tarp lashed between tree trunks. The wind raged, and flailing trees groaned in protest. Branches and leaves showered around the flimsy shelter. Rain blew sideways, soaking the three men to the skin. Their eyes widened as a crashing sound came closer and closer; a huge aspen slammed into the earth, its crown thrashing the underbrush not twenty feet away. The three men jumped in terror. "Too close," McNaughton shouted.

Durant thought of their little boat, which they had pulled up on shore as far as possible before the storm hit. Silently he begged God to protect the boat, as well, for without it, they might be marooned on this remote island for weeks or months.

In the future, he wanted to observe such storms from the safety of his solid little house, holding Jane in his arms until the winds stopped blowing. *Lord, please soften her heart toward me. I'm willing to wait, to court her until she loves and trusts me. Just please don't let her send me away forever!*

Two days later, Durant steered the *Silver Moon* toward Mackinac Island, grateful for steady winds. Falling branches had scratched the little craft's hull, and rain had nearly swamped her; but the three fishermen bailed her out, and the warm sun finished drying her. "Nothing a coat of paint won't cure," McNaughton finally said, stepping back to observe the craft in relief and satisfaction. "She's a tough lady."

"The Lord put a watch over her and over us," August said, sliding his hand over the boat's gunwales.

At last, the island appeared in the distance like a great green turtle afloat on the lake. Durant's heart seemed to rise in his chest and beat too rapidly. How would Jane greet him? Had she worried about him during the storm?

Trees and branches littered the island's shores. Several buildings appeared to be missing shingles, and the sound of hammering drifted on the wind. "Look like storm hit Mackinac hard, too," Wildcat observed quietly. He pointed toward the bluff. "Woman come."

Durant squinted and saw a figure moving rapidly down the path from the fort. White petticoats flashed in the sunlight. He was obliged to focus on sailing until the *Moon* was safely berthed, but as soon as possible, he searched the shore for another sign of that running woman. She was nowhere to be seen.

Fighting back disappointment, he climbed ashore with the other men, hoisting his pack upon the quay. Their small catch, a few whitefish picked up that morning, must be unloaded quickly before the sun spoiled it.

"August!" That faint cry might be a seagull. He paused to listen.

"Woman call you," Wildcat observed. Durant detected a smile in his friend's deep voice. "Best go meet her."

There was Jane running toward the wharf. She tripped and nearly fell but staggered up and kept coming.

Amazed, Durant started toward her, his boots thudding on the wharf. As realization struck him, his pace increased to a run. He met her on the shore, swept her off her feet, and spun her in a circle. She clung to him, gasping for breath, laughing and crying. "You're safe!" she repeated over and over.

Her bonnet hung on her shoulders, and her hair spilled over Durant's arms in wild confusion. He kissed her face and her hair and her neck and her sweet lips.

"I was such a fool, August! I love you so very much."

At that, he broke down and wept, clutching her to his chest, savoring the sweetness and softness of her. He felt ready and able to conquer the world.

Chapter 14

One week later, Jane stood arm in arm with August, gazing up at Rev. Ferry's earnest face and repeating her vows. She wore her mother's wedding gown, a coral-pink watered silk she had restyled to her own taste. She felt beautiful, and judging by the expression in August's eyes, she also looked beautiful.

A clear blue sky arched overhead, and the murmur of an Indian chant from the encampment farther down the shore provided unique music. Only a few tribal members actually witnessed the ceremony, but others sang in August's honor.

As soon as Rev. Ferry pronounced them man and wife, August threw his hat in the air and gave a ringing whoop. Jane knew the more proper guests would be scandalized, but she didn't care. August picked her up and kissed her soundly.

For a moment, the world faded away, but when the kiss ended and August lifted his head and smiled, Jane became aware of approving whistles and shouts from his trapper friends. Gerard, Armbruster, McNaughton, and the other trappers crowded around, begging their turn to kiss the bride. Jane laughed like a young girl and kissed the cheek of each beaming man. Billy Armbruster sighed with satisfaction; then he kissed her noisily on the cheek in return.

She felt honestly fond of these rough, gruff men. They were so real and uncomplicated—virtues she was learning to value highly.

Jordan stepped forward and shook August's hand. "I suspect I could not have given my sister to a man who would love her more," he said with a suspicious break in his voice. Jane saw him quickly wipe his eyes before he gave her a quick hug.

Although Jordan's first reaction to his sister's betrothal had been unenthusiastic, he was learning to appreciate August's qualities.

Jane held him a moment longer. "I love you, little brother," she said into his waistcoat.

"I still wish you had married my father, but at least we're still sisters," Lucretia whispered into Jane's ear while the two women embraced. Approaching motherhood had softened Lucretia's spirit, and she was learning to accept August.

Jane patted her sister-in-law's arm and smiled into her eyes. "Always sisters."

Mr. Henderson avoided greeting the newlyweds, but Jane saw him speak with various important personages. She and August had agreed to forgive his interference and lies whether or not he ever apologized. Henderson's disappointment was punishment enough, August said.

Dr. Beaumont approached, smiling. "I claim credit for introducing the two of you," he said, bowing over Jane's hand.

August chuckled and thumped him on the shoulder. "You claim credit after describing my wife as fat and old with five grown children? Fraud."

The doctor's mustache twitched. He coughed into his hand to cover a laugh. "I trust our village isn't losing the services of our fine midwife."

"I will continue working as long as I am able, doctor," Jane said quietly. "You needn't worry. Mr. Durant is proud of my abilities."

Long before the wedding guests had finished congratulating them, August caught Jane by the hand and ran. Past the Indian encampment, along the shore, over sand and rock and grass and driftwood, they ran and walked by turns until only the murmur of wind and water disturbed the silence. Gasping and giggling, Jane begged him to stop. "You'll ruin my gown!"

"Never!" He scooped her up and whirled her through the air to stand upon a rock, then gazed up at her with adoration in his eyes. Jane reached up and removed her bonnet, then pulled out her hairpins and shook her head. Wavy brown hair fell around her shoulders and uncoiled to her waist.

She gazed down at August's beloved face. Sunlight bronzed his hair and gleamed on his tanned features. The wind caught her hair and swept it around him. His eyes met and held her gaze. Words failed her. She longed to share her beauty with her husband, to hold nothing back.

"So beautiful," he groaned. "My wife. My Jane." He pulled her close, and she wrapped her arms around his shoulders. He lifted her off the rock, letting her slide slowly through his arms until at last their lips met.

The hairpins fell from her hand, one after another to *ping* upon the rock.

Later that evening, Jane and August strolled along the shore, breathing deeply of fresh lake air. A bald eagle soared overhead. Sunlight sparkled on the waves, and the very earth seemed to share in their delight.

"How God has changed my life this past year! From despair to delight, from ruin to riches, from loneliness to love." August pulled his wife close to his side, matching his stride to hers.

"That sounds like a song." She pushed her hair from her eyes to smile up at him.

"A song?" He chuckled and began to sing. After the first line, Jane joined in:

"I would love you all the day.
Every night would kiss and play,
If with me you'd fondly stray
Over the hills and far away."

JILL STENGL

Jill Stengl is the author of numerous romance novels including Inspirational Reader's Choice Award- and Carol Award-winning *Faithful Traitor* and full length historical *Until That Distant Day*. She lives with her husband in the beautiful North woods of Wisconsin, where she enjoys spoiling her three cats, teaching high school literature classes, playing keyboard for her church family, and sipping coffee on the deck as she brainstorms for her next novel.

Lady-in-Waiting

by Erica Vetsch

Chapter 1

This mail-order bride venture wasn't turning out at all like Jane Gerhard had planned.

"How far is it to the next place?" She glanced at the sky, wishing the thin sunshine held some warmth. The wagon hit a rut, jostling her against the driver.

"Coupla hours by road to Garvey's." Reverend Cummings slapped the reins. The breeze ruffled his long whiskers. He continued to scowl as he had since he'd first picked up the four sisters in Sagebrush that morning to deliver them to their prospective grooms.

Jane glanced over her shoulder at the ranch buildings receding into the distance, the Kittrick ranch where they'd left their oldest sister, Evelyn, and her son, Jamie, with Evelyn's new husband and daughter. How many times on the journey from the East had they talked about what a blessing it was that the sisters would all be neighbors, helping, supporting, comforting one another in this cross-country move? But none of them had counted on the vast distances in this territory so far from the Massachusetts coastal town they'd grown up in. Now she would be two hours from her sister.

And if Garvey's ranch was the next on their journey, she would be the next to marry. Harrison Garvey, her soon-to-be husband. Her insides squirmed like kittens chasing a ball of ever-unraveling yarn.

I wish his ranch was last.

Not that she was afraid, exactly, or wanted to put off getting married. She'd long dreamed of being a bride, of having a husband and house of her own to care for, though she had never expected it to actually happen. No, she wasn't afraid. She just didn't want Harrison Garvey to be disappointed when he realized he was getting the plain sister. If she was last, he wouldn't have Gwendolyn and Emmeline to compare her to right off.

Evelyn, Gwendolyn, and Emmeline all possessed striking blond hair and brilliant blue eyes. Thick lashes, slender figures, beautifully curved lips. Their fair skin and delicate features were the epitome of feminine beauty and the picture of their departed mother.

Then there was Jane. Mouse-brown hair, eyes that were neither brown nor green, short, with a figure more curvaceous than willowy, and a chin that could only be described as stubborn. Jane was the plain sister, the one who melted into the background. The one who worked hard to be useful, since she couldn't be decorative.

Shrugging, she tried to turn her mind to more productive thoughts, like what her new home would be like. Evelyn's had been a log structure, sturdy and solid, with a wide, inviting porch. Would Mr. Garvey live in a log cabin? Scanning the stark prairie spreading in every direction, she couldn't imagine where logs could be found for any structure, though when she'd put the question to Reverend Cummings, he'd jerked his chin to the mountains far in the distance and said, "Up there."

Her thoughts returned to her groom, as they had nearly every minute since receiving his proposal by mail. Harrison Garvey. She ran quickly through the list of things she knew about him. Twenty-eight, four years her senior. Originally from Columbus, Ohio. In need of a wife.

Not much to go on. But then again, what did he know about her? Twenty-four, a spinster from Massachusetts, in need of a husband.

A familiar ache returned to her chest. It was all well enough telling oneself to be practical, but Jane knew, in spite of what her sisters thought, that she possessed feelings, fears, and dreams that weren't remotely practical, things she kept squashed way down inside, things that only came out in weak or stressful moments.

She tugged her shawl around her shoulders and surveyed the landscape. The terrain rolled in gentle hills covered with tall, waving grasses, showing a hint of spring green in their strawlike stems. To the right in the distance, blue-purple hills rose toward a pale, cloudless sky, reminding Jane of her Creator and Sustainer. Her mind prayed her most frequent prayer these days:

God, go before us. Sustain us, and bless our new marriages and homes. Smooth the way for us where You will, and help us over the rough patches. Remind us of Your goodness and our need of Your strength.

"Reverend Cummings?" Gwendolyn stood in the jouncing wagon, grasping Jane's shoulder for balance. "Can't you tell us anything about the men we are to marry?"

The preacher's scowl deepened. "I told you you'll find out soon enough."

"But what are they like? Tall, short, lean, stout, learned, ignorant?"

Jane hid a smile. Gwendolyn and Emmeline had been the most enthusiastic about the prospect of moving to Wyoming Territory and becoming mail-order brides, and Gwendolyn had speculated almost constantly about what their prospective husbands would be like.

"What does it matter now what they're like?" the reverend asked. "You're here and you're bound to marry them. You should've asked these questions before. All you need to know at this point is that they're good, God-fearing men." He hunched his shoulders, braced his elbows on his knees, and clamped his lips shut, an odd trait in a preacher to Jane's way of thinking. The pastor of their church in Seabury had been well known for his ability to talk the leg off a Yankee mule.

Gwendolyn blinked, started to say something but subsided, her brow puckered and her arms crossed.

The reverend had a point. They should've found out more about the men they were to marry, but there hadn't been any time. With money running out, the eviction notice hanging over their heads, and post–Civil War men in Massachusetts scarcer than honest politicians, when an answer to their advertisement in the *Matrimonial News* had come, they'd acted swiftly.

After an eternity of jostling and fretting, a dark dot appeared on the horizon.

"Garvey's place." Reverend Cummings unbent himself enough to speak.

Jane studied her hands and tried to quell the fluttering in her chest. The dot resolved itself into black squares that eventually turned into buildings. The vast wooden barn and corrals were easy to see. It was the smaller structures Jane couldn't identify.

"What is that?" Emmeline asked, disregarding her manners and pointing between Jane and Reverend Cummings.

"Soddy."

"Pardon?" Jane asked.

"Sod house."

She swallowed. "The house is made out of dirt?"

"Yes." He drew out the *s* sound in annoyance.

She ignored his rudeness by focusing on the notion that she was supposed to live in the dirt like a gopher or a mole. A prayer made it as far as her lips.

"Oh, Jane. I'm so sorry." Emmeline squeezed her arm.

They pulled to a stop, and from the wagon seat Jane could look directly onto the low roof. Grass grew on the roof of her house? Her knees trembled.

A short, bald-headed man came around the corner. He was so bowlegged, he couldn't have stopped a pig in a lane, and he limped badly. His mouth split in a grin that showed several gapped teeth, and his eyes looked like raisins tucked into a sour-cream pie. He couldn't possibly be her groom. Twenty-eight had come and gone for this man a few decades ago.

"Welcome, welcome. I'm Lem Barton. Which one of you lovely ladies is Harrison's bride?" His smile and welcome eased the knot under Jane's breastbone. His gaze passed from one Gerhard girl to the next and settled on Jane. The grin widened, and he dropped one eyelid in a quick wink. She sensed she and this wizened old man would be friends.

"Barton, no time for palavering. Where's Harrison?" Cummings clambered to the ground. "Bags?"

While Emmeline and Gwendolyn sorted out the luggage, Jane accepted Lem's help alighting.

Lem didn't seem affronted by the reverend's gruff manner. "Now, now, parson, you've surely got time to introduce me to the young ladies. Harrison's working the kinks out of a new horse." He poked his gnarled thumb over his shoulder. "You'll see him yonder. He's anxious to be getting on with the work, but he's had to hang about here waiting for his lady to arrive."

All eyes turned to the hill on the far side of the wagon. A horse and rider stood atop the rise, silhouetted against the early afternoon sunshine. Jane swallowed, and her heart sounded much like the hoofbeats thudding the earth when the rider started down the slope.

When he reached the house, he pulled up in a swirl of dust and swung easily out of the saddle. Lem came forward to take the reins of the snorting, skittering horse. "What's the verdict?"

"He's coming along." Harrison tugged off his gloves while Jane tried to regain her composure. At the sight of her soon-to-be husband, her heart had taken a dive. Broad shoulders, well-muscled arms, long, straight legs, and a confident air. He swept off his hat to reveal coffee-colored hair and eyes to match. He was one of the best-looking men she'd ever seen.

What a shame.

He shook hands with the preacher and tucked his gloves into his belt before turning to Jane and her sisters. He studied each one briefly, and Jane braced herself for the disappointment she knew would come when he realized he was stuck with her instead of one of her beautiful sisters.

His attention focused on her, and a hollow place opened in the pit of her stomach. *Stop staring and shilly-shallying.* She offered her hand. "Mr. Garvey, I'm Jane. I'm very pleased to meet you."

Would he mind the calluses on her hands? Would he think her ill-bred and unladylike? She needn't have worried, for he only touched her hand for an instant. A jolt shot up her arm and scurried through her veins. He blinked, and something flashed in his dark eyes. Had he felt it, too? Surely these flighty flutterings would subside in a moment, and she would return to her normal, practical self.

He didn't return her smile. "Ma'am." His eyes flicked between her sisters and herself, and her heart sank. She lowered her gaze to keep from seeing his disappointment and busied herself with straightening the fringe on her shawl.

Her trunk landed with a thud in the dirt. "I'm in a hurry, Harrison. Let's get this done." Cummings reached under the wagon seat for his Bible.

No music, no flowers, no friends, and only her younger sisters to support her. At least she had a little idea of what to expect, for the ceremony mirrored Evelyn's only hours before. Trembles raced down Jane's legs and made her knees wobbly. Her wedding looked nothing like the beautiful ceremony she'd dreamed of in that twilight time between waking and sleep when her handsome knight would ride out of the mist, declare his undying love, and carry her away with him to his castle.

You're going to be practical about this, Jane Gerhard. Pull yourself together and be sensible.

She squared her shoulders and lifted her chin. In a steady voice, she promised to love, honor, and obey Harrison Garvey. When it came time for Harrison's vows, she swallowed and dared a look at him. He had a straight nose and firm chin with just a hint of shadow showing. His dark hair had a bit of a wave and curled at his collar. Her eyes went to his mouth. Straight, not too full, and with a determined set. Everything about him seemed so. . .solid. Other than her father, she'd not spent much time in a man's company, and this man she was in the process of marrying exuded masculinity and strength.

Yet the clasp of his hand was warm and gentle, and his thumb moved disconcertingly across the back of her knuckles in a gesture that comforted her out of all proportion.

Before she was ready, the reverend closed his Bible and pronounced them husband and wife. "I forgot at the last ceremony, but if you want to, you can kiss the bride."

Jane's gaze collided with Harrison's, and his eyes darkened, but he made no move. Did he want to kiss her? Did he *not* want to?

Lem nudged his arm. "Go ahead, boss."

Harrison's hands came up to cup her shoulders, and he brushed a quick kiss across her cheek. He pulled back, blinked slowly, and bent his head again, this time kissing her lips.

So this is what kissing is like. It's very nice.

She was just getting the hang of it when Lem cleared his throat. Harrison broke away, and the older man grinned. "My turn, boss."

Jane registered the rasp of the old man's stubbly whiskers as he pecked her cheek.

"We're awfully glad you've come, ma'am." He clasped both her hands between his. "You'll be the saving of the place, I wager."

She struggled to find her voice, still affected by Harrison's kiss. "Please, call me Jane." What did he mean? How could she be the saving of the place?

Reverend Cummings stuffed his Bible into his pocket. "Time to go." He made a herding motion toward Gwendolyn and Emmeline. "Daylight's burning." He leaped aboard the wagon, stopped, and dug in his inside coat pocket. "Almost forgot. Letter for you." He passed a thick envelope to Harrison, who scanned the return address, scowled, and tucked it into his back pocket.

"We'll just be a minute saying our good-byes." Emmeline's voice sounded as if she was damping down tears, and linking her arms with Jane's and Gwendolyn's, she drew them a few paces away. The hard lump in Jane's throat almost choked her.

"I feel like we'll never see each other again." Emmeline squeezed Jane's hand. "It wasn't supposed to be this way." She whispered the last sentence.

"I know, but there's no help for it."

"How are we supposed to manage all alone?" Gwendolyn asked.

"We're not alone. God is with us, and we will see each other. We're not *that* far apart. We are neighbors, after all." Jane hoped her voice sounded more certain than she felt, because as the older sister, it was her duty to set the example. If she acted bravely, they would, too. She hoped. If they started crying, she would surely follow suit.

"How can you sound so calm? We might be neighbors, but the neighborhood we live in is bigger than the state of Massachusetts." Gwendolyn's hands flew out in a wide arc. "We might as well be living in different countries."

"Stop it. There's nothing we can do about it now. Evelyn's married"—Jane swallowed—"I'm married, and you two will be married before the day is out. We have to make the best of things. I'm sure we'll be able to visit one another from time to time."

Emmeline hugged Jane. "Your husband is very handsome, like Evelyn's."

He was. So handsome, he must've been expecting someone more his caliber than Plain Jane.

Gwendolyn embraced Jane, too, hugging her neck so hard it hurt.

Jane swallowed against the lump in her throat. "I'm going to be fine, and so are you two. Remember, God has led us this far. He'll be our refuge and strength."

As the wagon rumbled out of sight, she repeated that truth to herself.

Harrison rubbed the back of his neck. He'd expected some of the tension to bleed away once he said his vows, but his muscles remained taut. His bride wasn't at all what he'd expected—though he didn't know exactly what he had expected. In truth, he hadn't spent much time thinking about it. Once her acceptance of his proposal had arrived, he'd known a sense of relief and shelved the issue. The ranch begged all his time and attention, and he didn't have time to waste speculating about what his bride might be like. Time enough to cross that bridge when he got to it.

Now his new wife stood only a few paces away saying good-bye to her sisters. One thing was for certain, he hadn't expected to be so attracted to her. Her intelligent eyes—green-brown like forest moss—drew his attention, and though she was a bit on the short side, she had a figure that would turn any man's head. He could still feel her hand in his, small and yet strong. Her cheek had been so smooth when he'd given her that chaste peck after the ceremony, he hadn't been able to resist following it up with a kiss on the lips. He wasn't sure who was more surprised, his bride or himself. And he had to admit, it was a very nice kiss.

"I think you got yourself a good one, boss." Lem eased onto the bench beside the front door and stretched his bad leg out.

"Time will tell."

"Hope she settles in."

Harrison couldn't take his eyes off her, not even when Cummings started grumbling about time-wasting. The girls embraced. As an only child, Harrison couldn't imagine what they must be feeling, but he didn't like the sadness on Jane's face. He'd known her less than half an hour, so why did he want to put his arms around her and tell her everything would be all right?

He rubbed the back of his neck again. He'd been out in the wilds of Wyoming Territory for far too long. Cut off from all feminine company and influence. That's all it was. Any woman would elicit such a response from him.

And yet the other two hadn't. They looked too fragile, and he'd never been drawn to pale hair and eyes. Pretty enough, but it was clear Jane was the pick of the litter.

He stuck his hands in his back pockets, and his fingers brushed the envelope. A thrust of satisfaction shot through him. At last he'd have something to report, something his father would hardly expect.

As always, the sense of sand running through his hourglass seized him. Shifting from boot to boot, he went through the chores he still hoped to accomplish today.

Lem rubbed his leg and scratched his chin. "She'll add a bit of brightness about the place. Wonder what your father will say. With the deadline coming, I bet he figured you'd be admitting defeat and heading home soon. This will catch him sideways."

Jane held her sisters' hands after they boarded the wagon, and she walked beside them a few paces as they rolled away, still clinging to their fingers. When she halted, she hugged her arms at her waist and stared after them until they disappeared.

Harrison hardened his jaw. "Father should know better. I'm no quitter."

Lem pushed himself upright. "Hope she isn't too lonely out here. I'm thinking those girls expected to live a tad closer to one another. By the time the last one is delivered, they'll be spread out more than thirty miles."

"That's not far out here." Harrison ignored the tickle of unease scampering across his skin. Should he have been more forthright about the distances involved? Would she settle in? What if she didn't?

"No," Lem agreed, "but considering where she's from, it's a fair stretch of the legs. She's a city girl."

When she brushed tears from her cheeks, the tickle of unease became a poke. What he didn't know about dealing with women would fill several books.

She walked toward the house, and he looked over to Lem for guidance, but his friend and employee was headed around the corner of the soddy like his hair was on fire.

Harrison glanced up at the sun, calculated the length of his chore list, and was surprised to realize he didn't want to leave her in spite of all he needed to do today. "Would you like to see the house?"

An uncertain light came into her eyes as she considered the soddy, but she swiped at her cheeks once more and squared her shoulders. "Yes, please."

Relieved that she seemed to be getting ahold of herself, he nodded. He guessed he could spare a few minutes to show her around.

Chapter 2

Jane sniffed back the tears and swallowed against the hard lump in her throat. It was all well and good telling her sisters that everything would be fine, that God was with them, but it was another thing altogether to act accordingly after being stranded in the middle of nowhere with complete strangers—one of whom she was now married to.

Harrison carried her trunk as if it weighed nothing, his muscles stretching his faded chambray shirt. "This way."

She lifted her two valises and followed him as he ducked under the lintel. Her first impression of the interior of the soddy was that it was dark. Her second was that it was dank. An unmistakable musty smell came from the walls. For Jane, who prided herself on her housekeeping abilities, the task of keeping anything clean in a house made of dirt staggered her mind.

"It isn't much. I'm sure it's not what you're accustomed to at all, but you'll get used to it. It's warm in the winter and cool in the summer." He let her trunk come to rest on the hard-packed dirt floor beside a plank table. "There's just the one room, but we're outside most of the time anyway."

Jane tugged the grosgrain ribbon on her bonnet and slid the hat from her hair. The entire house couldn't be much more than twelve by twenty, with a low ceiling of poles and grass matting with sod overlaying the whole. A stove, the table with four chairs, a metal bed, and a chest of drawers took up most of the space. Crates, barrels, and boxes lined the walls.

"Those are what's left of the winter stores. We don't get to town too often, so we stock up." He motioned to the rear door. "Water comes from the creek out back, and there's a lean-to for fuel." Scrubbing his cheek, he shrugged. "We mostly burn cow chips."

Cow chips? *Manure?* Faintness crept over her, and the already close walls seemed to crowd in around her.

"If you're not too tired from your trip, I can show you the rest of the place."

She almost beat him to the door. Breathing deeply of the cool spring air, she tried to quell the panic sloshing in her chest. Harrison strode toward the immense barn, and she hurried to catch up.

"Have you lived out here long?" Perhaps the soddy was a temporary structure until he could build a house. That was it. Building a real house must be part of his summer plans. Surely she could camp out in the soddy for a few weeks until a proper house could be erected.

"Two and a half years."

Her heart landed hard against her stomach. He'd spent two long winters in that dirt mound?

"Lem came west with me, and before that we both worked for my father's company in Ohio. Reed, the other ranch hand, has been here about a year. He'll be riding in tomorrow, most likely. I sent him over to the fort with a few head of cattle."

They reached the barn, and he pulled wide the door. He breathed deeply, his eyes lighting with what she thought must be pride. What an odd thing to be proud of, a great cavernous barn.

"Biggest in the territory." He pointed right then left. "Milk cow over there, stalls for horses on the other side. Hay storage for winter here in the middle." A few wisps of hay littered the floor, while the barn roof soared overhead. "We have to do quite a bit of haying and feeding out in the winter. I learned that the hard way my first year. Getting cows through a winter out here takes quite a bit of feed, and I lost so many it set me back quite a ways. Last summer we cut and stacked hay and piled this barn to the top, but the herd survived."

Jane's feet crunched on the graveled floor. Sweet dry-grass smells mingled with dust, grain, and animal, and a stiff breeze swirled through the open doorway, stirring her skirts and ruffling her hair.

"Over here is Butterscotch." Harrison leaned against a partition and reached over to scratch the rump of a cow the exact color of her name. She turned her head, blinking huge, liquid black eyes fringed with long lashes. Her jaw ground contentedly.

"Probably the only Jersey cow in the Territory. She's a grand little milker, though she's dry at the moment. Due to calve any day now. I'll double my milking herd soon if she has a heifer."

Jane tentatively touched the warm hide. Butterscotch shifted her weight and swished her tail.

"After she calves, she'll need milking twice a day. I have to say, I'm glad you're here to take over the chore. Lem doesn't complain, but with his bum leg, getting up and down off the milking stool is pure torture."

Milk a cow? Her? Jane stepped away from the animal, clenching her hands. Still, how hard could it be? She gave Butterscotch one last look and hurried out after Harrison.

They stopped beside a small, square sod structure. Netting strung on posts created an enclosure on one side, and within, nearly a dozen rusty-brown hens clucked and scratched. In their midst, a rooster strutted, his head tilted, regarding them with one beady eye. His magnificent tail, iridescent green, plumed higher than his red-combed head.

"You'll want to watch out for Napoleon. He'll peck you every chance he gets." Harrison threaded his fingers through the wire and watched the birds. "The hens are gentle enough, don't seem to mind when you gather the eggs, but that rooster will come at you." He pointed to a twig broom leaning against the coop. "But if you carry the broom with you, he'll run the other way." He reached for the door to the sod structure. "We've set a couple of hens in here."

The door groaned when he tugged it open. Ducking inside, Jane wrinkled her nose at the pungent odor. Droppings littered the floor, the roosts, and the edges of the nesting boxes. When was the last time anyone cleaned out this henhouse?

"These two are each sitting on a nice clutch of eggs. The flock should double this year if we don't lose too many to coyotes, hawks, or some such. Feed's in a barrel in the barn. And always make sure you close the gates and doors." He scuffed some scattered straw on the floor. "It's not the tidiest in here. I've had a hard time keeping up with everything since the spring rush of work is on us."

Milk cows, feed chickens, live in a dirt house? What else could she be expected to do? She followed him into the sunshine once more. "What are in the other buildings?"

"That's the bunkhouse." Harrison gestured toward a sod hut identical to the house and glanced at the sun again.

"And that one?" She pointed to a long, low sod building set well away from the rest.

"That's the house." He frowned and tucked his hands into his back pockets.

"The house?"

"There's materials to build a house—boards, windows, nails, paint—all of it."

"But why—"

"I'd best get back to my chores." He turned away, heading toward the soddy, where his horse stood dozing in the sunshine.

She followed, wondering what she'd done or said to provoke that reaction. Why have house-building materials and not use them? Why get mad when someone asked? A quick glance over her shoulder at the storage shed revealed no answers.

As they approached the soddy, weariness swept over Jane. Too many new things, too much to process. They came to an awkward halt before the door, barely acquaintances, and yet married for better or worse. Her mind shot back to the wedding, and she touched her lips, remembering the warm tingle of their bridal kiss.

"That's about it, I guess. The creek's out there where the trees are. There's a cold store down there for the milk and butter when we have them."

A movement caught his eye, and she followed his gaze. A pair of pointed black ears and a long black tail stood above the prairie grass near the barn. He smiled for the first time, just a fleeting one, but a smile all the same, and her heart did a flip. He had dimples. Two adorable creases dented his cheeks for an instant and momentarily erased the burdened light in his eyes. "That's the cat."

Jane looked closer. Green eyes stared at her through the tawny grass. "Does she have a name?"

He shrugged. "We just call her the cat. She showed up a couple of weeks ago. Probably escaped from a wagon train. She hunts rats and mice in the barn at night, and she does just what she pleases the rest of the time. And if she gets near the rooster, there's a dustup. She doesn't seem to like people too much. A law unto herself.

I'd advise leaving her alone unless you want to get scratched or bit." He checked the angle of the sun and resettled his hat. "I'd best get back to work."

"Thank you for showing me around." How formal they sounded, husband and wife, yet strangers.

He shifted his weight, reached for his horse's reins where they trailed on the ground, and looped them around the animal's neck. The way he studied her, unsmiling, made her skin quiver. He was weighing her up, but was he finding her lacking? Was he sorry?

"I won't be back until suppertime. Lem's around somewhere, so if you need anything, just holler. He and Reed fend for themselves in the bunkhouse, taking turns cooking. I'll see you this evening." Harrison swung into the saddle, touched the brim of his hat, and put the animal into a lope.

As he galloped away, Jane wanted to sink into the prairie grass and give free rein to the tears welling behind her eyes. She was alone on her wedding day, and her husband acted like he couldn't get away from her fast enough. He must be disappointed; why else would he ride away only minutes after they were wed?

Though she'd braced herself for such a reaction, a spark of hope had remained—fanned by the clasp of his hand during the ceremony and his gentle yet fervent kiss—that perhaps he hadn't minded so much about her plain features.

Jane cast one last glance back over her shoulder to where her new husband had vanished, picked up her hem, and headed into the house.

❧

Harrison topped the rise and pulled his gelding to a halt. The animal was really coming along, the best of the three young horses he'd acquired this past winter. He swung his leg over the horse's neck and dropped to the ground, sweeping the horizon and the ranch spread below him. In the hours since he'd left the house, he'd pulled two cows out of quicksand created by the spring-swollen river, delivered one calf who'd decided to enter the world backward, and ridden more miles than he wanted to remember. And he still hadn't managed time over the forge to repair a broken branding iron, nor had he sharpened the knives they'd need during the roundup.

Smoke drifted from the soddy chimney. Jane was down there waiting for him. His new wife. Guilt twisted his gut. He should've stayed, but work had beckoned, and her eyes had been full of questions about the unbuilt house—questions he hadn't wanted to answer.

Everything had seemed so simple when he first saw that advertisement. A mail-order bride would solve several of his problems. He'd get someone to help with the household chores, someone to ease a little of the burden around the ranch and free him up to spend more time on the range, and as an added bonus, he'd get to mark something off his father's list of demands—though not the way his father anticipated, he was sure.

But now, with his decision a reality, he wondered if he'd made a mistake. She wasn't just an idea anymore. Jane was a flesh-and-blood woman with feelings and expectations. She was a reality more complex than he'd bargained for.

He swallowed, hard.

Digging in his pocket, he withdrew the letter Cummings had given him and squatted in the grass to read it.

Smoothing the pages on his thigh, he scanned the familiar handwriting.

Harrison,

Have you given up on this nonsense yet? I had hoped a second long winter in the primitive conditions of Wyoming Territory would have cured you of this ranching bug. Only a few months before the deadline. You should have a fairly good idea if you're going to make it or not. And if you know you're going to fall short, then end this farce now by coming back to Columbus.

Harrison grimaced, shaking his head. Every letter began the same: give it up and come home.

The factory continues to prosper, though Peterson isn't the manager you are. New orders pour in every day. I still can't fathom why you would turn your back on such a successful business, on an inheritance I've given my life's blood building up for you, for this pipe dream. The conditions you describe are appalling. I can't bring myself to even discuss them with my friends and business associates. Why are you still living in a dirt house when I sent more than ample supplies—at considerable cost and aggravation, I might add—to build a proper dwelling?

Harrison flicked a glance toward the sod structure housing the building materials. Rolled up in a trunk under his bed lay the plans, along with stern instructions from his father to see the house was erected as soon as possible. It was a disgrace for a Garvey to be living in a rabbit hole. Taking a deep breath, he resumed reading. His eyes lit on a name that made his gut clench.

I dined with the Norwoods this week. Sylvia is still waiting for you to come to your senses, though I fear her patience (and her mother's) is wearing thin. Last week Sylvia was seen walking out with one of Rankin Booth's sons, and Mrs. Norwood went to considerable pains to tell me of all the invitations her daughter has been receiving of late. If you're not careful, you'll lose that girl to someone else. She's too beautiful a woman and has too much of a dowry behind her to go unclaimed for long.

Sylvia Norwood. The little black barn cat had nothing on Sylvia when it came to claws and stalking. The Columbus socialite had set her sights on Harrison years before—

or rather Harrison's family fortune—and nothing he did seemed to convince the woman he wasn't interested in her. At least a part of his reason for fleeing Columbus could be laid at Sylvia's feet.

But not all of it. The rest came from within himself, this burning desire to be his own man, to be free, to make his own way. Here, on his own property, away from the city and boardrooms, the factory and the demands, he felt a solace and completeness like nowhere else. Working with his hands, bending his back and making something solid out of a wilderness, pitting his strength and will against whatever challenge rose up to meet him, this was what he'd dreamed of since he was a small boy.

And it was almost within his grasp.

I can only hope and pray that once you return, you'll have gotten this wildness out of your nature and will embrace the role you were born to. But if you continue to be stubborn and insist on the full three years, I can't stop you.

Rutherford Garvey

Never "Dad" or "Pa" or even "Father." He always signed his letters "Rutherford Garvey." Harrison refolded the pages and slipped them into the envelope. If he was stubborn, at least he had come by it honestly.

He swung aboard his horse and pointed the animal's nose toward the ranch. He could put in a couple more hours before dinner and perhaps formulate a response to his father's letter. His father was going to have a conniption when he found out Harrison had married. And a mail-order bride at that.

Chapter 3

Jane surveyed her new domain. Though the bed had been spread up, one couldn't exactly call it tidy, and the ugly wool blanket covering it made her wrinkle her nose. Dust covered every surface, and boxes, crates, and cans tilted along the perimeter of the room.

She pursed her lips. What this place needed was a good cleaning and organizing. Well, she wasn't afraid of hard work. Refusing to be daunted, she rolled up her sleeves. If Harrison was going to be gone until supper, she had some time to get unpacked.

And to poke around a little to see what she could find out about her new, if absent, husband. A twinge hit her conscience that she might be prying, but she laughed it off. In a one-room house barely larger than her bedroom back in Seabury, it would be difficult to keep any secrets from each other.

She paused, realizing anew that she was indeed married, and to a man she barely knew. Her muscles tightened. Perhaps unpacking should come first. Her valises sat on the bed, and her trunk took up a fair portion of the available floor space. Time to get to work.

Opening the top dresser drawer, she knew a glimmer of hope. Half the space lay empty. And in each of the lower three drawers, his belongings had been placed to one side.

He'd made room for her things.

He'd made room for her.

That thought warmed her heart even as her cheeks heated at the intimacy of laying her clothing next to his and organizing her toiletries near his shaving mug and razor on the dresser top. A small mirror hung over the dresser, suspended from wire tacked into a roof brace. She studied her face, wishing once again she could be classically beautiful like her sisters. But her own ordinary face looked back at her, pale brown hair and green-brown eyes.

With earthen-block walls, there were no shelves or hooks, so she left her books and bonnets in her trunk. The one thing she did take out was her sewing basket. At least she'd have her knitting and her reading to occupy her hands and mind in the evenings.

She drew in a deep breath. Perhaps she'd best leave the rest of her belongings in the trunk and concentrate on putting a meal on the table. Cooking she could feel confident about. At least he had a proper stove with an oven and water reservoir. She propped the soddy doors open for more light and headed to the fuel shed.

Wrinkling her nose, she kicked a few of the dried cowpats into a bucket. Ugh. What she wouldn't give for a hod or two of coal or a few sticks of wood. Getting the fire to light was no easy task, and she managed to fill the soddy with smoke before she got the dampers adjusted correctly. She prayed the haze would dissipate before Harrison returned.

An examination of the stores turned up basic staples and a few pleasant surprises. She could work with these, and perhaps her wedding dinner wouldn't have to be plain fare after all.

Harrison headed for the house as the last of the sun's rays slipped below the horizon. His heart beat a quick tattoo.

The smell of hot biscuits and frying meat drifted toward him as he approached the soddy. On the doorstep, he scraped his boots as best he could and whacked some of the dirt and sand from his clothes.

Jane turned from the stove at his arrival. Her glance meshed with his. A flush colored her cheeks, and several wisps of hair curled at her temples. An apron covered her skirts, and his eyes were drawn to the bow in the back, so perky and feminine. When he realized he was staring, drinking in the contentment of not coming home to an empty house to prepare his own meager supper and fall into bed, he forced himself to look away. Her presence wasn't the only change in the soddy. A handful of grass-flowers stood in a glass of water on the windowsill, and a colorful patchwork quilt covered the straw mattress.

Jane flipped the ham in the skillet as if she knew her way around a stove, and he swallowed as his mouth watered.

"Smells good."

She smiled and took a pan full of golden brown biscuits from the oven. "Sit down. I'll have this on the table in a jiffy."

The table had been scrubbed and was set with stoneware dishes and steel flatware. He usually ate right out of whatever pan he cooked in. Glancing down at his work-stained clothes, he realized how accustomed to bachelor life he'd become. "I'll just wash up first." He ducked out the backdoor to scrub up at the washstand there. He grinned. Married half a day and already things were changing for the better. He returned just as she set the final dish on the table, and he didn't miss the surprise in her eyes when he held her chair for her.

"Thank you."

He took his seat and spread his napkin in his lap, a ritual he hadn't performed in so long it seemed foreign. And because he couldn't resist the impulse, he held out his hand to her. Though she raised her eyebrows, she hesitantly placed her fingers in his. Warm, strong, small fingers. She was so tiny his hand swallowed hers up. Her fingers quivered, and she sucked in a breath as if trying to calm herself.

"I'll say grace."

Comprehension entered her forest-colored eyes, and she bowed her head.

"Lord, I thank You for Your leading, and for bringing Jane here. I ask Your blessing on our union, and I pray that You'll help me to be a good husband to her. I thank You for this food, and I thank You for the hands that prepared it." His fingers tightened around hers. "Amen."

"Amen," she whispered, then busied herself dishing up his food and hers.

He almost closed his eyes again when he bit into a biscuit. So light it almost floated off his tongue, and perfectly cooked. His efforts at biscuits usually resembled granite lumps. Slowly he chewed, savoring every bite.

"Is it all right?" Her fork poised over her plate.

"That's the best biscuit I've ever had."

She exhaled and smiled. "I've never used this particular brand of fuel before. I wasn't sure how they would turn out."

"I'd say you did a fine job."

All through dinner she kept glancing past his shoulder, a pensive expression in her eyes that puzzled him. The lamplight picked out highlights in her hair and lashes and turned her skin to gold. Everything about her intrigued him, from the softness of her skin to the gentle curve of her cheek. Baby-fine hair wisped along her slender neck, and his fingers itched to touch it.

She stared at her half-eaten meal. "I hope you don't mind. I unpacked a few of my things and put them in the dresser."

He shook his head. "Jane, this is your home now. You can do whatever you want."

She swallowed and nodded, and when he reached for her hand again, she scooted her chair back. "I made dessert."

What had her so skittish? She was as jumpy as a jackrabbit with the hiccups. His attention went to the pan she set on the table. When was the last time he had peach cobbler?

"I thought, since it was our wedding day"—a delightful blush deepened in her cheeks, and her lashes swept downward—"that we should have something nice to celebrate. I couldn't manage a cake, so I made this."

As she lifted a square of syrupy, fruity goodness onto his plate, he realized how much she must've given up when she agreed to marry him. All the things a girl wanted in a wedding, all those things Sylvia Norwood and her mother had gushed about all the time—flowers, music, food, fancy clothes—Jane had missed out on all of those things. Instead, she got a wagon ride with a cranky preacher, a rushed ceremony with a total stranger, and an afternoon spent alone wondering if she'd overstepped her bounds by unpacking her bags.

Not knowing what to say, how to apologize or even if he should, he dug into the cobbler and tried to justify his actions. She knew what she was getting into becoming a mail-order bride. If she wanted all the fancy trimmings of a wedding, she should've stayed back East, right? The justifying didn't work. His conscience still jabbed him.

When he'd mopped up the last delicious crumb from his plate, she took it and started the washing up. Her movements were jerky, and more than once, something slipped from her hand to plop into the water. Finally, it dawned on him why she was so on edge. She finished the dishes, threw out the dishwater, and wiped her hands on her apron, all while trying to avoid looking at him.

He checked the clock on the dresser, rose, and put his hands on her shoulders to stop her bustling. She flinched, but he kept a gentle hold on her.

"Jane."

He lifted her chin to look into her eyes.

"You know this is going to be a real marriage, right?"

Though her eyes widened, she nodded, staring at his chin as if unable to look him in the eye. A tremble rippled through her.

"It's going to be all right."

An adorable blush started at her neck and crept upward, and she tried to lower her face, but he resisted gently. He brushed a tendril of hair off her temple, reveling in the soft strands that tangled around his fingers. "I know you're nervous, but everything will work out. We're married. Nothing that's going to happen tonight is wrong between a husband and wife."

"I know. I don't—" She swallowed and closed her eyes as if summoning her courage. "I don't know—"

Slowly drawing her into his arms, he rested his chin on her head, hiding his smile. She fit his embrace perfectly. He waited, and after a moment her arms came up to wrap around his waist, tentative and shy, but courageous, too, since he could feel her tremors and could only imagine how difficult this must be for her.

She was so strong and yet fragile, so tender, and yet he sensed the steel in her. She was everything he could've asked for in a wife, and so sweet his heart pounded, and he cautioned himself to go slowly, to not scare her. He brushed a kiss across the top of her head, said a prayer for wisdom, and led her to their marriage bed.

"How long will you be gone?" Jane folded a shirt and two extra pairs of socks together, and Harrison took them to stuff into his saddlebags. They'd been married less than a week, and already she couldn't imagine her life without him—though he spent nearly every daylight hour working. All the love she'd been holding on to for such a long time had found a place. Her whole world now revolved around her husband.

He shook his head. "Depends on how much the cattle have drifted. I could only afford to hire a handful of extra riders, so roundup might take a month or better." He glanced up from his list. "We'll be as quick as we can."

Reed Foster knocked on the open soddy door. "Boss, we're all set." Sunshine flashed on his reddish-yellow hair and made every one of his hundreds of freckles stand out. Barely out of his teens, he was Harrison's other full-time ranch hand. The three lounging beside the packhorses in front of the soddy were temporary hires, men who had ridden in together looking for work.

Harrison hoisted his bedroll and saddlebags and strode out into the sunshine.

Though Jane wanted to sag onto the side of the bed and wallow in her sorrow, she forced herself to smile and follow him. She wouldn't make a spectacle of herself, especially not in front of his men. If only their good-bye wasn't so public, she might be able to do more than just wave and ask him to take care.

Lem tightened the ropes on one of the packs and stepped back, rubbing his chin. "Sure wish I were going with you, boss."

Harrison secured his belongings behind his saddle. "I do, too, but I'll feel better if you're here looking after things. There's plenty that needs doing."

Jane felt the scrutiny of the men. Reed, who had returned safely from Fort Laramie with laden packhorses, was no trouble, frank, open, and sunny. But the other three were older, harder men, unlike any she'd encountered in Massachusetts. She wouldn't mind at all when they left for the roundup. She only wished Harrison didn't have to go with them.

"Let's move out." Harrison swung aboard his saddle and waited while the men followed suit. Saddles creaked, horses sidled, and bits jingled. They formed up with Harrison in the lead, and Jane swallowed against the lump in her throat, blinking hard. She would *not* cry.

Turning away, she entered the soddy. She needed to get to work, her favorite outward antidote for inward turmoil. Clacking dishes and cutlery together, she barely registered the sound of hoofbeats. A shadow blocked the light from the open door, and she whirled.

Harrison. He crossed the room in two strides and swept her into his arms. "I forgot to kiss you good-bye." He suited actions to words, crushing the breath out of her while filling her heart brim full.

He was gone as abruptly as he'd come, and she sagged onto a chair, sighing. Surely he must care for her at least a little. Perhaps eventually, he might even come to love her as she longed to be loved. As she loved him.

Everything was perfect. She only hoped her sisters were as blissfully happy as she was right now.

Chapter 4

The first order of the day was to get the soddy thoroughly cleaned and organized, which entailed enlisting Lem's help and moving everything out onto the grass.

"I'm not spending another night in this gloomy place until I have something between me and the dirt." Jane stood on one of the chairs and held the stretched canvas so Lem could nail it to the rafters. "Dirt sifts down onto everything, and this morning, a spider dropped smack on the table." She shuddered. "The canvas should stop a lot of that, and it brightens the place up. This afternoon, I'll need you to bring me the ash bucket from the bunkhouse and a couple of wheelbarrows of that clay you used on the chimneys."

"What do you want that for?" He spoke around the nails clamped between his teeth.

"I'm going to plaster the walls in here. Clay, ashes, and a little hay for a binder. That will lighten things up and seal out the dirt." She grappled with another fold of tough fabric. "If it works, maybe we can do the same in the bunkhouse."

"I wouldn't mind something between me and the dirt wall, that's for sure, but it seems like an awful lot of work. You're going to tucker yourself out."

"One of my mother's favorite expressions was 'Nobody ever died of tired.'" Jane smiled. "I want everything as nice as I can make it before Harrison gets back."

The plastering took two days of backbreaking toil. Every muscle ached from mixing the clay, toting the buckets, and slapping the mixture on the walls, but when she had finished applying two coats, the inside of the soddy looked fresh and clean. Even Lem had to agree it sure spruced the place up. He helped her haul things back in, following her orders as to where to place the furniture.

"Glad you'll be sleeping inside tonight. I don't know why you wouldn't use the bunkhouse. I offered to sleep in the barn." He grappled with the bed frame.

"I didn't mind. I've never slept outside before, and besides being a little chilly, I wouldn't have changed a thing. The stars were amazing." She pushed the table under the window beside the door, where it would get the most light. "Would you nail together a few crates to make some storage cupboards?" She set the chairs under the table, lining them up just so. "I want to unpack my books, and I'd dearly love to get the foodstuff up off the floor."

"Harrison won't know the place when he gets home."

She certainly hoped not. Making their bed, spreading her patchwork quilt over the mattress, and plumping the feather pillows before tucking them into linen shams, her thoughts returned again to her husband. Where was he right now? Was he safe? Did those rough men he hired follow his orders? When would he be home?

"This is the last of it. Where should I put them?" Lem stood in the doorway gripping two fancy leather suitcases.

She tapped her chin. "I found them way back under the bed. A mouse or something has already been chewing on them, which is a shame, since they're so nice." She surveyed the room, which, while it was now much brighter and neater, didn't abound in extra space. "Put them here on the bed for now."

"I'll fetch some water for coffee. I think we've earned a break." He picked up the bucket by the door and limped away.

Jane spooned coffee into the pot and poked up the fire before she unlatched the first suitcase. If she could consolidate the contents, she could nest the suitcases one inside the other safely in one of the trunks.

Opening the case, her eyes fell on a beautiful broadcloth suit, snowy shirts, and several silk ties and handkerchiefs. Her fingers brushed the navy silk as a hundred questions leaped to her mind. How had her husband, who wore homespun and buckskin and denim every day, come to own such fine clothing?

She quickly opened the second suitcase, expecting more of the same, but was surprised when papers and books filled the space. Letters, photographs, books on raising cattle, on farming, and several history books. Rolled up along one edge were large sheets of paper that proved to be blueprints for a house. In one corner of the drawings, bold and scrawling, someone had written, *Stop being so stubborn and build the house. I won't have you living in the dirt. Rutherford.*

Curious.

A picture caught her eye. A beautiful young woman with soft, creamy shoulders rising from an evening gown, and dark ringlets piled high stared back at her with large, luminous eyes fringed with heavy lashes, a saucy tilt to her bow-shaped mouth. Jane turned the photo over.

Something to remember me by, Harrison darling. I won't wait forever. Sylvia.

Who was this gorgeous creature? She must know Harrison very well to call him "darling." Jane studied the face in the portrait, a green feeling sloshing in her middle. Sylvia. An unusual name for an unusual face. Her own name, Jane, was as plain as pudding. Her father had insisted on medieval monikers for each of his daughters, and where her sisters had received beautiful names—Evelyn, Emmeline, Gwendolyn—she'd been given Jane. Plain old Jane.

Another photograph, this one of two men, lay in one corner of the suitcase. The younger one was clearly Harrison in city clothes with his hair brushed neatly. He stood behind an older, seated man with piercing eyes and an uncompromising set to his jaw. Her fingers curled around the frame as she studied her husband's face.

A shadow fell across the doorway. "That's Harrison and his father." Lem set the bucket of water on the table and ladled some into the coffeepot. "Two more stubborn individuals, I don't know that I've met."

"Help yourself to some corn bread if you like." She waved to the pan on the table before returning the photographs to their place and latching the case. A heavy feeling, as if she'd been prying into secrets, pressed on her chest, but her curiosity about the man she married shoved it aside. She had so many questions that needed answers.

When the coffee boiled, she poured them each a cup and sat opposite Lem at the table. "Tell me about Harrison. You've known him a long time, haven't you?"

He took his cup, blew across the steaming, dark liquid, and sipped. "Since he was a kid. I worked for his family back in Ohio, and when he wanted to head out West, I tagged along."

She cradled her cup and breathed deeply of the rich aroma. "I want to know everything about him. How he came to be in Wyoming, why he wanted a mail-order bride, what his childhood was like. He's got a suitcase of city clothes and another full of books on how to raise cattle and live on the prairie. He's got the plans and materials for a house, but it's sitting in a pile in a sod storage shed. Nothing seems to fit."

Lem chuckled. "All those things are tied up together. One thing you need to know about Harrison is that he's a strong man. Not just physically, though he could work most men to a standstill every day of the week. He's strong inside. When he sets his mind to something, he doesn't quit until he's accomplished it. Gets it from his father, Rutherford Garvey."

"Rutherford?" The one who had written the dictatorial note on the blueprints.

"Yep. That's him. Rutherford Garvey owns a factory in Columbus. They make sewing stuff. Pins, needles, thread, trimmings."

"The Garvey Sewing Company? That's Harrison's family?" Every woman who had ever sewn on a button had heard of Garvey's. "How on earth did he wind up out here?"

"Stubbornness mostly. All his life Harrison has wanted to be his own man, make his own decisions, and all his life his father has tried to hem him in, force him to be the man his father wants him to be. Rutherford had the boy's whole life planned out from the minute he was born, right down to the kind of girl he should marry and where he should live."

Jane set her cup down carefully. "The kind of girl he should marry?"

"That's right. Rutherford had a real beauty picked out for Harrison. Sylvia Norwood. A face to rival one of those Greek statues. Everyone expected them to announce their engagement, but Harrison bucked against the old man's maneuvering. He wanted to make his own way in the world. I don't know where he got the notion, but since he was a kid, he's wanted to farm and raise cattle. That's where the contract came in."

"The contract?" Jane could hardly concentrate, she was so stunned.

"Yeah, old Rutherford finally decided Harrison wouldn't settle down until he got this ranching lark out of his system, so the old man drew up a contract. He would loan Harrison the money to get started out here, to buy cattle, build the barn, hire hands. Harrison would have just three years to pay it all back with interest and show a profit. If he doesn't, then he agrees to return to Ohio and work for his father in the family business. Rutherford put all kinds of clauses in it, I guess. I haven't seen them all. Harrison doesn't talk about it much. I do know Rutherford heard Harrison was living in a soddy and shipped that house out here. Harrison won't build it though, because he doesn't want to incur more debt. He won't build it until he can buy the materials outright from his father. I don't imagine that will be anytime soon, since everything he's got is going into fulfilling the contract. It's due soon."

Her mind reeled. What kind of man was so ruthless as to treat his son this way? "And will Harrison make it?" She suddenly wanted him to succeed, to show his father he wouldn't be ruled, that he would be his own man.

Lem shrugged, his face sober. "I don't know. The first year out here was a rough one. We lost a lot of cattle over the winter, and that set him back. Since then, he's worked himself nearly to a frazzle every day trying to make it up."

"What about this Sylvia Norwood? Is she waiting for Harrison to get ranching out of his system and come home?"

"Doesn't matter much now, does it? Harrison's already married." Lem refilled his coffee cup. "You could've knocked me over with a gesture when Harrison said he was answering that advertisement. I don't think the notion ever hit him until Parker brought the paper over. They talked about it a long time, and I guess Harrison figured if he got married, that would be one less hold his father could have on him. Though he wrestled with the idea for a while, especially since he would need to pay your expenses out here, I guess he thought having a wife to do some of the chores would help him get the ranch. He could spend a lot more time on the range if someone was keeping the home fires burning, so to speak."

Jane studied the red and white checks on the tablecloth, heat swirling in her ears and cheeks.

"You're the right sort for here. I can't see that fancy Sylvia lasting a day in a soddy, much less slapping clay on the walls or feeding chickens or the like. No sirree. You're just what Harrison needs to help him meet that contract. I reckon he knew he'd need someone strong and healthy to share the load, who won't expect pampering. Someone plain and sensible."

Lem had no notion that his words hit like hammer blows, smashing all of Jane's fragile dreams. While she'd known Harrison hadn't married her for love, she had cherished the hope that love might grow between them. But if he'd only married her to spite his father and to have someone to do the chores, what hope did she have of happiness with him?

That night she curled on her side, pressing a pillow to her middle. She wanted to cry for her lost dreams, but the tears wouldn't come. Sylvia's beautiful face mocked her. Had Harrison loved her? Had she refused to follow him West? What was she,

Jane, going to do?

Her hand drifted to the empty side of the bed, and mortification coursed through her. She'd responded wholeheartedly to Harrison's advances. What must he think of her behavior? She'd assumed he was at least beginning to care for her, but if he only saw her as a scullery maid, cook, and gardener, then their coming together had nothing to do with tender feelings.

She drew a shuddering breath and clutched the pillow with more force.

The only thing she knew to do was to work hard. Perhaps if she helped Harrison get the one thing he wanted above all others, he might come to care for her a little bit, to see her more as a woman than as a hired hand.

But unless or until he did, there would be no more intimacy between them.

Harrison let his weight up off the calf, and it sprang away with a bawl of protest. The smell of singed hair, smoke, cows, and hot metal swirled around him like dust. He shoved the branding iron back into the coals and swiped his forehead with his sleeve.

"Here come a few more." Reed coiled his rope and prepared to cut out another calf. "Do you want me to spell you?"

"No, I'm fine." He motioned the boy toward the bunched cattle. Digging in his shirt pocket, he withdrew his tally book and pencil. The calf crop, though decent considering the winter they'd been through, wasn't near what he'd hoped for, not nearly what he needed it to be. He blew out a breath and prepared to tackle the calf bucking at the end of Reed's lasso.

The new men were working out all right, though they kept to themselves. He'd been lucky to hire them, considering he couldn't afford to pay top wages and he didn't even have a chuck wagon. But these fellows hadn't seemed to care, only wanting to find work. Harrison looked forward to the day when he could afford to keep a full crew on year-round.

By nightfall of the twenty-third day, they'd finished. They'd ridden every corner of his range, they had branded every HG calf they could find, and their supplies were running low.

Fletcher, the leader of the trio of temporary hands, let his saddle plop into the dirt beside the campfire. Reed stirred yet another pot of beans and rice, squatting on his heels, his face and hair illuminated by the flames. Harrison stretched out on his bedroll and went over his figures again. No matter how many times he added it up, he was still going to be short.

"Come and get it before I throw it out." Reed ladled out for everyone and piled his own plate high. The boy had lost weight, like Harrison had himself, over the course of the roundup. They could both use a rest.

But judging from the bottom line in the tally book, a rest was just what they weren't going to get. Harrison had worked too hard, come too far to fall short this close to the end. As he shoveled the bland food into his mouth, he racked his brain for a way to make up the deficit.

"Be good to get back to the ranch tomorrow, huh?" Reed flopped beside Harrison. "Bet you're looking forward to some good cooking. I thought you were crazy when you said you were sending off for a bride, but those cinnamon rolls she gave us before we left. . . It was enough to make me think about getting hitched myself."

Harrison smiled. He *was* looking forward to getting back to Jane, but a twinge of apprehension feathered across his chest. The time was coming soon when he'd have to explain to her about his situation, about the contract with his father and all that went with it. He should've told her in his letter, so she would have known what she was getting into, and he certainly should've told her when they met, but he'd taken one look into those hazel, trusting eyes and couldn't. If she knew about his life back east, she might start badgering him to give up the ranch and return to civilization.

"How'd the tally go? I've seen you scowling at that book." Reed set his plate on the ground and stretched his boots toward the fire.

"Not as good as I'd hoped. We'll have to find a way to make up the difference."

"Like how?"

"Dunno. I'll have to think on it."

"Sure hope you come up with something. I'd hate to see you lose everything after coming this far." Reed took his plate and Harrison's now-empty one and headed to the creek to wash up.

Harrison's hand clenched into a fist, and he pounded his thigh. He wasn't going to lose this ranch. There had to be a way.

Chapter 5

Harrison paid off the three temporary hands, broke camp, and with Reed and the packhorses in tow, headed home. Finally, near midday two days later, they topped the last rise, and his ranch spread out before him. Pride of ownership, the pride of knowing he'd worked by the sweat of his brow to build something out of nothing, welled up in his chest. He was so close to fulfilling his dream.

He frowned and pulled to a halt. Something was different.

"What's that?" Reed pointed with the hand that held the packhorse leads.

A large square of broken ground lay between the soddy and the creek. At least an acre? Gray-brown earth, tilled and harrowed smooth. Two figures bent over the dirt. Lem and Jane. He kicked his horse into a lope, leaving Reed to bring the packhorses.

Down the slope, around the soddy, and to the edge of the plowed dirt he rode, and the whole way he remembered his parting kiss and anticipated Jane's welcome.

Jane straightened, pressed her hand to the small of her back, and leaned on her hoe handle. He swung down from the saddle and strode across the broken earth, ready to embrace her, but her expression changed from surprised relief to. . . something else. Something wary and. . .hurt? He stopped a few paces away.

She swiped the back of her wrist across her forehead. Was it his imagination, or did she look thinner? "Welcome home."

Harrison blinked at the cold tone. Every day, several times a day, while they had been apart, he'd remembered the ardor of her embrace and looked forward to taking up where they'd left off. And now she looked every bit as self-contained and remote as the moment she'd climbed down from Cummings's wagon.

Lem shouldered his shovel and sauntered over. "Boss. What do you think?" He waved toward the expanse of dirt. "When your wife does something, she does it thoroughly. She said she wanted a garden patch, and she's had me digging for the past week." He stuck his spade into the earth. "With all she's planting, I don't reckon you'll need to buy much in the way of supplies this fall. You'll probably have enough to sell at the fort."

Jane pushed a strand of hair off her cheek. "That's my hope."

Why wouldn't she look at him? Was she shy in front of Lem? Relief trickled through him. That must be it. She just didn't want to show affection in front of an audience. Later then, when they were alone. He almost chuckled. He could wait.

Lem turned his attention up the hill where Reed plodded down with the packhorses. "I'll go help the kid."

As he shuffled away, Harrison stepped closer to Jane. "I missed you. You look tired. The garden is a surprise. Not that you're planting one, but the size. Are you sure you can keep up with such a large plot?"

Her back straightened. "Don't worry about me. I'm strong, and I can take care of a garden. How was your roundup?" She whacked her hoe blade into a stubborn dirt clod.

"Fine. Well, not as fine as I'd hoped. Not as many calves as I would've liked, though the herd seems to have wintered fairly well. All that extra feeding out we did helped." A pungent odor drifted up from the dirt, and he realized she was incorporating fertilizer into the soil. She'd need it, since the dirt out here wasn't the best for gardening.

"Are you hungry? I can leave off here for a bit and fix you something." *Chop, chop, chop.* She sounded as if she didn't care one way or the other.

Baffled by her remoteness, he shook his head, though his stomach gurgled at the thought of a decent meal. "I'd best see to my horse."

She never looked up, just nodded and continued working the soil.

Entering the barn, Harrison shrugged. Women were indeed a mystery, though he hadn't thought Jane the moody type.

Reed and Lem worked at the far end of the barn, slipping packs off and stowing equipment. Lem opened one of the packs. "She's worked herself to a standstill every blessed day you all were gone." He sorted the branding irons and hung them on hooks on the wall. "I rode over to Gareth's and got a plow and team to turn most of that field, or I swear she'd have done it all with a hand spade. As it is, she's hoed it over twice and planted most of it by herself. She had me ride clear into Sagebrush for seeds, too. I offered to take her with me to Gareth's. Figured she'd want to see her sister, but she said she'd go next time, that there was too much to do before you got back from the roundup. Never seen a woman work so hard."

Reed coiled a length of rope. "Guess she'll fit in with the boss pretty well then. He works from dark to dark himself."

"How was the calf crop?"

"Boss said it was fine, but his face was awful long every time he counted things up."

Harrison cleared his throat, and they both jumped. "Be sure to give those horses a good rubdown and feed now."

"Sure thing." Reed got busy, but Lem limped over to Harrison.

"You got time for a little walk? There's something I want to show you."

Harrison removed the saddle from his mount and led him into a stall. "Let me take care of this fellow first." He curried the animal while Lem doled out feed and made sure the water bucket was full.

"Look in here." Lem pointed into Buttercup's stall.

He looked over the partition into the eyes of the most perfect little jersey calf he'd ever seen. A smile tugged at his mouth. Big kneed, round-bellied, moist-nosed, the little heifer was the picture of bovine beauty.

"She came about a week after you left. Hard calving, though. Breech. Your missus helped with the birthing, though you could tell she was scared to death. Kept talking to Buttercup like the old girl could understand every word while I delivered the calf. And Jane's been down here every day teaching the calf to drink from a bucket. She's taken over the milking, too, though I had to teach her how."

As he emerged from the barn, Harrison checked the garden plot, but Jane had disappeared. A wisp of smoke trickled from the soddy chimney.

"Boss, that Jane is a wonder, but I'm worried about her."

Lem had his attention. Maybe he could give Harrison a clue as to why Jane was so distant. "She's not ailing, is she?" Was she homesick? Missing her sisters? Maybe he could take time out to let her visit one of them. But when? Work piled up every day as it was.

"No, that's not it. At least I don't think it is." He scrubbed his jaw and hitched his suspenders. "She found your city clothes and papers and things when she was cleaning out the soddy, and she started asking questions. I didn't think much about it, since it isn't exactly a secret, and I told her about the contract with your father. She also found a photograph of Sylvia Norwood and asked about her."

Harrison grimaced. He'd much rather have told Jane about his past himself, and he'd very much rather she had never known about Sylvia at all. They strolled in the direction of the chicken coop.

"How did she take the news?"

"That's just it. I thought everything was fine. She didn't seem upset at all, just a little quiet, but considering all the work she'd put in on the house that day, her being quiet and tired made sense. But ever since that day, she's about killed herself working. Look in here." He opened the henhouse door.

Pristine white greeted his eyes. The roosts and nesting boxes had been scrubbed and scoured, and the dirt walls whitewashed. A layer of fresh hay covered the floor, with not a feather or dropping to be seen.

"Look at the pen." Lem pointed to the fenced yard.

Raked clean, pans of mash and water immaculate. Even the birds looked cleaner. And fresh netting surrounded a smaller pen inside where two hens and more than a dozen chicks scratched and pecked.

"She rakes it every morning and hauls the droppings to the compost heap, and she's treated all the birds with delousing powder. You should see those crazy chooks. The minute she steps into the coop, they all squat down to be petted. Even that old rogue Napoleon eats out of her hand and almost purrs when she picks him up."

The rooster tilted his head and regarded them with a beady eye. His tail feathers shimmered in the sunshine as he strutted.

"And I don't know if you noticed, but the barn's cleaner than it's been since we put it up. No loose hay, no tools out of place, and every last piece of leather has been soaped and polished. She had me haul the manure pile to the garden and harrow it in, and bless me if she didn't strike out across the creek to gather cow chips, some for fuel and the rest for fertilizer. I've had to chase her out of the garden or the barn in the evening. If I didn't, I think she'd work all night."

"Why?" He scratched his head. "Not that I'm not pleased with the improvements."

"Beats me. I thought you might know. Maybe she was just filling in time. She seemed to miss you something fierce."

Harrison smiled. That was good to know. Her cool reception of him had set him back a bit. "Then I guess she'll taper off now that I'm home."

He couldn't believe the transformation inside the soddy. Clean, organized, and homelike. Little touches that said a woman lived there—everything from curtains at the window to the pretty shams on the pillows. A couple of rag rugs covered the floor, and she'd managed a set of shelves for the books he'd never unpacked. Her own books stood beside his, and atop the dresser, a chessboard and pieces stood perfectly ranked. How long had it been since he'd indulged in a game of chess? A feeling of contentment, of knowing himself blessed, settled around his heart.

She stood at the table, kneading dough. Though he needed a shave and a bath, and he wore the marks of three weeks out on the range, he didn't care. He needed to feel her soft skin and recapture the bond he'd felt with her the moment he'd said his vows. He needed to fill the void created when he'd ridden away from her more than three weeks ago.

"Careful." She turned her shoulder to his offer of an embrace, punched and rounded the pale ball one last time, and set it in the pan to rise.

He pushed his hat back, contentment giving way to puzzlement. "Jane, what's wrong?"

"Nothing."

"Lem says you've done nothing but work the whole time I was away. I think you could slow down for a few minutes to at least say hello."

She took a deep breath and folded her hands at her waist. "Hello. Welcome home. Your dinner will be ready in about half an hour."

"There something interesting about the floor?"

Her chin jerked. "What?"

Impatience at the change in her made him brusque. "You keep looking at the floor. Is there something interesting there? Most folks look at each other when they talk."

She raised her lashes, and he found himself staring into her pretty eyes, mostly brown at the moment, and still with that hurt look in the shadows.

"Is something bothering you?" If she'd just tell him what was wrong, he'd fix it, but he wasn't a mind reader.

"No. There's nothing bothering me. I've just got work to do." She turned away and grabbed a skillet, clanking it onto the stovetop.

He shrugged. "I'll go clean up then."

Women. What was a man supposed to do?

❧

Not a word about the improvements. Jane blinked hard and sliced ham into the skillet. What good did it do to work herself to a nubbin if he didn't even notice? Her gorge rose a bit, and she swallowed. Only halfway through the day, and already she wanted nothing more than to crawl into bed and sleep, to forget for a while that her husband had only married her to spite his father.

Harrison sat up to the noon meal and tucked in to the food as if he hadn't had a decent meal in weeks. He looked thinner, more worn. She dished out another helping of ham and beans for him and added another slice of bread.

"Are you pleased about the garden? I've put in beans, peas, corn, turnips, carrots, and potatoes. Oh, and onions."

He nodded. "The garden's fine."

Something stirred under the bed, and he jerked around. His hand closed around the broom by the door.

"Don't. That's just Boadicea." Jane rose, scraping her chair on the dirt floor.

"Boadi—who?" His forehead wrinkled.

"The cat. Actually, it's cats now. Come and see."

She knelt beside the bed and lifted the edge of the quilt. He followed suit, but tentative, as if he expected a cougar to leap out. Instead, over the edge of a box, two green eyes blinked, and a rumbly purr rolled out accompanied by some squeaks and mewls.

"They're waking up. I found them one morning in the barn, and she was spitting and yowling, trying to keep a coyote away from them. I brought them into the house to keep them safe, though Lem warned me she might move them out again. But she didn't. I think she was just starved for some attention, and she knows I won't hurt her babies. Aren't they sweet? There are three of them." She reached into the box and withdrew a black kitten with four tiny white feet and a white vest. "I named the mama Boadicea. It just seemed fitting, since she was so fearless defending her babies." The kitten curled in her hand, and she raised it to her cheek, nuzzling the fur and crooning.

"First the rooster and now the cat. Is there anything you can't tame?" His voice rumbled in his chest like the cat's purr and sent a shiver through her. He reached out and stroked one of the kittens in the box, and she found herself longing for him to touch her that way.

She swallowed and returned the baby to its mother. "If you don't want her in the house, I understand. Lem said they would take them into the bunkhouse."

"Do you want them to stay?"

She stroked Boadicea's head. "Yes. She's good company."

"Then she can stay." They returned to the table, and Harrison knew he couldn't put things off any longer. "Jane, we need to talk."

She rested her hands in her lap, trying to keep her composure.

"Lem says he told you about the contract between my father and me for this land."

"Yes. It came as quite a shock. I wish you'd told me yourself." Though she tried not to sound accusing, she winced at the chiding in her tone.

He pushed his plate away. "I should have. I meant to, but there never seemed to be a good time. But I don't want you to worry. I'll meet the contract demands if it kills me. I've worked too hard for this and sacrificed too much."

"Including Sylvia Norwood?" The words were out before she could stop them. She hadn't been going to mention Sylvia at all, but the image of the beautiful woman he could've married had stalked her dreams for the past three weeks. The Sylvias of the world were crystal chandeliers, while the Janes were the tallow candles. One beautiful, fragile, exquisite; the other utilitarian, ordinary, and plain.

His forehead bunched. "Sylvia? You saw her picture. Can you imagine her living out here? It would be a disaster."

But he could imagine her, Plain Jane, living here. Jane wanted to pick up the pot of coffee and dump it on his insensitive, practical, blind-as-a-mole head.

Harrison went on. "My father might think he has the upper hand, but he's going to get quite a shock when I write and tell him I'm married."

I bet. He'll be horrified when he finds out Harrison Garvey of Garvey Sewing Company married a nobody because she could work hard and survive living in a dirt house in the middle of nowhere. Somebody stupid enough to believe that her husband might come to care for her.

"What happens if you can't meet the contract?" She was proud of herself for sounding so calm when inside she hurt more than she'd ever thought possible.

"I will." His hand fisted on the table.

"But if you don't." She kept her voice firm.

"The contract stipulates that if I don't meet the demands, I will return to Columbus and take up my position in the family business."

Return to Columbus. Return to Sylvia? What about her, Jane? If he left Wyoming Territory, would he leave her, too? She was part of his life out here, not back east. If he returned to the world of business, power, and the company of socialites as beautiful as Sylvia, surely he wouldn't want a wallflower like Jane holding him back. Would he seek a divorce? What about the scandal? What about her sisters?

Her weary mind refused to contemplate a future in Columbus with Harrison or a future in Wyoming without him, so she changed the subject. "If the calf crop was less than you expected, how are you planning to make up the difference?"

His lips pressed thin, and he shook his head. "I'm not sure. I can't sell cattle. Keeping the herd up is part of the contract. I've cut expenses to the bone. I can't run the ranch without Reed and Lem, and they're taking less than standard wages as it is. What I need is cash."

"What do you have to sell?"

"That's just it. I don't have anything. I wouldn't make enough over the next few months hiring myself out to make it worthwhile, and I can't afford to be away from here that long. And I've got to cut hay for this winter."

An idea sparked. "Do the other ranchers around here cut hay?"

He shook his head. "No, most of them just let the cattle fend for themselves. I learned the hard way that winters here can decimate a herd, and I promised myself I'd never be caught out like that again. There were plenty of ranchers who came knocking last winter, though. I could've sold a barn full of feed." He sucked in a deep breath.

"Exactly. What if you cut and stacked hay, not just for your herd but to sell? Your neighbors would buy hay if it was available, wouldn't they?"

"They might. They just might." A smile spread across his face, bringing out those devastating dimples. "I could send Lem to make the rounds, see who would be interested. And Reed can keep an eye on the cattle while I cut and stack hay." He bounced out of his chair, grasped her hands, and pulled her to her feet. "That's brilliant, girl."

He hugged her, lifting her from the floor, but when he bent his head to kiss her, she turned her face so his lips just brushed her cheek. Though she longed to stay in his embrace, to savor his kisses and more, she forced herself to ease out of his arms. "I'd better clear the dishes."

Late that night, when he reached for her, she rolled onto her side away from him and feigned sleep. If he succeeded in winning the ranch, then she might be willing to risk her heart again, but until then, she had to be on her guard.

Chapter 6

Harrison pulled the whetstone from his pocket and ran it along the curved blade of his scythe. Bits of grass and dirt clung to his sweaty skin, and he swiped a rivulet from his temple. His shoulders burned, his muscles aching from the constant motion of swinging the scythe, and all around him the smell of fresh-cut grass rose up. Swallows darted over the hay field, feasting on the bugs stirred up by his passing.

Across the creek, Jane toiled in the garden, surrounded by knee-high corn plants. She toted yet another bucket of water. Cold, chilly spring had given way to hot, dry summer. Enough rain fell to keep the grass fairly green and thick, but her garden needed more. Her first crop of peas had come up like hair on a dog, and she'd spent hours shelling and drying them.

His chest pinched. He needed to send Lem to town to get Jane some canning jars, but he didn't want to spend the money. Every precious dime needed to be saved. The deadline, only four months away, stalked his dreams and pressed on his shoulders every waking minute.

As did his concern for Jane. She remained as remote as ever, and if he wasn't so dead tired every night that he could hardly muster the energy to fall into bed, he'd break down those walls and find the loving, generous girl he knew lived inside her, the girl he'd married.

Returning the stone to his pocket, his fingers brushed the latest letter from his father. He pushed his hat back on his head, set the scythe on the ground, and eased himself down to the warm grass. He unfolded the letter and squinted when the sunshine glared off the white pages. Short and right to the point, it opened with a bang:

Married? What were you thinking, son? Who is this girl? What am I supposed to tell the Norwoods? To say you've put me in an awkward situation would be an understatement. I can only ask again, what were you thinking? I've half a mind to come out there and see for myself just what you're up to.

Harrison sighed and shook his head. He couldn't imagine his father jolting across the prairie aboard a stagecoach. He'd never make good on that threat. As to what to say to the Norwoods, his father could hold his own with the Norwoods or anyone else he came in contact with. Harrison wasn't worried there. It was his father's own fault if he'd made promises on Harrison's behalf. He should've known better.

You sent no word on the progress of the house. I imagine now that you're married—I still can't believe it—your new wife will want the house put up as soon as possible. Any woman who'd be happy living in a dirt house can't be a suitable bride for you, though at this late date in the contract, building the house seems like throwing good money after bad. Still, if you build it, I can sell the property for more money once the deadline passes.

His father's lack of faith in him was galling. And his sideways swipe at Jane set Harrison's teeth on edge.

The house. His eyes strayed to the shed where the building materials lay under canvas shrouds. A fetter and a promise, an obstacle and a goal, a blessing and a curse. Someday, when the land was his, when he could pay his father for the building materials, he would build that fine house, but until then, knowing it was there waiting in the dark shed, it taunted him, accused him of being a poor provider.

He shoved the letter back into his pocket and picked up his scythe. Enough time wasted.

❧

Jane poured the last of the bucket of water onto the thirsty corn plant and straightened her aching back. Pressing her hand to her temple, she tried to still the dizziness. The sun baked everything, and she could well believe the nation's Independence Day was less than a week away.

She toted the empty bucket back toward the spring. Only half a row to go and she could be done with the watering for today. She'd have to remember to move the stick—her memory stick, she called it—to remind her where to start watering tomorrow. Dividing the garden into six parcels, one for each day, helped her keep up with the weeding, thinning, watering, and picking.

Boadicea stalked down the row, her tail erect. She stopped when she reached Jane and rubbed against her ankles. Jane lifted the animal into her arms and cuddled her, loving the hearty purr and the sleek fur. Gone was the wary, skinny, combative feline she'd first encountered. Satisfied, she set the cat down. "How are the babies?"

The triplets had quickly outgrown both the box and the soddy and spent their days prowling around the ranch buildings and wrestling one another in the high grass. The wagon rattling out of the barn drew her attention, the hayrack jostling and tilting over the ruts created by so many trips to and from the hay field. Lem slapped the lines on the team's rumps and waved to her.

She followed his progress back to the piles of hay he and Harrison had raked together yesterday and beyond to where her husband, with what seemed tireless strokes, sliced swaths of long grass into rows. With such a favorable response from the surrounding ranches, he had hope that he might be able to make up the difference between his resources and the contract's bottom line. But it was taking everything they all had. From before sunup to well past sundown, he drove himself. And she and Reed and Lem worked alongside him, as driven as he to achieve his goal.

Jane refused to let herself hope, though. Until the deed to the ranch was in Harrison's hand, there was always the chance they would fall short, that he would leave her.

She picked up her bucket and headed toward the house. Halfway there, she stopped, holding her side, low down. For days, off and on, she'd experienced twinges and aches in her abdomen, some sharp, some persistent. Shrugging it off as the result of toting so much water from the creek, she rubbed the spot and resumed her journey. Her favorite part of the day was fast approaching, and she wanted to be ready for it.

Harrison moved steadily, but he glanced at the angle of the sun frequently. His favorite time of day would be here soon. Step. Slash. Step. Slash. Keep up the rhythm, keep moving forward. Every swipe, every row, haycock, load, and stack meant he was closer to reaching his goal.

Another check of the sun, another glance toward the creek.

There she was.

His heart tripped. With a basket over one arm and a brown earthenware jug in the other, Jane crossed the stubble. Her bonnet hid her face from the merciless sun, but he knew when she arrived she would slide it off her silky hair so she could survey the landscape.

He waved across the field to Lem, who forked hay into the wagon. The older man waved back, flung his pitchfork into the pile of hay beside the team, and limped toward Harrison.

They arrived at the same time. Harrison reached for her basket while Lem took the jug. As anticipated, her bonnet slid off, and she swept the terrain. "I can't believe how much you've gotten done."

She said it every day, but every day it made his heart swell. Peeking under the napkin in the basket, he found his favorite sugar cookies. He took one, letting the sweet, sugary goodness melt on his tongue.

"We're going to have to start stacking in the field, boss. The barn's full." Lem took a long drink from the jug and swiped the back of his hand across his mouth. "I can't get so much as one more blade of grass in there."

Harrison traded him the basket for the jug and shook his head. "I don't want to stack it out here on the range. That's asking for trouble. We'll put the horses in the barn and stack hay in the corral. That way none of the cattle can get at it, and it will be handy for when the buyers come."

"We sure could use an extra hand or two. Stacking's a two-man job." The older man rubbed his hip. "Having to climb on and off that wagon is wearing me thin."

Familiar guilt settled in Harrison's gut. Lem couldn't swing a scythe all day. With his bum leg, he couldn't get the proper leverage. And yet, he was right.

He wouldn't last long climbing on and off the hayrack like he'd have to do if he was stacking the hay.

"I wish I could afford to hire someone to help us, but I'd just be paying out in wages everything we were earning selling hay." Harrison took off his hat and tunneled his fingers through his hair. "Maybe I can help stack after I'm through cutting for the day."

Lem grimaced and shook his head. "You can't cut all day and stack all night. You'll kill yourself. I'll manage somehow."

"I can help." Jane twirled her bonnet string around her finger. "The garden work is well ahead. If you'll show me what to do, I'm sure I can manage."

Harrison's immediate response was to say no. She had enough to do with her own work without doing his, too. And yet, what other choice did he have? "It's hard labor. Lem would pitch down the hay from the rack, but you'd have to rake it smooth and walk it down tight."

"I can do it." She straightened her spine and tugged her bonnet into place.

The stubborn light in her eyes made him smile. The newest member of the Garvey family just might be the most determined of them all. He couldn't deny the relief her offer gave him. "I'll let you help on one condition. If it's too much for you, you'll say so. No standing on pride. And I'll rope Lem in on the decision, too. If he thinks it's too much for you, he has the authority to stand you down and take your hay rake away."

She tugged her sunbonnet into place and took the now-empty basket and jug. "I'll just take care of a few things at the soddy, and I'll be ready when Lem brings the next load."

Harrison followed her with his eyes, thankful for her and puzzled by her. Lem nudged his elbow.

"She's a fine woman. Reminds me of my wife."

Harrison's head swiveled to the older man. "I didn't know you were married."

"It was a long time ago. My Deborah passed away when you were just a youngster, before I came to work for your dad. She was a hard worker, always looking to my comfort. Her passing left a big hole in my life. I always felt bad that I never told her how much she meant to me. I think she knew, but I never said it. I guess it was the way I was raised. I took her for granted and didn't realize what a treasure I had until she was gone."

Harrison didn't know what to say. He picked up his scythe and slipped the whetstone from his pocket once more.

Lem shrugged, hitched up his pants, and took a couple of steps away before pausing. "I'd hate to see you make the same mistake I did, son."

Chapter 7

Jane adjusted the kerosene lamp, slipped out of her wrapper, and eased her aching body into the tub. A glance at the clock told her Harrison wouldn't be in for another hour yet, so she had plenty of time for a good soak.

And a good think.

For the past month, she'd been too busy and too tired to think, but a rare rainy day had put a halt to the haying and endless garden work and allowed a respite. Harrison, ignoring the chance to rest, had donned his slicker, saddled up, and gone out to check on his herd, spelling Reed and giving him his first day off in weeks.

She rested her head against the back of the tub and closed her eyes. They were so close. Ranchers had already started sending hands to buy winter feed, wagonload by wagonload. With each purchase, Harrison added to his reserves, making notes in his ledger. If she could just hold out until the deadline, this endless round of toil would ease off. Harrison would've won his ranch, and her future here with him would be secure. She would be safe to let herself love him.

Raising her hand to the lamplight, she studied the hard-earned calluses. Though she couldn't remember a time when her hands had been soft and beautiful, they'd never been this rough and work-worn. In spite of wearing gloves, the daily toil with the hay rake had raised blisters. She'd had to keep her hands hidden from Harrison until new calluses formed, though with as little as she saw of him these days, it wasn't difficult. He left before sunup, returned after dark, ate whatever she left for him in the warmer, and fell into bed.

Not that her days looked much different from his. Early mornings she hurried through her housework and cared for the cows and chickens, picked whatever was ripe in the garden and spread it to dry between layers of weighted cheesecloth, and then it was off to the corral to stack hay, walking in endless circles, spreading what Lem pitched from the hayrack. In the evenings she pulled together a simple meal for herself and Lem, who helped her put up whatever foodstuffs she hadn't gotten to from the garden that morning, and then to bed to fall asleep before Harrison came in.

Today, in spite of the rain, she'd done laundry. Lem had protested that she should rest, but she pointed out that since they couldn't work outside this was the perfect opportunity to catch up on other chores. Now garments hung drying from lengths of rope stretched across the soddy, shirts lay over the backs of chairs, and her delicates draped over the foot of the bed.

In the midst of all this splendor, she let the hot water soothe her aches. Boadicea rose from the quilt, stretched, and wrapped her tail around herself, regarding Jane with accusing eyes. Or at least they seemed accusing to Jane's tender conscience.

"I know. But how am I going to tell him? And when? He's never here." The suspicion nagging at the back of Jane's mind for weeks now had become a certainty. She counted backward to her wedding day, to that first week of happily wedded bliss. Almost four months. Guilt tightened her chest. The timing couldn't be worse. Her desire to linger in the warm water waned.

Scrubbing quickly, she got out, dried, and donned a nightgown and wrapper. Placing her hands on her abdomen, she couldn't deny the thickening at her waist. It was time to acknowledge that she was carrying Harrison's child. She drew a shuddering breath, not knowing whether to laugh or cry and too tired to do either.

How would a child affect Harrison's plans? They had never spoken of starting a family, and since their first week of marriage, it hadn't even been a danger. He'd apparently taken her touch-me-not demeanor to heart. That and they were both too exhausted every night to do anything more than collapse. A baby was the last thing on Harrison's mind right now, and the very last thing he needed to worry about.

She couldn't tell him. He'd forbid her to work on the haying. Not that she would mind never picking up a hay rake again, but he needed her. Harrison was focused on his goal, throwing all his effort into winning the ranch. He didn't have the time or energy to be burdened with anything else.

Thunder boomed as she climbed into bed and scooted over toward the wall. Boadicea protested with a meow and settled herself near Jane's feet. Jane pressed her hand against her stomach. A tiny fluttering under her palm made her freeze. Had she imagined it? Lying perfectly still, she waited. . .

There it was again. Like butterfly wings. Faint, but insistent.

Her throat tightened. Nothing in her marriage was right. Her husband, who was supposed to be her gallant knight and rescuer, needed her hard work but didn't love her, was even now riding through a downpour to check on his herd instead of snuggled beneath the covers with her, and what should've been the most exciting and happiest news she could share with him was now her secret burden to bear.

Lord, I feel so alone.

Sleep dragged at her eyes, and her last thought was to wonder if the wait to be loved would ever end.

❧

The rain finally slackened off, just in time for Harrison to make it back to the barn. Soaked to the skin, hungry, and more tired than he could ever remember being, he stripped the saddle from his wet horse. Mechanically, he rubbed the animal down with a grain sack and fed him.

Not a glimmer of light shone from the soddy. Jane must be in bed already. His heart sank. He'd hoped that with a day to herself with no outside chores, she might've been rested enough to at least stay up until he got home. He headed toward the bunkhouse to check in with Reed and Lem. His boots squelched with each step along the path.

Warm lamplight spilled over him as he knocked and opened the door. The smell of hot coffee and biscuits made his mouth water and his stomach rumble.

His two hired hands sat at a plank table playing dominoes. Reed stood as Harrison entered and removed his drenched hat.

"Evening, boss. Everything all right with the cattle?" He motioned for Harrison to take his chair and perched on the end of his bunk.

"Right as can be. With all this rain you'll have to watch the trouble spots along the creek over the next few days and make sure none of them bog down."

Lem tipped his chair back and snagged a tin cup. "Coffee's hot."

Harrison helped himself, inhaling the warm fragrance. He stripped out of his slicker and pulled the chair up to the stove. "Sure hope things dry out quickly."

"The rain isn't all bad. The grass will grow, and we could use the break." Lem ladled up a plate of stew and biscuits. "Tuck in to this. Jane brought it over this afternoon, so it's edible, not like Reed's cooking."

The kid shrugged. "I never claimed to be no cook. I can only make beans and rice anyway." He picked up a lariat and twisted the rope until it creaked. "We got all the tools sharpened and went over the wagon and all the harnesses. Everything's tight."

"You've done well, both of you. I know I've asked a lot, and there's still plenty to do, but I never would've gotten this far without you."

Lem grunted and laced his fingers on his belly. "Or Jane. Best thing you ever did, marrying that gal. I don't know how she does it. Even today, instead of resting like she should've, she was scrubbing laundry, mine and Reed's, too. Said a rainy day was the perfect day to catch up on other chores."

Harrison's fork stopped halfway to his mouth. "Laundry?"

"Yeah, and she had me string a couple of ropes for her so she could hang clothes up to dry."

"Boss, two riders from the Circle M passed through with word that their foreman wants to buy some feed. He says it's plain foolishness to pay for grass, but the ranch owner says better safe than sorry. They'll take a couple of tons, and they'll send the wagons and hands to load it."

Harrison managed a smile. Word was spreading.

"That will help, won't it? Will we still be here ranching come spring?" Reed tossed the rope onto the bed. His blue eyes held the same worry Harrison knew lingered in his own.

"If hard work and praying can do it, we will."

Letting his chair fall back onto all four legs, Lem inclined his head to Reed, who nodded. "Boss, me and Reed have been talking, and there's something we want to say."

Harrison stilled. Lem's sober face and tone sent a chill racing through him. If they quit, he'd lose the ranch for sure. *Please, Lord, don't let it be that.*

"We know you've been about killing yourself trying to meet your dad's demands, and we know every penny is precious. So we have a proposition for you. Me and the kid have been talking it over, and we've decided we don't want any wages for the next little while."

"What? No. Absolutely not. You can't work for nothing."

"Sure we can. And it wouldn't be for nothing." Lem eased his suspenders over his shoulders. "If you lose this ranch, we lose our jobs. Neither of us has forgotten how you brought us out here and gave us jobs when nobody else would. Since the accident that mangled up my leg, I had to quit the factory. But you still thought I could be useful, and that means a lot to me."

Reed nodded. "And you didn't listen to all the folks who told you I was too dumb to work. You taught me to read and write, which nobody'd ever been able to do before, and you gave me a job and your trust. I ain't forgetting that."

Harrison studied his hands, humbled to his core. "I don't know what to say." Their wages, though modest, added back into the total would go a long way toward reaching their goal. "When this is over, I'll pay you both back. I promise." He held out his hand to shake Lem's then Reed's.

"We ain't worried about that."

Harrison knew a lightening of heart as he made his way to the soddy, something that hadn't happened in quite a while. He had the best crew in Wyoming Territory.

As quietly as he could, he eased open the door and slipped inside. Jane had left the firebox open on the stove, and pale orange light illuminated the lines of drying clothes. Boadicea's green eyes glowed from the end of the bed.

He let the cat sniff his fingers and stroked her furry cheek. She rumbled a purr, stood, and walked to the door to be let out. Navigating the clotheslines and the still-full bathtub, he got ready for bed.

The minute he slid between the sheets, Jane turned toward him, as she always did when she was asleep. His arm went around her, and she tucked her head under his chin. The pillow she clamped to her middle pressed against his side, and her soft breathing feathered across the base of his neck.

He brushed a kiss across the top of her head and closed his eyes, his muscles relaxing by increments. She might remain aloof during the day, but at night, she slept in his arms. He yawned, his thoughts already evaporating into sleep. But one notion persisted. The minute the ranch was his, the instant he could finally relax and think of something besides that contract, he was going to start courting his wife like she deserved. He was determined to find that sweet, spontaneous, loving girl he'd caught a glimpse of the first week they were wed.

Chapter 8

Jane walked another round on the haystack, careful of the edge now that she was several feet off the ground. The wheatgrass slipped and slid under her feet, seeds and chaff floating around her, sticking to her skin and clinging to her clothes. Sweat trickled between her shoulder blades.

Lem pitched the last forkful of hay from the wagon and stopped to swipe his handkerchief over his face and neck. "Sure wish that rain would come back. Hot enough to fry a stove lid."

She let the heavy rake fall from her fingers and shaded her eyes. Harrison was a tiny dot on the hillside across the creek, a perfect picture of how far her heart felt from him. Her hand started for her waist, but she stopped, not wanting Lem or anyone else to guess her secret.

She dropped to her seat and slid off the partially formed haystack, her feet thudding on the baked earth. The shade cast by the barn beckoned her, and she straggled to it, aching from head to foot and fighting a wicked headache. Lem hefted the water jug from under the wagon seat and toted it to where she leaned against the barn wall.

"Here, take a few sips of this. Not too much now. Don't want you getting sick."

She tilted the earthenware jug and let the lukewarm water trickle into her parched mouth. Though she wanted to gulp it down, she heeded Lem's advice. Her bonnet slid off her hair, and she welcomed the breeze on her face.

"Who do you reckon that is?" Lem stepped around the wagon, shaded his eyes, and squinted. A plume of dust followed a dark carriage.

Jane blinked. Heat made the landscape shimmer, and she wondered if she was seeing things. As the vehicle grew larger, sunlight glinted off glass. A carriage with glass windows? Out here?

Lem let out a chuckle. "Awful fancy rig. Somebody got lost. Must've made a wrong turn at Saint Louie." He took the jug from Jane and wet his handkerchief, swiping the damp cloth over his reddened face. "Looks like Harrison sees it, too."

Her husband was headed down the far hill, scythe over his shoulder. It almost appeared as if he and the carriage were on a collision course. She shook her aching head. The heat was making her giddy.

Blinking away odd, black spots on the edges of her vision, she took the jug from Lem, but it seemed too heavy for her leaden limbs, and she dropped it. "I'm shorry." She cleared her throat. "I'm sorry." But she made no move to pick up the container, and the water glugged onto the parched ground.

Hooves clattered, harness jingled, and a horse snorted. Jane took all this in, keeping her eyes closed against a wave of dizziness.

"That you, Barton? Where's Harrison?" An imperious voice forced her eyelids open, and she stared into a face that seemed acutely familiar, though her mind didn't seem to be working well and she couldn't place him. "Is this her? The girl he married?"

The gray-haired man, immaculate in a dark suit, climbed from his coach. He pointed with his cane. "Where is that son of mine?"

"Mr. Garvey?" The name slipped out between her stiff lips, and she had just a glimpse of Harrison rounding the corner of the corral when the ground rushed up and smacked her in the head.

❧

Harrison pulled his chair closer to Jane's bedside and bathed her face with a cool, damp cloth. When she'd fainted, he'd died about a hundred deaths, and his heart still *whumped* erratically. Fear stalked him, armed with spears and arrows of guilt.

This is your fault. How stupid could you be? You had no business letting her help with the haying.

"Where is that doctor?" His father smacked his cane-head into his palm.

"It's a long ride into Sagebrush, and the doc might've been out on his rounds." Harrison brushed baby-fine wisps of hair off Jane's temples. Her skin was so pale and clammy. "Thank you for sending Lem in your carriage."

His father waved aside the thanks. "How is she?"

"I don't know. I wish she'd wake up." He wrung out the cloth and placed it against her forehead. Hours had passed since Lem had pelted it to town, and she hadn't so much as flickered her eyelashes.

His father grunted and pursed his lips, making his mustache poke out. "This is utter nonsense. Look at this place." He waved toward the clay-plastered walls and canvas ceiling. "What kind of hole is this to live in? It's a wonder you aren't all sick in bed. I wish you'd listen to reason. And another thing. . ." He levered himself up from the table. Hampered by the small space, he could only pace two steps before having to turn around. "I don't like it that you've ignored my letters. I haven't heard from you in weeks, not since you told me you got married. What was I supposed to think? Regular communication, you promised. I don't like being ignored. Now I arrive to find you looking like a scarecrow, down to skin and bones, and that girl beyond the brink of collapse. And what for? Hardheaded mule."

"Not now. We'll talk about all that later." Harrison glanced out the open doorway at the gathering dusk. Pushing himself upright, he stretched his back and worked the kinks out of his shoulders, stiff from bending over the bed. Digging into the matchbox, he withdrew a match and scratched it on the heel of his boot. Raising the glass on the lantern, he touched the flame to the wick, inhaling the pungent kerosene-smoke smell. "I need to go take care of the stock. Will you sit with her?"

"Of course." His father leaned his cane against the table and took Harrison's chair. "I'll be right here."

Harrison headed toward the barn in the fading light. The cow had to be milked, the animals fed and watered, but the whole time he worked, his mind was back in the soddy. If Jane didn't recover, he would never get over his guilt. Driving her so hard. And for what? A few acres of land?

He knew a flash of anger. Why hadn't she told anyone she didn't feel well? Why had she pushed herself so hard? She'd promised to tell him if the work was too much for her.

His conscience shoved him. Hard. Jane wasn't to blame for this. It was his fault. And the minute she woke up, he was going to tell her so, beg her forgiveness, and make plans to return to Columbus. Life here was too difficult, even for his redoubtable Jane. His shoulders sagged, and he leaned against Buttercup's warm flank. Though he hated to admit defeat, he would, for Jane's sake.

At least his father would be pleased at getting his way.

He set the entire bucket of milk into the calf pen, not wanting to bother with straining and storing it. The calf could enjoy it instead.

Emerging from the barn, he drew in a deep breath, contemplating the faint stars emerging as the sunlight faded. He loved this ranch, this wide-open land, and it would be a wrench to lose it. But the truth was, he loved Jane more, and he would give it all up to have her love. He only hoped he got the chance to tell her.

Chapter 9

Why couldn't she seem to open her eyes? She frowned and tried again, this time rewarded by a sliver of lamplight before her heavy lids fell again.

She ached. From the top of her head to the soles of her feet, everything hurt. And her brain felt as if someone had wrapped it in wool. She moistened her lips, or tried to, but her mouth was so dry she only snagged her tongue on her chapped lips.

What time was it? She needed to get up. She needed to get to work, to help Harrison keep his ranch, so maybe he would love her. Feebly, she tried to move aside the quilt, but firm, gentle hands stopped her.

"Here now. You need to lie still and rest."

A strange voice. With every ounce of energy, she forced her eyes to open, but they didn't seem to want to focus.

"Harrison?"

"He's gone to stretch his legs. We're waiting for the doctor, and Harrison's been glued to your side for hours. I thought he needed a break. He hasn't left you except to do the chores since you first passed out."

"Thirsty." A desert fire raged in her throat, rasping her voice.

Awkwardly, he held her head up a bit and pressed a tin cup of water to her lips. Thankfully, she gulped the refreshing liquid until no more remained.

"Is that sufficient?"

She nodded and closed her eyes, fatigue rolling over her in waves.

"What time is it?"

"About two in the morning. The physician should arrive any time."

"Who are you?" she whispered.

"I'm your father-in-law, Rutherford."

Jane bit her chapped lip but couldn't stem the rush of tears that leaked from her eyes. She hiccuped on a sob.

"Here now. Here. What's wrong? Are you in pain?"

"This is all my fault."

"You can't help being ill." He patted her hand, rough and tender at the same time, this man she'd labeled a dragon to be battled in the quest for Harrison's ranch and happiness.

His gentleness seemed to open the floodgates where she'd stored up so much fear and pain and sorrow. Tears ran into her hair, and she couldn't muster the strength to wipe them away, nor could she seem to stop them.

"Do you want me to fetch Harrison?" Rutherford pressed a handkerchief into her hand, his voice gruff.

She shook her head. "No, please." Here she was supposed to be helping Harrison reach his dream, proving to him that she was a good helpmeet, and look at her. A bedridden, sobbing mess, not only failing to help him but taking him away from his work all afternoon and evening to care for her. What kind of impression was she making on his father?

She pressed the handkerchief to her lips. "He must be so disappointed in me." The words came out all broken, half-stifled. "I'll never earn his love now." Her heart cracked wide open.

"What kind of nonsense is this? Harrison isn't the least disappointed in you. That boy is besotted, judging from the letter he wrote me just after you married. He filled page after page about you. I couldn't have been more pleased. That's half the reason I came all this way. I wanted to meet the woman who could make my son wax lyrical."

She blinked, smearing tears with the back of her hand. "You're mixed up. He wouldn't wax lyrical about me. Sylvia Norwood maybe, but not Plain Jane."

"What's Sylvia got to do with anything? Proper little baggage. Everything has worked out perfectly. I couldn't have planned it better." He rubbed his hands on his knees, smiling like a cat with canary feathers decorating its whiskers. "I know my son better than he thinks I do."

"What do you mean?" The tears abated in the face of her curiosity. If only she had the strength to get out of bed, or even to lift her head off the pillow.

"My son is as stubborn as his father. I knew if I crammed Sylvia Norwood down his throat, she would be the last woman he'd marry. And I was right. Not only did he not marry Sylvia, he found himself a bride all on his own." Rutherford cackled and slapped his leg. "Yep, I know Harrison. I'm tickled to death he defied my wishes and came out here to make his own way. Seems to be a family tradition. I did the same with my father. Do you think he owned a factory? No he did not. He owned a fleet of barges on the Ohio River, and he expected me to take over for him, but I struck out on my own, built my own empire. And I wanted Harrison to do the same."

Trying to make sense of this incomprehensible man, she asked, "But what about the contract?"

"What good would it do him if he had it too easy? If he had too much money too soon, it would ruin him. He needed to fight, to prove to himself that he could do it, that he didn't need family money to reach his dreams."

His reasoning baffled her, but she was too tired to sort it out. Her eyelids fell, and she rushed toward sleep.

L

The doctor arrived just before dawn, yawning and blinking. Harrison greeted him at the door and brought him to Jane, who still slept soundly.

Rutherford jerked awake from dozing in a chair. He'd refused to go to the bunkhouse to sleep, though Harrison had encouraged him to.

"Tell me what happened." Dr. Iverson shrugged out of his jacket and rolled up his sleeves. "How long has she been asleep and what brought on her faint?"

His eyes were so piercing, Harrison was taken right back to his schoolboy days, caught in some prank or other. "She passed out yesterday just after noon. We were putting up hay, and I guess the heat got to her."

"She woke up a few hours ago, cried her eyes out, and fell asleep again." Rutherford rubbed his bristly cheek.

The doctor frowned. "All of you go out. I want to examine her."

Once on the other side of the door, Harrison couldn't stand still. He paced the grass, and while he paced, he prayed:

Lord, please let her be all right. I'll get her out of here as soon as possible, just let her wake up and be fine. I have so much I need to tell her.

Lem brought a pot of coffee and plate of biscuits from the bunkhouse.

"How is she doing?" The worry in the old man's eyes bespoke his affection for Jane. "It's my fault. I should've noticed she was ailing."

Harrison bit into a biscuit and grimaced. What had he made these out of? Damp wool and sawdust?

"She's still sleeping. Doc kicked us out so he could take a look at her."

After what seemed half of forever, the door finally opened. Doc stood there, wiping his hands on a towel.

Harrison wheeled. "How is she?" His heart acted like a jackrabbit with a coyote on its tail.

"You two need to talk. She'll tell you."

"She's awake?"

"She is. And my prescription is for the two of you to get things straightened out between you. She's got some odd notions that need disabusing. Beyond that, she needs bed rest and building up. She's underweight and overworked in addition to being overwrought. No more fieldwork and not much of any kind of work for at least a month."

"But she'll be fine?" He hardly dared hope.

"Eventually, if you go carefully." Dr. Iverson smiled. "What are you standing there for? She's waiting." He stepped aside and Harrison took a deep, steadying breath before entering the soddy.

The time had come. Jane pushed herself up against the pillows, so weak her limbs shook. Harrison closed the door and leaned against it, crossing his arms. She needed to get in first, before he said anything.

"I'm sorry. The last thing in the world you needed was to be pulled away from your work to tend to me. And now you have the added expense of the doctor. I'm sure I'll be fine in a day or so." She swallowed, trying not to sound as pitiful as she felt. "This won't set you back from meeting the contract, will it?"

"I don't care about the contract. My father can have the place. I won't need it."

"What?"

Harrison left the door and came to her side, dropping to his knees and taking her hand. "Jane, I'm not keeping the ranch. That contract has done nothing but drive us apart. When you first came here, you were so happy, and you made me happy. You filled a place in my life and heart that I didn't even realize was empty. Then Lem told you about the contract and you changed. All that joy and hope disappeared." He lifted her hand and brushed a kiss across her fingers. "I want the old Jane back. The one I married. And I won't have her killing herself to help me get a ranch. It isn't worth it."

She stared at the quilt. Was he really willing to give everything up, everything he'd worked for, just for her? She raised her eyes to examine his face.

"Jane, darling, I love you. I think I've loved you from the minute you first set foot on this ranch. Look at this house." He swept his arm to encompass the small room. "You took a hovel and made it a home. You bring light and joy wherever you go. You're loving and giving, and so sweet it makes my chest hurt. My father said you called yourself Plain Jane." He squeezed her fingers. "I don't ever want you to even think that again." His hand came up to touch her cheek. "You are the most beautiful woman I've ever met. I could willingly get lost in your beautiful eyes. I want to spend the rest of my life proving my love and earning yours."

Afraid to hope, yet unable to deny him, she leaned into his caress. "You love me? Me, Plai—" His hand stopped the words.

"I love you, beautiful, sweet, adorable, strong, amazing Jane Garvey." Gently, but insistently, he gathered her into his arms. His lips found hers, giving and taking, healing and renewing. Love for him overwhelmed her. This was what she had waited for all her life. When he broke the kiss, she rested her cheek against his strong chest, thrilling to the erratic beating of his heart.

"Harrison, there are a few things you should know."

"What?" He brushed a kiss across her hair.

"I don't want you to give up the ranch. We've got so much invested here. All your dreams."

"Not all. My dreams are bound up in you now."

"Well then, my dreams are here. I want to stay. To see this through." She cupped his stubbly cheeks and stared into his eyes, willing him to understand how important this was to her. When he still seemed unconvinced, she said, "I want our baby to be born here, on his father's ranch."

His eyebrows rose. "Baby?"

She nodded, her throat too thick for words.

He exhaled on a half laugh, blinked, and shook his head. "You're sure?"

"Yes, the doctor confirmed it."

He was off the floor and resting beside her on the bed before she could blink. His arm went around her, and he cradled her close. Reverently, he placed his hand on her abdomen and kissed her temple. "Ah, Jane, I didn't think I could love you more, but you're proving me wrong. I think I've been waiting for you my whole life."

She wrapped her arms around his neck and leaned in to him. "Me, too."

When they broke the news to Rutherford, he couldn't stop grinning. "How about that? A grandchild. Your mother would be so proud if she could see you now." He tapped his fist against the edge of the table.

Jane sipped chicken broth from a cup, resigned after much haranguing and negotiation to being on bed rest for the next couple of weeks. Harrison hovered, anxious and loving by turns.

Rutherford dug inside his suit pocket and withdrew a long envelope. "This is yours, son. My gift to you and Jane. It's the deed to the ranch. Enough of this standoff. I'm tickled to death at the start you've made here. Now it's time to bury pride and be done with that foolish contract. I only cornered you into signing it because I knew you'd get your back up and determine to make good on it."

Harrison froze. "Are you serious?"

"Never more so. The place is yours. Though you can do me one more favor."

"What?"

"Get that house out of storage and get it built. I don't intend to sleep in a dirt house when I come to visit my grandchild. Jane"—his eyes twinkled—"Harrison has been too stubborn to accept my gift of a house, but I know you're smarter than he is, and you'll see reason. I'm giving you that house, and I'm trusting you to convince him to get it built before the snow flies."

She leaned her head against the pillows, tickled at the outraged expression on her husband's face that quickly turned to sheepish pleasure.

"I think I can manage that."

Late that night, cradled in her husband's arms, Jane sighed.

"What's that for?" Harrison smoothed her hair back from her face and brushed a kiss across her brow.

She savored the security of his embrace. "All my life I dreamed of a gallant knight who would come and sweep me off my feet, carry me away to his castle, and love and cherish me forever."

"Huh, too bad you got stuck with me."

She levered herself up to look down into his eyes in the glow of the lamplight. "How can you say that? You are a gallant knight. You brought me all the way to Wyoming Territory to your castle on the plains, made me fall in love with you, then made me the happiest woman alive by loving me back. You're a wonderful husband and provider, and you're going to be a wonderful father. What more could a woman ask?"

He caressed her cheek and let his hand drop to cup her shoulder through the thin lawn of her nightgown. "Jane Garvey, you're amazing. I knew it the first time I saw you, and you've been surprising me every day since. I can hardly wait to see what you'll do next. If I'm a knight, you're my lady." He brought her down for a gentle kiss.

She snuggled close, wrapping her arm across his flat stomach and pressing her swelling abdomen against his side. As her eyes drifted closed, she envisioned her knight holding a little lord or lady in his arm, his other encircling her waist, and a smile curved her lips. Her wait for love had finally come to an end.

ERICA VETSCH

Even though Erica Vetsch has set aside her career teaching history to high school students in order to homeschool her own children, her love of history hasn't faded. Erica's favorite books are historical novels and history books, and one of her greatest thrills is stumbling across some obscure historical factoid that makes her imagination leap. She's continually amazed at how God has allowed her to use her passion for history, romance, and daydreaming to craft historical romances that entertain readers and glorify Him. Whenever she's not following flights of fancy in her fictional world, Erica is the company bookkeeper for her family's lumber business, a mother of two, wife to a man who is her total opposite and yet her soul mate, and an avid museum patron.

Shining Armor

by Erica Vetsch

Chapter 1

Would her soon-to-be husband be a knight or a dragon? In just a few moments, she'd find out. A cluster of buildings in the distance grew larger, as did the ball of anxiety in her middle.

Gwendolyn Gerhard twisted a piece of string around her index finger, unwound it, and wound it again, all the while jolting and jostling in the wagon next to the crankiest preacher she'd ever encountered.

Reverend Cummings hunched over, his elbows on his knees, his face set in a scowl. Had he ever heard of the joy of the Lord? At least he wasn't talkative. Not that she would've minded getting a little information out of him, but every time he opened his mouth, crabbiness flowed out.

Her sister Emmeline rode in the wagon behind her, taking in everything about their surroundings. After Gwendolyn got married, Emmeline would have to go on alone to her own wedding without the benefit of any of her sisters in attendance. Though she didn't seem worried. Of all the Gerhard girls, Emmeline had most embraced the notion of coming West as a mail-order bride.

Gwendolyn wound the string again, noting the ridges it caused in her finger. The shock of leaving her two oldest sisters just moments after each of their weddings hadn't quite worn off. This morning when they set out from the town of Sagebrush in southeastern Wyoming Territory, they had all been single women. Now Evelyn and Jane were married, Evelyn had acquired a stepdaughter in addition to her son, Jamie, and Jane was living in a dirt house.

That might've been me. After all, the selection of husbands had been a bit haphazard, with each sister picking a name from the list of four who had answered their advertisement. If she had chosen Gareth or Harrison instead of Zebulon, she might now be the mother to an angry young hellion of a girl or residing in a sod hut. According to Cranky Cummings, she was next on his mail-order-bride delivery route, and who knew what fate awaited her there? Of the four applicants, she knew the least about hers. Where her sisters had all received letters, she had only a telegram.

> *Sending train and stage fare. Stop. Come as soon as possible. Stop. Warmly, Zebulon Parker. Stop.*

At least he'd included the word *warmly*. Not exactly a love letter to melt a girl's heart but better than nothing.

In spite of the shocks of reality, she couldn't quite bring herself to be downhearted. For the first time in her life, she felt as if the doors had flown wide open. Living with a widowed father and three older sisters was like having three mothers. One or all of them usually had some correction, suggestion, or instruction regarding her appearance, her posture, or almost anything else she could name. With Evelyn a Civil War widow, the house had been somber and structured most of the time. And her father, while giving them all a deep appreciation for medieval history and classical literature, had often been distant and distracted, living in some castle in Camelot in his head and only surfacing to the real world periodically.

Of course, Camelot was a fine place to escape to. How often had she dreamed of Sir Gawain or Lancelot riding to her rescue, scaling ramparts, slaying dragons, laying siege to her heart? A man who would want her for the rest of her life, who would offer love, laughter, and a life together?

She pressed her palm against her skirt pocket, crinkling the telegram. Being a mail-order bride had little to do with the romance of her girlish fantasies, yet she couldn't help hoping—dreaming—just a little, that she was traveling to meet her knight.

The buildings were growing uncomfortably and excitingly near. A lump lodged in her throat, and her heart beat double-time. Pressing her lips together, she tried to sort out the structures ahead. A barn, sheds, and outbuildings, and oh, praise be, a house.

A two-story, wooden clapboard house. She threw a quick glance over her shoulder at Emmeline, who grinned back. No soddy or log cabin for Gwendolyn. She'd have a proper house, with a wide porch that wrapped around two sides, glass windows, and gables. There were even saplings planted in the yard and a picket fence with a gate. Though the barn and outbuildings bore some signs of age, the house looked surprisingly new and well kept.

Several figures moved between and around the buildings. Which one was *him*? She swallowed. Soon, she'd meet her intended, her knight in shining armor. *Please, Lord, let him be a knight and not a dragon.*

Reverend Cummings pulled the wagon up in front of the house with a grunt. "Parker's place."

A long, sloping ramp led to the porch—the boards even newer than the house appeared to be, still yellow and filling the air with a sawdust-and-pine redolence. A hundred questions popped into Gwendolyn's head, colliding and bouncing off one another. She gathered her skirts and her courage and climbed from the wagon on the side away from the house. Emmeline joined her, clutching Gwendolyn's hand with chilly fingers. The wagon box was so high, they could barely see over it. Movement caught her eye. The men working near the barn and in the corral all headed their way.

Cummings rounded the back of the wagon and unpinned the tailgate, muttering and grumbling.

The men, six in all, approached and formed a half circle around the wagon, staring and shifting their weight. She searched each of the faces, praying for a glimpse of recognition, hoping she would know Zebulon Parker when she saw him. But though she surveyed each one carefully, nothing special happened, not on their faces or in her heart. They were just men.

Some looked away from her scrutiny, some reddened and shrugged, and one grinned and raked her with his gaze. Though handsome, with black hair and mustache and glinting green eyes, he wore an insolent expression that diminished his good looks. *Please, Lord, don't let this be him.*

She'd been saying a lot of "Please, Lords" over the past few weeks.

The screen door squeaked. A man's voice—she couldn't see him over the heads of the other men gathered around—broke the silence. "What're you doing standing around? I'd think, heading out on the range like you are tomorrow, there'd be plenty to keep you boys busy."

The men parted, and Gwendolyn sucked in a breath.

Broad shoulders, lean hips, long legs, and brilliant eyes so blue they seemed to sparkle, even from this distance. She grabbed hold of the side of the wagon and peeked over the edge at him.

"Oh my," Emmeline whispered. "Do you think that's him?"

He strode across the porch, scorned the ramp, and leaped to the ground in a lithe movement. "Padre, what brings you out this way?"

Cummings dragged a trunk toward himself, cocked an eyebrow at the girls as if to ask "is this the right luggage?" and at their nod, hefted it from the wagon box. "I don't have time to palaver. I brung your bride. Let's get this wedding over and done with."

The blue-eyed man laughed and shoved his hat to the back of his head, revealing a forelock of reddish-brown hair. "Right. Tell me another while you're at it." His thumbs went into his belt loops. "Seriously, it's been awhile since you've been through. On your way to Dellsville? Need a place to stay, or are you going to try to make it before nightfall?"

"I *am* on my way to Dellsville. I don't need a place to stay, and I'm serious about the wedding." The trunk hit the dirt. "One of these two gals. Not sure which. You'll have to ask them which is which. Where's Zeb? He knows all about it."

"You can stop kidding around, Cummings. We're not much in the mood for it around here. I don't know anything about a bride, and you can't talk to Zeb. He isn't here."

Gwendolyn bit her bottom lip, gripping the side of the wagon box until her hands ached. Obviously this young man couldn't be her intended. Odd that she should feel a little swoop of disappointment when she didn't even know the man. But where was Zebulon?

Grimness stole over the young man's face, and his voice lowered. "Zeb passed away two weeks ago."

This brought Cummings to a halt. His perpetual scowl deepened. "I hadn't heard." He adjusted his jacket and scratched his chin. "His heart?"

"We've known for a while that he could go at any time, but it's still a shock."

"Too bad, but the wedding can go on just the same."

The man's hand shot out in a throwaway gesture. "What wedding? Make sense, man."

The reverend motioned toward Gwendolyn and Emmeline. "Come around here. Which of you is supposed to marry a Parker?"

Emmeline's grip on Gwendolyn's arm made her fingers tingle, but Gwendolyn rounded the wagon. "I am." She hoped her voice didn't sound as small and bewildered as she felt. If it was true that her intended had passed away, where did that leave her? "Zebulon's dead? Are you sure?"

The tall young man's gaze raked her from bonnet to boots. "Don't you think I'd know if my own grandfather was dead?"

She flinched at his harsh tone and the cloud of grief in his eyes. "Of course. I'm so sorry for your loss—wait. Your grandfather?" Her voice squeaked. "Zebulon Parker is—I mean, was—your grandfather?" Her mind cartwheeled.

"Just who are you, anyway?"

The reverend nudged the trunk out of his way and reached for a valise. "This one yours, missy?" He hefted it. "Zeb asked me to wait around Sagebrush until these gals arrived. I watched Zeb send the telegram myself, six weeks ago. I thought he looked poorly then but figured he'd just had a hard winter. She's one of those mail-order brides, her and her sisters. Zeb fetched her out from back East. Massachusetts, I think it was."

The cowboy jammed his fists on his waist and widened his stance. "That's ridiculous. Granddad would never send away for a bride. What kind of hoax are you trying to pull, Cummings?"

"No hoax. Gareth Kittrick, Harrison Garvey, Zeb, and Joe Barrett all worked it out together. One bride apiece. All sisters."

His narrowed eyes angled toward Gwendolyn then back to the preacher. "We've been bitten by this particular bug before, remember? And we all lived to regret it, though some not as long as others."

"It's true as I'm standing here. Lightning don't strike twice. This one won't be like Edith. Let's get to the marrying."

"Maybe you didn't hear me, Reverend. There's no marrying, because there's no groom. Zeb's dead, remember? You can just take this"—he jerked his thumb toward Gwendolyn—"this woman back where she came from."

"Then you marry her. I'm due in Dellsville, and you ain't my last stop before then. Won't take but a few minutes to say the words, and I can be on my way."

The scowl on the young man's face could've started a fire. "Whatever scheme you and Granddad and this money-grubbing female have cooked up, count me out. I'd rather be shot like a rabid coyote than marry a mail-order bride, especially a gold digger who would come all this way to marry a man three times her age."

Gwendolyn blinked, her ire rising to replace her bewilderment. It appeared knights in shining armor were singularly lacking on the Wyoming plains. She marched over to him and poked him in his well-muscled chest. "Sir, I'll admit to being flummoxed at this turn of events, but at least I haven't resorted to wild accusations or name-calling. For your information, I wouldn't have you if you were hung from top to toe with diamonds."

Matt Parker couldn't have been more stunned if she'd walked up and slugged him. For such a dainty-looking female, she had some grit, standing up to him that way. He stepped back and resisted rubbing the spot where she'd jabbed him. "Fine then. We're agreed. Nobody's getting married here. You can put those things back in the wagon, Cummings. The lady isn't staying."

Reverend Cummings got an even more mulish set to his jaw. "She surely is. I told Zeb I would pick her up, deliver her here, and see to the ceremony. He promised her a wedding, and a wedding is just what we're going to have."

"But how? Thankfully, a dead man can't get married, no matter what promises he made or what plans this finagler dreamed up." Matt ignored the indignant gasp from the girl.

"Zeb might be dead, but you ain't. You can hold up your granddad's end of the bargain. And don't give me that look. You'll keep his word, because there's no other help for it. I can't take her on with me, so get that notion out of your head."

Stepping between them, the girl glared from Matt to the reverend. "I'm not staying." She pushed her bonnet back, revealing hair the color of ripe wheat that curled around her face and looked as if it wanted to romp free of the pins holding it high on the back of her head. When she turned the full force of her gaze on him, he couldn't help but notice the deep purple-blue of her eyes, like the east sky just after sunset. "But I'll have you know, I came all the way from Massachusetts in good faith." She waved a piece of paper under his nose. "I have a telegram inviting me to come and asking me to hurry. I'm not in the habit of trapping men into marriages they don't want, nor am I after anyone's money. It's shameful of you to cast aspersions on my character when you don't even know me." She turned to the preacher. "Please return my things to the wagon."

Matt's men had stepped closer, eyebrows raised, smirking and elbowing one another. Having them witness this little set-to wouldn't do much for his authority around the place. "Don't you boys have something else you should be doing?"

"Nothing more interesting than this." Jackson tugged off his gloves and stuck them into his belt. "If you don't want her, boss, I'll have her. She's a looker. I wouldn't mind coming home to a pretty filly like her every night."

Matt scowled. "Watch your mouth, Jackson."

"Matt?"

The soft voice pulled his head around.

Betsy. He'd forgotten clean about her. "Be right there." Leaping to the porch, he held the screen door open. "Can you manage, or you want some help?"

"I've got it, I think." She wheeled herself through the opening, clunking down over the threshold. "Whoa, a bit bumpy."

"I'll fix that for you as soon as I can." Why hadn't he thought to ease that threshold when he built the ramp the other day? He added that task to his already gargantuan to-do list. At least the chore would keep him close to the house. With Granddad gone and Betsy confined to this contraption, he couldn't stray far from home these days.

"I know, Matt. Don't worry so much. We're all adapting as fast as we can." Her sweet smile ripped through his gut. How could she be so calm, so brave and accepting? How could a barely fifteen-year-old girl be so mature? He wanted to yell, scream, kick something, demand God tell him why. Why would He afflict such a gentle creature as Betsy with a disease that robbed her slowly of even the ability to walk? Why had He taken Granddad so suddenly, just when Matt needed him the most?

"Matt?"

He shook his head, clearing his thoughts, and let go of the door. It slapped, bounced, and settled.

She maneuvered her chair awkwardly toward the ramp. "Oh, hello, Reverend Cummings. How are you? Is your lumbago better?" Just like her to ask after someone else's ailment instead of dwelling on her own. Cummings grunted and kept rootling around in the wagon.

Matt guided her chair down the ramp and along the path to the gate. "Betsy, are you sure you should be outside? You aren't supposed to tax yourself, remember?"

"Don't fuss. I'll be fine." She extended her hand to the two women. "Hello, I'm Betsy, Matt's sister."

Matt held his breath. Folks could be so cruel, assuming just because someone was in a wheelchair, she must be an idiot who should be in an asylum. If this woman who claimed to be Granddad's bride so much as sneered, he'd pack her into Cummings's wagon like a bag of feed and send her on her way before she could say "rags to riches."

When she smiled with real friendliness at his sister, his breath snagged in his chest. In one thing at least, Jackson was right. She was a looker. But then again, Edith had been, too.

"How do you do? It's a pleasure to meet you. I'm Gwendolyn Gerhard." She took Betsy's hand. "I'm so sorry about your grandfather."

"I've been looking forward to meeting you." Betsy let her head rest against the wheelchair's high back. "I'm only sorry Granddad can't be here. I know he would've loved meeting you. He was really anticipating your arrival."

Matt rounded the chair. "What do you mean, you've been looking forward to meeting her? You knew she was coming?"

Betsy swallowed and nodded. "Granddad told me he was sending for someone." She toyed with the end of her braid, the coppery-red hair gleaming in the sunshine. "He said not to mention it to you just yet, that he would do it when the time was right. I guess he didn't get around to it before. . ." She let her words trail away.

Matt ground his back teeth. So this was real and not a hoax. Cantankerous, foolish old man. "Just what was his game? Didn't he learn anything from Edith? Why would the old man want to get married again?"

A peal of laughter caused every head to turn Betsy's way. "You didn't think Granddad brought her out here to marry *him*?" Again she laughed, such a rare sound these days, he wanted to bottle it. "He brought her out here for you. Said you weren't getting around to the job quickly enough, that Edith had soured you on women, and he didn't like the way you were headed." She grasped Matt's hand. "You aren't going to send her away, are you?" Her eyes pleaded with him. "I've been holding on, just waiting for her to arrive."

He'd been hard pressed to ever deny Betsy anything, and now with her trapped in that chair for the rest of her life, he found it even more difficult. But marriage was asking a bit much of a man.

Cummings thumped one of the girl's bags onto the porch. "Now see here, Parker. I'm in a hurry. I can't take the girl with me. I've got to take her sister out to Barrett's range, and you know he can't board her there. And Dellsville is no place for a decent woman. I'm supposed to be preaching a funeral service the minute I can get there, and daylight's wasting. Let's get to the marrying."

"I am not marrying her."

Every head turned their way, and Matt realized he'd all but shouted the words. Diamond-hard light glared in Cummings's eyes, and Matt had a feeling fire and brimstone might pour out of his mouth at any second. Not too many men cared to defy Cummings, who—it was whispered—had been a companion of John Brown's and contributed personally to giving Bleeding Kansas its nickname.

Jackson left his place among the drovers and sidled toward the girls. Though a good cowhand, he had a well-earned reputation as a skirt chaser, and the sight of him ogling the sisters tightened Matt's muscles. He stepped between his hired hand and the women.

Cummings crossed his arms. "I can't take her on with me."

Aware of the stares and anticipation hanging in the air, he found himself looking at the woman. Gwendolyn. What kind of an outlandish name was that? She clenched her fists and chewed her lower lip. She looked so vulnerable, standing in this circle of men like a filly being auctioned off.

"Reverend Cummings?" Betsy eased her chair forward. "When will you be coming back through this way?"

He scowled, his bushy eyebrows thrusting outward. “Six weeks, give or take. I have some business to transact over in Medicine Bow, and then I’ll have to make my regular circuit. Why?”

“I thought, maybe, Gwendolyn could stay here until you come back. There’s a spare bed in my room, and we could all get to know one another. Then, if it didn’t work out for her to marry Matt, you could pick her up on your way back through here.” Betsy lifted her face toward Matt, her eyes filled with appeal. “Please, Matt, can’t she stay, at least for a little while? She would be company for me.”

He found himself giving in, all the while deriding himself for being a fool.

Chapter 2

"That's settled. I'll see you in six weeks or so to sort this whole thing out." Pointing to Emmeline, Reverend Cummings motioned toward the wagon seat. "We're squandering daylight, so no dillydallying."

Emmeline ignored the cleric grouch and gripped Gwendolyn's hands, drawing her away from the crowd. "Gwendolyn, what are you going to do? What happens in six weeks when the reverend returns? Where will you go?"

"I don't know." Her eyes stung, her windpipe constricted, and she clutched her elder sister's hands as if they were her only lifeline in a tossing sea. While she hadn't expected hearts and flowers, she certainly hadn't expected to be treated like a leper in the place that was supposed to be her new home. The Parkers acted as if she were goods received on approval. *We'll try her out for a few weeks, and if we don't like her—and I expect we won't—you can take her back where she came from.*

"Hurry up!" The reverend slammed the tailgate shut.

Emmeline hugged her tight. "You're the smartest one of us all. You'll think of something." Her whisper did little to bolster Gwendolyn's confidence, and within moments, she found herself watching her sister disappear with the preacher. Emmeline waved and looked back until dust and distance obscured her.

Blinking and swallowing against the lump in her throat, Gwendolyn reminded herself that she had vowed to embrace the adventure. The reminder didn't work, and a tear slipped over her lower lashes. She swiped at it, aware of the stares. Nobody seemed to know what to say or where to look now that a stranger had been tossed into their midst like a rock in a pond.

At last, Betsy broke the silence. "Matt, why don't you bring the luggage in, and we'll show Gwendolyn the house?"

Her words broke him free of whatever had him trapped. . .probably shock, if her own reaction was anything to judge by. "Good idea. You men, get back to work. Those chores aren't going to do themselves." He hoisted her trunk. Her valise sat beside the gate, but when she picked it up, Betsy reached for it.

"I'll help. Set it on my lap." She reached for the bag, laughing. "Really, I can do it." Plumping the carpetbag, which wasn't all that heavy, onto her knees, she grabbed the wheels on the chair.

Gwendolyn relaxed a bit at this show of friendliness and took hold of the handle across the back of the chair. "I tell you what, you carry, and I'll push."

Aware of Matt's scrutiny, she maneuvered the chair carefully up the ramp and into the house. She stopped just inside the door, stunned.

The front room was crammed with furniture, settees, chairs, tables, lamps. Rugs lay over the top of one another, and bric-a-brac crowded shelves and tables. Heavy drapes blocked out the sunshine, and from what she could tell in the low light, dust cloaked every surface.

A narrow aisle led between the furnishings, and Matt stalked ahead, through a doorway in the far wall, refusing to offer any explanation as to the condition of the parlor. "This way."

Maneuvering the chair after him, Gwendolyn arrived at what she sensed was the hub of this home. Stark in comparison to the ornate parlor, the kitchen contained plain furnishings and an immense black stove. Dirty dishes sat on the table and counter. And a bare, glass-paned window let in light.

"We just finished lunch." Matt's defensive tone flicked her, but he continued. "Betsy isn't up to much housework, and I've been busy. I didn't exactly know we were going to have company." He trod heavily on the last word, emphasizing the temporariness of the situation. Her trunk landed with a thud on the floorboards. "You'll bunk with Betsy through here."

Gwendolyn shot Betsy a quick glance and was rewarded by a warm smile. Someone at least was glad she was here. Sharing a room with Betsy would be like sharing with Emmeline back home.

"You're going to love it here." Betsy gripped the valise handle. "When Granddad said he was sending for someone, I was so happy. I've always wanted a sister."

Matt stiffened. "Hold it right there, young lady. I am not getting married, so don't get any ideas. This is a mess of Granddad's making, and it's going to take some time to sort out, but six weeks from now when the reverend returns, you and I will be on the porch waving good-bye to this whole problem, understand? Anyway, you heard her. She wouldn't have me if I came dipped in diamonds."

Gwendolyn's ire flared. "Would you stop referring to me as a mess and a problem? It's not my fault your grandfather didn't explain things to you, or that he isn't here to do so now." She crossed the room and planted herself squarely in front of him. "If I had my druthers, I'd have been out of here so fast you wouldn't have seen me for dust." She snapped her fingers under his nose.

He blinked, taking a step back.

Betsy giggled. "You sound a little like Granddad standing up to Matt that way. I'm so glad you're here. Let's get your things put away, and don't mind him. He hates change of any kind, and things have been changing around here rather rapidly."

"I do not."

"Yes, you do."

He carried her trunk into the bedroom, and Betsy followed with the valise, both of them bickering in a way so familiar to Gwendolyn, a giant aching loneliness for her sisters swept over her. Though she chafed at her sisters' strictures, she missed them and would've given anything at that moment to have them here to boss her around.

"Are you coming?" Matt stuck his head through the doorway. She stopped woolgathering and entered the bedroom.

A chest of drawers stood between two iron bedsteads, though only one bed was made up. A china ewer and bowl painted with lavender flowers sat atop the dresser. A thin, limp set of curtains hung at the window. A feed store calendar adorned one wall, the only nonutilitarian object in the room. A chill went through Gwendolyn.

Matt slid the trunk toward the foot of the unmade bed. "Betsy can tell you where to find clean sheets and such, and you can unpack some things, but don't settle in too deep. As soon as I can make arrangements, I'll get you on your way back to where you came from." He took the valise from Betsy's lap and set it on top of the trunk.

Gwendolyn bit back the sharp reply that rose to her lips. He didn't have to keep reminding her that he planned to throw her out like used dishwater. "Very well."

"I'll help. It's going to be so nice to have another girl to talk to." Betsy noticed the ribbon holding her braid was coming loose, but when she tried to tie it, her fingers stumbled. Frowning, she tried again, but the shiny ribbon slipped from her grip. "Fiddlesticks, I'm all fumble-fingered today."

"Maybe she could leave the unpacking until later. You're tired." Matt stepped forward and tied the ribbon for her, his voice gruff. "You need to rest. You know the doctor said your symptoms get worse when you're tired."

Betsy submitted, and relief passed over Matt's face. He patted her shoulder awkwardly, and she smiled, covering his hand with her own for an instant. Gwendolyn tugged her bottom lip as she left them alone and returned to the kitchen.

A man like Matt, capable of such tenderness toward his sister, would make someone a wonderful husband. He clearly cared about Betsy, was protective of her. Somewhere under that gruff, contrary, dragonish exterior, there might be a knight in shining armor with a chivalrous heart.

But how did one go about exposing it?

Matt lifted his sister from her chair and eased her down on top of the covers. "You take a good nap." He brushed the red curls on her forehead. "I'll be close by when you wake up."

Betsy grabbed his hand. "Matt, she's nice, isn't she? And pretty. Did you see the way she took my hand and looked right into my eyes? Like I was a real person."

"You *are* a real person, and I'll clobber anyone who says different." He gave a mock growl, but he knew just what she meant. How many times over the years had people's eyes just slid right over Betsy? First the leg braces and canes, and now the wheelchair. Even the ranch hands were uncomfortable around her, not knowing what to say or do.

In that, at least, he couldn't fault their visitor. She'd certainly spoken to Betsy with more friendliness than she'd directed his way. Not that he could blame her. He hadn't been exactly cordial himself.

"It's been a long time since I had a girl to talk to." Betsy sighed, her eyes beginning to drift shut. "I really couldn't talk to Edith. She acted as if I wasn't even there." Her words slowed as she fell asleep.

Maybe, for the time being, having Gwendolyn here wouldn't be all that bad, not if she could bring a little happiness into Betsy's life.

He shook his head and left the room, easing the door almost closed so he could still hear if she called out. One glance into the crowded parlor brought him back to reality. No way was he going to be made a fool of. Women like Edith and Gwendolyn were only after one thing by marrying a man they didn't even know, and if that little miss thought she was going to sink her claws into him the way Edith had done to his father, she had another think coming.

When he returned to the kitchen, he stopped in the doorway. Gwendolyn stood at the dishpan, up to her elbows in soapy water.

"What are you doing?"

She glanced over her shoulder. "Is that rhetorical, or have you never seen anyone wash dishes before?"

Leaning against the door frame, he crossed his arms. "Got a little vinegar to you, don't you? And quite a vocabulary. You don't look old enough to have been a schoolteacher." He didn't know why he felt compelled to taunt her, unless it was to show her he wasn't fooled by her pretty ways and willingness to help out. Edith had been a new broom that swept clean, too. Before the rot set in.

"A schoolmaster's daughter." Cups sloshed through the soap and into the rinse water.

"And what does he think of you moving out here to marry an old man?"

"Like your grandfather, my father is dead, and fairly recently, too. That's why I, along with my sisters, was forced to advertise for a husband. We were being evicted from our home in Massachusetts at the boarding school where my father taught. I didn't know Zebulon Parker was a grandfather. I didn't know anything about him except that he lived in Wyoming Territory and was—I thought—looking for a wife. There wasn't time to learn anything else about him. We had no other options open to us. His telegram and the letters from the other three men were godsends, or so we thought."

He didn't miss the wry twist to her voice, but he wasn't going to rise to the bait. He wasn't anyone's godsend, thank you very much, nor did he want to be. "You didn't ask any questions or try to find out anything about the man you thought you were going to marry? No exchange of photographs, no letters? Not even an inquiry into his financial situation? You might've been jumping out of the frying pan and into the fire." Nobody would be that naive. Surely she'd probed Granddad's prospects before agreeing to marry him.

"My correspondence with your grandfather was by telegram only, and long telegrams cost more than I had to spend. I assumed that if he had the money to pay for my train fare, he couldn't be on his beam ends, and if he was a friend to the other gentlemen who wrote to my sisters, he must be all right. All we asked was that the gentlemen be God-fearing and live close together. Reverend Cummings assured us of the God-fearing part, though we're coming to realize a bit too late that our interpretation of 'close together' doesn't exactly match those of the ranchers out here."

He marveled that she didn't even try to hide her penniless state. Well, she wasn't going to get her hands on any Parker money, no matter what Granddad might've promised her. He glanced over his shoulder toward Betsy's bedroom door. His sister had taken an immediate shine to Gwendolyn, something she didn't normally do. Of course, she didn't have much of a chance to meet folks out here.

"I appreciate the way you've treated Betsy, but I've cautioned her, and I'll caution you again. You're not staying. Don't encourage any of her fancies. She's got a head full of romantic notions, and I don't want to see her get hurt."

Her hands stilled, and her shoulders drooped. Guilt at his harshness plucked his conscience. She had to be bone weary, coming all the way from Massachusetts to Sagebrush, bumping across the prairie in Cummings's wagon since before daybreak, and then landing in the middle of the Parker woes where all her plans had burned to cinders.

Before he did something stupid like apologize for telling the truth, he wheeled and headed up the narrow stairway to the top floor. He braced himself before the door to the bedroom across the hall from his. This room, like the parlor, went unused, tainted by the memory of Edith. He thrust those thoughts aside and entered. Her stamp was everywhere in the ornate furnishings. A four-poster bed with velvet drapes, dressing table, fly-spotted and dusty mirror, rugs—he should've tossed out the lot when Edith scarpered.

Ignoring the oppressive, cloying feel of the room, he crossed the carpet and pulled open the wardrobe. A set of plain sheets lay on the top shelf, but he pushed them aside and withdrew the set of bed linens farther back. Fine, expensive, snowy material with fancy stitching on the pillow slips. He might not've given her the warmest of welcomes, and he might have no intentions of letting her stay, but the Parkers could show a bit of hospitality to the stranger in their midst.

He returned to the kitchen, where she had finished washing the dishes and now leaned over the table, wiping it down. The nape of her neck caught his eye, vulnerable, soft, with wisps of golden hair teasing it. He swallowed. She'd removed her jacket, and to his way of thinking, her blouse fit her just fine. She straightened, and he wrenched his gaze away, chagrined to be caught staring.

"You can make up your bed with these." He held out the bundle of bedclothes. "I'd best go see about fixing that threshold." Thrusting the sheets at her, he stalked out the back door toward the barn. What on earth had come over him? He was acting as if he'd never seen a pretty girl before.

Chapter 3

So legend has it that's why the Knights of the Round Table wear green sashes, in honor of Sir Gawain's adventure with the Green Knight." Gwendolyn finished buttoning up Betsy's shoes for her and pushed herself up from the kitchen floor. Betsy insisted on doing as much as possible for herself, but this morning the buttonhook had refused to cooperate.

"That's the most wonderful story. How do you know all these tales?" Betsy brushed her hair, slowly separating it into three hanks to braid.

"I've heard them for as long as I can remember. Tales of Guinevere, Arthur, Lancelot, St. George. Father was a medieval scholar and professor, and my sisters and I just mopped it up." She quickly made Betsy's bed and straightened up the room for the day. "I used to dream of a knight coming to my rescue, saving me from the dragons and declaring upon his sacred honor his everlasting devotion to me." She laced her fingers under her chin and batted her eyes.

Betsy snickered. "Can you imagine Matt clanking around the ranch in a suit of armor?"

Gwendolyn grimaced and shook her head. She affected a gruff, deep voice, one hand on her hip, the other pointing at the window. "Hark, fair maiden, hast thou not been forbidden to settle thyself in at this castle? What is this I espy? Draperies?"

More laughter from Betsy as they relived the moment yesterday morning when Matt had caught them hemming pretty yellow fabric to adorn the kitchen panes. The fuss he'd kicked up over something so innocuous had baffled both the girls, but Betsy had declared the whole enterprise her idea, and he'd collapsed his protests like a stepped-on bellows.

"What is going on in here?" Matt eased the half-open door aside.

Gwendolyn jerked around, lost her balance, and grabbed for a chair back to steady herself. How much had he heard? She fought to keep her color down.

Betsy covered her mouth, but helpless giggles escaped. Matt's cheeks creased in a rare smile, and he laughed. The rich, mellow sound did strange things to Gwendolyn's insides, and she forced herself upright, smoothing her skirts and hair. He tugged on Betsy's newly fashioned braid. "It feels good to hear you laugh again, Bets. What's so funny?"

"Gwendolyn." Betsy's shoulders quivered, light dancing in her brown eyes.

"We were just talking." Gwendolyn hustled to the stove, chagrined to be caught giggling like a schoolgirl. "I'll have breakfast ready in two shakes."

A breeze fluttered the curtains at the kitchen window, but she hid her grin. He really had been grumpy about them. But what harm could it do? Aside from that chock a block full parlor, the other rooms in the house were rather stark and uninviting. Surely a few womanly touches wouldn't hurt anything.

Matt washed up and sat down at the head of the table. Gwendolyn turned the bacon and cracked a couple more eggs into the skillet. The warm, inviting smell of biscuits curled through the room when she opened the oven door. Neither Matt nor Betsy had complained that she had taken over the meals, and Betsy tried to help as much as she could.

"Ah, perfect." She whipped the biscuits onto a platter and set them on the table then slid the eggs and bacon onto plates before placing them in front of Matt and his sister. She took her own chair and bowed her head.

Matt offered his hands to each of them and bowed his head. A flutter started just under Gwendolyn's heart, the same way it did every time they happened to touch, and she chided herself to keep her mind on the blessing.

His simple prayer of thanks warmed her as it always did. There was something so straightforward about Matt. Hardheaded, but straightforward. He hadn't budged on the idea of her staying, but at least he no longer looked at her as if she might steal his wallet.

As he tucked into his food, she observed him from under her lashes. Square jaw, straight nose, and that thick, slightly wavy reddish hair that just begged her to touch it. His muscles moved under his worn blue shirt when he reached for the jar of honey, and a light dusting of ruddy hairs sprinkled his forearms and the backs of his strong hands.

His lips, which could be hard and uncompromising one moment and soft and smiling the next, drew her attention. Then there were his eyes. The same shape as Betsy's. Brilliant blue and slanted a bit at the corners, often filled with care or concern when he looked at his sister and consternation or confusion when he looked at her.

What would it be like to have him look at her with tenderness, or even just friendliness?

"Do I have dirt on my face?" He sat back and rested his knife and fork on the edge of his plate.

She blinked and looked away. "Um, no. I'm sorry. My thoughts were wandering." And into a region she should keep them well away from. "What are your plans for the day?" She helped herself to another biscuit, though she hadn't finished the first—anything to cover up being caught staring like an infatuated twit.

"I thought I'd slap another coat of paint on that fence today." He resumed his breakfast.

Betsy, who had been quietly pushing her food around on her plate, frowned. "Isn't it about time for the spring roundup? Shouldn't you be out on a horse somewhere?"

He shrugged. "The boys are handling it. They rode out a couple of days ago."

Her brow scrunched further. "This is because of me, isn't it? You're staying here because you're afraid to leave me now that I'm stuck in this chair and Granddad isn't here. You should've gone with the men. You always go on the roundup." Tears filled Betsy's eyes, a surprise to Gwendolyn, for she had a feeling Betsy fought hard to always be cheerful and staunch. "I don't want to be a burden to you, Matt. You have a ranch to run, and you can't do it from inside this house."

"You aren't a burden, so get that notion right out of your head. I've got plenty of work to keep me busy around the ranch, and I have a whole crew of men to help me do it. I just feel like painting today, that's all." Matt frowned.

Betsy sat back, letting her fork clatter to her plate. "Matthew Parker, you're lying. You hate that picket fence. When Edith insisted on it, you called it the most nonsensical contraption ever to hit Wyoming Territory. 'A maintenance headache that serves no useful purpose.'" She tugged a handkerchief from her sleeve and dabbed her eyes, her lip quivering. "And you're lying when you say I'm not a burden. I can't even button my own shoes." Tossing the handkerchief into her lap, she backed her chair up and turned, bumping into the table leg and rattling the dishes before rolling toward her room.

Matt shoved back his chair to go after her, but Gwendolyn touched his arm. "Leave her be."

His shoulders slumped. "What did I say? She was so happy just a while ago, giggling and laughing with you. Now she's crying. Betsy never cries."

Gwendolyn tugged on her lip, unsure how far to go. "I don't know her as well as you do, but I suspect she might cry more often than you think; she just doesn't want you to know it. She would rather stifle her feelings than ever cause you hurt. I suspect she's already regretting tearing up in front of you."

"She's not a burden." He sat back, an indignant scowl creasing his brow.

"Well, she is and she isn't." She rose to clear the table. Clearly they'd all lost their appetites. "It's true there are plenty of things she can't do for herself, and it's also true that because you love her, you don't consider doing things for her a hardship. From the little bit Betsy has told me, her illness has been advancing gradually for the past several years?"

He relaxed a little and leaned forward, turning his coffee cup in circles on the tabletop. "It started a few years back as a bit of weakness, then numbness, and now she can't feel much of anything in her lower limbs. The sickness is affecting other places, too. Her fingers won't always do what she tells them to. At first, she could get around with a cane, and she still went to school, but as things got worse, the doc switched her to leg braces and crutches. Just a couple of weeks ago, the day before Granddad passed away, in fact, she had to go into the chair. We knew it was coming, but that didn't make it any easier. Then Granddad died, and since then, I've been afraid to leave her. I've been working around the house so I can keep an eye on her, and I'm doing all I can to make things easier for her."

"Like building the ramp?"

"Yes, and moving her clothes out of the top drawers in her dresser and putting her brushes and fripperies on that low table in her room so she can reach them. I just wish there was more I could do."

"I know."

"No offense, but how could you possibly know what it's like?" He raised one eyebrow, draining his coffee cup as he stared at her over the rim. Scraping back his chair, he rose and brought his dishes to the dishpan.

She shaved some soap chips into the pan and lifted the kettle from the stove. "My father had something similar, though not until much later in his life. He was in a wheelchair for the last five years, since I was about Betsy's age. I'm just glad the school kept him on. So often people seem to think if someone can't use their legs, they can't use their brain either. They get cast aside or relegated to the poorhouse. I'm thankful that didn't happen to him and he was able to keep teaching right up until the day he died. His work was his life."

A few lines in Matt's forehead cleared. "So that's why you were so natural around Betsy right from the start. I guess I don't need to tell you how cruel folks can be, just through pure ignorance sometimes. Last time I took Betsy to town, I promised myself I'd never do it again. Several folks said right out in front of her that I should send her to an institution back East." His lips hardened.

He stood so near, her concentration wavered. The care of an invalid was a huge burden to shoulder alone. She had shared the task with three sisters, and it hadn't been easy. His troubled eyes scanned the horizon through the curtained window, and his compassion for his sister touched her heart and gave her courage.

"Matt, Betsy is right in one respect. You do have a ranch to run, and if you neglect it to care for her, she's going to feel terrible, not to mention see right through your feeble smoke screen." She smiled. "That picket fence is already whiter than a summer cloud. It needs a new coat of paint like the sky needs more blue."

"I know, but what can I do?" He shrugged. "She needs me." Sinking onto his chair once more, he rested his forehead in his palms. His plight and his posture made her offer easier to voice.

"Of course she needs you, but what about me? I can take care of her while you're working. I've had plenty of practice, and even though you harbor doubts as to my motives in coming out here, I promise you I'd never do anything to hurt Betsy."

He appeared to wrestle with her words, his shoulders stiffening and his back straightening. "I don't have any right to ask it of you. It's not as if we were married or anything."

That reminder stung, but she forged on. "You're not asking for anything. I'm offering."

For a long moment, he studied his hands, and she was afraid he would refuse her, but then his muscles slackened and he sat back.

"It surely would take a load off my mind." He raised his head and smiled at her for the first time, his eyes captivating her. "I could pack and head for the cow camp today. And Pete and Mike would be here if you got into trouble. They stayed behind to take care of the livestock and chores." She could see his mind was already racing with things he needed to do, but then he stopped. "You're sure? I don't have to go. And roundup lasts for at least two weeks, but closer to three. That's a long time. Maybe I should just ride out there and check on them and come right back."

"Nonsense. You need to be where the work is, and Betsy and I will be fine. As you say, there are two ranch hands here if we need anything, and it's only for a couple of weeks."

"This sure would help me out of a bind."

She grinned, warmed through to be able to help him. "Then it's decided."

He headed toward the back door, plucking his hat off the peg beside it. He halted with the door half-open, tilted his head, and regarded her. "I appreciate the help, but it doesn't change anything. This is only a temporary situation, until roundup is over. Then I'll see to getting you a return ticket back East."

Gwendolyn ground her teeth and considered hurling the wet dishrag at his retreating back. Stubborn man. She was foolish to entertain any hope he might come to care for her and want her to stay.

Matt joined his crew at the cow camp, fitting himself into the roundup with the experience gained from punching cows since his early teens, first in Texas and then in Wyoming Territory. Cattle bawled and churned the dust, men shouted, dogs barked, the smells of smoke and burnt hair filled the air. After being chained to the house for so long, he relished the labor, the wide-open skies, and the camaraderie of the cowboys.

By nightfall, every muscle ached, but it was a good ache. The calf tally looked promising so far, and his skill with his rope had not gone unnoticed by his crew. Not even Jackson could beat him when it came to throwing a loop.

In spite of how well things had gone today, an unnamed guilt sat heavily on his shoulders. As he waited for supper to be ready, he unrolled his bedding and sat down to sort it out. Snatching up a stem of wheatgrass, he broke off little pieces to aid his thinking. Being back at work felt good, and yet, as he thought about it, the guilt stemmed from those feelings and got all mashed up with thoughts of Betsy. It wasn't fair that he could ride away from the house, rope, flank, and flop calves all day, walk his own land if he so chose, while Betsy was bound in that chair, her world hemmed by a picket fence and her body wasting away before an ever-advancing illness. How soon before the sickness forced her into a bed and finally took her very life? His gut twisted at the thought. He'd already lost so much—his mother when Betsy was born, his father when Edith exploded all their lives, and Granddad just over a fortnight ago. When God took Betsy, who would he have left of his own?

Which thought sent his mind racing to Gwendolyn. Was he right to leave her in charge of his precious little sister? What did he really know about her? Heartjoltingly pretty for sure. She admitted she had no money, that she had nowhere to go.

All courtesy of Granddad. It was just like the autocratic, bossy old man to try to maneuver Matt into getting married. He'd certainly harped on it often enough, but Matt had resisted, not willing to put his neck into that noose. Edith had sickened him on the idea of marriage, especially to a high-stepping Easterner.

But Betsy really liked Gwendolyn, which made him even more wary. This was a temporary situation. When Gwendolyn went back East, it might break Betsy's heart. And how could he be a party to that?

"Vittles!" The cook, a Russian, pronounced it "wittles" and clanged on an empty pot. Cowboys scrambled to grab tin plates and get in line for their chuck. Matt held back, waiting his turn. As the men squatted with their full plates, he took his own serving from the cook.

Jackson lounged on his bedroll near Matt, scooping the beans and bacon into his mouth. "Surprised to see you out here, boss. Thought you'd be at home with that pretty gal." He gave a knowing leer, and several of the younger men chuckled and elbowed one another. "She as nice as she looks? Nice for you to be holed up in that house with just a kid sister to chaperone."

Matt lowered his fork and studied Jackson. "What I do isn't any concern of yours, Jackson. Miss Gerhard is our temporary guest, that's all."

Shrugging, Jackson took another bite. "Still, she's mighty pretty. A fellow could hardly be faulted for making the most of the situation. I know I wouldn't mind letting her warm up my bedroll, even if it was only for a little while."

Matt's jaw tightened, and his fingers gripped his fork so hard the skin showed white over the knuckles. A stillness passed over the group, as if everyone held their breath, waiting to see what his reaction would be.

Jackson seemed to pick up on the fact that he might've gone too far and shrugged. "Well, you know what I mean. No offense or anything."

Before Matt could answer, the cook lifted the lid on one of the pots.

"Sucamagrowl's done. Bring your plates."

Again a scramble for this camp delicacy. Sugary, vinegary aromas mingled in the air as the ranch hands held out their plates for the sweet dumplings—a rare treat, and one that Jackson hustled to get in line for. Matt forced his muscles to relax, grateful for the distraction, and took the chance to confer with the foreman, Melton.

"The cattle look to be in good shape."

Melton—whether this was his first name or last name, Matt didn't know and had never felt comfortable asking—nodded, his primary form of communication. The toothpick he kept permanently clamped in the corner of his mouth twitched a fraction.

"How're the men working together? The new men fitting in all right?"

Another nod. Granddad, a talker if there ever had been one, had questioned Matt's choice of ranch foreman on several occasions for his lack of conversational skills, but not even Granddad could fault the man's cow sense. Or his ability to get the most out of a crew.

"Walk?" The foreman discarded his toothpick and dug another from his pocket.

"Sure." They rose and headed for the rope corral, where their mounts grazed.

When they were well out of earshot of the men, Melton stopped and looked at the night sky, breathing in as if testing the weather. A horse stamped and swished his tail, his teeth ripping through the grass.

"That yellow-haired gal, she taking care of the little girl?" Concern colored his question.

Matt went still. Melton had never given the slightest indication that he even knew Betsy existed, much less asked after her health. "That's right."

"Good idea. Good you're back to work. Best if the men see you leading from the front." The toothpick switched sides. "Men haven't talked of much else besides that gal. Taken with her, especially Jackson."

It was the longest speech Matt had ever heard Melton make. While he loathed the men's curiosity, he couldn't really blame them for wondering. It wasn't exactly a usual situation. "She's pretty enough, I guess." Though *pretty* seemed a weak word to describe her.

"She after money?"

"She's made no bones about the fact that she's broke." The willing way Gwendolyn had pitched in around the house and the easy manner she had with Betsy had distracted Matt from the crux of the issue, but Melton's question brought it home again. Edith had made them all gun-shy, and with good reason. "I'll send her on her way as soon as I can."

"What about your sister?"

Matt rubbed the back of his neck. "I don't know. I'll have to think of something. Betsy can't stay alone. It was all right when Granddad was here." A fresh pang of grief seared his chest. "I miss the old codger."

"Natural."

"We fought hammer and tongs every day of my life. He could get under my skin worse than a cactus spine. Stubborn, bossy, hardheaded. His passing leaves a big hole, you know?" He shoved his hands into his pockets. "I feel stuck, no matter which way I turn."

For a long time, they stood looking at the stars, listening to the horses cropping grass and the lowing of cattle as they bedded down for the night.

Finally, Melton stirred himself. "Man has to be careful around women. Be they stepmothers, sisters, or wives." He strode away into the darkness, but his brief words lingered in the night air, a reminder and a warning. Matt shouldn't let his head be turned, or he'd find himself in a pickle.

Chapter 4

Gwendolyn tightened the kerchief covering her hair and handed Betsy a cloth. "If ever a room needed some attention, this parlor takes the prize." She swiped her finger through a layer of dust. "You're sure Matt won't mind?"

"If he does, I'll take the blame. Matt never talks about this room, and he mostly avoids it, uses the back door. But this parlor is hideous and a reminder of a time we'd all like to forget. Nobody's touched anything in here in almost a year. The sooner it's cleaned out, the better, to my way of thinking."

Both Matt and Betsy had alluded to past trouble, but how it connected to this overstuffed room remained a mystery. Gwendolyn didn't want to pry, especially since Matt had made it clear that hers was a temporary stay, but curiosity as to how an ostentatious parlor had come to be in a simple ranch home this far from civilization nagged at her.

She threaded her way to the front windows and pulled aside the heavy drapes, coughing and waving her hand in front of her face when a cloud of dust erupted from the velvet folds. Turning, she examined the room in better light.

"We need to remove at least half of this furniture, and the rest needs to be arranged so you can maneuver. A garter snake couldn't edge his way through here without bumping into something."

Betsy dusted figurines and china pieces while Gwendolyn shoved tables out of the way, rolled up rugs, and planned the new arrangement. "Any idea where we can put the extra furniture?"

"There's a storage area under the eaves. Pete and Mike will carry things upstairs for us."

"Perfect. Let's figure out what stays and what goes, so they can move it all at once."

Hours later, the girls surveyed the results. Though the front porch shaded the windows from the bright glare outside, enough light came in to glint off the newly polished surfaces. More than half the furniture had been relegated to the attic, and Gwendolyn had placed what remained into an inviting arrangement that left plenty of room for Betsy's chair.

"There. That's a good job done. It will be so much easier to care for, and you can be comfortable in here." Wiping her hands on her apron, she glanced at Betsy, noting her pale face and the way she rested her head against the chair back. "I'm tuckered out. We deserve a rest."

Betsy lifted her head and tried to appear less tired. "You're the one who did all the work. I just dusted a little. How about if we sit on the porch for a while?"

Gwendolyn fetched shawls for them both and a lap rug for Betsy, since the spring wind was still a bit fresh. Easing herself into the rocker beside the wheelchair, she tugged the kerchief from her head.

"You have beautiful hair. I wish I had golden curls." Betsy flicked her braid. "Better than this old carroty color."

"How can you say that? You have lovely hair. It glows like burnished copper." Gwendolyn fingered the end of Betsy's braid where it lay on her shoulder. "Two of my sisters have yellow hair like me, though mine's the curliest. Jane's hair is a soft, smooth brown that shines like silk. I always wanted raven-black hair or glorious red like yours. I guess we always want what we don't have."

"You must miss your sisters."

The ache that was never far below the surface rose afresh. "I do. We all thought we'd live closer together and be able to see one another often, but we didn't count on the distances out here. I can't help but wonder how they're getting along with their new husbands." At least they all had husbands. Neither Gareth nor Harrison had shouted in front of everyone that they weren't getting married, or that they would ship their mail-order bride off at the first possible moment. She crossed the ends of her shawl over her chest. "But having you here makes everything so much easier. I don't know what I would've done otherwise. I'm used to having someone to talk to. If you weren't here, I guess I'd just have to talk to myself." She laughed.

Betsy's eyes, so like her brother's, sobered. "I wish Matt wasn't so stubborn about you staying. I can't tell you how much better things are with you here. I feel like we've known each other forever."

Gwendolyn reached over and squeezed Betsy's hand. "I feel the same way."

"Then we should figure out a way that you can stay. You do like Matt, don't you?"

She did. And if she was honest with herself, she could easily come to love him, stubbornness and all. He had proven he could be caring and chivalrous, and he was a good provider. He put the needs of others ahead of himself. As if all these qualities weren't enough, just the sight of his handsome face and physique was enough to give her heart palpitations.

"I like him. And I'd like to stay." She recognized the longing in her voice, the unspoken desire to be Matt's wife and not just his temporary guest cum housekeeper. How had it happened so quickly? She was wise enough to know she had been ripe to fall in love, but the fact that it was actually happening and she couldn't seem to stop it surprised her.

"Then we have to get Matt to change his mind. He needs someone like you. He just doesn't know it yet. Granddad would've liked you, too. And you'd have liked him. He and Matt were very alike. So alike that they fought over just about everything. But that never bothered me, because I knew they each cared for the other one so much. They'd start out discussing something, and before you knew it they were pacing and jabbing the air, and then they'd start yelling. Finally, one or the other would throw up his hands and walk away." She chuckled. "That famous redheaded temper, I guess. But under it all, they loved each other, and they would work it out eventually. I know Matt's grieving something terrible. He thinks he's hiding it from me, but I can tell it hurts. I don't think he's ever really gotten over Father's death, especially since they were on the outs when he died."

Gwendolyn turned her face into the quartering breeze and let it blow the hair back from her temples. Her father's passing was recent enough to still ache. "Sometimes grief is so personal and deep, you can't share it. Everybody grieves differently. My sister Emmeline couldn't keep her sorrow at my father's death bottled up. She had to talk about it, to cry and grieve aloud. When she asked why I didn't cry, she quoted Shakespeare: 'Give sorrow words. The grief that does not speak whispers the o'er-fraught heart, and bids it break.' But I couldn't talk about it. Sometimes sorrow is too deep to express, especially when it is new. Perhaps that's why Matt doesn't give voice to his grief."

Betsy nodded. "See, you understand him so well already. Surely there must be some way to convince him to let you stay." She fisted her hands, resting them on her frail legs.

"If he's as stubborn as you say he is, I don't see how we can change his mind."

"We're two fairly smart women, aren't we? Between the two of us, we'll figure it out." The girl smiled. "Now that I have a sister, I don't intend to let you go."

❧

Matt rode toward the ranch, weary but content. After seventeen days of hard work, the new Circle P calves were all branded, the herd tallied, and the crew worn out. He rubbed his rough chin, conscious of his cow camp dishevelment.

He shrugged and grimaced. Nothing a bath, shave, and clean clothes wouldn't fix. Why should he care how he looked? He'd never cared before.

"Sure will be nice to have a bed instead of a bedroll." Jackson rode beside him. "And the sight of some feminine beauty would sure be nice. You must be eager to get home."

Weary of Jackson's digs, Matt legged his horse into a canter. Though after the first night in camp Jackson had minded his words to keep them just this side of insolent, he still managed to reference Gwendolyn at least once a day.

Not that Matt's mind wasn't already centered on her most of the time. He couldn't believe how often she traipsed through his thoughts, how often he wondered what she was doing or how she was caring for Betsy, and what sort of financial compensation he would have to offer her. At the very least, he owed it to her to pay her passage back east, and she deserved something for her trouble and the way she'd pitched in to help him out of a bind.

And yet, the idea of her departure brought him no joy. Not like he'd anticipated. And more than once, he found his thoughts straying to the mind-boggling notion of what it might be like if she actually stayed. Not for himself, of course. Only to help out Betsy.

At least having Gwendolyn to think about managed to distract him from some of his grief and kept him from brooding on Granddad's death.

The house and barn came into view, and his horse picked up the pace of its own accord. Matt's heart picked up the pace, too. A smile tugged his lips, and instead of riding to the barn, he headed straight for the house.

Tying the reins to the picket fence with a quick jerk, he opened the gate and started up the path. With the warmup to the weather, he wasn't surprised to see the windows open to catch the breeze, but he'd have to be extra quiet if he wanted to surprise them. A thump and giggle reached him.

"Good thing the picture will cover that mark. You can't hammer a nail worth anything." Betsy's laugh wrapped around him. He'd missed his little sister something fierce, worried about her the whole roundup, but she sounded happy. Creeping up the ramp, he eased to the open front door to peer through the screen.

Across the parlor, Gwendolyn stood on a chair with her back to him, her arms stretching up to hold a nail over the fireplace. Her posture caused the hem of her skirt to come up several inches, and he glimpsed snowy petticoats and a very trim ankle in a high-buttoned boot. Her apron strings nipped in her shapely waist, and glory, her hair hung down her back in a curtain of golden curls. The sight snatched the breath from his chest and turned his mouth to a desert.

The chair wobbled, and Betsy squealed, reaching out to grip Gwendolyn's leg. Before he could open the screen, Gwendolyn grabbed the mantel, and the hammer clattered to the floor.

"Botheration," she muttered, steadying herself.

"Are you sure you should do this? Maybe we should wait for Matt. Or call Pete or Mike to help." Betsy eased back, holding something in her lap.

"I can do it. I just hadn't counted on a teetering chair." Gwendolyn flipped her hair over her shoulder in a motion that captivated Matt. So feminine. Had she gotten prettier since he was away? "Never let it be said Gwendolyn Esmeralda Gerhard was daunted by a mere nail. My motto is *Excelsior*, and my course is onward. I want this done before Matt gets home." She lifted the hammer and gave the nail a couple of whacks. "There. Now hand me that picture, young lady."

She hefted the frame—a painting?—and eased it along the wall until the wire caught on the nail. Leaning back, she studied it, straightened it, and put her hands on her hips. "There. What do you think?" She had her attention on the picture and didn't turn when Matt drew the screen door open and stepped in, his finger pressed to his mouth to still Betsy's squeal.

When he stood right behind Gwendolyn, he made his voice as gruff and stern as possible. "What are you two doing?"

At his words, she whirled, arms flailing, and his hands shot out to grab her. The chair teetered, and she gripped his shoulders to steady herself. "Matt!"

A feeling of inevitability swept over him, and without thought, he tightened his grip on her waist and eased her from the chair. But somehow, she didn't make it all the way to the floor. Instead, he held her against him, wrapping his arms around her waist. Forgetting everything around him, he found himself staring into her wide, violet eyes. Her arms wound around his neck in a move that felt way too good for his peace of mind. She blinked, her lips parting.

"You're back."

Her smile slammed into his heart and got it beating again, and bless him if she didn't squeeze his neck.

Kiss her.

The notion came out of nowhere, but once it arrived, he could think of nothing else. His eyes zeroed in on her pink lips, so close to his. He halved the distance between them before he realized what he was doing.

Betsy's chair squeaked, reminding him of her presence and the folly of what he was thinking about. He glanced over to see his sister trying to back out of the room. She stopped. "Welcome home, Matt." Her innocent expression couldn't hide the glee in her eyes.

Reluctantly he released Gwendolyn, letting her feet reach the floor. He tried to ignore the empty feel of his arms and the regret at not getting a taste of those sweet lips as she stepped away and smoothed her hair. He turned from her purply-blue stare, trying to gather his scattered wits.

"What have you two been up to in here?" He scanned the room that had been off-limits for even conversation for the past year. Though some of the furnishings were the same, it was as if all traces of Edith had been removed. Open, bright, and without the clogging clutter, he might even be able to sit in here without feeling as if Edith might spring out from behind the drapes.

Betsy rolled her chair closer. "You aren't mad, are you? If you are, it was all my idea. But if you're not mad, then we thought it up together." She gave him a gamine grin. "Do you like it? We've worked so hard. And look." She turned the chair left and right. "Plenty of room for my chair now."

He rested his hand on his sister's shoulder, noting the color in her cheeks—cheeks that had a bit of roundness to them again. How could he be mad when Betsy looked better than she had in months? "It's nice."

"We were just putting on the finishing touches. Isn't it beautiful?" She motioned toward the painting. "Gwendolyn brought it all the way from Massachusetts."

Gwendolyn had laced her hands and laid the sides of her index fingers against her lips—those soft, pink lips. He dragged his mind back to what she was saying.

"My sister Evelyn painted it. It's of the shore near Seabury, where we lived." She took a deep breath. "I can almost hear the waves hitting the beach. I can't remember a time when I didn't know the sight and sound and smell of the sea. Sometimes, when I close my eyes, I imagine I'm walking along the rocky shore, leaning into the breeze, gulls keening overhead. I knew becoming a mail-order bride meant leaving the sea, but I never knew I would miss it so much."

The wisp of homesickness in her voice jarred Matt, as did her reference to being a mail-order bride, reminding him that her stay here was temporary, that soon enough she'd be on the train back to her beloved ocean. High-stepping easterners only caused trouble, changing everything to suit themselves then running off without a backward glance once they'd bled a fellow dry—and broken his foolish heart.

She still had a wistful smile on her face when she asked, "What do you think, Matt?"

He hardened his voice to bring them all back to reality. "What it looks like to me is that you're settling in. I told you there was no point in unpacking that kind of stuff. You'll just have to take it down again." He avoided looking at either of them, knowing he'd see hurt and confusion at his harsh tone. But the sooner they accepted the truth, the easier it would be on all of them. "I'd best see to my horse."

Gwendolyn sank onto the settee, staring after his departing form. All the happiness, the hope of belonging and companionship she'd built up during his absence, evaporated like a snowflake on a hot griddle.

Betsy pressed her lips together and narrowed her eyes, watching Matt through the screen as he untied his horse and led the animal toward the barn. She fingered the end of her braid, a sign Gwendolyn had come to recognize as meaning she was deep in thought.

"Well, that didn't go too well, did it?" Gwendolyn ran her fingers through her hair. It was finally dry now from the early morning washing she'd given it, and she pulled a ribbon from her pocket. With the dexterity of long practice, she divided and braided the heavy curls, winding and tying the ribbon. She coiled the braid, slid her hairpins from where she'd tucked them along the edge of her collar, and jabbed them into the knot of hair to secure it.

"Actually, it went better than you think." Betsy grinned. "If he wasn't starting to care about you, he wouldn't have reacted so strongly. I saw the way he was looking at you, like he was a starving man and you were the last cookie in the jar. I just wish my chair hadn't squawked when it did. He looked like he wanted to kiss you senseless."

Gwendolyn shook her head, convinced she was already senseless. The way he'd held her for an all-too-short eternity. . . Her blood zinged in her veins. She hadn't been able to resist winding her arms around his neck, and the instant it flashed in her head that he might actually kiss her, she realized she wanted nothing more. She was afraid to put too much stock in what Betsy said. The way he'd backed away, and worse, the wary look that had crept into his eyes were more reliable than anything his fanciful sister might read into his actions.

"We'd best get supper started." She rose and picked up the chair to return it to the kitchen.

"And get some water heating. Matt's going to want a bath." Betsy followed.

Gwendolyn had just slid the pan of corn bread into the oven when the back door opened and Matt came inside. He hung up his hat and began dipping water from the reservoir into a bucket to carry upstairs for his bath. She wiped her hands on her apron. "The bread should be ready in about half an hour. If you're all right, Betsy, I'll be back in a few minutes."

Returning to the parlor, she picked up the hammer from the mantel to take it back to the barn. It was nice to be able to leave the house for a while without worrying about Betsy being alone. She let herself out onto the porch and walked toward the barn. The prairie rolled away from her in all directions, the only trees a few stunted individuals clinging to the creek bank. In the northern distance, lavender hills rose. What had Cummings called the tallest one? Laramie Peak?

She breathed deeply of the grass-scented air. Hanging Evelyn's painting had made her a bit homesick, both for her sisters and for the sea. How often had they rambled along the shore together, watching the waves roll in like a great ocean heartbeat? What would her sisters advise her now about Matt? What if he really did send her away? Where could she go? Jane's place was much too small, and Evelyn's cabin housed four already.

Lord, I don't want to go. I want to stay here. Betsy needs me, and though he isn't ready to admit it, so does Matt. He's everything I could ask for in a husband.

She chuckled.

Except that he doesn't want to be married. What made him so skittish, and how can I change his mind?

She could almost feel his arms around her again, and she knew without a doubt that she wanted him to hold her like that again. Soon. She wanted him to want to be married to her.

Entering the barn, she let her eyes adjust to the dimness. The tools were kept in a room on the far side next to where they kept saddles and such. Her footsteps crunched on the dirt floor, and the smells of hay and livestock wrapped around her. The men must've stowed their gear and headed to the bunkhouse for supper. She entered the toolroom, grateful for the small window high in the wall that let in some light. A neat row of tools hung along the back of a wooden workbench, and she placed the hammer back where she'd gotten it.

"Evening."

She whirled, clutching her throat, and found the cowhand who had been so insolent her first day here blocking the doorway. A quick glance told her nothing about him seemed to have changed in the intervening days. He wore the same intent expression, his gaze roving over her from hair to hem and back again.

"Good evening." She gripped the edge of the workbench behind her.

"Didn't expect to see you here."

"I was just returning something."

He stretched, gripping the top of the door frame and leaning a bit into the room. "You're sure a sight for this cowpoke's weary old eyes. Don't believe I've ever seen a woman as pretty as you." His smile made her shiver.

"I need to get back to the house, if you'll excuse me." She waited, but he didn't move.

"There's no rush. I imagine you've been cooped up while we've been gone, what with looking after the cripple. That can't be very pleasant for a woman like you. I'd think you'd be looking for something a little more—shall we say, stimulating?" He studied her, letting his eyes linger far too long on certain parts of her anatomy. "My name's Jackson, by the way."

She crossed her arms at her waist and tried to ignore the prickles dancing across her skin. "I'm sorry, but I really do have to go. I left something in the oven."

He moved to the side of the doorway but not quite enough for her to get by. "I bet you're a fine cook."

The way his eyes glittered in the dusky light made her think of a gull. Dark, beady, watchful eyes, waiting for an opportunity to snatch up any morsel that happened to land in its path. He'd positioned himself so she would have to brush against him to get out of the toolroom, and his smirk said he knew it.

"Jackson?" A voice she didn't recognize came from behind him. A man with graying hair and a grizzled beard stepped from the gloom.

Jackson straightened and stepped back. "Melton. I was just"—he broke off—"you know."

The older man removed a toothpick from his mouth and stared hard at Jackson until the cowhand fidgeted and finally ducked his head and left.

Relief coursed through Gwendolyn, and she blew out a breath.

The man returned the pick to the corner of his mouth, clamped down, and spoke around it. "Trouble?"

"Uh, no. Everything's fine." She had no desire to try to explain Jackson or his behavior. "I'd best get back to the house, Mr. . . . ?"

"Melton. Circle P ramrod." He jerked his head toward where Jackson had disappeared. "Best stay away from the men, ma'am." With a tip of his hat, he was gone, as silently as he'd come.

"Stay away from the men?" she muttered on her way back to the house. "I'd love to stay away from that Jackson for the rest of my life."

Chapter 5

Everywhere he turned, she had invaded his life. In the week since he'd returned from the roundup, Matthew's world had been subtly and not-so-subtly altered. First it was the parlor, the painting over the mantel, the new curtains in the kitchen. Then it was cushions on the chairs, a chess set on the sideboard, and now, of all things, a flower garden along the picket fence.

Matt hooked his thumbs into his belt loops and stared at the scraggly plants in the newly dug soil. Yarrow, Indian paintbrush, Queen Anne's lace. Weeds, every one of them. What did a body want with extra work like tending flowers when there was plenty to do with the vegetable patch and looking after the house? Not to mention the fact that in just a couple of weeks, Reverend Cummings would be back through here, and she'd be on her way somewhere else.

"Stop scowling." Gwendolyn passed him with a sloshing bucket of water, pouring around each plant carefully before moving on. "What harm can a few flowers do? It pretties up the place a bit." Her shrug and ultra-innocent expression made him want to smile.

Grasping for a hold on his irritation, he tugged the kerchief from his neck, removed his hat, and wiped the sweatband. "You realize you've planted a row of weeds."

"Wildflowers," she corrected. "I didn't notice any nurseries around here where I could get roses and pansies. I had to make do." She bent to touch the ivory blossoms of a Canada milk vetch and trailed her fingers over a tiny cluster of harebells. "Aren't they pretty?"

Pretty. If anything in this yard could be called pretty, it was her. The afternoon sun bathed her face, bringing out honey strands in her hair and the smooth surface of her skin. He busied himself with retying his kerchief to keep from reaching out to stroke her cheek. What was the matter with him?

"What's going to happen to them when you leave here? I don't have the time to weed and water them, even if I wanted to, which I don't."

Her happiness at the flowers faded, and she gave him a reproachful glance that lanced his gut. More and more, the thought of her leaving gave him a hollow feeling under his heart. He had to remind himself why she couldn't stay, and it seemed she needed the reminders, too. Everywhere he turned, she was going against his orders not to settle in. He decided to change the subject.

"Where's Betsy?"

"Reading in the parlor. She's enamored of Chaucer's *Canterbury Tales* at the moment."

"One of your books?"

"Yes. My father used to read it to us in the evening, and we'd discuss it bit by bit. Even Jamie, my nephew, joined in, though he preferred Mallory's tales of King Arthur. He even had a stuffed dog he named Glastonbury Tor." Her smile flashed, and there was a faraway, remembering look to her eyes. "I miss Jamie. I wasn't yet ten when he was born, and I was sure Evelyn produced him just so I would have someone to play with. I wish I could see my sisters for just a little while, so I could make sure they were all right."

"You sound like a close family."

"Very. We've never been apart like this before. Every time things have been hard, we've always had each other to lean on. When Mother died, and when Evelyn lost Jamison in the war, when Father passed away. Then when we were being evicted from our home." She watered another weed. "Hard times remind you of who you can count on. God and my sisters have always been faithful. Our adversity brought us closer together."

"Adversity doesn't always bring people together. Sometimes it tears them apart." Sadness coated his words. Adversity, distrust, deceit, despair. He'd felt them all over the past year.

Her brows inched together. "But you and Betsy have a beautiful relationship."

"It's not Betsy I was thinking about."

She smoothed her hands over her hair, trying to tame some of the wispy curls that escaped the knot on the back of her head. Remembering the way her hair fell down her back in a glorious cape of curls when she was hanging that picture in the parlor, he swallowed. What would it be like to bury his hands in her hair, to let those curls twine around his fingers? He found himself stepping closer to her, close enough to touch, close enough to see the purple flecks in her blue eyes.

Her pulse beat in her throat. "Betsy told me how you used to argue with your grandfather."

He pulled his attention back to what she was saying. "We did. But neither of us was much for holding a grudge. Flare up and forget about it. Granddad knew just what to say to get my back up. He loved a lively debate. There for a while, after my father died, I wondered if Granddad would ever care about anything enough to argue again. He just sort of drifted for a few months. Then one morning he lit into me about something, and instead of getting mad, all I could do was grin. That made him madder, and he really erupted. It was nice to have things back to normal."

She fetched a sigh. "I wish I could've met your grandfather. He sounds like quite a character."

"That he was. I still can't figure his sending for you, but—" Matt just stopped himself from saying he was glad she'd come. Was he glad? She'd lifted his load considerably, and there was no denying she was the prettiest thing he'd seen in a long time. Fun, cheerful, and easy to talk to as well. He couldn't resist reaching out to tuck a stray curl behind her ear, and it just seemed so natural to let his fingers trail down her cheek. Softer than a sage leaf. Before he really knew what he was doing, he'd bent his head to brush his lips across hers. He pulled back to gauge her reaction.

Her eyes widened, and she looked so bewildered he had to kiss her again. Everything he'd been dreaming about since the day she arrived, all the questions he'd been asking himself about how soft and sweet she'd be got answered in that kiss. His arms came around her, and he angled his head to deepen the kiss. After her initial gasp of surprise, she delighted him by kissing back. The bucket fell from her hand, *thunking* to the ground and splashing his boots.

Reluctantly aware that they were standing in the yard in full view of anyone on the ranch, he ended the kiss and stepped back. Her lips were rosy pink, and a delicate coral color graced her cheeks. He had a sense of having taken a giant step across a line he'd drawn in the sand. There could be no going back to a time when they hadn't kissed. But did he want to go back? Maybe things would work out, maybe he could trust her after all.

She tucked her lower lip in and studied the horizon, clearly bemused. He smiled. She was so adorable, he wanted to kiss her again, just to fluster her.

He picked up the bucket she'd dropped. "I best be getting into the house. I've got some paperwork to finish. If there's one thing I hate, it's keeping track of the accounts."

"What kind of accounts?" Her voice sounded distracted, as if she was having a hard time gathering her thoughts.

He shrugged. "Wages, expenses, taxes, herd tallies, bills, sales receipts. Sometimes I feel like I'm drowning in paperwork. My father was the one who used to take care of it all, but over the last year, it's fallen to me." They walked up the path, and he could almost imagine she really belonged here.

"There's so much more to running a ranch than I ever thought, especially one as prosperous as this place appears to be." She paused halfway up the ramp and put her hand on his arm. "I'm pretty good with figures. If you'd like, I could help you." She turned the full force of those blue eyes on him. Her lips parted, expectant.

He glanced down at her hand on his forearm. Warning bells jangled in his head, and he flashed back to another time, another woman. A woman who barged into their lives and destroyed so much. A woman with a powerful attraction, who used her feminine wiles to trap and disarm. A woman who had caused catastrophic harm.

A woman who had offered to help with the bookkeeping.

Plucking her hand from his arm, he hardened his features. What a fool he'd been, letting her charm him, lowering his defenses, letting history repeat itself.

"The finances of this ranch are none of your affair. You can forget whatever notion you have of getting your hands on any Circle P property, and that includes me."

He dropped the bucket onto the dirt and stomped into the house. Brushing off Betsy's cheerful greeting, he marched to his room.

Gwendolyn stood still, as shocked as if he'd struck her. A chill rippled across her skin, followed hard by a wave of anger. Her hands fisted. How dare he? How dare he kiss her one moment and accuse her of trying to steal from him the next? Of all the hard-headed, mule-stubborn, moody men, he took the biscuit.

Her breath came fast, and her heart thundered in her ears. She wanted to scream, to throw something, to give vent to the frustration raging inside. Knowing she couldn't go into the house, couldn't face him until she got her feelings under control, she turned toward the gate. Halfway there, she stopped and went back to the door.

"Betsy," she called through the screen, "I'm going for a walk." She tried to keep her voice nonchalant and light, though she couldn't quite hide a tremor. "I'll be back."

The crooked branches of the stunted cottonwoods along Sagebrush Creek beckoned her, and she strode toward them, arms swinging, feet hitting the dirt with force, trying to expel the anger Matt's accusations had aroused. As she walked, she fought a mental battle with him, crossing verbal swords. His behavior was inexcusable.

But, oh my, how he could kiss.

She touched her lips, still sensitive, and tears pricked her eyes. *Oh, no, you don't. You're not going to cry over that despicable louse. From this moment on, he isn't the only one counting the days until Reverend Cummings returns to free you from this untenable situation. Matthew Parker is no knight in shining armor. He's a dragon, through and through.*

She waded through the waist-high grass until she reached the stream bank and the cottonwoods there. She leaned against the rough bark of a tree trunk. The water flowed slowly here, sluggish and sleepy in the growing dusk. A bird called from the tall grass on the far bank, and the wind skittered through the leaves, as unsettled as her thoughts.

The anger trickled away, leaving her tender. An overwhelming rush of loneliness, of longing to see her sisters, swamped her, and she slid down until her back rested against the tree and she could draw her knees up. Wrapping her arms around her legs, she pressed her forehead into her knees.

Lord, where do I go from here? I don't understand any of this. You led us to Wyoming Territory, You gave us all husbands, except me. I have no family, no husband, no home, nothing. I have nowhere to go when I leave this place. I can't trust anyone or anything here, not even my own feelings. What can I do?

She squeezed her eyes shut, and a memory flashed across her mind. Jane's cross-stitch sampler that had hung in the parlor at home, stitched with her favorite Bible verse:

The Lord *is my rock, and my fortress, and my deliverer; my God, my strength, in whom I will trust; my buckler, and the horn of my salvation, and my high tower.*

Gwendolyn raised her face, letting the breeze cool her hot skin, and contemplated the verse that had been a part of her life since she was a little girl. How many times had she flown past that sampler with only a cursory glance? And yet, the truth of the verse seeped into some hitherto unlit corners of her heart, illuminating her lack of faith in a God who had never failed her yet. Her heart might've been broken by Matthew Parker, but God had not abandoned her. He had a plan, and she could trust Him.

Perhaps He had needed to remove from her all that was dear and familiar in order to show her how she needed to rely on Him. Perhaps that had been His purpose all along for each of the Gerhard girls. He wanted to be her high tower, her rock and refuge. He wanted her trust.

Swallowing hard, she leaned back until her head rested against the tree. "All right, Lord. I choose to trust You. I don't know what is going to happen to me, but I know nothing happens that is not in Your control. Nothing surprises You. If it is Your will that I not stay here, then I'll go where and when You direct. If Matthew Parker isn't Your will for me, then I accept that."

As hard as the words were to say, there was tremendous freedom in them as well. As stubborn and confusing as Matt Parker was, he was beyond her ability to sort out. She closed her eyes, listening to the murmur of the water and the sighing of the wind until she slipped over the edge of sleep.

Chapter 6

"What is wrong with you? You're as cranky as a badger with a blister." Betsy dished up the half-burnt bacon and beans—her attempt at cooking the evening meal.

Just like a woman to sulk and stay away. Matt poked at the food. Beans weren't his favorite, burnt or not, and his appetite was nil, thanks to Gwendolyn's duplicity.

"I'm not cranky. I've just got a lot on my mind."

"Like what? Maybe I can help." Betsy wheeled her chair to her place and held out her hand for the blessing.

He mumbled through the words and released her fingers.

"It's nothing for you to worry about." He glanced at the clock and the angle of the shadows on the ground outside the back door. Gwendolyn should've been back by now. Where was she?

"If it concerns you and Gwendolyn, then I think I will worry about it, thank you very much. You do realize you're making more of a hash of your relationship than I made of cooking dinner?"

"We don't have a relationship." Being chastised by his younger sister wasn't on his to-do list this evening.

"Perhaps that's the problem. You're like the man who got bitten by a mustang, and now he hears hoofbeats everywhere. Gwendolyn isn't Edith."

"I never said she was."

"No, you just treat her like she is. I don't know why she'd ever want to marry you with the way you act, so suspicious and snarly."

"I'm not snarly." He paused, modulated his voice, and took a deep breath. "And who said she wanted to marry me? She's waiting for Cummings to come back the same as I am, so she can leave. Until that time, I have every right to be suspicious. Do you know what she asked me? She asked if she could help with the bookkeeping."

"And?"

"Do you remember what happened the last time we let an outsider look at the accounts? She fleeced us like a flock of sheep."

"How many times do I have to say this? Gwendolyn is not Edith. Her innocent offer of help was just that, innocent. Did you know she kept the household accounts for her family for years, even though she was the youngest? She has a knack with ledgers and figures. It's perfectly natural that she'd offer to help."

He wasn't ready to let go of his wariness, though his sister's logic and information put a dent in the wall of his suspicions. Had he jumped to the wrong conclusion? Had he misjudged Gwendolyn's offer? Had he been wrong about her all along?

If he had, if he'd kissed her and held her and then thrown her sincere offer back into her face. . . Shame wriggled through his chest. What kind of a beast must she think him?

"Matt, I'm getting worried. She said she was going for a walk, but she's never been gone this long before."

Glancing at the clock, he pushed back his plate. "Do you know where she might go?"

Betsy shook her head. "She goes to the rise just east of the house sometimes. Pete and Mike put a bench up there for her. But I can see the bench from my bedroom window, and she isn't up there. Maybe she needed to walk off her temper. She might've gone farther."

He rose and plucked his hat off the peg by the door. "You'll be all right while I look for her?" Though what he'd say when he found her, he didn't know.

"I'll be fine. Go."

"The rise east of the house, you said?"

"That's the only place she's mentioned walking before."

"I'll start there."

Matt left the house, his long strides eating up the ground. Betsy's assertion bored through his brain. *Gwendolyn is not Edith.*

He supposed he'd best practice his apologizing.

❧

Gwendolyn awakened, confused at first, memory trickling back as she straightened and rubbed her stiff neck. The sky, no longer a pale, hot blue, now showed streaks of rose and gold and gray. The breeze had died away, and the stalks of grass and sage bushes stood still. She'd been gone way too long. Betsy would be worried.

Scrambling to her feet, she brushed the dirt and grass from her skirts. A hank of hair slid over her ear, and she tightened a couple of hairpins.

A rustle in the grass off to her right caught her attention.

Jackson rose from the grass, grinning. "Hello, Gwendolyn." Her name rolled off his tongue like syrup.

Her heart quickened, as did her breathing. A glance over her shoulder told her no one from the ranch complex could see her here, down over the creek bank. She could just make out the roof of the house, a hundred yards away beyond the rise.

She gripped the tree trunk behind her, the rough bark biting into her skin. Jackson had always had a too-familiar gleam in his eye, but now that gleam burned white-hot. Her mouth went dry. "I should be getting back to the house."

"There's no hurry. It's a nice evening." He stepped closer, edging aside a sage bush, crushing the stems beneath his boots and releasing their herbaceous scent.

"Really, I'm overdue. It must be well past suppertime." She edged around the tree, hoping to put it between herself and Jackson, but he moved like quicksilver, his hand clamping down onto her wrist.

"I said there was no hurry." He loomed over her, the last rays of the sun glinting in his dark eyes. "Why do you skitter away every time I get near you?"

Because you remind me of a snake? "I'm sure Matt and Betsy must be expecting me now."

"Why do you care about them? The cripple is useless, and Matt's a real dog-in-the-manger. He doesn't want you himself, but he doesn't want anyone else to have you." He bared his teeth in a sneer. "I sure enjoyed sticking it to him on the roundup, digging at him about you." Grinding the bones of her wrist together, he jerked her toward him. "He's so almighty arrogant, walking around here like a little plaster saint, but I know better." He laughed. "Bet you didn't know he was cheating on his old man with his stepmama, did you?"

Gwendolyn gasped. "No."

"Why do you think his dad killed himself?" Jackson flung his arm toward the creek. "Ended it all right here. Shot himself and landed in the water. Heartbroken."

"Let go of my arm."

"I don't think so. I've bided my time, but I'm tired of waiting." He brought his face within inches of hers. "I saw you, you know. Out in front of the house. I knew you two had something going on, just like him and Edith. Those were some kisses you were giving him. I figure one man's as good as another to you, just like one woman's as good as another to him." He shifted his hold on her, gripping her upper arms and hauling her up against his chest. She struggled, sucking in a breath to let out a scream, but before she could, his hard lips came down on her mouth, stifling any sound.

The disgusting touch of his lips on hers made her want to retch. So different from Matt's kiss. Jackson wanted to punish, to take, where Matt's embrace had been safe, a giving and a receiving, everything a kiss should be.

Pinned against the tree as she was, she couldn't even draw back her leg to kick him. Her struggling seemed to fire him up, so she went limp in his arms, hoping to surprise him into dropping his guard long enough for her to break free.

The instant she drooped, he raised his head, a triumphant laugh escaping him. "I knew you'd give in."

As he shifted his grip, she steeled herself to slap his face, but before she could raise her now-free arm, a roar split the air. Jackson was flung away from her, and the sound of a fist hitting a jaw cracked.

Matt stood over Jackson's sprawled form, gasping, his hands clenched. Without a word, he bent and grabbed two fistfuls of shirt, hauling Jackson to his wobbly feet. Another punch sent him reeling into the dirt, his lip split and his nose bleeding.

"Jackson, get up to the bunkhouse and draw your pay. You're through here." Matt's chest rose and fell rapidly, his hands fisted at his sides.

Gwendolyn clutched the tree for support for her shaky knees. Blinking, trying to catch her breath, she couldn't help the rush of gratitude and something else, something stronger, that overwhelmed her. Matt stood there like an avenging angel... no, like a knight in shining armor, defending her honor against a scoundrel.

She crossed to him, holding out her hand as Jackson scrambled to his feet and backed up. "Matt, thank you. I'm so glad you came when you did."

He turned cold eyes to her for a brief second before swinging back to watch Jackson's retreat. "Are you? I don't know why. I'd think you'd be disappointed, having your little rendezvous interrupted. I want you off this property, and I'm not waiting for Cummings to come back for you. You can either leave with Jackson, or I'll take you to town first thing in the morning."

A strange, this-can't-be-happening icy shudder rippled through her. He'd gone from knight in shining armor to fire-breathing dragon—again. She swallowed.

"Matt, I didn't have any rendezvous with that...that animal." She pointed to a quickly retreating Jackson. "He caught me by surprise."

"That's not what it looked like to me."

"Then you're wrong. And if anyone should know what it feels like to be wrongly accused, it's you." Jackson's taunts about Matt rang in her ears. But she couldn't—wouldn't—believe them.

"What are you talking about?" The question jerked from him, deepening his scowl. "Never mind, I don't want to know." He jammed his fists on his waist. "I almost fell for it. Betsy *almost* had me believing I'd made a mistake, that I'd misjudged you. I was all set to apologize, to ask you to stay." A bark of mirthless laughter shot out. "What a fool I am." He turned on his heel and marched up the hill toward the house.

When Matt reached the house, he knew he couldn't go in, couldn't face Betsy's questions until he got himself under control. Glancing over his shoulder through the growing dusk, he spied Gwendolyn approaching, bold as polished brass in the noontime sun. He ground his teeth. When was he going to learn that women were nothing but trouble from a man's first breath to his last?

The bunkhouse door opened and Jackson emerged, saddlebags over his shoulder and a defiant set to his jaw. Melton edged out after him and, seeing Matt by the picket gate, strolled his way, hands in pockets. He came to a stop a few feet away, dug a toothpick from his pocket, and went to work on it, silent as usual.

Gwendolyn didn't come to the front yard, instead disappearing around the back of the house. The kitchen door slapped shut.

Matt waited, watching Jackson head to the corral and lasso his horse, saddle up, and ride away. Though he should've been relieved, his heart felt like it had been replaced with a fistful of horseshoes, cold, heavy, lifeless.

"Good riddance." Melton slipped a rifle bullet from a loop on his belt and used the point to clean under his fingernails. "Madder'n a skunk-bit coyote. Busted nose, too."

Matt flexed his hand, wincing at his bruised knuckles. "He deserved it."

" 'Magine so. Wanted to punch him myself a time or two. Had to hold the boys back just now. Wanted to tenderize his hide, spouting off about you and that girl. And Edith."

Matt flinched. "What did he say?"

"Claimed you were dallying with that gal. And the real reason your daddy kilt himself was because he caught you and Edith together."

Closing his eyes, he took a deep breath. "It's not true."

"Figured."

This must've been what Gwendolyn meant about him knowing what it was like to be falsely accused. But he'd seen what he'd seen. Her in Jackson's arms, not struggling, not fighting him in the least.

"Don't usually give advice, but you and her need to talk. Deserves to know about Edith. And you deserve to be rid of Edith and her trouble. Weighing you down. Holding you back." Melton placed the cartridge back in his gun belt and shifted the toothpick. "Plain she's not like the other one and that you're in love with her."

Matt's mind rebelled at the thought, even as he embraced it.

"If I had to believe Jackson or that gal, I reckon I'd choose the gal. Shame to let her get away." With that, Melton turned and sauntered back toward the bunkhouse.

Matt gripped two of the pickets, hanging his head. His gut muscles clenched. The scene by the riverbank played itself over and over in his mind. Had he made a mistake? Was she telling the truth, that Jackson had caught her unawares and forced his attentions on her? Was he being unfair by lumping her in with Edith without giving her a chance to explain? Would she believe him if he told her the truth, and would she forgive him if he did?

The last thing he wanted to do was dredge all that up again. And yet, he wanted to be free of Edith and all the hurt she'd caused. He wanted peace and a chance to be happy. And he wanted to hold Gwendolyn in his arms, with no suspicions or accusations between them.

Edith's ivylike vines had imprisoned him for far too long, binding his thoughts and actions. Guilt, disgust, anger, bitterness, and no matter how he slashed at them, they grew back with longer thorns and stronger boughs.

And at first, he'd seen Gwendolyn the same way, trapping, scheming, plotting. But now, when he thought of her, there were no entangling thorns or entrapping vines. Gwendolyn meant wildflowers in the breeze, sunshine and light, laughter and hope.

His heart craved some hope. It had been a long, dry spell.

Chapter 7

"You can't leave." Betsy reached out her fragile, pale hand and stopped Gwendolyn from putting another folded garment into her valise.

"I have no choice." She choked back the tears that wanted to fall. No way was he going to see how he'd hurt her. She refused to cry. This very day she'd promised to let God be her refuge and tower. Well, she would. If it killed her. No more trusting in men.

"But where will you go?"

"Evelyn's, I suppose. After that, I don't know."

"This is ridiculous. If you're going, I'm going with you."

Gwendolyn stopped cramming things into her luggage and sagged onto the side of the bed. "You can't. Matt needs you here."

"He needs you here, too; he's just too dumb to see it."

Weary beyond anything she'd felt before, Gwendolyn wrapped her arms around her waist. "I can't do this anymore. I'm fighting shadows, wild accusations, and half-spoken thoughts. I'm left to imagination and supposition. He doesn't trust me. How can I win against something I can't see, someone I don't even know? Nobody will talk about this Edith woman and what she did. At first, I didn't want to pry, and then I was afraid to. It was almost as if she was still here, still holding sway. I have so many questions, but Matt's locked everything up behind a wall of prejudice I can't break down."

The bedroom door eased open. She raised her eyes. Matt stood in the doorway, his expression sad and watchful. Jumping to her feet, she began packing once more, blinking hard and commanding herself not to cry.

"Matt, this has gone on long enough. Either you tell her about it or I will." Betsy backed her chair up to make room for him to enter.

"You don't have to preach anymore, Betsy." He sounded weary, beaten down. "Gwendolyn, we need to talk."

Gwendolyn's heart went out to him, captured by the sorrow in his blue eyes and the way his shoulders drooped, but she steeled herself, not wanting to get hurt further. He stepped aside to allow her to pass through the doorway and motioned for her to head toward the kitchen.

"Can we go outside? I have a few things to say that I'd rather Betsy not hear." He held the back door open for her.

Instead of stopping in the backyard, with its washtubs and clothesline, Matt grabbed her hand and took off walking, heading away from the house and the creek to her favorite rise a few hundred yards from the buildings. He followed the path her feet had created on multiple trips up the hillside. The long twilight held, but a few stars peeked from the eastern sky.

When he finally stopped, he let go of her hand and walked a few paces away. She waited, running her fingertips across the airy fronds of wheatgrass stalks. She was finally going to get some answers, but her heart quailed at the thought that they might not be the answers she wanted to hear.

He stood with his thumbs in his belt loops, legs braced apart, staring out over the prairie. The wind rippled through the grass and fluttered his shirtsleeves. She couldn't help but step closer and only just refrained from putting her hand on his back to offer solace. Fear of being rebuffed kept her from touching him.

"I owe you an apology. Several of them, actually." His voice rumbled in his chest, as if the words had to work hard to come out.

She took his elbow and tugged gently. "Come sit." Leading him to the little bench Pete and Mike had built for her, she braced herself and told herself not to hope. She turned so she could see his profile, put her hands in her lap, and waited.

He took a deep breath and plunged into his story. "Three years ago, right after we moved here from Texas, my dad made a trip down to Denver to buy cattle. He left me and Betsy and Granddad here to look after things. Betsy wasn't so bad then. She could get around with a cane most of the time. We had a little cabin, just a couple of rooms. Betsy slept on a bed in the front room and me and Granddad and Dad had bunks in the other room. It wasn't much, but we were happy. We'd saved and worked hard to get started ranching here, away from the divided loyalties and backlash of the war in Texas. A place where we could start over."

He had a faraway look in his eye, and his voice held a touch of longing.

"Dad came back from Denver with a herd of cattle, a half-dozen ranch hands, and Edith, his new bride." His hands fisted on his thighs. "She was about ten years older than me and about as ready to rough it on a ranch as she was to sprout wings and fly. Fancy clothes, fancy talk, fancy manners. Real handsome, and Dad was head over heels. At first she gushed over everything and played nice, but the rot set in pretty quickly. She hated it here, hated the people, the prairie, the animals. The cabin appalled her, even though Granddad and I moved into the bunkhouse with the ranch hands to make room for her and all her belongings.

"The first thing she demanded was a new house. Dad tried to put her off, get her to wait a while so we could build up the herd, but she wouldn't let up about it. Finally, he gave in, had all the materials freighted out here, and hired builders. For a while she seemed happier, picking out wallpaper and paint and rugs and such, supervising the construction. When it was finished, Granddad and I moved in with them and Betsy again. She wanted to go to Denver on a shopping spree to furnish the place, but Dad told her the house had cost more than he'd anticipated, and she could only decorate a couple of rooms. The rest would have to wait until we had cattle to sell. She pored over the catalog and spent right up to the limit."

That explained the parlor.

He seemed to read her mind. "Yeah, the parlor. And one bedroom upstairs. The places Edith was most likely to be. The rest of the house looks like the kitchen and Betsy's room did when you first got here. No decorations, nothing soft or pretty. We weren't even allowed into the parlor, not that any of us wanted to be in there. We weren't good enough."

She held her tongue, not wanting to interrupt him. The longer he spoke, the easier the words seemed to come.

He pursed his lips and shifted on the bench. "You know Granddad and I used to argue about pretty much everything? We knew it didn't mean anything, flare up and be done with it. But Dad was different. He never argued, just kept everything bottled up inside. And the more Edith complained, the more silent he got. She whined she was wasting the best years of her life in this forsaken place and wanted him to leave the ranch. He'd tell her his life was here and that she'd get used to it after a bit. She just needed to 'settle in.'"

Gwendolyn flinched at this phrase that she'd come to loathe. No wonder he'd said it to her so often.

He glanced her way. Grim lines bracketed his mouth. "A few months after the house was finished, Edith started acting strange. I couldn't put my finger on it, but she seemed to be there every time I turned around. Watching me, paying compliments, using any excuse to be close. At first, I didn't want to believe it. I mean, she was my stepmother. But after a while, I couldn't ignore it. I ended up putting a lock on my door." A dusky red crept up his neck. "I was afraid she'd come into my room one night.

"I couldn't talk to Dad. He defended her at every turn. In spite of how unsuitable she was for the life here, he was in love with her. Then one day when I was coming in off the range, I forded the creek down where I found you today. I stopped to water my horse, and. . .I'd made up my mind to have it out with Dad about Edith. I knew she was giving Betsy a rough time, though Betsy didn't say anything, and I'd had enough of Edith's maneuvering." A shudder rippled through him.

"I was just getting ready to mount up and head for home when I heard someone crying. It was Edith, huddled in the grass, bawling." A grimace twisted his lips. "I wanted to ride away and leave her there. I wish now that I had."

Gwendolyn squeezed her laced fingers together. Pieces of the puzzle began to fall together, creating a picture of tension, conflict, misery, and mistrust. Poor Matt.

"Like a fool I squatted down beside her. I wanted to make sure she wasn't hurt. She threw herself into my arms, crying about how miserable she was, about how she'd never loved my father, she'd just wanted to get out of Denver." He shook his head, shrugging. "I didn't know what to say to her, and I tried to get loose, but she held on tight. Then she came at me, trying to kiss me." He swallowed.

"I shoved her away and tried to leave, but she came after me, saying she was in love with me, that her marriage was a mistake. When I wouldn't give in to her, she got ugly, screaming and calling me names. Then she went all quiet. I don't know how to describe it. It was like she went cold inside, her eyes kind of glittered. Then she said real loud, 'We'll have to tell your father. I can't go on deceiving him like this. He deserves to know we're in love.' I know now that she'd seen my dad coming down the bank. I was so stunned I couldn't move. And then she kissed me again." He rubbed his hands down his face. "I'll never forget the look on Dad's face. I pushed her away, and she fell down. Dad turned around and headed back toward the house. Edith started laughing, and I went after Dad, to explain."

Gwendolyn's chest squeezed as if caught in a vise. Biting her lip to keep back the questions, she kept her eyes glued to his profile in the fading light, his chiseled lips, straight nose, stubborn chin. She loved every plane and angle of his face, and her heart ached for what he'd been through.

"He didn't believe me. I suppose he couldn't bring himself to. I guess it was easier to believe his son had betrayed him than to believe his own judgment had been so flawed. I knew I couldn't stay here. Dad left the house, and I went upstairs to pack. When I came down, I went to say good-bye to Betsy and Granddad. I prayed I wouldn't run into Edith, because I don't know what I would've said or done. Then I heard the shot."

Gwendolyn took his hand between both of hers. "Matt, I'm so sorry. You don't have to say any more."

"I do. I have to tell you the rest of it, so you can decide what you want to do." He studied the horizon. "I've never forgiven myself for not trying harder to convince Dad of what really happened. I should've gone to him the minute I first suspected what Edith was up to. I should've cut and run when I found her crying by the creek."

"This isn't your fault, Matt."

"I never thought he'd do something like that."

"Is there any chance that it was an accident?"

"I don't know. That's what folks assumed, and I never told anyone until today what really happened between the three of us, though I think some of the ranch hands suspected."

"What happened to Edith?"

He heaved a sigh. "Dad had turned over the ranch bookkeeping to her pretty early on, because she asked if she could help. By the time we found Dad's body downstream and got back to the ranch house late that night, she'd cleaned out the cashbox and disappeared. We found out she rode straight to Sagebrush and withdrew every last cent from our account there. Last I heard, she was back in Denver, married again."

"And Betsy knows none of this?"

"How could I tell her? She was just a kid, still is, and she has her own problems. I didn't want to disillusion her about our father, and I didn't want her ever to have any doubts about me. I never even told Granddad, though I think he suspected there was more to the story. Then he died, and Betsy got worse." He gave a rough laugh. "And before I could hardly draw a deep breath, you landed on my doorstep out of the blue." Giving her hands a little shake, he released her and stood, pacing the area in front of the bench. "A mail-order bride I didn't order. I thought you were like Edith, grasping, conniving, finagling your way into an old man's affections, coming out here to see what you could bilk him out of."

Gwendolyn moistened her lips, for the first time seeing things from his point of view.

"Every time you tried to help, I accused you." He stopped pacing. "I thought history was repeating itself. But gradually, you were winning me over. The way you took care of Betsy and the house, the way you never asked me for anything or complained that the house wasn't big enough or that you were lonely. You seemed to get joy from such simple things, like those ridiculous weeds you planted today." He chuckled. "I was falling in love with you, but I was still fighting it."

Her heart swelled, and her breath snagged in her throat.

"Then, I went and ruined it by throwing your offer of help with the bookwork back at you." He closed his eyes, turning his face toward the darkening sky. "Then I found you with Jackson, and it looked like all my suspicions were being proved. I was so angry, I wasn't thinking right."

She rose and went to his side, touching his arm. His eyes opened, and he looked down at her. "You do believe me, right? That it was Jackson forcing his attentions on me?"

His hands cupped her shoulders. "I do. I of all people should know what it's like to be falsely accused. Jackson and Edith sound like two of a kind. But I don't want to talk about them anymore. Gwendolyn, I want to start over. I'm tired of fighting how I feel about you." He shoved his hat to the back of his head and starlight illumined his eyes. "I love you, and I don't want you to leave. I regret every harsh word I ever said to you. Please say you'll forgive me and that you'll stay." His grip tightened. "Tell me that when Cummings comes back, you'll marry me. I don't want to live without you."

Tears burned the backs of her eyes. "Oh, Matt, I love you, too." She went into his embrace, wrapping her arms around his waist and pressing her cheek into his chest. The thundering of his heart and the harshness of his breathing matched her own. Now that she knew the whole story, forgiveness came easily. She raised her face to stare into his eyes. "I've been waiting forever for you to ask me to stay."

He lowered his lips to hers, and her eyes fluttered closed. Gathering her even closer, he kissed her with all the ardor and passion her heart could hold. As starbursts of happiness broke behind her eyelids, she knew she'd found her knight in shining armor after all.

ERICA VETSCH

Even though Erica Vetsch has set aside her career teaching history to high school students in order to homeschool her own children, her love of history hasn't faded. Erica's favorite books are historical novels and history books, and one of her greatest thrills is stumbling across some obscure historical factoid that makes her imagination leap. She's continually amazed at how God has allowed her to use her passion for history, romance, and daydreaming to craft historical romances that entertain readers and glorify Him. Whenever she's not following flights of fancy in her fictional world, Erica is the company bookkeeper for her family's lumber business, a mother of two, wife to a man who is her total opposite and yet her soul mate, and an avid museum patron.

A Birthday Wish

by Darlene Franklin

There is one alone. . .yea, he hath neither child nor brother;
yet is there no end of all his labour;
neither is his eye satisfied with riches. . . .
Two are better than one;
because they have a good reward for their labour.
Ecclesiastes 4:8–9

Chapter 1

Gladys checked the baskets on the kitchen table. Red calico bows she'd festooned with small white flowers peeked out between juniper branches. Such cheerful decorations should improve even crotchety widower Norman Keller's spirits in the middle of the miserable Kansas winter.

Ma carried a couple of baskets to the family wagon, together with garlands of fragrant juniper branches. "Maybe it would be good if I came with you."

Gladys came close to agreeing when she remembered the last time she had knocked on Mr. Keller's door. The growl with which he had greeted carolers could have passed for Ebenezer Scrooge's. "I'll see how it goes today. I'd like to do this on my own, if I can. I'll be back in time to help with supper."

Grateful for the January thaw that made an outdoor project possible, Gladys buttoned up her winter coat and drew on her mittens before heading out to the wagon. When she'd decided to reach out to Norman Keller, she hadn't considered how to keep her activities a secret. To avoid attention, she would keep her wagon off Main Street.

A few minutes later she came to a stop in front of the imposing three-story structure that Norman Keller called home. As far as Gladys knew, he was the only one who lived there. His wife had died, and his children never visited. Rather than knocking on the front door and risking Mr. Keller's rejection before she even started, Gladys approached the house from the back. She tied the horse to the railing and carried the baskets to the wraparound porch. A closer inspection of the once-magnificent structure revealed sagging boards and peeling paint. Such neglect by the richest man in town befuddled her. She hoped he would feel better after she'd hung enough baskets for him to see one no matter which window he looked through.

As she walked down the porch, a basket in each hand, she realized she had miscalculated the number needed to adorn the rafters. She'd start from the front and work her way back. She tiptoed to the corner and put the baskets down. She returned for her stepladder, and as she carried it to the front, it bumped along the floorboards. She froze, expecting Mr. Keller to shuffle out the door to check on the noise. When he didn't appear, she continued until she had unloaded everything in the wagon.

From the corner, she studied the overhang. With a hammer in one hand and two nails in the other, she climbed the stepstool, reached high overhead, and tapped a nail into the wood. A thin crack appeared. Would a section of the overhang split and fall? Mr. Keller wouldn't appreciate it if she destroyed his property in the process of decorating it.

Tucking her tongue behind her teeth, Gladys waited and the nail held. Next she centered the basket handle on the nail. She stepped down to study the effect. *Good.* Setting another arrangement on the railing, she climbed the stepstool to hammer the second nail in place.

As she adjusted a couple of ribbons around the berries, she wondered what else she could do for Mr. Keller. Fashioning a few bows hardly qualified as a mission project, and she wanted to do more. She tapped the nail in and reached for the basket.

Behind her, the front door banged. "What are you doing?"

The edge of the door caught the stepstool, throwing Gladys off balance. Her arms windmilled, her feet slipped, and she fell backward.

Into two strong arms.

"Oomph."

The arms lifted her and held her steady while she regained her footing. The basket had fallen, crushing the bows and scattering the juniper branches across the floor.

Falling into Mr. Keller's arms wasn't the introduction Gladys had hoped for.

Slowly she turned around to meet the man she wanted to help. And looked up. . .and up. . .and up. Long legs, straight limbs, strong arms. . .brown hair.

Definitely not Norman Keller.

Haydn stared at the person who had been making all the noise. Her cheeks gleamed bright red beneath a green knit cap, and brown curls bounced on her shoulders. Her mouth opened just far enough to reveal straight white teeth. This little thing didn't weigh much more than a hummingbird. "Are you all right? Did you hurt yourself?"

"No." She brushed her hands on her coat and glanced at the porch, covered with greens and ribbons and straw baskets. What was this stranger doing on the porch on a ladder in the middle of winter? The Old Man hadn't mentioned any guests.

"I apologize for making such a mess." She gestured helplessly at the scattered items on the floor. "If you give me a broom, I'll clean it up."

The Old Man's pride demanded Haydn refuse. As he stepped to the side, a board moved underneath his foot, a reminder of all the repairs needed on the house. Whoever this stranger was, at least she wanted to help. "Let me get one for you." He paused at the door. "But who are you?" *And what are you doing here?*

"I'm Gladys Polson." Shivering, she slipped on a pair of gloves. "Who are you? I haven't seen you before."

"I'm Haydn. . ." He hesitated in mid-introduction. "Haydn Johnson." He used the name he often gave in his newspaper work.

Miss Gladys Polson was as pretty as a Christmas angel, standing there against the backdrop of the winter-white world, and whatever her purpose in coming to the house, she surely meant no harm. He smiled. "Look, it's a miserable day. Come in and get warmed up before you do any more work."

Her mouth opened, and he thought she was going to refuse. Tilting her head, she touched her lips with a mittened hand. "I'd like that."

Haydn held the door open.

"Who was it making all that blasted noise?" The Old Man's petulant voice carried across the living room.

"It's Gladys Polson."

"Don't know her."

Gladys crossed the room to greet the man sitting in the straight-backed chair by the low-lying fire. "Good afternoon, Mr. Keller. You may not remember me, but I want to introduce myself. We're members of the same church."

Haydn hid a smile behind his hand. The Old Man didn't know how to respond to this force of nature. "So you were the one making all that racket out there?"

Pink tinged Gladys's cheeks. "I apologize for the noise. I had hoped you might not hear me inside. I wanted it to be a surprise."

She shivered, and Haydn remembered how cold the living room had seemed when he first arrived. He added a couple of logs to the fire, and soon the flames leaped merrily. "I'll fix us some hot tea while the room warms up some."

Gladys nodded. "Thank you."

As she unbuttoned the top button of her coat, he started forward. "I'm sorry. Let me help you." He stood behind her, his arms easing behind her slim shoulders, ready to take the coat as it slid from her back. This close, she smelled like rosewater and cedar needles. Draping the coat over his arm, he pulled the chair closer to the fire. "Sit here by the fire until the room gets warmer."

She glanced at the man in the chair, huddled beneath a thick blanket. Noting her silent interest, Haydn scooted the Old Man's chair closer to the fire.

"What the fool do you think you're doing?"

"Putting your feet to the fire. Doesn't that feel better?"

Scowling, the Old Man stared at the fireplace. "It's a waste of good firewood, that fire is."

Yes, Mr. Scrooge. "We want our company to feel welcome, don't we?"

Gladys stared at her hands, folding and unfolding them in her lap. "Go ahead and fix the tea while Mr. Keller and I visit." She flashed a smile full of genuine warmth at Haydn, and he relaxed.

"Three cups of tea, coming up. I wish I could offer you some cookies, but all we have is a couple of slices of bread." He grinned.

Walking into the kitchen, Haydn questioned why he had offered tea instead of coffee. Maybe because tea seemed like the kind of thing he should offer a lady. Hot cocoa sounded even better on a cold day, but he didn't know how to make it, some slow process of heating milk and adding cocoa powder and sugar. He'd prefer coffee, but they only had the dregs of the pot from the morning.

He couldn't mess up boiling water and adding tea leaves. He opened the cabinets to the usual collection of blue enamelware but then changed his mind and headed instead for the china cabinet. If he was going to entertain a stranger, even one up to an unexplained errand on the front porch, he might as well do it in style. A silver tray nestled at the back of the china cabinet; he brought out three cups and saucers that looked like they hadn't been touched in a month of Sundays. He cleaned them with a dishrag, filled a sugar bowl, and poured fresh cream into a small pitcher.

While he waited for the water to boil, he listened to the quiet murmurs of conversation from the living room. Gladys spoke in a pleasant cadence, and the Old Man answered in short, one-word answers.

After the water came to a boil, Haydn poured it over the tea leaves in the pretty china teapot.

"I have a question of my own." A querulous voice broke the quiet murmurs. "What are you up to, disturbing my peace and doing all that hammering on my front porch?"

Chapter 2

The tray tilted in Haydn's hands, and he righted it. Waiters and hostesses might handle trays with a single deft hand, but he kept all ten fingers on this one. His host would never let him hear the end of it if he dropped any of the china. Through the open doorway, he watched the tableau unfolding before him. The Old Man had his hands on the arms of his chair, his face set in an angry mask.

Across from him, Gladys leaned forward, perfectly at ease in this awkward social situation. "Why, I'm obeying our Lord's command."

"Speak up, young lady. I can't hear you."

"I'm obeying our Lord's command." The girl spoke louder and slower, as if used to speaking to someone who was hard of hearing.

"Which one is that? The one that says to trouble a man in his own home?" The Old Man waved Haydn into the room. "Come on, young man. Stop hovering."

Haydn laid the tray on a small table with a marble top.

"Shall I?" Gladys reached for the teapot as if she was the hostess, ignoring the outburst. "What do you like in your tea, Mr. Keller?"

"A teaspoon of sugar."

She stirred in the sugar. "The command to love our neighbors as we love ourselves."

"You don't live next to me." He looked through the windows on either side of the parlor. "I would recognize you."

"No, I don't. How do you like your tea, Mr. Johnson?"

The Old Man looked up sharply at that, an appreciative gleam in his eyes. He covered his chuckle with a sip of tea.

"I'll take it black, please."

Handing the cup to Haydn, Gladys continued her explanation. "But everyone in Calico is my neighbor, don't you see? God brought you to my mind. I realized I don't know much about you except your name. And I thought I should remedy the situation."

"Busybody." The word came out under the Old Man's breath.

If Gladys heard him, she ignored him. After she fixed her own cup of tea, adding both sugar and cream, she leaned forward and chafed her hands together in front of the fire. "A fire cheers up a room, doesn't it?"

The temperature had risen a few degrees. The Old Man no longer looked so drawn. It was a surprise he hadn't come down with a cold before now. Haydn would keep the fire going after Gladys left.

"You still haven't explained all the hammering."

Gladys's face turned bright pink. So this question came closer to revealing her true purpose for showing up this morning. Haydn leaned forward, awaiting her answer.

"I had some bows left over from last Christmas that look good against greenery." She dabbed at her mouth with a napkin. "From what I could see from the outside, you didn't have a Christmas tree. I thought some hanging baskets might cheer up the house."

The Old Man harrumphed. "Seems a waste to cut down a tree just so's to decorate a house for a couple of days a year."

"We each may celebrate the birth of our Lord in whatever way we wish, that is true. But I didn't notice you at church any time during December." She batted her eyelashes, making her stinging statement into innocence reborn.

"I don't have to go to church to know the Savior."

"That's true. But God wants us to love each other. It's hard to do that if we never see each other. That's why I'm here." Gladys smiled, having brought her argument full circle.

Haydn felt the indictment. He, who had good reason to love the Old Man, hadn't bothered to spend much time with him at all since he started college four years ago. This slip of a girl was practicing the heart of the law: to love the Lord God and to love one's neighbor as one's self.

She poured both men a second cup of tea before standing. "Now, with your permission, I will return to hanging the baskets." She slipped on her coat and headed outside.

"Well, go after her. Make her stop."

A smile sprang to Haydn's lips. "What, and stop her in her God-given mission in life? You have to admit, it's kind of sweet." He stood behind the curtain, watching Gladys move the precarious stepstool. Soon the banging of the hammer resumed.

"Sit down, why don't you," the Old Man said. "We haven't yet had that conversation I promised you."

"Very well, Grandfather." Haydn settled in his chair. "You do have some interesting neighbors."

"Sweet, I think you said." A calculating look brightened his dark brown eyes. "That's just as well, given the nature of my proposition to you."

Haydn arched an eyebrow. "I thought since I graduated from college, it was high time I came for a visit."

"Your father and I have been in communication. Believe it or not, we do write to each other."

Haydn did know. Something in the Old Man's most recent letter had scared his father enough to insist his only son come straight to Calico. Haydn leaned forward. "I'm here to help in any way I can, Grandfather."

"Humph." Grandfather's gnarled fingers tapped the arm of his chair. "It's more what I can do to help you. I understand you're interested in the newspaper business."

Haydn nodded. "I was the editor of my college paper my last two years at school. I've applied for an internship at the *Topeka Blade*. The editor who interviewed me said I have a good chance." That news had brightened Haydn's Christmas holidays considerably.

"What would you say if I told you that in spite of its amenities, one thing Calico sorely needs is a newspaper?"

Was the Old Man suggesting. . . ? It was out of character from what Haydn knew of him. "That's good news for someone who has capital to invest." He closed his mouth before he mentioned his financial constraints. From what his father had said, the Old Man believed each man should make his own fortune.

"Or someone who has an investor willing to back the enterprise." The words fell into a dead silence in the room.

Haydn slowly leaned forward, clenching his hands in his lap. "What do you mean?" He reached for a log, ready to add it to the fire.

"Don't do that. Can't waste good money."

Haydn tamped his impatience. The Old Man's idea of a warm room barely kept water from freezing. Why he wasn't sick remained a mystery, but they could talk about that later.

"Sit back and look me in the eye."

Haydn did as his grandfather requested, resting his hands on the arms of the chair while the silence lengthened.

At last his grandfather put on a pair of glasses he only used when he was reading his Bible. "There's a folder on top of my desk. Bring it out here."

Haydn walked down the hallway, growing chillier the farther he moved from the parlor. A single thick folder sat on top of his grandfather's desk, newsprint curling over the edges. He started to pull back the cover then decided against it. His grandfather had taken effort planning this surprise; Haydn wouldn't ruin it.

The Old Man gestured for Haydn to lay the folder on the end table by his arm. "They're all in there." He opened the folder and pulled out a piece of paper about a foot long and two inches wide—a newspaper article from the looks of it. Grandfather peered over the top of his glasses then brought it in closer and read from it. TRENTON RUNS FOR TOWN COUNCIL.

The words sent a shiver of shock through Haydn. He had guessed that the file held his articles, but not that one. He had been so proud when his first piece appeared in his hometown paper when he was sixteen years old. He had been joyfully surprised when the *Topeka Blade* picked up the story.

"You weren't expecting that, were you?" The Old Man chuckled. "Your father sent everyone he knew a copy. He was so proud." He cleared his throat. "So, for that matter, was I. So I asked him to keep me apprised if you had anything else published. I have watched your burgeoning career with interest. You have a gift with words, my boy."

He paused, inviting Haydn to respond. But what could he say? "I didn't know. . .thank you."

"It seems that Calico's need and your talent intersect." The Old Man hammered his fist on the arm of the chair. "So, tell me, are you interested?"

Haydn drew in a deep breath. His dreams, handed to him on a silver platter. "Yes."

Grandfather's dark eyes so like his own glittered in the darkening room. "Since you are my heir, it is a fitting use of my capital."

Haydn hadn't thought he'd ever hear those words. "I would appreciate the opportunity, sir."

"Wait until you hear my conditions." The Old Man scowled. "It is only right for me to help you. Frankly, I'd like to see how you handle money. I had to earn mine the old-fashioned way."

Haydn had heard the same song when his father insisted Haydn pay for his own college education. "I've kept my books balanced while I worked my way through college, sir. Running a business can't be much more difficult than paying tuition and bills on a part-time salary."

"Perhaps." The Old Man grunted. He had left school after eighth grade and didn't hold much use for college education. "Be that as it may. I will help you launch a newspaper in Calico and give you twelve months to make it a profitable enterprise. But I do have one condition. One that is nonnegotiable."

The Old Man gazed at the fire's glowing embers. Haydn waited patiently, his mind awhirl with possible demands Grandfather might make of him. Starting with the fact that he would have to live in Calico to run a newspaper here.

"I'm not getting any younger, and I have regretted the distance separating me from my family since your father moved away. The newspaper would allow me to spend time with you, but I want more." The Old Man looked at Haydn, mirth dancing in his eyes. "I want to see your children before I die. My one requirement is for you to become engaged before my next birthday and to marry before year's end."

Of all the. . . Haydn's father had warned him the Old Man could be unreasonable and demanding, convinced he knew what was best for everyone. But surely Haydn's future wife was a matter between Haydn and God—and the young woman in question, of course.

Grandfather looked expectant. Haydn schooled his features not to reveal his shock at the demand.

"Are you courting anyone at the moment?" The Old Man managed to make it sound like a job interview.

"No." Haydn thought about the coeds who had caught his eye during college. None of them returned his interest, however. The debutantes his mother paraded for his inspection lacked intelligence or beauty or spunk. Haydn was in no rush to marry; he figured God had exactly the right person out there when the time came.

Gladys Polson's face floated through Haydn's mind. That one had plenty of spunk, climbing stepladders and hanging baskets on a near stranger's porch in the dead of winter. Her comments suggested both intelligence and spiritual hunger.

Don't be ridiculous. Only Grandfather's suggestion brought Gladys to mind.

"Well, what do you say to my proposition?"

Haydn stood and looked down at his grandfather's upturned face. "The price you demand for your gift is too high. I will marry if and when the right woman crosses my path."

"There's another thing." The Old Man continued as if he hadn't heard Haydn's refusal. "I'm not going to tell anyone that you are my grandson, and I don't want you to tell them either. I don't want any money-grubbers making eyes at you just because they think you'll get my money." Cackling, he settled back in his chair with a self-satisfied grunt.

What arrogance.

If only finding a wife was so simple.

Chapter 3

"You went inside the Keller mansion?" Annie asked as soon as she arrived at the Polsons' home.

Gladys groaned. "I might as well have announced my plans at church. I made so much noise hammering that everyone knew I was there. Why don't I think things through?"

They heard a soft knock on the door. Gladys opened the door to Ruth, Birdie standing behind her.

Gladys hadn't known whether Birdie would join their mission projects or not, but she rolled out the welcome mat for her guest. Birdie took her seat, placing a bag filled with yellow flowered calico beside her. Since she had left the Betwixt 'n' Between Saloon, she had taken up sewing to earn a living.

Gladys brought out a cup and plate and fixed Birdie a tea serving. Dressed in a quiet slate blue dress and with her hair pulled back in a simple bun, the former saloon girl looked much closer in age to herself than she had guessed. Gladys resolved to make her feel at home.

"I was just telling Annie about my disastrous attempt to meet up with Mr. Keller." Gladys took out her quilt block.

"I wouldn't call it disastrous." Ruth was hemming tea towels. "You met Mr. Keller. That's more than any of us have ever done."

"And you met a handsome stranger." Annie wiggled her eyebrows. "A *young* handsome stranger."

"Haydn Johnson." The name tripped off Gladys's tongue in a single breath. "He was very kind."

Annie's knitting needles continued clacking together. She wanted to send more socks to her brother who was serving with the cavalry up in Wyoming. "He caught her when she fell off the stepladder. And he built up the fire—"

"Brrr, it was freezing in there. I'm surprised Mr. Keller hasn't caught cold." Gladys shivered.

"—and he fixed tea. A man serving tea!" Annie giggled.

"He sounds like quite a gentleman." Birdie took out a length of calico and began working on a seam.

"I doubt I'll see him again. I hope Mr. Keller doesn't slam the door in my face when I go back." Gladys tied off a quilt knot beneath the fabric.

"God led you to Mr. Keller for a reason. I'm sure He'll show you the way." Birdie spoke with a quiet faith.

"Thank you for that reminder. I'm not doing this all on my own, am I?"

"At least you've started. So far, God hasn't answered my prayers for guidance."

Ruth flattened out the bottom of the towel and changed the thread in her needle to embroidery thread.

Conversation flowed back and forth while they continued work on their projects. Gladys finished her quilt block first. "It's time for me to get to the diner for my shift. Is anyone in the mood for some of Aunt Kate's pie?"

"I've got to get home. Ma's expecting me." Annie finished her row and put away her knitting needles.

"I'll come with you." The upper half of a fancy *F* appeared on the tea towel Ruth was working on. "Birdie, would you care to join us?"

Birdie shook her head. "No, not this time, thank you."

Before they left, Gladys rinsed the dishes and slipped into her coat. Soon the four of them walked down the street, the ground beneath their feet the perfect firmness of a sunny winter day. At the corner, Gladys and Ruth bid good-bye to Annie and Birdie and headed for the town square. The Keller mansion was on the way.

"It looks very festive." As always, Ruth found something nice to say.

Gladys stared as they approached, trying to decide. "It looks half finished." As they neared the house, the front door opened, and Mr. Johnson stepped out.

Although Gladys immediately turned her attention aside, he bounded down the lawn to the street. "Miss Polson! How nice to see you again." He joined the two of them without asking permission.

Gladys slowed down. She couldn't outrun him. "Good day, Mr. Johnson." She managed a weak smile. "This is my friend Ruth Fairfield. She's our local schoolteacher."

"Nice to meet you." Mr. Johnson dipped his head to acknowledge the introduction before turning his attention back to Gladys. "I hoped you were returning to finish hanging the baskets. When you do, I want to help."

Gladys's cheeks grew warm enough that the cold air stung her heated skin. "I would love to. When would be a good time?"

"My—Mr. Keller is an early riser. Anytime during the day is fine."

"Are you staying with Mr. Keller, then, Mr. Johnson?" Ruth asked the question that was weighing on Gladys's mind.

"Yes." Haydn didn't offer a reason for his visit.

They reached Aunt Kate's diner. "This is our destination." Gladys paused, unsure if Mr. Johnson planned to join them.

He opened the door for the ladies and followed them inside. Gladys headed for the counter and draped an apron around her neck.

"Who is that tall drink of water?" Aunt Kate, Gladys's plump, pleasant relative, inquired while she exchanged her apron for a coat. "Is he someone you know?"

Rather than get into a lengthy explanation, Gladys simply said, "He's staying with Mr. Keller." Aunt Kate headed out the back door, and Gladys brought a copy of the menu to the table where Mr. Johnson had taken a seat with Ruth. They looked so cozy, she wished she could join them. But she helped at the diner to give Aunt Kate a break. The pocket change was welcome as well.

"What do you recommend?" Mr. Johnson lifted his eyes from the menu. "I wouldn't mind a meal. I've been fixing most of our food, and I'm not fond of my own cooking."

Gladys laughed. "You fix a good cup of tea, at least. I believe Aunt Kate has chicken and noodles left over from lunch."

"I'll take a bowl, then, with a slice of dried apple pie with sharp cheese."

After Gladys waited on the other customers in the diner, Mr. Johnson called her to the table. "Are you allowed to sit with the customers?"

"For you she'll make an exception," Aunt Kate said as she bustled back into the room. One of the friendliest souls in Calico, she would gladly encourage Mr. Johnson's acquaintance with Gladys. She refilled their coffee cups.

Gladys brought a cup of coffee for herself as well as food for Ruth and Haydn. She slipped onto a chair next to Ruth, across from Mr. Johnson.

Goodness, he was handsome. And to think she might never have met him if she hadn't decided to hang baskets on Mr. Keller's house.

To think he would never have met these two lovely ladies if he had never come to visit the Old Man. Some good had come out of the journey, after all. With a shake of his head, Haydn chided himself. Thinking like that would put him right in his grandfather's clutches. Find the girl he wanted to marry, indeed, before the middle of April.

"Do you want anything else to eat?" The owner—Aunt Kate?—reappeared at their table.

Haydn couldn't help smiling. "Just the pie. My—Mr. Keller doesn't keep many sweets in his house."

Aunt Kate retreated behind the counter.

"No wonder he's so thin." Miss Polson shook her head. She looked apologetically at Haydn. "His hands and fingers were so bony."

Haydn chuckled.

Miss Polson covered her mouth. "Oh, I'm sorry. I didn't mean any offense."

"None taken."

Aunt Kate returned with a slab of pie big enough to be a quarter of the whole. "Here you go, Mr. . ."

"Johnson. Haydn Johnson." Haydn dug his fork into the tip of the pie and took a bite. "Mm, this is good. Is it possible to buy a whole pie that I can take back to Mr. Keller?"

Miss Polson's beam matched Aunt Kate's. Any woman he knew liked to have her cooking praised. She motioned for her aunt to lower her head, and she whispered into her ear.

"I have an extra peach pie today," Aunt Kate said. "I'll send it along with you. It's the neighborly thing to do."

Haydn shifted in his seat. He had concerns about his grandfather's health as well, but the old man had insisted he was fine, nothing worse than old age. "He might not be sick if I could convince him to keep the house warm."

Miss Polson shook her head in an exaggerated shiver. "I hope you didn't suffer any ill effects from your exposure to the cold yesterday," Haydn said.

Her cheeks grew pink. "Of course not." She sipped her coffee.

Miss Polson's curls spilled down her neck and dusted her cheek. She looked very different from her friend the schoolteacher. Even without their earlier introduction, he would have guessed Miss Fairfield's occupation by the precise bent of the tie around her neck and the exact fixture of her hair on top of her head.

The schoolteacher might know the answer to his question. Haydn thought it a good time to ask what was on his mind. "Is there a place in town where I can pick up a newspaper?"

Miss Polson curled her nose. "Calico doesn't have a paper of its own."

"But you can get the *Topeka Blade* at the mercantile," Miss Fairfield said.

Haydn relaxed. He hadn't realized how dependent he was on his regular dose of news until he'd landed in Calico. He might have to start a newspaper just to give himself something to read.

Miss Polson tapped her fingers on the table. "I believe the library carries the paper as well."

A library but no newspaper? Haydn raised an eyebrow. "I didn't realize Calico has a library."

"Yes." Miss Polson threw her shoulders back like a crow fixing to tell a story. "When Calico was settled, the founding mothers decided to put all their books together so they would have a larger pool of books to choose from. Now we pay a small fee if we want to join. It's the best library in the county."

Small-town pride. "Kansas would still not be much more than a string of trading posts if it weren't for those founding mothers." Kansas actually had a good education system, and Haydn had enjoyed the coed education at the university.

Miss Polson nodded enthusiastically. "What is your occupation, Mr. Johnson?"

Haydn hid behind his last bite of pie while considering his answer. "I just finished my university education. I've been helping with the family firm back in Kansas City."

"So does your family conduct business with Mr. Keller?" she asked.

"Some." "Business" described the state of relations with his only grandfather better than "family." "My father authorized me to spend time here in Calico, to improve communication with Mr. Keller."

The bell above the door jangled, and several people came in. Miss Polson glanced around the rapidly filling diner. "Aunt Kate needs my help. It's been lovely to see you again, Mr. Johnson. Will there be a time when Mr. Keller isn't home? My presence seemed to upset him, but I'd like to finish what I started out to do." Her eyes pleaded with him.

Haydn opened his mouth to say yes before he thought about the true answer. "He almost never leaves the house." Haydn's fingers drummed the table. "But I've learned he usually takes a nap right after lunch. Can you come by then?"

"I'm working at the diner all day tomorrow, but I'll be finished after midday the next day. I can make it then."

A few minutes later, Aunt Kate came out with the peach pie tied up in a box. She refused payment. "Consider it my welcome present to you, Mr. Johnson. I hope we'll see you again soon."

Miss Fairfield excused herself, saying she had papers to grade from school, and Haydn headed back to the Old Man's house. The baskets of greenery welcomed his approach, although the porch looked half-dressed with baskets hanging on only one side of the steps. Gladys's colorful baskets would bring cheer to the cold house. But if she returned, the Old Man might decide Haydn took his condition to find a wife seriously.

Of the two of the women he had met today, Ruth Fairfield was much more what Haydn sought in a wife: a heart for children, well educated, soft spoken.

So why did his traitorous mind keep returning to Gladys Polson?

Chapter 4

After Gladys returned from work the next day, she started on a buttermilk pie.

Ma took out the rolling pin. "Who are you baking for? I planned on the leftover applesauce cake for a sweet tonight."

Gladys continued stirring the custard for the buttermilk pie. "It's for Mr. Keller."

Ma rolled out the pie dough. "For Mr. Keller—or for his guest?"

Gladys's cheeks warmed. "Mr. Johnson did say he liked having a slice of pie with his meals. But Mr. Keller doesn't keep any in the house." She poured the mixture into the waiting dish and slipped it in the oven. "I've got a basket ready. Do you mind if I add jars of honey and apple butter?" After she washed her hands, she joined her mother at the table.

Ma's laughter rang across the kitchen. "Of course not. They always say the way to a man's heart is through his stomach." She sniffed. "Something smells good. But it's not the pie. It smells like. . ." She turned back the cloth covering one of Gladys's baskets. "Needles from a cedar tree?"

Gladys took small squares of fabric out of the basket. "His living room smells musty, like no one has opened any windows for years. I thought about making cedar sachets. He didn't have a Christmas tree, either." She held a sewing needle up to the window light and pushed a thin strand of green thread through the eye. "It's sad, really. That big house and no one to share it with." Except for the surprising Haydn Johnson.

"I think it's wonderful how you're reaching out to Mr. Keller. I've only seen him once or twice since his wife's death. I admit, he struck me as a grouchy sort."

"He wasn't that bad." Gladys ran small, even stitches down the sides of the fabric. She used a soup spoon to fill the small pouch with needles before cutting a length of cheery red ribbon to tie it closed. "One down, nine to go."

"Do you plan on redecorating the entire house?" Ma lifted the sachet to her nose. "Such a lovely scent. Can God smell things?"

Gladys was used to her mother's sometimes whimsical thought processes. Her mind ran through the five senses. "The Bible says He sees us. He hears us. We're told to 'taste and see that the Lord is good.' Jesus told Thomas to 'touch and see.' Smell, hmm, I remember something about prayers smelling like incense." She picked up the Bible Pa read from every evening and leafed through the book of Revelation. "Here it is. 'And another angel came and stood at the altar, having a golden censer; and there was given unto him much incense, that he should offer it with the prayers of all saints upon the golden altar which was before the throne.'"

Ma laid the sachet back in the basket. "Of course God was using words we could understand to explain things. I wish I could have been a fly on the wall at creation."

Gladys finished another sachet. "I want to finish these tonight. I told Haydn—Mr. Johnson, I mean—that I would come over tomorrow to finish hanging up the baskets."

"It's Haydn now, is it?" Ma's eyes twinkled. "I'll have to meet this young man. I've never seen you this interested in one of our local boys."

Gladys chewed her lip. "I'm doing it for Mr. Keller, Ma. But Ruth and I ran into Mr. Johnson at the diner. After I made such a nuisance of myself the last time I went to the house, I thought it was best to warn them of my visit."

Ma only nodded and smiled.

Gladys finished the last of the sachets after the evening meal. The pie was cooling on the windowsill. When she finished, she cleared off the table. After she dressed for bed, she found Ma studying the contents of the baskets she had prepared. "Why don't you fix them some fried chicken while you're at it?"

Gladys's heart sped at the thought of fixing her special cinnamon chicken for the two bachelors at the Keller house. Then she caught herself. "I've done enough already. As far as I know, they have plenty to eat, even if they are basic dishes."

In the morning, Gladys checked the knot on the back of her head—no one wanted hair served with their food—and headed out the door. "I'll be back after lunch to pick up the food."

"I'll make sure the children leave the baskets alone," Ma called after her.

"Thanks, Ma." As Gladys headed for the diner, she hoped a brisk walk would clear her head of troublesome thoughts of Mr. Keller's young guest. Instead, her anticipation grew, hoping he might return to the diner while she was at work. *Shame on you, Gladys Polson.* She wanted to engage Mr. Keller, not his guest, with people.

Even though the walk didn't take care of her wayward thoughts, it did provide a nice break between the kitchen at home and the kitchen at work. She wasn't sure which she enjoyed more, cooking a good meal or sewing, especially quilting. Ma said Gladys was practicing for a whole passel of children someday. The only problem was she needed a husband first, and not one of the eligible young men in Calico had ever caught her fancy.

Her thoughts strayed again to Haydn Johnson. He interested her because he was someone new, that was all. A college graduate and city dweller wouldn't look twice at a small-town girl like her.

After lingering during the walk, she sped up to reach the diner on time. As she opened the door to the jingle of the bell, she spotted a familiar profile, head thrown back in laughter. She smiled at the sound.

Aunt Kate spotted her first. "Come over here and sit a spell." She winked. "Don't worry. It counts as work."

Since the diner was emptier than usual for this time of day, Gladys took advantage of the offer. "If anyone comes in, I'll wait on them. Why don't you join us?"

"Don't mind if I do." Aunt Kate sat down with a *whomp*. "Mr. Johnson—"

"Haydn, please. And Miss Polson, please, call me Haydn also."

"And you may call me Gladys." *Haydn.* Gladys loved the way his name sounded. She noted with amusement that Haydn was eating the breakfast special. Did Mr. Keller only serve toast?

"It's lovely to see you again. I understand you have business with Mr. Keller. How long do you expect to be in town?" Aunt Kate asked.

Her aunt sounded like a cross between a busybody and a father interrogating a suitor, but Haydn didn't seem to mind. He pulled his attention away from the newspaper at his elbow. "Do you mind if I take this with me?"

"Of course not."

He folded the paper and tucked it beside his plate. "I expect to remain in town several weeks. We are discussing our arrangement."

"Norman always did like a good bargain. He was active in the community when he was younger." Aunt Kate nodded. "Don't look so surprised. Something happened with his son that created an estrangement between them. He took it hard, and then when his Minnie died, he took to staying by himself. It was sad. He turned away from the very people God intended to help him through hard times."

The food lodged in Haydn's throat at Aunt Kate's statement. The only grandfather he had ever known was the aloof and forbidding Old Man, someone who seemed to have no interest in his only son and grandchildren. But perhaps the estrangement could be blamed on both sides. Haydn determined to start thinking of him as "Grandfather."

Coughing, Haydn swallowed some water. He took up another spoonful of stew and blew on it, pretending that the heat of the previous mouthful had caused his spasm.

"How is his health? Is he faring well?" Aunt Kate asked.

The grandfather Haydn knew wouldn't welcome that question, not even from his grandson.

Gladys said, "I confess I wondered the same thing. You will let us know, won't you, if he could ever use some help?" She smiled.

"He does have a bad cough. I asked him about sending for the doctor, but he refused."

Gladys exchanged a look with her aunt. "I'll fix chicken soup for him," Aunt Kate said.

Grandfather would throw the soup across the room if he learned that Haydn encouraged the people of Calico to intrude on his privacy. "That may not be such a good idea."

"I'll bring it with me when I come over this afternoon. He doesn't have to know where it came from." Gladys glowed with goodwill, and Haydn couldn't say no.

Aunt Kate snapped her fingers. "Even if he objects, maybe you can coax him to eat the soup. That will put some meat on his bones." She disappeared into the kitchen.

Gladys giggled as the door shut behind her. "If I know Aunt Kate, tomorrow she'll come to your place with two loaves of bread and a fresh crock of butter and claim she made too much."

"You're the one who showed up at the house ready to hang baskets. I guess helping others runs in the family."

"Whether they want it or not." She paused, sipping on her coffee. "I confess, I baked a pie to bring today. And I added jam for corn bread or biscuits." A pretty pink infused her cheeks. "I sensed you have a sweet tooth and don't get much to satisfy it."

"Bread and water, that's it." Haydn winked at her.

Mischief shone from her eyes. "You're making fun of me."

"No, I admire your reasoning. You were able to deduce my sweet tooth from only a few clues."

The kitchen doors swung open, and Aunt Kate appeared carrying a box. "Now, you can't refuse. It's only a small crock with hot stew in it."

A snicker escaped from Gladys. Haydn didn't dare look at her for fear he would break out laughing. "I'll have a hard time convincing him these are leftovers." He knew she would ignore his feeble protest.

"Nonsense. Mr. Keller knows I'd feed an entire cavalry if they stopped by. I love feeding a man with a good appetite."

The bell over the door jangled, and Gladys slid out from the booth. "It's the mayor. I'd better put my best foot forward."

Haydn finished his food, but it didn't taste nearly as good without Gladys's company. Rather than going to the register, he calculated how much he owed for today's meal and left three times the amount—for today, yesterday's free meal, and the basket of food Kate had prepared. He would have left more if he thought he could get away with it. Tucking the box under his arm, he headed out before either Gladys or Kate could catch him.

Haydn stole home as quickly as he could and headed straight for the back door so he could leave the food in the kitchen.

"Haydn? Is that you?"

Haydn spun around at the sound of Grandfather's raspy voice. "Yes, Grandfather?"

"What's that?"

"I didn't finish all my food at the diner. Aunt Kate sent it home with me. Let me dish some out for you." Haydn's speech was rushed, but Grandfather didn't seem to notice.

"Kate, huh? That woman is never happy unless she's cooking for someone." Grandfather chuckled, as if he knew the cook well. He sniffed the bowl. "Beef stew. Smells good enough to make me hungry." He sat down and dug into the bowl, finishing quickly. "I'd like some more." His eyes brightened at Haydn's surprise. "I know the woman. I'm sure that crock is full."

Laughing, Haydn refilled his grandfather's bowl. "Do you want me to heat it up for you?"

"Nah." The word scraped the bottom of Grandfather's throat. He spooned more stew into his mouth. "Her stew is good even when it's cold."

Haydn sat down across from his grandfather. Questions spun through his mind, ones he didn't know how to ask.

Grandfather took longer on the second bowl. Haydn pushed a piece of pie across the table. "Help me eat the pie she sent over yesterday."

Grandfather lifted the plate and stared at the filling. "This calls for some cream." His eyes gleamed with pleasure, and he went to the icebox. He brought out a small bottle of cream. "Betcha thought I didn't know where to find it."

"You sound like you've had her pie before."

Grandfather set down his fork. "She kept the house going when your grandmother was sick." The bleak expression on his face told Haydn not to intrude on his memories. Sure enough, he changed the subject. "Keep going to the diner. That place is gossip central. A good place for a newspaperman to pick up on local news."

Haydn hadn't accepted his grandfather's offer to start a newspaper—yet. But it wouldn't hurt to learn more about the town. Gladys had occupied so much of Haydn's attention that he hadn't noticed much happening around him. The next time he returned, he would have to open his eyes and ears.

Grandfather began to cough in midbite, spitting out crumbs of pie in the process. He gestured wildly. Haydn poured him a glass of water, and he gulped it down. "More." The word came out as a croak. Haydn emptied the pitcher before the coughs subsided.

Grandfather pushed away the plate, the slice of pie half-eaten. "That teaches me to accept handouts."

"You can't blame your cold on the stew." Haydn bit his tongue to keep from saying any more. If Grandfather got worse, he would send for a doctor. For now, he heated water. Tea with honey and lemon should help.

Grandfather scowled. "Maybe not. But it didn't make it any better either."

Chapter 5

Confidence bolstered Gladys as she prepared for her second visit to the Keller mansion. Knowing that Mr. Keller was probably resting and that she had an ally in Haydn made the afternoon's task seem less like a siege and more like a social call.

"I've used all the baskets. I need to get some more with my next pay." The only basket left in the pantry was the one Ma used for summer picnics.

Ma waved away her concern. "Go ahead and use the picnic basket, I can get another one before summer. Now get the sachets out of here before our lunch smells like cedar."

Laughing, Gladys carried the first two baskets to the wagon. As she packed them in, Haydn came up behind her. "I thought you might need help carrying your pretty baskets, but I see you have it all organized."

"You can help me bring things out from the kitchen." She walked with a light step as Haydn held the door open for her.

Ma greeted Haydn with a bright smile. "You must be Mr. Johnson."

"And you must be Gladys's sister."

Ma colored prettily at that bit of flattery. "That's kind of you to say, Mr. Johnson, even if it is a bit of foolishness. Gladys is our eldest."

Gladys handed Haydn the heavier baskets with glass jars and then lifted more greenery baskets.

"You'll have to come for dinner one night while you're in town. You and Mr. Keller must take a break from your business discussions from time to time. Can you make it Saturday evening? Or perhaps Sunday after church?"

Ma was clever to give Haydn a couple of choices and make it harder for him to say no.

But then Gladys had another thought, and her face grew warm. With such an impromptu invitation, Haydn might feel like they viewed him as a potential suitor.

But Haydn took the offer in stride. "Provided it's acceptable to Mr. Keller, I'll come over after church." Tipping his hat, he took the baskets outside, and Gladys followed him.

Haydn placed his baskets in the wagon then helped Gladys with hers. After they finished loading the wagon, and as she lifted her leg to get up, he slipped his arms around her and whisked her onto the passenger's seat. Never before had her spine tingled at the courteous gesture in all the times Pa had done the exact same thing.

By the time the momentary surprise had passed, Hayden had swung onto the driver's seat. "Are you ready?"

At her nod, he snapped the reins over the horse's head.

During the short ride to the mansion, Gladys glanced at Haydn's profile out of the corner of her eye. Brown hair streaked with lighter colors, strong, handsome, clean cut—a man who would look right at home in a city. She couldn't imagine him settling down in a small town the size of Calico.

Where had that thought come from? Haydn had no intention of staying in Calico. As soon as he finished his business with Mr. Keller, he would leave. She mustn't expect any romance from that corner.

Her spirits sank at that thought, but there was no reason she couldn't enjoy an afternoon in his company. He rushed, however. When she dawdled with every basket, he sped up, and they finished the project faster than Gladys thought possible.

Haydn dusted his hands on his Levi's, flecks of snow melting on the denim. "After all that work, we've earned a warm beverage, don't you agree?" He opened the door and swept her inside before she could say no.

He settled her in the front parlor before heading to the kitchen. When she rose out of the chair to follow, he shook a finger at her. "You are not to help me. This kitchen is a man's domain." He smiled his devastating smile and disappeared.

Gladys took advantage of the reprieve to explore. Tinkling noises confirmed Haydn's presence in the kitchen, and she scooted out of her chair. The personality of the parlor should reveal something about its owner. She almost hoped Mr. Keller would wake up so they could visit some more. Their verbal sparring had given her pleasure, and she suspected Mr. Keller enjoyed it as well. Besides, he was the man God had called her to reach with His love, not his more-than-amiable guest.

The room was considerably warmer than it had been on her last visit, thanks to the cheery fire in the grate. Mr. Keller's wife had probably provided the homey touches. Two samplers took pride of place on one wall. In addition to a wedding design, a birth sampler included a verse about the blessing of a quiver full of children. Maybe they had hoped for a large family. As far as Gladys knew, the Kellers only had the one child. And he had moved away before his mother had died. No wonder Mr. Keller seemed so sad, angry even.

More surprising than the samplers was the collection of whittled creatures on the mantel. Birds and rabbits, a train car or two. She ran her hands over the smooth wood, thinking how much her little brother would enjoy them.

"I used to play with those when I was little." Haydn had returned with a tea tray.

Gladys swiveled, embarrassed at being caught snooping. "You were here as a child?" She wondered about the exact nature of the business between the two families. The question was hovering on the tip of her tongue when one of the rabbits fell on the floor with a clattering sound. Swooping down to pick it up, she discovered a tiny piece of his ear was broken off.

"So it's you back here, bothering my peace and quiet."

Mr. Keller stood at the bottom of the stairs, one hand on the railing, the other on a sturdy walnut walking cane. In his brown-eyed glare, humor gleamed. But Gladys couldn't return his banter. She felt like a naughty child, holding the mutilated rabbit behind her back.

"Caught!" Smiling, Haydn reached for the creature she was holding. "Are you worried about that little broken place? I did that when I was a boy."

"That he did," Mr. Keller grumbled. "He threw those things every which way and that. I made a bunch more of them, but those are the sturdy ones that survived a boy's hard play." He crossed the room, his cane tapping the floor. He took the rabbit from Haydn and examined it before setting it back in its place on the shelf. "Silly thing for me to spend my time on."

After that brief glimpse into a happier time, Mr. Keller sat down. As he pulled a blanket over his lap, a cough seized him, knocking the cover to the floor. Gladys and Haydn sprang forward at the same time, their hands brushing. Haydn draped the blanket over the older man's shoulders while Gladys poured a cup of tea and added enough cream to cool it. She held it to Mr. Keller's lips. "Drink this. It should help."

He slowly drained the cup, and the coughing subsided. She glanced at Haydn, worry written on her features.

"Mr. Keller, you really need to see a doctor."

Haydn read the signs of the coming explosion even as his grandfather coughed into his handkerchief. "Nonsense. Just because my—Mr. Johnson—has brought you into my house, doesn't give you the right to tell me what to do."

"She's right, you know." Later, when the Old Man had settled down, Haydn would slip out and ask a doctor's advice. For now, all he could do was sit and watch. And pray.

Gladys fixed a second cup of tea. "Did you add any honey? It always helps me when my throat hurts." When Haydn shook his head, Gladys held the cup for Mr. Keller to drink.

The Old Man brushed it away. "I'm not so helpless that I can't feed myself. Why don't you leave a man alone to enjoy his privacy?"

"You know better than to treat a lady that way," Haydn said. Every unkind word Grandfather spoke diminished his chances of seeing Gladys again. Even if Haydn met someone he might marry and he chose to remain in Calico, who would want to stay around a man who could change his mood at the drop of a hat?

Grandfather rose out of his chair, shaking his cane at Gladys. "And don't bother coming back."

With a final desperate look at Haydn, Gladys stumbled toward the door.

Haydn dashed across the floor in two giant steps and held her cloak for her. Leaning close enough to whisper, he said, "I would still like to join you for Sunday dinner. If that is acceptable after today. I'll bring the dishes Aunt Kate sent over. You might not believe it, but he ate every bite of the stew."

She nodded. "Get him to see a doctor if you can, will you?"

He opened the door for her. "I'll let you know on Sunday. I'm so sorry things turned out this way today." He helped her into the wagon and watched her drive away, disappearing down the street. Her departure leached some of the color from the brightly colored baskets hanging on the porch.

"Shut the door, boy, before you let all the heat out."

All the warmth had fled the room with Grandfather's outburst, but Haydn did as requested. He crossed the room and climbed the stairs.

When Grandfather coughed this time, it sounded forced, a plea for sympathy. Haydn made himself turn around and return to the living room. Grandfather picked up his teacup. "Get me some honey, will you? You'll find it behind the jams on the shelf underneath the counter at the back of the pantry."

Haydn smelled the chicken soup he had left steaming on the stove. Bless Aunt Kate. This was perfect for Grandfather. Deciding to risk his anger, Haydn dished out a deep bowl and brought it out on a tray along with the honey.

"Here's the honey. And something extra you don't deserve, not after the way you treated Gladys today." He opened the jar of honey and poured a bit into Grandfather's tea.

"Tea with milk tastes like child's pabulum." In spite of his complaint, Grandfather drank it. "I suppose Kate sent over the soup. She seems to think she can cure every ill in the world with some chicken soup."

"A lot of women agree with her. Including my mother." Haydn itched to get away, to go upstairs, but he made himself wait. This was a time to prove Paul's statement that "love is patient, love is kind" and to continue helping when everything in him wanted to run.

The heated red of Grandfather's cheeks subsided, and he didn't cough again while he downed the bowl of soup. Neither one of them spoke until he finished.

Now that the immediate danger had passed, Haydn spoke his mind. "I'm ashamed of you, for the way you treated Gladys. All she's done is offer friendship, and you attacked her."

Grandfather threw back his head and laughed. "That's the spirit."

Haydn stared.

"I was waiting for you to show some backbone, something to light your fire about that young thing. I guess I did it, didn't I?"

It was Haydn's turn to frown. "You frightened her so bad, she may never return."

"No worry about that." Grandfather chased a final chunk of chicken around his bowl. "She's too much like Kate to give up easy." He placed the bowl back on the tray. "When are you seeing her again?"

"Sunday. Her mother invited me to join them for dinner."

"Excellent." Grandfather rubbed his hands together. "Time to meet the family."

The remainder of the week passed quietly enough. Occasionally Grandfather's coughing woke both of them up in the middle of the night. Haydn had taken to leaving a mug of tea with milk and honey on Grandfather's dressing table when he went to bed. Downstairs, hot water simmered in a teapot over low heat for the night, in case he needed more. If he needed help, he had a bell he could ring to call Haydn. He didn't get any worse, and although he didn't get any better either, Haydn decided the doctor could wait for now.

Grandfather shooed him away earlier than usual on Saturday night. "Stop fussing over me like an old mother hen. I've got my bell here if I need help." He picked it up and shook it. "If you want to make a good impression on Gladys's father, you'll put on your best suit to go along with your fresh haircut. If you want to get her mother on your side, you'll praise her cooking, even if it's charred, and her wonderful children, even if they run on top of the tables."

Haydn had to smile at that. He'd never cared enough about a woman to worry about what impression he made on her family. But Gladys, she just might be different.

Haydn didn't know how Grandfather had guessed about his trip to the barbershop. His mustache was trimmed about a quarter of an inch, the hair at the back of his neck shaved, the irksome cowlick at the top of head cut short and tamed with pomade. Would it be obvious to Gladys as well? He shook the thought away. No need to dwell on it. Every man got his hair cut sooner or later.

The season kept Haydn from taking flowers to offer his hostess, so instead he'd stopped by Finnegan's Mercantile and asked the owner for any candies he carried. As he paid for the candy, he spotted a silver hair comb that had ruby-colored stones set in the handle. On an impulse, he added that to the purchase. He could imagine it holding Gladys's dark curls in place.

Sticking the items in his pocket the next morning as he prepared for church, Haydn debated the wisdom of giving Gladys the comb. He might as well ask her father for permission to court his daughter if he gave her such a personal gift. Despite Grandfather's conditional promise to fund the newspaper, or maybe because of it, Haydn wasn't ready to commit to courtship.

When he saw Gladys enter the sanctuary in the company of Ruth and two other women he hadn't met before, her hair sparkled in the light. He wanted to rush over and give the comb to her right then and there. The girls disappeared into the cloakroom before he caught up with them, and he stopped himself. He waited, ready to greet Gladys as they came out.

"—since he's so rich."

Haydn thought it was the blond who said that. "Oh, Mr. Keller is rich enough to buy himself ten carriages if he wanted to," Gladys said.

The words hit Haydn like a slab of ice, and he stumbled away. Maybe Gladys Polson was nothing but a money-hungry schemer after all.

Chapter 6

Gladys wasn't sure what she had said about Haydn that got her brothers so excited.

The youngest, Georgie, in his first year at school, couldn't wait to play trains with their guest. On Sunday morning he was pushing two small blocks of wood across the floor. "Choo-choo, chugga, chugga. Do you think Mr. Johnson will bring his caboose with him?" He had latched on to Gladys's mention of the carved toys.

"I don't think so. They belong to Mr. Keller, not Mr. Johnson."

Georgie shrugged. "I bet he'll play with me. I'll ask."

Whether he would or wouldn't, Gladys didn't know. "Maybe. Now put those away and stand up before you get your Sunday clothes dirty."

"He won't want to play trains with you," Glenda, the youngest girl in the family, huffed. "He's going to come outside and throw snowballs with us."

Gordon, Glenda's twin, told Georgie, "You can play with us if you want to."

"Why do you all think he's going to play with you?" Gladys asked. "Maybe Ma invited him so she and Pa could visit with him."

"They're all excited about meeting him because you haven't stopped talking about him." Grace, closest to Gladys in age at fifteen, grinned. "You start every other sentence with 'Haydn.' 'Haydn caught me when I fell off the ladder,' and 'Haydn helped me hang the baskets.' Ma only invited him so you could see him again."

After that too-close-to-home statement, Gladys didn't ask any more questions. When she'd left the Keller mansion a few days ago, she could have sworn Haydn was every bit as upset as she was at Mr. Keller's outburst. The way he asked if he was still welcome in their house had warmed her heart. His question hinted that he was eager to see her again, even to spend time with her family.

If she'd thought her family was bad, the sewing circle was even worse. Annie wormed the story of Gladys's last visit out of her in less than fifteen minutes.

"He's sounds mean as an ogre. I wouldn't go back." Annie shook her pretty blond curls.

"That's what I thought at first." Gladys struggled to put her thoughts into words.

"But God called you to love Mr. Keller, even when he's grouchy and mean?" Ruth guessed.

Gladys squirmed uncomfortably and stopped stitching for a moment. "Something like that. Only I don't know what to do next."

"Ask Mr. Johnson if Mr. Keller ate the soup you brought to him. Maybe you can bring more over," Ruth said. "Isn't there a verse in the Bible that talks about heaping coals of fire on your enemy's head? Not that Mr. Keller is your enemy."

"That's a good idea. I'll ask Haydn tomorrow."

That statement started the speculation all over again.

Gladys hoped her friends had worked the teasing out of their systems at their Saturday meeting. But on Sunday, when they all arrived at church about the same time, Annie started in again.

"It's a pity that Mr. Keller is so unhappy, since he's so rich."

"Oh, Mr. Keller is rich enough to buy himself ten carriages if he wanted to." Gladys fingered the lace on her collar and wondered why she had gone to so much trouble. "But money hasn't made him happy."

When they left the cloakroom, Gladys spotted Haydn across the sanctuary, and a smile leaped to her face. She lifted her hand to wave, but he didn't acknowledge her presence in any way. She wondered if he had forgotten about the invitation.

Ma came up beside her. "Don't worry, Gladys."

How mothers sensed these things was beyond Gladys.

"I'll remind Mr. Johnson of our invitation." Ma made her way through the crowd like a cat weaving its way through a maze of feet. Gladys couldn't see over the tops of heads well enough to see what happened, but he joined them at their house after the service.

But something was wrong. The ease that had fueled conversation between the two of them disappeared, and their words fell into uncomfortable gaps at the dinner table.

Haydn covered it well. He talked with Georgie about all kinds of train cars, from engines to hoppers to the little red caboose.

"Can you whittle one for me, Mr. Johnson?"

"Not me." Haydn smiled. "Mr. Keller made those for me. I'm not any good at it."

"Then you can come outside and throw snowballs with us." Gordon sounded like Haydn's visit was for his special benefit.

"I will if your mother doesn't mind." The two of them discussed strategy, whether to use loose or hard-packed snow to throw.

Grace didn't say much to their guest, blushing whenever he glanced in her direction.

With Pa, Haydn discussed the finer points of Pastor Fairfield's sermon, taken from the love chapter in 1 Corinthians. "I try to love my wife like that. The way Christ loved the church." Pa pointed a fork at Haydn. "That's what I will expect from the men who marry my daughters."

Gladys could have sunk through the floor at that statement. What would Haydn think?

Haydn gave her a passing smile. "I don't blame you, sir." He didn't say anything to suggest he had any intentions toward Gladys at all.

The boys more than made up for Haydn's lack of interest in her, monopolizing his time from the moment they finished eating.

"Go ahead and talk with our guest." Ma tried to shoo Gladys out of the kitchen.

"I can't." Gladys pointed out the window. "He's out there playing with the boys already." Touching her collar again, she thought of the extra minutes she had spent on dressing this morning. Waste of time, as it turned out.

About the time Georgie tired of the game and stomped his boots at the door to shake off the snow, Pa met Haydn at the door and led him to the barn. Gladys took her time drying the dishes, her glance darting to the window more times than she wanted to admit.

When the two men exited the barn, Haydn headed down the street without returning to say good-bye to Gladys or her mother. Gladys stayed rooted to the spot until Pa came in.

At a single shake of his head, Gladys ran up to her room, holding back her tears until she could sob into her pillows.

When Haydn first overheard Gladys's comment, he decided to excuse himself from his visit to the Polson house. But faced with Mrs. Polson's friendly insistence and Gladys's hopeful face, he'd felt helpless to refuse. Maybe he had heard Gladys's words out of context.

Unwilling to risk his heart, he sat as far as possible from Gladys at the dinner table. He spoke to her only when he had to. He never expected her to be money hungry, but Grandfather's warning had turned out to be prophetic.

In spite of his resolution to keep his distance, Haydn couldn't help being drawn to the family. Who could resist little Georgie, who clung to his arm and sent snowballs across the yard with great abandon and bad aim? Or young Gordon, eager to prove his coming manhood? Even the two girls, Grace and Glenda, had charmed him with their blushes and giggles. They were the kind of younger sisters Haydn wished he had.

Not a one of them seemed curious about how much money he had or didn't have. As Haydn whisked the boys back into the house to dry off before they got too cold, Mr. Polson appeared. "Care to join me, Mr. Johnson?"

Although phrased as a question, the gleam in Gladys's father's eye told Haydn he'd better not refuse. Inside the barn, Haydn's horse neighed a greeting, and Haydn stroked its nose.

After Mr. Polson's comments about loving his wife as much as Christ had loved the church, Haydn could guess what was coming. What timing. The first time a father took him aside to ask, "What are your intentions toward my daughter?" happened within days after Grandfather laid down the stipulation that Haydn marry before year's end.

Gladys's father took his time getting around to the point. At last he took a seat on a bale of hay and gestured for Haydn to join him. "When I was courting my wife, I was a bundle of nerves. I never imagined what it was like for her father. Now I think it's even worse." He smiled. "Gladys is our eldest, my firstborn. I love all my children, but for three years, until Grace was born, we poured all our love and energy into Gladys. So if anyone were to hurt her in any way. . ." He left the sentence dangling.

Haydn gulped. What had Gladys said to give her father reason to think he was courting her? All he had felt was a passing interest, a curiosity, no more, a feeling born of proximity and new surroundings and his grandfather's impossible demand.

Mr. Polson continued. "I also want to be sure my daughter and any children she may have will be taken care of. What kind of business are you in, Johnson? Do you have the means to support a family?"

Money, again. Haydn's heart dropped. Even if it didn't matter to Gladys, it did to her father. Maybe she felt compelled to marry money.

"I'm afraid there's been a misunderstanding, sir." Haydn used all the skills he had picked up in elocution class at the university. "Gladys is a fine woman, but all that lies between us is a joint interest in making life better for Mr. Keller."

Mr. Polson frowned. "I had the impression, from what my wife said. . . More than that, I've seen the way Gladys looks when she mentions your name. I've never seen her like that, and there have been several young men who've come calling."

The conversation had taken an awkward turn. Haydn offered an olive branch. "I have, however, enjoyed working with Miss Polson to get Mr. Keller involved with the community again. He has shut himself away from people for too long." He paused, wondering how much he could say without revealing too much. "I don't know how much your daughter has told you about her last visit. After she left, Mr. Keller expressed regret over his harsh words." That wasn't exactly true, but Grandfather hoped for something to develop between Haydn and Gladys. "Please tell her that she is welcome at the house anytime."

Mr. Polson stood, brushing off his pants, his back straight, as if relieved of a heavy burden. "You may stay and tell her yourself." His eyes were at peace again. Did the man think Haydn was courting Gladys after all? Wasn't he listening?

Haydn didn't want to talk with Gladys privately where she could read the doubt in his eyes. "Mr. Keller is awaiting me. In fact, I told him I expected to return before this. Please tell Mrs. Polson how much I appreciated the wonderful meal."

When Mr. Polson opened the barn door, only gray light greeted them. "It looks like it's going to snow," he said.

The temperature had plummeted, turning the afternoon much colder than the morning. The first flakes of snow fell as Haydn returned home. His mind sped across the contents of their pantry. Even without more of Aunt Kate's food, they had plenty to last for several days.

At the house, Grandfather was chopping wood. What was he thinking? Haydn hustled down the side path, but Grandfather disappeared before he reached the woodpile. He filled his arms with logs and headed for the house. During the short walk home, the fury of the snowfall had increased. Haydn shivered inside his thick coat.

Grandfather reappeared with a wheelbarrow. "What are you carrying all that wood for? Put it in here with the rest of what I chopped." He grabbed the top logs from Haydn's arms and dropped them in the wheelbarrow, glaring at Haydn.

"I'll get them inside. You go on in before you get cold." Haydn glared back.

"I'll have you know I've been cutting my own wood since before you were a speck in your father's eye." Grandfather's chin jutted out. He tossed two more logs onto the wheelbarrow before he grabbed his arm in pain. As he doubled over, his breath wheezing, he began coughing. Haydn dropped the wood he was holding into the wheelbarrow and put his arm around Grandfather's shoulders, helping him into the house.

Chapter 7

On Tuesday morning Gladys awakened to a white world with a shining blue sky. Snow covered the limbs of trees and the ground, in spite of Pa's attempts to keep the path to the barn clear.

With the blizzard's onslaught coming on the heels of Haydn's Sunday visit, Gladys hadn't had a moment's peace to herself to think about her conversation with Pa on Sunday night.

He had evaded Gladys after Haydn left until the children went to bed. In the quiet, she sought him out in his refuge, his study. Standing in front of his desk, she asked, "What did you and Haydn talk about for so long out in the barn?"

"Now, Gladys, don't jump to any conclusions."

A quiet knock on the door interrupted them, and Ma came in.

"I'd like to hear what you have to say." She took a seat. "And Gladys. Pull up a chair and talk like a sensible young woman." Once everyone was situated to her satisfaction, she settled back in her chair. "Now, Herbert."

"Did you ask him what his intentions toward me are?" Gladys spoke crisply.

"Not in so many words." Pa squirmed a bit. "I think he felt threatened when I warned him not to do anything to hurt you. And I asked him if he had enough money to support a family."

Taken aback, Gladys almost laughed. Of course Haydn had work. He had come to Calico to conduct business with Mr. Keller.

"Gladys," Ma said. "You've wandered away from us."

Blinking, Gladys brought her thoughts back to the conversation. "What was Haydn's answer?"

Pa cleared his throat. "I don't want to disappoint you."

"Stop beating about the bush." Ma's voice held firm, but her hand cushioned Gladys's in its grip.

"He said he had no interest in you in that way. That what brings the two of you together is your desire to bring Mr. Keller out of his solitude."

Gladys had come to the same conclusion about their relationship. So why did it hurt to hear the truth come from her father's lips? "He's right, you know." She squeezed Ma's hand.

Ma's gaze pinned Gladys, daring her to speak the truth. "If you say so, Gladys. I will confess"—she cast one of "those" looks at Pa, the kind that always reassured Gladys that her parents loved each other and everything was all right with the world—"the way you look at Haydn when you think no one is watching reminds me of the way I used to look at your pa when we were courting."

Shame flamed heat into Gladys's cheeks. "You're the ones who taught me there's a difference between wishing and the truth." Not wanting to say any more on that topic, she added, "But I do believe God has more for me to do with Mr. Keller."

"Then all is well." Pa looked as relieved as a dog who escaped a scolding after licking his master's face. "That is exactly what Mr. Johnson proposed: that the two of you continue to partner in your work with Mr. Keller."

As always, Ma knew all was not well with Gladys. She kept the younger children out of her way as much as she could with the seven of them housebound. Gladys didn't know if she could take another day inside. Now, with the storm ended, she determined to get to the diner, even if she had to shovel the path herself. She donned several layers before she walked to the kitchen. Ma was already there, stirring up eggs and oatmeal. "You'd better eat a hot breakfast before you go out in this cold."

At least Ma didn't argue with Gladys about heading to work today. Even though Gladys's insides felt like burning fire, she wouldn't refuse the food. She added a bit of butter and milk and honey and cinnamon to the oatmeal and took a spoonful. Delicious, soothing, especially with the light-as-air eggs that were even better than the ones Aunt Kate cooked at the diner. The warm coffee finished the job. "Thank you, Ma. For everything." She threw her arms around her mother and hugged her. "You knew I'd head to work today." She buttoned up her coat.

"Of course." Ma grinned. "You have to get more soup for Mr. Keller."

Haydn hadn't slept much since Saturday night. After Grandfather's foolish hours spent chopping wood outside, he had turned really and truly sick. Haydn had never experienced a storm quite like this. Wind and snow blew so hard, a person could get lost walking from his house to the barn and back. With Grandfather so ill, Haydn did what he could and prayed for the best until the storm ended.

Dozing in the chair beside his grandfather's bed, Haydn woke with a start in the middle of the night. Peering through the snow crystals on the window, he saw that the storm had stopped. Grandfather's breathing had eased. As long as he was resting, Haydn would take advantage of the opportunity to clear a path to the street. Grandfather needed a doctor, although Haydn felt uncomfortable leaving him alone in the house for the time it would take to fetch one.

Haydn grabbed a shovel from the mudroom and opened the front door. The snow had drifted higher on the porch than he expected, in spite of the protection of the overhang. He stayed in the doorway only long enough to clear a place to stand then he shut the door behind him, trapping the heat inside. Soon enough the effort he expended left him warm, and he worked with a will.

When he left the porch, the snow reached Haydn's knees, and moonshine sparkled on the diamondlike surface. He continued until the first rays of the sun reminded him of the passage of time. As much as he wanted to finish the job, he needed to check on his grandfather. He tramped up the steps and opened the door, carrying his boots and snow-soaked garments to the adjacent mudroom.

Haydn added another log to the fire. The extra wood Grandfather had chopped had come in handy after all. Upstairs, the Old Man slept so peacefully that Haydn put his head to his chest to make sure he was still breathing. Pioneers lived like this all the time, with no medical help available except what they could do for themselves, locked up in a single-room hovel with no way to reach the outside world.

Haydn's experience hadn't prepared him for this kind of isolation. He didn't mind taking care of Grandfather or clearing the path, but he couldn't do both at once. Padding down the stairs to the kitchen, he scraped the last of Aunt Kate's chicken soup into a bowl. They'd reached the end of the food she had provided. He'd have to cook their next meal, maybe sausage gravy and biscuits.

Grandfather managed to eat the small amount of soup and drink a few sips of tea before he slipped back into sleep. His breathing rasped, and he felt hot to the touch. Thrashing, he threw his quilts on the floor. Every time Haydn replaced them, he flung them down again.

Haydn didn't know if he should keep Grandfather covered or allow him to cool down, without the quilts. The front parlor seemed like a good solution. With the fire, Grandfather would stay warm even if he kicked off every cover. Haydn placed one arm under the Old Man's neck and another under his knees. Amazing how insubstantial his grandfather felt in his arms, his body emaciated by illness. He picked his way down the stairs and laid Grandfather on the couch. Plumping the pillow under his head and covering him with a quilt, Haydn looked into his face. Seen like this, the man inspired pity and even love. He had lived and loved and survived.

If Haydn wanted to please his oldest living relative, he was supposed to find a wife within the next two months. So far the only women of marriageable age he had met in Calico were all members of Gladys's sewing circle. The ones who gossiped about Grandfather's money. "Lord, what am I supposed to do? Are You going to send a bride my way by special delivery on a train?"

Grandfather grunted at that, and Haydn rushed to his side. "What is it?"

Grandfather opened those dark eyes, clear for the first time since his collapse. "God will provide." His eyes drifted shut, and Haydn almost thought he had imagined those few words.

Because of checking on Grandfather so often, Haydn scorched his oatmeal. Bringing a big bowl out to the parlor, he ate it quickly and set it to one side. The family Bible sat on a nearby shelf, and he reached for it. With interest, he read the family record: his grandparents' marriage, his father's birth, the birth and death of a younger sister, his parents' marriage, his own birth as well as his younger brother's.

Of his grandmother's death, no record had been made. Looking at the flowing script, Haydn wondered if she had kept the records up to that point. He found no mention of his youngest brother, born twelve years ago. Haydn found writing materials in the study. No one else was available to bring the family record up to date.

He added Grandmother's name but laid down the pen when he couldn't recall the exact date of her death. Maybe he could find it on her gravestone. After adding his brother's birth date, his eyes drifted to the page set apart to record marriages. With only two entries, the blank lines called to him. Whose name would be joined with his?

Haydn turned to the gospel of Mark, hoping Mark's active writing style, rather like the way he wrote for the newspaper, would hold his interest. But before he could even finish the account of John the Baptist preaching in the wilderness, the Bible dropped into his lap and he fell asleep.

Loud knocking awakened Haydn, and a familiar voice called, "Mr. Keller? Haydn?"

Gladys. How had she made her way to his doorstep through the snow?

Gladys held Aunt Kate's basket on her arm. The unrelenting freeze continued even without wind-whipped snow driving icy pellets into her face. Pastor Fairfield was with her. He had rallied the men who made it to the diner to sweep through the town, stopping at every house not yet dug out from the storm. Gladys came with him as far as the Keller mansion, wanting to deliver food.

"Just a minute," Haydn called to them through the door. A light wind had scattered a thin blanket of snow over the porch boards she assumed Haydn had shoveled. She shivered and hoped he had convinced Mr. Keller to keep the front room warm. The doorknob rattled, and the door swung open with a welcome *whoosh* of warm air. "Gladys, Pastor Fairfield. Come in. What brings you out on such a cold day?"

"We're checking all the houses that haven't dug out from the snow yet," Pastor Fairfield said. "I see you started but didn't have a chance to finish."

"And I brought you some soup." Gladys pointed to the basket on her arm. She glanced into the parlor, where she could see Mr. Keller stretched out under a quilt. "Is Mr. Keller ill?"

"Yes." Haydn conveyed a lot of emotion with that one word. "What about the doctor? Is he available?"

Pastor Fairfield nodded. "He was one of the men at the diner whom we recruited to go door-to-door. I'll hunt him down and tell him he's needed over here." He patted the top of his hat. "I'll move on, then. Are you able to see yourself home, Miss Polson?" He shook Haydn's hand. "I'll ask my wife to come by later to see if you need any additional help."

Gladys nodded. "I'll go back to the diner. That's the first place people head when they get out of the house. Aunt Kate will need my help."

"Come in and sit a spell, if you care to." Haydn acted pleased to see her, as if they had parted on the best of terms. He helped her out of her coat and took her basket. "You're an angel sent by God Himself. We were down to my biscuits and gravy for supper, and I'll warn you, that's not too good."

Gladys smiled politely. She walked closer and stood over Mr. Keller, assessing his condition. His cheeks were flushed, and his breathing was raspy.

A quilt molded into the shape of a man filled the chair next to the sofa. Haydn drew another chair close to the sofa and held it for her.

"How long has Mr. Keller been sick?" Gladys settled into the roomy chair. She could barely touch the floor with her toes.

"When I got home on Sunday, the foolish man was outside chopping wood. He got very sick not long after that."

"And you've been by his side ever since?" She shook her head. "You can't do that night and day."

"It hasn't been so bad." The droop to Haydn's eyes suggested otherwise. "I've slept in snatches."

"And you stayed awake long enough to start clearing that path."

"I was trying to figure out how I could finish the path, get to the doctor, and keep an eye on Mr. Keller all at the same time." He leaned forward and tugged the quilt over the older man's shoulders. "I don't know what I would have done if Pastor Fairfield hadn't stopped by and offered to get the doctor."

Haydn was one special man, taking such good care of a business associate who could be as grouchy as a mama bear with cubs when roused. Gladys made a snap decision. "I'll stay here with him. If we need extra help, I'll ask the sewing circle. Mrs. Fairfield, too. You can't stay in Calico forever, not with business back home to attend to."

Haydn fell back against his chair, disappointment stamped on his face.

Chapter 8

Haydn's eyes strayed to the family Bible, which had fallen open to the page for recording family marriages. A couple of times recently, when his heart tried to cast Gladys in that role, he'd remembered what she said about Grandfather's riches. He still didn't know how important money was to her or what to expect if she learned about his relationship with his grandfather.

He realized his brief silence had distressed her. "My family's association with Mr. Keller is of long standing. They would not want me to return as long as he is ill." He stopped short of reminding her that his business concerns weren't any of her concern. That would be rude, when all she had done was offer to help.

The clouds in her eyes cleared, and she smiled. "The offer to help still stands. You can't continue to take care of him twenty-four hours a day. Let me at least help with that." She leaned forward, brushing his grandfather's hair back from his temples. "He has lovely, thick hair. Sleeping like that, he doesn't look sick. Like he could jump off that sofa and stomp down the walk and join us at the diner. I know Aunt Kate would like to see him."

When Gladys acted as solicitous as a granddaughter might, Haydn didn't know what to think.

Someone knocked at the door, sparing him. He opened the door to a welcome figure carrying a black bag

Gladys sprang to her feet. "Dr. Devereux! I'm so glad Pastor Fairfield found you."

The doctor knocked snow off his boots. "I would have been here sooner except I had to go back to the diner for my bag. Now, what seems to be the problem?"

Haydn described the past few days while the doctor examined his patient. "There's not much to do beyond what you are already doing. Medicine has made some remarkable discoveries, but we still don't have a cure for the common cold. Let me see how bad he is." Dr. Devereux placed his stethoscope against Grandfather's chest.

"Get that thing off me. It's cold enough to freeze my skin." Grandfather pushed away the instrument and glared at Devereux. "I don't like doctors. All you do is say a bunch of words and charge a lot of money."

The doctor continued checking him. "I don't like the sound of his lungs. If he gets too restless, you can give him some of this laudanum." He poured a small amount into a bottle. "Only a teaspoon, and only if he really needs it."

"Dr. Devereux, should we use a cold compress? Or do they do more harm than good?" Gladys asked.

"I'm not sure what the scientists say. But I figure remedies folks have used for years must have some value. Otherwise, people would stop using them. Steam, too, can help clear his sinuses."

Gladys nodded. Haydn would ask for an explanation about a cold compress later. "One more thing I can recommend. Mr. Keller has a strong constitution, and I expect him to get better. But in case this takes a turn for the worse, perhaps you should inform his family of his condition. I've heard him mention a son. Do you know whom to contact, young man?"

Haydn stammered a bit. "Yes, I believe so." *Me.* "I'll send a letter to his son as soon as I find out if the postal service is working." He'd do that, too. His father would want to know.

"Good." Dr. Devereux shifted his bag into his left hand. "Unfortunately, family business demands that I leave town as soon as possible. My daughter is expecting a difficult, um, confinement. There is an excellent physician over in Langtry. He'll be here next week, but if you need a doctor before then, you can contact him and see if he can come."

The doctor must have seen the terror that Haydn felt at his words. "As I've said, most of the time these illnesses work themselves through the system. Mr. Keller is a strong individual, and I expect him to rebound. I'll keep you both in my prayers."

Haydn asked, "How much do we owe you for the visit?"

"I'm not going to pay that charlatan a single penny," Grandfather rasped.

"Don't worry about that now. You just focus on getting him better." The doctor disappeared through the door.

"I'll go home and gather my things before I return." Gladys stared at Haydn, as if daring him to disagree. "I'll let my parents know where I'm going to be, and I need to get word to Aunt Kate not to expect me. I'll set up a schedule with Mrs. Fairfield." As she ticked off the things she would do, Haydn alternated between wanting to hug her and to shoo her away.

By the time she came back, Haydn had started on biscuits to eat with Aunt Kate's soup. Gladys carried a small valise with her. "Where can I leave my things?" She headed up the stairs as if she planned to stay awhile.

"There's a room to the left of the stairs," he called after her. "Do you want to eat?"

"Yes." She peered down the stairs. "Let me finish those biscuits for you. Give me a minute." She returned a few minutes later, her feet encased in warm slippers. "You go out there and stay with Mr. Keller while I finish up cooking."

Haydn wished they could linger over the table, enjoying bowls of soup and biscuits slathered in butter. But that defeated the purpose of watching over Grandfather.

Pulling his chair away from the fire, where the warmth tempted him to slumber, Haydn opened his Bible to Mark's gospel again. What would Jesus do if He showed up in Calico today? Would He have stilled the snowstorm that cut Grandfather off from a doctor's help when he needed it? Would He accept an invitation to supper and heal Grandfather as long as He was in the house? Sometimes the Jesus of the

Gospels seemed remote from life almost nineteen hundred years later.

Except for someone like Gladys, who loved people the way Jesus loved them. She brought out a tray with three bowls and a platter of biscuits. "I have an apple cobbler and whipping cream for dessert. Mr. Keller might not be able to eat it, but we can enjoy it."

Haydn spared a thought to wonder who had canned the jars in the pantry. Aunt Kate was probably behind the food. Gladys didn't touch her bowl; instead, she woke up Mr. Keller and fed him vegetable broth one spoonful at a time. She didn't stop until he emptied the bowl. "I bet a glass of milk would taste good, but I wonder if it would curdle in his stomach when he's sick like this." She lifted his head so he could drink from a glass of water.

Mr. Keller opened his eyes and roused enough to look around. "Minnie, is that you?" Lifting a shaky finger, he pointed it at Haydn. "Young man, you take good care of my Minnie, now." Refusing Gladys's offer of more water, he closed his eyes again.

"Minnie was his wife." Gladys's voice shook a little. "That was sweet." She exchanged the empty bowl for a full one.

"Do you want me to heat that for you?" His own empty bowl made him embarrassed. He hadn't waited on Grandfather; he hadn't even said a silent word of grace.

"This is fine." She gestured with her spoon. "Feel free to get yourself some more soup, or if you're ready, bring out the cobbler."

"If you don't mind, I'll take a second bowl of soup." He had given Grandfather the rest of the chicken soup yesterday. For himself, he hadn't eaten more than that bowl of charred oatmeal since then.

"Good. Then we can eat together."

After they finished the meal in companionable silence, Gladys insisted she would stay up that night with Mr. Keller. "You need to get some rest yourself, before you come down with whatever he has."

When she volunteered to share his burden like that, it was hard not to think of her as a potential partner in more than taking care of his sick grandfather.

On Wednesday night, Mr. Keller was restless enough to need laudanum. "I think it's gone into his chest," Gladys told Haydn.

"Do we need to go get that other doctor?" Haydn asked.

"Stop talking about me as if I'm not here." Coughing broke up Mr. Keller's words. That last bout of chest-racking coughs had awakened him. For the past twenty-four hours, he hadn't been able to sleep more than half an hour at a time. "I told you. No doctors. I hauled Minnie all the way to Topeka to see a doctor, and he didn't do her any good."

Gladys couldn't combat that argument, even when Haydn looked at her so pleadingly for an answer. "You heard what Dr. Devereux said. There's not much more the doctor could do." Taking Mr. Keller's hand, she made him look at her. "Mrs. Fairfield promised to ask Ma to bring over our medical book the last time she was here. It'll have some ideas we haven't tried yet."

She didn't add that she had asked Ma to also bring the small box where she kept her savings from work. She'd intended to use it for setting up her own house when she married, but she would willingly spend every penny if it would help Mr. Keller get better. Of course he had plenty of money, but she didn't know where he kept it. And she wouldn't feel right if she took it without asking him, even if it was to pay for his own supplies.

Someone knocked. "There she is now." Gladys hurried to the door.

Ma entered. "Mr. Johnson." She nodded at Haydn. Walking closer, she sat by Mr. Keller. "And Mr. Keller. It's good to see you again, although I wish it was under different circumstances."

"Is that Gladys your gal?"

Ma nodded, and Mr. Keller nodded with satisfaction. "She's a good one. I've told Haydn to hold on to her." He coughed and sank back against the pillows.

Ma handed Gladys the medical book. "I've marked a few remedies I've found work best. Go on, both of you, and look them over, while I visit with Mr. Keller."

Hugging the tome to her chest, Gladys walked into the kitchen, Haydn following behind. Neither one of them mentioned Mr. Keller's continued references to a match between the two of them. Keeping her tone brisk, Gladys turned to the first marker. "Here the author's talking about tea. Tea with honey—we're already doing that—and lemon." Her nose wrinkled. Lemons in February were as rare as fourteen hours of daylight. "Also peppermint is a good flavor for the tea. Maybe we can melt peppermint candy in hot tea. I wonder if that would work the same way. Maybe lemon drops, too." They'd be easier to find than an actual lemon.

Haydn nodded. "Those sound too simple."

"There's more." She turned to the next section that described what to feed their patient. "It does recommend chicken soup. But listen to this. It says to cook it with cayenne pepper. And even to add hot peppers with the vegetables." She hadn't cared for green peppers the one time she'd tried them. "I might be able to get hold of some green peppers."

Haydn shook his head. "Green peppers aren't hot. It's talking about chili peppers or something like that. I had some once when I went to Texas. They burned my mouth. Maybe it's supposed to burn away whatever is troubling his chest."

"I'll ask Ma." Flipping to the last marker, she found the section on steam treatments and scanned the article. "It says oils can make steam more effective, eucalyptus and lavender in particular." Now, those things Mr. Finnegan probably carried. Some women used oils to add scent to bath soap or to make perfumes.

Gladys made a list of things to look for at the mercantile. She grabbed a pencil to figure out an estimated cost. She should have enough, although it might cut her savings in half.

"I haven't been able to find Mr. Keller's money," Haydn said. "And I didn't bring that much with me. Will Mr. Finnegan put it on account?"

Gladys covered the total with her hand. "You don't have to worry about the cost. It's something I want to do."

"You really mean that, don't you?" Surprise stamped Haydn's face as he sat back. "You're willing to spend that much money on a man who's done nothing but yell at you?"

And say you should marry me. Gladys didn't point that out. "He's my brother in Christ. He's someone God loved enough to die for. I figure it's the least I can do."

She stomped out of the room before he could rile her even more by refusing her money.

Chapter 9

While Haydn waited, he heard Mrs. Polson say good-bye. He whirled on his heels and left the kitchen. Time after time, Gladys tore down his defenses with a simple act or gesture. He had seen the total for the supplies the medical book recommended. He didn't know where she could get her hands on that kind of money. Add to that all the money she lost by taking off the week to spend with Grandfather.

It was time he accepted her for who she was: a beautiful young woman who loved the Lord and for some reason known only to her and God, loved Grandfather no matter how he acted.

Haydn tossed his suitcase onto the bed and dug out his slim wallet. After his extended stay in Calico, he had spent most of the money he had brought with him. Paying for the last delivery of wood, a delivery Grandfather had insisted they didn't need, had nearly wiped him out. But what he had left, he would give to Gladys. It was *his* grandfather who was sick. He counted out the money, not nearly enough, and went back downstairs.

He pushed the money at Gladys. "Take this."

"You don't need to do that. I told you—I want to pay for this." She didn't touch the money.

"And so do I." He held out his hand, willing her to accept the money in spite of her earlier rejection.

"Why—so your business with Mr. Keller doesn't suffer?" He had hurt her.

The words hung between them. Haydn considered telling her the truth—*because he's my grandfather*—but his reasons were more complex than that. "Because I love him, too. I've grown up thinking of him as a loveless Ebenezer Scrooge of a man. But because of you, I've learned to love him, too." He pressed the money into Gladys's palm. "Take this from me. Please. Let me have a part in getting him well."

Gladys chewed her lip. "When you put it like that, what can I say?" A grin replaced her worried look. "And if there's any extra money, I'll get more food. Some of your supplies are running low."

Haydn glanced at the sleeping figure on the sofa. "Can you carry everything by yourself?" He wished he could go down to the mercantile with her, to enjoy a few hours of her company away from the sick man's bedside.

"I can." Gladys reached into her pocket and pulled out a change purse. "But why don't you go ahead? You haven't been out of this house for days."

The prospect sorely tempted Haydn, but he decided against it. "You need to do the shopping. You send me for eucalyptus oil and I might come back with castor oil instead."

"I'll be back before you know it."

❧

Gladys didn't know if it was the steam treatments, the vegetable broth spicy enough to strip green from copper, or the dried-up lemon Mr. Finnegan found for her. But by Sunday Mr. Keller had improved to the point where she and Haydn could leave him alone and go to church together.

She rejoiced that it was Palm Sunday, the beginning of Passion Week. Ruth led her schoolchildren in a reenactment of Jesus' triumphal entry, waving pine branches instead of palms, and Jesus riding a pony instead of a donkey. Ruth had recruited Gladys's brother Gordon to hold cue cards for the congregation.

With Gordon's encouragement, the rafters of the church rang with shouts. "Hallelujah! Blessed is he who comes in the name of the Lord." Heart lifted in praise and worship, Gladys could hardly believe the same crowd had cried, "Crucify Him!" less than a week later.

On Monday morning, the doctor from Langtry pronounced Mr. Keller well enough to get up if he wanted to. Speaking with Gladys and Haydn in the front parlor, he said, "You've done an excellent job, both of you."

"It was all Miss Polson's doing." Haydn reflected the credit back to her.

"All I did was follow the suggestions in my mother's medical book." Telltale heat raced into Gladys's cheeks.

The doctor nodded. "Since I'm not needed here, I'll go check on a couple of Dr. Devereux's other patients."

Gladys's valise waited under her cloak by the front door. "I'll say good-bye to Mr. Keller before I leave." She headed up to his room, where they had moved him earlier when he improved enough to climb the stairs. Knocking on the door, she called, "Mr. Keller?"

"That you, Gladys? Come on in." Mr. Keller sat up in bed, a pillow at his back. "It's about time I said thank you for all you've done. That young doctor said you had a lot to do with me getting better."

Gladys sat beside him, hands crossed in her lap. "It was God. I was only His instrument."

"You healed more than my body, young lady. You healed my heart. This next Sunday is Easter, isn't it?"

Gladys nodded. "My favorite time of year. I love Christmas, but Jesus' resurrection completes the story."

"You may be right." Mr. Keller patted her hands. "I plan on going to church with Haydn next week. We'll be looking for you."

"You will?" Joy spread through Gladys's body from the inside out. "That's the best news I've had since the first time I came to visit."

❧

Gladys called the sewing circle together to finish one final project for Mr. Keller. Late Saturday night, she knotted the final stitch on the surprise and wrapped it in plain brown paper with string.

Early Sunday morning, about the same time the women headed to Jesus' tomb, Gladys put the package in the bottom of a basket and added several of her mother's hot cross buns in a towel. Ma hugged her. "Have I told you lately how proud I am of you?"

"Too many times." She returned her mother's hug. "I'll see you at church if not before."

"If they invite you to stay for breakfast, go ahead and eat with them."

As Gladys headed out the door, her mother said, "He is risen!"

"He is risen indeed!" Gladys returned the greeting then picked her way down the street, a muddy morass from the melted snow. She knocked boldly on Mr. Keller's front door, none of the fear that had troubled her on her first visit stopping her this time.

She was about to knock a second time when Haydn opened the door, surprise evident on his face. "Gladys! What are you doing here so early?"

She followed him into the parlor. "I come bearing gifts. Ma sent boiled eggs and hot cross buns for your breakfast."

"That wasn't necessary."

"We wanted to." She continued into the kitchen, where Mr. Keller sat at the table. "Happy Easter, Mr. Keller." She removed the food from the basket and then lifted the package from the bottom. Feeling suddenly shy, she laid it in front of the old man. "This is for you."

Mr. Keller smiled. He *smiled.* "I got a present, and it isn't even Christmas. Get me some scissors, Haydn, so I can cut the strings. They're in the drawer next to the silverware."

He stripped the strings away and unwrapped the brown paper. "It's a quilt of some kind. That's a lot of work."

"A small one. My friends helped me finish it." Gladys tugged the two top corners and stretched the quilt out, revealing a log cabin design in shades of blue. "You can use it as a lap rug. That way you can always be cozy and warm. I thought you might like it, going out today."

Haydn bent over it, studying the stitches. "You do amazing work." He had set the table with three plates. "You will join us for breakfast, won't you?"

"Gladly."

Before Gladys could sit, Haydn blocked her chair. "Will you join me in the parlor for a few moments?"

Did he have a gift for her? Gladys's heart beat faster. She hadn't brought a gift for him.

Once in the middle of the room, Haydn dropped to one knee. After stumbling back a step, Gladys steadied herself, and Haydn caught hold of her fingertips. "Gladys Polson, you opened my eyes to a love I had never known. How could I help but fall in love with the woman who showed me the love of the Lord every day since I've met her? Although I'm not worthy of you, I still dare bare my soul to you. Will you marry me? Be my wife and share my life and my love?"

"Yes. I'll even follow you back to Topeka, if that is where God leads you."

The tap of a walking cane announced Mr. Keller, carrying his new quilt. "That won't be necessary."

Gladys wondered why Mr. Keller was interrupting this private moment, but she decided she didn't mind. They waited until he joined them and placed his hands on their arms. "Haydn won't be going anywhere. He'll be staying right here and starting a newspaper." He settled in his chair, and Gladys darted forward to tuck the new quilt around him. "Gladys, I'd like to introduce you to my grandson, Haydn Norman Keller."

Haydn grinned somewhat sheepishly. "You don't object to being a Keller and living here with my grandfather?"

Gladys looked from one man to the other, comparing those identical sparkling brown eyes. How had she missed it?

"Gladly. Tomorrow and for the rest of my life."

"Kiss her, boy."

And Haydn did.

DARLENE FRANKLIN

Bestselling author Darlene Franklin's greatest claim to fame is that she writes fulltime from a nursing home. She lives in Oklahoma, near her son and his family, and continues her interests in playing the piano and singing, books, good fellowship, and reality TV in addition to writing. She is an active member of Oklahoma City Christian Fiction Writers, American Christian Fiction Writers, and the Christian Authors Network. She has written over fifty books and more than 250 devotionals. Her historical fiction ranges from the Revolutionary War to World War II, from Texas to Vermont. You can find Darlene online at www.darlenefranklinwrites.com

The Spinster and the Cowboy

by Lena Nelson Dooley

Dedication

This book is dedicated to James Allen Dooley,
who married me fifty-one years ago and still loves me.
My life has been richer because you have been in it.
You are the one person who can come to my office door
and interrupt me when I am writing.
I love you more every day.

A good man leaveth an inheritance to his children's children.
PROVERBS 13:22

Prologue

San Francisco, Spring 1894

When the sharp rap on his closed office door roused him, Joshua Dillinger raised his gaze from the legal document he had been studying with intense concentration. He hated distractions, and Charles Ross, his secretary, knew it. Only something of great urgency would cause this interruption.

"Enter." Joshua realized that his command sounded abrupt, but he wanted to get this interruption over with so he could discern any flaws in the contract that had to be ready for signatures in less than an hour.

Brandishing an envelope, the thin man walked briskly across the rug that swallowed the sound of his footsteps. "This was just delivered by messenger, sir. I have a feeling it's important."

He handed the missive to Joshua and hurried out of the room, pulling the door closed behind him. Joshua studied his father's scratchy scrawl on the front of the letter. He wondered how the post office even knew where to send it. The older Father became, the worse his handwriting grew. If Joshua hadn't been used to deciphering the letters he received from his dad, he wouldn't have been able to tell what the address was.

Joshua placed the packet on top of the stack of documents that needed his attention today and turned back to his contract. He returned to the place where he held his finger on the paper, then went back to the beginning of the sentence and started over.

For the next forty-five minutes, he had a hard time keeping his mind on his task. Every few moments, his eyes strayed to the slightly wrinkled envelope. Joshua wondered what it contained, but he had to finish with the contract and send Charles over to the client's office with it.

After his secretary left with the completed document, Joshua stood and stretched. While he concentrated on a hard task, his muscles became more and more knotted. He rubbed his neck with both hands and rotated his shoulders, trying to loosen them, as he stared out across the bay from his perch most of the way up one of San Francisco's many hills. Joshua had chosen this office because of its view of the water. Not only could he keep up with the comings and goings of ships, but watching the bay in all kinds of weather proved soothing. He loved this city and once again thanked the Lord for the opportunities that had led him here.

Finally, Joshua turned around and picked up the letter from his father. He hoped it wasn't bad news. Using the opener with the beautifully carved scrimshaw handle his grandfather gave him when he first opened the law office, he slit the paper and removed the contents—a sheet of paper and an already-opened envelope with papers inside. Father had forwarded a letter he'd received from his best friend, Fred Cunningham. In his included note, his father added his own request that Joshua do what Fred asked of him.

Now curious, Joshua pulled out the other papers. Before he read the words, his memory revisited a time when he was twelve and his family traveled by coach from Texas to Arizona to visit the Cunninghams. Their ranch spread for hundreds of acres from the base of the Rincon Mountains toward a tiny town, really not much more than a few huddled buildings surrounded by tall cacti with arms that spread toward the sky. What was the name of those plants? Something that started with an *s* and sounded foreign to his young ears.

He had enjoyed that trip. The ranch was larger than the one his father owned in Texas. Much of the time, Joshua had accompanied Mr. Cunningham's nine-year-old daughter on wild rides around the vast acreage. With her brown braids flying in the wind, India could ride better than most of the cowboys. He often wondered about the girl. A few years after that trip, they'd received word that her mother had died. Did her death calm India or make her even wilder? He never heard anything more about them, because soon after that, he left home to study law.

Joshua turned his attention to the message. Fred Cunningham wanted Joshua to go to Arizona and help his daughter run the ranch for a time.

While perusing every piece of paper in the envelope, Joshua discovered that Mr. Cunningham had died almost a year ago. The message shouldn't have taken so long to reach him, but the man's lawyer had forgotten to mail it to Joshua's father until recently. Father had sent it on from Texas.

At first, Joshua decided that he should ignore the appeal. He was a city lawyer, a long way from the young man who grew up on the plains in Texas. He hadn't ridden a horse in years, preferring to use a buggy in the city. However, throughout the long afternoon, his mind kept returning to the request. Mr. Cunningham had been his father's best friend, and he wouldn't have asked something like this if he hadn't believed that India needed help. How could Joshua refuse?

When he finished work for the day, he stood watching the lights flicker on one by one up and down the hills that spread from his office toward the shoreline. Soon many of them reflected in the water of the bay, sending sparkles that looked like stars in the inky liquid.

In the last year, Joshua had taken two partners into the fast-growing firm. Because he worked so hard to build the business, he hadn't taken any time off. With the partners and a couple of junior lawyers to keep things going, maybe he could take an extended leave and fulfill Mr. Cunningham's dying wish.

Chapter 1

Arizona Territory

India Cunningham tried to blow away the curls that fell across her right eye. She didn't want to stain her white-blond tresses with the rich red barbecue sauce concocted by one of her ranch hands, Hector Gonzalez. India had no idea what all Hector put in the mixture, but she knew it left a mark on anything it touched. She would have to rub a lot of lemon juice on her hands before they would return to their natural color. Even then, it might take a day or two for the crimson stain to wear off.

Today should have been a good day for the fund-raiser for the Cactus Corner Orphanage. This time of spring was usually cool and mild. Not today. A blazing sun beat down, bringing a river of sweat that rushed down India's spine. She had worn a brown blouse in case some of the sauce splashed on it while she basted the whole steer her foreman, Nathan Hodges, butchered yesterday. While he slowly turned the spit holding the beef over the fire pit, India painted the side nearest her with sauce, making sure every inch of the carcass would absorb the tantalizing flavor.

Hector's sauce almost guaranteed the success of the event. Cowboys from every ranch for miles around flocked to get their share of the feast and add to the coffers of the orphanage. Today most of the cowhands' pay would be spent to help people instead of wasted in the saloon across from the general store.

The milling crowd kept even a hint of a breeze from reaching India. She had hoped to escape to the hotel and clean up before the festivities began, but the time for that was long past. Maybe no one would notice how terrible she looked since she was by the fire pit at the edge of the crowd. Wrinkling her nose, she shrugged her shoulders, trying to dislodge the fabric that was plastered against the moisture on her back.

"India Cunningham!" Jody McMillan pushed her way through the nearby crowd. "What are you doing still back here?" A frown replaced the questioning expression Jody had worn just a moment ago. "I thought you were going to clean up at the hotel. Didn't you take a room for that very purpose?"

India watched her good friend try to brush away some of the dust that had settled on the skirt of her own dress. Why ever did Jody wear such a light color to a picnic? Didn't she know it would show all the smudges? And all those ruffles would just hold in the heat.

After putting the sauce brush on a plate to catch the drips, India tried to push her hair back with her forearm. The attempt only dislodged the curls for a moment before they fell again. "I haven't had time to get away."

"Surely you don't want everyone to see you like that." Jody's hands fisted on her hips as she glared at India.

Just what she needed, to be reminded of how awful she looked after toiling over the barbecue most of the morning. If only Martha had been able to help her husband with the beef. Donating the steer should have been enough of a contribution for India to make, but lately, nothing came easy. For some reason, many of the men in the surrounding area didn't believe that a young woman could run a ranch as large as the Circle C. She had to prove her abilities to everyone except the hands on the ranch. They knew that ever since she returned from finishing school back East, she had been more in charge than her father.

"Do you want me to do that while you go clean up?" Even though Jody offered to take over painting the luscious-smelling beef, India could tell that she really didn't want to.

"And get this red stuff all over that dress?" India couldn't help laughing. "You'd never be able to wash it out." She thought about what else Jody had said. *Besides, there's no one I want to clean up for.*

The loud blast of the train's whistle announced the arrival of the eastbound in Cactus Corner, Arizona. Joshua stood and lifted his carpetbag from the seat beside him. He would pick up his larger luggage at the baggage car after he stepped down from the stuffy passenger compartment. He ducked his head and stared out the grimy windows. Cactus Corner was not the tiny village he remembered from the summer when he was twelve, but the mountains in the background held the same purplish cast against the clear blue sky. His family had come about this same time of the year, but he didn't remember it being so hot.

He pulled his attention to the surrounding area. A thoroughfare that intersected the tracks not far from the depot had a sign reading MAIN STREET. People milled around, but many of them seemed to be headed the same direction.

When he stepped down onto the platform, he asked the stationmaster, "Is something special going on today?" Then he noticed the heavenly aroma that made his mouth water and reminded him that it had been too long since he'd eaten.

"Sure is." The man nodded, and his prominent Adam's apple bobbed in tandem with his head. "A big barbecue and auction—to benefit the orphanage." As Joshua approached the baggage car, the man walked right beside him. "You might want to go over there and get something to eat later. It's the best barbecue this side of Fort Worth, Texas."

After retrieving his small trunk and hefting it onto one shoulder, Joshua turned back toward the shorter man. "I have a couple of questions. Where is the hotel, and which way to the barbeque?"

A frown marred the man's face. "You might not be able to get a room tonight. Lots of folks from outlying areas have come in for the festivities. They take every opportunity to get together when one comes along, since they are few and far between." He turned and looked down the street. "The hotel's that way, and a boardinghouse is up there." A thumb thrust over his shoulder accompanied the last comment. "You might get a place there if not at the hotel. If they're full up, I believe there's some rooms over the saloon."

"Thank you." Joshua wasn't sure the information was very helpful, but his mother had taught him to be polite. However, he was certain that he wouldn't take the man's last suggestion. He'd sleep outside under the stars with his trunk for a hard pillow before he would go into that place.

"I could tell you to just follow your nose to the barbecue, but the smell pretty much covers the whole town." The white-haired man laughed at his own joke. "If you go past the hotel and turn right at the next corner, the church is a couple of blocks down that street. Most of the activities will take place in the open field behind the building. I'll probably see you there later."

❧

Getting his name in the hotel registry almost proved the dire prediction of the station agent. After talking until he thought he would lose his voice, Joshua finally procured a room, such as it was. A tiny space the size of a closet in the house he rented in California. The single bed sat beside the wall opposite the door, with both the headboard and the foot almost touching the sides of the room. The space barely allowed the door to open all the way, and a chair sat in one corner. He dropped his trunk on the chair and placed the carpetbag on top. Evidently he would be expected to retire by dark, since the hotel didn't have gaslights on the wall, and no table to hold an oil lamp or candle could be wedged into the meager space. He hoped he would only spend one night here.

Since he'd left his business suits back in San Francisco, getting ready for the festivities didn't take him long. After making a stop in the washroom to get rid of some of the travel grime, Joshua set out to find the church. Stretching his legs after his long journey felt good. He took the indicated street and strode on the wooden sidewalk. Even if the stationmaster hadn't told him how to get there, he would have figured it out. Probably every person who lived within twenty miles of this town headed the same direction he did.

By the time he reached the church grounds, several people had introduced themselves and welcomed him. Maybe they hoped he would contribute to the cause in a big way. . . . Maybe he would.

Cactus Corner must have been built around a spring. Even though he had passed through arid country, this town looked more like an oasis. Trees and sparse grass surrounded the houses he passed, and many of the structures had a few colorful flowers in pots on their porches. He smiled. A pleasant place, for a small town.

A large crowd milled around. People stopped beside several tables laden with handmade items, such as quilts, hand-carved knickknacks, and even furniture.

Many of the women congregated around a display of lacy things and frippery. They chattered and exclaimed over each item they picked up.

Joshua studied the younger ladies, trying to decide if one of them was India Cunningham. When he last saw her, she wore her hair in braids, but strands escaped and curled around her face. Freckles had peppered her nose and cheeks, becoming more pronounced the longer she spent time in the sun. Since she had to be in her twenties now, she might have lost the freckles. He hoped some of them remained. They looked cute on her.

What color were her eyes? He couldn't remember exactly. She had been like a whirlwind, always in motion. Well, it didn't matter. Joshua stood to the side and studied every woman with brown hair who passed him. Somehow, he didn't see anyone he thought was India Cunningham. Should he ask someone if she was here?

Chapter 2

India picked up a long-handled cooking utensil with two thin, pointed tines and thrust it into the hindquarters of the rotating steer. It slid right through and quickly encountered bone. When she pulled out the special fork, bits of the barbecued beef stuck to the metal, and savory-smelling juices seeped out. She picked off a juicy piece and popped it into her mouth, realizing almost too late that she should have let it cool a bit more. But it did taste wonderful.

"Is it ready, Miss India?" Nathan Hodges had added *Miss* to her name when she came back from Mrs. Collier's Finishing School. Even after all this time, it still sounded funny.

The spicy meat almost melted in her mouth. India nodded. "Just right. Do you think you can take care of slicing it?"

The older man reached for a large sharp knife that waited on the table behind him. "Sure thing. Just keep the platters coming."

India wiped her hands on a towel hanging on the waistband of her voluminous apron. When she had been at the general store last week, Mr. Lawson received a crate of lemons from California. More of the citrus fruit made it, in these modern times, without spoiling since trains delivered them now. India had been tempted to buy the whole box, but she only took half of the fruit, leaving the rest for other shoppers. Her ranch hands liked lemonade, and most of the yellow orbs were gone, even though she was able to store them in the cool springhouse. Four lemons waited for her to return to her hotel room and clean up the mess on her hands. Since Nathan took over slicing the meat, maybe she could finally get away. She motioned Hector to take her place. Giving her a wide smile, the man complied. India knew he took pride in providing the sauce for the beef.

She turned to make her way through the growing crowd, and her gaze connected with that of a man she had never seen before. He wore the same kind of clothes the other cowboys did, but his still looked new and stiff instead of faded and soft, and he moseyed with a similar ambling walk. Something else set him off from the others, but she wasn't sure what. Aside from his good looks, and he had plenty, he towered over most of the people around him. His curls glinted blue-black in the sun as they blew in the gentle breeze and tumbled down on his forehead. From this distance, his eyes looked almost as dark as his hair, but more on the brown side. India's heart skipped a beat, and her hands itched to coax those curls back from his face. *Where did that thought come from?*

Letting out the breath she had held momentarily, India wished she were anywhere but here looking like some carcass her ranch dog had dragged up from the desert. She pushed an errant curl out of her eyes, then remembered the sauce that stained her hands. Hopefully none of it had transferred to her hair. India didn't want the man, who seemed to be making a beeline toward her, to see how horrible she looked. Why hadn't she listened to Jody earlier? She should have left immediately to freshen up.

India glanced down, made a face at her clothes, which were covered with a fine sprinkling of dust and irregular splatters of red, and raised her chin in a defiant gesture, glancing toward a large tree that shaded the opposite side of the dusty field. What was she doing letting the most handsome man she had ever seen rattle her so? For all she knew, he could be an outlaw.

Out of the corner of her eye, she noticed the stranger stop and start talking to Reverend McCurdy. India knew her pastor would gently ferret out all kinds of information without the man even recognizing what he was doing. Maybe she should plan to spend some time visiting with the clergyman later that day.

While the two men were deep in conversation, India slipped around the other side of the crowd and hurried toward the hotel.

❧

As Joshua made his way through the bustling crowd toward the barbecue pit, a shorter gentleman in a black suit stepped in front of him. How in the world could the man stand to wear a suit in this heat?

"I'm Gavin McCurdy." Gavin's strong voice belied his slight stature. He thrust out a hand, and a smile lit a twinkle in his eyes. "I'm the pastor of this church. Welcome to our community. Are you just passing through?"

Joshua vigorously pumped the outstretched hand. "Glad to meet you, Reverend McCurdy. I just arrived in town about half an hour ago, and the wonderful smells led me straight to the church."

"If you're here Sunday, I'd love to see you in our services." The pastor's hearty welcome brought interested glances from many bystanders in the crowd.

The next few minutes, the clergyman asked many questions that Joshua chose to sidestep. As a lawyer, he was adept at answering without giving any information. He knew what the man was doing, but he didn't resent the questioning interest. He supposed a stranger was somewhat of an oddity in this corner of the world. You had to be looking for Cactus Corner to find it, even though the railroad now connected it to other towns.

When the man of God moved on to greet other people, Joshua's eyes sought the woman he'd glimpsed near the roasting steer. She'd been standing near an older man swathed in an apron. He was now slicing the meat and piling it on large platters held by a wiry Mexican whose smile spread across his face. Joshua's stomach gave a loud rumble, reminding him once again of just how long it had been since he had eaten. He worked his way through the mass of people toward the food, all the time scanning the crowd.

He couldn't find the woman dressed in dark clothing with hair that looked like moonlight shining on a clear lake. He had never seen that color of hair before. She wore it in a careless bun on top of her head with wispy curls forming a halo around her lovely face. Some of the barbecue sauce had smudged her cheeks, but not enough to mask her loveliness. Where could she have disappeared? Oh well, with his luck, she was married to one of the cowhands forming a line at one end of the table loaded with a bounty of food besides the platters of beef.

Past the other end of the long table stood a smaller lady who held a large earthenware crock. Another woman dipped from it and poured the liquid into all manner of drinking vessels—tin cups, heavy mugs, even a few glasses. He was surprised she didn't spill any with all the kids who were darting through the crowd and even ducking their heads to scoot under the table as if it were some kind of tunnel. As Joshua watched, his parched throat felt like the desert the train had traveled through. He probably should try to get a drink before he thought about eating, or he might not be able to swallow any food. He made his way toward the shorter line at the drink table.

With a smile, the woman handed him a heavy mug. He took a long swig. Joshua hadn't expected the sweet, tart taste of lemonade, but it did quench his deep thirst. Too bad there wasn't some ice to cool it more. Living farther north where people experienced winter definitely had added blessings. Some folks cut ice into large chunks and buried them underground surrounded with sawdust. That ice often lasted until the next winter. Thinking about the coolness only intensified the dry heat he was immersed in, but the lemonade soothed his parched throat. At least he wasn't wearing a business suit.

Joshua took his drink and joined the long line for food, glad that it moved quite fast. Soon he leaned against a scraggly tree on the edge of the open field, shoveling food into his mouth. His mother would be aghast at his lack of manners, but he didn't think anyone here noticed. A lawyer learned to study people, so he enjoyed watching the other people interact. In a small community like this one, everyone seemed to know everyone else. That might be a good thing.

After a while, movement on the street side of the crowd drew his attention. A woman glided through the group almost like Moses parting the Red Sea, and everyone gave her attention. He didn't blame them. She was breathtaking. Although her hair was the same color as that of the woman working with the meat earlier, the resemblance ended there. This woman's hair was arranged in a style that would have been fashionable in San Francisco, and she dressed with understated elegance. Her dark brown skirt didn't have any of the extra ruffles some of the women wore. He imagined her clothing was cooler than theirs. The light-colored blouse wasn't really white, but looked more like the cream he used to skim off the milk back home. It accentuated her smooth complexion, which was more tanned than that of any woman he knew in California. Joshua figured she must spend a lot of time outdoors.

He couldn't pull his attention from her. Then it hit him. She was the same woman. Evidently she had gone somewhere to clean up.

Joshua would have loved to know who she was, but he didn't want to cause ripples by asking too many questions. He would bide his time and keep his eyes and ears tuned to what was going on around him.

Once again, the parson approached. "Have you seen the desserts on the table by the church?"

Joshua had just sopped up the last of the barbecue sauce with a hunk of bread before he stuffed it in his mouth. It took him a moment to chew it up. Mother would have a conniption if he talked with his mouth full.

"I sure didn't." He took the last swig of lemonade. "I thought this was a fund-raiser for an orphanage or something like that. No one has asked me for any money."

The preacher's laugh had a rich resonation. "Indeed it is. There's a bucket on the corner of the dessert table for people to put in their donations. The women thought that after people enjoyed the wonderful food, they'd be more inclined to be generous."

Joshua nodded. "Good thinking. I've never tasted meat as tender or delicious as this."

The two men headed toward the whitewashed frame building crowned by a steeple.

"They put the desserts in the shadow of the church so they'd be out of the sun." Reverend McCurdy patted his stomach. "I don't really need anything else, but I have to have a piece of Miss Mabel's buttermilk pie. It's the best I've ever tasted. She always brings it anytime we have a church dinner."

"So did the church start the orphanage?" Joshua shortened his stride to fit the other man's.

"No, but most of the women in the church help the orphanage all they can."

Closer to the building, the ground was covered with sparse grass. Joshua was sure that would keep the dust down. Another reason to put the desserts there.

India had seen the stranger leaning up against a tree when she returned from the hotel. How could she miss him? Even in dungarees and a chambray shirt, he had a commanding presence. Just what was it about the man that made her feel unsettled? Granted, he might be an outlaw, but would a wanted man stay out in the open like that? Hopefully she would get a chance to talk to Reverend McCurdy later.

During the rest of the social, India felt the man's presence, even across the field from her. No matter how she turned or whom she talked to, she knew when he moved from one place to another, almost as if he had some connection to her. For a woman who owned a huge ranch and was the boss of a large crew of cowboys, she didn't understand why she didn't feel in control. Nothing she did could break that nebulous link.

He went with the pastor over to the dessert table and sampled plenty of the sugary sweets. She wondered why he wasn't flabby if he ate like that, but when he walked, his body was poetry in motion. Before she got up the nerve to join the two men in the shade of the church, the newcomer sauntered away, heading back toward Main Street. She took a deep breath and gave a relieved sigh. She was glad he was gone. Wasn't she?

Other strangers had come to town, especially since the railroad tracks were laid. None of them had put her off balance with their presence. He shouldn't have either.

As the crowd thinned, India went to help clean up. She also wanted to see if any of her lemon pound cake was left. She hadn't had time for dessert yet. Only one piece remained. As she slid it onto a saucer, her pastor stepped near the table, perusing the contents.

"We're almost cleaned out, aren't we?" He glanced at the small plate in her hand. "At least you got a piece of something."

She took a bite, savoring the tartness of the lemon mixed with the sweet, buttery flavor of the cake. The morsel tasted wonderful all the way down. "I just love fresh lemons." She turned to face the minister. "So who was the stranger I saw you talking to earlier?"

"Didn't you get a chance to meet him?" The older man's eyes searched her face as though he was looking for something specific. "Nice fellow."

India hoped her expression didn't reveal what she had been feeling. She didn't want him to think she was too interested. "So who is he?"

"You know, come to think of it, he never did tell me his name." Reverend McCurdy scratched his chin.

"What's he doing in Cactus Corner?" She took another bite.

"He didn't really say." Deep grooves between the man's brows indicated his frustration.

She set the saucer on the table and put her fists on her hips. "He might be an outlaw for all we know."

Her pastor laughed. "I don't think so, India. In my profession, I've had to learn to size up a man pretty well. I don't know his name or why he's here, but he isn't running from the law."

She picked up the cake again and took another bite, frowning as she did.

The man beside her reached into the bucket and pulled out a wad of bills. He unrolled them and riffled through them. "This is the donation he made. It's a goodly amount, India. Don't judge a man before you know anything about him."

After spending a few minutes in the hotel washroom freshening up, Joshua returned to his broom-closet room. He took off his stiff outer clothing and stretched out on top of the covers. At least there was a tiny window that let in a slight breeze. Tomorrow he would see if the livery had any horses for sale. He wanted to ride his own mount out to the Circle C.

Even though he had studied every woman at the social, he didn't see anyone who might be India Cunningham. Maybe he was too late. Since the letter had taken a year to reach him, maybe she had already lost the ranch. Now he wished he had asked the parson about it. He could be going on a wild goose chase. He might have to rethink buying that horse. Perhaps he should rent one and go to check things out first.

After having chased that rabbit, his thoughts returned to the blond he'd seen at the barbecue. For some reason, he'd felt an invisible connection to her, almost as if they'd been tied by strong rope. The feeling didn't release until he started back to the hotel. She was a vision of loveliness, but he didn't know anything about her. He probably wouldn't even see her again. That thought gave his heart a little hitch.

This new obsession would have to stop. After he was sure that India Cunningham didn't need his help, he would board the train for the westward journey back to civilization. He didn't need to leave any complicated ties in this town. He pulled his worn Bible out of his carpetbag. Maybe feeding on the Word would take his mind off her.

When he had finished eating a big breakfast in the hotel restaurant the next morning, Joshua quickly found the livery stable. A beautiful palomino stallion caught his eye. He made a deal to hire the horse for the week, then headed out of town toward the Rincon Mountains. He felt sure he could remember the way to the ranch.

Even though the countryside was mostly desert, splashes of beauty were all around him. Joshua remembered the tall cacti that looked as though they were reaching for the sky. A few of them sported blossoms on their outstretched arms. The ground wasn't bare; it was covered with a different type of vegetation from what he was used to in California. Off in the distance, a line of varying shades of green indicated where the river meandered through the ranch. The two-story ranch house was built on a knoll not far from that river. If Joshua missed the turnoff, he could just ride across country and follow the stream.

The trip took longer than he remembered, but eventually he reached the cluster of buildings. There were more of them than he recalled, though. The house looked much the same. White paint glistened in the bright sunlight, and the shutters and outside trim wore a coat of dark green. Instead of one barn, three stood sentinel far enough behind the house that the barnyard smells shouldn't reach there. A few smaller houses probably indicated that some of the hands were married, and twice as many bunkhouses as before flanked the barns.

Joshua wondered if all this happened before Mr. Cunningham died or if maybe a new owner had expanded. He rode up to the corral beside the first barn. The man who had turned the steer on the spit yesterday stood with one booted foot hiked up on the bottom rail. He leaned his crossed arms on the top rail and watched a young hand working with a skittish horse.

When Joshua brought his horse to stop by the hitching rail, the man turned around. "You looking for a job?"

Joshua didn't know how to answer that.

"I only put the notice up at the feed store in town yesterday when I went to the barbecue. I didn't expect any takers this soon. Miss India will be glad."

Well, that answered one of his questions. India Cunningham was still here. Maybe he should hire on while he scouted out the lay of the land, so to speak. "Sure, I'd like a job." He stuffed his hands into the front pockets of his dungarees and hunched his shoulders.

The man dropped his foot onto the ground and walked toward him. "I'm Nathan Hodges, the foreman of the Circle C. I do all the hiring and firing, so you don't want to rile me." His laugh took the sting out of the words. "When can you start?"

"Right away. I'll need to go back to town and get my things from the hotel."

"You got much gear?" Nathan held out a hand, and Joshua shook it.

"A trunk and a carpetbag." Joshua was glad the man didn't seem surprised. He knew a cowboy usually traveled with only his horse, a saddlebag, and maybe a bedroll.

Nathan gazed over Joshua's shoulder and called out, "Come over here, Miss India. We already have a taker for the job."

Without turning, Joshua knew whom he would see. He felt *her* approach.

Chapter 3

India had watched the man ride in on the palomino—the handsome stranger who could have been an outlaw but was just a cowboy needing work. Why should she care if the man showed up at her ranch for a job? Twenty or thirty men inhabited the large bunkhouses at any given time. Just because he sparked a special awareness at the barbecue yesterday didn't mean anything.

As she walked toward the two men, the stranger slowly turned and looked straight into her eyes. Her heart took another hitch. This would never do. She had to let him know that she was the boss on this ranch and not give him time to even think about having to work for a woman.

The way his eyes widened was barely perceptible before his face became a stiff mask. She would have missed it if she hadn't been looking straight at him. His flinty gaze seemed to take in everything about her without raking her up and down. She was thankful for that. Maybe having him around wouldn't be so bad, if the man could do the work required of him. The ranch did need another hand in the barn when many of the men went out to round up the heifers with calves that were scattered all over the outlying pastures. She hoped the fact that he was wearing new, instead of well-worn, clothes didn't indicate that he was inexperienced on a ranch.

Joshua studied the woman walking toward them without making it too obvious. Today she wore a no-nonsense split riding skirt and matching long-sleeved shirt. Her hair hung in a braid over one shoulder; wisps framed her face under a well-worn cowboy hat.

He had known of a couple of women whose hair had lightened to blond by the time they reached adulthood, but neither of them had almost snowy hair. Why hadn't he considered that possibility? He wouldn't have wasted so much time looking at every woman with brown hair when he would rather have spent his time getting reacquainted with this beauty.

When she stopped beside the foreman, Joshua noticed a faint sprinkling of the freckles he had wondered about. If he had gotten close enough yesterday, he might have recognized those blue eyes as the ones he remembered from her childhood, but maybe not. Her lashes were thicker and longer than any he had seen on any other woman.

India held out her hand. "I trust Nathan's judgment. Welcome to the Circle C."

Joshua engulfed her hand in his before he shook it. "Thank you. I'm glad to be here."

Before he had a chance to say anything else, she quickly withdrew and turned toward the foreman. Joshua felt as if he had been dismissed—something he wasn't used to—and he hadn't even told her his name.

He stepped back so they wouldn't feel he was eavesdropping. Maybe he should continue to be just a hand until he could see how well she was doing with the ranch. From the way the foreman listened to her, he must respect her and trust her judgment. Did the other men? If he hired on without the other hands knowing why he was really here, perhaps he could learn the truth about how they felt about India.

When the two finished their conversation, India went back into the main house while the foreman turned toward Joshua. "You can take the wagon into town to pick up your gear. When you get back, we'll settle you into one of the bunkhouses." The foreman called over his shoulder to another hand. "Bring the wagon out here, Clint."

In less than half an hour, Joshua headed away from the ranch with the palomino tied to the back of the wagon. He went straight through town to the livery, which was on the other side of the business district, such as it was.

Joshua took off his hat as he walked into the cavernous stable. "I need to talk to you." He wished he had asked the liveryman's name earlier.

The tall, thin man looked up from mucking out one of the stalls. "You didn't stay away long. You aren't going to turn the horse in, are you?" He stuck the pitchfork in the dirt and leaned both hands on the end of the handle. "I don't give any money back."

"No. Actually, I wanted to know if this horse is for sale." Joshua dusted his Stetson against one leg.

The man leaned the pitchfork against the railing of the stall and pushed back the hair that had fallen over his forehead. "Funny you should ask today. That there horse belongs to Elmer Brody over at the freight line. Just this morning, he said he was thinking about selling him. You'll need to talk to him, though."

Joshua nodded. "Okay, I'll do that. But what about the saddle? I like a saddle that's been broken in, and this one fits me just fine. I'd like to buy it."

After they completed that transaction, with the man offering to make an allowance for some of the money already paid to him, Joshua headed toward the freight office—an unpainted building that had weathered to a smoky gray. When he came back out into the bright sunlight, he owned the stallion. He'd have to rename him, though. The animal seemed smart enough to learn a new name quickly. Goldie sounded more like a mare's name, or even a dog's. King was more masculine.

Joshua walked to the stallion's head and began stroking his forehead and neck while whispering into his ear. "You look really regal, boy, so I'm going to call you King. Before we go back to the ranch, I'll see if the general store has some carrots or apples for you."

Joshua climbed into the wagon seat and looked back toward his new horse. King held his head higher as if he understood every word.

At the hotel, Joshua paid his bill and loaded his trunk and carpetbag in the back of the wagon. Now he was glad he had thought to pack several books. His evenings might be a little lonely out in the bunkhouse. Most of the cowboys his father hired at his ranch in Texas had been rather solitary until they got to know a man. Those books would come in handy.

Before he headed back to the ranch, he stopped by the café for lunch. While he ate, he listened unobtrusively to as many conversations as he could, trying to get a feel for what was going on in the town.

A couple of tables over, two older men talked to the waitress about yesterday's festivities. They made a few comments about India Cunningham, but they were all complimentary. It sounded as if she was well liked in Cactus Corner.

India had turned one of the downstairs rooms in the main house into an office. She liked to see what was happening on the ranch through the windows that wrapped around two sides of the room. While sitting at the desk working on the books, she heard the wagon rumble by on the way to the barn. India had wondered why Nathan sent the newcomer to town in the wagon. Maybe he needed something from the store. She went to the window and leaned close to the glass so she could watch the two men. A large trunk sat in the bed of the wagon, and the same palomino followed the conveyance.

She'd never before known a cowboy to want that much encumbrance. Why did the man have a trunk with him? India wished she could see what he kept in it. Her father always told her that her curiosity would get her into trouble one of these days.

Even though there were things about that cowboy that didn't make sense, India had never found any reason not to trust her foreman. If Nathan thought the man wouldn't make a good hand, he wouldn't have hired him. One of the things she learned when she first started running the ranch without her father was that she needed to be able to trust other people. Since Nathan and Martha had been on the ranch almost as long as India could remember, she knew from their long association that her trust wasn't misplaced.

All this woolgathering wasn't getting the books done. She turned from the window and delved back into the finances of the ranch. She wouldn't relinquish this task to another person. Her father always knew exactly what was going on with the finances. He taught her that a good rancher had to, and she wanted to be a good rancher.

India had ridden across the vast acres and helped with roundups by the time she was a young teenager. That's why she could take over running the ranch when she returned from back east. All through her father's last months, she had kept an eye on everything while letting him feel that he was still in control, making it an easy transition for everyone when he was gone.

Since Joshua had more possessions with him than most cowboys, Nathan Hodges offered one of the empty cabins to him, but he wouldn't be able to get a feeling of what was going on with the cowboys if he moved in there. When he declined, the foreman assigned him an empty bed at one end of a bunkhouse. His trunk would fit in the corner by the wall.

"Since it's Saturday, most of the boys will go into town this evening." Nathan leaned against the wall and crossed his booted feet. "Were you planning on going, too?"

Joshua slid the heavy trunk from his shoulders and put it into place. "I didn't realize this thing weighed so much." He stretched his neck and rotated his shoulders. "I should have let you help me carry it like you offered."

Nathan chuckled. "What's in there? Rocks?"

Joshua gave a sheepish grin. "No, books. I like to read."

The foreman nodded.

"About your first question, I've been in town twice today. That's enough for me."

The other man stood up away from the wall. "Martha told me to ask if you would like to eat supper with us. She didn't feel too good yesterday, so she didn't go to the shindig in town, and she'd like to meet you."

Joshua stuffed one hand into the front pocket of his dungarees. "I wouldn't want to be any trouble."

Nathan hooted a loud laugh. "Trouble for Martha would be if she didn't get to meet you today. Besides, she likes to cook."

Joshua pulled out a pocket watch. "It's already four thirty. Do you have any work for me this afternoon?"

The foreman shook his head. "Naw. Everyone's off on Saturday afternoons."

"What time do you want me to come, and you'll have to tell me which house." Joshua slipped the timepiece back into the small opening just below one of his belt loops.

Nathan started toward the front door. "We usually eat at six."

Joshua followed the foreman. "I won't be late."

When they reached the porch, Nathan pointed toward the largest of the cabins behind the main house. "India's father built that house for Martha and me when he hired me to be his foreman."

After Joshua watched the man amble toward his home, he went to the wagon and retrieved his carpetbag. He stowed it on top of his trunk, then drove the wagon and King to the wagon yard beside the main stable. First, he took King to the stall Nathan had told him to use. He soothed the stallion and filled his trough with feed. He rubbed down the two horses that pulled the wagon and returned them to their stalls.

A flurry of activity around the bunkhouses indicated that the other cowboys were cleaning up. A few even made use of the outdoor shower. Joshua hoped they didn't use all the water in the tank, because he wanted to get rid of some grime before he went to eat with Nathan and Martha. Of course, it was a large tank, and probably the men knew how to conserve water so everyone could have a turn.

By five thirty, all the cowboys had ridden out in groups of three or four toward town. He took a quick shower, wishing he had asked Nathan about how to get hot water for shaving. He'd just have to go to supper with stubble on his face, something he never would have done in San Francisco, but he really didn't like a cold shave.

When he left the bunkhouse to start toward the foreman's home, he noticed India step from her porch. He stopped and waited to see if she was headed toward him, but she didn't even look his way. She did, however, go straight toward Nathan and Martha's. Evidently she hadn't recognized him, and he'd told Nathan his name out of her hearing. Maybe Joshua could keep it a secret from her until he knew the lay of the land. Tonight could be interesting.

Nathan answered his knock. "Since all the other hands are gone, Martha invited Miss India to eat with us, too."

The older man stepped back, opening the door wider. Joshua searched the room until he saw India standing in the archway between the kitchen—where another woman bustled around—and the dining room.

Her startled gaze collided with his, and a slight blush colored her cheeks. "I thought you went to town. . .with the other hands." The last phrase was almost a whisper.

She glanced at Nathan before looking at Martha.

The other woman wiped her hands on her apron. "I told Nate to ask him for supper. I didn't get to meet him yesterday." She smiled at her husband. "He didn't tell me how handsome the new hand is."

The blush on India's cheeks deepened and bled across her neck. Joshua almost laughed. So she wasn't the self-possessed woman she seemed to be yesterday at the barbecue.

"I don't know any of the men yet, so I decided to stay on the ranch tonight." He wasn't ready to tell her that he wouldn't be caught dead in a saloon.

Maybe he was being too harsh in his judgment. Perhaps the hands had other things in mind for their evening entertainment, but he doubted it.

Nathan laughed. "Some of them won't ever want you trailing along with them. I believe they've gone courting."

Okay, so he *was* being too harsh about some of them. Time would tell about the others.

"Come on. Let's be seated." Martha set a couple of bowls on the almost full round table. "Don't want the food to get cold."

Joshua planned to pull out India's chair for her, but she slipped into the nearest seat before he reached the table. After they were all sitting down, Nathan pronounced a word of thanks to the Lord. Joshua was glad the foreman shared his faith. He wondered about India. He couldn't remember them going to church when he was here as a boy.

While they passed the food, Nathan started the conversation. "I haven't seen any of the other hands carry timepieces, and that's a really fine watch you have."

Joshua pulled it out of his pocket and stared at the etching on the cover. He opened it and peered at the face. "This was my father's watch. It belonged to my grandfather before him. He gave it to me for my eighteenth birthday."

"May I see it?" India reached her hand toward him, and he snapped the timepiece shut and unhooked it from his belt loop before giving it to her.

She studied it on one side, then turned it over. "The workmanship is beautiful. It reminds me of something I've seen before, but I can't remember when or where."

When she returned it to him, the gold felt warm. Joshua was sure her hand would feel just as warm, only much softer. For a rancher, her hands were exceptionally smooth with no calluses. Either she wore gloves, or she didn't do much of the heavy work.

The next morning, India hurried to dress for church. She hoped she would see the new hand riding to town for services, too. But when she harnessed one of the horses to the surrey, no one besides Nathan and Martha headed the same way.

Jody had invited Anika, Elaine, and her for dinner after church. She hoped being with her best friends would take her mind off that man. Unfortunately, during the service, her thoughts often wandered. She was sure Pastor Gavin preached a wonderful sermon as usual, but she hoped no one asked her what he said.

Soon the four women sat around the small kitchen table. Jody's cooking was legendary, and today was no exception. While they partook of the bounty, the friends talked about inconsequential things. All too soon, someone asked the question India didn't want to hear.

"So did you see the stranger who came to the barbecue on Friday?" Jody made eye contact with India.

After swallowing what she was chewing so she wouldn't choke, India nodded. "He was hard to miss."

"Aren't you glad you went back to the hotel and changed clothes?" Elaine's auburn hair was pulled up into its usual bun on top of her head, and it wobbled when she turned her head quickly.

"Of course." India tried to make light of her answer. "I wasn't really wanting anyone to notice me while I took care of the meat." She shoved another bite into her mouth, hoping the other women would change the subject.

Jody picked up on what she said. "Did the man notice you?"

"He'd be crazy if he didn't." Anika scooped some mashed potatoes onto her fork.

Jody stared at her. "So you noticed him, too."

"Just because I believe in women's suffrage doesn't mean I can't appreciate a good-looking man, does it?" With a dainty motion, Anika placed the food in her mouth.

"I didn't mean anything by what I said." A look of contrition wrinkled Jody's brows.

India decided she might as well tell them the rest of the story. "He came to the ranch yesterday looking for a job. . .and Nathan hired him."

Three pairs of eyes stared at her.

"I suppose Nathan knows what he's doing, but that man has secrets." By their raised eyebrows, India could see that her statement surprised her friends.

Jody clasped her hands in her lap. "What do you mean?"

India thought a minute so she would get all the details right. "For one thing, his clothes are too new. If he's been working as a cowboy, why aren't his clothes broken in?" Jody looked as if she might defend the man, so India rushed on. "And he travels with a trunk and a carpetbag. How many cowboys have you seen carry more than just their saddlebags?"

With a deflated look, Jody leaned back. "He came into the freight office yesterday and bought Goldie from Mr. Brody. It seems odd that he didn't already own a horse. If he's a cowboy, why didn't he ride his horse to town?"

"Martha invited both of us for supper last night. I had hoped to learn more about him, but even though we talked a lot, and Nathan asked him a lot of questions, he didn't give us any information in his answers." Each time India said something else about the man, she felt worse and worse. "He even carries a pocket watch. A very elaborate gold one. Have you ever seen a cowhand do that? I just know I'll have to keep an eye on him to make sure he's who he says he is."

Anika, ever the lawyer, stood and took her plate to the dry sink. "I could have him checked out for you. What's his name?"

India stared at each of her friends before she answered. "I don't know," she whispered with a sinking heart.

Chapter 4

Joshua Dillinger. His name was Joshua Dillinger. For some reason that sounded vaguely familiar, but India couldn't remember why. That vagueness only added to her discomfort with the man. When he was around, all her old insecurities flooded back. Because her father never had a son, she had done all she could to prove to him that she was just as good, but Daddy had never recognized that fact.

Then after he was gone, India had to prove herself all over again. The regular hands who stayed on the ranch year-round knew her abilities, but every time they had to hire extra hands, the discrimination happened again. No one wanted to work for a woman. If Nathan hadn't been so loyal, she never would have been able to run this ranch. He gave her the respect she needed, and the other men finally followed his lead.

India looked down at the ledger spread open on the desk in front of her. She should work on the books, but that new man distracted all her thoughts. She huffed out a deep breath and picked up her last stubby pencil. The next time Nathan went to town, he would have to buy her some more.

A knock sounded at her open office door, and she looked up. "Come in, Nathan. I was just thinking about you."

The man crossed the waxed hardwood floor in a few long strides. "I hope I didn't put those frown lines on your forehead."

India laughed. "No, you didn't." She held up the flat wooden pencil. "I need you to get more of these when you go into town for supplies."

Nathan sat with one hip on the front corner of her desk. "I'm thinking about sending Joshua for the supplies."

She leaned back in her wooden swivel chair. "Do you think that's a good idea?"

He crossed his arms. "I've seen you watching him like a hawk. Almost as though you're waiting for him to make a mistake. You're not usually like this. How long has he been here now?"

"Two weeks and four days." After she said the words, she regretted them. She didn't want her foreman to know how often she thought of Joshua, and that answer made it sound as if she had counted every day. So what if she had?

"Right, and he's a hard worker." The grooves between Nathan's eyes indicated his seriousness. "When are you going to give him a break?"

India rubbed the ache in both sides of her forehead with the thumb and middle finger of one hand, then looked straight at her foreman. "Okay. You've told me more than once that you trust him. I promise I'll take your word for it."

Nathan stood up. "Good. I'll send him to town right away."

After the foreman exited the house, India went to the window and watched him walk across to the corral. Joshua was helping one of the younger hands practice roping the cows that milled around inside. When Nathan reached him, they started talking. She knew exactly when Nathan told him that he was going to town, because Joshua's gaze turned toward the house as if he questioned whether she agreed.

Before Joshua made it to the barn to hitch up the wagon, India opened the ranch house door. He hoped she wasn't coming to tell him that she didn't want him to run this errand. He planned to check if there was anything in the mail for him, especially from his partner telling him how everything in San Francisco was going.

Joshua turned toward India and smiled. She hadn't said anything about remembering who he was, and he hadn't brought it up yet. Perhaps it was time, but he didn't want to rush the moment. He hadn't found out as much as he wanted about how well she was doing with the ranch. When his anonymity was destroyed, he felt sure the other hands would clam up around him.

India stopped in front of him. Remnants of the girl he remembered still lingered, but the woman had almost overtaken them. She shaded her eyes with one hand. "I have a few more things I'd like you to pick up for me." She thrust a list toward him.

When he took it from her, he nodded, tempted to grasp her fingers in his. All kinds of feelings ran through him, but he couldn't pursue them until he finished the job he'd come to do. Joshua stuffed the paper into his shirt pocket before climbing up on the wagon seat. He could feel her gaze boring into his back as he rode away.

After Joshua picked up all the things on both lists and left them on the counter for the clerk to add up, he headed toward the post office in the back corner of the general store. "Got anything for the Cunningham ranch?" He couldn't believe how quickly he'd slipped into the vernacular of a cowhand. No one in his law office would believe it if they heard it. He was known all over northern California for his oratory skills.

"Sure do." The sandy-haired man reached for a packet tied with twine. "It's been a while since anyone from the ranch came to town. Miss India usually helps at the orphanage a couple days a week."

As Joshua walked back toward the counter in the store, he pondered that information. Why had she stopped? Was something wrong with the ranch? Or did she not trust him and want to keep an eye on what he was doing? He chuckled at that thought. If she only knew.

On the ride back to the ranch, Joshua stopped the wagon when he was far enough from town for no one to see what he was doing. He picked up the mail and carefully untied the package. Sure enough, a fat envelope was addressed to him. He stuck it inside his shirt and retied the packet. He would take time to study the papers later.

India must have been watching for him, because she came out on the porch before he reached the house. "Did we get any mail?"

Joshua held it up before stepping over the side of the wagon. She met him halfway with her hand outstretched. After he placed the bundle in her hand, she quickly untied it and began to shuffle through the pieces of mail before looking up.

"Do you know where Nathan is?"

"When I left, he was going to help the hands get ready to ride out for the calf roundup in the morning." Joshua waited to see if she wanted anything else from him.

Instead, she turned and strode toward the large bunkhouse.

India forced herself not to look back as she walked away from Joshua. She tried to force him from her thoughts, too, but had less success with that. She almost regretted her last trip to town, but she hadn't been in a while.

She hadn't wanted to talk about Joshua. But her friends had asked about him the whole time she was with them. She had attempted to avoid all that questioning. When she had answered, the three of them seemed greatly amused about something that completely eluded her.

She didn't know what she felt. On the one hand, he worked hard, but she still didn't truly trust him. He was keeping some secret from her. And that bothered her . . .more than she wanted to admit.

Another thing India didn't want to admit to anyone was her attraction to the man. Not just to his good looks, and he had plenty. Something about him tugged at her heart, while her mind wanted to push him away because of his air of mystery.

Her boots kicked up dust as she stomped toward the bunkhouse. Nathan had a letter, and she needed to give it to him, but sometimes she felt that he could see what was going on inside her. That would never do. How would she keep control of the ranch if he knew that she was so double-minded about Joshua? All the men, including Nathan, needed to see her strength and leadership, not some dreamy-eyed woman. India didn't even notice Nathan coming toward her until he stopped right in front of her.

"Did you want to see me for something?" He hooked his thumbs through his front belt loops and studied her face from under the brim of his hat.

She nodded and shuffled through the envelopes again before pulling out one of them. "This letter came for you. I thought you might like to see it."

He took it and smiled. "It probably could have waited until I came to the office." However, Nathan quickly tore the end off of the letter, blew into it, and slid out the paper.

India watched him a moment before turning toward the house.

"Wait a minute, Miss India." Something in his voice stopped her. "This here has some bad news in it."

She whirled around. "I'm sorry, Nathan. Who is it from?"

The paper in his hand shook. "My brother." He gulped, and his Adam's apple bobbed up and down. "He says Dad's dying. He says I need to come home quickly, or I might not see him again."

India put a comforting hand on his arm. "Then you and Martha must go."

A lone tear made its way down his wrinkled cheek. "It's time for calf roundup. I can't go."

India could take over the complete running of the ranch if she had to. She could be the foreman in his place. "I can do it."

"You shouldn't have to." He covered her fingers with his calloused hand. "You're the ranch owner, and there are plenty of men who can do the work."

"And I can ride and rope with the best of them."

Nathan stood in thought for a long moment. "Joshua could fill in for me while I'm gone."

India's heart thumped out of rhythm. She worked very closely with her foreman. Could she work that closely with Joshua? "Isn't there anyone else who could do it?"

He shook his head. "None of the rest of these yahoos could handle it. They're good wranglers, but none of them can see the big picture like Joshua can."

She stepped away from him, but she had to try one more time, so she turned back. "But won't the other men resent a new man bossing them around?"

"I don't think so. He has a good relationship with every one of them."

Joshua stood beside India while Nathan told the hands that he was leaving for a while. When he announced that Joshua would be the foreman while he was gone, not a single man blinked an eye. Joshua was thankful that Nathan had made it easy for him to fit into his boots. The man had everything planned for him.

After driving Nathan and Martha to the train station in Cactus Corner, Joshua quickly settled into his new job. He followed Nathan's suggestions when he assigned men to teams and sent them to different parts of the ranch.

The next morning, he watched the hands leave at early light, wishing he could go with them but understanding the reason Nathan didn't want India left alone. Then he strode toward the main house. India had told him she would fix his meals while the cook was out with the chuck wagon for roundup.

He stepped up on the porch, and the tantalizing aroma of sizzling bacon mixed with the fragrance of biscuits made his stomach rumble. Although the grub he'd been eating had been filling, this breakfast held more promise. Before his knuckles connected with the door, it swung open.

"Come in, Joshua."

He hadn't heard India say his name very many times since he'd come. The throaty musical quality of her voice gave it a special sound that went straight to his heart. "Something sure smells good."

She hurried into the kitchen and grabbed a bundle of toweling before lifting the pan of biscuits from the stove. "I'm not as good a cook as Martha is, but I get by."

Joshua watched her for a moment. Stray curls fluffed around her face, which held a becoming blush. A longer lock of hair lay down the back of her slender neck. For a moment, he wished he could plant a kiss in that exact spot. He shook his head to clear his thoughts and walked over to the sink. "May I wash up here?"

After her nod, he lifted the handle and pumped vigorously to fill the pan. If they were going to work closely until Nathan got back, Joshua would have to curb his growing fascination with everything about India. A moist bar of soap sat in a bowl in the window. He used it to lather his hands before plunging them into the water for a rinse. Although he didn't look toward her, he knew she watched his every move.

He turned while drying his hands. "Thank you for allowing me to take Nathan's place while he's gone."

Her eyes widened. She probably hadn't expected him to bring that up. "You're welcome."

"I won't do everything exactly as he does, but I'll do a good job."

She lifted her chin. "So Nathan told me."

Joshua couldn't tell if she agreed with her foreman or not. With nothing else to say, he pulled out the chair across from where she stood. Everything within him wanted to pull out her chair first, but he wasn't sure what she would think about that. He didn't want to upset her at this juncture.

Surprisingly, the meal went well. Soon they were exchanging pleasant conversation about the workings of the ranch and what was going on in town. Even though India only went on Sundays lately, she kept up with what was happening.

About the time Joshua decided to tell her why he was here, she stood and picked up her dishes. "If you have everything under control here, I'm going into town today. It's been a while since I helped at the orphanage."

He quickly stood, too. "That's fine. Nathan left me with lots of written instructions. It will give me time to study them again." And also give him time to read all the papers his partner had sent him.

India couldn't get out of the room quickly enough. She hadn't realized that having Joshua share her meals would upset her equilibrium. She enjoyed watching him so much she almost forgot to eat. What was it that pulled her heart toward him while her mind told her to be careful?

On the way into town, India was glad the horses knew the way without being driven. She spent most of her time going over the breakfast with Joshua. Since he'd been at the ranch, Joshua's hands had grown some calluses, but he kept them well groomed. *Graceful.* His hands were graceful as they pulled apart a biscuit and slathered it with butter and mesquite bean jelly at breakfast. And he had perfect table manners, much better than those of most of the cowhands. Perhaps when she returned she should ask him where he came from and why he looked for a job at her ranch. With that resolution, she raised the reins and urged the horses a little faster.

"India, there you are." Jody arrived at the orphanage at the same time. "We've been missing you." She glanced in the back of the wagon. "What did you bring today?"

"Martha has been making beef jerky. The older kids like to chew on it while they do their lessons." India went around to the back and picked up a small barrel.

Jody looked in a wooden crate that sat beside it. "Has she been making more clothes for the babies?"

India nodded. "You know Martha. She doesn't waste a minute." She hoped maybe she and Jody would be the only ones to help today.

When they walked into the large main room of the orphanage, her hopes were dashed. Anika leaned over the top of a large wooden barrel. Elaine watched her, jiggling a baby on her hip.

Anika rose, bringing a pretty frock with her. "This mission barrel has some nice things in it." She held the dress up to Elaine. "I believe this would fit you."

Elaine's face turned red. "I don't usually take anything from the mission barrels."

Anika placed her hands on her hips, one of them still holding the garment. "And why not? These things are for the orphanage, and you work here. It's way too large for any of the girls and too grown-up of a style, as well."

India set the small barrel on the table and joined them. "I agree. Its color would look good with your hair."

She reached out and took the baby and pulled her into a hug. "Aren't you just growing so much?" She planted a kiss on a chubby cheek, and the little girl laughed out loud.

While they worked, the four women took turns holding the youngest orphan, tickling her and cooing to her. Just as India feared, it didn't take long for the questions to start.

Anika stood folding the clothes from the barrel and separating them by size on one of the tables. "So how is your new ranch hand working out?"

Before India could think of how to answer, Jody added, "Have you found out his name yet?"

"Joshua." At least that was an easy question. "Joshua Dillinger."

Even Elaine was curious. "He's still there, isn't he? I thought I saw him in town yesterday."

India took a deep breath, willing her body not to betray her, but it did. "Yes, he went to town for supplies." She could feel a flush creeping up her neck and cheeks.

All pretense of working stopped as they crowded around her, bombarding her with questions and comments. Maybe staying on the ranch might have been a good idea. As soon as she could do so gracefully, she'd leave.

After Joshua read all of Nathan's instructions and the papers from the law firm, he decided that now would be a good time to check on the finances of the ranch. All the other hands were out on roundup, and India should be gone most of the day. He stowed his personal papers in his trunk and hurried to the house.

India kept the ledger in the top right drawer of her desk. Joshua pulled it out and started making his way through the entries for last year. Although he used an accountant for the law firm, he had helped his father keep the books for the ranch in Texas. It didn't take him long to figure out exactly how they did their accounting.

When he reached January of this year, Joshua heard the wagon stop in front of the house. He should have noticed it sooner, but when he was concentrating on something, he had learned to block out distractions. In all the noise of a city, that was important.

Joshua looked out the window to discover India stepping up on the porch. He quickly shut the ledger and pushed it into the drawer. By the time she entered the front door, he was halfway across the office, trying to walk quietly. Maybe he could slip out if she went upstairs or toward the kitchen.

She must have heard him, because she jerked open the office door. "Joshua Dillinger, what are you doing in here?"

Her question hung in the air like a diamondback rattlesnake about to strike.

Chapter 5

The air in the office tingled with suppressed tension, making it hard to breathe. India stared at Joshua. Why had she trusted him? *Because Nathan does.* She ignored the quiet voice that whispered in her mind.

"I asked you a question." She bit out the words, then hesitated only a split second. "But I have another one for you. Why aren't you out with the roundup?"

Joshua shifted position, almost as if he relaxed. He took so long answering, she figured he was formulating something believable without revealing his true colors.

"Aren't you going to answer me?" She thrust fisted hands against her hips and added heat to her glare.

"India"—he left off the usual *Miss*—"Nathan didn't want me to leave you unguarded while all the men are gone. He told me that he stays here during most of the roundup, too."

Well, that much was true, but India hadn't realized Nathan thought she needed guarding. "I can take care of myself." She stretched as tall as she could and took a deep breath.

"Of course you can." A tentative smile lit his face. "I'm not trying to say you can't, but you have to admit the ranch headquarters are rather isolated. Plenty of outlaws might take advantage of that fact. The success of the Circle C is well-known in this part of the country, which could make you a target."

"We're getting away from the subject of my first question." India crossed her arms and gave him her fiercest stare.

Joshua strode toward two leather chairs that sat near the windows. He pointed at one. "Sit down and we'll talk. I've been needing to tell you some things anyway."

The man sure was bossy. She didn't want to give him the impression that he was in control, but she did perch on the edge of the chair, without uncrossing her arms. "Go ahead." A nod accompanied her terse order.

When he dropped into the other chair, he relaxed against the back. "You don't remember who I am, do you?"

Where is he going with this discussion? "Should I?"

Joshua leaned forward with his forearms on his thighs and clasped his hands. "I visited the ranch when you were nine and I was twelve."

What he said triggered a long-forgotten scene. "Joshua. . .Dillinger." The words came out in a whisper.

India dropped her hands to her lap and closed her eyes to bring up the memory she had often revisited for a few years after his family left. When had she stopped dreaming about the boy who joined her when she rode like the wind across the dusty plains of the ranch? His high spirits almost matched hers.

"No wonder the name sounded familiar." She opened her eyes and looked at him in a new way, studying the black curls that now fell across his forehead.

Her attention moved to his eyes. India should have recognized those eyes that had shared in her fun so long ago. Maybe it was because Joshua was now so serious. She remembered him as a happy boy, who laughed a lot. Where had that daring boy gone?

"So why did you come to my ranch looking for work?" She needed to get to the bottom of why he was here. . .in this room.

Her gaze traveled around, trying to see if anything was out of place. She couldn't find anything that looked disturbed. She hoped he would have an explanation she could accept.

Joshua stood and shoved his hands into the back pockets of his dungarees. She'd seen him do that several times since he'd been on the ranch.

"I didn't really come looking for a job, but when Nathan assumed I did, I took the opportunity."

Why did he need an opportunity? India wasn't sure she liked the sound of this, and she didn't like him hovering above her or nosing through her business. She needed to let him know that she was still boss of this ranch. She stood and crossed her arms again.

He cleared his throat. "I received a letter from your father's lawyer."

"Daddy has been dead for over a year."

He nodded. "I know. His lawyer forgot to mail it any sooner, and it went to my dad in Texas. He forwarded it to my law offices in San Francisco."

"You're a lawyer?" This was getting complicated. "Then why would you want to work on a ranch?"

Joshua raked one hand through his hair, forcing his curls away from his face. "Your father wanted me to make sure you could run the ranch on your own. Besides, I've enjoyed revisiting the things I grew up doing."

"You didn't think I could run the ranch!" India stomped over to her desk and leaned against the front of it. "What were you looking for in this office?"

Almost as if he were mimicking her, he crossed his arms. "I wanted to see if you were in any financial trouble."

She stood up in his face. "How were you going to find out?" When he didn't say anything, the answer slid into her mind. "You looked at my books, didn't you?"

India knew she was almost screeching, but she didn't remember when she had been so angry. The look on his face was all the answer she needed. "Let me tell you something, Joshua Dillinger." She thumped her forefinger against his muscled chest. "I do not need a cowboy—lawyer—or whatever you are sashaying in here trying to take over my ranch. I was running it before my father died, and I can run it now."

Her throat clogged with tears of frustration, but she didn't want him to see them. He might think she was weak. She whirled and started toward the door.

Joshua's strong hands closed around her shoulders, halting her progress. "Please, India, listen to me." When she stopped her headlong plunge away from him, he moved around in front of her. With one finger, he lifted her chin until she was staring into his eyes, which held a look of tenderness. "I'm not trying to take over your ranch. I just wanted to know if you needed my help. Because of the close ties our dads shared, I thought I owed your dad that much."

India couldn't stop the two tears trailing slowly down her cheeks.

"Oh, India, I didn't mean to hurt you." Without thinking, Joshua pulled her against his chest, enclosing her in his arms. "I really only wanted to help."

He felt her relax against him, and more tears stained his shirt, but he didn't care. He stroked her back and murmured soothing words against her hair. Why didn't he tell her sooner who he was and why he was here? Maybe she would have been able to accept his presence. He whispered prayers for her while she continued to sob in his arms.

A long time later, she finally stopped crying and pulled away, mopping her face with both hands. "I'm sorry I broke down." She moved toward the front windows and stared out. "I've had to be strong ever since Daddy died. I haven't really cried." She turned a rueful expression toward him that arrowed straight to his heart.

Joshua leaned against the front of her desk and crossed his ankles. "I didn't want to add to your pain, but I'm glad you finally cried. That's the only way to release your grief."

She swiped at her eyes. "I imagine I look a mess. Sorry your shirt's wet."

"You could never look a mess." He wasn't sure he uttered the words out loud until her eyes widened. "You're a very beautiful woman, not at all like the pigtailed hellion who rode like the wind. I just miss all your freckles."

India burst out laughing. "I don't. . . . What do we do now?"

He stood up and walked toward her. "What do you want to do?"

This time when she crossed her arms, the gesture looked defensive, not defiant as she had been earlier. "I'm not sure. I suppose you looked at the ledger."

He wished he could take her in his arms again. "I'm not going to lie to you. I did go over all of last year's pages. I was just getting to this year when you arrived. So far everything looked good to me. Has this year been good, too?"

She nodded. "We're doing fine."

"If you want me to leave, I will." *But I don't want to.* "Will you let me stay until Nathan comes back? I'd feel better if you would."

He could think of other things that would make him feel better, too, not the least of which was tasting her trembling lips. When had he moved from being fascinated by her to longing to make their relationship something permanent? How could that ever work out with her in Arizona and him in San Francisco?

Chapter 6

Joshua finished cleaning up and headed out of the bunkhouse. With the men coming back from roundup today, he had expected Cook to prepare the evening meal, but India insisted on taking over for him. She said that Martha usually did supper after roundup to give Cook time to clean out the chuck wagon. Joshua would miss his evening meals alone with India. Over the last two days, they had spent a lot of time catching up on each other's lives. All he learned about her fascinated him, except the side of her that had to be in control of everything. She sounded as if she feared losing everyone's respect if she let down her guard even a bit. This troubled him.

He knew she went to church regularly, but where was her trust in God if she had to have such tight control of everything—the ranch, her emotions, her grief? Maybe they would have to have a serious talk about spiritual matters. Joshua wasn't looking forward to upsetting her, but he feared that kind of discussion would.

After stepping up on the porch of the cookhouse, Joshua reached for the handle but didn't need it. The door swung inward of its own accord, and the tantalizing aroma of rich beef stew wafted around him, causing his mouth to water. India was a woman of many talents.

He spied her in the other end of the large room, just outside the kitchen, and hurried toward her. "I'll help you serve the men."

The look she gave him would have been comical if it wasn't so serious. "Now, why would you do that?"

"It will give me a chance to thank each of them." He even tied one of the large utilitarian aprons around his waist. "I'll dish up the stew while you take care of the biscuits."

The first of the hands sauntered in, followed by several more in quick succession. The men picked up a bowl and a plate. Tin cans scattered along the length of the two tables held eating utensils.

Joshua ladled a big scoop of the savory soup. "Good job on the roundup, Hankins. Thank you."

The man studied him through squinted eyes, then gave a nod.

The next few minutes passed in the same manner. After getting a serving of stew, each man went to India for two or three of the fluffy biscuits. Joshua had eaten enough of them the last few days to know how good they tasted.

When all the men were seated, Joshua filled a bowl for himself and one for India and set each in front of one of the two empty chairs at the end of the table. India started a heaping plate of biscuits down each table before bringing some more to share with him. While the men ate and talked to each other, Joshua enjoyed his own food.

"So when are you going back into town to work at the orphanage, India?"

She looked up from her plate and gave him a questioning look. "I told you why I haven't been going so much. I'm really tired of all the questions and insinuations."

Joshua took a drink of the cool well water. "How about if I go help you and your friends tomorrow? Then they can get to know me, too. That way I won't be such a mystery to them."

India studied him thoughtfully before answering. "Don't you need to stay here with the men?"

"I'll give them assignments before we leave. None of these men are slackers."

She studied him for a moment. "If you're sure you want to do that."

"I'd like to get a look at this orphanage, since I contributed to it the day of the barbecue."

India had a hard time deciding what to wear to town. On any other day, she would have just slipped into the first skirt and blouse she picked up. For some reason, knowing that Joshua was accompanying her made her pause and consider before she chose something. She stared into the looking glass above the bureau. What did he think about her nearly white blond hair? He had told her he missed her freckles, but when she leaned closer to the mirror, she saw plenty of them. Maybe he hadn't been close enough. Just the thought caused heat to start in her midsection and make its way into her cheeks, leaving a blazing path on her skin. She pulled the neck of her unmentionables away from her chest and used it as a fan. She shouldn't be thinking about the man as anything but an old friend who would leave when Nathan came back. Didn't most people consider her a spinster? He probably did, too. Although she was only in her early twenties, most young women around here wed in their late teens.

After giving her head a quick shake to dislodge these thoughts, she picked up a navy blue skirt, sprigged with tiny white flowers. The light blue lawn blouse brought out the color of her eyes. After turning the long braid that hung across one shoulder into a figure-eight bun at the nape of her neck so it wouldn't interfere with her Stetson, she took a deep breath and ventured out on the porch.

Joshua was hitching the horses to the wagon. For a moment, India watched the sun play across his muscles, bunching and releasing as he worked. The man was strong. . .and good-looking. The fluttering that settled in her stomach brought a sigh to her lips. Why couldn't she control these feelings as well as she took care of everything else?

When he finished his task, Joshua looked toward the house and gave a wave of his strong, tanned hand. "I'll be right there."

India picked up the wooden crate she had filled earlier with things for the orphanage. The wagon stopped in front of the house as she made her way carefully down the three steps. Joshua's long stride brought him quickly up the line of flat stones that led from the house to the gate.

"Here, let me carry that."

He took it from her arms before India could tell him that she was doing fine. He even crooked the arm closest to her as if he wanted to escort her. She started to tell him just what she thought about that but decided not to. Instead, she slipped her hand into the space beside his elbow. The muscles of his forearm felt hard as rock. How could a man who worked behind a desk most of the time develop these kinds of muscles?

The man was an enigma.

Joshua enjoyed the ride into town. Since he shared the wagon seat with India, he made sure he sat close enough that when they hit a bump, their arms touched. The first time, she flinched, almost as if it hurt. He glanced at her out of the corner of his eye. She tightened the muscles in her jaw and turned her attention to something off in the distance ahead. This gave him the opportunity to study her. With skin that looked soft and smooth despite the fact that she was often out in the sun, India was by far the most beautiful woman he'd ever seen. He could imagine her holding her own in any society gathering in San Francisco.

But did he want to see her there? This wild, sometimes desolate land was part of who she was. Could he take her away from all of this?

Did he want to stay here with her? The more he thought about it, the more feasible it sounded.

"So what's so interesting out there?"

She turned startled eyes toward him. "I was just watching the green trees that line the river bordering the ranch. We really need its water in the late summer."

Always the ranch. Did she ever think about anything else?

Before he could decide how to bring up her need to control everything, he noticed four men riding toward them. As a precaution, he had strapped a pistol on his hip before they left the ranch. He never knew when he would need it for protection from snakes—of many kinds.

"Do you know those men?"

India studied them as they got closer. "That's another rancher with some of his men."

When the men drew close enough, Joshua raised a hand in a friendly salute. The cowboys pulled close to the wagon and stopped their horses, raising a large cloud of dust. If it had been Joshua, he would have slowed his horse gradually in consideration of the other travelers.

"Have you been to town?" India gave the first greeting.

The taller man took off his hat and fanned himself with it. "Yes, my wife had several things she wanted us to take to the orphanage today, and the boys had a little business they needed to take care of."

Joshua could smell what kind of business they had been participating in. The fumes of alcohol wafted toward the wagon. He was glad India wasn't alone. Maybe he should make sure she didn't ride into town alone again.

After India told the rancher to greet his wife for her, the men rode on, and Joshua clicked his tongue as he picked up the reins. The rest of the way to Cactus Corner, he tried to figure out how he would broach the subject with India. He knew she wouldn't welcome his interference.

India felt relieved when they arrived at their destination. The ride hadn't been comfortable. The attempts at conversation during the ride had fallen as flat as her first pancakes. Where had their easy comradery gone?

Every time their arms brushed against each other, that silly sensation once again rushed through her. If she didn't know better, she would think she was a young teenager just becoming aware of the masculine gender. Then she realized that it was the first time she had ever been interested in a specific man.

When she came home from back east, none of the young men sought her out. Although her father did what he thought was best for her, he couldn't have been more wrong. No one in this area of Arizona Territory wanted someone from Mrs. Collier's Finishing School. They wanted a woman who knew how to thrive in this part of the country. That might have been one of the reasons India tried so hard to prove she could run the ranch—even before Daddy died.

After stopping the horses, Joshua rushed around the back of the wagon to help her alight. The gold flecks in his dark brown eyes glistened in the bright sunlight, and his fingers splayed around her waist made her feel breathless.

Unfortunately, Anika, Elaine, and Jody came through the open door of the orphanage and witnessed her exit from the vehicle. Hopefully they would think her cheeks were red from being in the sun, but she knew different. His touch sent a blush to her cheeks as quickly as the bumps on the ride made her stomach jumpy.

"So"—Anika stood arms akimbo—"this is *the* Joshua Dillinger that I've been hearing so much about."

Joshua released his hold on India and turned around, but not before she heard his soft chuckle. "Just what have you been hearing about me? You're Anika, aren't you? India described you exactly."

He held out his hand, and Anika gave him the firm handshake she always used, almost like a man's. "Yes. I'm a lawyer, also. Maybe we can compare the differences in practicing law in a small place like Cactus Corner as opposed to a city like San Francisco."

His questioning gaze targeted India. "So what have you been telling her about me?"

Thankfully Jody intervened. "Oh, she's not the only one in town talking about you."

Joshua pulled his Stetson from his head and brushed it against his leg as he often did. "Don't you work in the office of the freight company?" After Jody nodded, he continued, "I remember seeing you there when I bought King."

"King?" Jody wrinkled her brows. "I thought Elmer sold you Goldie. I don't remember him having a horse named King."

Joshua's rich laugh pealed forth. "Goldie isn't a very good name for a stallion, so I renamed him King. He took to it pretty quickly."

The group moved around to the back of the wagon and started carrying in the things India and Joshua brought from the ranch. Cook had sent a few cuts of the steer he butchered yesterday, which they kept in the springhouse overnight. Elaine took it to the kitchen so Carla, the cook at the orphanage, could start chopping it into smaller pieces for the stew they would eat at noon.

India couldn't believe how much they accomplished that day. With Joshua helping, they completed many of the needed repairs. He promised to come on his next day off and give the building a new coat of paint.

She and Joshua started home in plenty of time to reach the ranch before dark.

When they were away from town, India turned toward him. "I didn't want to say anything back at the orphanage, but we don't have enough extra money to buy paint." When he turned to face her, she read the surprise in his eyes.

"I gave a pretty substantial amount at the barbecue." He cleared his throat as if the admission had a hard time coming out.

She nodded. "Pastor Gavin showed me the wad of bills you dropped in, and we are thankful."

"Then what's the problem?" He looked back toward the road.

"Well, the fund-raiser wasn't for the day-to-day running of the orphanage. Didn't you notice how crowded it is?"

"It did seem so." He certainly wasn't wasting any words. "So what was the money for?"

"We're saving to buy the empty mercantile building next door." Just the thought made India happy. "We'll have more room for the kids we have now, and we can even take in more, if we need to."

They rode along in silence for a while. India spent the time thinking about what needed to be done at the ranch when they got back. She almost missed his next softly spoken sentence.

"Then I'll pay for the paint myself."

Chapter 7

Over the next two weeks, whenever India went to town, Joshua accompanied her. Soon everyone she knew seemed to be in cahoots, figuring out ways that she and Joshua would have to spend time together. Pastor Gavin along with the rest of them. Not that she minded, but the time would come when he would go back to his law practice in San Francisco. She tried not to think about that.

Anika, Elaine, and Jody each found a chance to talk to her alone. Every single one of them told her not to let him get away, as if she were trying to snag him for a husband. She didn't want to think about that either. Sorting out her jumbled emotions would take more time than she had to give to it.

All too soon, India received the letter she had been dreading. Nathan and Martha would be home today. As she read the words, her heart pounded in panic. What would she do now?

India took a deep breath and squared her shoulders. She would run the ranch just as she did before that man rode back into her life. That's exactly what she would do. Unfortunately, the thought settled like a huge stone in the pit of her stomach.

Pasting a smile on her face, she went out to the barn to give the news to Joshua. Within half an hour, they were headed toward town in the wagon with their horses tied to the back. She hadn't wanted to ride in the back of the wagon on the way from Cactus Corner to the ranch, and she wouldn't think of asking Nathan and Martha to do it either.

Evidently Joshua was affected by the news, too. Neither of them talked on the way to town. They arrived just in time to hear the train whistle as it approached the depot. To India's heart, it sounded mournful, a death knell to hopes she hadn't even admitted she harbored.

After all the greetings, Joshua helped Nathan load the baggage into the wagon. Then he invited them to go to the café with him and India. He would buy everyone a meal before they returned to the ranch.

Nathan looked rested. As a matter of fact, so did Martha. Even though he'd lost his father, the trip must have been good for them. Over a meal of smothered steak and mashed potatoes, Nathan told all about his family. Martha inserted that they were glad to be back home.

India was just as quiet as Joshua during the delicious meal that went down like sawdust in his throat. The time for a decision was here, and he wasn't sure what India would think of his ideas.

After getting Nathan and Martha situated in the wagon and started toward the ranch, Joshua turned to India. "Let's take a detour by the river on our way back." He stuck his fingers in the hip pockets on his dungarees. "Maybe we could sit on that big rock that juts out over the water and talk awhile."

For some reason, her eyes held a wary expression, but she agreed.

The summer sun beat down on them as they rode across the arid land, but their speed whipped up a wind that cooled them. When they slowed near the river, the canopy of sheltering branches gave comforting shade. After walking the horses to the span of grass that lined the riverbank, Joshua quickly dismounted. How he wanted to help India down and encircle her with his arms, but that would have to wait. . .hopefully not forever.

India sat on the rock and arranged the split skirt to cover her legs completely. She stared across the water that shimmered with reflected sunlight. Joshua lowered himself beside her.

He waited a minute or two before he broached the subject on his mind. "We need to talk, India." She turned her gaze toward him, and he found it unreadable.

"Okay. What do you want to talk about?"

"You. . .me. . .the future." He felt like a stammering schoolboy.

The wall of her defenses strengthened visibly. "So what about me?"

He took her hand, and she didn't pull away. "Can we pray together first?"

She nodded her assent and bowed her head.

Lord, help me. Joshua cleared his throat. "Lord, we're at a crossroads here. We need Your wisdom to help us see the way You've set before us. We ask for that wisdom, in Jesus' name. Amen."

When she raised her head, she still didn't take her hand from his. That was a good sign, wasn't it?

He might as well plunge right in. "I've noticed that you always have to be in control."

India clenched her other hand but still didn't remove the one he held. "And?"

"Maybe you're not trusting God enough." The expression in her eyes hardened a little. "I know you're a Christian. I'm just saying that maybe you should trust Him to fight your battles for you." What else could he say to get her to understand? Maybe he should just let her think about it for a bit.

They sat in silence with India staring across the river for quite a while before she spoke. "Maybe you're right." She turned to look at him. "I understand that He knows best, but it took a long time for the men around here to accept me as a ranch owner—not only because I'm young, but also because I'm a woman."

He smiled into her eyes. "Yes, you are."

A blush stole over her cheeks, giving her a special glow.

"When I was a boy, my father had me memorize a Bible verse that has carried me through many hard times. It tells us to trust in the Lord with all our hearts, instead of leaning on our own understanding. If we acknowledge Him in all our ways, He will direct our paths. I believe that's one of the reasons that I've been so successful."

India glanced down at their hands and gently pulled hers away before clasping both hands around her upraised knees. She stared into the water flowing below them. "Do you think God brought you here, Joshua?"

He liked the sound of his name on her lips. "Yes, I do."

"You know I thought you came here to try to take over the ranch, don't you?"

He needed to be totally honest with her. "I guessed as much. Do you still believe that?"

"No." The soft word floated toward him on the breeze. "What are you going to do now? Go back to San Francisco?"

"Is that what you want?" He watched her intently, trying to discern her thoughts.

Finally, she turned to look back at him. "I'll really hate to see you go."

That was all he needed. "I don't have to."

She stood and walked to the back edge of the large rock before she turned around. "What are you saying?"

He scrambled to his feet but stood where he was, afraid to approach her yet. He'd be tempted to pull her into his arms and smother her with kisses.

"That I love you, India."

A spark lit her eyes. "But you live in San Francisco, and I own a ranch in Arizona Territory."

And never the twain shall meet. He'd see about that. "Would you be willing to go to San Francisco with me?"

Their gazes locked, and it almost felt like an embrace.

"What would we do with the ranch?"

India said *we*, as if they were a couple. Hope sprang forth full-blown in his heart. "*We* can decide that together."

Mischief colored her expression. "Are you asking me to marry you, Joshua, or are your intentions dishonorable?"

He took a step in her direction. "I offer nothing but marriage."

"Yes." She flung herself toward him, and he enclosed her in his embrace.

"India." Joshua was so full of emotion, he couldn't say anything else for a moment. "You won't have to give up your beloved ranch. In my Bible reading this morning, I came across a proverb that said a good man leaves an inheritance to his children's children. When I look into your smiling face, I see the foreshadowing of our children, and they need to grow up on their grandfather's ranch."

Her bright eyes trembled with unshed tears. He hoped they were tears of happiness. Gently he kissed her forehead, and her eyes drifted shut, spilling a tear on each cheek. He dried each of them with his mouth on the way to her luscious lips. They tasted of honey and sunshine and ignited a depth of love he'd never imagined.

He had only planned to give her a gentle kiss to seal their engagement. When India's arms crept across his shoulders and she relaxed against his chest, he deepened the kiss. She responded with passion. Joshua felt as if heaven opened and God placed His seal on their promise to each other.

Epilogue

India stood in a bedroom on the upper floor of the boardinghouse. So much had happened in such a short time. Today was her wedding day. In only three weeks, her best friends had helped her make a wedding dress and a trousseau to take on a honeymoon to San Francisco. They would soon be here to help her prepare for the ceremony.

Joshua had spent last night at the hotel so he wouldn't see her until she arrived at the church. His parents arrived last night, too. She was sure they were having a good time with their son.

Probably everyone for miles around Cactus Corner would attend the celebration today. India's head swam from the speed with which everything was accomplished. She thought about the land that she had inherited from her father—her heritage.

Those musings were interrupted when she noticed her helpers driving down the street in a carriage. She quickly finished her ablutions so she would be ready when they came upstairs.

The first one through the door was Jody, who rushed to give India a hug as if they hadn't spent the last twenty-one days working together. "So are you excited?"

India placed a hand on her stomach to try to stop the flutters there. "Of course."

Anika and Elaine came in carrying the dress, being careful to protect it from being soiled. When India was back east, many of the women had taken up the tradition started by Queen Victoria of England of wearing a white wedding dress. The practice hadn't really made its way this far west, but she had decided that if she ever married, she'd wear white. She had been pleasantly surprised when the general store had a bolt of white silk in its dry goods department.

The women bustled around helping India. Jody arranged her hair in an elaborate upswept style with long curls falling over one shoulder.

As she finished India's hair, Jody asked, "So you're going to San Francisco? Will you go today or tomorrow?"

India felt a blush move across her cheeks. "Joshua didn't want to spend our wedding night riding the train, so we'll go tomorrow."

"A wise move." Elaine helped Anika drape the dress carefully across the bed. "But are you moving there? You haven't really shared any of your plans with us."

Joshua's wise decisions under the leadership of the Lord had brought a satisfying answer to their dilemma. "No, we'll live on the ranch most of the time, but we'll go to San Francisco from time to time. And when we're gone, if Nathan needs to get in touch with us, there's always the telegraph. Joshua is still the senior partner in the law firm."

Anika raised her eyebrows at that statement. "Is Joshua planning to practice law here?"

India laughed. "Of course not. There's not enough business to keep both of you busy. His legal expertise will help with things at the ranch, though."

While her friends held the dress, she stepped into it before they pulled it up over her hips. After slipping her arms into the sleeves, they started fastening the long line of buttons that went up the back. How would she ever get out of the dress? A vision of Joshua standing behind her, carefully unfastening it, sent heat rushing all through her. She needed to keep her thoughts on the next few minutes, not the wedding night.

Joshua waited at the front of the church with Pastor Gavin McCurdy. He never dreamed when he decided to fulfill Mr. Cunningham's request just how much it would change his life. . .for the better. He knew God had sent him to this place, and he was glad he had listened to the Lord's direction. The most wonderful woman in the world was soon to be his wife. *His wife.* The words still felt strange, but wonderful.

Mrs. McCurdy came in the back door and walked down the side of the room toward the piano. After she sat down, she began to play the "Wedding March." India had chosen the music because she came to love it when she was in finishing school. However, Joshua wondered if the woman at the piano had ever played it before. It didn't matter, because the back door opened and Nathan escorted India down the aisle toward him. Everything else faded from his consciousness. He couldn't take his eyes off his bride—looking like an angel as she slowly walked toward him. *Thank You, Lord, for the gift of this woman.*

LENA NELSON DOOLEY

Award-winning author Lena Nelson Dooley has had more than 800,000 copies of her books sold. She is a member of American Christian Fiction Writers and the local chapter, ACFW - DFW. She's a member of Christian Authors' Network, CROWN Fiction Marketing, and Gateway Church in Southlake, Texas.

Lena loves James, her children, grandchildren, and great grandsons. She loves chocolate, cherries, chocolate-covered cherries, and spending time with friends. Travel is always on her horizon. Cruising, Galveston, the Ozark Mountains of Arkansas, Mexico. One day it will be Hawaii and Australia, but probably not the same year. Helping other authors become published really floats her boat, with over thirty having their first book release after her mentoring. Three of her books have been awarded the Carol Award silver pins from American Christian Fiction Writers, and she has received the ACFW Mentor of the Year award at their national conference. The high point of her day is receiving feedback from her readers, especially people whose lives have been changed by her books.

Her 2010 release *Love Finds You in Golden, New Mexico,* from Summerside Press, won the 2011 Will Rogers Medallion Award for excellence in publishing Western Fiction. Her next series, *McKenna's Daughters: Maggie's Journey* appeared on a reviewers Top Ten Books of 2011 list. It also won the 2012 Selah award for Historical Novel. The second, *Mary's Blessing*, was a Selah Award finalist for Romance novel. *Catherine's Pursuit* released in 2013. It was the winner of the NTRWA Carolyn Reader's Choice contest, took second place in the CAN Golden Scroll Novel of the Year award, and won the Will Rogers Medallion bronze medallion. Her blog, A Christian Writer's World, received the Readers Choice Blog of the Year Award from the Book Club Network.

In addition to her writing, Lena is a frequent speaker at women's groups, writers groups, and at both regional and national conferences. She has spoken in six states and internationally. She is also one of the co-hosts of the Along Came a Writer blog radio show.

Lena has an active web presence on Facebook, Twitter, Goodreads, Linkedin and with her internationally connected blog where she interviews other authors and promotes their books.

The Spinster and the Doctor

by Frances Devine

Dedication

For Mom—I wish you were here.
Special thanks to my friends:
Carol, Patty, Della, Evelyn, and Doris.
Your prayers help make this possible.

Marion and Megan,
I couldn't finish anything without your help.
Thanks to Vickie, Jeri, and Lena
for letting me be a part of this exciting book.
My kids and all my angel grandkids, you make me believe.
And to my heavenly Father, thank You for giving me this.
I love you all.

For God sent not his Son into the world to condemn the world;
but that the world through him might be saved.
John 3:17

Chapter 1

Elaine Daly gathered a deep breath and filled her lungs with early morning air. After five years in Cactus Corner, she still hated the heat and dust, but she loved the calm and quiet of the desert morning. The half-mile trek from the orphanage to the church and back had offered a nice stretch of the limbs and allowed for contemplation and reflection.

She crossed the dusty street, clutching the tied-up bundle of donated clothing tightly as she almost tripped over a rut. All she needed was to drop them and have to wash them out in the hot sun today. She stepped up onto the board sidewalk and headed past the bank. As she neared the café, the familiar sound of laughter and banter broke the silence and the aroma of strong coffee wafted out through the open door. Elaine glanced in. Etta Stephens was said to make the best flapjacks and eggs in Arizona Territory, and the packed café testified to that.

Elaine walked on, slowing her steps as she approached the vacant mercantile. The building had been empty since John and Rebecca Lane moved back east. Elaine's friend Jody McMillan had it in her head to buy the place, which was right next to the town orphanage. There was no denying they needed more space. The overcrowded children's home's large front parlor had recently been converted into a dormitory, relegating the visitors' area to a small room in the rear, formerly used for storage. But whether the church board would agree to expansion was anyone's guess.

A sudden scream pierced the morning air. Elaine froze in her tracks. Whirling, she turned and peered through the abandoned store's dingy window. Another scream rent the silence. She jerked back around as she realized the sound was not coming from the mercantile. Hitching up her skirts, she bounded up the wooden sidewalk toward the large adobe house that sat at the end of the dusty street. One more nerve-shattering shriek knifed through her as she reached the door of the orphanage. Her survival instinct kicked in and, dropping her bundle, she snatched a broom from the porch—it would have to serve as a weapon.

Elaine warily crept through the door, prepared to swing the broom with all her might if anything threatened. The hallway was clear. She tiptoed to the door on the left and peered into the room just as another scream issued forth. The daytime staff, mostly volunteers, stood in a circle in the middle of the new dormitory. Carla, the cook, glanced around, her brow furrowed.

"What in the world is going on?" Elaine flung the broom down and made her way over to the circle. She squeezed between Carla and the parlor maid.

Jody knelt on the hardwood floor, patting the golden curls of a tiny girl who sat holding a cornhusk doll. The child couldn't have been more than two. Suddenly the girl clutched her doll tightly, opened her rosebud mouth, and screamed.

Elaine's mouth dropped open. "Jody, who is this child, and why is she screeching like a banshee?"

Jody's blue-green eyes swam with unshed tears as she met Elaine's gaze.

"We're not sure. John Turner brought her in and just dropped her. We think she may belong to"—a crimson flush washed over her face, and she swallowed—"one of his saloon women."

Elaine's knee popped loudly as she knelt beside Jody. She sighed. At forty, she felt much younger, but her right knee apparently didn't agree.

"Does she have any injuries?"

"None that we could find. And no signs of illness either. She just screams." Jody inhaled deeply, then let the air out in a whoosh. "We've tried everything to reach her. She doesn't respond to anything."

"Did you send for Doc Howard?"

"Yes, but apparently he's gone to Tucson to pick up the new doctor."

Elaine let out a little breath of exasperation. "If only the Jacobsons were here." The couple who served as house parents for the orphanage had gone to San Francisco to visit relatives. A much-needed vacation.

"I know. When will they be back?"

"Not until tomorrow. We'll have to deal with this ourselves."

Jody stood and smoothed down her skirt, throwing a glance of regret in Elaine's direction. "Elaine, I'm so sorry to leave you with this situation, but I can't stay. I promised to sit with Mrs. Wright today while Mr. Wright runs some errands. He's afraid to leave her alone."

"Then of course you must go. And don't worry. We'll just have to do the best we can until the doctor gets back." Elaine rose, then bent and picked up the child, watching closely to see if there was any reaction. When the little girl remained silent, Elaine glanced at Jody, who smiled and shrugged.

Elaine spent the morning in the parlor, rocking the child, who didn't utter a sound as long as the back-and-forth motion continued. But every time Elaine grew fatigued and stopped for a moment, a scream would issue forth from the little pink lips. No sign of agitation, just the ear-piercing scream.

The soft little body curled into Elaine's arms, and as she gazed at the child, an unfamiliar warmth spread through her chest. Of course, she had always loved children. Why else would she have spent fifteen years of her life raising her brother and sister after her parents died? And she certainly would not have left her comfortable home in Chicago five years ago to come out to this despised desert to help the Jacobsons if not for the love she had for children. No, right now she would be enjoying the fragrance and beauty of the May flowers that bloomed each spring on the green, green lawns of her friends and neighbors there. And soon she'd be enjoying summer picnics by the cool lake. The season she missed most was autumn. Nostalgia washed over Elaine as her mind conjured up pictures of red and gold leaves sparkling in the morning sun. She could almost feel the crisp, cold air coming off Lake Michigan. Elaine sighed. Even more important than these pleasures, she could be cradling her infant niece in her arms, or she might, perhaps, even have a family of her own.

An unaccustomed wash of hot tears filled her eyes. Shaking her head, she blinked them away and sat up straight. She had chosen this life and did not regret her decision. Not in the least.

The child screamed again, and Elaine, who had been wrapped in her thoughts, realized she had stopped rocking. She began to move vigorously back and forth. *Then who would have been here for this little one?*

At noontime, Elaine carried her charge to the dining room and coaxed some soup into the little mouth. When the toddler smacked her lips with obvious enjoyment, Elaine and Carla exchanged pleased grins. As long as a child could enjoy food, the situation wasn't hopeless.

"What shall we call her? Until we find out her name, I mean."

"Hmm, how about Sunny? To match that hair."

Elaine thought for a moment and smiled. "No, let's call her Autumn." She reached over and turned the little face toward her. "You're my Autumn for now. Is that okay?"

For a moment, Elaine thought the deep blue eyes showed awareness, but then the soft lids came down and the child's lips opened wide. Elaine braced herself for the scream. When it didn't come, she cast a puzzled look toward Carla, who grinned widely.

"What?"

"She's waiting for another bite of that soup."

Dr. Dan Murphy jumped down from the buggy, hefted his trunk from the back, and followed the white-haired man into a small adobe house.

"You can just toss your things into the storage room off the side." Dr. Howard waved his hand toward a door. "I put a cot up in there. Guess you won't mind that until I get moved out of here." The aged doctor's mouth twisted up into a grin.

"Not at all. From what you've told me about that cabin in the mountains of Wyoming, I'm sure you can't wait to get out of here and take it easy."

"Well, I can and I can't." A pensive look crossed the doctor's face. "Hated it here when I first came, but I've gotten used to Cactus Corner. I'm probably going to miss it at first. I've patched up a lot of ranch hands. Doctored a bunch of kids. Most of them are grown-up now." He chuckled. "It was wild country when I came out here in '52. Belonged to Mexico back then. I was a young pup like you and just about scared out of my britches at all the goings-on."

Cactus Corner's newest citizen smiled at being thought of as a young pup. He had just turned forty-five last month. "I'd like to hear all about it sometime, sir, if you don't mind."

"Oh, you will. If not from me, from someone else. Still a lot of old-timers around." He threw his hat on the table. "Well, I'm sort of tuckered out after that long buggy ride. Think I'll take a nap, and then you can go with me on my rounds. Meet some of the people you'll be caring for. They're good folks, albeit a little rough around the edges."

A loud pounding caused both men to turn. The door flew open and a young boy of about eight or nine crashed into the room. A large calico cat clutched beneath his arm wriggled furiously and made its escape, running out the open door.

"Doc! You must go to the orphans' home. I promise Miss Jody I tell you as soon as you got back."

Dr. Howard grabbed his medical bag and headed for the door, motioning for Dan to follow. "What's wrong, Pedro? One of the young'uns sick?"

"Don't know, Doc. Miss Jody, she say to tell you she needs you. I wait on your porch all morning." His dark eyes crinkled with laughter, and he flashed a dazzling grin. "But I get so very hungry, I run to my *casa* to get some grub."

Dan held on to the side of the buggy as Doc Howard raced through town. The doctor pulled the horse to a stop in front of a large adobe house. Dan looked on in amusement as the older doctor jumped down, waving his buggy whip at two boys playing beside the railroad tracks. "Hey, you young rascals! Ray and Charlie!"

Two guilt-filled faces turned their way.

"Get away from them tracks. You want to get yourselves killed?"

"No, sir!" the boys yelled in unison, then ran in through the side gate and took off around to the back of the house.

Dr. Howard shook his head. "I've been telling folks we need to move the children to another location ever since the railroad came through. I hope someone doesn't have to get killed before they'll listen to me."

Dan nodded. "It does seem hazardous." *Just another case of folks not caring.* He followed Doc Howard up the stone walk and stood to the side as the older man tapped on the door. A little girl with bronze-colored skin and long black braids opened it. She stared at the doctor with wide dark brown eyes, then scooted aside for them to enter, yelling loudly, "Miss Elaine, the doctor is here."

"All right, Rainsong. I'm coming."

Dan stared at the woman who came through the door. Her deep auburn hair had come loose on the sides and hung in bouncy curls on each side of her face. She appeared to be in her midthirties. Her dark blue eyes stared into his, and a delicate pink flush washed over her very attractive face. Lowering her gaze, she shifted the child she carried in her arms and turned quickly to the older man.

Elaine swallowed with difficulty. She couldn't believe she had been staring at the stranger. What must he think?

"Dr. Howard, thank the Lord you're here at last. We have a situation."

"A new child, right?"

"Yes, but more than that."

She led the men down the hall and into the parlor. Her glance shifted to the stranger, and she blushed as she caught Dr. Howard's amused smile.

"Elaine, let me introduce you to Cactus Corner's new physician, Dr. Dan Murphy. Dan, this is Miss Elaine Daly. She assists Mr. and Mrs. Jacobson in the care of the children."

Elaine offered her hand to the new doctor and instantly wished she hadn't. His strong hand enveloped hers, and heat rushed through her palm and up her arm. A little involuntary gasp escaped her throat, and she felt heat rise to her face.

A scream reverberated through the room. Elaine started, jerking her hand free as both men looked at the little girl with concern.

"And that," Elaine said, her voice shaking, "is one of the problems." She moved to the rocking chair and sat down with Autumn on her lap. She motioned for the doctors to take a seat on the sofa. Once they were seated, she quickly apprised them of the details.

"Hmm, well, let's get her onto a cot, and I'll take a look." Doc Howard rose from the sofa and picked up his bag.

"Er—maybe I'd better hold her. She screams every time I put her down."

He blinked in surprise and peered at her through his spectacles. "Nevertheless, I think you'd better put her down so I can examine her. I've attended to screaming children before."

Elaine rose reluctantly and led the way to the toddlers' nursery.

Apparently one of the volunteers had taken the two- and three-year-olds outside to play, leaving the room vacant. Elaine laid Autumn down on a small cot and, after giving the child an encouraging pat, stepped back.

Elaine glanced at the stranger and felt a twinge of pleasure when he smiled at her sympathetically. She let her lips form just the tiniest smile, then looked away.

Dr. Howard gently examined Autumn, seemingly undeterred by her screaming. After a while, he stepped back, snapped his bag shut, and motioned for Elaine to pick the child up.

They went back into the parlor, and Autumn quieted as soon as Elaine sat down and began to rock her.

"Doctor, what's wrong with the poor little thing?" Elaine waited anxiously for his answer.

"Not exactly sure. No sign of injuries, anyway. And the child isn't ill." He twisted one side of his mustache. "She could be deaf. Or it could be some sort of shock. I'll know more about that after I talk to Turner." He shook his head and sighed. "To tell you the truth, Elaine, I think the child is just spoiled."

Elaine stared at Doc Howard, then down at the little girl who sat peacefully looking up at her. Laughter tickled her throat, and she chuckled. *Well, the little stinker.* "Spoiled? Do you really think that's all it is?"

"Mm-hm. Of course, I don't know for certain. But I'd just about be willing to bet on it." He stood up. "Send for me if you need me, and I'll let you know what I find out from Turner."

"I will, Dr. Howard. Thank you. At least she's not ill or injured."

Both men headed for the door, where Dr. Murphy turned and smiled.

For the first time, Elaine noticed the enticing gold flecks that sparkled in his dark brown eyes. *Stop it, Elaine. They're just brown eyes. Stop it before you make a fool of yourself!*

Tipping his hat, he said, "Good day, Miss Lainey. Don't let little Autumn wear you out."

She gasped as he turned and followed Dr. Howard down the path. He called her "Lainey." No one had called her that since she was eighteen. A smile tugged at her lips. *Lainey.* She liked it.

Chapter 2

Dust swirled around Dan's boots as he walked down the street. When he neared the saloon, a cacophony of noise assailed him. He paused and gazed at the swinging doors. Drawing in a deep breath, he took a determined step forward and pushed his way into the smoke-filled room.

Men in various stages of intoxication stood at the bar and sat at the tables. A garishly painted woman tripped across the outstretched boot of a customer at a gaming table. Ribald laughter reverberated against the walls. Loud angry voices floated down from the upper rooms, and something crashed to the floor. Dan blinked against the acrid smoke that burned his eyes. He clenched his teeth as memories assaulted him.

Five-year-old Dan squirmed and twisted, trying to see his mother's face, but her arms held him tight against her. She coughed, and a glob of blood hit Dan's hand. A jolt of fear pierced him as she fell to the floor, pulling him with her.

"Ma!"

She hit the floor with him still clutched tightly to her chest. Terror held him in its grip as her loud, rasping breaths suddenly stopped. Burly arms pulled him from his mother's grasp, and he struggled against them.

"No! Ma!"

He twisted and turned, striking out at the tall figure who held him captive. Bending forward, he bit down hard on the man's hand. The man cursed, and then a blow landed on Dan's head. . . .

A loud guffaw brought Dan back to the present. A shudder ran through his body. Maybe it hadn't been such a good idea to volunteer to do this for Doc Howard. Clenching his fist, he strode to the bar.

"What'll it be?" The surly bartender didn't bother to turn around as he continued wiping down bottles.

"I'm looking for a woman named Mary."

"Yeah? Well, we got three of 'em." The bartender faced Dan and gave him the once-over.

"The one I'm looking for was taking care of a baby until recently."

The man raised his eyebrows, and his lips turned downward. "What interest would you have in that baby?"

At the suspicious tone, Dan held up both hands. "Nothing except pure concern. I'm the new doctor in town. I need some information about her medical history."

"You mean if she's been sick or something?"

"That's right." Dan smiled.

"Ain't never been sick as far as I can remember. Mary took good care of the kid."

The man narrowed his eyes and glared at Dan.

Dan nodded. "I'm sure she did. But most children have some sort of childhood disease at one time or another. I really need to speak to Mary, if you'd just tell me where she is."

"Charlie, quit bein' so contrary." A frowsy-looking redhead with kind eyes sauntered over and grinned at Dan.

"So you're the new doc, huh?"

"Yes, ma'am. Just arrived yesterday. Would you by any chance be Mary?"

The woman chuckled. "Nope, name's Lottie." She tilted her head toward the stairway and grinned. "Mary's busy right now. But I could probably tell you anything she could. We all took care of Baby."

"Well, Lottie, that's kind of you. Any information would be greatly appreciated by me as well as the good women at the orphanage."

Lottie frowned. "Humph. Good women, eh? And what does that make us girls in here? I can just imagine what they think and say about us." She slid onto the stool next to Dan. "You might want to buy me a drink. Turner don't take too kindly to idleness."

Dan smiled. "I'll tell you what, Lottie, how about if I just pay for your time and we forget the drink? Will that satisfy your boss?"

"Don't know why it wouldn't." She motioned the bartender over. "Charlie, the doc wants to talk and is willin' to pay for it. So you just mark down two drinks every fifteen minutes or so."

"I dunno, Lottie." Charlie scratched his chin and frowned.

Lottie gave a huff and retorted, "Never mind what you dunno." She smiled and softened her voice. "It'll be okay, Charlie. Just do it."

"Well, okay. If you say so." He cast a sideways look at Dan. "But you call me if you need me."

"Come on, Doc. Let's sit over at that corner table. It's a little bit quieter there."

Lottie slid off the bar stool, her red and white satin skirts swinging around her legs, and motioned for Dan to follow.

A half hour later, satisfied that Autumn was a healthy little girl, Dan left the saloon. As he stepped outside the doors, his eyes met those of a woman just coming out of the general store across the street. He tipped his hat. She gave him a cold stare and turned away.

Uh-oh. I've only been in town one day and I've already given the good ladies of Cactus Corner ammunition against me.

"Miss Elaine, Miss Elaine. That baby won't hush up, and I'm tryin' to do my 'rithmetic."

"*A*-rithmetic, Charlene."

"Yes, ma'am, that's what I said—'rithmetic."

Elaine sighed and brushed the stringy blond locks from the girl's forehead.

"All right, Charlene, bring her to me. I'll take care of her." She looked into the girl's face. "Why are you doing your homework in the toddlers' room anyway? You're supposed to use the dining room table."

"Grace asked me to help watch them while she went to fix bottles. But those babies are makin' me crazy."

"Get your things and go into the dining room. I'll watch the toddlers until Grace gets back."

"Yes, ma'am." The girl made a beeline for the door.

"And go find your ribbon. It seems to have fallen out of your—" Elaine stopped talking, as the girl was already out of the room. She groaned. This was the most hectic day they'd had in a long time. There were usually at least two volunteers each day to help the Jacobsons and Elaine with the children as well as to oversee the younger volunteers who came in from time to time. But Mr. and Mrs. Jacobson's train would not arrive until late afternoon.

Anika was in the middle of a legal dispute of some sort, and India was busy at the ranch. Elaine was tempted to ask Jody to come in, but her friend's boss had been keeping her so busy lately that Elaine hated to disturb her on one of her few days off.

Elaine entered the toddlers' room and found not only Autumn screaming but seven more youngsters, as well. Grace's helper, Jane, sat in the rocker with two crying babes in her arms. She cast a frantic glance at Elaine. Several older toddlers sat on the floor in obvious distress.

Grace came through the door, huffing and puffing and carrying a basket full of milk bottles. "Sorry, Miss Elaine. Cook was busy and couldn't help." She set the basket down and handed bottles out to the little ones who were not yet weaned.

"I understand, Grace. It's been a difficult day for all of us. I really think we need to move the children who are off the bottle into the next dormitory. The others' screaming just gets them all going, and nap time is almost impossible."

Elaine went over to Autumn's crib. The little girl drank peacefully, with a tiny stream of milk running from the corner of her mouth. Elaine glanced around the room. It was finally quiet now that the babies were eating. Breathing a sigh of relief, she waved to Grace and Jane and headed for the kitchen to help Carla.

She passed through the hall just as someone knocked on the front door. *What now? It had better not be those rascal boys playing tricks again.* She opened it to find herself standing face-to-face with the new doctor. His eyes crinkled as he flashed a smile.

"Dr. Murphy—" Elaine cleared her throat and tried again. "May I help you with something?" She reached up and patted at her wayward curls. *Why can't they ever stay in the bun where they belong?*

He looked down at her from his considerable height. Again that smile about knocked her off her feet.

"As a matter of fact, I think perhaps I can help you. I have some information about your newest charge."

"Oh." Elaine stepped back. "Do come in, please. We're rather at sixes and sevens around here today, but I'm sure I can find a few moments."

He followed her to the small parlor, and they sat on the sofa. A lock of sandy hair had fallen across his forehead, and Elaine could almost feel her fingers brushing it back. She forced the thought out of her mind, wishing she had sat on the chair across the room so she wasn't so close to this man who left her flustered.

"It seems Miss Autumn's mother was one of the. . .er. . .entertainers at the saloon. She died shortly after the baby arrived. Since the mother had never mentioned family, there was nowhere for the child to go."

"Well, for goodness' sake! Why didn't they bring her here instead of waiting nearly two years?" Elaine felt the creases between her eyes and consciously composed her face.

He raised one eyebrow and said, "It seems some of the ladies in the establishment thought she would be better off with them than here."

She gasped. *They thought the child would be better off in a saloon than with godly Christian people?* "How could they possibly believe a child should be raised in a saloon?"

A painful look clouded his eyes, but the next moment his mouth twisted in a sardonic smile. "Ah. . .well. . .Lainey, there are worse places than saloons."

Heat warmed her cheeks. *Lainey.* That name again. She glared at him. "What exactly do you mean by that?"

"Nothing personal, my dear. I was merely stating a fact." He rose and picked up his hat.

"Wait. What caused them to change their minds?"

"They didn't. Turner didn't want the child around anymore, so he took matters into his own hands."

"Did you ask about the screaming?"

"As a matter of fact, that was the clincher. Turner told them they'd spoiled her so much he couldn't stand to have her around anymore. Apparently her tantrums and screaming were hurting the business. There's not a thing wrong except she's been spoiled rotten." He gave a nod in her direction. "Well, Miss Lainey, I'll get out of your way. Don't work yourself to death."

"Thank you, Dr. Murphy. I do appreciate the information." She reached out her hand, which he took and held for a moment.

"You're more than welcome. I'll do anything I can for these orphans. And I'll do anything I can for you, as well." Turning, he left her standing in stunned silence.

Now what did he mean by that?

❧

Dan ran his hand over the mare's glistening chestnut flank and gave her a final pat. He had run her harder than he liked to, but he'd wanted to see how she would do in an emergency.

"She's a beauty, Mrs. Dillinger. I'm surprised you can part with her, but I'm glad you are." He tied the reins to the back of the buggy. His newly purchased horse had rested enough for the slow trot back to town.

The young woman smiled and tucked a loose strand of blond hair behind her ear. "Just take good care of her. And please call me India. After all, we are neighbors now."

"I'm sorry I missed your husband. Maybe next time."

"I'm sure we'll see you in church. You can meet Joshua then."

The lovely young woman smiled broadly and waved to him as he pulled away in Doc Howard's buggy.

Dan whistled as he rode through the saguaro and other cacti, which grew profusely in the area. Mrs. Dillinger was a beautiful woman. She'd grace any big-city drawing room. He couldn't help but wonder why she chose to live in this hot and dusty country. Of course, Arizona Territory had its beauty. Like now with the sun setting behind the mountains. If a man didn't know better, he'd think the mountain itself was on fire. He had to admit he'd never seen a sunset like this in San Francisco. Still, life wasn't easy here. Especially for the women and children.

He had wondered about Miss Elaine Daly. It was obvious she came from back east somewhere. He grinned. The prim and proper Miss Daly hadn't said a word about his familiarity with her name. He had no idea why he was deviling her the way he was—trying to get under her skin. He couldn't deny the attraction he felt for her. A grin quirked his mouth. He had to admit he enjoyed the reaction he got when he called her Lainey.

Amazing, the difference in women. These ladies, although obviously used to hard work and no-nonsense lifestyles, were nevertheless genteel and gracious.

Then there was Lottie and her kind. Dan frowned, and his body tensed into the familiar fighting mode. Most likely Lottie's life had been a lot different from Miss Daly's or Mrs. Dillinger's. It wasn't her fault she hadn't had the same advantages as the other ladies. No doubt they snubbed her and made her feel like dirt under their dainty little shoes when they saw her on the street.

Dan took a deep, cleansing breath and relaxed. He wouldn't let the past mess up the chance of a fresh start here in Arizona Territory. He was going to stay on the straight and respectable path here. The "Lotties" would have to fight their own battles this time.

Chapter 3

The small visitors' room was stuffy—too stuffy. Elaine pulled at her collar, then grabbed her fan and waved it furiously.

Anika Truesdale shook her head and narrowed her hazel eyes. "Really, Elaine, I'd think after nearly ten years you'd be used to the weather here."

"Well, I'm not. It's not natural for it to be so hot in May." She gave another sharp pass with her fan to make her point.

"Well, it's natural for Arizona, honey," Anika drawled.

The four friends tried to meet at least once a week, although it wasn't always possible now that India and Anika were married. Today's meeting had begun with a lot of friendly banter and catching up on each other's events of the week. Elaine didn't know why she'd gotten so tense all of a sudden. But the weather wasn't helping.

"Are you sure it's the heat, sweetie?" India grinned, then ducked as Elaine's fan flew through the air, bounced against the wall, and almost landed on her head. A startled look crossed her face, and she stared at Elaine.

Elaine gasped in horror. What in the world had she done? "I'm so sorry, India. I don't know what came over me."

India nodded her forgiveness. "I think I know. Why don't you admit you're smitten with the good-looking new doctor?"

"Oh no! You can't be!" Jody lifted her hands to her cheeks, her eyes wide.

"Why, Jody, what do you mean?" Elaine asked. "Not that I care a whit about Dan Murphy, of course." Her heart fluttered, and she felt warmth creeping up her face.

Jody bit her lip. "Oh dear. I hate passing on gossip, but. . ."

"But what?" Anika leaned forward. "Just get to the point, Jody."

Elaine couldn't help but smile. Anika and her lawyer mind could never abide beating around the bush.

"Well—" Jody hesitated, then rushed on. "Mrs. Sanders thinks Dr. Murphy might not be quite nice."

Elaine's heart pounded. Why would Mrs. Sanders say such a thing?

India looked at Jody, a surprised expression on her face. "What's that supposed to mean? I've met him and I think he's very nice." She grinned. "My horses even like him."

"I hate to spread gossip, but for Elaine's sake, I think I must. Mrs. Sanders saw him coming out of the saloon week before last, and a few days ago, Mr. Sanders spotted him standing outside the saloon doors, talking to one of those. . .women." Jody blushed and bent her head over the small garment she was sewing.

"Well, maybe someone was sick," India said.

Jody glanced up. "That's what I said, but Mrs. Sanders said no respectable doctor would treat those women and take a chance on spreading their disgusting diseases to the decent folk in Cactus Corner."

"Hmm." Anika tapped her fingers against the wooden arm of her chair. "She may be right. The bartender usually does their doctoring."

"How in the world would you know that?" India jerked her head up and stared at Anika, wide-eyed.

Anika grinned. "I am a lawyer, you know. We have ways of finding out things."

Elaine felt numb. She couldn't speak because of the lump in her throat.

"Elaine, you don't really care about that man, do you?" Jody asked.

"No." The word came out with a croak, and Elaine ducked her head and concentrated intently on the small shirt she was mending. "Of course not. I barely know him."

Mercifully, at that moment, India took pity on her and turned to Jody. "By the way, Jody, has Elmer proposed yet today?"

Anika and India exploded with laughter as Jody rolled her eyes and didn't bother to answer. Her employer made no secret of the fact he intended to make Jody his bride. Not that Jody thought him repulsive, but she simply wasn't interested, and Elaine knew his constant wooing was about to drive Jody insane.

Just then, Grace peeked her head through the door.

"Everyone's tucked in. Do you mind if I join you?" A few months ago, Anika had recruited the girl to women's suffrage, and since then, Grace had almost become Anika's shadow.

"Grace, what in the world are you wearing?" Elaine stared at the pant-covered legs.

"It's a bloomer outfit, ma'am. I waited until I went off duty to put it on."

Elaine heard a muffled snort coming from India's direction and had to press her own lips together to keep from laughing. Jody had turned her head and coughed into a hanky.

Anika stood and took the girl's hand, leading her over to a chair beside them. "Pay no attention to them, my dear. You look absolutely delightful. I've been thinking of making a bloomer outfit for myself. I hear they're all the rage among the suffragettes in England and even New York."

Elaine was thankful for the laughter and the change of subject.

A short while later, when everyone had left, she stepped outside and watched the moon rise above the mountains. She shivered as cool air tickled her skin. She should have remembered to wear her shawl. That was one good thing about the desert. Although she was burning up a short time earlier, nighttime always brought a cool breeze.

She went back inside and said good night to Mrs. Jacobson, who was just coming out of the kitchen. Once in her room, she fidgeted as she tried unsuccessfully to keep her mind on her devotions. Finally, she gave up and went to bed.

Thoughts of Dan Murphy's kind eyes pressed into her mind, and she tried fruitlessly to block them out. He seemed so nice, and she had to admit her pulse raced whenever he was near.

"Oh Lord, I almost fell in love with a scalawag."

Through her open window, the cicadas seemed to mock her. She could almost hear them chiding, "You did, you did."

Slinging her coverlet back, she strode to the window and slammed it shut. "There," she muttered, brushing her hands together.

But as she lay back on her soft pillows, a sob caught in her throat as her own thoughts echoed the words. *I did. I did fall in love with him.*

Dan patted little Sam Carter on the shoulder and handed him a piece of licorice. "You're a trouper, Sam. I think you may be the best patient I've had all day." He didn't mention that the little boy was the only patient he'd had all day.

Mrs. Carter's tired eyes rested kindly on Dan as she clutched the bottle of cough syrup he had given her for her son. "I wish I had the money to pay you, Dr. Murphy." She bit her lip, and Dan could see embarrassment written all over her lined face.

"Don't worry about it, Mrs. Carter. I can't wait to sink my teeth into this wild plum cobbler. It's payment enough."

A hint of a smile touched the woman's lips as she lifted her toddler from the cot. She headed for the door, then stopped and turned. "I don't believe them rumors about you, Dr. Murphy. And my man don't, either."

Dan stared after her as the door swung shut behind her. Rumors? What rumors? He'd wondered why he'd had only a handful of patients all week. The first few days after Doc Howard left, the office had been full almost continuously. He'd thought maybe no one was sick, but it was highly unusual not to at least have headaches or rashes to treat. Come to think of it, the few folks who had come in had been from the Indian camp a few miles away or miners' families. Not one of the upstanding citizens of Cactus Corner had darkened his doorway this week.

Now that he recalled, he'd received some cool nods from the ladies of the town, and not a few skirts were swept aside as he walked down the street.

What were the rumors? And who started them? He inhaled deeply, then let the air out with a *whoosh*. So it had begun again. Only this time, he was innocent of any wrongdoing.

He washed up and changed his shirt, then grabbed his bag and headed out the door. He hadn't checked on the children at the orphanage in a few days. Besides, a visit with Miss Elaine was just what he needed to lift his spirits.

Grace answered his knock.

"How are you today, Miss Grace? Lovely as ever, I see."

The girl blushed and stammered, "I'm fine, Doc. Brother and Sister Jacobson are at a church board meeting. I'll tell Miss Elaine you're here." She scurried from the room, leaving Dan standing in the hall with his hat in his hand.

A few minutes later, Elaine walked in. How she managed to look so cool and crisp in this heat was a mystery to Dan. Unfortunately, the expression on her face was even cooler.

"Yes, Dr. Murphy? How may I assist you?" Not a trace of friendship or congeniality appeared on her face. In fact, she seemed to struggle with some emotion he couldn't identify.

"I thought I'd check in on the children," he said, attempting a smile.

"The children are all fine, Doctor. So if you'll excuse me. . ." The words trailed off, and she glanced toward the door.

He nodded and turned away, then with resolution wheeled back around to face her.

"What's going on, Miss Elaine?" He took just a tiny bit of satisfaction at the shocked look on her face. Apparently she hadn't expected to be confronted.

"I don't know what you mean."

Dan quirked an eyebrow. "Well now, let's see. I have very few patients, none of whom happen to be the so-called respectable citizens of the town; I'm getting the cold shoulder from said citizens; and now you're treating me as you would a rattlesnake getting ready to strike."

He watched with interest as Elaine's face flamed. She opened her mouth, shut it, and then opened it again.

"Miss Elaine, one of my patients tells me rumors are going around town about me. I think I have a right to know what they are so I can either admit to them or defend myself."

Elaine felt tension clamp down on her from her head to her toes. She realized she was twisting a section of her skirt and forced herself to open her hand. Uncertainty gripped her. It had never occurred to her that the stories were untrue. After all, why would anyone make up such atrocities? But he looked so confused and even a little hurt as he stood facing her. What if he truly was innocent? It was easy to jump to conclusions. Elaine had been guilty of that herself at times.

She swallowed and took a long, shuddering breath. "Dr. Murphy, would you like to come in for a moment? Perhaps we should talk."

A look of surprised relief passed over his face, and he followed her to the small receiving room in back.

Elaine sat down next to a small table, motioning him to the chair on the other side. Could she really do this? Maybe one of the men should be talking to him. But then, most of them believed he was guilty. Still, such a delicate subject. She could feel warmth on her face just thinking about it, but having admitted to herself that she was in love with him, she felt she owed it to him to push through her embarrassment.

She glanced at him and was surprised to see sympathy on his face.

"Miss Lainey, if this is too difficult for you, don't feel that you have to tell me anything."

She straightened her back and looked him in the eye. "I'm fine, Dr. Murphy."

She began with the incidents at the saloon. "I realize the first time was probably when you went to find out about Autumn."

"Yes, you're right. It was."

"Well, what about standing in the doorway with one of those. . ." She stopped and blushed again, then, frustrated at her own emotions, she took a deep breath and exhaled loudly. They wouldn't get anywhere if she couldn't stop blushing.

"Her name is Lottie," Dan said, coming to her rescue. "I was giving her instructions on how to care for one of the girls who'd come down with a very bad case of tonsillitis."

"Oh." Elaine paused. "But. . .should you be treating those women? I mean, after all, you could pass something on to other people."

"What exactly could I pass on to these 'other people'?" Dan scowled. This was the first time she'd seen him with anything less than a pleasant expression on his face.

"Well, I don't know." She frowned and blew a strand of hair from her eyes. "Mrs. Sanders said some kind of disease could be passed on."

"My dear, the type of disease the good Mrs. Sanders was referring to can't be passed from patient to patient by a doctor."

"Oh." She wasn't sure what to reply, since she had no idea what sort of disease he was referring to.

"Didn't Dr. Howard give medical treatment to the folks at the saloon?"

Elaine shook her head. "My friend Anika said the bartender took care of them."

Anger washed over his face. "Well, just so you know, physicians take an oath to give medical care to all who need it. And I intend to do just that. If anyone, including you, has a problem with that, I'm sorry, but that's the way it is." He stood, gave her a short bow, and then strode from the room.

Elaine listened to his boots as he walked up the hallway. Suddenly she jumped up and ran out into the hall just as he reached the front door. "Doctor, wait."

He stopped and turned, his brow raised, a question in his eyes.

"Don't you want to hear about the other things being said?"

His lips turned up slightly at one corner. "Not particularly. I think I have a pretty good idea of what's being said. I hope in the future you'll give me the benefit of the doubt before you believe the rumors, Miss Elaine. I may be rough around the edges, but I'm not immoral."

Elaine's heart fluttered. She could feel the throb of her pulse in her neck as relief washed over her. She held her hand out to him. "I believe you, Dr. Murphy."

With two strides, he was standing in front of her, her hand in both of his. Warmth filled his eyes as he gazed into hers. "Thank you, Lainey. But are you sure you want to be my defender? It may cost you in terms of friendship."

Elaine jerked her chin and gave a tight little smile. "My friends won't turn against me." Gently she slipped her hand from his warm grasp. "Good day, Doctor. I'll be praying for you."

Chapter 4

Elaine stopped and stood gaping at the crowd gathered around the door of the general store. What in the world was going on? And how would she ever get through the shoulder-to-shoulder throng? Well, the flour bin was almost empty, so she really had no choice.

"Excuse me." She squeezed between two strange men at the edge of the crowd. Twisting and elbowing her way, she managed to get to the door, where she slipped inside. The crowd there wasn't as large. Mrs. Granger locked the door and motioned for her to follow her into their private quarters in back of the store.

"Elaine, you shouldn't have come out. It's getting pretty bad on the street."

"But what's going on?" Elaine followed the storekeeper's wife to the corner, where they sat in high-backed rockers.

"You didn't hear about the copper strike last week?" Mrs. Granger fanned herself and gazed at Elaine through wide blue eyes.

"Well, yes, I did hear that someone had found copper up in the mountains. What does that have to do with this?"

Mrs. Granger sighed. "Unfortunately, it seems everyone from a hundred miles around has heard about it, too. They've been pouring into town like ants since yesterday. Many of them came without any mining gear at all, expecting to buy it here. And expecting credit. We sold what we had on a cash basis, but we've run out. We simply weren't prepared for the rush. Some of them are getting downright ugly."

Elaine gasped. "Isn't the sheriff doing anything to control them?"

The woman gave a short laugh. "He's trying. But the jail won't hold them all."

"Can't you get more supplies?"

"Fred's heading to Tucson today. He's tried to reason with the miners, but some of them can't be reasoned with. Like that crowd outside." She brushed hair from her forehead and breathed deeply. "I was just getting ready to lock up and put the closed sign on the door when I saw you coming. I suppose you need something for the orphanage."

"Yes, tomorrow is baking day, and we're about out of flour." She looked questioningly at the older woman.

"Sorry, dear. That's gone, too. I'll have someone bring some over from my own supply—enough to make a few loaves." She peered at Elaine. "But you really shouldn't go back through that crowd. And it wouldn't be safe to go out the back way either. No telling who'd be out there."

"Well, no one bothered me on my way in. I'm sure I'll be fine, and I really have to get back." Elaine rose. "Anything you can send will be fine. We'll get by."

They walked to the front of the store. Mrs. Granger put the Closed sign on the door, and the crowd began to thin out just a little.

Mrs. Granger unlocked the door, and Elaine slipped through. Seeing the angry faces of the men in the throng, she almost turned around and knocked on the door. But no, she had to get back to the orphanage. Taking a deep breath, she stepped forward and began to make her way back through the jumble of sweating, mumbling bodies.

"Hey there, pretty little lady." A hand grabbed Elaine's arm and yanked her around. She found herself nose to nose with a grinning, bearded round face. She almost retched from the foul smell emanating from between the man's broken, rotted teeth.

"Let go of me." She jerked her arm, then yelped as he squeezed it tighter, pulling her close to him. Laughter met her on all sides, and she felt herself getting dizzy.

"Let her go. Now!" She heard Dan Murphy's voice and felt strong arms catch her just as darkness overcame her.

❧

"Elaine, dear, wake up."

Elaine's eyes fluttered open as gentle hands patted her cheeks. Martha Jacobson's worried face looked down at her. As she raised herself onto one elbow, she saw that she was lying on her bed at the orphanage.

"What? How did I get here?"

"Dr. Murphy carried you here after he rescued you from that mob of ruffians."

Elaine's heart raced as the memory of her assailant flashed through her mind. "Oh, I need to thank the doctor. Is he still here?" Her hero. Her knight in shining armor. Warmth rose from her chest to her face, and she felt the corners of her lips tilt upward.

Martha smiled and cast a knowing glance toward her. "I guess you're feeling better. But you'll have to wait to thank the young doctor. As soon as he knew you were all right, he slammed out of here. He was quite angry."

Elaine stood and smoothed her skirt, then went to the small mirror over her washstand and arranged the hair that had come loose.

"You lie back down, now. The girls and I can manage."

"Nonsense. I'm fine. I was just overcome from nerves and the lack of air. Oh, Mrs. Granger will send some flour over later. They're out of everything in the store."

"Yes, I heard. I'm afraid our sweet little town won't stay the same now that the miners are here. A few of them will bring families, of course, but most of the miners are a rough bunch."

They left the room, and Martha headed for her desk in the kitchen while Elaine went to check on the children. Grace was rocking Autumn, and the little girl seemed contented as she lay with her head against Grace's chest, her thumb in her own little rosebud mouth.

Elaine smiled and ran her hand over the soft curls. "We really need to make her stop sucking her thumb."

"Yes, ma'am. That we do." Grace looked at Elaine, and they exchanged knowing smiles. Little Autumn had almost stopped the screaming. They weren't about to upset her just yet.

Jane rushed in carrying a stack of diapers. When her eyes rested on Elaine, they lit up with mischief. "Miss Elaine, you are so lucky."

"What do you mean, Jane?"

"What do I mean? Well, I would give just about anything to be carried in the strong arms of a handsome man like Doc Murphy."

"Jane Andrews, that's not very nice. I was unconscious."

"Yes, ma'am." The girl giggled and put the stack of diapers away.

Elaine let out a huff and walked out of the room. There were several volunteers helping out today, so she mostly went from one group to the other making sure all was well and giving occasional instructions. This, of course, left too much time for free thinking, and Elaine found her mind wandering to Dan Murphy. Her cheeks flushed as she thought of Jane's words. She couldn't help but wonder how those arms would have felt if she'd been awake. *Stop it, Elaine.* All she needed was to get people gossiping about her, too.

The rumors about Dan seemed to be getting worse instead of dying down. Elaine knew most of the *respectable* folks were going to a doctor in another town and continued to snub Dan every chance they had. She'd made several of the ladies angry when she defended him at the last sewing circle. Since then, she'd gotten the cold shoulder from a few people herself, although most folks stood by her even though they thought she was deceived.

She was happy the Jacobsons hadn't been swayed by the gossip. They liked the new doctor and didn't care who knew it, although they thought he was unwise to continue to give medical treatment to the saloon girls. Elaine had to admit to herself that she agreed. Those creatures had done fine with the bartender to take care of their medical needs, and she simply couldn't understand why Dan couldn't see it, as well. After all, they'd chosen the sort of life they lived, hadn't they?

❧

If he aimed a little to the left, he'd make it this time. Dan leaned back in his chair with his boots propped up on the desk, then aimed the wadded-up paper and sent it sailing, giving a satisfied grunt when it landed in the can on top of the bookcase.

Pushing his boots against the desk, he slid his chair back and got up. How pathetic was he anyway to be so easily entertained?

He grabbed his hat and slung it on his head as he went out and locked the door. If anyone needed his services after hours, they could come looking for him. He intended to go to the hotel and check on the miner who'd come down with a fever earlier in the week. It probably wasn't anything serious, but with so many strangers crowding into town, he didn't want to risk an epidemic.

The town was quiet today. Since getting their supplies a couple of days ago, all the miners were up in the mountains searching for copper. He passed the dress shop, which was closed for the day, and sauntered through the door of the hotel.

"Howdy, Doc. What can I do for you?" The desk clerk ran a feather duster over the long counter.

"Hello, Bob. I just came to check on the miner who was ill."

Bob stopped dusting and scratched his ear. "He hightailed it out of here with the rest of them."

"Hmm. Did he appear to be all right?"

"As far as I could tell. Didn't seem sick to me. He probably just had a touch of the sun or something."

Dan frowned. "Maybe." Shrugging, he said good-bye and left. He stood outside the hotel with his hat in his hands, running his fingers around the brim. He wondered if he could get by with going to the orphanage to see Elaine. Probably not. Since she'd agreed to let him call on her last week, he'd already been over there three times. He grinned. No sense in pushing his luck. He'd never imagined he'd feel this way about any woman.

He crossed the street and headed down the sidewalk to the café. *Might as well eat supper,* he supposed. Etta usually closed up by seven on weekdays. She had a huge crowd for breakfast and lunch, but it was pretty slow at supper, except for Friday night. Today was no exception. There was only one other customer in the place.

Dan sat at a table near the door and looked over at the menu on the chalkboard.

"What'll it be, Doc?" Etta's cheerful voice rang out through the room.

"I'll have the meat loaf dinner, Miss Etta. It's been a while since I had it, and I think I hear it calling me. A cup of that great coffee, too."

Etta laughed and went to get his coffee. She placed it on the table and headed back to the kitchen to get his food. He knew she did all the cooking and serving. The girl who'd worked for her had quit, and now she was stuck with it all.

"When are you going to get some help, Etta?" He took a sip from the steaming mug. "You can't run this place by yourself forever."

"Matter of fact, I just hired someone. She came in looking for work this afternoon. Starts in the morning."

"Well, that's good. Who is it?"

"She's not from around here. Came in on the train this morning, looking like a little lost kitten. Had a tiny baby in her arms. She didn't say why she landed here in Cactus Corner, but I guess that's her business. I put her up in my spare room."

"Are you sure that's wise, Etta? Moving a stranger into your place?" Dan shook salt on his potatoes, then put the shaker down. No insult to Etta's great cooking. He just liked a lot of salt.

Etta wiped the dusting of white granules off the red-and-white-checkered tablecloth. "Maybe. But she and that baby looked as though they needed help even more than me. And sometimes you just have to trust people." She grinned. "Besides, she's not big enough to do me any damage even if she tried."

Dan shook his head as she walked away. He ate his meal, then sat back with a slice of apple pie and another cup of coffee.

A murmur of voices drifted in from the kitchen, then footsteps. Dan inhaled sharply as an all-too-familiar scent pervaded his nostrils. "Dan, I'd like for you to meet Lila, my new waitress."

"Well, small world, isn't it, Dan?"

Dread surged through him, and he knew the women he'd see before he even raised his head. His heart thumped loudly, and he felt sick as he glanced up at the familiar blond hair and curvaceous figure of the woman who stood over his table, smirking at him.

Would it never end? Would trouble follow him wherever he went?

Chapter 5

What was the use of even trying? Just when he'd begun to think maybe there really was a loving God up there somewhere, the same old garbage came raining down on his head. Dan let the door of the orphanage slam shut behind him and mounted his horse, slinging his medical bag over the saddle horn.

Sure, she'd allowed him to give medical treatment to the children, but he could tell she'd rather have had a witch doctor had one been available. She at least could have listened when he tried to tell her about Lila. But no, she stood there with that frozen look on her face and handed him his hat.

Pain shot through him. Pain he thought he had gotten rid of years ago. And all because Lila had decided to get her revenge. Apparently it was time to move on again. He had hoped it would be different this time. *Thanks a lot, God. If You're really up there, You're not doing much of a job taking care of my life.*

Elaine choked back tears as she peered through the lace curtains and watched Dan ride away. Uncertainty nibbled at her mind.

"Do you think you might have been a little bit too hard on him?"

Elaine turned and stared at Anika. "Too hard?"

"You might have listened to his side of it." Sympathy was written all over Anika's face.

Oh no, she'd heard it all.

"Sorry. I didn't mean to eavesdrop. The walls are thin."

"But, Anika, that woman came right out and told Etta he'd run out on her. After getting her. . .well, you know."

Her friend pursed her lips and looked thoughtful. "I know. I heard all about it. But who's to say she's telling the truth?"

"Oh, I don't know." Elaine dropped onto a settee. "But why would anyone lie about something like that? And besides, what about all the other rumors?"

"I thought you didn't believe the other rumors."

"Well, I didn't, but. . ."

Anika sat next to her and patted her hand. "Honey, it's not my place to give you advice. Especially when you didn't ask for it. But even criminals get a chance to defend themselves."

Elaine sat frozen as she watched Anika get up and leave the room. Was she really being unfair to Dan? Respectability was as much a part of Elaine as the color of her hair. So much so, that the very hint of a lack of virtue was enough to fill her with horror. Her decision to believe Dan when the rumors had first started had surprised her as much as anyone else. She'd had little experience with men and, even when she was a young girl, had never fancied herself in love. And now, the possibility that she'd been foolish in her defense of him, especially since the whole town knew she'd agreed to let him call on her, sent waves of embarrassment through her veins.

But what if he *was* innocent?

The banging noise wouldn't go away. Dan threw the pillow off his face and sat up, groaning. The pounding continued, but now he was awake enough to realize it came from the front door.

"Coming!" He pulled his pants on and limped into the front office, carrying his boots. As he yanked the front door open, Joshua Dillinger dropped his fist, which had obviously been ready to pound on the door again.

"I've got a miner in the wagon. He's unconscious and burning up with fever."

"Let's get him into the examining room." Dan followed the rancher to the wagon and looked at the man lying there. Immediately he recognized the sick miner from the hotel. They carried the limp figure inside and laid him on an examining table.

"How long has he been like this?" Dan ran a practiced eye over the unconscious miner and stuck a thermometer into his mouth.

Dillinger swiped a hand through his hair. "I've no idea. I found him like this on my property early this morning. A pack-laden mule was grazing nearby. The miners have been filing across our land headed for the mountains all week. This one, obviously, didn't make it."

"His temperature's raging." Dan laid the thermometer down and opened the man's mouth with his fingers. He gazed at the white-coated tongue and red throat, then probed the man's neck. "I remember seeing him in the crowd around the general store one day. And he was staying at the hotel—which means others have been exposed." Dan spoke quietly, reflectively, to himself and was surprised when he heard Dillinger's voice.

"Exposed to what?" The man stood in the doorway to the outer office, frowning.

"I can't say for sure until I examine him more thoroughly, but I'm afraid it may be influenza." He dipped some water into a glass and managed to get a trickle down the man's throat.

"That's serious, isn't it?"

"It can be if left untreated. Hopefully we've caught it in time."

"But if it should become an epidemic?"

Dan's lips tightened, and as he spoke, he could hear the grimness in his own voice. "Let's hope it doesn't come to that."

"What are you going to do?"

Dan sat silently for a moment. What should he do first? He made a sudden decision. "I'm going to get someone to stay with the patient while I go up in the hills and check for signs of the sickness among other miners."

"I wish I could stay, Doc, but I have pressing matters at the ranch."

"One of the women from the Indian camp helps me out occasionally. If you could stop by there on your way home, I'd appreciate it."

"Consider it done." The two men shook hands, and the rancher left.

Dan lifted the miner and placed him on a cot against the wall. He took a bottle from a cabinet in the corner and managed to get a spoonful of medicine down the man's throat, then dipped a cool cloth in water and washed the hot, red face.

Sighing, he spread a blanket over the man's body and stood. He washed his hands, then went into the main office. His packed suitcase, in the middle of the floor, caught his attention. He'd forgotten he planned to leave this morning. It seemed the right thing to do yesterday, but now, with a patient in the other room, his plans would have to wait. He carried the bag to his quarters and stowed it, then made a pot of strong coffee. It seemed as though he wouldn't get to run from his troubles this time. At least not yet.

When he rode into one of the miners' camps a couple of hours later, he found no sign of sickness. As he went from site to site, he breathed a sigh of relief as no more cases of influenza appeared. Perhaps it was just an isolated case.

He went back to town to discover the miner awake. His fever had broken and he appeared to be recovering. Perhaps he'd get to remove himself from his place of torment after all.

Elaine's face crossed his mind, and he hesitated. Maybe he wouldn't leave just yet. This time he had something to stay and fight for.

❧

"Miss Elaine, wake up." The insistent voice penetrated Elaine's sleep-fogged brain, and she opened her eyes to see Jane bending over her bed.

"What is it, Jane? Have I overslept?" She yawned and looked at the girl, who still wore her nightdress with a shawl thrown over her shoulders.

"No, ma'am. It's only three o'clock. Two of the children are sick, miss. Mrs. Jacobson says you need to come now."

Wide-awake, Elaine got up and dressed quickly. When she got downstairs, she could hear coughing coming from the small infirmary. Martha Jacobson was bending over Rainsong, wiping her face with a wet cloth.

Elaine hurried to her side, glancing at the next cot, where Grace was holding Pedro's hand as he moaned in his sleep. "What seems to be wrong with them?" She reached over and brushed the little girl's damp hair back from her forehead.

"I'm not sure," Martha answered. "They are running fevers and coughing. Maybe it's merely a summer cold. But I really think we need to send for the doctor and have him check them over." She glanced at Elaine with an apologetic little smile. "With George in Tucson picking up the new wagon, I'm afraid you'll have to go, dear."

A knot formed in Elaine's throat, and she forced herself to relax and swallow. Her heart sped up. *Stop it, Elaine. He is the only doctor in town. You can do this. For the children.*

Hastily twisting her hair up, she grabbed a shawl and headed down the dark street. As she neared the doctor's office, she heard voices raised in what sounded like an argument. Peering ahead in the darkness, she gasped. The young woman, Lila, stood with her arms tightly around Dan's neck.

His eyes met Elaine's, and he jerked away. "Elaine, this isn't what it looks like. I promise you."

The Lila creature cast an amused glance at Elaine. "Don't believe a word he says, honey. Trust me." With a laugh, she sauntered off down the dusty street toward the café.

Dan took Elaine's hand. "Please let me explain." The pleading in his voice made Elaine's heart race, and a sick feeling clutched at her stomach.

She jerked her hand away and stood stiffly, speaking through tightened teeth. "Dr. Murphy, what you do is of no concern to me. We have sick children in the infirmary who need your assistance." She turned and hurried toward the orphanage. As she neared the sheriff's office, she crossed the street and broke into a near run.

Before entering the orphanage, she brushed away the tears that flooded her eyes and spilled down her cheeks. This time she had seen the truth with her own eyes. There was no denying now that the only man she'd ever fallen in love with was a scoundrel.

Chapter 6

Dan sat by Pedro's bed and felt his pulse again. It was too fast—much too fast. He looked up at Mrs. Jacobson, who stood with a pan of water and some clean cloths. The worry on her face matched the concern on his.

"I think I've done all I can for now, Mrs. Jacobson. Keep the children cool and give them the medicine every four hours. Try to get clear liquid down them." He paused. "Pedro came and got me when the miner accosted Miss Elaine. Was Rainsong, by any chance, with him that day?"

"Yes, as a matter of fact, she was. I sent them to tell Elaine to add white thread to her list. Why?"

"One of the miners was ill. It's obvious they were exposed at that time." A sick feeling washed over him. "Has Elaine shown any symptoms?"

She shook her head slowly, frowning. "No, none that I'm aware of."

"Do you know where she is?" He intended to find out for sure. Whether she wanted to see him or not.

"Probably in the kitchen. Or perhaps in the toddlers' room. She spends what time she can with Autumn."

He closed his bag and stood. "Thank you, ma'am. I'd better talk to her."

Elaine wasn't in the toddlers' room or the kitchen. He found her in the backyard hanging sheets out to dry. She looked both directions when she saw him as if searching for a way to escape.

"How are the children?" She averted her eyes and gazed at the railroad tracks as though watching an invisible train go by.

"About the same. I'm afraid it's influenza. One of the miners came down with it. He's doing better, but it's much more dangerous for children. You'll need to watch them carefully."

She nodded and bit her lip, then bent down and pulled another sheet from the basket at her feet.

"I believe they were exposed the day the mob was outside the general store."

"Oh no. They'd been sent with a message for me, but I didn't see them in the crowd." She concentrated on the sheet, two little furrows between her eyes.

"Have you had any symptoms? Sore throat, headache?"

"No."

"Elaine, please look at me."

She lifted her face and looked straight into his eyes. The pain and accusation he saw there overwhelmed him. She cared about him. But she didn't trust him. Well, why should she? The evidence against him was pretty strong.

"Listen. I couldn't sleep last night. I went outside to get some air. Lila was there before I knew it. She'd been drinking. She tried to talk me into. . .well, never mind. The next thing I knew, she had thrown her arms around my neck. That's when I saw you. I know it looked bad, but I had nothing to do with it."

A shadow of doubt crossed her face, then straightening her shoulders, she glared at him. "Well, perhaps she loves you. Perhaps she's desperate for her child's father to marry her. Although I don't know why any woman would want a scalawag who walked out on her when she was—" She stopped and blushed.

"I'm not her baby's father, Elaine."

"Oh, then why would she say it's you?" She placed her tiny hands on her hips and tapped her foot on the ground.

"Because she hates me and wants revenge."

A startled look crossed her face. "Revenge for what? Walking out on her?"

Dan sighed. "No. We never were together. She wanted a relationship. I didn't. So she drifted on to someone else. She hates me because I killed her lover in a gunfight." There. He'd said it. She'd turn and run now. But at least it would be for the truth.

Her mouth opened slightly, and his eyes were drawn to her soft lips. Oh, how tempting to take her in his arms and claim those lips as his own.

Gasping, she drew back. Apparently she'd read his expression too well.

"So you're a cold-blooded killer? You killed the man out of jealousy?" Incredulity was written on her face.

Okay, so maybe it wasn't the passion in his eyes that had caused her to gasp.

"No, Elaine. It wasn't like that. It's a long story. But I was protecting someone when I shot the man."

"Mm-hm. Well, Dr. Murphy, I'd say that's a pretty wild story, and it's your word against hers. Since she has a little baby as evidence, and I can't imagine anyone claiming a killer as her child's father, I'd say her story rings a lot truer than yours." She picked up the empty basket and headed for the house.

"Elaine, please send for me if you have any sign of illness."

Tossing her head, she went in and shut the door firmly behind her.

Dan inhaled and blew out a loud breath. He didn't know what it would take to convince her of his innocence, but he'd be blamed if he'd give up trying.

Elaine straightened and wiped her sleeve across her perspiring face. She'd been bending over the ironing board longer than she wanted to think about, and the muscles in her back and shoulders were screaming at her. With sick children in the house, everyone had a little more work to do. She put the iron away and took the stack of shirts and dresses to the dormitories.

Three days after the children became ill, they still weren't over the sickness. Elaine had managed to avoid Dan each time he'd come to check on them. He had stressed extreme cleanliness, and they had complied, boiling everything they used and scrubbing their hands with strong lye soap dozens of times a day. Thankfully none of the other children were showing symptoms, but several miners and a few of the townspeople were ill. Dan had told India and Joshua that the sickness was definitely some strain of influenza and was reaching epidemic proportions.

That wasn't the only thing India had told her. In no uncertain terms, she'd informed Elaine that her husband believed totally in the doctor's innocence, and many of the townspeople were also rethinking their original position on the subject. Even Etta, who had championed the young woman in the beginning, was starting to be disenchanted with her. In fact, she had told Jody that if it weren't for the baby, she'd send the girl packing.

Elaine sighed. She dared not get her hopes up again. And besides, if he was innocent, he'd probably never forgive her. She'd been pretty hard on him.

Deep in her thoughts, she headed down the hall toward the kitchen. Just as she reached the kitchen door, Dan walked out, almost running into her.

She drew in a sharp breath and stammered, "I d–didn't see you c–come in."

"Apparently not, or you'd have hidden again." A sad smile appeared on his lips.

"Excuse me? I most certainly have not been hiding from you." She could feel her cheeks flaming. A dead giveaway.

He leaned against the door frame, and the gold in his eyes flickered as he looked at her. "You don't need to hide from me, Elaine. I won't force my attentions on you."

Elaine's heart raced as she watched him walk away and out the front door. She went into the kitchen and sank into a chair at the table.

Carla looked up from the dishpan. Removing her dripping hands, she dried them on a white cloth. "Miss Elaine, I think you need a cup of strong coffee. You've been going like a wildfire all day."

"Thanks, that sounds wonderful." She leaned against the tall ladder back of the chair and watched the wiry cook as she poured strong, black coffee and set the steaming mug on the table in front of her. Elaine added sugar and cream, then inhaled gratefully as she lifted the mug to her lips and let the sweet, milky liquid trickle down her throat.

"Oh, that's heavenly. Who would think coffee could be so refreshing on a hot day like this?"

"Hmm, you need to get off those feet more often. I see you scurrying all around the place day and night."

"Well, we all have to do our part. The volunteers are working hard, too." In fact, India and several of the ladies from the church had helped nearly every day. They couldn't always stay long because of other responsibilities, but they did what they could. Anika and Jody had come at night a couple of times and promised to help out on the weekend if the children were still ill. Elaine breathed a prayer of thanks for her friends.

She stood and stretched. "I'll send Mary and Charlene in to help with supper. They should be finished with their studies by now."

After locating the girls and sending them to the kitchen, she headed to the toddlers' room.

Children in varying stages of walking and running tripped around the room. One little boy stood firmly and let out a yell as another child attempted to take a wooden horse from his hands. Ellen, one of the volunteers, settled the argument by distracting both children with other toys. Autumn lay in her crib with her arm around a stuffed bear and her thumb in her mouth.

"How in the world does she sleep with all this noise going on?"

Ellen shook her head. "I was wondering the same thing. She must have been tired. She's been asleep since right after lunch. She's usually the first one up after nap time."

Elaine walked over to Autumn's crib and placed her hand on the soft curls. She didn't feel hot. Ellen was probably right. The child was merely tired. Still, Elaine determined to check on her later to make sure. As tiny as she was, influenza could be especially dangerous.

Dan opened a can of beans and poured them into a bowl. He wasn't too excited about eating cold beans, but he didn't want to build a fire on a hot day like this. He thought longingly of Etta's hot bread and beef stew. She always had stew on Tuesdays. He crumbled a piece of two-day-old corn bread into the beans and tossed in some stewed tomatoes a patient had given him for payment. Cutting some onion into the mix, he sat at the table and tried to enjoy his meal. Actually, it wasn't bad.

I'll bet Elaine's a good cook. Dan threw his spoon down. Couldn't he do anything without thinking about Elaine? Her blue eyes appeared in his dreams. The sound of her laughter would ring out across the street when he went outside. He'd turn only to find some other woman laughing outside the dress shop or walking a child. Often he'd feel a wave of anger that anyone should dare to have Elaine's laugh. Then he'd direct the anger at himself for being such a fool.

He scraped his bowl, then washed and dried it and the spoon and put them away. He went outside and stood on the weathered board sidewalk. The air was beginning to cool. Maybe he'd take a walk.

"Doc! Doc!" Startled, Dan looked down the street. Charlie and Ray came up the street in a dead run. This didn't look good. He met them halfway down the block.

"What's wrong?" He grabbed each boy by an arm as they skidded to a stop.

"Miss Elaine says come fast." Ray gasped and choked out the words. "That baby, Autumn. . .she's been taken with the sickness."

Chapter 7

But why can't we help? We ain't tainted, you know." The plump redhead stood outside the door wringing her hands, frustration and indignation written all over her face. Her companion stood quietly, with her head down.

Elaine had never experienced embarrassment the way she did at this moment. She knew the women were from the saloon. What in the world should she do? With eight sick children and several of the staff down sick, she desperately needed the help. But these creatures? Surely not. On the other hand, to send them away would be depriving the exhausted staff and volunteers of extra helping hands.

"Look, lady, I know you think we're trash. But we heard Baby was sick, and we're the ones raised her, you know. Mary here was the closest thing to a mama the little one had. Please, if you'd at least let us see her for a minute."

Elaine glanced at Mary, who lifted soft brown eyes filled with pleading. She couldn't have been more than eighteen or nineteen, and beneath the paint, Elaine could detect a vulnerability she wouldn't have expected to see in a saloon girl.

Surprising herself, she pulled the door open wider and motioned them in. She hardly knew why and knew even less what to say to the two. Should she offer them chairs?

She ran the back of her hand across her forehead and felt herself sway. A pair of firm hands grasped her arms and lowered her to the settee.

"Mary, find someone and fetch some water. Honey, stay with me, now. Don't faint."

Elaine could hear the words but couldn't find the voice to answer. The room was spinning wildly, and she closed her eyes and gave in to the darkness.

"Elaine, wake up."

Someone was shaking her. She wanted to tell the person to stop but didn't have the strength to form the words.

"Elaine, can you speak?" She recognized Jody's voice, filled with worry.

She opened her lips and breathed. "Jody? What happened?"

"You fainted. That's what." Relief filled her friend's voice. "Nearly scared me to death. I thought it was influenza."

Fear clutched her. She couldn't be sick. The children needed her.

"It's not, is it?"

"I don't think so. You don't have any of the symptoms. Seems like plain old exhaustion to me." Jody stooped beside her and patted her hand. "But just to be sure, we sent for Dr. Murphy."

Elaine tried to sit up, but Jody pushed her back down. "Don't even think about it until the doctor gets here."

"But, Jody, I don't want to see him."

"Well, that's too bad, because you're going to." She stood and looked down at Elaine. "You know, you're just about the only one in town who still believes the rumors about Dan Murphy. Don't you think it's about time to consider the possibility that he may be innocent?"

Elaine pushed herself up and glared at her friend. "I have work to do. Let me up."

"Sorry," Jody said with a triumphant grin. "Martha says you're not to do anything till the doctor looks you over."

Elaine jerked her head around, and her gaze fell on the two women from the saloon. They were standing in the corner of the hallway self-consciously but looked at her with sympathy. Whatever was she going to do about them?

The door opened and Dan burst in. His eyes widened at the sight of the saloon women, but when he saw Elaine, he hurried over to her. Before she had a chance to protest, he lifted her into his arms and started up the stairs.

Unfamiliar feelings coursed through Elaine. Her skin felt hot where his hands gripped her arm, and the scent of his cologne made her head reel. She snapped to herself. "What are you doing? Put me down."

"You need to lie down while I make sure you're not ill. Miss McMillan, will you come with us and help her get into bed?"

"I'd be more than happy to, Doctor." Was that a tinge of glee in Jody's voice? Oh, would she get an earful when Elaine was strong enough to deliver it.

An hour later, Elaine lay propped up on soft pillows while her friend fed her sips of soup. "For heaven's sake, Jody, I can feed myself."

"Dr. Murphy said you're not to do anything until morning." Jody held the spoon up to Elaine's lips.

"Well, he didn't mean I have to be fed like a baby. Give me that spoon."

Jody laughed and relinquished the utensil. "Okay, I'll let up. But promise me you'll stay in bed until morning. I'm going to stay overnight so you can rest."

"What about church? Who's going to teach your Sunday school class?"

"They've canceled church tomorrow due to so much sickness. Dr. Murphy said there shouldn't be any more public gatherings than are absolutely necessary."

"But, Jody, I'm needed to help."

"Well, we have two new volunteers."

"Really? Who?" At the look on Jody's face, she knew. "Not those—"

Jody interrupted her friend. "Mr. Jacobson says we need everyone who is willing to help. After the initial shock, Martha agreed." A peculiar expression crossed Jody's face. "Dr. Murphy said not to worry. They don't bite."

Elaine pressed her lips together. "He would."

Jody sighed and shook her head. "You're making a mistake, Elaine. Dr. Murphy is an honorable man."

Pain jabbed at Elaine's stomach. She pushed the tray away and turned over onto her side. Jody's footsteps whispered across the floor, and Elaine heard the door shut softly as her friend left the room.

Thoughts whirled around in her mind like fireflies, darting here then there. So the whole town was coming around to Dan's side? But they'd all been just as adamant before that he was guilty, so who was to say they were right about his innocence? Did she dare believe in him?

She tossed her head back and forth in an attempt to clear the thoughts away. A pair of gold-flecked eyes made their way into her mind. "Oh, go away and leave me alone." She crammed a pillow down over her head, but somehow she knew those eyes would find her there, too.

Dan chuckled to himself as he rode up the rocky mountain path. What a sight it had been to see Lottie and Mary working side by side with the upstanding ladies of the town. He cut the laughter short and frowned. He wondered how often those upstanding ladies stopped to scrub their hands to make sure something didn't rub off on them. Well, he hoped something would rub off. Maybe something like Lottie's full-hearted kindness or Mary's sweet compassion. Dan sighed. It wasn't that he thought their lifestyle was right. The Lord knew he didn't think that. But he knew that most of them had become trapped by one thing or another and would give anything to be able to settle down and live decently and respectably.

He didn't know Mary's story, but Lottie had told him her father had sold her when she was thirteen. She'd been beaten and almost killed before she lost her will to fight. It didn't take long after that for her to completely give up any thought of things changing for the better.

It was another "Lottie" he'd been protecting when he killed Lila's lover. Dan had been walking by a saloon on the outskirts of San Francisco when a scream pierced the air. He took the outside stairs two at a time and crashed through the door just in time to see Tom Furley's fist land on Annie Carter's face, causing blood to gush from a two-inch gash. The ensuing fight had ended in Furley pulling his gun. Dan drew his own and fired before Furley had a chance to shoot.

He'd lived with the guilt ever since. Maybe he could have talked the drunken man into putting the gun away. Dan sighed. He'd never know. All he knew was he hadn't worn a holster since. Like Lottie, he just wanted to settle down and live a decent, God-fearing life. But trouble seemed to find him wherever he went. People judged harshly. Even then, when he'd saved the woman's life, folks pointed fingers and raised their eyebrows. And Lila had vowed to get revenge. Dan supposed it was easier to turn her rage on him than on the lover who'd betrayed her.

After searching for an hour, Dan found another miner down with the sickness and managed to get him into town with the help of the man's friend.

They'd turned the hotel into a makeshift hospital for the miners and others who had no one to care for them in their sickness.

Finally, when he'd treated the last sick miner and everyone was as comfortable as possible, he headed home to get a couple of hours of sleep. If he didn't get some rest, he wouldn't be any good to anyone.

Sun was streaming through his window when he awoke. He jumped up and quickly washed up, not bothering to heat the water. After he was dressed, he headed out the door. His stomach felt hollow, and after a moment's hesitation, he turned and walked to the café. Lila or no Lila, he was stopping for a hot breakfast.

The café was locked, and a CLOSED sign hung on the door. Puzzled, Dan went around to the back entrance and knocked. After a moment, he heard footsteps and muted coughing. The door opened. Etta stood holding Lila's baby. Lines of tiredness crossed her face.

"Dan, I'm so glad you're here. I couldn't leave the baby and didn't want to take him out with all the sickness. But I don't know how much worse it would be. His mama's down with something. I think it's this influenza that's going around. I've been taking care of her the best I can, but. . ."

Another fit of coughing erupted from the cot across the room, where Lila lay writhing and moaning. When Dan touched her face, the heat was almost enough to burn his hand.

He looked at Etta. "Are you or the child sick?"

"No, thank the good Lord." She shook her head. "What can we do, Doc? Can you move her to the hotel?"

Dan frowned. The hotel was full of sick miners. He hated to take a woman there. Even Lila.

"Are you willing to take care of the infant until Lila's well?"

"Sure. Got nothing else to do. No sense in opening up. People are scared to leave their houses anyway."

"Give me a few minutes to check with the Jacobsons. Since the sickness is already there anyway, maybe they'll agree to care for one more. I don't know where they'll put her, but a pallet on the floor would be better than the hotel right now."

Elaine watched as Dan carried Lila into the house. She'd only seen the woman once, and it had been dark, but she tried to restrain her curiosity. What did she care what the woman looked like?

She led the way to the small visitors' room, where three cots had been set up. One of the staff members lay on one of them, her small form still as death.

Elaine pulled down the blanket on one of the cots and watched as Dan placed the woman gently between clean white sheets. He checked her pulse, then straightened up and turned to the woman on the other cot. After checking her vital signs, he looked at Elaine.

"Thank you for taking Lila in. I wouldn't have liked to leave her around the baby any longer. He's already been exposed to the influenza, and at his young age, he'll have little chance to survive if he catches it. We can only pray he hasn't already."

Elaine stood frozen, unable to speak. Between the extreme tiredness and the emotional stress of being in Dan's presence, she was feeling dizzy again.

"Elaine, are you all right?"

Her heart leapt at the concern in his voice. "I'm fine. I'm just tired." She pulled at the button on her throat. "Of course, it was the Jacobsons' decision to allow her to stay here. But I'd like to think I wouldn't turn a sick woman away from the door."

A tender look crossed Dan's face, and he placed his thumb on her chin, turning her face up so that she had to look at him. "Of course you wouldn't, Lainey. I know that."

Tears filled her eyes and threatened to overflow. Blinking, she cleared her throat and clasped her hands behind her back before she could make a fool of herself by flinging herself into his arms. The thought warmed her cheeks, and she cleared her throat again. "Would you like to check on the other patients while you're here?"

He looked at her silently for a moment, tenderness and yearning in his gaze, then a veil seemed to cover his expression. "Yes. Have you seen any improvement in anyone?"

A twinge of disappointment gripped her. Then she firmed her chin. "Rainsong doesn't seem as feverish today. But she still can't keep any nourishment down."

Side by side they walked to the infirmary, where three people kept around-the-clock vigil with at least one staff person in the room at all times. In addition to Rainsong and Pedro, nine more patients tossed restlessly in the infirmary, including three toddlers and one infant.

Elaine and Dan walked over to the crib near the window. Little Autumn lay still and silent.

Mary sat by her side, constantly dipping cloths into cool water and sponging the child's hands, arms, and legs. She looked up at Dan as he and Elaine stopped by the crib. Her eyes were brimming over. "Please, Doc, don't let Baby die."

Chapter 8

The night breeze fluttered the lace shawl that lay across Elaine's shoulders and caressed the skin at her neck. She shivered, and a sigh of pleasure escaped her lips. Fifteen minutes had passed, and she knew she had to get back inside, but the thought of facing the stifling heat and the smells of sickness inside the orphanage was almost more than she could bear.

At least the epidemic seemed to be dissipating. There had been no new cases for the past few days, and some of the earlier victims were showing signs of improvement. Thankfully they hadn't lost anyone. Dan had said Rainsong and Pedro should be well enough to leave the infirmary in another day or so. Autumn was also getting better, much to Mary's delight—although she still had to be practically hauled away from the child's bedside to get a few hours' sleep each day.

Elaine inhaled deeply and attempted to rein in her thoughts. Her intention had been to spend a few moments mentally preparing for the chores that must be done before she could retire for the night. Her thoughts, however, had taken on a mind of their own, and no matter where she tried to guide them, they skipped and danced right back to Dan Murphy. She had stopped denying, at least to herself, her feelings for the handsome doctor. But she was so ashamed of herself for believing all the rumors that she couldn't bring herself to spend any more time than necessary in his presence.

How could I have thought he was capable of such deeds? He's proven his character over and over again.

"Elaine! Come quickly!"

At the sound of Martha's frantic cry, Elaine rushed into the house and down the hall to the infirmary. *Lord, please don't let it be a new case of sickness.*

The fear on Martha's face caused Elaine's heart to race.

"What is it? What's wrong?" The sound of her own voice matched the expression on Martha's face.

"Lila's taken a turn for the worse. I've sent for Dr. Murphy, but I need you to sit with her until he arrives." She paused and inhaled deeply. "It's really bad. I don't know if she'll make it."

As Elaine's hand rested on Lila's face a few minutes later, she wasn't sure either. The young woman's skin was hot and as dry as parchment. She moaned and thrashed from side to side. Suddenly the thrashing stopped, and she grew still.

"Please, Lord, no. Don't let her die without knowing You." Elaine hardly knew she was praying aloud. She leaned her head down to Lila's chest and breathed a sigh of relief when she detected a heartbeat. "Heavenly Father, forgive me. I've been so bitter toward this woman, I haven't even prayed for her. I don't know her heart, but

You do." She sobbed the last few words. "If you'll give me another chance, I'll tell her about You."

A gentle hand touched Elaine's shoulder, and she glanced up to find Dan gazing tenderly at her. She stood and moved aside so that he could attend to Lila.

"Elaine, will you hold the lamp close so I can get a better look at her throat and eyes?"

She complied, all the while watching Dan's hands as he examined his patient. Such strong hands, and yet so gentle.

Finally, Dan stood and washed his hands in the clean water one of the staff had brought, then turned to Elaine and motioned her out into the hall. "Continue with the medicine and keep her as comfortable as possible. Try to get water down her. At this point, that's about all we can do."

"Do you think—" Elaine stopped, unable to voice her fear.

Dan rubbed his eyes and took a deep breath.

He's exhausted. He needs to get some rest.

"I really don't know. Her condition is poor, but she has a couple of things going for her. She's a strong woman. And she has you to pray for her." He looked at Elaine intently, searching her face. "Take care of yourself. Get plenty of nourishing food and make sure you don't overtire yourself." He reached down and brushed back a strand of hair that had fallen across her cheek.

Elaine closed her eyes and sighed. If only she could stand here like this forever. Suddenly she felt his lips brush against her forehead. Startled, she opened her eyes. The love in his eyes almost took her breath away. With sudden resolve, she decided it was time to let him know she trusted him.

"Dan, I'm so sorry for my attitude lately. I was terribly confused. I shouldn't have condemned you the way I did."

A look of tenderness crossed his face. "Shh. It's okay. I know things looked bad. I don't blame you."

She bit her lip, and her eyes filled with tears. "I want you to know I believe in you. You're a good man, and I know you're innocent."

The gold in his eyes flickered, and his smile was warm. "Thank you. You don't know how happy it makes me to hear you say that. I could handle everyone's doubts but yours."

Elaine sat and stitched as she watched over Lila. She laid the small shirt she was mending aside and reached over to feel the young woman's forehead. The skin was cool and moist to Elaine's touch. *Thank You, Lord.*

"Could I have some w-water, please?" Lila's cracked voice wasn't much more than a whisper, but Elaine's heart jumped with excitement.

"Of course you can." Elaine poured a little bit of water from the pitcher on the bedside table. "Here, let me lift your head a little."

Lila took a few sips, then lay back on the pillow. Her eyes still appeared tired as she looked up at Elaine. "I could hear you praying for me." Her words held a measure of wonder. "Why would you care if I died?"

Elaine struggled to find the right words. "I just couldn't bear the thought of you dying. Especially when I wasn't sure if you even knew about Jesus."

"I do." Her voice seemed stronger now. "My mother took me to church when I was little. I accepted Jesus when I was thirteen." She stopped speaking and took several breaths before continuing. "Mama died of the typhus a few months later. I guess I blamed God. My granny tried to keep me straight, but I was so bitter. By the time I was sixteen, I'd just gone wild, I guess."

"You know God will forgive you, Lila. You can start over."

"I know. I'm a little scared at the thought of what I'll do with my life, but I'm going to give it back to God right now and ask Him to help me."

Lila closed her eyes, and after a few moments, Elaine thought she'd gone to sleep. But she stirred and her eyes opened slightly. "All that stuff about Dan wasn't true. We never were together."

"I know." Elaine smiled. "But thank you for telling me."

❧

It was over. Finally. Dan yanked off his boots and fell across the bed, not even feeling the wrinkles in the rumpled sheets. He was going to sleep the rest of the day and all night. Then he'd get cleaned up and go have a long talk with a certain auburn-haired woman.

❧

Dan and Elaine stood side by side and watched as the train pulled out of the station. They stood silently until the last car was out of sight.

"Do you think they'll be okay?" Elaine squinted, trying to see the caboose in the distance.

"I think they'll do marvelously."

"Lila showed me her grandmother's letter. She sounded so happy and excited to see her first great-grandchild." Elaine frowned. "Of course, Lila did lie to her and tell her she was a widow."

Dan laughed. "Well, she hasn't been back with God for long. Give her time."

The real surprise was Mary. During Lila's convalescence, the two young women had become friends, and Lila had led Mary to the Lord. Then, to be sure her friend didn't go back into a life of sin, she'd insisted on taking Mary home with her.

"I wonder how Lila's grandmother will react to Mary."

"Well, my dear, that's where you come in. Pray. A lot." He took her hand and placed it in the crook of his arm, gently leading her away from the empty platform.

"I will, Dan. I promise I will. And for Lottie, too. She has such a big heart and worked so hard to help the children." She felt tears rise to the back of her throat. "Now she's right back at the saloon. I had so hoped. . ."

A shadow crossed his face. "I know. I did, too. But remember, as they say, Rome wasn't built in a day. And now, Miss Lainey, what's this I hear about a Fourth of July picnic?"

She started at his sudden change of subject. "Oh yes, we have one every year. It's so much fun, Dan. You'll have to be sure and attend."

He chuckled, and she looked up into his eyes. Oh, those gold-flecked eyes.

"Yes, of course I intend to go. But I meant would you do me the honor of attending the event with me?"

Elaine's breath caught in her throat. She had begun to think she'd imagined his interest in her. In the weeks since the end of the epidemic, he'd not spoken of anything personal. In fact, he'd only come to the orphanage a couple of times a week to check on the children. But now his eyes seemed to burn into hers.

Oh, stop it, Elaine. There you go again, imagining things. He's just being friendly.

Realizing he was waiting for an answer, she swallowed. Well, she had planned to go to the picnic anyway. But she couldn't let him think she was expecting anything but friendship.

"That would be nice, Dr. Murphy. Thank you for asking me."

He threw back his head and laughed.

Now why is he laughing?

Chapter 9

Dan knew he needed to tell Elaine about his past. He'd imagined it dozens of times, each time changing the words and location. In one scenario, she looked at him tenderly with tear-filled eyes and assured him it didn't matter a bit. She was only sorry he'd had to endure so much. Then, in another, a look of disgust crossed her face and she turned and ran away from him.

Night after night he'd tossed and turned, weighing the cost of telling her. And tonight was no different. He knew, before their relationship could go any further, he had to be honest with her. If he asked her to marry him, and that was his intention, she had the right to make a decision based on the full knowledge of who he was.

Groaning, Dan turned over and sat up on the side of his bed. He lit the lamp on his bedside table and picked up his watch. He groaned again and flung himself back onto the bed. Four in the morning—another sleepless night.

"So, Elaine, dear, who will be escorting you to the picnic?" Mrs. Granger's lips tilted in a teasing smile as she added a spool of white thread to Elaine's sack.

Elaine blushed and tried to concentrate on the money she was counting out. "Why would you think anyone is escorting me? I usually walk over with the children and staff." There. She hadn't actually lied.

"Mm-hm. A number of things don't seem to be as 'usual' lately, do they, now?"

"Mrs. Granger, really. . ."

"Oh, all right, then. I'll stop teasing. But everyone knows you and the doc are sparking."

"Wh–what?" Elaine almost dropped her reticule. Grasping it, she yanked the strings tightly.

"Well, there's no shame in being courted, you know. And personally, I think it's about time you two continued what you started a couple of months ago."

Elaine mumbled good-bye and left with her purchases. How mortifying. Was the whole town talking about her and the doctor? Because other than being kind and attentive, he certainly hadn't made any declarations of affection toward her. True, he'd asked to court her at one time, but that was before Lila came to town and the rumors got so bad. Then the epidemic hit right afterward.

Early this morning he'd dropped some medicine off at the orphanage for one of the children, and he'd asked if he could come over tonight to talk to her. Maybe he wanted to tell her he'd made a mistake when he'd asked to court her. At the thought, a knot formed in Elaine's stomach.

"Elaine! What's wrong with you? I've called your name twice."

Startled, Elaine looked up to see Anika standing in the doorway of the office she shared with her husband.

"Sorry, I didn't realize I was here. I guess I was daydreaming."

"Hmm. Do you have time to walk over to the café with me? I was just about to take a break."

"I'm afraid not. I told Martha I'd start the ironing this morning. We did laundry yesterday, so there's a lot." Elaine puckered her forehead and bit her bottom lip. "Oh, fiddlesticks. Maybe I will go with you. A few minutes won't hurt."

The two walked in perfect step, their heels clacking against the boards. As they turned into Etta's place, the smell of coffee and fresh-baked pastries assailed Elaine's senses.

They found a table near a window and sat facing each other.

Anika groaned. "Etta's baking is wonderful for the palate but murder for the waistline."

"Like you have anything to worry about." Elaine grinned at her friend, whose statuesque form was the envy of just about every woman in Cactus Corner.

"Well, I have to be careful not to get too sure of myself. You know how trim May Johnson was, and she's big as a cow since she had her baby."

"Anika! You don't mean you're—"

Anika glanced at her and laughed. "No, silly. But we do plan to have a family someday."

Elaine felt her face go hot. "Oh. Well, we shouldn't talk about such things."

"Excuse me if I offended your maidenly ears," Anika teased.

Elaine stood, her hand knocking over the saltcellar. Fumbling, she brushed the spilled granules off the cloth.

"Anika, I really should go on home. I'd forgotten I have to help Rainsong with her arithmetic before I can do the ironing." Elaine rushed out, feeling a twinge of remorse at the hurt and bewildered look on her friend's face. But she couldn't take the teasing and banter today. Not until she knew what was going on with Dan.

Dan and Elaine stood in the moonlight and listened to the night sounds. He reached over and took her hand. From their position on the stone patio behind the orphanage, they gazed out across the desert.

An ache began in the depths of Elaine's being at the sweetness of the moment. *Father, whatever happens next, no matter what Dan says, let me remember this sweetness.*

When she knew she couldn't bear another moment, she glanced up at him. "Whatever it is, Dan, you can tell me."

A sound between a sob and a groan escaped from his throat. He raised her hand to his lips, then with a sigh released it and let it fall to her side.

"I know you've questioned my championing of the women who work at the saloon. I don't blame you. Maybe it's not the wisest course to take. It surely hasn't done my social life much good in the past."

He looked down into her eyes, and she could see the pain in his.

"Until I was five, I lived with my mother in a room above a saloon. She worked there, you see."

Elaine blinked, trying to absorb his meaning. "She was a cleaning lady?"

"No, a saloon girl."

A shock passed through her body, but Elaine took a deep breath and steeled herself against whatever might be coming next.

"I grew up being bounced on the knees of gamblers, drunks, and women of questionable morals and had no idea it was not an ordinary life for a child." Dan ran a hand over his face. "To this day, I don't know why my mother was reduced to such a state. I only know she was an angel to one small boy. She cared for me, protected me, and loved me. When I was five years old, she was killed. She'd picked me up to get me out of harm's way but never made it to the stairs. When the bullet hit her, she fell with me in her arms."

He stopped, and Elaine knew from the horror on his face he was reliving the moment from the eyes of that small child. The blood rushed from her face, and she fought the dizziness that tried to overcome her. She couldn't faint. Not now. Dan was hurting. She could see the pain written all over his face, feel it in the trembling of his body.

She reached up and touched his cheek. "How horrible for you. I'm so sorry, Dan. What happened to you after that?"

"I was placed in an orphanage in a nearby city. Years later, when I was eighteen, I went back to try to find out more about my mother and why she was killed, but no one remembered her. Or if people did, they wouldn't admit it. I couldn't even find her grave."

He took her hand, which still rested on his cheek. "I'm not telling you these things to get your sympathy, Elaine. I want you to know why I am who I am."

He led her to a small bench at the back of the house, and they sat down.

"A benefactor, knowing my desire to study medicine, paid my way to medical college. I threw myself into my studies, and my benefactor, an established physician, took me in. Over the next eight years, I became quite successful. Then a typhoid fever epidemic hit the city. We eventually got it under control, but there were many deaths. Most of them on the docks and in the saloons. You see, the upstanding folks had to be taken care of first. When I realized what was happening, I headed down there, but it was too late. I did what I could but saved very few. One girl, not more than sixteen, died in my arms. I'll never forget the look of fear on her face."

He leaned back and closed his eyes, and Elaine thought her heart would break for him. She wanted to take him in her arms and comfort him, but somehow she knew his story wasn't over.

He opened his eyes and sat up straight. "After that, I left the city and opened up a practice in a small town. But before long, some of the good ladies there decided

I was worthless and had no morals because I tried to help the unfortunates in the saloons. I realized some of them were there by choice, but most weren't. Besides, I had taken an oath. Of course, my practice dropped off, and I couldn't make a living, so I headed out to another town. And then another. But trouble followed me everywhere I went. I'm so tired of it all. I want respectability so badly. But I just can't seem to stay out of trouble."

"But, Dan, you haven't done anything wrong." Surprise filled Elaine as the words left her mouth. She really meant them.

"Do you mean that, Elaine? You're not shocked?"

"I probably would have been two months ago. God has changed me, Dan. I thought I had compassion before, but I know now the compassion I had was conditional. It took working with Mary and Lottie and being around Lila to show me the truth about myself."

Dan reached over and traced his thumb along her jawline and looked into her eyes, searching. Elaine looked back without trying to hide her feelings from him.

"Lainey." The word was only a whisper. He touched her face, caressing her cheek, and raised her hand to his lips.

When he lifted his head, Elaine realized that she was trembling from head to toe.

"Lainey, my Lainey. This isn't the moment for the question I want to ask you. You have the right to think over the things I've told you. And maybe you'll decide I'm not the man you want to give your heart to—the man you'd want to be a father to your children."

He bent down and kissed the top of her head. "I love you. Whatever you decide, I'll accept and understand."

❧

Dan brought the buggy to a stop in front of the orphanage and turned to Elaine.

"It's been a wonderful day, hasn't it?"

"Yes, but I'm afraid you and I were perhaps the main attraction. I hope you weren't bothered by all the stares and knowing grins." Elaine shook her head at the memory. India and Anika had been the worst, but even Jody had done her share—the traitor.

He threw back his head and laughed. "Not at all. I rather enjoyed it."

She gave him a sidewise glance. "You would, you rogue." She smiled to soften the words. "It seems you've been accepted as a full-fledged upstanding member of the town."

He laughed again. "Yes, well, now if it only stays that way. I hope you didn't mind leaving while the fireworks were still going on."

"No, I was getting a little tired. And anyway, we can still see and hear them from here." She smiled secretly. She was pretty sure she knew why he'd suggested they leave early.

He jumped down and came around to help her out, and they walked hand in hand around the building and sat on the bench on the stone patio.

He turned to face her and looked intently into her eyes.

This is it. Oh God, please let this be it.

Before she knew what was happening, he'd slipped off the bench and knelt in front of her. Her heart fluttered wildly. *Yes, this is it. It has to be.*

"Elaine, will you do me the honor of becoming my wife?"

She gazed into his gold-flecked eyes, her mind racing as wildly as her heart. Could this really be happening to her? Surely she must be dreaming. But the hand that held hers was warm and strong. Yes, it was a dream. A wonderful dream come true.

"Yes, Dan. With all my heart, I will." Her words were strong, true, and sure.

Joy washed over his face. He examined her face as though wanting to make sure she'd really said yes. Then with a cry of jubilation, he jumped up and pulled her to her feet.

"My darling." His voice shook with emotion as he drew her closely to him. "I'll spend the rest of my life making you happy."

He lowered his head, and she lifted her face to his, eager, with joy in her heart. And as his lips claimed hers, she could hear the fireworks in the distance.

Or maybe it wasn't the fireworks at all.

FRANCES DEVINE

Frances grew up in the great state of Texas, where she wrote her first story at the age of nine. She moved to Southwest Missouri more than twenty years ago and fell in love with the hills, the fall colors, and Silver Dollar City. Frances has always loved to read and considers herself blessed to have the opportunity to write in one of her favorite genres, historical romance. She is the mother of seven adult children and has fourteen wonderful grandchildren.

Frances is happy to hear from her fans. E-mail her at fd1440writes@aol.com.

The Spinster and the Tycoon

by Vickie McDonough

Defend the poor and fatherless:
do justice to the afflicted and needy.
Psalm 82:3

Chapter 1

Autumn 1895

"Please, Lord, let someone other than Elmer buy my box dinner this year." Jody McMillan sighed and set the ACME Paperworks box that held her fried chicken meal on the table in her boardinghouse room and adjusted the frilly bow. She'd picked the blue gingham ribbon on purpose, hoping to entice someone other than her boss, Elmer Brody, to bid on her meal. Everyone in Cactus Corner knew by his trademark plaid flannel shirts that Elmer loved red.

She smiled to herself. In a moment of unabashed orneriness, she had even affixed a little bird that had fallen off her favorite hat to the bow, because her boss had hated birds ever since he was seven, when he'd been pecked by a crow. Every box social, her boss had purchased her dinner, and this year she was determined to dine with someone else.

She peeked out the window, delighted to see that a large crowd had gathered in the churchyard. A flash of red snagged her attention, and she dropped the curtain as if she'd been burned by a hot coal.

Elmer owned Brody Freight Line, and his marriage proposals were as regular as his freight deliveries. She had no intention of ever saying yes to him. If he continued asking her to marry him, she just might have to seek other employment. Even though the town was growing because of a recent copper strike, few people in Cactus Corner had need for a female bookkeeper.

Jody sighed, picked up her decorated container, and covered it with a towel. If she could keep Elmer from seeing it, just perhaps she could dine with some other lonely bachelor.

She closed the door to her room at the boardinghouse and hurried down the hall, her shoes clicking on the shiny oak floor. If she was the last to arrive, Elmer would for sure notice which box was hers.

Couples moseyed arm in arm toward the church. Adolescent girls giggled, excited about a chance to spend some time with a young man, and blatantly displayed their boxes for all to see.

She drifted along with the noisy crowd. When had she lost the desire to be wooed by a handsome man?

At twenty-six, she'd long ago come to grips with her spinsterhood and had given up on marrying, even though her three closest friends had found love and married in the past year and a half. India, Anika, and Elaine, though spinsters for years, all now sparkled with a newlywed glow.

Jody was sincerely happy for each of them, although she felt left out and missed their weekly get-togethers. And now India was expecting a baby.

Jody attempted to swallow as her throat tightened. Would she never know what it was like to be a mother?

At least she had the children at the orphanage to cuddle, and they all needed cuddling. She would soon be able to lavish India's baby with kisses and hugs. Shouldn't that be enough?

She shook her head in an effort to shake off her melancholy. This was an exciting day—she felt it in her heart. Something good was going to happen, and she wasn't about to let self-pity ruin it.

As she neared the crowded area outside the church, her gaze landed on India waddling toward her. Most women who were in the seventh month of their pregnancy wouldn't dare be seen in public, but India didn't mind. In fact, if Joshua hadn't put a temporary halt to it, her friend would probably still be riding horses and herding cattle on their ranch.

Jody sighed, knowing that deep inside, she wanted the happiness her friends had found. But she wouldn't settle for marrying someone who didn't make her insides tingle.

"There you are." India smiled and rubbed her back with her fist. "I had just about decided you'd chickened out on attending today."

"Well. . .I can't deny I considered it."

India looped her arm around Jody's and tugged her toward the front of the crowd. She flashed a mischievous grin. "Elmer has been asking about you."

Jody emitted a very unladylike grunt. She spied Anika and Elaine chatting near the table holding a whole slew of colorful boxes with lavish decorations. It had been a good year since the last box social, and it looked as if the ladies in town had gone all out in their decorating.

This gathering had been her idea, and she fervently hoped they would earn enough money today to finally be able to buy the mercantile property next door to the orphanage so the children's home could be expanded. She and her friends had been saving money and organizing fund-raising events for two years now.

As she glanced at each container, Jody added up the amount she thought it would sell for. Like a dust devil spinning up a cloud on a hot day, a giddy excitement swirled in her stomach. They would make their goal today; she was certain of it.

Keeping her back to the crowd, she looked both ways, relieved not to see Elmer. She lifted off the towel, set the box on the table, and then put two others in front of it. If Elmer was watching, he'd think that one of those was hers.

Lucinda, a little girl from the orphanage, squealed and darted past her, dark pigtails flying. Pedro, another orphan, dashed by close on her heels.

Jody snagged Pedro's collar as he tried to slip past her. She gave him a stern glare. "Take that lizard to the other side of the church and let it go. You need to be on your best behavior today."

"*Sí*, Señorita McMillan."

She watched him head toward the church building and bit back a smile at the boy's attempted regret, knowing this wasn't the last time today she'd probably have to warn him about his behavior.

"Pedro at it again?" Elaine smiled as Jody approached her. "What kind of varmint was it this time?"

"A lizard."

Anika shook her head and chuckled. "That boy does love his critters."

"But Lucinda hates them—and he knows it." Jody moved into the shade of one of the huge saguaro cacti, for which the town was named, and her friends followed. Anika's and Elaine's husbands stood a short distance away, chuckling about something. Jody turned so she couldn't see them. Watching her friends' spouses only made her loneliness greater. Each of her three best friends had found her soul mate and true love, leaving her the only unmarried woman left in the town of Cactus Corner, except for the Widow Classen, who was in town visiting her sister.

The church bell clanged, and everyone quieted, turning in unison to face the front. Elaine leaned toward Jody. "Elmer's been looking for you. He asked me what your box looked like."

The eager anticipation making Jody nearly bounce on her toes slammed to a stop like a locomotive squealing to a halt at a washed-out bridge. She spun around to face her friend. "You didn't tell him, did you?"

Elaine's eyes twinkled as she shrugged. "Perhaps."

"Oh, Elaine. . ." She bit back her comment, knowing her friend was teasing.

As the pastor stood and began auctioning the boxes, Jody kept a running tally. After the tenth sale, she glanced around the crowd, wondering who might buy her container. Her gaze collided with Elmer's, and he lifted his straw hat. Jody quickly turned to face the front as the pastor lifted up a box decorated in red fabric. Perhaps Elmer would bid on this one. She considered turning and giving him a coy look so he'd think it was hers, but she shrugged aside the thought—tempting as it was. She wasn't one to play games with another person's emotions.

It wasn't that she didn't like Elmer—he just didn't make her heart sing. Only an inch taller than she, he was more than three times wider. His straw blond hair stuck out from under his hat in straight spikes that reminded her of a scarecrow's. He was a kind, albeit persistent, man, but she simply didn't love him. She wanted to like him, but the pressure of his constant marriage proposals had driven a wedge in their onetime friendship.

She shivered at the thought of them marrying. Her new name would be Jody Brody.

No, she'd rather spend the rest of her days as a spinster than marry Elmer.

❧

Aaron Garrett surveyed the deed in his hand again. There had to be a mistake.

He had bought the old mercantile, sight unseen, on the recommendation of a business associate. The property wasn't nearly as large as he had been led to believe, and the man had stated explicitly that the mercantile bordered the railroad.

But that wasn't the case.

A run-down children's orphanage sat between his newly acquired land and the railroad tracks.

His father's investment company had devoted a fair amount of money to buy the old mercantile, which Aaron planned to tear down so he could build a hotel. The recent copper strike in the mountains north of town had brought an influx of miners, investors, and businessmen into the small town. If his instincts proved right, Cactus Corner would soon be on the map.

Aaron rubbed the back of his neck as he walked along the property line. Things were worse than he'd first thought. The property was almost too narrow for a hotel, and behind it, the land dipped swiftly down to form a gulley.

He longed to prove that he was just as sharp a businessman as his father, but what would he do now? Phineas Garrett had told him many times location was everything in real estate, but Aaron had messed up in a big way.

That was the last time he'd allow an agent to buy property for him. If a man wanted something done right, he had to do it himself.

He rolled up the deed, tapped it against his leg, and glanced around the town. The few people left on the street all seemed headed in the same direction. He'd noticed a huge crowd at the churchyard as the train rolled into town. Some kind of shindig was going on there. He hoped whoever worked at the land office hadn't left yet.

Smacking the deed against his thigh, he strode south past the closed café. The only building after that was the bank, so he crossed the street to check the buildings on the east side of Main Street. He passed a dress shop, a doctor's office, and the general store—all closed. Evidently when Cactus Corner held a gathering, the whole town showed up.

He stopped at the train depot, grateful to see the clerk still there. The man was removing his black cap as Aaron approached the counter. "Excuse me. Could you please tell me where the land office is?"

The clerk tapped on his straw hat. "Ain't got one. Tucker Truesdale, the town attorney, handles most all land deeds around here. 'Course there was the time when him and his wife—"

"Where can I find this Truesdale fellow?" Aaron wasn't in the mood for a rambling story. His reputation was on the line.

"Why, most everyone's at the box social over at the church. I'm headed there myself."

"Excellent. I'll walk with you, and perhaps you can point out Mr. Truesdale."

The skinny clerk nodded, put a board behind the grill in his window, then closed and locked up the depot office. They walked the short four blocks with the clerk talking the whole time.

Aaron just wanted to finish his business so he could find something to eat and get a room at the boardinghouse. He'd traveled from Phoenix and was tired and dirty from the train soot. He knew the previous hotel had burned down a few months ago, and he hoped building a new one in Cactus Corner would earn his father's stingy praise, but so far, things didn't look good.

"That there's Truesdale."

Aaron watched a tall man stride to the front, drop some coins in the preacher's hand, then pick up a box covered in yellow ribbon and fripperies. The man's smile came easily as he held up the box and the crowd cheered. Mr. Truesdale sidled through the horde and stopped beside a pretty dark-haired woman. She looped her arm through his and gave a smile that sent a surge of longing through Aaron.

He'd love to settle down and get married, but he'd never met a woman who intrigued him enough to make him cease his endless work. Building hotels took up most of his time, and no woman wanted to come in second to a man's occupation.

As he made his way toward the lawyer, the man noticed his approach and handed the fancy box to the woman. She glanced curiously at Aaron, smiled, and then headed toward an empty quilt spread in the shade of the church building.

The lawyer held out his hand as Aaron stopped in front of him. "Tucker Truesdale."

Aaron shook hands and introduced himself. "I'm terribly sorry to bother you at a time like this, but I have a huge problem."

Mr. Truesdale's brows lifted. "What kind of a problem?"

Aaron held out the deed. "I bought the mercantile property through an agent but was under the impression that it bordered the railroad."

"No, it doesn't." The lawyer took the deed and looked at it.

"I know that now, but that doesn't help me." Aaron heaved a frustrated sigh.

Mr. Truesdale glanced over toward the woman and then back at Aaron. "I fail to see how I can assist you."

"I need to acquire the land by the railroad. I'm planning to build a hotel there."

"The orphanage is located next to the railroad."

Aaron restrained himself from sighing out loud. "I know that now. I don't suppose the land the orphanage is on is for sale."

Truesdale shrugged. "I doubt it. You're fortunate you bought the mercantile when you did. Some women—my wife included—have been raising money to buy that property so the orphanage could expand. They'll be sorely disappointed to find out it's been sold." He pressed his lips together and glanced toward his wife again.

Aaron wasn't sure if he'd been deliberately misled or if it was an honest accident, but either way, he'd lost money and his father would be furious.

Truesdale started toward his wife, but Aaron stepped in front of him. "I was deceived about that property. There's not enough room to build a decent-sized hotel, and there's a gulch in back." He waved his rolled-up deed in the air, more annoyed than he could ever remember. He knew his behavior wasn't Christian-like and lowered his arm.

Could things get any worse?

The animated pastor pointed his direction and held up a box dinner with a frilly blue ribbon tied around it. "Sold to the gentleman in the back for four dollars."

Chapter 2

Tucker Truesdale crossed his arms and stared at Aaron with upraised brows and an amused smirk. "Looks like you just bought yourself a dinner, Mr. Garrett."

"What? No, I didn't." Aaron darted a glance at the minister, who was looking across the crowd straight at him, motioning him forward with his finger.

The man hoisted the frilly box in the air. "Come on up and claim your dinner, stranger. Your generous donation will help our orphans."

Aaron groaned under his breath. He was starved, but a picnic with some farmer's wife or an old spinster wasn't what he had in mind.

Truesdale patted him on the shoulder. "Aw, don't look so troubled. It's for a good cause."

Mrs. Truesdale's shoes scuffed against the dry ground as she hurried to her husband's side, hazel eyes alight with excitement. "That's Jody's box."

Truesdale lifted his brows again and looked Aaron up and down. "Is it, now? Elmer will sure be disappointed."

With the whole town turned in his direction and suddenly silent, except for a squalling baby, Aaron had no choice but to accept his fate like a man. He plodded forward, hoping this Elmer fellow wasn't the beefy husband of the woman whose box he'd accidentally purchased.

He shelled out the money and claimed the container, surprised at how heavy it felt and at the delicious fragrance of chicken emanating from it. His stomach gurgled. For a moment, he considered letting the pastor keep his money and offering the box to be auctioned off again, but he didn't want to hurt some old woman's feelings or embarrass her in front of the townsfolk.

Sighing, he glanced around, and the crowd seemed to be waiting as a whole to see the box's owner. A loud murmuring erupted in the crowd as a woman of average height and slender build stepped forward, looking both curious and hesitant. Her honey blond hair glistened in the sunlight like a shiny gold coin. Her long blue dress swished around her legs, and as she drew closer, he saw that her eyes were a pretty blue-green. Surely she wasn't a farmer's wife.

Apprehension surged through him, and he glanced around the crowd to see if he'd upset some hulking husband. People visited in small groups, no longer paying them any attention now, except perhaps the lawyer's wife and two other ladies chattering beside her.

The pretty woman gave him a hesitant smile. "Um. . .that's my box."

Aaron grinned. Perhaps his luck had just changed.

Jody's heart still pounded a frenzied beat. Watching several men bid on her box had been nerveracking, but when the handsome stranger topped all offers, she'd been both relieved and thunderstruck.

How could she be expected to dine with a stranger?

She glanced at her three friends. Anika, Elaine, and India had their heads together, ignoring their own dinners, most likely scheming and matchmaking.

The gentleman cleared his throat and held out his hand. "I'm Aaron Garrett from Phoenix."

Jody shook his hand, trying to ignore its warmth. "Jody McMillan."

"Uh. . .would that be *Miss* or *Mrs.* McMillan?"

"Oh, it's *Miss.*" She pulled her hand free and glanced past Mr. Garrett to see Anika motioning them to join her and Tucker. The last thing she wanted was to have her friends questioning this stranger and making him uncomfortable with their pointed questions. When she saw that Dan and Joshua had moved their quilts next to the Truesdales, Jody knew she had to get Mr. Garrett away from them.

He stood with her box under one arm, jingling some coins in his pocket with his other hand. He seemed as uncomfortable as she felt. Was he disappointed in her?

Jody swallowed the lump in her throat. "Um. . .why don't we see if we can find some shade?"

He nodded and looked around, then pointed to a place near several saguaro cacti a little ways past the adobe church. Jody took his offered arm and allowed him to lead her.

Behind her she heard Elaine call out in a singsong trill, "Jody, come and eat with us."

With her free hand, she waved off her friends and could hear their not-so-subtle laughter as she and Mr. Garrett walked away. Tension tightened Jody's neck. Her irritation with her friends surged. Why couldn't they leave well enough alone instead of embarrassing her?

Mr. Garrett stopped in front of a tall cactus and stared at the ground. "Will this do?" He kicked away several small rocks, then glanced up.

Her gaze collided with his, and she thought she'd never seen brown eyes as intriguing as his. He wasn't especially tall, probably just under six feet, but his curly dark brown hair and hat made him seem taller. Dressed in his stylish business suit, he stood out in the casually dressed crowd. Jody realized she was staring and forced her gaze away. *What's wrong with me?*

Perhaps she *would* have been better off dining with Elmer. At least she knew what to expect with him.

Mr. Garrett set her box down and peeled off his suit coat. She shifted her gaze away, knowing she was blushing.

He spread the jacket on the ground with the lining side against the dirt, then offered his hand. "Allow me."

Jody realized he meant for her to sit on his coat, and her insides turned to mush at the thought of such an intimate action. "Oh, that's not necessary. I'm used to sitting on the ground."

One of his dark brows lifted; then he pressed his lips together as if holding back his amusement. "I'm afraid that comment intrigues me so that I can't allow it to pass without further elaboration."

"Uh. . .well, I mean, I sometimes sit on the ground when playing with the orphans."

"Ah. . .sounds delightful." He chuckled, then held out his palm. "Please have a seat, Miss McMillan. I insist."

"All right, then." She took his hand, sat down, and rearranged her skirt, just wanting this afternoon to end. When she got back to her room, she'd kick herself for organizing this event. What had she been thinking?

"So how does this work? I've never eaten at a box social before."

Jody tilted her head up, holding her hand over her eyes to block the sun. "Well, first you have to sit on the ground."

"Ah. . .point taken." Mr. Garrett tugged at his pant legs and eased down. He smiled, and Jody tried not to notice how white and straight his teeth were.

Focusing on their dinner, she dragged the heavy box toward her, untied the bow, pulled off the lid, and spread open two cloth napkins. Then she laid a plate on each one. "I hope you like chicken."

"Love it." The gleam in his eye told her he was telling the truth.

She loaded his plate with three pieces of chicken, green beans still slightly warm in their canning jar, and buttery new potatoes.

"Mmm. . .it looks wonderful. I haven't eaten since this morning before I left Phoenix."

Jody handed him his plate and silverware, wondering what business he had in Cactus Corner. She'd never seen him here before—she was sure she'd remember him.

He took a bite of chicken and closed his eyes. "This is positively delicious. I'm going out on a limb here, but this might even be better than my mother's. Please don't ever tell her I said that, though." One corner of his mouth quirked up, and he winked.

She couldn't help the delight that coursed through her. Elmer never seemed to notice her food that much, because he was always gawking at her. A shaft of concern for her boss speared her, and she glanced around to see where he was. She didn't want to marry Elmer but hated the thought of his being left to himself without dinner. When she noticed him eating with the Widow Classen and her sister's family, she blew out a sigh. Thankfully, he didn't look as if he missed her at all.

"Have you lived here long?"

She turned back to Mr. Garrett and nodded. "Most of my life. I was raised in the local orphanage after my parents died."

"Oh, I'm sorry." His dark gaze softened.

"It was a long time ago."

He pressed his lips together in a sympathetic smile.

Who was this man? And why were her insides in such turmoil at his nearness?

She picked a piece of the chicken's crisp buttermilk coating off her skirt and flicked it away. "So. . .are you in town on business or pleasure?"

Aaron couldn't help feeling sorry that Miss McMillan had lost her parents at such a young age. His father might be tough and expect a lot out of him, but his mother was the heart of his world. He couldn't imagine growing up without her encouragement and support.

He realized Miss McMillan was waiting for his response to her query.

"I'm here on business. Looking to purchase some land."

The pretty woman across from him brightened. "Oh, then we have something in common. I—well, I mean, the orphanage committee—will be buying land soon so the dormitory can be expanded. That's the whole reason for this gathering, and if my calculations are correct, we've finally reached our financial goal."

Two youngsters ran past them, squealing and laughing. He watched them, wondering if perhaps they were orphans. They looked happy enough, but what was it like for them to grow up without parents to love and guide them? He pulled his attention back to the comely woman across from him. "So you're looking to buy real estate?"

"Yes. We've been raising funds for two years to buy the old mercantile property."

He could tell by the way her lovely blue-green eyes glimmered that she was ardent about her cause. A shaft of guilt surged through him as he realized she'd be terribly disappointed.

As much as he didn't want to admit it, he liked her. But that was dangerous with both of them wanting the same property—property he'd already bought. He shook his head. What did it matter if this woman piqued his interest more than any other had lately? If he couldn't buy the land the orphanage now occupied, he wouldn't be in town long.

She chattered on and on about her cause, making him feel even guiltier. He'd purchased the land in good faith, not knowing she also wanted it. He decided to try a different approach.

"Have you ever considered relocating the facility? I mean, it can't be safe for the children with it being in such close proximity to the railroad tracks."

Miss McMillan blinked. "Why. . .no. They know not to play around the tracks, and the location is a perfect one, being so close to everything."

"But children need a place to run and play. Surely being located in town is a hardship for the youngsters. Wouldn't they be better off on an acreage where they could stretch their legs without fear of the railroad or town riffraff?"

"Just what is your interest in the orphanage? Are you some kind of inspector?" Miss McMillan hiked her cute chin and glared at him. "Because if you are, I can assure you the children are well cared for and loved."

He lifted his hands in surrender. "Now, don't get your feathers ruffled, Miss McMillan. I'm just curious. I noticed the orphanage when I came into town and thought to myself that a railroad and children were a dangerous mix."

"Well, it's never been a problem. The orphanage was there before the railroad, and it will remain in the same location for many years."

Aaron sighed, even though he couldn't help admiring her spunk and determination. He glanced at the sky as his hostess scraped the remains of his meal off his plate. *What do I do now, Lord? Just give up? Or see if I can't help Miss McMillan understand that moving would be a wise decision?*

His concentration was pulled away from his prayers as she laid a huge slice of apple pie on his plate. With his mouth watering at the sight of the fat, juicy apples, he reached out, taking hold of the dish and a clean fork. For the next few minutes, he savored each delectable bite, wondering why such a good cook hadn't been snatched up by some local bachelor.

Miss McMillan ate her pie, taking dainty bites and occasionally wiping her appealing mouth with the corner of her napkin. For a moment, he could only watch her, fascinated with her mannerisms and capriciousness. She was all lady, but underneath her frilly layers, a passionate fire burned.

If he could spend time with her, he was sure he could change her view about moving the orphanage. It was in the children's best interest every way he looked at it.

"Will you be in town long, Mr. Garrett?"

"Well. . .that all depends." He pinned her with a smile. "Will you have dinner with me tomorrow night?"

Chapter 3

Jody's shoes tapped against the polished wood floor, then quieted as she stepped onto the braided rug. She paced to the window and back to the door of her small room in the boardinghouse. Mr. Garrett was probably waiting downstairs. She should have told him she lived at the boardinghouse, but it hadn't seemed a proper thing to be discussing with a stranger.

What was she thinking, agreeing to dine with him again?

She wasn't thinking. She'd been lost in those expressive brown eyes of his and listening to his wonderful voice. That and trying to avoid glancing at her friends, who'd stared at her and Mr. Garrett the whole time they ate.

She heaved a sigh, thinking about how withdrawn Elmer had been at work today. He'd looked wounded and asked her who that man was she'd eaten with. At least he hadn't pestered her and Mr. Garrett at the box social. She was thankful he hadn't even seemed to miss her with the Widow Classen stuffing him full of her homemade sausages and sauerkraut. Jody had been relieved to have Elmer's attention focused on someone else for a change.

She'd cringed this morning when Elmer had said, "Just remember, I staked a claim on you first. You tell that city feller I intend to marry you."

She'd tried to set him straight by informing him that she belonged to no man, but he'd simply glared at her and stomped off.

Oh. . .I have to find another job.

Jody rolled her head to one side and then the other, working the tension out of her neck as she pulled her thoughts back to the man she was to meet. Part of her desperately wanted to get to know Aaron Garrett better, and another part wanted to run the other way. Surely she was mature enough to have dinner with a man without making a big to-do about it.

There was no point in prolonging the inevitable. She stepped into the hall and closed her door, unable to deny even to herself that she was attracted to the suave, handsome stranger. But what could come of such an attraction? He lived in Phoenix and she in Cactus Corner.

Holding on to the railing with one hand and lifting her skirt with the other, she made her way downstairs. At least being seen around town on Mr. Garrett's arm would help refute Elmer's claim on her.

Jody's breath caught in her throat at the view of Mr. Garrett standing in front of the window with his back to her. He was a sight to behold all decked out in his fancy suit, his dark hair curling along his collar. Broad shoulders narrowed to a slim waist, and one hand in his pocket jingled his impatience.

Had her three close friends felt such a strong attraction to the men they'd married when they first met them?

Jody twisted her lips and forced that thought out of her mind. She would enjoy spending the evening with this handsome man, but that was all. She'd most likely never see him again once he concluded his business in town.

Aaron paced the foyer of the boardinghouse where he was staying. He stopped at the open front door and stared out, hoping to see Miss McMillan coming his way. She'd been hesitant to agree to dine with him, but when she learned he was staying at the boardinghouse, she'd finally relented and told him she'd meet him there.

But she was five minutes late, and he couldn't help wondering if she'd changed her mind. Perhaps he'd come on too strong the previous evening at the box social. He should have just told her he'd bought the mercantile, but he hadn't wanted to see the disappointment in her eyes.

A woman behind him cleared her throat. He spun around and stood face-to-face with the very female who'd occupied his mind all day. A faint rose color stained her lightly tanned cheeks as he stared at her.

"Good evening, Mr. Garrett. I trust you had a productive day."

Aaron gave a curt bow and smiled. "Let's say it was an interesting day. Cactus Corner may seem like a sleepy little town, but there's a lot going on here."

She smiled, making Aaron's stomach quiver. He'd found a rose blooming in the desert. He offered her his arm and rejoiced silently when she looped her hand around it. "I explored the town earlier and found a quaint café that serves some delicious food."

"Oh yes. Etta Stephens is a wonderful cook. I occasionally eat lunch there. Gives me a break from the boardinghouse fare."

"Obviously you live here." Ah, that explained how she managed to slip up behind him.

Her cheeks turned pink again. "Yes. I suppose I should have told you, but it didn't seem a proper topic of conversation."

"Think nothing of it." Aaron escorted Miss McMillan out into the warm sunshine, ignoring the sweat trickling between his shoulder blades. One would think that this close to sunset the temperature would drop.

"That's my place of employment."

Aaron looked across the street to where Miss McMillan was pointing. "You work for the freight lines?" He chuckled. "Don't tell me, you're a driver?"

Mirth danced in her eyes as she shook her head. A faint scent of something floral drifted past on the hot breeze. "No, although there are days I wish I were. I'm the bookkeeper and process most of the paperwork."

"Ah, I see."

They passed the attorney's office, and Aaron helped her cross over the railroad tracks. Children ran around yelling and playing outside the orphanage as they approached the building.

"Miss Jody!" Several youngsters squealed her name and charged toward them. Dirt flew behind their little feet. Three Mexican girls and two boys of Indian heritage, who all looked to be about seven or eight, huddled around Miss McMillan.

She released her hold on him, opening her arms to envelop the whole group in a big hug. Aaron stood back and watched, mesmerized. The children were dirty and sweaty, while Miss McMillan was spotlessly dressed. She didn't even grimace at handling the grubby kids. Most women would have been put off, but not her.

And he admired her for it.

After she touched each child and greeted all of them, she sweetly sent them on their way, then glanced at him apologetically. "I'm sorry about the disruption. I volunteer at the orphanage, and they all know me."

"And love you, I'd say." Aaron tucked her hand back around his arm and proceeded toward the café.

She peeked at him out of the corner of her eye. "I suppose it's only natural for them to care for me since I love each of them. I, better than most people, can empathize with them, since I, too, grew up in the orphanage."

As they passed in front of the mercantile, an arrow of guilt drove its way into Aaron's conscience. He needed to tell her that he'd purchased the old store, but if he did, would she still dine with him? Perhaps he'd tell her afterward.

"Oh!" Miss McMillan suddenly stopped and let go of his arm. She glided over to the filthy mercantile window, cupped her hands beside her eyes, and peered in. "This is the property we're going to buy."

Stepping back, she waved her arm to the right. "This purchase will enable us to greatly expand the orphanage. It will take a while, though, because we'll need to raise money for the building." She turned back to face him, excitement glowing in her eyes. An enchanting smudge of dirt covered the tip of her nose.

Pushing his guilt aside, knowing he would be the source of her disappointment, he pulled out his handkerchief. When he held it out to her, she gazed at him questioningly with those beautiful aquatic eyes. He tapped his finger on his nose, and her brows lifted.

"You—uh—have dirt on your nose."

"Oh my!" She grabbed the clean handkerchief and rubbed her whole face.

He couldn't help smiling, as all she'd done was smear the dirt. "Please, allow me." He retrieved his kerchief and grasped her shoulder, ignoring her trembling, then gently wiped the end of her nose. He hoped she wasn't afraid of him, but it wasn't fear in her gaze, more like. . .wonder.

Aaron swallowed and stepped back, needing to put some distance between them. He wasn't sure, but he thought he might be shaking a bit himself. How was it this particular woman had such an effect on him?

"Is it gone?" She looked in the window and tilted her chin up as if trying to see her reflection.

He nodded and returned his handkerchief to his pocket, then started jiggling his coins. It was a bad nervous habit that he was trying to break. Closing his hand around the coins, he held it still.

"How mortifying!" She pressed her lips together and looked at two cowboys riding their horses down Main Street.

Aaron chuckled. "Think nothing of it, Miss McMillan."

She swirled around, cupping her fingertips together. "We don't hold much to formality here in Cactus Corner, and I realize we've just met, but would it be too forward of me to ask you to call me Jody?"

"Not at all. And you must call me Aaron." He bit back a smile when her cheeks turned pink again.

"All right, then, Aaron. Shall we continue on? I had an early lunch, and the fragrant aromas coming from the café are just about to do me in."

He bowed and held out his hand. "After you."

They placed orders for Etta's special pot roast and mashed potatoes, then Aaron studied his dinner partner. She waved at a couple sitting at the corner table, and he didn't miss their curious stares as they waved back. Jody's honey-blond hair was braided and twisted into a becoming bun. Soft wisps fluttered around her face. She had an appealing habit of tucking the rebellious strands behind her ear, even though they refused to stay.

Glancing down at the table, he forced his thoughts back to business. He'd asked around town and learned that Jody held some position of respect with the board that managed the children's home. Winning her over to the idea of moving the facility could help his cause tremendously.

"So how long did you live at the orphanage, if I might be so bold as to ask?"

She glanced at him with those beautiful eyes that he could easily lose himself in. He straightened and leaned back in his chair, arms crossed over his chest.

"Oh, it was about twelve years. First I lived there as a child until I turned sixteen; then I lived and worked there until I got the job at the freight office when I was nineteen."

Aaron pressed his lips together. "That's quite a long time."

She nodded and smiled at someone he hadn't met across the café. He wished he could just enjoy this time with the lovely Miss McMillan, but he was a businessman and had decisions that needed to be made concerning the hotel.

"Miss—uh, Jody, have you thought any more about moving the orphanage?"

She glanced at him, confused. "Why, no, I haven't. I see no reason at all to relocate. I believe I clearly stated my opinion yesterday."

Aaron sighed. She was as stubborn as she was beautiful. His gaze landed on a plate piled high with roast beef, potatoes, and carrots the waitress was carrying to another table, and his stomach grumbled. One thing he agreed with Jody on—the fragrant odors of the café were tantalizing him.

He regrouped his thoughts and tried a different approach. This morning he'd poked around town and learned that there had been several close calls with the train and the orphans. One time, two brothers had even stowed away and weren't found until the train reached the next town. Aaron imagined Jody and the orphanage staff must have been frantic to find the boys. Perhaps if he hinted at those incidents. . . "Surely there have been events with the train and the children."

Jody grimaced and avoided his gaze. She toyed with the corner of her cloth napkin. "Well, of course there have. You know how children are fascinated with anything that is forbidden."

"Then I rest my case. It would be in their best interest if the orphanage was moved."

She stared at him wide-eyed. "Uh. . .no, that's not what I meant. You can't remove all temptations from young ones but rather must teach them how to handle such circumstances. Surely if you had children of your own, you would teach them to stay away from the railroad tracks, wouldn't you?"

He nodded. "Of course—if I had any. But I also wouldn't build my home next to the tracks where they would be tempted daily to rebel against my authority. It's the nature of youngsters to test rules. I fear one of these days, one of them could meet disaster by tempting fate. Besides, they would have fresher air away from the train, and you wouldn't have to worry about the noise waking the little ones from their naps. They'd have land to raise animals and grow a bigger garden. As far as I can tell, there are only positive reasons for moving."

Jody pressed her lips together and eyed him with a narrowed gaze. "Just what's your interest in all this? Why are you so concerned about the orphans?"

His heart lurched. He hadn't been prepared for her pointed question. Silverware clinked and the soft hum of voices distracted him. He knew he should just tell her the truth.

"Mr. Garrett, I asked you a question."

Aaron sighed. Just like that they were back to using surnames. He turned to face her. "My job is to scout out towns and find property to build on. I'm sure you're aware that the only hotel in town burned down."

Jody nodded. "Of course."

"With the recent copper strike and the influx of people, Cactus Corner is a good investment, and the town needs a new hotel. I wouldn't have even been able to get a room in the boardinghouse if it wasn't for the fact that someone else was checking out the same day I arrived."

"But I still don't see what this has to do with the orphanage."

Aaron leaned back in his seat as the waitress placed two steaming plates of aromatic food in front of them. His mouth watered, but he needed to finish explaining.

"I believe that the orphanage land is the best place to locate a hotel."

Jody gasped. "You can't be serious."

"Yes, I am. But I wouldn't even consider such a thing if I didn't feel it was also in the children's best interest to relocate."

Jody pushed her food around on her plate, having suddenly lost her appetite. So Mr. Garrett was merely a fortune hunter. A scalawag who didn't mind putting orphans out on the street to accomplish his goal. Disappointment coursed through her like a raging creek after a heavy rain. She had hoped something might develop between her and Aaron, but now that would never happen. She should have known better than to be swayed by a charming gentleman. He was merely a wolf in sheep's clothing.

Like a mother bear, she would defend the orphans and their home. "The current location has sentimental value since it was the only real home I can remember having. It may be in need of repairs, but that doesn't mean it should be torn down." She wanted to add, "just so you can build your swanky hotel," but didn't.

He lifted one hand in surrender. "I understand that, but surely the children's welfare is more important than sentiment."

Jody was too upset to reply. He made it sound as if she was thinking only of herself. She pushed her plate back, ready to get away from the infuriating Mr. Garrett.

Chapter 4

Aaron stood back, watching the three-man crew he'd hired dismantle the old mercantile. Their fervent pounding made the ache in his head worse. He needed to succeed at this job to earn his father's respect. Phineas Garrett was as stingy with his admiration and praise as he was with his money, and if it hadn't been for the inheritance left Aaron by his grandmother on his mother's side, he would most likely be working as a clerk for his father instead of building the hotels that made him and his father wealthy men.

He sighed, again regretting buying the mercantile land without first looking it over himself. He wouldn't make that mistake again. Once he got the crumbling building out of the way, he could more accurately measure the land and determine if there was room for a small hotel. He might have to build out over the gulch in the back, but that might not be a bad thing. The area underneath the hotel there would allow a place where guests could tether their horses out of the sun. It might work, if the slope wasn't too steep.

What he really wanted to do was make Jody happy and let the orphanage have the property, even though he still felt the children would be better off in a different location. But if he failed to accomplish his goal, his father would only chastise him further and deepen the chasm between them that Aaron had prayed God would close. He only wanted his father's love and respect, but so far he'd been unable to earn it.

Aaron rubbed the back of his neck and looked at the orphanage property. He hated going behind Jody's back, but it was time to approach the Jacobsons to see if they felt the same way about moving the orphanage as Jody did. He wouldn't have waited this long, but he had hoped to sway Jody to his way of thinking. The woman was as stubborn as his father.

He sighed and turned his gaze next door. If only he could purchase that land, too, then he'd have the perfect hotel location and plenty of room.

But that was a big *if only*.

Jody stomped toward the old mercantile, her footsteps pounding on the boardwalk like Indian war drums. She was certainly angry enough to start a war.

Here she'd let herself become enamored with Aaron Garrett, even though she tried to resist his polished charm, but now she was sure she was just another victim in a long line, probably all the way from Cactus Corner to Phoenix. She clenched her fist as she caught a glimpse of him standing in the middle of the street, surveying the building that was being torn down.

She clenched her teeth together and furrowed her brow. Of all the nerve!

Jody stepped off the boardwalk onto the hard-packed dirt street and bypassed a rancher on horseback. So far, caught up in his work, Mr. Garrett had failed to see her approach.

She marched up behind him and stopped, trying hard to ignore the delicious scent of expensive cologne wafting from him. She shook her head. It didn't matter if he smelled better than anything she could think of. Of course, as upset as she was, she couldn't think clearly anyway. "How could you?"

Mr. Garrett jumped and spun around. "Miss McMillan, you gave me a start. I was rather engrossed in this project and didn't hear your approach."

"Well. . .you know I'm here now, so you might as well answer my question." She crossed her arms over her chest, waiting.

His dark brows darted upward. "Sorry, but I didn't hear your question. What was it again?"

He tipped his hat to her and gave a smile that made her heart quiver. She and that heart would just have to have a talk later. Aaron Garrett was too nice-looking for his own good—but she wouldn't fall for his charm again.

"I said. . .how could you?" She welcomed his confused stare, which allowed her a moment to catch her breath and push aside her attraction to him.

"How could I what?"

The obvious fact that he had no idea what she was talking about irritated her even more. She flung her arm out and pointed toward the mercantile. "That! How could you not tell me that you'd bought the property after you learned how hard I'd worked to raise money to buy it?"

"Ah, that's what's gotten your feathers so ruffled."

Jody looked sideways at the sounds of a harness jingling and a wagon creaking. A mule brayed as if telling her to get out of its way.

Aaron took hold of her arm. "Let's clear the road before we get run down."

Jody allowed him to help her up the boardwalk steps, then jerked her arm free of his. Each pound of the hammer knocking boards loose only reemphasized her failure. A plank squealed as a worker pulled it free, and then it tumbled down with a loud clatter, sending up a puff of dirt when it hit the ground. This should have been a day for rejoicing; instead, it nearly broke her heart. The town might have a nice, new hotel—and she wouldn't argue that it was needed—but the orphans would lose out.

"Miss McMillan, I know this causes you distress, and that's the very reason I was hesitant to tell you about my purchase."

Jody narrowed her eyes and glared at him. "It would have been the courteous thing to do, especially once you knew *I* planned to buy it."

"I was going to tell you the night I took you to dinner, but then we argued, and the time never seemed right. I do apologize. I probably should have told you the day of the box social when I accidentally bought your dinner, but—"

Jody held up her hand. "Wait! You mean you never planned to buy my box?"

"Uh. . .no. It was an accident. I was waving a paper in the air, and the parson mistook it for a bid. That said, I'm most delighted I did purchase your dinner. I enjoyed the meal and my time with you very much."

She didn't want Aaron being nice to her or his voice softening when he talked about their time together. Jody stared into the eyes that reminded her of coffee and could read his sincerity. For a fraction of a second, she was tempted to forgive him. She knew for sure that was what the Lord wanted her to do.

Perhaps this *was* just an honest mistake, but now Aaron knew how much she wanted that land, and he was still going ahead with his plans.

Well. . .she had other plans. And she was sure Aaron Garrett wouldn't like them.

❧

Jody smiled and looked around the partially dismantled mercantile where she and her friends were staging a protest. She could only imagine Aaron's expression of surprise and frustration when he and the crew returned from their dinner break and found the women camped out in the middle of their work area. She chuckled to herself at her ingenuity. Surely Aaron would see how determined she was and would sell the land to the board.

"Jody, I have to tell you this is the most outlandish idea you've ever come up with." Elaine settled into the rocking chair that she'd borrowed from her husband's office. "If I hadn't planned to work on these squares for a quilt for Autumn, I'm afraid I wouldn't have been able to join you." Her gaze landed on the doctor's office across the street. "I just don't know what Dan will say about this when he returns from the Johnson ranch."

"I agree. This *is* a crazy idea, but you inspired me, Jody, when you came out to the ranch yesterday, begging for my help." India lowered her cumbersome body into the chair Jody had scrounged from the orphanage. "I left Joshua a note, but when he gets back to the house, he'll be livid. Ever since I started showing, he's been so bossy, wanting to keep me close to home. I'm about to go stir-crazy. I needed a good mission to concentrate on." She flashed an ornery grin.

Elaine shook her head and focused on stitching two fabric squares together. "He's only trying to watch out for you, India."

"I know, and I love him for it, in spite of the fact that it sometimes frustrates me." She fanned herself with a cardboard advertisement for the funeral home in neighboring Baxter Bluff.

Jody glanced across the street at the café, feeling both guilty for coercing her friends to stage this protest and glad that they'd so willingly come to her side to help the orphans. Delicious odors emanated from the café, reminding her that she'd skipped breakfast, and now the dinner hour was quickly passing. Perhaps once the ladies were settled, she'd ask Etta to fix a tray for them.

India squinted and pointed down the road. "Here comes Anika."

Anika was struggling to carry a side chair Jody recognized as coming from Mr. Jacobson's office. Jody stepped out from under the shade of the mercantile and hurried to help her. Anika handed the heavy chair to Jody. "I have a surprise. Be right back."

Her friend's skirts swished as she hurried away. Jody hoisted the chair over a small stack of boards pulled from the building and set it next to India's.

"Where's she off to in such a hurry?" India asked.

Jody shrugged. "Said she had a surprise."

Simon Fitzgerald, the banker, slowed his steps as he passed in front of the old store and gawked at them. "Just what are you ladies doing?"

Jody stared back. "We're declaring a protest to stop Mr. Garrett from building a hotel here. Everyone knows this is our land, and we're not giving it up without a fight."

Mr. Fitzgerald chuckled and shook his head. "Miss McMillan, I fear you're starting something here you won't be able to finish. Mr. Garrett is one determined man."

Jody crossed her arms and hiked her chin, ready for battle. "Well, he doesn't know what he's up against."

He laughed out loud as he crossed the street and entered the café at the same time the three men Aaron had hired moseyed out. They crossed the street, their voices getting louder the nearer they came. Suddenly, one glanced at Jody and grabbed one of his cohorts by the arm. Jody braced herself for another skirmish.

"Hey! What do you think you're doing?" John Simmons, a local carpenter and the tallest of the three, stepped forward, hands on his hips. "Get out of there before you get hurt."

"We're not leaving. And that's that."

John glanced at his coworkers, then back at her. "We don't get paid if we don't work."

Jody shrugged and stood her ground. "I'm sorry, but we're staying put."

John motioned to Clay Stuart. "You and Sam go work out back for a while. I'll go tell Mr. Garrett we got us a problem."

The two workers disappeared behind the back of the mercantile, while John spun around and headed back to the café. A moment later, Jody could hear pounding coming from behind the building. She heaved a sigh and readied herself to face Aaron.

"Whatever you have there, Anika, sure smells good." Elaine stood to help Anika with the crate she carried.

"Oh, what is it?" India asked.

Anika smiled and lifted her head as regally as a queen. "I thought since we were going to sit out here, we might as well try to raise some additional funds for the orphanage while winning people over to our way of thinking." She lifted a towel and revealed a platter of sugar cookies and a dozen muffins. "We'll have a bake sale."

India clapped her hands together. "What a wonderful idea. I'm famished. I need to sample some of those cookies."

They all laughed in unison.

"You're always hungry," Jody said, smiling at her friend.

"Well, I am eating for two."

"True." Anika placed the basket on what used to be the store's counter. "Now all we need is a table of some kind."

"Here." Jody crossed the room and picked up the end of a board. "We can use these."

"Good idea." Anika hoisted up the other end, and they placed the board on two crates, blocking the open doorway. They added another plank, then set out the items for sale.

Anika straightened and looked at Jody. "You do realize we're trespassing on private property. We could get in a lot of trouble."

"I don't believe Mr. Garrett is the type of man to press charges. I just hope he'll see reason."

Anika looked Jody squarely in the eyes. "You don't know what type of man he is. You've only just met him a few days ago. Or is there something you're not telling us?"

Jody glanced away. How could she explain her feelings? She was more attracted to Aaron than she'd been to any man she could ever recall meeting, but they were practically enemies now. Or would be soon. A measure of doubt niggled at her. This morning she'd been so certain of her plan, but now. . .perhaps they should just call off the protest.

"Oh, I see." Anika's lips twisted up in a wry grin.

"See what?" Elaine looked around as if she'd missed something.

Anika sashayed over to where India and Elaine were sitting. "She likes him."

"Who?" India furrowed her brows.

"Jody likes Mr. Garrett."

"I do not." Jody stomped to the middle of the room. "Don't go telling tales, Anika."

"But you see, it's not a tale. The truth is written all over your face and in your fervent denial."

Jody turned away and stared at the café door, her friends' soft chuckles echoing behind her. It wasn't true. It couldn't be. Perhaps she admired Aaron's fine looks and citified bearing and manners, but that was all. Wasn't it? She couldn't afford to like him.

Jody leaned against a pillar and sighed, wondering again if she was making a mistake. Had she once more plowed ahead without seeking God's guidance?

Yesterday she'd been so sure of her plans. So sure the protest would stop the work on the mercantile. But it hadn't.

She heard a loud crash out back, and the whole building shimmied. Jody swallowed and peeked at her friends to see if they'd felt it, too. None of them seemed concerned, and their happy chatter continued. They were probably planning how to matchmake her and Aaron.

Jody sighed. She'd prayed about what to do and had thought of the protest, but had that been only her idea and not the Lord's?

Peering over her shoulder again, she saw Stanley Becket looking over the baked goods. He selected several items, then handed Anika some coins. She turned and smiled, lifting her hand in the air. The coins in her fist jingled.

More money for the orphanage, but what did it matter now?

❧

The banker pulled out a chair at Aaron's table and sat down without even asking permission. The little hairs on the back of Aaron's neck stood up. Trouble was brewing; he could feel it.

Had there been a problem getting his money from the bank in Phoenix? He had some working capital on hand but not a lot.

"There's a hen party going on at your mercantile." Mr. Fitzgerald motioned to Etta, who came and took his order.

Aaron waited until she left, then leaned forward. "Hen party?"

The banker rumbled a deep belly laugh and nodded. "There's a quartet of pretty women staking their claim on your property."

Aaron looked over his shoulder and out the window and saw the flash of a green skirt inside his building, just as John Simmons stomped into the café. Aaron's heart ricocheted as he recognized Jody's slim form inside the mercantile. What was that gal up to now?

His scowling crew foreman stopped beside the table, his hands on his hips. "We've got trouble, boss."

Chapter 5

Aaron stood on the boardwalk outside the old store with his hands on his hips, staring at the ground. Just how was he supposed to deal with this situation? He couldn't exactly stomp in and throw out the four ladies, especially with one being in a delicate way.

He glanced up at the sky. *I could use some help here, Lord.*

A tiny part of him wanted to laugh at the ridiculous situation. Jody had to know her little hen party wouldn't get her what she wanted, but in spite of the irritation and inconvenience it caused him, he couldn't help admiring her gumption.

She saw him staring and crossed her arms, glaring at him as if daring him to confront her. He thought of the scripture in Proverbs: *"A soft answer turneth away wrath: but grievous words stir up anger."* He'd try reasoning with her first.

With the doorway blocked with an array of baked goods on wooden planks, Aaron climbed in a window that had already had the glass removed, then dusted off his hands as he looked around. The women had quite a setup, with chairs, food, and things to occupy them.

"We're not leaving." Jody uncrossed her arms and sashayed toward him. "So don't bother to try making us."

Aaron sighed. "You do know what you're doing is against the law?"

When he got no response from Jody, he glanced at the lawyer's wife. She fidgeted and looked away. She knew he was right.

"Some things are higher than the law." Jody stared straight at him.

"That's not for you to decide. I own this land, and you and your friends are trespassing. I could have you arrested."

Panic widened Jody's eyes for a moment, and then she glanced at her friends. Obviously they hadn't considered that factor. The doc's wife stopped her sewing and dropped her hands into her lap. Mrs. Truesdale glanced at the woman with child.

"That's not necessary. If you'll just sell us this property, we'll gladly leave." Jody's lips turned up in a smug smile that didn't quite reach her eyes.

Aaron lowered his head and shook it. He reached in his pockets, found some coins, and started jiggling them. Perhaps the best thing would be to sell out. But he didn't like losing, and deep in his heart, he felt the orphans would be safer and better off in another location. If he gave in now, they'd most likely never get to move.

He blinked. When had Jody's mission become his?

Behind him he heard the sound of rapidly approaching hoofbeats and turned to see what was happening. People rarely charged into town unless there was an emergency. A cowboy reined his horse to a stop so fast, the poor animal practically sat on his rump. Farther down the road, he could see the doctor's buggy coming their direction at a fast clip. Perhaps this little showdown would be over more quickly than he'd thought.

The cowboy leapt off his horse with an agility that left Aaron awestruck. He stomped onto the boardwalk and stopped at the blocked front door. His brow was tucked down in a severe scowl.

"India, you've done a lot of crazy things, but this one takes the prize. Get your things. We're going home." He reached down, snagged a sugar cookie, and bit it almost in half, glaring at Jody the whole time. "You ought to have more concern for your friends than to ask them to participate in such a harebrained stunt."

Jody walked up to him like a royal queen. "We're selling those cookies to raise money for the orphans. That will be two bits, please." She held out her hand.

Aaron didn't know the man but gave him credit for not punching her. He must have had a lot of self-control, although it looked as if he was at his boiling point.

He reached into his pocket, pulled out a handful of change, and dropped it on the table. Several coins spun around before falling down with a *clink*. Glaring at Jody, he helped himself to two more cookies, then looked across the room. India was on her feet.

"I'm sorry to jump ship, but I really do need to go. By the time I get back to the ranch and rest a little while, it will be dinnertime." She pressed her fist into her back. "Oh, I'll be so glad when this child comes."

Jody walked up to her. "You won't get in trouble, will you?"

India smiled and glanced at her husband. "Oh, you know how overprotective Joshua is. He's just worried about the baby and me. And probably a bit put out for having to ride to town when he's so busy with the ranch."

Jody leaned forward and hugged her friend around the neck. "Thank you for coming. I hope it didn't tire you out too much."

India waved a hand in the air. "No, it was wonderful to get to visit with you all, even for a short while. I've missed working at the orphanage. Come visit me soon, and let me know how all this pans out."

India glanced at Aaron with a knowing smile, and it made him wonder just what it was she knew.

The lawyer's wife removed the cookies and muffins from the planks in front of the door, while the cowboy lifted the boards and set them aside. As India stepped outside, she turned and waved.

"Where's the buggy?" her husband asked as he helped her down the steps and into the street.

Aaron didn't hear her answer because the doctor was tramping his way inside. The older woman who'd been sewing stood up. "Uh-oh, looks like I've been found out, too."

The doctor stepped farther into the room and looked around. "Elaine, what's going on here? I was halfway back to town when I heard about this little soiree. Pete

Mayberry stopped me on the road and told me about it. Said he'd bought a couple of muffins from you gals."

"It's for a good cause." The woman gathered up her sewing. "I would appreciate it if you could carry this chair back to your office. I had quite a time getting it over here."

"Of course, dear." The doctor rolled his eyes and stepped forward, his hand held out. "I'm Dan Murphy, the town doctor."

Aaron shook his hand. "Aaron Garrett. A pleasure to meet you."

"I'm sorry about this." Doc Murphy waved his hand in the air. "When these women get together, they can nearly move mountains."

They shared a chuckle that made Jody scowl. The doc hoisted up the chair and made his way out. As soon as he passed through the doorway, Jody placed a board on two crates, just inside the doorway, probably hoping to keep her last hen from fleeing the coop. Mrs. Truesdale laid out the cookies, then smiled at two men who stopped at the door.

Aaron turned to Jody. "You can't stay here. You've made your point, but now it's time to go."

As if she had more to prove, Jody glided over to a rocker and plopped down. "I don't intend on going anywhere."

Aaron heaved a sigh and stooped down right in front of her. Jody's lovely blue-green eyes widened.

"What do you hope to accomplish by this stunt?"

Jody stared at Aaron's handsome face. She'd expected him to storm in ranting and raving, but when he gently climbed in the window and didn't even raise his voice, she'd been taken off guard. How does one fight when the other person remains so calm?

She needed to answer him, but the truth was she didn't know what she'd hoped to accomplish when she had planned this protest. The dismantling hadn't stopped, and work was still going on out back. There was banging and the squealing of nails being pulled out of wood and the clatter of boards falling to the ground.

She sighed and looked at Aaron, so patient, so close. "I don't know. I just knew I had to do something."

He laid his hand on her arm. "This isn't the way to go about it. You're getting your friends in trouble with their husbands, and you could get hurt. It's not safe to be in this building." He ran his hand through his hair. "I should have told the workers to stop."

A sliver of guilt worked its way into her conscience. Aaron was a good man, only trying to build a hotel, which the town needed. But the orphans had a greater need. Why couldn't he see that?

Jody jumped at the sound of a loud bang out back. The building gave a huge shudder and groan, and then the whole back side caved in. Aaron dove forward, shocking her as he covered her body with his. Boards clattered all around them as if an earthquake was in progress. Finally, the noise ceased, leaving behind a cloud of dust that had them all coughing.

Jody pushed Aaron off and looked for Anika. She'd been talking to the men at the door, and evidently one of them had hauled her outside when the cave-in started.

Aaron shook his head, sending a shower of dust plummeting to the ground. He hauled her to her feet, looking worried. "Are you all right?"

His concern touched a deep place in her heart. It would be so easy to love this man, if they weren't adversaries. For a fraction of a second, she wanted to lean against his chest and let the security of his strong arms make all of this go away.

A crowd had gathered outside, and Jody saw Tucker shoving his way forward. She knew he'd been out of town and was due to arrive on the train today. It looked as if she'd be losing her last ally.

"Surely you see now that this escapade of yours is unsafe." Aaron brushed off her shoulders, sending a delicious shiver charging down her spine.

Jody closed her eyes, willing herself to be strong. She couldn't give in now and let him win. "I suppose you'll just have to tell your workers to stop."

The incredulous look Aaron gave her would have melted many a woman's resolve, but she held her ground. Keeping one hand over her nose and mouth to keep the dust out, she slid her chair closer to the front door.

"Are you all right?" Anika leaned in the doorway, her arm around her husband's waist.

The lawyer glared at Jody. "You all could have gotten badly injured. This is one of the craziest stunts you've pulled, not to mention it's illegal. Mr. Garrett is well within his rights to prosecute you for trespassing."

Ashamed for raising her friend's ire, she studied the ground where the remaining cookies lay amid a pile of debris. She sincerely hoped she hadn't gotten her friends in trouble with their husbands as Aaron had said.

But wasn't that all the more reason to stay? If she left now, it would all have been for naught.

"You go on, Anika. And thanks for being here today. I appreciate the support."

As Tucker led his wife away, Jody tugged her chair as close to the door as possible without actually going outside, then sat down.

"Jo–dy!" Aaron ground out. "You cannot stay here. I won't allow it."

She hiked her chin. "You can't make me leave."

He clenched his fist. "I could pick you up and haul you right out that door."

She glared at him and tightened her grip on the arms of the chair. "You wouldn't dare."

He looked as if he were seriously considering it. She smothered that small, rebellious part of her that wished he would and maintained her stare.

Suddenly he pivoted and fled outside, down the stairs. Jody didn't know whether to be relieved she'd won or disappointed that he'd given in so easily.

Leaning her head back, she fought the tears that stung her eyes. Or perhaps it was just all the dust. Was she doing the right thing?

When Aaron had asked what she hoped to accomplish, she had no answer to give. She just charged in, barely even asking God what to do and not taking time to listen to His answer. Why did she always do that?

Was Aaron right? Would moving the orphanage be the best thing for the children?

Now that her anger had subsided, she could see the benefit of such a move. But there were no funds for such a venture even if they had land.

Yawning, she laid her head back. The heat of the day and the stress on her emotions, not to mention their near miss, had left her tired and unsettled. A little rest would make the long day pass more quickly.

Jody jumped at the sound of someone marching up the steps and realized she must have dozed off. A shadow darkened the doorway. Aaron stood there, along with the sheriff.

"There she is, Sheriff, just like I said. I've tried to reason with her, but she's the most unreasonable female I've ever met. I want her arrested for trespassing."

"Arrested?" Jody's heart stumbled, and her parched mouth suddenly went desert dry.

Aaron nodded, but it looked as if the sheriff was trying not to laugh.

"Are you going to come peaceably, Jody?" the sheriff asked, amusement lighting his eyes and making his thick mustache dance.

Jody clung to the arms of the chair. "I'm not going anywhere, and you can't make me." She winced, knowing how childish she sounded.

Aaron looked at the sheriff, and he nodded. Faster than greased lightning, they hoisted up her chair and carried her outside. The gathering crowd cheered and burst out in a gale of hoots and laughter.

"That's showing her who wears the pants," a man hollered.

"Git 'er, Sheriff," someone else cried out.

Jody gripped the arms of the chair and wrapped her feet around its legs, hoping she wouldn't tumble to the ground. Any other time this might have been fun, but now she was absolutely mortified. She knew her cheeks were flaming. How would she ever show her face in town after being thrown in jail?

After some jiggling around, Jody found herself in the adobe jailhouse. The thick wooden door clicked shut, and the hot, stuffy room darkened. She sat there in stunned disbelief.

How could Aaron do this, just when she was starting to care for him and even beginning to see how moving the orphanage might possibly be a good thing?

She'd been on the verge of giving in, but not now. Even though the town would benefit from a new hotel, she would fight Aaron Garrett tooth and nail.

Chapter 6

Aaron fiddled with his hat while he waited at the orphanage office to talk with Mr. Jacobson. The sheriff had suggested he'd have far better luck with the orphanage director than he ever would with Jody.

He pressed his lips together and sighed. It had been two days since Jody had spent those three hours in jail, and she still wouldn't give him the time of day. He was certain he'd agonized over the event far more than she had.

A flash of color caught his gaze. Outside the window, he saw Jody marching into view with a half dozen orphans following her like ducklings in a row. She tossed her head back and laughed at something a young boy said. Taking the boy's hands, she spun around in a circle, looking lighthearted and carefree.

The thought of that smile dimming when she saw him weighted him down. In spite of the trouble she'd caused, he couldn't help liking Jody. In fact, he much more than liked her; he was deeply attracted to the stubborn yet feisty spinster. That in itself amazed him, since he was usually so busy he only admired most women in passing.

But Jody wasn't most women. She had ridden in and made her mark on his heart faster than a cowpoke could brand a calf, and she wasn't even aware that she had.

The front door opened, and the children hurried in on a gale of chatter and clomping feet. Aaron's heart picked up speed. Jody entered right behind the youngsters.

"No running, and you all need to get cleaned up for supper." As she passed the doorway where he stood, her head turned, and her gaze collided with his. The smile on her face wobbled, then slipped. Her brows dipped. "What are *you* doing here?"

Jody crossed her arms over her chest and leaned against the door frame. In spite of her attitude, he was glad she hadn't run off at the first sight of him, though he couldn't help wishing she was happy to see him.

"I have a meeting." He stepped closer and didn't miss the apprehension in her gaze.

"With whom?"

"Jacobson." Aaron stopped a few feet away from her, admiring her wind-tossed appearance. "I wouldn't mind having dinner with you again."

Surprise widened her eyes, and she stared at him in disbelief. "Why in the world would you want to spend time with me after what I did?" She straightened, looking as if she were ready to flee.

Aaron shrugged, then allowed a smile. "Perhaps I'm a slow learner."

Her brows dipped. "Well, I'm not. I haven't forgotten the way you embarrassed me in front of the whole town and had me thrown in jail."

She'd never forgive for him for that. Perhaps it *had* been a mistake, but it was the only thing he could think of at the time to protect her. That building could have collapsed at any moment, right on top of her.

A door behind him clicked open, and Aaron turned to see Mr. Jacobson and another man he didn't recognize. After the two shook hands, the stranger nodded as he walked past Aaron and out the door.

"Come on in." Mr. Jacobson waved his hand toward the open door of his office.

Aaron looked over his shoulder, disappointed to find Jody gone. He knew he shouldn't cling to hope that she'd ever like him.

Taking a seat, he prepared himself for another battle. Perhaps he ought to just cut his losses and leave town, but he couldn't. The image of a new orphanage, located just outside of town, had engraved itself inside his mind, and he couldn't shake it loose. The children needed a champion.

Mr. Jacobson sat down behind his old walnut desk and rested his hands on its top. "So how can I help you, Mr. Garrett?"

Aaron shot a prayer heavenward. *Lord, if You're the One who put this plan for the children's home in my head, then I need Your help to bring it to pass.*

"I won't mince words, sir. I'd like to purchase the land the orphanage is on and help you relocate."

Mr. Jacobson's brows rose, and an amused smile tugged at his lips. "Jody isn't enough of a challenge for you? Now you have to take on the whole board of directors?"

Aaron wasn't sure if the man was teasing or serious, but he wasn't going to back down. Mr. Jacobson lifted his hand in the air when Aaron pressed his lips together.

"I'm well aware of your agenda, Mr. Garrett. I've talked with Jody—several times, in fact." Jacobson tapped his fingertips together. "This might surprise you, but I've actually been praying that God would make a way for us to move."

Aaron's heart skittered, then pounded a ferocious beat. He leaned forward, his elbows on his knees.

"This town has tripled in size since copper was discovered nearby. It's not the sleepy little town it was when Jody was young." Jacobson swiveled around and stared out the side window for a moment, then turned back. "I've talked with the board already. When I heard what you were about, I suspected you wouldn't waste much time in coming here. The board has agreed that we will sell you this property under two conditions."

Aaron sat up, smelling victory—both for himself and for the orphans.

Mr. Jacobson held up a stubby finger. "One—you *and Jody* must find a piece of land priced no more than what she and her friends have already collected. And two—you must persuade Jody that the move is in the children's best interest. Expanding the orphanage has been her dream for a long while, and she needs to be involved."

Aaron slumped back in his chair. The first item was more than reasonable, but the second? Was it possible to reason with Jody McMillan?

A smile tugged at his lips. Then again, he did love a good challenge.

"So you gonna marry me or not?" Elmer stood in front of Jody's desk, smelling like rank onions and covered in dust. His pudgy face was scrunched up, and a loud squeak sounded as he sucked on his eyetooth—a habit that never failed to irritate her.

She sighed and glared back. "Not."

Elmer's furry brows dipped. "Not what?"

How did the dense man ever run a successful business? Jody grabbed her handbag, thankful the workday was over. "I am *not* going to marry you. Why don't you ask the Widow Classen?"

Elmer stroked his chubby jaw. "Perhaps I will. That sauerkraut of hers is right special."

Jody shut the door and hurried across the street toward the boardinghouse, hoping he wouldn't follow. Her emotions had been swirling like a cyclone the past week. The board of directors had informed her that they'd told Aaron they would sell him the orphanage land if she and he could find a suitable place to relocate. Why did *she* have to help *him* find land?

She felt as if her family had betrayed her. Tears burned her eyes, and she bypassed the front door and headed down the alley to avoid questions from well-meaning folks. Fifty yards behind the boardinghouse, she stopped near a large cluster of beaver-tail cacti. She loved their vivid pink flowers that bloomed every spring, brightening the barren landscape, but now the prickly pear cactus was just thick, rounded pads with sharp spikes.

Like me.

As if she'd pricked her finger on the barbed bristles of the cactus, she flinched.

She wanted to argue with herself, but she knew the truth. She *was* as prickly as the beavertail around Aaron.

The man both attracted her and infuriated her. She wanted to flee his presence, and yet she longed to run into his arms. How was that possible?

She was fighting a losing battle. Tears burned her eyes and overflowed onto her cheeks. Was she upset about losing the home she'd been raised in? Or losing to Aaron?

Tilting her heard back, she looked up at the light blue sky. *Help me, Lord. Show me what to do. I don't want to be a stubborn, prickly cactus.*

The memory of Reverend McCurdy's Sunday sermon danced in her mind. He'd talked about having the faith of a tiny mustard seed. She knew the truth—ever since her parents had died, she'd had trouble trusting God. Oh, she believed in Him, but giving over control of her life and trusting Him were another thing.

Now she'd been boxed in. She had no choice but to search for property with

Aaron. She loved volunteering and working with the children too much to resist the board's request and risk developing a chasm between her and them.

She picked up a rock and tossed it at a yucca, relieving some of her frustrations. A roadrunner darted out from behind the spiny plant and took off across the barren landscape as if a coyote were on its tail. Nearby, a Gila woodpecker peeked its red-capped head out of the hole it had carved in one of the old saguaros. It flitted around, then took flight.

Being around nature helped clear her mind and soothe her restlessness. Even though this part of the country was dry and desolate, God had created beautiful creatures and plants for His people to enjoy.

She had longed for this freedom during her three hours in jail. Being shut away from the sun and wind had been horrible. Still, she knew Aaron would have been every bit within his right to have her locked away for a longer time, but he hadn't. He'd only wanted to teach her a lesson.

And he was right about moving the orphanage, too, although she still didn't want to admit it. Since Aaron had come to town, she'd paid closer attention to the children playing around the train tracks. Twice, older boys had taunted the engineer and stood right on the tracks as the locomotive was approaching. Its loud, plaintive whistle had cried out a warning, and the boys jumped off the tracks only a moment before the train squealed to a stop. As if it had just happened, her heart pounded out a ferocious tempo.

She looked heavenward. "All right, Lord. I'll help Aaron search for a new site for the orphanage, but You're going to have to do something about Elmer Brody, or I'll be looking for a new job."

Chapter 7

Jody fiddled with her skirt and tried not to let her shoulder hit Aaron's as the buggy dipped into another ridge in the rough road. She'd had a nice time riding around with him this afternoon, but she wouldn't admit it to anyone.

"So did you prefer any particular property over another?" Aaron made a smacking noise that sounded like a kiss to the horse to encourage it to keep moving.

A delicious shiver charged up Jody's spine. She shouldn't be thinking of Aaron and kisses in the same thought. After all, she was still upset with him, wasn't she?

She heaved a sigh. Arguing with herself could be *so* exhausting.

Aaron nudged her shoulder. "You awake?"

Jody hiked her chin. "Of course I am. I was just thinking." *Yeah, about the wrong thing.*

"So?"

Jody shrugged. "I don't know. I suppose the Nickerson farm is the best choice. It's close to town, near the creek, and has plenty of room for the children to run and play."

"Not to mention the farm has that big, fenced-in garden."

"It's sad the Nickersons died from that influenza epidemic we had here."

Aaron nodded. "Must have been tough on the people who found them dead."

Jody glanced at Aaron. "You don't suppose there could be any disease lingering there, do you? I'd hate for any of the children to get sick."

"I seriously doubt it. Besides, the children will be getting a new dormitory. The Jacobsons could live in the old farmhouse—or perhaps use it for the office."

As they pulled into town, ideas were flying in Jody's mind. Now that she'd caught the vision, she was starting to get excited about moving the children's home.

Aaron stopped the buggy in front of the café. "Supper?"

A heat other than the sun's warmed Jody's cheeks. She probably should say no, but they'd had such a nice time that she couldn't refuse. She nodded. "Dinner would be nice."

Aaron helped her down and kept his hands on her waist far longer than necessary. His gaze penetrated hers. She loved the color of his eyes. His tempting lips turned up in an enchanting smile.

"I had a nice time today. You'll have to favor me with another buggy ride soon, Miss McMillan."

Giddy—that was the only word that described the way she felt. When she wasn't arguing with or being mad at Aaron, she truly liked him. His impeccable dress and fine manners made him stand out in this little country town, yet it was his kindheartedness and gentle spirit that truly attracted her. Still, it wasn't proper to stand in the road staring longingly into a man's eyes. She stepped back and bumped into the buggy.

Aaron took the hint and offered his arm. "Shall we?"

Jody returned his smile and looped her arm through his. As he reached for the café door handle, the church bell started clanging, and her heart jumped into her throat. What could be wrong?

"What's that mean?" Aaron looked down at her, his brows furrowed.

"Something must have happened." She tugged him back into the street and toward the church.

Holding up her skirt, Elaine hurried toward her. "Oh, Jody, Pedro and Ray are missing."

Jody's heart all but stopped. Pedro, ornery as he could be, was one of her favorites. "How long?"

"No one has seen them since breakfast. They didn't come in for dinner or *siesta*, so we started searching but to no avail." Elaine wrung her hands together.

"Has the train been through? Could they have hitched a ride?" Jody couldn't stand the thought of the two young boys so far from home.

"No. This is Tuesday. No train today."

Jody clenched her eyes shut. Where could those rascally boys be? "We'll just have to search the whole town."

"Mr. Jacobson is doing that exact thing now." Elaine hurried toward the gathering crowd.

Jody sought out Mr. Jacobson and found him near the train depot. Aaron followed her, and as they drew near, she heard the orphanage director organizing a search party.

"You men"—he pointed to Elmer and two of his freight workers—"you search the north end of town. Doc, you, Parker, and Lane take the east side. Me and Truesdale will take the west." His concerned gaze fixed on Jody. "Jody, you and Mr. Garrett check south of town and be sure to check the livery well. You know how those boys love horses. The rest of you fellers pick a building and search it. Just make sure none of them get left out. All right, folks, let's find those boys."

The murmur of the crowd died down as people trotted off in different directions. Jody allowed Aaron to take her arm and guide her to the southern end of town. As they approached the weathered barn of the livery, Homer Sewell rode up on a bay mare.

"What's all the ruckus?" He dismounted and held the mare's reins in his big hand.

"Two of the orphanage children are missing." The words nearly stuck in Jody's throat. What if something happened to them before they could be found?

"I've been riding south of town, exercising my mounts, but didn't see hide nor hair of any young'uns." The big man lifted his hat and ran a dirty hand through his thin, greasy hair.

"Mind if we check in the livery?" Aaron asked.

Sewell shook his head. "No, sir. Not at all." He turned toward the livery doors, opened them, and stepped into the shadowy recesses.

A blast of heat that smelled of leather, hay, and horses slapped Jody in the face. She lifted her hand to her nose and allowed Aaron to guide her inside. As her eyes adjusted, she looked around. There were plenty of places a boy could hide, but she couldn't imagine them staying for so long somewhere this hot and stuffy.

Mr. Sewell opened the double doors at the back of the livery, allowing more air and light in. A gentle breeze drifted in, making the heat slightly more bearable.

"Pedro? Ray?" Jody slipped into the dark corners of the building, searching the shadows.

"I'll check the loft." Aaron headed for the ladder and deftly climbed upward, as if it were something he did daily.

Ten minutes later, their search unsuccessful, they stood behind the livery, watching Mr. Sewell ride off on another of his horses. He looked back over his shoulder. "I'll keep an eye out for them boys."

Aaron waved to him. Tears stung Jody's eyes. "What if we never find them? What if some mean miner kidnapped them to use as slave labor?" She sniffed.

"Hey now." Aaron took her shoulders and turned her to face him. "Don't even think that way. We'll find them."

Jody's throat burned, but Aaron's gentle massaging of her upper arms soothed her. "How can you be so sure?"

"I've been praying for the boys ever since I heard they were missing. The Bible says that not even a sparrow can fall without God knowing. He even knows the number of hairs on our heads, so He knows where the boys are. We just need to seek His counsel on where to find them." Aaron's lips turned up in a sympathetic grin. He tucked a strand of hair that had escaped her bun behind her ear.

Jody shivered with delight at his gentle touch but also with chastisement as she realized she hadn't even thought to pray about the boys. As usual, she'd charged forth in her own power. Would she never learn? Jody ducked her head, shamed to the core.

"Hey, stop fretting. We'll find the boys. Trust me." He lifted her chin with his finger and gazed into her eyes, pleading with her.

Her rebellious heart leapt at his nearness. She wanted to absorb his strength, but she'd had to rely on herself for so long that it was hard to lean on someone else.

"Jody." Aaron pulled her into his arms, and her tears gave way.

She clung to his shirt and cried, feeling good in the release of her fear and frustration.

He gently rubbed her hair. "You don't have to be tough all the time. It's okay to lean on people who care about you."

She wiped her eyes and tilted her head up, not quite ready to step from the security of his arms. "You care for me?"

Aaron grinned so widely her heart nearly stopped beating. "Isn't it obvious?"

She sniffed, thinking that throwing her in jail surely didn't prove his affection.

"Perhaps I've been too subtle." His eyes flamed with passion, and Jody's mouth suddenly went dry. He leaned forward, gazing intently at her as if waiting for an objection. Her eyes drifted closed of their own accord. His lips were warmer and softer than she'd expected, and his kiss set every speck of her being on alert. When he pulled back, his lips looked damp and his eyes warm.

Jody suddenly realized the inappropriateness of the situation and stepped back. As much as she enjoyed her first kiss, this wasn't the time for romance. Aaron seemed to sense that, too.

"So where now?" He lifted his hat and ran his hand through his dark, curly hair.

"I don't know." They wandered back down Main Street, listening to the calls for the boys coming from all directions.

Suddenly, like a light in a fog, a memory began to take shape in Jody's mind. She grabbed hold of Aaron's sleeve, and he turned toward her.

"What is it?"

Jody kept her eyes shut as the memory came into focus. Suddenly she opened her eyes and stared at Aaron, hope blossoming. "I know where the boys may be."

She grabbed Aaron's hand and dragged him down the street.

"Where are we going?"

"The boys used to play in the root cellar at the old mercantile."

"Root cellar? I never saw one there."

Jody glanced at him as she hurried on. "It's around back, where your workers were dismantling the day I—"

A tiny smile twittered on Aaron's lips. "Ah, yes. The day of the protest."

She scowled at him for finding amusement in something she took so seriously.

"I've had the men working out front since then, but they finished and were going to resume work on the back again today."

The thought of the boys lying hurt or worse flashed across her mind like lightning. Hoisting up the front of her skirt, she hurried around the side of the old mercantile, noticing how little of it remained standing. Her heart ricocheted inside her chest. *Please, God, let them be there and not hurt.*

She skidded to a halt near the cellar, but disappointment slowed her steps when she saw the doors had been covered with aged lumber from the building. There was no chance the boys could have gotten into the cellar with all that wood covering it.

Aaron must have noted her disappointment. He put a comforting arm around her shoulder and gave it a little squeeze. "It was a good idea, Jody."

She wiped her damp eyes. "Where do we look now?"

John, Aaron's lead worker, tipped his hat and tossed another board onto the pile, making a loud clatter. Jody jumped and gazed up at Aaron.

His eyes sparked, and he turned toward the man. "How long has this pile of wood been here?"

John wiped his sweaty forehead with his sleeve. "Not long, boss. We started piling it there this morning after we started working back here."

Aaron grabbed a board and slung it aside. "Get the other men. We need to clear these boards away."

"But why?" John brushed his arm across his sweaty forehead.

"Jody suspects the missing boys could be in the root cellar." He stopped tossing boards and glanced at John. "Were the doors open when you first started work this morning?"

John peered up at the heavens as if he was thinking hard, and then he nodded. "Why, I believe they were."

Aaron glanced at Jody and smiled. She was certain once the boards were cleared, they'd find the missing scamps down there. She just hoped they weren't injured.

Half an hour later, a crowd had gathered. Aaron tossed aside the last of the boards. The cellar door creaked open with a loud groan. An echoing clatter erupted when the door dropped to the ground.

Anxious and brimming with hope, Jody hurried to the steps and cupped her hand around her mouth. "Pedro? Ray?"

The crowd waited with hushed silence. Jody's hope wavered when there was no response.

"Hand me that lantern." Aaron motioned to Clint Stevens. Clint climbed over some of the discarded boards and passed the lantern to Aaron. He struck a match and the wick flamed to life.

Aaron gave Jody a wobbly smile. "You wait here."

He made his way down the rickety stairs, holding the light in front of him. As soon as his head disappeared in the dark hole, Jody hoisted her skirt and followed. If the boys were hurt, they'd need her comfort. The stairs screeched as she made her way down.

"They're here, thank goodness, but you don't mind too well." Aaron lifted up the lantern, illuminating the two boys huddled together asleep.

Her heart soared with relief when Pedro rubbed his eyes and looked up.

"Who's there?" he called in a hoarse voice.

"It's me, Jody. And Mr. Garrett."

"I'm hungry." Pedro shoved Ray. "Wake up. We can leave now."

Ray yawned, rubbed his eyes, and glanced around in confusion. "I'm thirsty."

Jody hurried across the dirty floor and pulled the boys into her embrace. "You had us all scared."

"Ray was scared, too."

The smaller boy shoved Pedro. "Nuh-uh. I wasn't."

"They found them!" Mr. Jacobson's voice boomed, setting off a chorus of muted cheers upstairs.

"Let's get out of here." Aaron raised the lantern, illuminating the small room. Go on up, boys. I imagine you'd like some supper."

Both children cheered and charged up the stairs. Jody looked at Aaron, gratitude warming her heart, though physically she was exhausted from their long day in the sun and then their searching.

"I had a feeling they'd be all right. God was watching out for them."

Jody nodded. "You were right."

Aaron grinned. "I could get used to hearing that. I suppose this reinforces my theory that moving the orphanage is the right thing to do."

Her initial happiness turned to irritation. "Well, you don't have to gloat."

His smile dimmed, and he lowered the lantern. "I'm not gloating. Just trying to get you to see the truth."

Jody stomped toward the stairs. She was tired, hungry, and dirty and wanted only to eat and then soak in a tub of cool water. "Well, you should be happy. You're getting what you want."

He grabbed her arm. "Wait a minute. This isn't about me or what I want. It's what's best for the children."

Jody yanked her arm from his grasp. "Yes, well, you won. You will have your hotel."

Aaron sighed. "This isn't a competition, Jody. I'll admit at first I may have felt that way, but once I saw the need for a new children's home, that's what drove me."

"And what happens when your hotel is built? What then?" She didn't want to hear his answer. She'd opened her heart to Aaron Garrett, and just like everyone she'd ever loved, he'd leave her. Her parents died, leaving her scared and alone. When she was fourteen, her best friend died from a tiny scratch that became infected. The children she loved either got adopted or moved away once they were old enough to live on their own, and even her spinster friends had all found love and left her alone.

Aaron's hand made a bristly sound as he rubbed it across his chin. "It will take quite a while to build a hotel. A lot can happen between now and then, but in the end, I suppose I'll return to Phoenix or search out another town to build in."

Jody closed her eyes against the stinging sensation. It was just as she thought. Aaron was leaving. She couldn't afford to lose her heart to a man who'd ride off someday and leave her behind. She was the only person who could protect herself.

"Well"—she hiked her chin—"it seems to me you're getting everything you want, Aaron. You ought to be quite happy." She stomped up the stairs, blinking back her tears.

"Not everything. . ." she thought he murmured as she stepped onto the hard ground.

Chapter 8

Aaron paced his small room at the boardinghouse. Rubbing the back of his neck, he stopped at the window and stared out. His own scowling reflection glared back.

Why had Jody reacted that way after finding the boys? She should have been happy, but instead, she seemed more irritated with him than ever.

Women! Who could understand them?

He pushed away from the ledge and flopped onto the bed, lying back, staring at the ceiling. A water stain marred the whitewashed wood. He pressed his lips together as he contemplated what to do.

Jody had responded almost eagerly to his kiss, but later she was as mad as ever at him.

And he had no clue why.

He hopped off the bed and crossed to the window again. Shoving aside the curtain, he stared at the inky pane as dark as his dreams.

"Lord, why did I have to give my heart to a stubborn, fickle woman who doesn't want it? Did I miss Your guidance?"

He was fooling himself to believe Jody could ever care for him. He'd allowed himself to hope, and now his heart was aching because of it. He paced to the door, pivoted around, and strode back.

A pair of laughing green eyes teased his memory. Once before he'd dared to love a woman. Florence had turned the heads of most men in Phoenix with her unparalleled beauty and lively personality. She'd done more than just snag his attention; she'd stolen his heart when he was but seventeen, then stomped on it when she quickly married a wealthy businessman. The joke was on her when Aaron unexpectedly inherited nearly a quarter of a million dollars from his grandmother on his eighteenth birthday.

He pulled out the desk chair and dropped into it. Jody and Florence were almost complete opposites in every way. He shouldn't be comparing them, but the one thing they had in common was that both women had staked a claim on his heart.

Aaron growled and jumped up. He jerked his suitcase out from under his bed. Jody had made her feelings clear. She had no interest in him—could barely tolerate him. He couldn't spend months in Cactus Corner building a hotel and seeing her all the time. The pain would be too great.

He slapped his belongings into the case and clicked it shut. Only one more thing to do.

Aaron pulled an envelope and a sheet of company stationery from his briefcase, then sat at the small desk and picked up the pen.

Dear Father,

After careful consideration, I have decided to use the alternate location as a hotel site. I will be leaving tomorrow for Banner Ridge. I have workers here clearing the property I purchased. With the vacant land being so near the railroad, it should sell for as much as I have invested in it. The orphanage next door is interested and will most likely purchase the property to expand their facilities.

I hope you and Mother are well.

I remain your loving son,
Aaron Garrett

He set the pen down and blew on the ink, then stuffed the missive into the envelope. Tomorrow morning he'd catch the train to Banner Ridge, leaving his heart behind in Cactus Corner.

Jody swirled the coffee in her cup and glanced around the café, knowing she wouldn't see the man she'd come to love. She'd looked for Aaron at the boardinghouse at breakfast the day after they'd found Pedro and Ray, hoping to apologize for her appalling behavior, but he never came downstairs. That evening she learned he'd checked out and left town.

"I still can't believe Aaron is gone."

Anika gave her a pensive stare, then a sympathetic smile. "I knew you cared for him."

Jody snorted. "Lot of good it did me."

Elaine patted her arm. "At least Elmer has turned his attentions on the Widow Classen. You no longer have him pestering you to marry him."

"Yes, that's something to be thankful for." Jody toyed with her fork, doubting she'd be able to eat the plate of food Etta would soon deliver to their table. Why had she been so mean to Aaron that night when they'd found the boys?

She was a coward, that's why—frightened that Aaron would up and leave town, breaking her heart, so she had tried to keep him at arm's length. She sniffed, and her lower lip trembled. The very thing she dreaded had happened sooner rather than later.

"Stop it." Anika lowered her brows, giving Jody a stern glare.

Jody blinked, her mind swirling. "Stop what?"

"All the what-ifs and why-didn't-I's."

Jody glanced at Elaine, who nodded her head. "You can't rationalize everything—wondering if the situation would have turned out better if you'd done things differently."

"But I drove Aaron away."

Anika squeezed Jody's fingers. "You need to leave all this in God's hands. If you and Aaron are meant to be together, God will work it all out. Fretting won't help."

Jody sighed, feeling the tension leave as she accepted her friend's advice. "You're right. I'll try harder to leave things in God's hands."

She took a sip of coffee, the cup clinking as she set it back in the saucer. "So are we in agreement to ask the board's permission to purchase the Nickersons' farm? It could be quite a long while before we raise enough money to build a dormitory, though."

Both Elaine and Anika nodded.

"Good. On Saturday I'll drive out to visit India and make sure she's favorable to the idea." Jody leaned back to allow Etta room to set down her meat loaf dinner. Suddenly her appetite returned. She might have lost Aaron, but he'd been right about moving the orphanage, and the children would be the real winners in the long run. Now all she needed were some creative ideas for raising some more money. . .and something to soothe her aching heart.

Monday morning, Jody grasped the arms of the wooden chair across from Tucker's desk, her heart dropping to the floor. "But I don't understand. How could the Nickerson farm be sold? Didn't Anika tell you we wanted to buy it for the orphanage?"

"Actually, no. She mentioned you all had decided on a place but never said which property. I'm terribly sorry, Jody, but there are other places that would probably work almost as well."

"But nothing as close to town that wouldn't need lots more work." Jody's hope sank as if it were trapped in quicksand. How could this be happening?

Fearing she'd burst into tears, she hurried from Tucker's office and made her way behind the building to avoid stares. Feet dragging on the ground, she wandered through the cacti, stopping in the shade of a giant saguaro. The shadow this particular cactus made reminded her of a cross with its stubby arms upturned, as if in praise to God.

Unshed tears burned her eyes, then dripped down her cheeks. Were all her dreams doomed to failure?

Aaron had been gone a week, and she missed him more than ever. Why hadn't she realized the treasure God had given her before she'd cast it away?

Leaning into her hands, she allowed her tears to flow. After a few minutes, she looked up, struggling to gather her composure. A woodpecker tapped at a nearby cactus, and the warm breeze teased her cheeks but did little to soothe her.

"I've made a mess of things, Lord. I thought I was doing what You wanted, but obviously I haven't been. Forgive me for rushing ahead with mule-headed stubbornness and not spending enough time seeking Your will. I don't know what You have planned for the orphanage, but I will continue to pray that You will direct and guide us. And if it's Your will, please bring Aaron back."

As if a cleansing rain had blanketed the parched land, Jody felt refreshed and relieved. She didn't always have to be the one to work things out. God was in control.

Chapter 9

Aaron held his breath, staring at his father. Instead of traveling to Banner Ridge as he'd planned, on a whim, he'd come home. "So what do you think?"

He'd just explained how he'd bought the Nickerson farm and donated it to the orphanage. Jody and her friends could use the money they had collected to build the new dormitory, since they wouldn't have to use it to buy land.

"I have to say I'm proud of you, son." Smiling, Phineas Garrett leaned back in his chair and laced his fingers over his midsection.

Aaron's heart leapt, and he sat numb with stunned delight. He'd finally heard the words he'd longed to hear for so many years, and they had come about not because of a successful building project, but simply from giving to someone in need.

"I know I've been hard on you, Aaron, but I didn't want you to grow up wealthy and spoiled. You're my only heir. I needed to know you would be a man of character and could run things after I'm gone." His father stared out the window for a moment, then captured Aaron's gaze again. "This whole orphanage deal proves to me that people are more important to you than money. You did a good thing."

A warmth like a steaming cup of coffee on a cool morning flowed through Aaron's being. His father was proud of him. This moment would always be one he cherished as a high point in his life.

Perhaps that was God's purpose in sending him to Cactus Corner—not to build a hotel, but to help the orphans and gain his father's respect.

If only he could get Jody out of his mind and heart.

Phineas leaned forward, a twinkling gleam in his dark eyes. "So tell me about this gal that's got you all hornswoggled."

Aaron blinked. Was it that obvious?

His father chuckled. "I may have been married thirty-five years, but I still recognize that look. Tell me what happened, son. Perhaps I can offer some advice."

Two days after his talk with his father, Aaron stepped off the train at the Cactus Corner depot. A nervous excitement surged through him at seeing Jody again. His father had said if he loved Jody so much as to mope around like he was, then he owed it to himself to make amends and see if they had a future together.

With carpetbag in hand, he crossed the street, and his gaze automatically swerved toward the old mercantile land. His crew had done a good job of clearing away the building. Behind the orphanage were tall piles of lumber he had donated to be used for firewood.

He turned around and headed toward the freight office—and Jody. But as he passed the orphanage again, his pace slowed as he noticed the words *For Sale* painted on the side of the adobe building. His heart jumped. This was what he'd wanted all along. He glanced at the freight office and then across the dirt road to Tucker Truesdale's office. Perhaps a quick detour was in order.

Aaron stepped into the lawyer's office and was suddenly assailed with the scent of beeswax.

Truesdale glanced up from his shiny walnut desk and smiled. "Good to have you back in town, Mr. Garrett."

They shook hands, and Aaron took the seat the lawyer indicated.

"So what can I help you with?"

Aaron leaned back, willing his insides to settle. Just perhaps, he'd win the woman he loved and get the land he'd wanted. "I'd like to buy the orphanage property if it's still available."

Truesdale smiled. "It is."

He named a price. For a brief second, the businessman in Aaron considered dickering over the sale price, but the money was going to a good cause. He quickly signed papers, put down a deposit, and agreed to have the remaining funds forwarded.

"So what did Jody say when you told her about the Nickerson farm?" Aaron laced his fingers to hold them steady. Had she been happy about someone buying that property and donating it to the orphanage? Had she figured out it was he?

Truesdale's brows dipped, and he sighed. "She wasn't too happy. Had her heart set on getting that property for the children."

Aaron blinked. "I don't understand. That's the whole reason I bought that land. Was there some misunderstanding?"

Truesdale leaned forward, head cocked to one side. "You may not remember, but you were rather upset and in quite a hurry to leave town that day. You purchased the land but never indicated it was to go to the orphanage. I couldn't breach confidence and simply told Jody the farm had been sold."

Aaron rubbed the back of his neck. Oh brother, what a fine mess!

A few minutes later, he stood outside Truesdale's office, staring at the Brody Freight Company window, thinking about all that had happened. He had given up on purchasing the orphanage land when he left town, but now God had turned things around and blessed him with the property. Would the same be true with Jody? Would she even be happy to see him?

Anxiety made his belly swirl. His heartbeat sped up as he stepped off the boardwalk and crossed the road. He hoped the woman he loved was in the building straight ahead.

He thought of how Jody's blue-green eyes sparked with excitement as she talked about her vision for the orphanage. He loved her fiery passion and loyalty to her cause. If only she were that passionate in her feelings toward him. His steps slowed as doubt crept in.

Before he informed Jody that he'd bought the Nickerson farm, he wanted to see her response to his presence. He wanted her to care for him, not because he was wealthy or had the means to make her dreams come true. He wanted her to love the man he was.

"Hey, clear the road!"

Aaron jumped at the gruff voice and the sound of harnesses jingling. He moved out of the road and put his foot on the first step up to the boardwalk. The freight office door jingled open, and an angel dressed in blue stepped out.

The sun shone down on Jody's golden hair, making it gleam. She squinted against the outside glare and pulled the door shut. He stepped onto the boardwalk just as she turned around. Her hand lifted and covered her brow. Suddenly her gaze shifted from questioning to surprised.

"Hello." Excitement mixed with unnatural shyness made his legs tremble.

"Aaron," she whispered. "You came back."

He flashed her a soft smile. "I couldn't leave things the way they were. You need to know how I feel."

Jody glanced around. Two scruffy miners passed by, giving them quick, curious stares. "Not here."

She grabbed his hand and pulled him behind the freight office and out onto the desert floor. Cacti of various sorts littered the barren land, along with a stubby tree or two. Closer to the creek, greenery grew in abundance. At the sight of Jody and him, a lizard darted under cover of a yucca.

Jody dropped his hand and turned to face him, looking as shy and anxious as he felt. "So what was it you wanted to say?"

Sweat trickled down his back as he stared into the eyes he loved so much, hoping to see affection staring back. "I couldn't just leave things as they were. I've been miserable since I left here. You have to know I care for you. Love you."

Something flickered in Jody's eyes, and she started crying. "Oh, Aaron. I'm so sorry for driving you off. I tried to find you to apologize for my irrational behavior, but you were already gone. Can you forgive me?"

"All is forgiven, sweetheart." He took his beloved's hands. Jody's warm smile took his breath away. "I love you, Jody. I know we haven't known each other long, so I won't mention marriage yet, but could I court you? Should I ask Mr. Jacobson's permission?"

Hope soared in his heart at her expression.

"I'm a twenty-six-year-old spinster, Mr. Garrett. *My* permission is all you need." Jody squeezed his hands and smiled. "You may come courting—and you may also talk marriage, if you're so inclined."

Aaron was sure his smile nearly reached his earlobes. "I'll have you know I aim to retire your spinsterhood status."

"That's perfectly fine with me." Jody laughed and fell into his arms.

Aaron wrapped his arms around her, holding her tight against his chest. His heart surged with love for Jody and gratitude to God. He gently set her back a little and leaned down, and their lips met. For a few too-short minutes, Aaron was in heaven on earth.

With regret, but knowing it was necessary, he pulled back. "I have a surprise."

"Another one?" Jody grinned, her pretty lips looking puffy and thoroughly kissed.

Aaron nodded. "I bought the Nickerson farm. Truesdale was supposed to notify the orphanage board that I purchased the land as a donation, but obviously I failed to make that clear to him."

He didn't think Jody's smile could get any bigger, but it did. "Oh, Aaron. That's so kind of you. We can use the money we've collected to start a dormitory right away."

He nodded. "I thought we could also buy a place in town to live when we're not traveling. That way you can still help out at the orphanage and visit your friends."

"Oh yes. That sounds perfect." Tears gleamed in her eyes, and she lunged back into his arms, but Aaron didn't mind one bit.

VICKIE MCDONOUGH

Vickie is an award-winning inspirational romance author. She has written four Heartsong Presents novels and five novellas. Her second Heartsong book, *Spinning Out of Control,* placed in the Top Ten Favorite Historical Romance category in Heartsong's 2006 annual contest. Her stories have also placed first in several prestigious contests, such as the ACFW Noble Theme, the Inspirational Readers Choice Contest, and the Texas Gold contest. She has also written book reviews for over five years and enjoys mentoring new writers. Vickie is a wife of thirty-one years, mother to four sons, and a new grandma. When she's not writing, Vickie enjoys reading, gardening, watching movies, and traveling. Vickie loves hearing from her readers at vickie@vickiemcdonough.com.

Harvest of Love

by Janet Lee Barton

Chapter 1

Roswell, New Mexico Territory, 1895

Liddy Evans flounced out of the bank, muttering to herself, "How dare he suggest such a thing? How could he even think I would agree to such an arrangement?"

At the end of the boardwalk, she gathered her skirts in one hand and slid a protective arm around her growing abdomen. Her mutterings continued as she stepped down onto Roswell's dusty main street and crossed over, dodging horse-drawn wagons and surreys. Safely across, she stepped up to the walk in front of Emma's Café, all the while fighting the tears that threatened.

Dear Lord, what am I to do? How can I save the farm Matthew worked so hard for?

Nothing had been easy since he'd been killed by a rattlesnake while watering his horse down by the creek. Now this. A whole different sort of snake to contend with. There would be an answer. *There just has to be,* Liddy thought as she entered her friend's establishment.

Liddy was relieved to find the café nearly empty. Since Matthew's death, and as her delicate condition became more obvious by the day, she dreaded the pitying looks she received from the townsfolk. They meant well. She knew they did. Still, she was not one to pity herself, nor did she want the pity of others.

She sat at a table and looked around. Cal McAllister was the only other person in the café. Well, at least she'd get no pitying looks from him. He had suffered his own loss a couple of years back and kept pretty much to himself. As soon as Emma finished serving him, she hurried over.

She took one look at Liddy's face. "It didn't go well, did it?"

Liddy untied her bonnet and shook her head.

"You just relax while I fetch you a cup of tea and a piece of one of your pies." She hurried to the kitchen before Liddy had a chance to tell her that she didn't have much of an appetite.

Liddy leaned back in the chair to ease her aching back. Closing her eyes, she took a deep breath and prayed silently. *Dear Lord, please help me find a way to keep the farm for my child.*

Emma set a cup of tea and a large wedge of apple pie in front of her as Liddy breathed an *Amen* and opened her eyes.

"What did old Harper say to drain the color from your cheeks, Liddy?" Emma asked as she took the seat across from her.

"He won't grant an extension. If I can't make the payment by next week, he'll foreclose." Liddy shrugged and took a welcome sip of tea. "You know what chance I have of meeting that deadline?"

Emma pounded her fist on the table. "That man! He hasn't given you a moment's rest since Matthew died. I'd like to have him run out of town."

Liddy managed a small smile. "Oh, wait. You haven't heard the worst of it. He say's he's willing to pay off the loan himself, if. . ."

"If what?"

"If I'll marry him."

Emma jumped to her feet. "What? Is he crazy?"

"Well, *he* says it's the only way out."

"Liddy, you aren't thinking of—"

"No. No!" Liddy shook her head adamantly. She shuddered and closed her eyes as though attempting to shut out her pain. "I could never do that. Not even to save the farm for my child."

When she opened her eyes, she saw Calvin McAllister at Emma's side. His gaze rested on Liddy, and his eyes were full of concern.

"I couldn't help but overhear part of your conversation, Mrs. Evans. Is Harper giving you problems?"

Liddy wasn't sure what to say. "I. . .he's. . ."

Emma turned to Calvin. "He's giving her problems all right, Cal. Harper is threatening to take away Liddy's farm unless she comes up with the payment she owes by next week."

Calvin looked closer at Liddy. "Are you that much past due, Mrs. Evans?"

Liddy opened her mouth to reply that the matter was really none of his concern, but Emma didn't give her a chance.

"She's not really behind at all. She's managed to make the payments from the small amount she and Matthew had saved before he died. But that money has run out, and for the last two months she's struggled to pay, but. . ."

"Emma!" Liddy was appalled that Emma was telling Calvin McAllister her life story. He was a neighbor of sorts, but she'd never really gotten to know him. Since his wife's death, he kept pretty much to himself. About the only time she did see him was when he brought his girls to church.

She'd sent Matthew over with food when his wife passed away, and he'd been at Matthew's funeral. Other than that, she knew nothing at all about this man. Thanks to Emma, he was learning an awful lot about her.

Emma only paused for a moment. "I'm sorry, Liddy. But you aren't going to be able to keep up this pace forever. I need the pies you make and the eggs you sell me. But that heavy laundry you are taking in is going to be too hard on you before long."

Liddy barely noticed when Cal sat down at the table. Emma just kept talking. "And the gardening is going to be too much soon."

"Emma! Stop. Please." Liddy could feel the heat radiating from her face. She'd never been so embarrassed.

Finally Emma stopped her tirade and slumped back into her chair. "I'm sorry, Liddy. I just hate to see you go through this much stress so close to the baby's coming" She clamped a hand over her mouth as if to keep herself from saying anything more.

Liddy sighed in exasperation. She looked up to find Cal's warm gaze on her, a half smile on his lips. She lifted her chin a notch. "I'm sorry Emma has subjected you to my boring life, Mr. McAllister." She glared at her friend. "She's usually more discreet."

Cal chuckled and shook his head. "I don't think we know the same Emma, ma'am. She's always been one to speak her mind to me." He sat up straight. "But I regret that you've been made to feel embarrassed. I know Emma worries about you, and I'm sorry that Harper is giving you such a hard time by threatening to take your land away. His practices leave much to be desired."

"Oh, you haven't heard it all. He'll pay off the loan if she'll marry him! That's. . ."

"Unethical." Calvin squared his shoulders and sat straighter in the chair. "Maybe I should go have a talk with Harper."

Liddy could stand no more. "No! I couldn't ask you to do that, Mr. McAllister. He'd only get mad and might decide to foreclose now."

"He can't do that, Mrs. Evans. Not legally. Not if your payments are up-to-date." His warm brown eyes met hers, and Liddy wondered why she had never noticed how good-looking he was.

She dismissed the thought with a shake of her head. "I can't let you do that. It's my problem. I thank you for your offer, though."

"Have you thought of applying for a loan at another bank?"

"Mr. McAllister, I'm a widow, with a farm that's too big for me to handle on my own. Who would give me credit?"

Cal leaned forward and propped his arms on the table. "Don't give up hope, Mrs. Evans. I think it's possible to get you out from under this stress. I'd like to help if I can."

Liddy was speechless. Calvin McAllister didn't know her. Why would he even want to try to help her? She watched as he unfolded his long legs and stood up. He dug in his pocket and pulled out some coins and laid them on the table.

"Mighty good lunch, Emma. And that was the best apple pie I believe I've ever tasted, Mrs. Evans. I'll be in touch with you soon." With that, he put his hat on and walked out the door.

Liddy looked across the table and watched a huge grin spread across Emma's face. Her friend got up and came around to hug her. "Oh, Liddy. I know Cal will come up with something! I don't know why I didn't think to ask him to help you before now."

"Emma, I can't believe it. You've been talking to him about me? Before today?"

Emma hugged her once more before reaching for their cups. "I just worry about you, Liddy. I thought he might have an idea of what to do. He's a good man. He'll come up with something. I just know he will."

Liddy couldn't think of a reply as she watched Emma head for the kitchen. She felt dazed. It'd been a long day. She'd been up gathering eggs at dawn, after putting six pies in to bake. She'd tended her garden and picked only the best and freshest produce to bring in to Emma. After she'd delivered it all, she'd gone to the bank to ask Mr. Harper, one more time, to give her an extension on this month's payment.

She sighed deeply. What good would an extension have been anyway? Another payment would still be due next month. . .and the month after that. There was no end to them. She wanted to keep the farm for the child she was carrying, but, at the moment, there just didn't seem to be any way to do that. Unless she married Harper. A shiver slid down her spine at the very thought and she shook her head. There was no way she could or would agree to that.

Emma returned with fresh tea, and Liddy welcomed it without speaking. After several sips, she felt the anger at her friend drain away. She met Emma's smile with one of her own and shook her head.

"What am I going to do with you, Emma? You shout my life story to anyone who'll listen; make a man I barely know feel that he has to help me, then you sit here grinning like the cat who caught the canary!"

"I'm grinning because, for the first time, I feel that you may be able to keep that farm you love so much. And that Douglas Harper might be thwarted in his plans to have that farm—and you."

Liddy hid her smile behind her teacup. Emma was the best friend she'd ever known, and as exasperating as she was right this minute, she wouldn't know what to do without her. "I can assure you. Douglas Harper may well end up with my farm. But he will *never* end up with me."

Emma chuckled. "That's a relief. For it would only be over my dead body that I would let you make such a deal."

"Thank you for wanting to help me, Emma. I really do appreciate it. But unless I can figure something out, I think I may have to take you up on your generous offer to stay with you until after the baby is born."

As though on cue, the baby kicked within her. Liddy smiled and placed her hand over the movement.

"My offer still stands. You know that. But now that Cal is trying to figure something out, I don't think it will come to that."

"You seem to have gotten to know him well." Was there something going on between Emma and Calvin? She'd thought that Emma was sweet on the new deputy in town, but. . .

"I think he just gets tired of his own cooking. And he brings the girls in a lot, too. He's really good with his girls, Liddy, but I think they need a woman's touch."

"How old are they now? I see them in church, but it's hard to tell."

"Grace is six, and Amy is nine, I believe. They're very sweet, but I think he could use some help with them."

Liddy arched her back, trying to ease the ache she frequently felt. "I'm sure it's not easy to raise children by one's self. I know the thought scares me at times."

Emma reached out and patted her hand. "You're going to do just fine. Any child of yours will be very lucky, indeed."

"I'm the lucky one. I have a part of Matthew left with me. I'll have someone to care for and love. I just wish that Matthew could have known a little one was on the way." Although she had suspected that she was in the "motherly way," she hadn't voiced her thoughts to Matthew. Her suspicions were confirmed only a few weeks after he died.

"I'm sure he does, Liddy," Emma tried to reassure her.

Liddy nodded. "Yes, I'm sure, too." She didn't need to sit here turning maudlin. She had work to do at home. "I'd better be on my way. You've got your supper crowd to get ready for. I'll get those pies and cakes to you first thing tomorrow." She eased to her feet and retied her bonnet.

She'd left her buckboard tethered around back, so Emma walked Liddy through the kitchen. The fragrant aroma of simmering stew greeted her as she entered the swinging door. Old Ben, who helped in the kitchen, looked up from his work. "How do, Mrs. Evans. Those sure were some pretty pies you brought today. They'll be gone in no time."

"Thank you Ben. I'm glad they sell well."

Emma called out after Liddy as she clambered up into the wagon. "You be careful, you hear? I think I might have to start sending Ben out after your deliveries soon. You could hurt yourself climbing in and out of that wagon."

"I'm fine, *Mother,* I promise." Liddy grinned at her friend. "I'll let you know when it gets to be too much for me."

"You'd better."

Liddy waved good-bye, and with the flick of the reins, the horse started for home. She told herself she was being silly. There was nothing Calvin McAllister could do. But, hard as she tried, she couldn't stop herself from feeling a small glimmer of hope. Maybe, just maybe, he *could* find a way to help.

Chapter 2

Calvin finished loading into the back of his wagon the last of his purchases from the Jaffa-Prager Company, Roswell's large general store. The girls would be out of school soon and he would need to pick them up. He wondered if Mrs. Evans was still at the café. He still had time to tell her what his banker had said. She might, just possibly, get out from under that swine, Harper. Too bad her husband hadn't known what kind of man he was dealing with when he bought the farm.

Cal had checked out both banks in town before he'd settled on one. Douglas Harper at Harper Bank had rubbed him the wrong way the very first time they met. The men at the Bank of Roswell had always been fair in their dealings. They were good Christian men. But Douglas Harper was another breed altogether. That man made his skin crawl.

He turned to cross the street just as Liddy Evans pulled her buckboard onto Main Street and headed out of town. For a moment, Cal debated about going after her, but his news would wait, and she'd looked awful tired at Emma's. There was something fragile about her. Maybe it was because she was expecting a baby and, he knew all too well, that condition could be more delicate than he'd once realized. Maybe it was that she was a widow and had no man to handle things for her.

He didn't know the reason for sure, but he did know this: Douglas Harper adding extra worry in her life right now bothered him. Bothered him a lot. Her farm wasn't far from his and he knew the land was good and fertile. What would Harper do with the property if he foreclosed? A lot of people had been looking for land in these parts lately. Maybe he just wanted to jack the price up and get richer. Or maybe he wanted it for himself. The place wasn't far out of town.

Cal pulled out his watch and looked at it. He would like to talk things over with Emma at the café, but it was nearly time for the girls to get out of school. He untied his horse, climbed up onto the wagon seat, and headed for the schoolhouse, but his thoughts remained on Liddy Evans's problem.

❧

Liddy sat by the fire brushing the shine back into her light auburn hair and thinking back over her long day. She loved working in her garden, baking for Emma's café, and taking care of her home. But she could do without the heavy laundry she took in.

She leaned back in the rocker and looked around her home. She would hate to lose this place. Matthew had worked so hard to build it, and their life had been here in these rooms. The parlor and kitchen spread across the front with two bedrooms behind. The house wasn't large, but there was room to grow.

Liddy had enjoyed adding her own touches. She'd worked as fast as she could on her mother's old sewing machine to make curtains for the windows. The quilts on the bed came from her childhood home. Matthew had always taken pride in the fact that she was a good housekeeper and an even better cook.

She went to take the steaming teakettle off the fire to brew a cup of tea. She missed pouring Matthew that last cup of coffee in the evenings. They used to sit by the fire, and he would tell about his day and all the plans he had for this place.

Liddy crossed the room and eased into the rocker with her tea. She leaned her head back and sighed deeply. She missed her husband, still. She missed the companionship, the closeness of married life. The baby stirred and kicked as if to let her know that she wasn't alone. Liddy smiled and patted the spot where he'd moved.

She was sure she would always miss Matthew, but she thanked the Lord that she'd been left with his child. She would have someone to love and care for. It wouldn't be long now. Just a few more months and she'd know if she had a little boy or a girl. It didn't matter to her which, but she'd always thought of the baby as a boy. She knew she'd be happy with either and just prayed that he or she would be healthy.

Liddy took a sip of tea and put the rocker in motion. She'd provide the best she could for this child, farm or no farm. But, oh, how she wanted to be able to keep it, to let this child know how hard his father had worked to build the place up. To be able to leave the farm as an inheritance to that child one day. But that might not happen. The possibility looked less and less likely with each passing day.

Liddy admitted to a hope that Calvin McAllister could come up with a plan to help her keep the farm, but she didn't have a clue as to what that could be. Still, he was nice to even offer.

She wondered again if he and Emma were sweet on each other and wished she'd asked her friend. She'd always thought of Cal as a loner, but he and Emma certainly seemed to know each other well. She wondered how hard it was for him to be raising two daughters without a wife, and her heart filled with compassion for them.

His girls were pretty little things and were always clean and neat when they were in church. They obeyed their father and were well-behaved during service. She wondered if they took after their mother or Cal. They had his dark hair, but both had blue eyes and fair skin. Cal's complexion was darker, probably from working outside so much.

He was a very good-looking man, Liddy had to admit. He was tall and muscular, with such warm brown eyes. And he did seem a decent man. For a moment, she felt a little envious of her friend. Then she quickly chastised herself. Emma deserved happiness. She should be happy for her.

Liddy shook her thoughts away. Well, she was sure there was no way Calvin McAllister could help. Douglas Harper wasn't going to give her an extension on paying the rest of this month's payment. He'd told her that he'd been too lenient as it was by letting her pay by the month. And there was no way to be sure about the crop this year.

The alfalfa was there. Matthew had planted it two years ago, and they'd had a really good harvest last year. It was growing nicely now, and the future of a good crop looked bright. But there was no money left to meet the payments on the loan Matthew had taken out for farm equipment and improvements. And when it was time to harvest, what then? Liddy couldn't do it herself, and there wasn't enough money left to hire help.

Well, she couldn't hire anyone, and that was all there was to it. And she was doing all she could to bring in money now. She simply didn't have enough energy or hours left in a day to do more.

The clock chimed the hour, and Liddy realized that if she was going to get up early and get the wash on the line and her baking done before the kitchen heated up, she'd better get to bed. She banked the fire and picked up the lamp. After making sure everything was locked up tight, she went to her room.

She turned down her bed, slipped under the covers, and reached for her worn Bible. God's Word brought her comfort as nothing else could. After reading several psalms, she blew out the light and said her nightly prayers. She closed her eyes, knowing that her life was in His hands, and no matter what happened with the farm, He would see her through.

❧

The next day dawned bright and sunny. Cal hadn't slept well at all. He'd spent the better part of the night trying to figure a way to help Liddy Evans. After the restless night, he had to admit to himself that his offer to help was more than just trying to be a good neighbor.

He was attracted to her. Yet, considering her condition, he knew this fact was not something she would want to know. But he wanted to get to know her better and to find some way to help her keep her farm. He kept thinking about Mary and what if it'd been his wife who was trying to keep his place together for the girls. To think that a man like Harper would try to take advantage of a situation like that infuriated him.

Cal listened to the girls prattle as he took them to school. They were good girls, but they needed a woman's touch. Little Grace could barely remember her mother, and Amy was getting to an age where she needed a woman to teach her all kinds of things. She'd shown an interest in learning how to cook, but he was doing all he could do to get any kind of a meal on the table. And, the way he figured it, his cooking shouldn't be taught anyway. It simply wasn't that good.

The girls never complained, though. He grinned to himself. But they sure were happy when he fed them at Emma's place. He felt they needed better meals than he prepared, so he made sure they stopped at Emma's several times a week.

He'd tried to hire someone to come in and cook for him and the girls, but none of the ladies in town wanted to make the drive out to his ranch. Besides, the married ones had more than enough to do just taking care of their own families. There just wasn't a wealth of women in Roswell to begin with. Most of those that weren't married either had their own businesses, like Emma, or they simply weren't the kind of women he'd want his girls around. So, he plugged onward.

When he passed Liddy's place, the idea hit. A good idea. One that would help her out and certainly help him, too. Why hadn't he thought of it before? Cal flicked the reins and hurried the team along. He would drop the girls off and head for Emma's. He'd burnt most of the bacon this morning and given the best pieces to the girls. He could use some breakfast, and if need be, he'd wait out the rush hour so he could run his idea by Emma. But he knew already what she'd say. This idea was a good one. He just knew it was.

Liddy pulled up to the back of Emma's Café. Three cakes and three more apple pies sat covered with cloth on the floor of the wagon. Ben rushed out to help her carry them in.

"Just in time, Mrs. Evans. A few minutes ago, Miss Emma served the last piece of pie we had in the kitchen. She told me to ask if you would have time for coffee this morning."

Liddy set the last pie on the worktable in the kitchen and smiled at the old man. "I'll make time, Ben. She's out front?"

"Yes, ma'am, she sure is."

Liddy headed through the swinging door into the dining room. She knew Emma always had a crowd for breakfast, but by this time of day, the café would be clearing out, and only those who had time to savor a second cup of coffee would be left.

Emma looked up from the cash box and grinned at her. "I'm so glad you are here. Cal's been waiting for you."

Surprised, Liddy looked around the room and found him at a table by the front window, looking into his coffee cup as if he were a million miles away.

"Cal? You mean, Mr. McAllister?" She wasn't thrilled when her heartbeat sped up.

Emma grabbed her by the hand and practically dragged her across the room. "One and the same. He wants to talk to you."

Was it possible? Had he come up with an idea? Liddy was afraid to hope, but that was exactly what she did as Cal looked up at her and immediately got to his feet.

"Mrs. Evans. I was hoping to have a chance to talk to you. Would you join me for breakfast or a cup of coffee?"

Emma gave her a little shove and she found herself sitting in the chair across from Calvin McAllister. "I. . .ah. . .I'll take a cup of tea, thank you."

Emma immediately scurried away and was back in a flash with a clean cup and a fresh pot of tea. She filled Liddy's cup and then said, "If you'll both excuse me, I have things to do in the back."

Some friend, Liddy thought, as Emma disappeared into the kitchen. *She spills my life history to the man and then won't stick around to see what he has to say.*

Cal cleared his throat and brought her attention back to him. "Mrs. Evans, I think I may have come up with a plan to help you and myself in the process. I. . . uh. . .I have a proposition I'd like to put to you."

Liddy felt color flooding her face. Another one? What was wrong with the men in this town? She was a widow, not a year yet, not to mention, *she was with child.* She started to stand.

Cal got to his feet once more and held out his hand. "Oh, no, Mrs. Evans. Not like that. What I meant to say was. . .a *business* proposition. Nothing like Harper. Please. Stay and hear me out."

Chapter 3

Liddy looked into Calvin's eyes and saw the earnestness in his expression. Maybe she had jumped to the wrong conclusion. She hoped so. She settled back in the chair.

"All right, Mr. McAllister. I'll hear you out."

He sat back down and let out a sigh. "I'm sorry. I don't always think before I speak." Liddy's heart did a little flip at his smile. He looked like a little boy trying to talk his way out of a jam.

"First, I talked to my banker. He'd like to help, but you were right. His board of directors wouldn't consider you a good risk."

Liddy felt her heart drop. She knew that, but still she'd allowed herself to hope. She nodded. "I expected as much, Mr. McAllister. All the same, I thank you for trying."

"He did have another idea, though. He suggested that you lease part or all of the land."

Liddy's eyebrows drew together. "Lease it?"

Cal leaned back in his chair and grinned at her. "That's where you let someone else farm your land. They pay you for using it, usually after harvest, from the profits off the crops."

Liddy spread her hands out and shook her head. "That's something I wish I'd known earlier, Mr. McAllister. It won't help me now. I don't have time to wait for harvest."

Cal leaned forward and pushed his plate out of the way, propping his forearms on the table. "I realize that, but what if someone paid you half up front and the balance at harvest?"

Liddy leaned back in her chair and chuckled. "That would be wonderful, but I don't think that's likely to happen."

"If you'll agree to let me lease your land, it will."

"You? But, well, I—"

"I had a really good crop last year, and I've wanted to expand for some time now. I'd appreciate it if you would lease to me, Mrs. Evans. I'd give you a fair price."

Liddy could only gape at the figure he gave her. She wasn't sure she could believe her ears. This was the way out. With the advance on the lease, she could pay ahead until harvest, and with the final payment from Mr. McAllister, she would be able to pay the balance for the year.

"Mr. McAllister, I don't know what to say. Of course I accept your offer. I. . .thank you."

Cal rubbed the back of his neck and smiled at her. "I'm glad. I do have another favor to ask you."

A favor to ask her? After what he was offering to do for her? "Of course; what can I do for you?"

"You know I have two daughters? Grace is the little one and Amy is my oldest."

"They are very pretty little girls, Mr. McAllister." Liddy wondered where he was leading with this.

"Well, I'm not a very good cook. And I don't know how to teach them how. Wouldn't want to teach them to cook like I do, anyway. I tried to get a housekeeper. Even ran a few advertisements in the paper, but got no answer."

Did he want her as a housekeeper? He wasn't suggesting anything more, was he? After Douglas Harper's proposition, she was more than a little apprehensive.

"You want me to be your housekeeper?"

"No. No! I just want you to teach Amy a little about cooking and both of them how to help me keep house. I don't expect her to cook five-course meals or anything like that. Just maybe learn a few things that would help me out. And I don't expect them to do heavy cleaning, just maybe how to dust and pick up?"

Liddy couldn't contain the burst of relieved laughter that escaped. "Oh, that's it? That's all you want me to do?"

"Seems like quite a lot to me. I don't have the first idea how to go about teaching them the things their mother would have been teaching them."

Liddy's heart went out to the man. She wasn't going to have any idea how to teach her child, if it were a boy, all the manly things he needed to know.

"I'll be glad to take your girls under my wing, Mr. McAllister. It will be a pleasure."

"I'll pay you extra—"

"No, sir, you will not."

"Yes, ma'am, I will. With teaching the girls those things, you won't be having time to take in that laundry anymore. And I won't take charity from you any more than you would take it from me."

"But—"

"No arguments." Cal shook his head. "I'll not ask you to take on more work and give up income to do that, without paying you." He held out his right hand. "Do we have a deal, Mrs. Evans?"

Did they have a deal? Did he think she was crazy? Or was he crazy? Either way, there was only one answer as far as Liddy was concerned. "We have a deal, Mr. McAllister."

Her hand was swallowed by his larger, work-callused grip in a shake that sent little splinters of electricity up her arm. The jolt was an unwelcome surprise. Liddy quickly pulled her hand back.

"When, ah, when do you want me to start with the girls? After school today?"

Cal shook his head. "Not today. You need time to let the people you've been doing wash for know that you'll no longer be available. Why don't we start Monday? That will give you several days to get things in order and get some rest."

Dear Lord, thank You. I don't know why You sent this man into my life, but I thank You for this blessing.

"That will be fine, Mr. McAllister. I'll be looking forward to meeting your daughters." Liddy took a sip of tea, not sure what to say next. How did you say thank you to someone for saving your life?

"I think this is going to work out well, Mrs. Evans. I'll have my lawyer draw up the lease agreement, unless you'd prefer to have yours—"

"No, that's fine. I trust you, Mr. McAllister."

"I'll have a bank draft drawn up and bring it to you. Will you be in town for a while? If not, I can drop the draft by your place."

"I have some supplies to pick up. I'll wait, if you don't mind. Then I can take the payment to my bank and get that debt off my mind."

Cal grinned at her. "And I'll even accompany you, if you'd like. I wouldn't mind getting a look at Harper's face when you make that payment."

Relief replaced her dread of facing Douglas Harper by herself. "Thank you. I think I'll take you up on that offer. I don't like. . ." How could she say she didn't like the way the man leered at her? There was something about Harper that made her heart grow cold each time she was in his presence. She'd be glad for the company.

"I don't like him much myself. I'll find you around town and we'll go over together." Cal stood up and put coins down for his bill. He put his hat on and lowered the brim at Liddy.

"Ma'am, I'll see you a little later." With that, he turned and walked out the door.

Liddy willed her heartbeat to slow as she looked around for Emma, wanting to share the news with her.

Emma appeared at her elbow almost immediately. She poured them both a fresh cup of tea and set between them a plate of sweet rolls from the batch that Liddy had baked and delivered yesterday.

"Oh, Emma." Liddy felt dazed. She still couldn't believe what was happening. She shook her head, and then threw it back, her laughter filling the dining room.

"You said yes! Oh, Liddy, I'm so glad. This is the answer to your problems." Emma reached out and clasped Liddy's hands with her own. "I told you Cal would find a way."

"I can't believe it, Emma. Why didn't I think of leasing my land?"

"Well, there's not a lot of leasing done around here. I did hear that Douglas Harper has been buying up all the land he can. I guess some people would rather sell than lease, but for you it seems to be an answer to a prayer!"

"Oh, Emma, it is. Do you realize that I can pay several months ahead with the bank payments, and with the earnings from the harvest, I might be able to pay up until next year?"

Emma nodded at her. "And, what's even better, Douglas Harper will have to leave you alone."

"Praise the Lord! Oh, Emma, He does know our needs and finds the best ways to fill them. You're a very lucky woman, you know."

"Me? I've got a lot of blessings, to be sure, but I'd think you are the lucky one today, Liddy. To have Calvin McAllister taking up your cause. . ."

"Emma, are you upset that he's helping me?"

"Upset? Liddy, I'm delighted! You should know that."

"It won't cause problems between the two of you, to have his girls at my house, and him letting them off and picking them up?"

"Liddy, the day's events must have scrambled your mind." Emma looked confused for a moment, then burst into laughter. "So that's it? You thought Cal and I were interested in each other?"

Liddy grinned and nodded her head.

Emma wiped tears from her eyes and shook her head. "Oh, Liddy, you are such a goose. Cal is a wonderful man, but, no, we are *not* interested in each other that way. He's just become a good friend." She leaned closer to Liddy and whispered, "Besides, I have my sights set on that new deputy in town."

The relief Liddy felt was more than it should be, considering her current condition. Yet, knowing that fact didn't keep it from washing over her, just the same. "Well, when are you going to let the deputy in on how you feel?"

Emma snorted delicately. "Not until I'm certain the feeling is mutual. He's about as dense as a horse, that's for sure."

Liddy laughed again and, as she did, she realized that she hadn't done much laughing in a long time. It felt really good to join her friend in shared fun.

She gathered her purse and stood up, brushing crumbs from her dress. "I'd better get my shopping done. Cal—Mr. McAllister—is going to bring me a draft to take to the bank before I leave town. He's even going to go with me when I make the payment."

Emma stood, too, and began to clear the table. "Oh, wouldn't I love to be a mouse in the room. Douglas Harper isn't going to be very happy today."

"I know. But I surely am!" Liddy grinned at her. She waved to Emma and, though she felt like twirling out the door, she forced herself to step sedately out onto the boardwalk.

Chapter 4

Liddy took a deep breath and pondered how much brighter the day had become. The sky was a cloudless blue, the sun warm. Her heart was singing for the first time since Matthew's death. She would be able to keep the farm he'd worked so hard to start, and she would be able to take care of the child that grew in her womb. God was so good. Over and over again, she silently gave thanks as she made her way to Jaffa-Prager Company.

Letting herself relax, she wandered across the store selecting her purchases, and was only half-finished when Cal found her.

"Are you ready to take a load off your mind, Mrs. Evans?" He handed her the bank draft.

Liddy looked at the amount and her spurt of laughter brought curious looks from the other shoppers. "I'm ready, Mr. McAllister." She took the arm he offered and told the storekeeper that she'd be back shortly to finish her shopping.

The walk to the bank was short, but not too short for Liddy to feel protected in a way she hadn't in months. She missed the courtesies of having a man to guide her across the rough and dusty streets, to open a door for her.

They entered the bank, and it took a moment for Liddy's eyes to adjust from the bright outdoors to the dimness of the interior. She walked up to the teller.

"I'd like to deposit this into my account, please." She handed him the slip of paper. "And then I'd like to write a draft out to the bank for the balance of my note payment this month and also make next month's payment."

The teller looked at her and shot a nervous glance at Cal, before looking toward the back of the building. "Yes, ma'am. I'll. . .I'll get the amount of that payment and be right with you." He quickly hightailed it from behind the teller's cage to the door of Harper's office.

He'd barely entered before he reemerged, Harper shoving him out of the way as he headed toward Liddy and Cal.

"What's this, Liddy? You've come to pay your note? After our talk yesterday, I thought—"

"You thought there was no way I would be able to meet my obligations, Mr. Harper. But here I am."

"Yes, well, why don't we talk about it? If you'll just step into my office. . ." His pudgy hand motioned to the room he'd just left.

Liddy shook her head and smiled. "There's no need to talk. I have the payment right here. If your clerk will be so kind as to deposit this draft into my account and let me write my own out to the bank, I'll be on my way."

"But, Liddy, I'd be interested to know how you came into this money. Have you sold your land?"

Calvin stepped up. "No, Harper, she hasn't sold out. She's agreed to lease her land to me."

"Lease? To you?"

"That's right."

"I didn't know that you were wanting to expand, McAllister."

Cal cocked an eyebrow. "No reason I can see why you should know."

"Yes, well. . ." Harper looked away and glared at the teller. "Deposit Liddy's draft and let her write her own to the bank, Nelson."

Cal smiled at the clerk. "And please make sure *Mrs. Evans* gets a receipt for her payments."

Harper blustered. "Yes. . .well. Nelson, see to it." He turned on his heel and scurried back to his office.

Cal watched as the clerk finished the transaction and Liddy had the receipt firmly in hand. He crooked his arm and smiled down at Liddy. "I'll see you back to the general store, Mrs. Evans."

Once out into the bright sunshine again, Liddy turned to Cal and released a huge sigh of relief. "Mr. McAllister, again, I thank you. I believe I'll sleep well tonight."

Cal inclined his head. "I hope you do. If you're feeling up to it, we can walk over to my lawyer's office. He should have the contract ready by now."

Suddenly, the realization struck Liddy that he'd put his trust in her by giving her the draft before they'd even signed the contract. She wanted to honor that trust as soon as possible. "Let's go get those papers signed."

The attorney's office was light and airy compared to that of the bank. Cal's lawyer saw them both into his office and went over the simple contract. Liddy had no reason to feel apprehensive about anything. The agreement was for a year at a time, with options for her to agree or not, to each renewal.

After being asked if she had any questions, she signed over the right to farm her husband's land to another man. But she didn't feel the least bit bad. It was what Matthew would have wanted her to do, to keep the land for their child.

The lawyer shook their hands, and Cal took her elbow to lead her outdoors once more. He saw her back to the general store as promised, then turned to her. "Thank you for trusting me with your land, Mrs. Evans. I promise to take good care of it."

Liddy shielded her eyes from the lowering sun. "I know you will, Mr. McAllister." She smiled at him. "And I promise to take good care of your girls."

"Speaking of whom, I'd best be picking them up from school. I know they're going to be excited about having you teach them." He tipped his hat and smiled down at her. "I'll be talking to you, ma'am."

Liddy watched him walk toward the schoolhouse before she turned into the store. The realization that she no longer had to pinch her pennies quite so hard made her feel quivery on the inside. She still couldn't quite take it all in. She might actually buy a length of material to make another dress. She'd let out what she had as far as they would go. And she still had weeks to go before the baby was due.

However, as she looked at the colorful bolts of material, she realized how exhausted she was from the day's events. Or was it just the lifting of the worry that made her feel ready to drop? No matter. She just wanted to get home, to think about all that had happened, and to enjoy the knowledge that she wouldn't have to move.

She hurriedly gathered up the rest of her purchases, adding a tin of her favorite tea to the pile. The boxes were totaled, loaded into her buckboard, and she was on her way home.

Liddy passed the school on her way out of town and saw Cal helping his daughters into his wagon. They were both talking to him at once, and she could tell by the smile on his face that he was enjoying their excitement.

In her haste to get back home, she forgot to tell the hotel that she wouldn't be doing the wash for them anymore. *Oh, well,* she thought, *the matter can wait.* She had to deliver fresh linens to them tomorrow.

She grinned to herself. They would simply have to find someone else to wash their dirty laundry.

At home, she carefully unloaded her purchases. She must ask Mr. Carmack to make the packages lighter for a while. Her back was aching by the time she finished, but she knew if she sat down, she'd never get her afternoon chores finished.

After putting the kettle on for tea, she changed into her everyday dress and a fresh apron. She made a cup of tea and let herself pause to look out the front door at the land that she would now be sharing with Calvin McAllister. Things might not be working out the way she'd thought they should, but they were working out.

She hoped his daughters would be open to learning what she could teach them, and she prayed that the Lord would show her how to be sensitive to their feelings. They might possibly resent being taught by someone who wasn't their mother. Her heart filled with compassion for them. After the last few days, she was sure Calvin was a good and loving father to them, but still, he could only do so much.

Liddy sighed as the thought reminded her that she'd have the same problem soon. To try and be both mother and father to a child was a daunting thought. She must trust the Lord to lead her. She turned from the doorway and went to get her laundry basket. The sheets she'd washed that morning would be dry by now. She still had much work to do before she could relax.

Calvin pointed out Liddy's farm as he drove the girls home.

"That's it, Papa? That's where we're going to learn to cook and clean?" Amy asked, her voice rising with excitement.

"That's it, darlin', and I think you are going to really like Mrs. Evans. She's a nice lady."

Grace craned her neck as they drove by. "Is that her out at the clothesline, Papa?"

Cal turned his head and saw Liddy at the clothesline, struggling with a sheet. He turned the wagon around and pulled into her yard. "Stay here, girls."

His long stride took him quickly to Liddy's side, and he pushed her hands away from the sheet. "Didn't you let these people know you won't be working for them any longer?" he asked, his tone rougher than he intended.

"Mr. McAllister, what are you doing here? No. I didn't let them know. I was tired and figured to tell them tomorrow when I take this laundry in to the hotel." Liddy stood aside as he quickly added the sheet to the pile already in the basket.

He picked it up easily and headed for the house. "Where do you want these?"

Liddy hurried ahead of him. "On the kitchen table will be fine. Thank you."

"You shouldn't be doing this kind of work." Cal noticed her shortness of breath as she hurried beside him, the faint shadows beneath her eyes. She was exhausted.

He couldn't help but notice how neat and clean her home was. Next to his, it would have been impossible not to make the comparison. She motioned to the table, and he set the basket down. "You will tell them tomorrow? That you won't be taking in their wash anymore?"

Liddy smiled at him, but he didn't miss the fact that she'd placed a hand at the base of her back. Obviously, her back was bothering her. "I'll tell them, Mr. McAllister. And I have you to thank that I won't be needing to do it anymore."

Cal nodded. He just wished he'd been able to help sooner. "Well, I guess I'd best be getting the girls home."

"They're outside? May I meet them?"

"Of course. They were very excited to learn that you will be teaching them to cook and clean." He went to the door and motioned for her to go in front of him.

The girls were patiently waiting, but he could see them smiling as he and Liddy moved closer to the wagon.

"Mrs. Evans, I'd like you to meet my daughters. The little one is Grace, and the older one is Amy." A sense of pride swept over him as his girls both smiled at Liddy.

"Pleased to meet you, ma'am," Amy said. Grace nodded her head in agreement.

"It's very nice to meet you both. I'm looking forward to our time together."

"Are we really going to learn to cook, Mrs. Evans?" Amy asked.

"You certainly are."

Amy's smile lit up her face. "Oh, I'm so glad. Will we learn to cook something besides bacon and beans?"

Liddy chuckled and slid a glance toward Cal.

He joined the laughter. "Now you know what my girls live on, mostly."

"I promise I'll teach you to cook more than bacon and beans. Although those are things you'll need to learn, too. But we won't start with them."

Grace clapped her hands together. "Could we learn to make desserts? We only have them when we eat at Miss Emma's. Those sure are good pies at Miss Emma's."

"Well, you are in luck, Grace," Cal said. "Know who makes those pies?"

Grace shook her head.

Cal reached out and tousled her hair. "Mrs. Evans makes them."

Grace's eyes grew round with delight as she looked at Liddy. "You do? Really?"

"Will we learn to make pies, too, Mrs. Evans?" Amy fairly bounced in the seat.

"I promise to teach you to make pies."

Both girls clapped their hands. "Oh, I can't wait to get started, Mrs. Evans," Amy said.

Liddy smiled at both girls. "I'm looking forward to it myself."

"Well, I guess we'd better be on our way." Cal looked down at Liddy. He was pleased that she and the girls had obviously taken a liking to each other. Liddy Evans was going to be good for them.

"I'll look forward to Monday, Grace and Amy," Liddy said. "But I'll see you in church on Sunday, too."

Cal turned before he climbed into the wagon. "You try to get a little rest before then, you hear?"

He watched as a faint pink color crept up Liddy's cheeks. She waved a good-bye to them all as she nodded and replied, "I'll surely try, Mr. McAllister."

"Papa, she's really nice, isn't she?" Amy asked when their wagon turned onto the road.

"She really is, Amy."

"Papa, is she going to have a baby?"

Cal nodded. "Yes, she is. I want you girls to be very good for her and mind what she says, you hear?"

Grace leaned her head against him. "We will, Papa."

Amy met his eyes and smiled. "We will," she assured him. "Where's her husband, Papa?"

"She's a widow, honey."

"Oh. She must be very lonesome. But she will feel better when the baby gets here."

Cal hadn't let himself think about that. Liddy probably was very lonesome. He had his girls, yet still, he felt lonesome at times. Now he looked over at their shining heads and wondered what he would do without them. He smiled at Amy, wanting to reassure her. "You're right. She'll feel much better when the baby gets here, honey. I'm sure she will."

He knew from experience, this was true. But, while children could carve out their very own spot in one's heart, they couldn't fill that soul-deep void that came with the loss of a mate. Alone in her home, with her child not yet here, Cal was sure that Liddy Evans felt that emptiness very acutely. He hoped having his girls around would help.

Chapter 5

Liddy poured herself a cup of tea and carried it to the rocker. She sat down with a sigh of relief. Her work was done for the day. The sheets were ironed and folded and put neatly into the baskets. No longer would she have to do mountains of laundry for other people. She leaned her head back and smiled.

Calvin McAllister's daughters were delightful, and she found herself really looking forward to teaching them. He'd done a good job on his own. They were polite and well behaved. Seeing the job he'd done, she felt that there was hope for her to raise her own child alone.

He was a good man. It had felt good to have him carry in the basket of sheets. It'd been so long since she'd had anyone around to do the simplest things for her. She still couldn't quite take in the fact that she didn't have to worry about Douglas Harper foreclosing on her farm.

Dear Lord, I thank You for bringing this man into my life. For letting there be a way for me to keep the farm. You've always seen to my needs, and I'm sorry I worried so.

The Scriptures were right. One shouldn't worry about tomorrow; it would take care of itself. The Lord would see to tomorrow.

Liddy sipped her tea and thought about the next week, and how nice it would be to have the girls around. She would try to teach them simple, basic cooking at first. And of course, desserts. Pies had always been her favorite thing to prepare. She didn't find them difficult, as some women did. She hoped she could teach the girls in a way that would make it easy for them.

A huge yawn escaped her and she hurriedly finished her tea. It was time for bed. Tomorrow she would plan some more. She wished she knew what foods Mr. McAllister particularly liked. After all he was doing for her, she'd like to make sure the girls learned to make some of his favorite dishes.

Cal checked on his daughters and found them fast asleep. They had kicked off their covers, so he pulled the sheets back over them again, then he bent to kiss each girl gently on the forehead. He smiled to himself as he made his way back downstairs. They hadn't complained about the beans and bacon they'd eaten for supper, but they had said how it wouldn't be long until they would be cooking for him.

He was glad they were excited about learning from Liddy. He just hoped the girls wouldn't prove too much for her. She did look tired this evening. Still, her eyes had been shining. He was glad he'd helped to put the shine in them. He would have hoped that someone would have helped Mary out, had she been the one left alone.

Cal poured the last cup of coffee and settled down in front of the fire. He wondered if Liddy had been able to sit a spell before going to bed. He'd noticed she had a rocker pulled close to the fireplace, too. Was she sitting there now?

She was a pretty woman, glowing because of the child she carried. He wondered if she would have a girl or a boy. Would she name it after her husband if it was a boy? Matthew had been a good man, a hard worker. They hadn't known each other real well, but they'd exchanged pleasantries when they'd met at the general store or on the street. Cal hadn't really ever talked to Liddy until recently. But, then again, why would he? She was a married woman.

Now she was a widow. Expecting a child. He'd do well to remember that fact. He found it too easy to get lost in her green eyes. Not liking or wanting to admit the direction his thoughts were taking him, Cal gulped down his coffee and turned in for the night.

Sunday dawned bright and beautiful. After putting several pies in the oven to bake, Liddy hurried through her morning chores. She dressed in one of only two dresses that she could still fit into and promised herself that she would shop for material the next day. She took special care with her hair, pulling the locks up into a soft knot.

Liddy loved Sundays. She only did the chores that had to be done, and she looked forward to going to church. She loved the fellowship, the lesson, and the singing. Covering the pies with clean cloths, she placed them under the seat of the wagon, which she'd hitched earlier. Carefully climbing up onto the seat, she headed for town.

Greeted by several members as she entered the church, she was smiling as she took her seat beside Emma.

"You're coming home with me for dinner, aren't you?" Emma asked.

Liddy nodded. "I'm looking forward to it." They'd made plans when Liddy had come into town with the laundry on Friday. She hadn't relaxed fully until she'd told the hotel manager that she wouldn't be doing the laundry anymore. He hadn't been too happy, but he'd paid her and wished her well.

Liddy looked across the aisle as Calvin and his daughters arrived. The girls settled down quickly but caught Liddy's eye and smiled excitedly. Grace tugged at her father's arm, and he looked over at Liddy, nodded, and smiled.

She told herself that the racing of her heart was just excitement in looking forward to the next day, and turned her attention to the service. As always, the singing uplifted her. The lesson was a good one, on trusting the Lord in all things.

Liddy felt peace in her soul. She knew how well the Lord took care of her, and she said a silent prayer of thanksgiving. The service was over all too soon and Liddy and Emma stood to leave.

Calvin and his daughters stepped into the aisle at the same time. "Morning, ladies. I hope you have a nice day."

Amy smiled up at them. "Hello, Miss Emma and Mrs. Evans."

"Good morning, Amy and Grace. Thank you, Mr. McAllister. I'm sure we will.

I'm having dinner with Emma. But first, I have something for the girls, if you'd be so kind as to follow me out to my wagon?"

"For the girls? Mrs. Evans, you don't have to—"

"I know that, Mr. McAllister," Liddy said as they moved to the back of the church, the girls and Emma behind them. "It's not that much. Just something I wanted to do."

Calvin's daughters and Emma were whispering behind them, and Liddy turned just as Emma gave them both a wink.

"Cal, why don't you bring the girls over to the café for dinner, too? My treat today."

"You're closed on Sundays, Emma. You deserve a break."

"Having friends over is a break for me. Please come join us."

Cal looked at Liddy, and she smiled at him. It would give her a chance to know the girls better before tomorrow. "Please do. We'd love to have the girls and you join us." They drew alongside her wagon and Liddy stopped beside it.

"I made a pie for you and the girls, and one to take to Emma's. But we can all have ours for dessert, and you can take the other home."

Amy and Grace clapped their hands. "Oh, thank you, Mrs. Evans! What kind is it?"

The adults all chuckled at their enthusiasm. "It's apple," Liddy said. "Do you like that kind?"

"It's my favorite," Grace said.

"Mine too," Amy added.

"Well, good. And we can all enjoy it together." She handed one pie to Amy and one to Grace. "You be careful with them. We wouldn't want to eat dusty apple pie."

Both girls giggled, and each carried a pie as carefully as if they were glass baubles.

"That was very nice of you, Mrs. Evans."

"It was the least I could do, Mr. McAllister."

"Oh, for goodness' sake." Emma stopped in the middle of the street and put her hands on her hips. "When are you two going to stop this 'Mrs. Evans', 'Mr. McAllister' business? Takes you forever to get out what you are going to say. Liddy, this is Cal. Cal, Liddy."

Cal grinned at Liddy. "Hello, Liddy. I am pleased to make your acquaintance."

She smiled back. "Hello, Mr.—Cal."

Emma continued on her way. "Well, that's better. If you are going to be seeing each other nearly every day, it will make conversation much easier."

Liddy and Cal chuckled as they followed Emma and the girls into her restaurant.

Emma left them with orders to set the table while she went to check on the roast she'd put on earlier.

Liddy took off her hat and found aprons for her and the girls. She showed them how to set the table with the fork on the left and the knife and spoon on the right.

Cal found a two-day-old copy of the *Roswell Register,* one of the town's two newspapers, to keep him occupied while Liddy and the girls helped Emma finish preparing the meal and carry the food to the table.

Once they were all seated, Cal said the blessing, and Emma asked him to serve the meat as they started the meal.

Liddy couldn't remember the last time she had enjoyed a dinner quite so much. Grace and Amy's manners were wonderful, and she approved that Cal hadn't raised them to be timid as they joined in the conversation, regaling the adults with stories from school.

The afternoon passed far too quickly, and soon Cal and his girls were ready to take their leave. He'd left to bring Liddy's wagon from the church to the café, while she and the girls helped Emma with the cleanup.

Liddy made sure they took the rest of the pie with them, and Cal and the girls thanked her profusely.

She and Emma took tea out to the back porch as they wound down. "Emma, that was awfully nice of you to invite Cal and his family to join us. I enjoyed it immensely."

Emma gave her a grin. "I could tell. I did too. Cal has done a good job with the girls. They're a pleasure to be around."

Liddy took a sip of tea and nodded. "I'm really looking forward to teaching them how to cook and clean. They seem to be excited about it, too."

Emma chuckled. "I think they are a little tired of Cal's cooking."

"You know, Emma, I still can't believe that I don't have to worry about the farm being taken away. The Lord has answered my prayers a hundredfold."

Emma patted her shoulder. "I'm glad. I knew He'd see to it that you kept the farm. I'm just glad Cal was the one the Lord sent to help you. I trust him. He's an honorable man."

"Yes, he is." Liddy stretched, and then chuckled when the baby did a flip. "And it's such a relief that I can bring my child into the world and not worry if I'll be able to provide for him." She rubbed a hand over the child she carried.

"He or she is going to be a lucky little one to have you for a mother, Liddy."

"As would a child of yours, Emma. And that reminds me, how are things going with you and Deputy Johnson?"

Emma sighed. "They aren't. I asked him to dinner today, too, but he declined, saying there was no one to watch the jail if he were to come here. The sheriff is out of town."

"You could always take him a plate, Emma. I'm sure he would appreciate such an act of kindness."

"Do you really think I should? That's rather bold, isn't it?"

Liddy shook her head. "Think of it as an act of Christian kindness. You don't have to tarry. Just take the plate to him and leave." She grinned at Emma. "Let him taste your cooking and think about what a nice gesture that was and what a great cook you are."

"I could do that."

"Of course you can. And he'll have to return the plate and thank you." Liddy grinned at her friend.

Emma giggled. "Oh, Liddy, you do have the best ideas!"

Before taking her leave, Liddy accompanied Emma to the kitchen and helped her put together a plate to take to the deputy.

Outside, Liddy climbed into her wagon and looked down at Emma. "You be sure and let me know how it goes, you hear?"

Emma held the plate in her hand, ready to take it to the sheriff's office. "You can be certain I will. Let's just hope some other eligible female hasn't had the same idea."

"Well, you aren't going to know that until you take it to him. Go on, take that man some food." Liddy waved at her friend and turned her horse toward home.

It had been a wonderful day. She was really looking forward to the next afternoon. A tiny part of her acknowledged that she was looking forward to seeing not only the girls, but their father as well. She pushed the thought aside. She had no business thinking that way.

Yet, even after she changed her clothes and went about her evening chores, her thoughts kept returning to the tall, handsome farmer. She felt rather disloyal even thinking of him. She had lost her Matthew only seven months ago. Surely that wasn't long enough for her to be thinking about another man in this way.

Dear Lord, please forgive me. I know I'm lonely, but it's not time to think of someone else, is it?

She struggled to put Calvin McAllister out of her mind and began by planning what cooking project she would first attempt with the girls. A good stew might be nice. And biscuits. Those should be easy enough. The art of baking bread would come later.

Liddy busied herself until bedtime and, as she settled down with her Bible once more, she thanked the Lord again for taking such good care of her. But as she closed her eyes for sleep, she couldn't keep her heart from beating a little faster at the thought of seeing Calvin McAllister the next day.

Chapter 6

Liddy watched the clock the next afternoon as she waited for Cal to bring the girls out to her. Early that morning, she had baked several cakes and pies and delivered them to Emma. After that, she'd shopped for the material she'd promised herself. Today had been a good day, and a much easier one without the laundry to do for the hotel.

She heard the sound of horse hooves outside and went to the door with a smile on her face.

Cal helped the girls down from the wagon and turned to Liddy. "Don't let them tire you, all right? They don't need to learn everything at once."

Liddy shielded her eyes against the sun. "We'll be fine. How long do we have?"

"I'll pick them up at sunset, if that's all right with you?"

"That will be fine. We'll have plenty of time that way."

Cal tipped his hat to her. "I'll see you then. Girls, mind your manners now."

"We will, Papa," they chimed together.

Liddy led them inside and found a couple of aprons for them to put on. "How does a menu of stew and biscuits sound to you, girls?"

"Mmm, sounds wonderful to me," Amy answered.

"Me, too," Grace said. "It'll sure beat those old beans we eat all the time."

Liddy chuckled and set the girls to work. Grace scrubbed the vegetables and Liddy showed Amy how to cut them in uniform pieces. Then, Liddy showed them how to cut up a chunk of pork by doing it herself.

She cautioned them about the use of the cookstove, and how they had to be really careful with the fire.

Amy looked over Liddy's shoulder as she browned the meat and then she pulled up a stool for Grace so that she could watch as they added the chopped vegetables to the pot. Liddy added some water last, and they watched and waited until it came to a boil. Then she covered the pan and slid it into the oven.

"Oh, the stew already smells so good," Grace said, as she helped with cleaning up the table so they could use it once more to learn how to make biscuits.

"It really does." Amy agreed. "Won't Papa be happy to smell that when he comes to get us?"

Liddy smiled, listening to their chatter as she got out the ingredients for the biscuits. "We don't need to start these just yet. Let's see. We have the stew and there will be biscuits. You have the pie for dessert."

At their downcast faces and the shaking of their heads, Liddy chuckled. "You finished the pie already?"

Amy nodded. "It was just so good. Papa let us have some after supper last night."

Grace shook her head up and down. "And we had the rest for breakfast and our lunch. Papa put a piece for each of us in our lunch pails. He didn't even save a piece for himself."

Liddy smiled. "Well, maybe we can think of something else for dessert." Both girls smiled and nodded.

"We'll make a quick peach cobbler. That will be easy, and we can use some of the biscuit dough for that."

She led the girls down into the cellar and picked a jar of peaches she'd put up the year before. She pointed out where things were located, in case she sent either of them down for something. She was proud of her cellar. She'd canned everything she could get her hands on last year and would do the same in the coming months. She wanted to be sure that she'd have enough to take her through the winter so she wouldn't have to spend quite so much at Jaffa-Prager Company. Or, if she was snowed in, she wouldn't have to make the trip with a new baby.

The sun was lowering by the time they climbed the stairs once more. She showed them how to check the stew and prick the meat to see if it was done. Then they started the biscuits.

She let Amy cut the lard into the flour, baking powder, and salt, and showed Grace how to make a well and add the milk. Liddy cautioned them not to overwork the dough as she kneaded it lightly and turned it out onto a floured board. She let Grace roll out the dough and Amy cut out the rounds.

They both helped to put them in the baking pan. Liddy slid the stew out of the oven and put it to the back of the stovetop. The biscuits were slid into the oven. She talked the girls through opening the jar of peaches, adding a little sugar, cinnamon, and flour to thicken the juice, then mixing it well in a baking dish. Next, they rolled out the biscuit dough and cut it into strips to place over the peaches. The pan was added to the oven and they started cleaning up.

The smells wafting around them made Grace's stomach start to growl, and they were all laughing when Cal knocked on the door.

"Oh, I'm sorry, Mr.—Cal. Time got away from us. This will all be ready in just a few minutes. Let me dip up some stew for my supper, and you can go ahead and load it into your wagon."

"Papa, we made stew and biscuits and a cobbler from the leftover biscuit dough and, oh, I know it's going to be so good," Grace rambled.

"From the way my stomach is growling at those smells, I can tell it's going to be great," Cal said as he tweaked Grace's nose.

He looked at Liddy as she dipped up a bowl of the stew for her own supper. "They did all right?"

Liddy smiled. "Why, they did more than all right. They are naturals. They're going to learn very quickly."

Both Amy and Grace beamed at her compliment.

Liddy handed Amy a pot holder. "Amy, would you like to check the biscuits and the cobbler and tell me what color they are?"

Anxious to show off some of her newly learned skill for her father, Amy took the pot holder and eased the oven door open. "They're a beautiful golden brown, Mrs. Evans."

"Then it's time to take them out. Do you need some help?"

Amy shook her head and carefully lifted the pan of biscuits out of the oven. She placed them on the worktable and went back for the cobbler.

Cal sniffed appreciatively. "Oh, peach cobbler. That's one of my favorites. You've outdone yourselves, ladies."

Liddy took a biscuit for her meal and used clean dish towels to cover the rest and the cobbler. "There you go. A meal fit for a king. I hope you all enjoy it." She smiled as she handed a pot holder over to Cal and then handed him the pot of stew. "Let's get this to your wagon so that you can get home and enjoy it while it's hot."

They took the meal out to the wagon and carefully placed the pans so they would travel safely. Cal turned to Liddy. "Thank you. The girls look so proud of themselves, but I'm sure you did most of it," he said in an undertone.

Liddy shook her head. "No, I didn't. They had a hand in it all. I mostly talked them through the steps. I've found it's much easier to remember if one does instead of watches."

Cal helped the girls into the wagon, and they took turns in thanking Liddy for teaching them.

"What will we make tomorrow?" Amy asked.

"Yes, what?" Grace echoed her sister.

Liddy laughed. "I'm not sure. I'll give it some thought tonight."

Cal turned to her once more. "Oh, I forgot to give you extra money for the food. I'm so sorry. I'll get it to you tomorrow."

"Don't worry about it. I—"

"I'll get it to you tomorrow. You plan whatever you want," Cal interrupted her.

Liddy nodded. "I'll keep that in mind."

She waved good-bye to them and went to catch up on her chores before she ate supper. The cow wasn't too happy that she was late with her milking. Liddy promised Bessie that she'd do better the next day.

She went inside, pleased with the accomplishments.

As she ate her meal, she wondered how the McAllisters were enjoying theirs. She knew Cal would make his daughters feel wonderful about the meal they'd helped prepare. She could just imagine the proud and happy looks on their faces that they'd made their father a good supper. Liddy chuckled. A meal that didn't include beans.

After cleaning up the kitchen, she lit the oil lamp and pored over her old cookbook. Luckily, she could teach the girls how to prepare many recipes before they had to learn how to cook those old beans and bacon.

Cal and his girls enjoyed the supper they'd cooked for him. The girls took turns telling him just how they'd done it, and he felt beholden to Liddy, for she'd helped them in a way that made them feel they could repeat the meal on their own.

Amy decided that she wanted a record of the recipes, so she hunted down a piece of brown paper and wrote down the directions Liddy had given them.

Cal helped Grace with the cleanup, while Amy made notes of what she could remember. Then, he gathered all of Liddy's pans together to return them to her the next day.

He lit the lamp and put it on the kitchen table so that the girls could do the schoolwork they usually did while he was cooking supper. They didn't grumble about getting to their lessons late. It seemed as though the cooking classes were worth the delay to them.

Cal settled in his chair by the fire and let peaceful contentment settle over him. He'd had a wonderful meal, and his girls were happy, excited, and looking forward to the next day. The only thing that could make this evening better was a wife to share it all.

Now, where did that thought come from?

He knew. It came from the empty spot deep in his heart that had been there since the death of his Mary. She'd been carrying their third child, and it had been a difficult time for her. The baby had come too early. Roswell did have a good doctor, and Cal had rushed to get him. But even he hadn't been able to save either one of them.

The pain had eased through the years, but the loneliness he felt never quite went away. Cal usually just brushed it aside and got on with taking care of his girls.

And that's what he did this time, as he checked their lesson and sent them to get ready for bed. He listened to their prayers and locked up the house before heading to his room. But, as he lay awake in the dark, he couldn't help but wonder if Liddy Evans was as lonely as he was. Was it possible the Lord had brought them together for more than just to help her keep her land?

Cal remembered how pretty she had looked with her face flushed from the warmth of her kitchen, and those little tendrils of hair escaping around her face. Her green eyes sparkled as she'd watched Amy and Grace tell him about their afternoon. The girls liked her a lot, he could tell. And so did he. So did he.

The next few weeks sped by for Liddy. Cal dropped his daughters off right after school and picked them back up as the sun was going down. The girls were easy to teach and fun to be around, and while the evenings and nights were still lonely, Liddy kept herself busy.

She'd made herself one more dress, in a style that could be taken up easily after the baby arrived. Now she kept herself busy at night by sewing for the baby, baking for Emma's restaurant, and planning the next cooking class for the girls.

School had been dismissed for summer on Friday, and she and Cal had decided that he would bring the girls over right after lunch each day. Liddy was going to teach them a little more about housekeeping than she'd had time for with school in session.

Cal would work his land in the mornings and hers in the afternoons. He had checked out the alfalfa and told her he'd start the first cut in a couple of weeks. It looked to be a good crop. If the next few cuttings over the summer were of the same quality, Liddy wouldn't have to worry about making the rest of the year's payments to Harper.

She was feeling pretty good, except for a few twinges in her back now and again. But it was getting a little more difficult to do the normal daily chores. Gathering eggs was no problem, but she was beginning to wish old Bessie didn't need milking quite so often. Some of the items in her garden would be ready for picking soon, but keeping it clear of weeds was becoming quite a challenge. She was just finishing her weeding chores when she heard a noise. Thinking it was Calvin and the girls, she struggled to her feet and turned to find Douglas Harper standing in the middle of her yard watching her.

Liddy's hand flew to her throat. "Mr. Harper. What are you doing here?"

Chapter 7

I thought I'd come out and see how you are doing, Liddy. I haven't seen you in town lately."

"Since I was able to pay the note ahead by several months, there's been no need for me to come to the bank, Mr. Harper."

He nodded his head and looked around at the alfalfa ripening in the fields. "You've got some good land here, Liddy. But it's too much for a woman to take care of. Farming is a hard, unpredictable life for a man, much less for a woman on her own. It's a struggle you don't need, my dear. My offer still stands."

Liddy felt nauseous at the very thought of his *offer.* "You know that I'm leasing my land to Mr. McAllister. You'll be getting your money on time from now on. There's no need to worry."

Harper nodded. "Leasing might work, as long as you have a good harvest. Nevertheless, you have no control over the elements, my dear. A heavy rain or hailstorm could wipe you out, and take McAllister with you. He won't be able to pay you the rest of what he owes you, if that happens. And you won't be able to make your payments."

Liddy hadn't really thought of the risk Cal was taking. He'd already paid her a deposit. If something happened to both crops, he'd be the real loser, because she'd already paid much of it to the bank.

"She'll make her payments, Harper."

Liddy hadn't heard the approach of Cal's wagon, and the relief she felt as he walked up behind Harper was almost overwhelming.

Harper looked startled to find Cal standing there, but he recovered quickly. "You're guaranteeing that, McAllister?"

"Look around you, man. She's got a bumper crop this year."

Harper nodded. "First cut looks good. But a lot can happen between now and the final cut. I wouldn't count my chickens just yet."

"No, we won't. We'll count on the Lord to get us through. And, unless I'm mistaken, Mrs. Evans paid several months ahead on her loan. She isn't accountable to you until the next payment is due."

Harper held up a hand. "McAllister, you have me all wrong. I've offered to pay off Liddy's loan myself. Her well-being is of utmost importance to me."

The arrogance of the man sickened Cal. When he'd spotted the man rounding the corner of Liddy's house, he'd hurried his team as fast as he possibly could without alarming the girls.

Not wanting Harper to know how anxious he was that Liddy was here alone with him, Cal had rushed the girls inside and made it to the back of Liddy's house as fast as his long stride could take him. The sight of her with both arms wrapped protectively around her growing middle told him how uncomfortable she was in Harper's presence.

Cal slid a glance toward Liddy and his concern grew. Her eyes were huge and overly bright in a face that was much too pale. Hurrying to her side, he looked down at her. "I think you've been outside in this heat too long, Liddy. The girls are inside. Why don't you go in and rest for a little while?"

Liddy looked from him to Harper and swallowed hard. She met Cal's eyes again and took a deep breath. Then she nodded at him and headed for the house.

"You take care of yourself, Liddy. If you need anything, you just let me know," Harper called after her.

Liddy kept walking.

Cal clinched his fists to his side. *Lord, help me stay in control.* He took another step toward Harper.

"Oh, yes, I think I know how genuine your concern is, Harper. You try to force a woman into marriage just to get control of her land? That kind of concern, she can do without. You can take your leave anytime now, *Mr.* Harper," Cal said.

"Who do you think you are, McAllister? I can call in this loan anytime I want to."

"Mrs. Evans has paid ahead, Harper. It'd be unethical to call in that loan, and you know it."

"Still and all, I *can* do it."

"I wouldn't, if I were you." Cal took a step forward.

He wasn't sure if he was relieved or disappointed when the banker turned and hightailed it out of the yard. Much as he'd have enjoyed the feeling of his fist meeting Harper's chin, he knew it was better this way. No sense in making things harder on Liddy. She still had to pay off the loan. And the faster the better.

He unclenched his fists and watched as Harper drove his team away. He turned to find Amy running toward him.

"Papa! Something is wrong with Mrs. Evans. She's in a lot of pain. Do you think the baby is coming now?"

Cal ran into the house and found Liddy in her rocker. From everything he remembered when the girls were born, he was pretty sure Liddy's time had come. Her eyes tightly closed, she was gripping the arms of the chair, breathing in and out rapidly.

The pain seemed to ease, and her breathing slowed. She opened her eyes and looked at him.

"I think maybe—"

"It's time?" he asked. Liddy nodded at him. "I'll go for the doctor. Do you think you'll be all right? Until I get back?"

Liddy eyes met his, and he could see the fear in them. "I think so. It's a little early, though. Do you think it's really time?"

Cal could tell she needed reassurance, but what did he really know? Babies seemed to have a mind of their own when it came time to be born. He sent up a silent prayer that everything would be all right. But he needed to get the doctor. Now, he thought, as he watched another wave of pain wash over Liddy.

"Girls, you help Mrs. Evans to bed and get her as comfortable as possible. I'll be back with the doctor soon as I can."

"Yes, Papa," they both chimed.

Cal was out the door instantly. All the way into town, he prayed that Doc was in and that Liddy and her baby would be fine. If anything happened to them, he'd be looking for Harper. As far as he was concerned, the blame for Liddy's baby coming early rested squarely at the unscrupulous banker's feet.

Cal's prayers were answered, Doc Miller was in, and by nightfall, Liddy was holding her newborn son. Matthew Richard Evans was a little on the small side, but had a robust set of lungs. Doc said Liddy and the baby would be fine.

Emma had followed them out from town, leaving her café in Ben's charge. She would stay the night and several days with Liddy, and no amount of arguing from Liddy was going to change her mind.

Cal was relieved. He didn't want to leave Liddy alone with a newborn baby. He and the girls were allowed in the room after Doc had taken his leave. Liddy was glowing, and although Cal could tell she was exhausted, she looked beautiful with her newborn son in her arms.

"He's a fine boy, Liddy," Cal said, watching the baby as he curled a tiny finger around his mother's larger one. "You would have made Matthew proud."

"Thank you." Liddy brushed a kiss over her son's forehead and looked back at Cal. "Again. I think I'll be beholden to you for the rest of my life. I'm so glad you were here. I don't know what I'd have done. . ."

"I'm glad I was here, too, Liddy. No need to thank me. You'd have managed."

Liddy chuckled. "Maybe. But Bessie wouldn't have. Thank you for doing my chores, and. . ."

Cal held up his hand. "If I was sick, or down for some reason or another, wouldn't you make sure my girls were taken care of, and my cow milked, and my eggs gathered?"

"Of course I would."

"Okay, then." Cal could see that Liddy's eyes were starting to droop, and he knew she needed sleep. It'd be only in spurts for a while now, if he remembered right. "I'm going to take the girls home and let you get some rest. If you need anything at all, have Emma let me know. Otherwise, we'll be over tomorrow to check on you all."

Liddy nodded. She knew it would do no good to argue with the man. She let him get halfway out the door before she called, "Thank you, Cal."

He turned and found her eyes closed and her breathing steady. She looked beautiful sleeping, with her son cuddled close. He wasn't even sure she heard his next words. "You're welcome, Liddy. You did real good. He's a beautiful boy. Sleep well."

Looking back on the past week, Liddy didn't know what she would have done without Emma's help. But it was Cal's help that had been invaluable.

Being a new mother was intimidating enough, but between Emma's admission that she didn't have a clue what to do, and all the advice given from the wonderful church women bringing food and presents, by the end of the week Liddy had found herself almost in tears.

She'd convinced Emma to go back to her restaurant after five days, thinking she could manage on her own. And she did pretty well until nightfall. Baby Matthew fussed and cried and no amount of rocking, feeding, or changing could quiet him. It was then that she realized the depth of her love for him. Yet, she felt totally inadequate to provide all that he needed. How could she do this alone?

Dear Lord, please help me. I love this child You've blessed me with, but there's so much I don't know, she prayed as she rocked her son in the early morning light. When she heard the light knock on the door, she quickly brushed at her tears and went to open it.

"Liddy, I came to milk Bessie, and the girls insisted on coming to help you out, but I wanted to make sure it would be all right with you."

She hoped he couldn't see she'd been weeping, but her fussing son began to cry in earnest once more, and Liddy couldn't hold her own tears back. She shook her head. "It appears I can use all the help I can get. Obviously, I don't know the first thing about being a mother."

She looked so helpless standing there sobbing, holding her child in her arms, Calvin did the only thing he knew to do. He wrapped his arms around the both of them and led Liddy back to her rocker. He took the baby from her, and went to the door to call his girls in from the wagon.

"Amy, you brew Mrs. Evans a cup of tea like she showed you, and Grace, go find me one of those little soft blankets for the baby, please."

"No, Cal. You've got your own work to see to." Liddy looked up at him as he held her son so easily. "We'll be all right. I'm sorry. We just didn't have a good night—"

"I talked to Emma. She said Matthew hadn't been letting you sleep much, and she knew you were afraid to leave him in her care. . .no more than she knows about babies."

"Oh, dear. Now I've hurt her feelings."

"No, you haven't. She just wants to make sure it's not too much, you being here all alone." Cal took the blanket Grace brought him and laid it out on the settee. Then he laid the baby down and brought the ends around him, wrapping him snugly.

He sat back and jiggled him in his arms until the baby's eyes grew heavy and his lids closed.

Liddy watched closely as she sipped the tea Amy brought her. "How did you do that? Have I been wrapping him too lightly?"

Cal shrugged. "I don't know if there's a right or wrong way to wrap them. This is just the way my girls seemed to be happiest at first. Very snugly wrapped, even in warm weather. I guess it made them feel a little more secure. But I think what Matthew sensed was that I'm not afraid of him."

"And he knows I am?" Liddy couldn't help but chuckle.

"Well, he probably senses that you are unsure of yourself. But you know what, Liddy? I think God gives these instincts to mothers. And I think you just need to listen to them and trust that they come from Him."

"You think so?"

"I do." He brought her sleeping son over to her. "Why don't the two of you go back to bed? Amy and Grace said they'd like to help you, so I'm going to let them gather eggs and put some dinner on for you, if that's all right?"

Liddy let him help her up from the rocker and smiled at his daughters. "Thank you, girls. I'd appreciate your help."

She headed toward her bedroom with the baby. "I don't think I'll sleep long. Wake me if you have any questions."

Cal and his daughters grinned at each other, as Liddy yawned the last sentence.

❧

Liddy slept through the day, rousing only to feed her son when he cried from hunger. She awoke with a start when the setting sun shimmered through her window. The smell of biscuits and stew and the sound of a baby cooing greeted her as she quickly dressed and opened the door. There, sitting in her rocker was Cal, holding Matthew and talking to him as if the baby understood everything he said.

From the way the baby cooed, she wondered if maybe he did.

"It looks like I slept right through lunch. I'm sorry. I—"

"Liddy, you needed the rest. The baby has only been awake for about an hour. We figured you'd be up shortly."

"I'm sure he must be hungry again," Liddy said, taking her son from Cal. "I'll just go feed him."

Cal nodded. "I'll go milk Bessie, and by the time you are finished, the girls will have supper on the table."

Liddy held Matthew close and smiled over at Cal's girls. "It smells delicious. You must give me your recipe."

Amy and Grace giggled at her teasing and began to set the table while she headed for her room.

The baby fell asleep as soon as she fed him, full, clean, and content. Evidently, Cal had bathed and changed him earlier. Liddy wrapped him snugly and put him in the cradle that Cal had brought over for her use. He'd made it for his daughters.

Cal was just washing up from bringing in the milk when she came out of her room. The girls insisted she sit down, and they hurriedly dished up the meal. As Cal said the blessing, Liddy added her own silent prayer, thanking the Lord for bringing this family into her life.

That night marked the change in their routine. Cal and the girls started showing up right after lunch each day. Cal worked her land, the girls learned by helping Liddy, and they all shared the evening meal.

Then the girls washed dishes while Cal helped Liddy bathe baby Matthew and get him to bed. Only after Liddy was settled in her rocker, with a cup of tea by her side, did they start for home.

Each night, it became harder and harder to see them leave. Amy and Grace had already claimed a spot in her heart. Now, right or wrong, Liddy was sure she was falling more than a little in love with their father.

And where could that possibly lead? Why would any man let himself fall in love with a widow who was in debt? Not to mention one who'd just become a new mother.

Chapter 8

Cal wondered just how long he could wait to tell Liddy he loved her and ask for her hand in marriage. It was becoming increasingly difficult to leave her and baby Matthew each night.

Yet, how could he even begin to hope that Liddy might return his feelings when the baby must provide daily reminders of the love she and her husband had shared?

No, he'd best bide his time for now. He loved the woman; there was no denying that fact, and he prayed daily for patience. He'd put his trust in the Lord to let him know when to approach Liddy with a proposal of marriage. He just hoped it would be soon.

First cut of the alfalfa was finished, and it lay drying in the field. Cal hadn't needed any help with the mowing. He'd brought his own horse-drawn mower over the night before, but he had hired several men from town to help rake it into windrows. Tomorrow morning it would be turned, and if the weather held, by that afternoon it would be safely in the barn, out of harm's way.

He had cut his own fields the week before. Liddy and the girls had gone to his house to prepare the noon meal for the men, and today they had done the same at her home.

Now, as he watched them cleaning up after supper, while he entertained the baby, his love for Liddy deepened even more. She was unfailingly patient with his girls, and her son was thriving from her nurturing. She brought the coffeepot over to refill his cup, and bent to kiss her baby's cheek.

Cal wished he had the right to turn her face toward him and bring her lips to his. But he didn't.

"Thank you, Liddy."

"You're welcome." She smiled, and her eyes met his.

He watched a blush steal up her cheeks, and wondered if she'd read his thoughts.

"Thank *you,* Cal. Two months ago, I never thought I'd see those rows of hay in the field. I was sure I was going to lose all of what Matthew and I had worked so hard for. If he could, I know he would thank you for taking such good care of his family and his land."

So that's the way it is. He'd best face the fact that the timing might never be right to ask for Liddy's hand. Now certainly wasn't the right time. It seemed that, in Liddy's eyes, this house he was sitting in, this land he was farming, this child he was holding, and this woman he loved all still belonged to Matthew. Would she always feel that way?

"Liddy, you aren't the only one who's being helped by our arrangement. My girls have learned so much from you, not to mention how they are thriving by the attention you give them. And I stand to make a profit from leasing your land. It's not like I'm doing this all for nothing. The way I see it, we're helping each other." Cal knew his voice sounded rough, but he couldn't help it. He didn't want her gratitude. He wanted her love.

Liddy watched Cal's wagon until it was out of sight and sighed deeply. She went inside and bolted the door before easing into her rocker to enjoy her waiting cup of tea. He still made sure she had a fresh-brewed cup before he and the girls left for the night.

Taking a sip of the warm liquid, Liddy leaned back her head and closed her eyes. She'd upset him tonight. She hadn't meant to; she'd only wanted to thank him. She knew he was uncomfortable when she voiced her gratitude, but Liddy couldn't just let him think she took his goodness for granted.

She'd known many Christians, but not all of them acted on their beliefs, like Cal had when he saw to her and her son's needs. He might think he was getting something in return, but Liddy knew who was benefiting the most. And it wasn't Calvin McAllister.

He'd taken a huge risk in leasing her land. She realized that now. If her crop failed, he would be out the money, not her. With the alfalfa already in the field, she hadn't even had to buy seed this year. It looked like they were going to have a good crop, but, still, he was doing all the work.

As far as teaching his girls went, that was a pleasure, and they spent most of their day at her house, helping *her*. Besides, he was giving just as much attention to baby Matthew as she gave to Amy and Grace.

Liddy was sure he went home bone-weary each night, after taking care of both places during the day. Still, he always found time for his girls and to help her with her son. As good a husband as Matthew had been, he hadn't been as considerate of her, after working in the fields all day, as Cal was.

Liddy's heart pounded at her realization. She was in love with Calvin McAllister.

Oh, dear Lord. I did love Matthew. You know I did. But it's Cal I dream about at night. It's Cal I look forward to seeing each day. What is Your will for us, Father? What am I to do about my feelings for this special man?

Liddy went to bed with no answers, but she trusted the Lord to show her the way.

She was up before dawn, getting her chores out of the way so that she could prepare breakfast for Cal and the men he'd hired to help with the haying. She'd just finished milking Bessie when she heard what sounded like a whip cracking, and her heart fell.

Hurrying outside, she looked up at the sky and saw a flash of lightning. *Oh, dear Lord, not now. Please, keep this storm away until we can get the hay out of the field.*

She hurried to her house, watching the sky closely. This time of year was known for electrical storms. They didn't always have rain in them, but the lightning could be truly ferocious. Huge cloud-to-ground flashes began in earnest, and Liddy hurried in to a crying baby, who had been awakened by the loud booms.

Cal, his girls, and the men he'd hired all showed up at the same time. He rushed Amy and Grace in the house, and against Liddy's protests, he and the men started toward the field to try to save the hay.

Liddy and the children watched from the porch as the storm moved closer. She prayed silently, all the while, for Cal and the men to be safe, as she watched them hurry to load the hay into wagons.

Normally, it would be turned over and allowed to lay in the field until the afternoon. But with the storm approaching, it appeared that Cal had decided to get it into the barn as fast as possible.

Less than half the field's yield had been moved to the barn, when a huge bolt struck the field. Immediately, a row of hay ignited, the flames shooting down the row and across to the next.

Liddy quickly handed the baby to Amy and ran out to the barn. She gathered all of the burlap bags she could find and rushed to wet them in the watering trough.

Cal met her at the edge of the field and took them from her. "Stay here. I don't know that we'll be able to do much, but if it should come close to the house, you'll need to get what you can and get the children in the wagon."

Several other ranchers who'd seen the flames had joined in the fight. Some started digging a trench to keep the house and barn safe, while others were filling buckets from the water trough, and everyone was doing all they could to help. But there was no rain with this storm, and Liddy knew saving the crop was a losing battle. By the time the men had the fire under control, there wasn't much left of the crop to save. Their hopes for a good first cut were gone.

Liddy brushed at the tears running down her face as Cal approached, his own face sooty from fighting the fire.

He gathered her in his arms. "I'm sorry, Liddy."

She shook her head. "There's no more you could do, Cal. It's not your fault."

"I should have cut earlier."

"You had no way of knowing this was going to happen. It'll grow again. There'll be another cut."

Cal nodded and brushed her still-wet cheek.

"I'll have some breakfast for everyone shortly," Liddy said.

"You don't need to do that, Liddy. No one expects—"

"It'll keep me busy, Cal."

He nodded. "Ring the bell when you're ready."

L♥

Liddy and the girls were cleaning up after feeding the men who'd come to help. The storm had moved out of the vicinity, but someone had mentioned that they'd heard there'd been some hail toward Cal's place, and he and several of the men went to see if the reports were true.

Matthew was down for a nap and the girls were trying to be quiet. Liddy sent them to gather eggs and check on Bessie.

She prayed there hadn't been any damage to Cal's crops and thanked the Lord that, as bad as it seemed at the moment, they had managed to save some of the hay. Most importantly to her, Cal and the other men had been unharmed as they fought the fire.

She hated that he blamed himself. There was no way he could have known the storm would build up. Things like this happened.

Liddy poured herself a cup of tea, but found she couldn't sit still, and decided to go help Amy and Grace in the barn. But when she opened the door, it was to find Douglas Harper at the bottom of the steps. Her heart plummeted before seeming to stop.

"My dear Liddy, I heard in town about your misfortune and had to come see for myself. I'm so sorry about your crop."

How dare the man? She'd had about all of his sarcastic lying that she could take. Loan or no loan, she wasn't taking that kind of attitude from this man anymore.

"I'd appreciate your getting off my land, Harper." The man didn't deserve to be called *Mr.,* and Liddy couldn't bring herself to do so. She wanted to run, but she stood firm, as Harper took a step up.

"Whose land, my dear? I think you are mistaken in calling it yours. Because, you see, I'm calling in your note. With no crop, there is no way you can pay your next installment. And I've given you all the leeway I can."

"I'm paid up. And the next payment isn't due for two more weeks."

"Doesn't matter. You won't have the money then."

Liddy lifted her chin a notch higher. "I may."

Little Matthew had awakened and could be heard crying from inside the house. She headed back through the door but turned to Harper once more. "I don't have time to discuss this with you right now. My son needs me. You'll excuse me if I go see to him."

She went inside and shut the door, hurrying to pick up Matthew. She wouldn't rest easy until she knew Harper was off her property. The girls were in the barn, and she didn't want them to be frightened by his presence.

But when she turned, it was to find that Harper had followed her inside.

"Liddy, my dear. You have me all wrong," he said coming toward her. "My offer still stands. I'd like nothing more than to take care of you and your son. If you'll marry me, you'll never have to worry about paying off your loan."

She gathered her son close. "Get out of my house, Harper. You know your so-called *offer* repulses me. I'll lose my house and land before I'd marry you!"

"And that's exactly what you'll be doing, if you say no. I will call in the note tomorrow." He advanced toward her.

"Harper." There was no sweeter sound to Liddy's ears than that of Calvin's voice as he entered the house.

"Ah, McAllister." Harper turned to face Cal. "I should have known you'd be showing up. I figured there was something going on between the two of you. Well, you can't help Mrs. Evans this time, because I'm calling in her note first thing tomorrow."

"No, you are not." Cal was across the room in two strides and had the banker by the collar. "And you will apologize for speaking to my fiancée that way. *Now.*"

Liddy felt as if her heart somersaulted all the way to her feet and back. What was Cal doing?

"Your what? Did you say fiancée?" Harper turned first to Cal, and then back to Liddy. "Is this true?"

"I. . ." Liddy was at a loss for words.

Cal had no such problem. "Harper, we don't owe you any explanations. All you need to know is that Liddy and I will be in first thing tomorrow morning to pay off her debt. No. Better yet, we'll be in your office by closing time today."

He gave the man a shake before letting go of his collar. "Now, apologize nicely, and get out of this house and off the property."

"I'm sorry, Mrs. Evans," Harper said sarcastically as he turned and headed for the door. But he tried to get in the last word. "You be there. Or I will have the sheriff deliver foreclosure papers. And I'll have you arrested for accosting me, McAllister."

With that, Harper slammed out the door.

Cal followed him and called, "Well, you can try, but I don't think the sheriff will do your bidding, once he hears how you tried to blackmail a widow into marrying you."

He watched until the banker was safely off the property before turning back to Liddy.

As soon as Harper had gone out the door, she'd dropped into her rocker, holding her son securely in her lap. She was trembling like a leaf. What had Cal been thinking to tell Harper such a thing?

"Liddy?"

She looked up to find Cal smiling down at her. "Calvin McAllister. What have you done? What are we going to do now?"

Cal lowered himself to one knee in front of her. "If you'll have me, we're going to get married."

"Calvin, you can't marry me just to get me out of debt. And the crop is nearly gone anyway. There is no money."

"Remember, I told you I had a good crop last year? Well, I'm doing fine, Liddy. I have more than enough to pay off your loan to Harper. I don't want him spreading talk about you, Liddy. And he will if we don't get married. You know that."

Tears welled up in her eyes. This was what she wanted, but it was happening for all the wrong reasons. "Cal, you can't marry me to protect my reputation, either. And I don't want your pity."

Cal lifted her chin, so that her eyes met his. "Look at me, Liddy. Pity is *not* what I feel for you. And it's not what you see in my eyes. What you see there is love, Liddy. Pure and simple love."

"I know I've done this all wrong," Cal continued. "I meant to give you more time to get over losing Matthew. But, Liddy, if there's even a chance that, one day, you could learn to love me, I'll settle for that. I promise I'll try to be a good husband to you, and a good father to young Matthew."

"Shh. . .shh," she said, her fingers coming up to still his words. Her heart sang with the realization that Calvin did love her. She had never known this man to lie, and she knew he wouldn't lie to her about something as important as this.

"I've been falling in love with you for weeks, Calvin McAllister. If you mean what you say, then my answer is *yes*. I'll marry you. And I'll happily spend the rest of my days trying to be a good wife to you and mother to our children. Yours, mine, and ours, if the good Lord wills it."

Cal lifted her fingers from his lips and kissed her palm. Standing, he pulled Liddy and her son into his embrace and hugged them tightly.

Tipping her chin, he lowered his lips to hers and captured them in the kiss he'd only dreamed of until now. Tentative at first, he deepened the kiss to seal the promise of their love for each other.

It was still light when they returned from town. They had to go from one bank to the other, but before the afternoon was over, Liddy and Cal left Harper's bank with her note stamped paid in full and the knowledge that he would never be able to take her place away from her.

They celebrated with supper at Emma's. Once she found out they were going to be married, nothing would do her but to help plan the wedding.

By the time Cal pulled his wagon into Liddy's yard, there were only a few hot spots still smoldering in the field.

Thrilled that Matthew would soon be their baby brother, Amy and Grace happily took him inside, while Cal and Liddy walked hand in hand to the edge of the field.

Liddy sent up a silent prayer of thanksgiving—thanking God that only the crop had burned, that the Lord had kept Cal safe, and that His will for her and Cal and their children was for them to become a family.

Cal turned her to him and wrapped his arms around her. "You know, if this field hadn't caught on fire today, I'd probably still be wondering how much longer I needed to wait until I could ask you to marry me. But I think the Lord had plans for us all along, even before you agreed to let me lease your land."

Loving the feel of being in the circle of Cal's arms, Liddy smiled and nodded. "He planted the seeds of love in each of our hearts, when all we thought we were doing was helping each other out."

"We'll harvest this field over and over again," Cal said. "But the Lord intends for our love to last through all the harvests of our lives. I love you, Liddy, today, tomorrow, and forever." Cal bent his head toward her.

Their lips met, and the lingering kiss they shared convinced Liddy that Calvin McAllister did indeed love her. . .every bit as much as she loved him.

JANET LEE BARTON

Born in New Mexico, Janet has lived all over the South, but she and her husband plan to stay put in southern Mississippi, where they have made their home for the past six years. With three daughters and six grandchildren between them, they feel blessed to have at least one daughter, Nicole, her husband, Darren, and two precious granddaughters, Mariah and Paige, living in the same town. Janet loves being able to share her faith through her writing. Happily married to her very own hero, she is ever thankful that the Lord brought Dan into her life, and she wants to write stories that show that the love between a man and a woman is at its best when the relationship is built with God at the center. She's very happy that the kind of romances the Lord has called her to write can be read by and shared with women of all ages, from teenagers to grandmothers alike.

Hope's Dwelling Place

by Connie Stevens

Dedication

To my nieces and nephews: Kris, Brad, Matt, and Esther.
You are all so precious to me.

Chapter 1

Near Fredericksburg, Texas
February 1897

Amelia Bachman braced herself against the jarring ride of the stagecoach and peered out the window. The stage was scheduled to arrive in Fredericksburg before dark, but the deepening purple, gold, and magenta streaks in the western sky hinted the sun might be in deep slumber by the time she reached her destination. She'd had no way to notify Mr. Lamar Richter, chairman of the Fredericksburg school board, that her arrival was delayed by a broken wheel. She hoped he didn't interpret her tardiness as a change of mind.

Amelia pulled two letters from her reticule and held them up to the waning sunlight. The well-worn edges and bent corners testified to the number of times she'd unfolded and refolded each one. She'd nearly memorized the first, from her father. His disapproving frown the day she left home to attend Normal School in Austin lingered in her mind. He couldn't understand how she could ignore the opportunity to marry a prosperous rancher in favor of becoming a schoolteacher—a menial occupation at best, and one where she would be required to remain single. Her throat tightened as she read his berating words once again. If she'd followed the same path as her parents, she might live a comfortable life in a fine house with servants to do her bidding. But she couldn't erase the images from her childhood of the misery etched on her mother's face, trapped in a loveless marriage. She'd long ago promised herself she'd never marry for the sake of social status.

She folded the letter and stuffed it resolutely back into her reticule and opened the second letter. The words scrawled in this letter brought a smile to her face.

Dear Miss Bachman,

We school board of Fredericksburg, Texas, offer to you teach der school to end of der school year.

Amelia shifted her position on the hard, dusty seat, thinking of the teacher she was replacing. Mr. Richter had stated in a previous letter that their teacher had turned in her resignation just after Christmas. Seemed the woman was getting married and didn't want to wait until the end of the term. Well, Mr. Richter wouldn't have to worry about Amelia doing such a thing. She squinted at the rumpled paper once again.

You must stay at der Richter family Sunday haus. *There is a place for* schlafen *up der stairs side. Stagecoach bring you and der town familys is glad.*

A tiny smile tweaked Amelia's lips when she remembered struggling to recall the little bit of German she knew, relieved to translate *schlafen* to mean there were private *sleeping* quarters for her. She cast another glance out the window at the quickly disappearing sun and imagined Mr. Richter growing weary of waiting for her stage to arrive.

As she feared, darkness shrouded the town when the stage finally drew to a halt amid swirling dust. Amelia brushed the gritty film from her skirt and smoothed her hair the best she could. The driver grunted as he climbed down and opened the door, kicking a wooden crate over for her to step on. He didn't wait to help her down, but rather climbed back up to retrieve the luggage. She unfolded her stiff muscles, closing her lips to stifle an unladylike groan, and disembarked the conveyance. Lanterns flickered on either side of the depot, casting ghostly shadows across the boardwalk. Amelia glanced around but only the stage driver was within sight.

Where was Mr. Richter?

"Oh dear."

The driver lowered her trunk to the ground. "Beg your pardon, miss?"

She turned. "Do you know Mr. Lamar Richter?"

"Nope."

She bit her lip. "I wonder where I might inquire after him."

Her carpetbag plunked at her feet as the driver jumped down. "Iffen you can rattle the depot door loud enough, the old German fella that runs the place might can help ya. Name's Humble, Hurmole, Hummerol. . ." The man knocked his hat askew scratching his head. "It's somethin' like that."

He climbed over the wheel and collected the reins. His sharp whistle made the horses snort in protest, but they lurched forward, leaving Amelia standing alone in the chilled February night air.

She scanned up and down the street. The whole town seemed to have retired for the night. She longed to do so as well, but first she had to find this Sunday house of which Mr. Richter wrote.

She drew her thin shawl tighter and tapped at the depot door. No lights glimmered from within. She knocked harder, rattling the glass in the door window. "Hello? Is anyone here?"

A faint glow spilled from a back room and moved slowly toward the door. Candlelight never looked friendlier. A wizened old man clad only in a nightshirt shuffled to the door, holding the candlestick aloft.

"*Wer gibt es?*"

Wer? Amelia prodded her brain. . . . *Who*. No doubt he was asking who was knocking on his door in the middle of the night.

"My name is. . .um, *ich bin* Amelia Bachman." What was the German word for *teacher*? "Mr. Richter was supposed to meet me."

"Richter, *ja*." The man set the candlestick down, gripped Amelia's hand, and pumped it. "*Fraulein* Bachman. You am. . .uh, teacher, ja?

Relief rippled through her. "Yes! I mean, ja."

He drew his shoulders back and clapped his hand to his chest. "I is Humbert Schmidt." A beaming smile accompanied Mr. Schmidt's broken English.

"Very nice to meet you, Mr. Schmidt." She pulled the school board chairman's letter from her pocket. "Mr. Richter says I'm supposed to stay in the Sunday house, er, *Sonntag haus.* Can you tell me—" She furrowed her brow trying to think around the headache that had weaseled its way behind her eyes. "*Wo ist das haus?*"

"Ja, ja—" He pointed and gave her directions, half in English and half in German, but she caught the words *gelb haus*, so at least she knew the house she was looking for was yellow.

"*Sie brauchen*—" Candlelight danced against the elderly man's thick gray eyebrows as he shook his head. "Bah! Englisch, Schmidt!" An apologetic smile wobbled across his countenance. "You need lantern. *Hier ist.*" He scurried to a cabinet and returned with a lantern, lighting the wick with his candle.

"Thank you, uh, *dank*, Mr. Schmidt. I'll bring your lantern back in the morning." She picked up her satchel and pointed to the larger trunk. "I will send someone for the trunk tomorrow—*morgen*, all right?"

He nodded. "*Morgen ist fein. Gute nacht.*"

"Good night." Clutching her bag in one hand, she looped her small cloth purse over her arm and picked up the lantern. Its flaming wick cast a swath of light before her.

Unfamiliar with her surroundings and weary from the hours of travel, she couldn't be sure if the shiver that ran through her was from the cold or the eerie shadows. Either way, all she wanted was a warm bed behind a sturdy door.

Mr. Schmidt had told her to take the second street—that much she understood. She held the lantern higher to get a better look at the tiny houses that lined up for her perusal. She trudged on, her carpetbag growing heavier by the minute. Finally, the lantern light fell on a small yellow house. Amelia ventured closer and shone the light on the door. Above the lintel was an ornate sign that read: RICHTER HAUS.

Fatigue wilted her shoulders. "Thank goodness."

She climbed the steps to the narrow porch, but hesitated at the door. It didn't seem fitting to enter the house without knocking. Was the Richter family sleeping inside? She held the lantern up to one window. The light glared off the wavy glass.

She rapped on the door but there was no response. For good measure, she knocked again and listened for stirring from within. Satisfied the house was empty, she gripped the door latch and pushed.

"It's locked!"

Her arrival was expected. Why would Mr. Richter tell her she would stay here, and then lock the door without providing her a key? She worked the doorknob again to no avail.

The frustration of the day crawled up from her gut and she clenched her jaw. Leaving her satchel and reticule by the door, she tried the two front windows. Neither of them budged. She huffed out a breath of annoyance and took the lantern around the side of the house. She held the lantern high and continued to make her way along the side of the house.

Near the back corner, she stumbled into a pile of firewood stacked against the house. "Oh!" Pieces of split stove wood tumbled down with a noisy clatter. A yowling screech split the air as a cat scrambled off the unstable woodpile.

An involuntary scream strangled in Amelia's throat and a stabbing pain shot through her foot. She managed to hang on to the lantern as she hopped on one foot and leaned against the corner of the house.

Her breath heaved in and out as she waited for the pain to subside. Between the stagecoach's delayed journey and the turbulent ride, Mr. Richter's absence, struggling to communicate with Mr. Schmidt, and finding she couldn't gain access to her promised living quarters, seething tears burned behind her eyelids. She squeezed her eyes shut and forced the tears to retreat.

Drawing in a deep, steadying breath, she hobbled around the scattered firewood and found another window on the back wall of the house. She set the lantern on the ground and pushed at the window. It gave a piercing squeak as wood scraped against wood, but at least it opened.

"*Wer sind sie und was machen sie?*" The deep, masculine voice boomed through the still night air.

Amelia squawked and spun around. She understood the first part of the challenge: Who are you? "I'm Miss Amelia Bachman, the new schoolteacher. Mr. Richter?"

Two large, booted feet carried the man out of the shadows and into the lantern light. "You're a woman!"

Under the circumstances, his observation was so ludicrous she didn't know whether to laugh or throw the lantern at him.

He reached for the lantern and drew it up where it illumined both their faces. His disheveled sandy hair flopped in his eye. If this was Mr. Richter, he was a lot younger than she expected.

"What are you doing?" His tone lost a bit of its gruff edge, but his dark brown eyes still held an air of suspicion.

She was getting ready to climb through the window. What did it look like she was doing? "Are you Mr. Richter?"

Skepticism flitted across his face. "No. I'm Hank Zimmermann." He jerked his thumb over his shoulder. "My family's Sunday house is next door." He narrowed his eyes. "You didn't answer my question. What are you doing outside the Richter's' Sunday house in the middle of the night?"

Indignation pulled her chin up. She resented Mr. Zimmermann's accusing tone.

"Mr. Richter's letter said I would be staying in the Sunday house belonging to his family. The stage arrived late and nobody was at the depot to greet me. I had to find this house by myself in the dark, and the door is locked." The tears that threatened earlier returned to taunt her, but she refused to give in to them.

"Locked?" His frown pulled his eyebrows into a *V*. "Folks around here don't lock their doors."

Her voice cracked with emotion, but she latched on to the frayed edges of her composure and hung on. "Well, it wouldn't open and I have no way of getting in. I can show you Mr. Richter's letter if you don't believe me."

Chapter 2

"No, no, I believe you."

Hank had never called a lady a liar before, especially not one this beautiful.

"I know Mr. Richter and the school board have been looking for a new teacher since Miss Klein left. But I didn't know. . .that is, I didn't expect—" He couldn't very well say he didn't expect someone as pretty as her to be a schoolteacher. The teacher he'd had as a boy was as homely as a mud fence.

"Let me check the front door for you." He stepped back and allowed her to precede him. Before she took three steps, he blurted, "Hey, you're limping. Did you—" He clamped his hand over his mouth while heat filled his face. She might have some physical impairment that caused her to limp.

She lifted her shoulders. "I stubbed my toe on the woodpile when that silly cat startled me."

"Oh, good. I mean, it's not good that you stubbed your toe, but. . .I thought, that is, I was afraid I'd insulted you."

A befuddled look marred her features. Perhaps he could smooth over his clumsy remark by offering her his arm. To his surprise, she laid her gloved hand on the crook of his elbow while he held the lantern. They picked their way around the house and when he sneaked a peek at her from the corner of his eye, he caught her looking up at him.

"So you speak both English and German?"

He grunted. "Everyone around here speaks German. Most speak English, too. You'll encounter both in the classroom." He handed her the lantern and stepped up on the front porch, certain the door was not locked. He twisted the doorknob and pushed, but the door didn't budge.

"Hmm. The wood is probably swollen." He angled his shoulder and pushed hard against the stubborn door. It popped open. "It was just stuck. I can fix it if you like." He bent to pick up her satchel. "Would you like me to carry this upstairs?" He tilted his head to the side of the house opposite of the way they'd come.

Confusion flickered over her face as she moved the lantern inside the door and perused the small space. "There are no stairs."

He pointed to the end of the porch. "The stairs leading to the sleeping loft are on the side of the house."

She blinked and raised her eyebrows. "Oh."

Even in the dim lantern light, he saw a rosy blush steal into her cheeks and the impact of his statement struck him. "I'll—I'll just put the bag at the top of the stairs for you. If you have any trouble with the door to the sleeping quarters—"

Embarrassment cut off his words and they stuck in his throat. He plowed up the steps two at a time and plunked the satchel on the landing. When he descended the stairs, she finished the sentence for him.

"I'll push it open with my shoulder. Thank you, Mr. Zimmermann."

"Hank."

"Uh, yes, well, good night." She picked up her skirt and scurried up the steps as quickly as one could with a painful toe.

He stood in the shadows and watched until she was safely inside and had closed the door. Wisps of light drifted past the small upper window.

"What are you doing, Zimmermann?" Hank muttered, shaking himself back to consciousness. Sweat prickled out on his upper lip like it was a sultry July night instead of a frigid February eve. He prayed Miss Bachman didn't get the wrong impression of his offer to help with the door.

The front door of the house still stood open. He tried to pull it closed as quietly as possible, but the place where it stuck previously hit with a thud. He cringed and strode off the porch before the pretty schoolmarm hollered down, wanting to know what he was doing.

❧

Dawn's first rays had barely broken through the slate sky when Hank's feet hit the floor. He couldn't remember the last time he'd tossed and turned all night, but when he'd climbed into his cot after the encounter with Miss Bachman, he couldn't quiet his thoughts.

Her wide, hazel eyes lingered in his mind. How could a woman with whom he'd spent less than ten minutes drive away sleep and confound his thinking? She wasn't the first pretty woman he'd ever met, but there was something distinctly distracting about her.

He pulled on thick woolen socks and padded to the tiny kitchen. Coals still glowed in the small stove. A few sticks of kindling coaxed them to life. While he waited for the coffeepot to boil, he ran his hand over the cabinet he'd spent the past few days working on, the satiny smooth grain of the wood submitting to the will of his fingers. The result of his labor pleased him. He only hoped the customers of Horst Braun's general store agreed. If the samples of Hank's work generated enough interest, perhaps his father wouldn't look on him with disappointment.

Needles of guilt jabbed him. Tradition dictated that the eldest son worked side by side with his father and eventually took over the family business—in this case, their farm. But Hank's heart didn't find contentment in working the soil or growing crops. Instead, his hands itched to create fine pieces of furniture. His brother, George, on the other hand, loved planting and harvesting, and longed for their father's approval. George should be the one to partner with *Vater* on the farm.

He ran one finger along the curved edge of the intricate carving he'd done last night. The pattern mimicked the one on the cabinet in his parents' home, crafted by his mother's grandfather. His father had always admired the piece. Hank prayed for God to help him prove his skill so Vater would be more accepting of his chosen occupation. Would his father ever subscribe to the belief that a son could pursue a different vocation and still adhere to the fifth commandment?

"Must I be a farmer in order to honor my father? Lord God, please guide my hands and help me to show Vater that I can still honor him without following in his footsteps."

The coffee boiled over and hissed as the liquid hit the hot metal plate of the stove. Hank grabbed a towel and moved the pot to the dry sink. What a mess.

After a breakfast of dark bread, cold sausage, and strong coffee, Hank set to work on the cabinet. Thoughts of the pretty, new schoolteacher next door continually distracted his focus and had him peering out the window at the Richter's Sunday house.

He poured another cup of coffee and blew on the steaming liquid before taking a noisy sip. As he set the cup down on the windowsill, he saw her.

Miss Amelia Bachman stepped onto the porch and pulled her shawl around her. When she hesitated a moment, it gave Hank the opportunity to stare at her without her knowledge. Fascination arrested his attention. Even her name sang in his subconscious—*Miss Amelia Bachman*.

She set off resolutely down the street and Hank followed her with his eyes. As he watched, he realized she was headed toward the depot. Consternation filled him. What if she'd decided not to stay? What if she was going to buy a one-way ticket back to where she came from? He hoped she wasn't judging Fredericksburg by the awkward late-night meeting with her neighbor. Admittedly, he hadn't made a very a good impression last night, but Fredericksburg needed a teacher. He couldn't let her leave.

He grabbed his leather jacket and hat and ran out the door after her. By the time he caught up to her, she was knocking on the depot door.

"Mr. Schmidt?"

"*Ja, gut morgen, Fraulein Bachman.*"

"Good morning. I've come to—"

"Miss Bachman."

She turned and the moment she made eye contact with him, her cheeks turned bright pink. "Mr. Zimmermann."

"Miss Bachman, please don't leave. The town needs you. I apologize for surprising you last night and I hope you don't think—"

"Mr. Zimmermann, what are you talking about? I'm not leaving." She cast a dubious look at him. "I'm returning Mr. Schmidt's lantern."

Hank's tongue tangled around his teeth. "Oh." He took a step backward. "I, uh, suppose I should just mind my own business."

The tiniest of smiles twitched across her lips. "That's quite all right. It's nice to know I'm needed." She glanced past him and scanned up and down the street. "I was hoping to meet Mr. Richter this morning."

"*Nien*," Humbert Schmidt spoke up. "Richter don't come. . ." He cast a glance at Hank. "*Stadt?*"

"Town." Hank supplied the English word. "What Mr. Schmidt is trying to tell you is the Richters don't ever come into town except on the weekends."

"But I don't understand." Lines of puzzlement deepened across Miss Bachman's brow. "I sent him my itinerary. He knew I was arriving yesterday." She turned to the depot agent. "You mean Mr. Richter wasn't here waiting for my stage to arrive yesterday?"

The elderly man scratched his head and looked at Hank.

"*Wartete Richter hier gestern?*" Hank translated her question, but he already knew the answer. Richter wouldn't rearrange his weekly routine for anyone.

"Nien." Mr. Schmidt shook his head. "He work at farm. He come. . ." He scowled as if trying hard to think of the word he needed, then brightened. "Tomorrow. Richter come tomorrow. *Samstag*."

"Saturday?" The schoolmarm aimed her inquiry at Hank. "He wasn't planning on coming to town until Saturday?"

Hank shrugged. "Probably." Clearly, she didn't understand the life of a farmer in this area of Texas. "Most of the farmers live a ways out of town. For some, it's a two- or three-hour journey. So they only come to town on Saturday to do their trading, stay overnight at their Sunday house, attend worship and socialize, and then go back to their farm Sunday afternoon."

Mr. Schmidt nodded even though Hank knew the man only understood about half of what he'd said.

Miss Bachman appeared as if trying to hide her embarrassment. "I see. If I'd known, I wouldn't have made such a fool of myself."

Hank opened his mouth to assure her she had no need to be embarrassed, but Schmidt beat him to it. The older man shook his head so vehemently, his unkempt gray hair flopped over one eye.

"Nien, nien, I know das word, fool. You ain't fool." He patted her hand. "You is . . .*klug*."

"Smart," Hank supplied.

Schmidt nodded. "Ja, you smart. You teach"—he bounced his hand, palm down, indicating several young ones—"*kinder*." He poked his thumb into his chest. "Schmidt *dummkoff*."

He rapped his forehead with his knuckles. "Fraulein Bachman, you *sehr hubscher* . . .teacher."

"Mm." Hank murmured in agreement despite the expression on Miss Bachman's face that indicated she didn't understand the full meaning of Schmidt's statement. He ducked his head to hide the smile he couldn't suppress.

"Mr. Zimmermann, since you're here—"

Hank jerked his head up and met her enchanting hazel eyes.

"Could you give me a hand with my trunk?" She pointed to the battered piece of luggage that sat just inside the depot door.

"Sure." He grabbed one leather handgrip and hoisted the load, clamping his lips on the grunt that tried to escape. The thing must be filled with rocks.

She thanked Mr. Schmidt and led the way back to the Sunday house. Hank followed with the rock-laden trunk.

"I hope it's not too heavy." She glanced over her shoulder. "I packed quite a few books."

That explained why it was pulling his shoulder out of joint.

She tipped her head and looked sideways at him. "May I ask you a question?"

He nodded and hiked the trunk up a tad higher.

"What does *sehr hubscher* mean, and why did you find it amusing?"

Heat raced up Hank's neck. Sehr hubscher meant *very pretty*.

Chapter 3

Saturday morning, Amelia sat at the small table with her books. The *clip-clop* of hooves and jingling harness announced the arrival of a wagon, and moments later the door crashed open. A husky woman with ruddy cheeks nearly fell into the room. Amelia leaped to her feet.

"*Was ist dies?*" The woman's eyes widened. "The door is not stuck?"

"Hank Zimmermann fixed it."

The woman eyed her with suspicion. "You are the new schoolteacher?"

"Y–yes." Amelia didn't know whether to extend her hand or stand there like a statue. "I'm Amelia Bachman. May I help you carry anything?"

"I am Olga Richter." The woman eyes snapped and she pointed to the small table. "You may carry those books upstairs. There is no room for them."

Before Amelia could collect her things, another woman, as wide as she was tall, waddled into the room, fussing over the cluttered table and scolding Amelia in German.

A burly man stepped in behind her. "*Mutter, stoppen sie sich zu beschweren*—stop complaining. Pardon my mama, she speaks no English. I am Lamar Richter. This is *meine mutter*, my mother, Winnie. You are Miss Bachman, ja? So—you are here." The man didn't appear bothered in the least that Amelia had arrived with no one to meet her or escort her to the Sunday house, for he said little else.

Amelia spent the remainder of the day dodging out of the way as Olga and Winnie bustled around, her attempts at conversation rejected. Evening brought the uncomfortable realization that she was expected to share the tiny sleeping loft with the two women, while Mr. Richter slept downstairs on a pallet.

Sunday afternoon as Amelia helped Olga carry things to the wagon, agitated voices carried on the air. Next door, Hank Zimmermann stood beside his family's wagon while his father berated him.

"The Zimmermanns are famers. When will you stop with your playing and come back to the farm where you belong?"

Hank ran his hand through his hair. "Vater, building furniture is not playing. It's my hope that one day you'll respect my choice to be a carpenter."

"Respect! It is you who should respect your father and work the land as you were born to do."

Mr. Zimmermann's harsh tone made Amelia flinch with the memory of her own father's disapproval of her chosen vocation. Empathy trickled through her. Sometime after the Richters left, the Zimmermann wagon pulled out, but Hank wasn't on it.

❧

The first two days of classes required some adjustments. Most of the children were sweet, but some of the older boys attempted to play a prank or two, taking advantage of Amelia's unfamiliarity with the German language and culture. The class snickered when Bernard Braun tried to convince her that Mr. Richter went by the name *alte ziege*. Between the laughter and the devilish smirk in Bernard's eyes, it wasn't hard to figure out the reference wasn't flattering. She knew *alte* meant "old" and she was fairly certain *ziege* was some kind of animal. Bernard and his best friend, Paeter Lange, appeared panic-stricken when she replied that she'd make sure Mr. Richter knew the boys were kind enough to tell her his nickname. She ducked her head to hide her smile.

As she prepared to leave the little house on Wednesday morning, she heard the ring of Hank's hammer. Sending a furtive glance toward the Zimmermanns' Sunday house, she caught a glimpse of Hank perched on a ladder, hammering a board into place at the back of the house. She paused and watched for a moment, fascinated by the way Hank's tools seemed an extension of himself. Pieces of wood conformed to the mastery with which he used his skill.

What a wonderful lesson to teach her students—that their hopes and dreams could grow and develop when surrendered to the hands of the Master. She tucked the thought away, but before she stepped off the porch, Hank straightened and looked her way. He tugged the brim of his hat then raised his fingers in a slight wave.

Her heart hiccupped. There was no point in pretending she hadn't been staring at him. She returned a polite nod and scurried down the street.

She'd barely gotten the fire started in the potbellied stove in the middle of the classroom when a wagon rolled into the yard. She cracked open the door to see who was arriving early. To her surprise, Hank's father sat on the wagon seat and three blond heads peeked just above the sides of the wagon bed. The gruff farmer pulled the team to a halt in front of the schoolhouse and barked at the youngsters to get out while he climbed down.

Amelia met him at the door, glancing past his shoulder to watch a little girl with golden pigtails help the two younger ones slide off the end of the tailgate. The oldest child couldn't have been more than seven or eight years of age, yet Mr. Zimmermann left them to fend for themselves. They were undoubtedly siblings, their resemblance being too uncanny to miss.

Amelia disciplined her features to not show disapproval of the man's inconsideration. "Good morning, Mr. Zimmermann."

Instead of returning the pleasant greeting, he merely grunted and gestured to the children. "These are startin' school today. That one"—he pointed to the eldest—"is Elsie. Next is Joy, and the boy is Micah. Last name's Delaney." He almost sneered when the name fell from his lips. "You kinder mind what the teacher tells you, or I'll take a strap to you."

Three pairs of eyes glistened with tears and the little boy's lower lip trembled. Mr. Zimmermann climbed back onto the wagon seat. "You go find your uncle Hank when school's out." With that Mr. Zimmermann released the brake and whistled to the team.

The trio stood huddled together, eyeing Amelia with fear-filled eyes. Only then did she realize she was scowling, but the children had no way of knowing her displeasure was not aimed at them. She fixed a smile in place and stepped toward them. The little boy started to cry.

"Now, there's nothing to be afraid of." She reached to pat Micah's head and the child shrank from her.

She pulled her hand back and tried a different approach. "Elsie? You must be the oldest. It looks like you're doing a fine job of taking care of your sister and brother." She sent the little girl a beaming smile. "Come inside where it's warmer and you can tell me all about yourselves. I brought some sugar cookies to school today."

At the mention of cookies, Micah wiped his nose on his sleeve and followed his sisters into the schoolhouse.

Amelia glanced at the little watch pinned to her bodice. The other students wouldn't begin arriving for at least another fifteen minutes. She directed the three siblings to one of the front benches and retrieved a cloth-covered pail from her desk.

She offered each child a golden-edged cookie. Elsie and Joy whispered a thank-you, but Micah observed her with wide, solemn green eyes, as though weighing her trustworthiness. Her heart twisted within her breast. She wanted to take the little fellow and hug him. Instead, she held out a cookie.

"My name is Miss Bachman, and I'm very happy to meet you." They munched their cookies while Amelia continued. "Elsie, can you tell me how much schooling you've had?"

Elsie wiped crumbs from her mouth. "We ain't never went to school before, but Mama taught us letters and numbers, and I can read."

"I can read, too." Joy lifted her chin and straightened her shoulders.

Elsie clucked like a hen. "No, you can't. You just know all the letters."

Amelia smiled, but in the back of her mind, Elsie's reference to *Mama* intrigued her. Where was their mother, and why was Mr. Zimmermann carrying them to school? "Well, that's a very good start. Do you have a paper tablet and pencil?"

Elsie and Joy shook their heads in unison, their yellow braids flopping against their chins.

"That's all right. You can borrow mine today." Amelia's heart lifted just a little when a hesitant smile poked a dimple into Joy's cheek.

"Can I learn to read today?"

Amelia couldn't stay her hand from reaching out to cradle the side of Joy's face. "It will take more than one day, but we'll get started today." The glow in the little girl's eyes reflected her name.

Amelia instructed the three Delaney children to wait until she had cleaned the chalkboard and swept the floor so she could walk them to the Zimmermanns' Sunday house. Mr. Zimmermann's harsh tone and uncaring attitude still irked her, but she wasn't going to allow the children to wander the town searching for their uncle Hank alone.

Elsie wanted to carry Amelia's lunch pail, and Joy begged to carry her paper tablet, while Micah shyly tucked his hand into Amelia's. The four of them walked uptown and turned on Lincoln Street. As they approached the Zimmermann house, Amelia's eyes widened. The few boards and posts that Hank had nailed in place that morning had expanded into an extension off the back of the house. It still lacked a roof and one wall, but the structure was definitely taking shape.

"Mr. Zimmermann." Amelia raised her voice to be heard above Hank's hammering. Instantly, all three children halted and hung back.

When Hank poked his head around the corner to respond, Micah cried out, "Uncle Hank." The child dropped Amelia's hand and raced toward his uncle. The girls also relaxed and ran to claim a hug from the man whose blue-plaid shirt was speckled with sawdust.

Amelia's heart smiled.

Hank squatted to corral all three children in his arms. He tugged on the girls' pigtails and ruffled Micah's hair. "What are you rascals doing here?"

Amelia stepped forward. "Your father dropped them off at the school this morning and told them to *find you* when class was dismissed." She raised her eyebrows in a silent question.

Hank stood and pointed toward the door. "Elsie, there is some bread in the cabinet and a jar of jam on the table." The siblings trotted inside, leaving Amelia waiting for an answer to her unspoken inquiry.

Hank glanced over his shoulder and blew out a stiff breath. "First of all, let me explain. I'm not their *uncle* Hank. They are actually my cousins, but my father thinks it's disrespectful for them to call me Hank without some kind of title in front of it." He brushed sawdust from his sleeve. "My father's baby sister, Laurene, was fifteen years younger than him. My parents disapproved when she married an Irishman about nine years ago. Last week my father got a telegram saying Aunt Laurene and her husband had been killed in a wagon accident and the three children were being sent here."

Amelia's stomach clenched in sympathy for the three orphans, but misgiving filled her as well to think of them growing up under Mr. Zimmermann's harsh hand. "They were very frightened this morning."

"I'm not surprised." Hank muttered the remark that sounded more like he was talking to himself than to her. He shoved his hands in his pockets. "My father doesn't want them. He said he's already raised his children and doesn't intend to raise these.

On Sunday, he said he was going to send them to the orphanage, so I'm a little surprised to see they are still here."

The disturbing revelation made no sense to Amelia. "He told me they were starting school today. Maybe he changed his mind."

Hank snorted. "Nothing changes Thornton Zimmermann's mind." Instantly, regret softened his features. "I didn't mean that the way it sounded."

Amelia's insides churned at the uncertainty the children faced. At least they appeared to love their "uncle" Hank, and if the way he greeted them was any indication, the feeling was mutual.

Chapter 4

Vater, how could you say such a mean thing to those kids?"

Thornton Zimmermann thumped his coffee cup down on the table and turned to face his son with rage in his eyes. "I am the head of this house. I make the decisions. Der kinder are not my responsibility. My sister and her Irish husband whelped them and now I am expected to raise them? Nein! I already raise my kinder." He cast a withering look at Hank. "Ja, I raise my son to be a farmer and he wants to be a *woodcutter*."

Hank sucked in a breath. He would not shout at his father no matter how angry he was or how much he disagreed with him. Instead, he pointed across the room at his brother, who waited in silence for their father to head out to the fields. "Vater, can't you see how much George loves planting and harvesting? He's the one who should take over the farm one day. I came here this morning hoping I could make you understand the gift God has given me to craft things out of wood, but this isn't about me being a craftsman."

"Bah! Craftsman!" The elder Zimmermann turned away. "I have fields to plow."

Hank took three strides and blocked him. He pointed out the door where Elsie, Joy, and Micah huddled together, crying.

"Look at those children out there. They've already lost their parents. We are the only family they have. How could you tell them you're sending them to an orphanage?"

His father's face mottled beet red. "You do not question what I decide. I have fed them for over two weeks. The letter finally comes and says there is no room at the orphanage in San Antonio. The director says he writes to Austin and Abilene. Or maybe kinder will go to Dallas, but they will go! As soon as I have word from the place"—Vater pointed his finger in Hank's face—"they *will* go."

Hank stared at his father. When had the man become so hateful? Was this his fault? Was Vater so angry at him for not following in his footsteps that he'd take it out on innocent children? Hank clenched his fists at his sides as anger boiled within him.

Hank glanced across the room at his mother, but Lydia Zimmermann shook her head at him, a warning in her eyes. There was no point in trying to talk to his father like this. He turned and stalked out the door.

Three tear-stained faces tipped up to look at him when he approached. His heart splintered at the sight of their blotchy cheeks and red-rimmed, swollen eyes. A cool March wind stirred the dust, creating muddy streaks tracing their sorrow.

Hank pulled out his bandanna and dipped it in the horse trough. Lowering himself to one knee, he blotted each child's face, talking in low, soothing tones.

"We can't have you going to school with dirty faces. What will Miss Bachman think? Besides, if you climb up on old Fritz with stripes on your cheeks, he's liable to think you're a tiger and buck you right off." He wiped the last of the dirty tears away from Micah's cheeks and the little boy looked up at Hank.

"Fritz won't buck me off. You said he's too old to buck."

Hank feigned surprise. "Did I say that?" When all three children nodded, he forced a smile he didn't feel and stood. "Well, maybe I did. Now, if we don't hurry, you're going to be late for school."

"I don't want to go to school today." Tears again filled Joy's eyes.

"Here now." Hank bent to cup her chin. "Miss Bachman would miss you something fierce if you didn't go to school. She told me you're learning to read."

Joy nodded.

"How about if you come to the Sunday house after school and read to me what you learn today?"

Joy shrugged. "I guess so."

"All right, then. Do you have the lunch pail Aunt Lydia packed for you?"

Elsie held it up.

"Then we're ready to go." Hank scooped Elsie up and lifted her onto Fritz's swayed back while the gray horse dozed at the hitching rail. He positioned Joy behind her sister, and Micah sat in the front where Elsie could hold on to him.

"Everybody all set?" He swung up onto his own horse. "C'mon, Fritz. It's time to get these kids to school."

❧

Amelia led the first and second graders as they recited their addition tables in unison, but her gaze continually wandered to the three empty seats the Delaney children usually occupied. Although she tried to convince herself not to worry, her heart refused to listen.

"All right, first and second grade. Take out your tablets and copy the addition problems I've written on the chalkboard. Third and fourth graders, come to the front bench for reading. I want the older grades to go to the back corner where you will find some maps of the United States to study. When you've—"

The clopping of hooves cut her instructions short and she glanced out the window. A sigh of relief rippled through her.

"Freda Braun, you will be in charge of the reading group. Page thirty-seven. I must step out for a minute. Everyone has their assignments."

She exited the classroom in time to see Hank help the Delaney children off the swaybacked plow horse. The instant she caught sight of their puffy, red eyes, fear gripped her heart.

Hank bent to tuck Micah's shirt into his pants and smooth the boy's unruly straw-colored hair. "Come to the Sunday house when class is dismissed. I'll see you then."

Amelia touched the top of each child's head and gave them a reassuring smile.

"Go on in and find your seats. I'll be there in a minute. I want to talk to your uncle Hank."

Elsie took Micah's hand and led him toward the door, but Joy wrapped her arms around Hank's waist and clung.

"Are you gonna make us go away, Uncle Hank?" A fat tear trickled down her cheek.

Amelia met Hank's gaze, holding her breath and waiting for his answer. His smoky eyes were a study in anger. The fear she felt when she first saw the children doubled. What had transpired to make the children so late and upset them so? She was afraid to ask.

Hank stooped to speak to Joy at her eye level. He brushed loose tendrils of hair from her face. "If it was up to me, you wouldn't have to go anywhere, sweetheart. But it's not my decision to make." He cupped her chin. "Do you remember the Bible story we read last night?"

Joy sniffed and nodded.

Hank thumbed her tears away. "Jesus is the Good Shepherd and He knows His sheep. No matter where His sheep are, He looks after them." He folded her fingers within his. "That means wherever we are, Jesus promises to take care of us, even if we are far away from each other."

The child buried her face in Hank's shirt and mumbled, "But I don't want to be far away. I want to be here."

Amelia gently peeled her away from Hank. "Joy, sometimes hard things happen in our lives and we don't have a choice. But the hard things don't mean that our love for each other goes away."

A twinge of guilt stabbed her. Growing up watching her parents' cold hearts and resentful demeanor was hard, and when she left home she didn't have the love of her parents to take with her. But Joy didn't need to know that.

She pulled the child into a hug. "Suppose you go behind the schoolhouse to the pump and wash your face. Then we will have our reading lesson."

Joy dragged her sleeve across her soggy cheeks and sniffed again. "Yes'm." She trudged away to do her teacher's bidding.

As soon as she was out of earshot, Amelia spun to face Hank. "What happened?"

He turned away as though looking her in the eye was painful. "Micah heard my father say something this morning about an orphanage, and he asked what an orphanage was." The dejection in his tone made Amelia shiver. He removed his hat and fidgeted with the brim. "So my father told him and the girls that they weren't his children and he wasn't going to be saddled with them, and as soon as he could make the arrangements, they were going to live in an orphanage."

Amelia covered her mouth and a gasp slipped between her fingers. "Oh no. How could he be so heartless?" She bit her lip, fearing her outburst may have offended Hank.

He snorted. "I asked him the same thing. He just blustered that it was his decision. We argued—" He shook his head. "I don't know what else to do."

Amelia plunked her hands on her hips. "Couldn't you take the children?"

Hank jerked around to face her. "What?" His eyes widened. "You can't be serious. I don't know anything about raising children."

"What do you have to know?" She cocked her head. "You need to love them and provide for their needs."

Hank's fist crumpled the brim of his hat. "How am I going to do that? In case you haven't noticed, I'm working out of my family's Sunday house and I don't have customers beating down the door."

"But those children need to know they are wanted and loved. Who is going to do that?"

He opened his mouth but apparently changed his mind. He plopped his hat back in place. "Look, I can't do what you're suggesting. How am I supposed to take care of three little kids? Do you really think my father would let me move them into the Sunday house like I owned it? He doesn't even like me using the place for my woodworking." He heaved an exasperated sigh.

Discouragement wilted her posture. She shrugged and turned back toward the schoolhouse. "I just wish. . ."

"I know. I wish the same thing."

She turned to face him. "Wishing won't change a thing, but praying might."

He looped Fritz's reins over a low-hanging branch. "Sometimes I'm not sure God hears my prayers."

Amelia glanced over her shoulder. She needed to return to the classroom, but Hank's remark disturbed her. "Of course, He hears you. Why would you think otherwise?"

He turned to his own horse, gripped the saddle horn, and swung astride. "Sometimes I wonder if God is as angry at me as my father is." He spoke absently, as though more to himself than Amelia. "My father refuses to listen to me because I'm not doing what he wants me to do. Does that mean I'm out of God's will? Wouldn't He refuse to listen as well?"

As if suddenly remembering she was there, he straightened and reined the horse around, tugging on the brim of his hat before nudging the horse into a gentle lope.

Amelia watched him ride away and felt a check in her spirit. Unconsciously, wasn't she doing something similar? She felt like a hypocrite. She'd encouraged her students to trust God with the new skills and knowledge they were learning, and let Him be the Master of their hopes and dreams. But her own hopes and dreams remained tucked away in a secret place in her heart—like unplanted seeds.

"Lord God, I couldn't do what my father wanted to me to do. I just couldn't." She paused by the schoolhouse door and fingered the pull rope on the bell. Becoming a schoolteacher was a noble occupation, one in which she could influence young lives and mold their character.

And remain single.

She, too, had gone against her father's wishes. Did that mean she was out of God's will, and therefore beyond the reach of His ear?

Chapter 5

Amelia swept her tiny pile of dirt out the back door of the Sunday house, noticing as she did so that Hank was nowhere to be seen. She'd grown so accustomed to hearing the song of his chisel gliding along a length of wood, or his mallet beating out staccato taps, the absence of the sounds felt lonely. The lean-to addition he'd constructed off the back of his family's Sunday house testified to his skill. Amelia paused for a moment and studied the lines of the new space he'd created, and wondered if the inside was as efficient and functional as it appeared from the outside.

Her face warmed with the thought. Why in heaven's name was she so fascinated by this man? She ordered her attention back to her tasks. Now that the sun was up, she wanted to polish the windows before the Richter family arrived for the weekend. The Saturday morning air held a bit of a chill for late March. She propped open the windows so the house would smell as fresh and clean as the spring breeze.

As the sun climbed higher in the eastern sky, Amelia took rags soaked in a vinegar solution to the windows, angling her head to peer sideways, checking for streaks. She wanted to give Olga and Winnie nothing to criticize.

The sounds of wagons arriving to the melody of birdsong, children's laughter, and folks calling out greetings to each other began filling the air. Amelia hurried to finish her preparations. Her final chore was filling the woodbox. She picked up as much stove wood as she could hold, but as she turned to carry it into the house, the breeze blew the door shut.

She stamped her foot. "Drat!"

"Here, allow me."

Amelia jerked her head around. Hank stepped onto the small stoop and reached for the load in her arms.

"When I saw what you were doing, I came to help."

"Oh, th–thank you, Mr. Zimmermann."

"Hank."

"Mr.—Hank. I didn't realize you were. . .your house looked empty."

He cocked one eyebrow and his silent query caused flustered embarrassment to twine up her throat—she'd just told him that she'd been looking for him. She put her composure back in place.

"You don't have to do this."

He shrugged and grinned. "I'm setting a good example for my young cousins."

She allowed Hank to relieve her of the load of wood and she propped the door open.

He tipped his head toward the wood piled in his arms. "Toss me a few more pieces."

She obliged, and he carried the firewood inside and emptied his arms into the box beside the stove, filling it to the brim.

"Thank you, Mr.—Hank."

"My pleasure." He dusted off his hands as he exited, then paused on the stoop. "It's a beautiful day."

She murmured her agreement with his observation.

"Perfect morning for a stroll. If you aren't too busy—"

"Oh, but I am." A sliver of guilt over the fib poked her. She ignored it and continued. "The Richters will be here any time, and I still have things to do before they arrive. Thank you for your help. It was very kind of you. Good day." She pasted a polite smile on her face and closed the door on his disappointed expression.

Filling the woodbox was her last chore of the morning, but Hank's warm brown eyes sent strange ripples through her. The inclination to explore the feeling teased, but she purposefully shoved it into submission.

Reverend Hoffman stood at the door of the church and shook hands with the parishioners as they filed out. Amelia fell into line behind the Richters and expressed her appreciation to the pastor for a fine, inspiring sermon.

"I hope my students were listening as you spoke about compassion. It's a virtue I hope to instill in all the children." She didn't add that she hoped Thornton Zimmermann was listening as well. She'd seen the man, three rows ahead of her, thump Micah's head when the five-year-old squirmed.

"Thank you, young lady." Pastor Hoffman grinned broadly. "My daughter loves going to school since you began teaching. Whatever you're doing, don't stop."

The preacher's praise sent warmth scurrying into her cheeks. "Your Gretchen is a fine student. It's a pleasure having her in my class."

They bid each other good afternoon and Amelia stepped out into the early spring sunshine.

"Miss Bachman!" A joyful chorus of childish voices greeted her. The Delaney children ran to her with smiles. How good it was to see them happy, even if it was for only a few moments.

Elsie, usually the serious one, tugged at Amelia's sleeve. "I learned a Bible verse today."

"Why, that's wonderful, Elsie. I'd love to hear it."

The little girl twisted one braid around her finger and dipped her fair brows in concentration. "For He shall give His angels charge over thee, to keep thee in all thy ways. Psalm ninety-one, verse eleven." A grin filled her face as she finished.

"Excellent, Elsie. I'm very proud of you."

"You are?" The child's eyes widened with wonder.

"I am." Amelia bent and slipped her arm around Elsie's shoulder. "Do you know what the verse means?"

"I think so." The little girl cocked her head. "It means God tells His angels to take care of us wherever we go." She leaned close to Amelia and whispered, "Even if we have to go to the orphanage."

Amelia's throat tightened at the child's courageous spirit. "We're still going to pray that doesn't happen, but if it does, yes, God will take care of you wherever you are."

Elsie fingered the lace edging on the sleeve of Amelia's green, flowered dress. "I ain't never seen such a pretty dress." She tipped her face up. "Green was my mama's favorite color. She woulda looked beautiful in a dress like this."

Amelia pressed her lips together and forced the corners upward, blinking hard. She didn't dare try to speak.

"Good morning."

Amelia looked up to find Hank Zimmermann's deep brown eyes fixed on her. Had he heard Elsie's heart-wrenching appraisal? She gulped.

"Elsie was just reciting her scripture verse for me." She took Elsie's golden braid between her thumb and forefinger.

"Oh?" Hank bent down, his hands on his knees. "Will you recite it for me, too?"

Elsie leaned to one side and peeked around Hank to where Mr. Zimmermann stood talking with another man. "All right, but just you."

A smile stretched across Hank's face, but an ache invaded Amelia's heart. Elsie and her siblings had only been living with the Zimmermanns' for less than a month and already the child knew whom she could and could not trust.

Hank slid the last of the newly finished pieces of furniture through the yawning double doors of the general store and turned to face the proprietor, Horst Braun. The man grinned and slapped Hank's shoulder. "This is good work, ja. You will have many customers when they see this beautiful craftsmanship." Horst ran his hand along the intricate design at the top of the cabinet Hank had labored over for two weeks.

Hank swiped his sleeve over his forehead. "I hope you're right, Horst." He didn't add that if he didn't get orders for more pieces, he'd find himself back on the farm doing what his father wanted. Doubt swirled in his stomach and he besought God again for direction. A silent prayer ascended from his heart.

Lord God, I want to be certain this is Your will. Why else would You have put the skill in my hands and the desire in my heart if You did not intend for me to use it? Please make peace between Vater and me, Lord. Can I not honor him and still be a carpenter?

Horst positioned the smaller piece, a pie safe with punched tin door inserts and gingerbread trim, near the entrance of the store. "There." Horst turned to Hank and beamed. "The customers can't miss it when they come in."

"Are you sure you have room for the cabinet?"

"Ja, we just move a few things over." Horst's gap-toothed grin stretched the man's beard into a crescent. "You push *der* pickle barrel there, and I move *dies* display of boots."

The two men shoved and maneuvered items here and there, opening up a space into which they slid the cabinet. Hank stepped back to survey the position of the piece at the same moment the front door opened and hit him in the backside.

"Oh, pardon me. I'm so sorry."

Hank turned to see Amelia's contrite expression turn to one of mortification. Her eyes widened and color stole into her cheeks and for the briefest of moments, Hank thought she was prettier than the sunrise he'd admired that morning.

Amelia clasped her hand over her bodice. "Oh dear, I should watch where I'm going. Do forgive me."

A grin tweaked his face. "No harm done." His pulse quickened. "I didn't realize it was time for school to be out. Are the youngsters at the Sunday house?"

She shook her head and looked out the window. "They were headed out of town on their old farm horse. I believe they call him Fritz." When she turned back around, she'd regained her composure. A polite smile curved her lips.

"Ja, Fritz is too old to pull the plow, but he doesn't mind the kids riding him." Hank shuffled his boot against the rough-hewn floor, trying to find the words to ask Amelia to join him for a stroll. "Vater must have told them to come straight home." Perhaps she'd agree to walk down by the creek with him before going back to. . .

"The children are—"

"Would you have time to accompany—"

Nervous laughter bubbled from Amelia, and Hank gestured with his hand. "You first."

The rosy glow crept into her cheeks again. "I was just going to say the children are doing well with their studies. Joy loves learning to read, and Elsie excels in spelling and vocabulary. Micah needs a bit more help with his letters and numbers, but he's a bright little boy. He'll learn quickly."

Hank shrugged. "They sure seem to like school and I thank you for that, but I don't know how much longer they'll be here. My father is waiting for letters from the orphanages at Abilene and Dallas." He scowled and studied the toes of his boots. "I'm afraid he won't even try to keep the kids together."

"But the children *must* stay together." Her voice broke. "They've already been through so much. If they are sent away—all they have is each other."

Her plea carried with it a thread of challenge and Hank gritted his teeth. He would take all three children in a minute if he could, but he'd already told her he didn't have the means to support them.

Distress over the children's future pressed her lips together and tiny lines appeared across her forehead, but she straightened her shoulders and lifted her chin slightly. "You were about to ask me something."

Hank swallowed the sudden dryness in his throat. "Would you consent to walk with me to Baron's Creek? It's not far from the Sunday house and we'd be in plain view for propriety's sake."

Amelia's eyes widened and she blinked twice. Her lips parted but she hesitated to speak, and the same flustered expression he saw when she hit him with the door returned to her face.

"It's very kind of you to ask, Mr. Zimm—I mean, Hank. But I've come to Fredericksburg to teach, and I don't wish to give any other impression. Good afternoon."

She hastened down the steps, apparently forgetting whatever it was she came to purchase.

Chapter 6

Almost a week after Amelia's conversation with Hank in the general store, the words she'd spoken to him still haunted her. She hadn't lied to him—not exactly. Teaching school had brought her to Fredericksburg, but there was no denying the underlying motive. Becoming a schoolteacher afforded her a perfectly reasonable excuse for refusing invitations from would-be suitors, including the prosperous rancher with whom her father had attempted to marry her off.

As evening fell she crossed the small kitchen area to prepare her simple supper. A light winked from the window of the Sunday house next door, testifying to Hank's presence. She fixed her gaze at her neighbor's window and felt a whisper of defiance ripple through her.

"I came to Fredericksburg to teach."

A twinge of foolishness poked her since there was nobody to hear her repeat the declaration she'd already delivered to Hank. If she were honest, she'd admit her decision had as much to do with her desire to control her own destiny as it did with molding the minds and character of children. In the five weeks she'd been in Fredericksburg, she'd thrilled to see her students learn and grow, but Fredericksburg was also a refuge. She was safe here.

She released a soft snort. "Safe from what? Marriage? Or just life in general?"

She lit the oil lamp on the table and cut a thick slice of the dark bread she'd purchased at the German bakery and slathered it with peach preserves. A chunk of cheese and small piece of cold sausage rounded out her supper. She set the kettle on the stove for her tea.

An image tiptoed into her mind. What would it be like to put supper on the table for a husband and children? The silent suppers she'd endured all her life, with her father at one end of the table and her mother at the other, faded from her memory as a fascinating scene unfolded and drew her. Blond-headed children with smiles of anticipation welcomed the culinary offerings she placed before them, and the man at the head of the table beamed at his family and bowed his head to pray. When he said amen and lifted his head—it was Hank Zimmermann's face.

Amelia startled and covered her warming cheeks with both hands. "Mercy!" *Such nonsense.* But the more she tried to push the thought away, the more strongly it insisted on manifesting.

Amelia heaved a sigh. A distraction. That's what she needed. Her canvas satchel sat gaping open on one of the chairs. She dug deep past the books and folders, and felt around the bottom of the bag. Her fingers found the small cloth pouch and she pulled it out. While she waited for the kettle to boil, she untied the strings that held the pouch tightly closed and shook an assortment of seeds into her open palm. A dozen different kinds of wildflower seeds given to her by one of her professors when she graduated—to commemorate her new beginning and opportunity to blossom.

As she rolled the seeds around in her hand, a plan began to form. Why not use the seeds as a science lesson, coupled with an outing for her students before the end of the school year? She glanced at the calendar on the wall. First week of April. Plenty of time to plan. She smiled and slid the seeds back into the pouch, pulling the strings snug. Her thoughts were back where they belonged.

Steam rose from the kettle's spout in lazy wisps that fogged the window. Amelia wiped the condensation away and the lamplight from Hank's window became visible again.

❧

Amelia stepped out the door of the post office clutching two envelopes. The first one bore her mother's distinctive flowing script. The arrival of the letter—the first she'd received from either parent for more than six months—sent hope surging through her. But anticipation over the contents of the letter sparred with dread in her heart. The last conversation she'd had with her mother was not a happy one. She tucked the letter into her satchel along with her books, lesson plans, and papers to be corrected. The privacy of the Sunday house was the place to read the letter, in case her parents' opinion of her career choice had not changed.

She didn't recognize the handwriting on the second letter, and the return address was smudged. Pausing on the boardwalk, she broke the seal on the envelope and extracted the single sheet of paper, scanning downward to the signature.

"Uncle Will?" The corners of her mouth lifted. Her father's brother, widowed a year ago, was her favorite relative. He and his wife had worked together in his medical practice in McAlester, Oklahoma. She read his scrawled words.

> *I hope this letter finds my favorite niece happy and well.*
>
> *It's been difficult for me to continue living and working here in McAlester since your aunt's passing. I can't walk down the street without her presence accompanying me. Everything I see reminds me of her, and while I desire to cling to her memory, I seem to be bogged down in grief.*
>
> *I need a fresh start. After corresponding with a few colleagues, I've made the decision to close my practice here and move to Fredericksburg.*

"Uncle Will's coming here?" Happy anticipation lifted her heart. She read the last line of his missive.

> *It may take some time to finalize everything, but I hope to be there perhaps by late May. Fondly, Uncle Will.*

While she'd been sad for Uncle Will at the passing of her aunt, joy tickled her stomach at the prospect of him coming to Fredericksburg. She slid Uncle Will's letter into her satchel with the one from her mother and hurried toward the general store.

A brisk spring breeze flapped the brim of Amelia's bonnet as she stepped through the bright blue door. Two ladies stood admiring the pie safe near the entrance of the store while Horst Braun walked over to them, wiping his hands on his apron.

"*Das ist verkauft*—that one is sold, ladies, but I'm sure if you speak with the craftsman, he will be happy to build another for you."

One of the ladies examined the gingerbread trim. "*Wer ist es?* Who does this fine work?"

Horst grinned. "Hank Zimmermann. He is very skilled, ja?"

A swell of pride for Hank danced through Amelia as the ladies exclaimed over the piece of furniture. The instant she recognized the emotion for what it was, heat filled her face. She ducked her head and pretended to examine a bolt of dress goods.

Foolishness.

Certainly Hank would be pleased to know people praised his work, especially in light of the argument she'd overheard between him and his father. She'd caught glimpses of him working hard at his craft, but to experience prideful flutters in her belly over the compliments from Horst and the women was just plain silly. So why did an absurd smile insist on stretching across her face? She shook her head.

"What can I get for you today, Miss Bachman?" Horst's voice boomed directly behind her. Amelia jumped as if he'd read her thoughts and knew why she was smiling.

"Oh, uh..." Why *did* she come into the store? She gawked at Horst for a moment. "Thread."

His indulgent smile was punctuated by a slight arch of his thick eyebrows, and he remained in place. The ends of his mustache wiggled and he pointed to the shelf a foot away from her right elbow. She jerked her head around.

"Oh." Her face burned and she could have sworn it was the middle of summer. "Oh my. I admonish my students about daydreaming and here I am, guilty of the same pastime. Forgive me, Mr. Braun."

The burly man tilted his head back and belly-laughed. "*Es ist gut*—it is good, ja, to daydream sometimes. My little Freda, she likes to watch the clouds. Her mutter grows impatient with her when she imagines stories drifting across the sky instead of doing her chores." A wide grin elongated his mustache.

Amelia imagined her student cloud-gazing with her father. A tiny ache began in the pit of her stomach. She'd never known such frivolity as a child, and especially not with either parent. Amelia hastily chose spools of thread, one of green and one of white. She opened her reticule to pay, but paused and pointed to a glass jar on the counter.

"Please give me two scoops of those gumdrops. I think I'll let my students do some daydreaming and reward their creativity."

Horst shoveled two large scoops into a paper bag. "I won't tell Freda's mutter you let her daydream in school." A twinkle in his eye accompanied his conspiratorial whisper.

Amelia paid for her purchase and dropped the thread and confection into her satchel. She hesitated for a brief moment at the door to take a better look at the pie safe. Horst was right. Hank was a fine craftsman. The silly flutters began again.

Hank couldn't keep the grin from his face three days ago when Horst Braun told him the pie safe was sold and two other women were interested in having one made. But when Mayor Ehrlichmann knocked on the door of the Sunday house and inquired about having a rocking chair crafted for his wife's birthday, Hank's heart soared. This was God's answer. After countless prayers asking for heaven's affirmation of his dream, Hank had cash in his pocket from his first sale, an order in his hand, and the possibility of two more, lending true credibility to the choice he'd made. Gratefulness filled his heart.

A soft spring rain fell outside the lean-to workshop. Hank ran his hands over slabs of burr oak, choosing the best pieces for the rocking chair. Interesting waves and curves flowed along the wood grain, interrupted by an occasional knot. He carefully selected each cut for its beauty and strength. Once the chair was finished, rubbing linseed oil deeply into the grain would enhance its radiance. The classic lines and intricate detail came alive in his mind—a chair to hand down to the mayor's grandchildren and great-grandchildren.

The smile in his heart faded. If his young cousins were split up and sent to different orphanages, they would likely never possess a family heirloom like the one he planned to create for Mayor Ehrlichmann. A scowl tugged on his brow with the disturbing thought. Raising his heart heavenward, he sought God's ear.

"Lord, I know I got angry at Amelia for suggesting I take the children, but how can I do that without a way to support them? I'd have to sell a whole lot more pieces of furniture. Amelia doesn't understand how a man feels about taking care of a family, how he wants to give them everything they need and put a decent roof over their heads, to be able to feed them and clothe them, keep them safe and warm and protected."

He halted his list of things God already knew. Since God was already aware of every desire of his heart, it seemed futile to hide the one thing he'd neglected to mention.

"God, if it's not asking too much, could You send me a helpmate?" The entreaty had barely escaped his lips when he caught sight of Amelia fetching firewood from her back stoop.

Chapter 7

Olga and Winnie Richter each grunted a greeting to Amelia and brushed through the door of the Sunday house. Winnie muttered something in German Amelia didn't catch. Olga turned and sent a sour frown in Amelia's direction.

"She wants to know if you've been cooking on her stove."

Before Amelia could admit to using the stove to heat water for tea or to warm leftover stew, Winnie waved her chubby hand.

"*Sprechen sie auf Deutsch!*" She followed up the challenge with a torrent of German, none of it sounding the least bit complimentary in tandem with her derisive tone.

Amelia understood the first demand. Winnie wanted German spoken and became angry whenever Olga had to translate into English.

Lamar Richter entered, lugging a loaded crate. "*Mutter, beruhigen sie sich.* Calm down." He plunked the crate on the table and faced Amelia. "Der is a matter I must talk to you."

"Yes, sir?"

The school board chairman pointed to the back door. "Outside."

It wasn't a request.

Amelia sucked in a breath. Had she done something wrong? She hated the way her heart hammered, much the way it used to do when her father berated her for speaking her mind or disagreeing with him.

She exited the back door with Mr. Richter on her heels. He stepped in front of her the moment he closed the door. His bushy eyebrows resembled a fat, gray caterpillar wiggling over his hooded eyes, but she didn't dare smile.

Mr. Richter cleared his throat and thumbed his suspenders. "Some parents complain to me. You do not teach der class in German. This is true?

Was that all? "Yes, it's true." Amelia clasped her hands at her waist. Frankly, she didn't see the problem.

"You know our community is German. All der schools in every district always teach in our mother tongue." Mr. Richter lifted his chin and raised his voice a decibel, injecting a demanding tone into his words as if daring her to state otherwise. "Der parents"—he struggled to find the word—"expect der kinner learn in German. Der young ones must grasp their heritage."

Amelia lifted her shoulders and opened her hands, palms up. "You knew when you hired me that my German was very limited. I didn't make a secret of that fact. Neither do I recall reading anything in my teaching contract about German being mandatory."

"It is who we are." Mr. Richter's voice boomed through the cool spring air, disturbing a few birds in the overhead branches.

Lamar Richter's inflection and the pitch of his voice intensified, but Amelia refused to be bullied. "I agree. But you and your families are living in a country, and in a state, that speaks primarily English. These children will have to learn to function in an English-speaking society. If they don't, some unscrupulous person may try to take advantage of them or cheat them."

The man's face reddened and his jaw worked back and forth. "You refuse to speak German in der classroom?"

Amelia was certain most everyone up and down the street could hear him bellow. "I'm not refusing, and if speaking German is that important to the parents, I will do my best to improve my understanding of the language and conduct classes in both English and German."

"Nien! This is not acceptable."

"And what *is* acceptable, Mr. Richter? That I do exactly what you say, no more and no less?"

If the man's face grew any redder, he'd explode. Judging by his clenched fists and sputtering lips, he obviously wasn't accustomed to his word being questioned.

"Mr. Richter, you must remember, I have some students who do not speak German. All of my German-speaking students understand English. But the ones who speak no German would come to a standstill in their learning. I won't allow that to happen."

"You won't allow—? Who are you to decide what is allowed?"

Amelia lifted her chin and folded her arms across her chest. "I am their teacher. It is my job to see to it that they learn, and I will use whatever means necessary to impart knowledge to them. If that involves teaching in two languages, I'll do it, even though it will require a great deal more lesson preparation time."

Mr. Richter blustered. "You can take some of dat time you use now teaching foolish things and learn better German."

"Foolish things?" Amelia's ire tightened her jaw. "What have I been teaching that you deem foolish?"

"Some parents tell me der kinner must draw maps of der whole United States. And others complain about der kinner reciting poetry." He leaned slightly forward. "Paeter Lange's father say his son must know a long list of many dates. Foolishness!" Richter waved his hands as if erasing a lesson plan from the air. "None of those things teach a child to plant and harvest a better crop."

Amelia plunked her hands on her hips. "Are you suggesting that I don't teach geography or history or literature?"

"Ja! Dat is just what I suggest. The young ones, dey only need to know how to read and write and cipher." Mr. Richter's fingers clutched his waistband and he hiked up his britches and threw out his chest.

"I disagree."

Predictably, the red blotches mottling Mr. Richter's face turned purple. He huffed and stammered, his anger tying his tongue in a knot. Amelia took advantage of his rattled state and continued.

"The children will become much better citizens, and much better people, if they know how our country came to be. Understanding the boundaries and rights of each individual state teaches the children to respect the diversity among us. Literature and science help expand young minds. They are learning to be productive people."

She uncrossed her arms and held her hands out in front of her, beseeching the man to understand her point of view. "Don't you see? Some of these children will follow in their parents' footsteps and become farmers, and that's wonderful, if it's what they want to do. But some will become merchants or skilled craftsmen. Others will want to go to the university and become doctors or scientists. Some might grow up and learn the law or become part of our system of government. Some may even become teachers."

Mr. Richter started to open his mouth, but Amelia put her hand up. "Yes, teachers, Mr. Richter, because every *parent* should be a teacher."

Checkmate.

Exasperation etched hard lines in the school board chairman's face, and for now, he had no retort. He stared, unblinking, at her for several long moments. Finally, he waved a stubby, sausage-like finger under her nose.

"You think about what I said."

With that, he turned on his heel and returned to the house, slamming the door in his wake.

Amelia shook her head. "I wonder if he will think about what *I* said." She started to follow the man into the Sunday house but caught sight of Hank Zimmermann standing, arms akimbo, by his back door, staring in her direction. Dismay filled her when she realized he must have heard every word.

Hank lingered outside the front door of the church as the parishioners filed out. His three young cousins romped in a circle around him like colts in a spring meadow.

"Catch me, Uncle Hank!" Micah jumped up and down, shrieking with giggles when Hank grabbed the child around the middle and tickled him.

Elsie and Joy dodged out of his reach in a silly game of tag, their laughter spilling out to rival the singing of the birds.

Hank emitted a mock growl. "When I catch you two, I'm going to tie your pigtails together."

The little girls squealed and dashed between the parked wagons. Hank had just crouched behind one of the wagons, lying in wait to jump out and surprise the girls, when Lamar Richter rounded the corner.

"Zimmermann." The school board chairman leveled a glare at Hank crabby enough to wilt the spring flowers. Richter shifted his gaze to the children who stopped short, colliding into one another.

"Good Sabbath to you, Mr. Richter." He glanced down at his cousins. "Laughter is music in God's ears, is it not?"

Richter snorted. "Sacrilegious. Children should be seen and not heard."

"You know, Mr. Richter, I'm glad you brought that up, because there is something I'd like to discuss with you." He turned to the children. "Elsie, you and Joy take Micah and go to the wagon. Uncle Thornton will want to leave soon."

At the mention of his father, the smiles on all three children's faces drooped.

"Are you coming, too, Uncle Hank?" Joy tugged at his hand.

"I'll be along shortly. You three scoot now, and go get into the wagon."

As soon as the children were out of earshot, Hank returned his gaze to Richter. "I heard you yesterday—in fact, I think half the town heard you—bellowing at Miss Bachman for not conducting her classes in German."

Richter scowled. "It is no business of yours."

Hank leveled a steely gaze at the man. "You made it everyone's business hollering at the top of your lungs. And I beg to differ with you." He gestured in the direction the children had gone. "Three of the children Miss Bachman was talking about were my little cousins. Granted, they've picked up a few German words since they've been here, but if classes were taught purely in German, they would cease to learn. I don't think that's what you want, is it?"

"All der school districts teach in German. Der old ways are best." The volume of Richter's voice rose with each word until nearly everyone in the surrounding churchyard stopped what they were doing and stared at the school board chairman.

Hank cocked an eyebrow at the man. "Seems to me your first consideration should be to the children and their education. You have a teacher who is doing an excellent job. The children—*all* the children, are learning."

"*Was es ist*—What is it to you?" The veins in Richter's neck bulged. "You have no children in der school. You have no say in the matter. Mind your own business."

Pastor Hoffman hurried across the yard to where the two men stood toe-to-toe. "Gentlemen, please. It is the Lord's Day and we have just come from worship. Can this not be settled in a Christian manner?"

Hank turned to the preacher. "You're right, pastor. Forgive me. I only meant to clear up a misunderstanding. You see, it is my business to ensure that the children I love get the best education possible."

Richter smoothed one hand through his hair and drew in a deep breath. "Hank Zimmermann is not a parent—"

Pastor Hoffman held up both hands and spoke in a quiet but firm, even tone. "I'll not allow our day of worship to be disturbed by uncontrolled tempers. Both of you go home and examine your own hearts, and let God rule in this issue."

Hank chewed on his bottom lip and gave a curt nod. He turned on his heel and strode across the churchyard past the gawking parishioners. At the edge of the street, Amelia stood with her fingertips covering her mouth, and wide, unblinking eyes fixed on him. His step slowed as their gazes locked and his heart squeezed. He prayed he hadn't made things worse for her by confronting the pigheaded school board chairman, but a small voice within pressed him to take a stand for his cousins. In doing so, he supposed he also stood up for Amelia. The thought caused no small stirring in his heart.

Chapter 8

Hank waited outside the schoolhouse until the children came spilling out the door at the end of the school day. The Braun children, Pater Lange, the Hoffman girls, and the Werner twins chased each other around the yard in a dizzying game of tag, but Hank's cousins were apparently still inside.

"Hope they didn't get into trouble," Hank muttered to himself as he approached the door. Sometimes his father made the children do extra chores in the morning before they left for school, which made them late. The door stood open and Hank peeked in. His three cousins encircled their arms around their teacher in a collective hug.

"G'bye, Miss Bachman."

"See you tomorrow, Miss Bachman."

"I love you, Miss Bachman."

Hank's heart tumbled end over end. A twinge of jealousy nipped at him. The children held no inhibitions when it came to expressing their affection for their teacher. How Hank wished he could do the same.

"Uncle Hank!" Joy and Micah squealed their delight when they spied Hank standing in the doorway. Elsie, more sedate, held Miss Bachman's hand and walked like a little lady. Was it his imagination, or did Amelia's eyes light up when she saw him? Probably just wishful thinking.

He tweaked Micah's nose and tugged on the girls' pigtails as they clamored for his attention. "Did you three rascals behave yourselves today?"

"I learned to read some new words." Joy tugged on his arm.

Micah grabbed his other hand. "I can write the whole alphabet."

Hank raised his eyes and found Amelia's soft smile and tender eyes on him. The moment their eyes met, she dropped her gaze and her cheeks pinked.

He gathered the children and pointed them toward the door. "There is some apple *kuchen* on the table in the Sunday house. You may each have a small piece, but then you must go straight home. Uncle Thornton will expect you to do your chores."

The siblings grabbed their slates and McGuffey's, Elsie snatched the lunch pail, and they skipped out the door, calling out their good-byes to their teacher.

Hank watched them scramble aboard Fritz. "They're very fond of you, Miss Bachman. You've helped ease their grief with your kindness." He turned to face her. "Thank you for that."

She looked past him through the open door. "I have affection for all my students. But those three. . .I suppose as a teacher, I'm not permitted to have favorites, and I try to be impartial, but your cousins are very dear to me." Her voice quavered and she straightened her shoulders and marched back to her desk. "So, what brings you to school today?"

Hank gulped. Her sweet voice and enchanting eyes so mesmerized him, the answer to her question was momentarily lost in his fascination of her charm.

Why did I come to. . . "Oh yes. Mr. Richter asked me to see if I could repair a broken hinge."

Amelia's eyes widened. "I wasn't sure Mr. Richter heard me when I mentioned the cabinet hinge needed fixing." She walked to the cabinet in the corner and cautiously opened the door with both hands to prevent it from falling. "See? I hope you can mend it. The door almost fell off and hit Gretchen Hoffman in the head last week."

Hank gave the hinge a cursory inspection, but Amelia's nearness proved quite distracting. Some kind of sweet fragrance clung to her, like a field of wildflowers—those purple ones that bloomed in late May. He drew in a surreptitious breath, hoping she didn't realize he was drinking in her scent.

"Can you fix it?"

Hank startled and the door slipped from his grip onto his toe. He gritted his teeth and bit back the *ouch* that sprang into his throat.

Amelia uttered a soft gasp. "Oh my, are you all right?" She impulsively laid her hand on his arm.

No, I'm not all right, but it has nothing to do with the door falling on my foot. "Sure thing. I'll have to bring some tools back with me to fix this properly, but it shouldn't take more than a few minutes. In the meantime, I suggest you leave the door off."

"Of course. Thank you—Hank." A rosy blush accompanied his name on her lips.

His heart rat-a-tatted like a busy woodpecker. "I'll be back first thing in the morning." He couldn't stop the silly grin that pulled the corners of his mouth at the thought of seeing her again.

He walked the few blocks to his Sunday house with the memory of his cousins hugging their teacher and declaring they loved her. He glanced at the windows of the houses and shops he passed, certain the occupants could hear his heart proclaiming that he loved her, too.

❧

The rocking chair for Mayor Ehrlichmann came to life in Hank's hands. He savored the gratification of watching the grain of the wood take on a character for generations of the Ehrlichmann family. Inhaling the aroma of the freshly sanded burr oak, he stroked his fingers along the satin surface of the armrests. Tomorrow he'd begin coaxing linseed oil into the grain.

"Uncle Hank! Uncle Hank!"

Without pulling out his pocket watch, he knew it was three-thirty. Who needed a watch with his cousins around? He wiped his hands on a rag and met the children at the door of the lean-to. Elsie and Joy wore look-alike dresses of green calico he didn't remember seeing before. His mother sewed, but certainly Hank's father wouldn't allow his wife to spend money on yard goods for children that weren't his.

"Look, Uncle Hank." Elsie's eyes sparkled. "Look what Miss Bachman made for us." She held out the edges of her skirt and pirouetted, her straw-colored braids flying and her face beaming as if she'd just been given a precious treasure.

Hank's heart arrested as he gazed from one sibling to the other. There was something familiar about the dresses. "Miss Bachman made them?"

The sisters nodded and Elsie fingered her sleeve. "Green was Mama's favorite color."

Recognition rang in Hank's mind. Two Sundays ago, he remembered Elsie admiring Amelia's green calico dress, telling her teacher that her mama "would have looked beautiful in a dress like that." A tender ache tangled through Hank's chest when he realized what Amelia had done.

Micah sported a new white shirt. The boy tipped his beaming face up to Hank with a gap-toothed grin. "My shirt used to be Miss Bachman's apron."

Hank ruffled the boy's hair. "You look like a fine gentleman in that shirt. Don't get it dirty, all right?"

"I won't, Uncle Hank."

Amelia Bachman was an extraordinary woman. Was there no limit to her giving heart? How could anyone—his father or Lamar Richter or any of the parents who'd complained—doubt her love and compassion for these children? How many of them gave pieces of themselves to enrich a child's life the way Amelia did? Hank's heart groaned within his chest. How he wished he could declare to her the love God had already revealed to him.

Elsie hugged Hank's waist. "We have to get home so Uncle Thornton won't be mad, but we wanted to show you our new dresses." Even the thought of their tardiness stirring their uncle's wrath couldn't erase the smile from her face.

Hank boosted them up onto Fritz's back and made sure Elsie had a firm grip on Micah. "I'll see you tomorrow. Be careful going home."

Three small hands waved as Fritz plodded down the street. Their childish voices created a woven tapestry as they called out to him "Bye, Uncle Hank. I love you, Uncle Hank."

Hank's heart turned over. Those ornery, adorable youngsters had wrapped their fingers around him and there was no escaping their clutches—nor did he want to.

"Oh Lord, I hate the thought of those kids being sent to an orphanage—maybe separate orphanages. Please provide some way for them to stay together with a family who will love them."

Amelia wished she could stamp her foot to express her frustration, but she'd not give Lamar Richter the satisfaction of knowing he'd irritated her. All she wanted was to borrow the man's wagon for the outing she'd planned. Shouldn't the school board chairman be the greatest supporter of the teacher and her efforts to educate the community's children? The man's narrow-mindedness caused her no end of vexation.

"Reading, writing, and ciphering. Dat is all der pupils need to learn." He flipped one hand out in a derisive motion. "Planting flower seeds. Bah! Such foolishness."

"Mr. Richter, planting seeds and nurturing plants is a science. Every time a farmer sows seeds for his crop, the conditions have to be right to ensure a successful harvest. This exercise will show the children how seeds germinate, put down roots, develop into plants, and propagate new seeds." She paused, trying to read his facial expression. Surely he could see how beneficial the planned outing was for the students.

He muttered something in German she didn't understand. She bit her lip. She'd spent more time studying the language like Mr. Richter demanded, but her vocabulary was still lacking.

His thick eyebrows knit together into a deep scowl. "Der kinder learn about planting at home."

Amelia sucked in a breath. "I had planned to combine the science lesson with a picnic to celebrate the end of the school year. It's only for one day, Mr. Richter. Certainly you could spare your wagon for one day."

"Nein." He waved his hand as if shooing away the very idea. "I have no time for picnics. If you must do this, have your picnic in der school yard." A sharp bob of his head punctuated his declaration before he stomped off.

Amelia plopped her hands on her hips. She couldn't remember ever meeting a more stubborn man.

Amelia set the McGuffey's Readers on the front bench and then began writing arithmetic problems on the chalkboard, when a soft knock drew her attention. Hank filled the door frame, his toolbox in one hand.

"I've come to fix that hinge before the students arrive." He stepped into the schoolroom and left the door standing open for propriety's sake.

Butterflies danced in her stomach at the sight of his boyish face. She sent a silent reprimand to her heart and ordered the flutters to cease. They didn't. "Th–thank you, Hank. I appreciate this."

A lopsided smile pulled a dimple into his cheek. "My pleasure." He set the toolbox down and rummaged through it, extracting a chisel and hammer. "I'd like to thank you for what you did for the kids—the new dresses for the girls and the shirt for Micah. That was mighty kind of you."

Warmth skittered up her neck and tickled her ears. "I couldn't help noticing all three of them were outgrowing their clothes. It was nothing."

Hank's hands paused in their task. "I disagree. What you did meant a great deal to them." His eyes smiled at her and a shiver darted up her spine.

Stop that! You're a teacher. You aren't looking for a beau.

He tapped the hammer against the chisel and removed the broken hinge. "I wish there was something I could do to repay you."

"Actually there is." She pressed her lips together. Dare she ask?

He looked over his shoulder at her. "Name it."

She clasped her fingers together to stop their jittery fidgeting. "I'm planning an outing for the children in a couple of weeks to plant some wildflower seeds. It will be a combination science lesson and end of the year picnic."

Hank tipped his head in a most appealing way. "I'm not very good at frying chicken."

A nervous giggle escaped her lips. "No, the children will bring their lunches as always, but I need a wagon to carry all the children out to our picnic spot."

He took on a thoughtful pose. "When is this?"

"Sometime in mid-May."

He fit the new hinge into place. "I don't own a wagon, just a buckboard, but I'll see if I can borrow my father's wagon."

His smile tied her stomach into a knot.

Chapter 9

Hank rubbed linseed oil into the sideboard he'd been working on for Karl and Gerta Schroeder. Since finishing the rocking chair for Mayor Ehrlichmann, four new orders now hung on the workshop wall. Hank sent another prayer of gratitude heavenward for the way God was blessing his business. But in the midst of his joy, a dark cloud of gloom hung about his shoulders like a heavy cloak he couldn't shed.

He glanced at the afternoon sun. Amelia would be arriving home soon. The anticipation with which he normally watched for her was markedly absent today. He dreaded having to tell her about the letters Vater had received.

The linseed oil's pungent odor stung his nose. He watched the intricate detail of the wood grain emerge as he rubbed the oil deeply into the oak, as if the very tree that provided the wood left its fingerprint. He wished God would write His answer to this matter with which Hank struggled as clearly as the oil revealed the wood grain.

"Lord, I need an answer. I don't know what to do."

As if hearing the whisper of God's voice, Hank raised his head and looked out across the narrow expanse of yard that separated the Richter Sunday house from his. Amelia walked up the limestone path to her front door. A groan that started in the pit of his stomach rumbled past his lips.

"God, I'm not ready to face her. I've been turning this over in my mind for two days and I still don't know how I'm going to tell her."

The unmistakable impression of God's Spirit blew across Hank's conscious thought. *"Go tell her. You won't be alone."*

The assurance of God's presence fortified Hank's courage and he set the oil-soaked rag aside. Before Amelia could step inside her door, he jogged across the yard.

"Amelia."

She lifted her eyes in his direction when he called to her. The smile that glowed across her face felt like a punch in Hank's gut. His news would erase that sweet smile.

"Hello, Hank." Her cheeks flushed with pleasure. "My students are excited about the picnic. I'm looking forward to it as much as they are. In fact, we've been studying about—" The delight faded from her expression. "Is something wrong?"

He shoved his hands in his pockets. "I have something to tell you."

A flicker of panic crossed her face and she set down her book satchel. Breathlessness tinged her voice. "What is it?"

This is going to hurt her, Lord. Please comfort her.

Hank drew in a tight breath. "My father has received replies to his letters. The first is from the orphanage in Dallas. They have room for the girls, but their boys' dormitory is already overfull."

As he expected, distress carved furrows in Amelia's brow and she covered her mouth with her fingertips.

Hank went on to deliver the rest of the bad news. There was no gentle way to say it. "The orphanage in Abilene said they could take Micah."

Moisture glistened in her eyes and she shook her head mutely. She turned away from him. A slight shake in her shoulders defined her sorrow. He longed to wrap her in his arms to deflect the cruelty of his message. A soft sob reached his ears. He could stand it no longer. He reached out and ran his hand up and down her arm, despising his own helplessness.

"I wish I didn't have to tell you this. I know you love those kids as much as I do."

She didn't shrug off his hand so he slid his fingers up to her shoulder and squeezed. "The director of the facility in Dallas said to wait until the school year had ended. My father grumbled about it, but at least the children will be here another month."

She sniffed and wiped her eyes before turning around to face him again. But instead of the despair he expected to see in her expression, her eyes grew dark and stormy.

"Hank Zimmermann, I simply cannot understand why you don't take those children yourself. Even if your father doesn't want them, there's no reason for you to stand by and watch them separated and sent away."

Hank yanked his hand back. His earlier excuse of not having the means to support his cousins wouldn't wash anymore. The furniture orders he'd received the past few weeks kept him plenty busy. He'd even spoken to his father about the possibility of purchasing the Sunday house. Vater hadn't agreed yet, but he hadn't said no. Still, none of that meant he was in the position to take on three children.

"I can't take care of those kids by myself." He blurted out the retort before he could temper his words. "What about you?"

"Me?" Her brow dove downward in disbelief. "What are you talking about?"

Hank thrust his upturned palm in her direction. "How can you do something so loving for those children—making clothes for them out of your own clothing—and then do nothing to try and keep them together?"

She lifted her arms away from her sides. "What can I do? I'm only their teacher."

"You could marry me and then we could take them."

If every muscle in his body hadn't frozen at that moment, he would have turned around to see who had spoken those words. The realization that they'd come from his own lips startled him, but judging by the expression on Amelia's face, she was even more dumbfounded than he.

Her mouth fell open and wavered closed like a fish gasping its last on the end of a hook. Her wide, unblinking eyes nailed him.

"Wh–wha–what?"

Hank grappled with his composure. He couldn't say the idea hadn't crossed his mind before. Imagining Amelia as his bride had caressed his dreams more than once. But his dream hadn't included shocking her by blurting out a clumsy proposal of marriage.

"You've said yourself that you love the kids. We could adopt them, they could stay together, and they wouldn't have to go to the orphanage." The word *we* pushed past the growing lump in his throat and came out unnaturally high-pitched. He swallowed hard but the lump remained.

Deep red flushed her face and she gasped like she'd just finished a footrace. "Do you have any idea what you're saying? Lifelong relationships must be founded on something greater than good intentions." She leaned down to grab her satchel. "Yes, I love those children, but to make them the basis for a marriage is—it's. . ."

Something painful flashed through her eyes and she took a step backward. When she finally completed her sentence, Hank barely caught her strained whisper. "It's not right."

She turned and marched in the front door.

Anticipation and dread swirled in Amelia's stomach. Her students had enthusiastically prepared for today's outing, but after the heated exchange with Hank over two weeks ago, she now regretted asking him to transport her and the students in his wagon. Since Hank had uttered his "proposal" to her, Amelia avoided making eye contact with him across the yard and at church. She'd tried in vain to dismiss Hank's words from her mind, but her heart refused to comply. She muttered as she slipped her lunch and the wildflower seeds into her satchel.

"Lord, You know I grew up watching my parents endure a loveless marriage. Joining with Hank in such a union for the sake of the children might be unselfish, but they would grow up seeing the same resentment in both of us that I observed in my parents."

A deep sigh whooshed from her lungs. She couldn't deny her attraction to Hank, beginning with the night she arrived in Fredericksburg. Despite trying to push the unintended feelings away and refuse them acknowledgment, they persisted. Hank occupied her thoughts more than she wanted to admit. She repeatedly asked God to remove this unreasonable captivation, for surely it was nothing more than admiration, or perhaps infatuation. But God allowed the feelings to persist and grow. Certainly her secret feelings for the man didn't mean he reciprocated.

She couldn't shake the nagging prick of melancholy over Hank having asked her to marry him with no expression of tenderness. Not that the children staying together and having two parents who loved them wasn't important, but she refused to become the woman her mother was—trapped in a marriage with a man who would never love her.

"God, I became a teacher so I could remain single." She suspected her adamant statement only caused God to smile. She huffed and snatched her shawl from the peg. "This is foolish. Why am I arguing with God? He knows why I became a teacher." She stepped toward the door, but stopped short. Talking to herself was as foolish as arguing with God.

Hank halted the wagon near the door of the schoolhouse. Amelia had the children lined up by grades. Hank had to admit that, despite their excitement, Amelia maintained order and discipline as she directed one group at a time to the wagon. Hank boosted the younger ones up to the tailgate.

Amelia had avoided him ever since the afternoon of his awkward proposal and she didn't appear anxious to converse with him now. Once again he berated himself for the bumbling manner in which the words had fallen from his lips. After spending considerable time communing with God, he determined that he didn't regret his suggestion at all, only the way he'd spoken it. In fact, the longer he thought about it, the deeper and more steadfast his conviction that he was in love with Amelia Bachman. He'd spent the last week praying God would grant his petition to make Amelia his bride. The opportunity to speak privately with her today didn't seem likely with twenty-two children listening. If only she'd look in his direction, he could at least offer her a smile.

The last student scrambled into the wagon bed and Hank held out his hand to the teacher to help her up to the front seat. She hesitated momentarily, deep pink flooding her cheeks. She gathered her skirts and accepted his hand to aid her up over the wheel.

He settled himself beside her and picked up the reins. "I'd like to speak with you later, Amelia."

She folded her trembling hands primly on her lap. "As you wish."

He drove out past the edge of town and turned the team northwest toward his parents' farm.

Amelia jerked her head in his direction. "Where are you going?" She pointed northeast. "The spot I found is that way."

He smiled sideways at her. "If you'll allow me—there's a hillside lined with oaks and mesquites about halfway to my folks' place that has a beautiful view of a small lake. I think you'll agree it's a perfect spot to plant your wildflower seeds."

She arched her eyebrows and he half-expected her to argue, but she nodded. "All right. I'll concede that you know the area better than I."

Forty-five minutes later the wagon rounded the curve of a hill, bringing into view a little pristine lake reflecting several burr oaks along the water's edge.

"What a beautiful spot." It was the first time he'd seen her smile since he'd told her about Vater's letters. Hank's heart pinched. How he wished she'd smiled in response to his proposal.

He set the brake and aided her down from the wagon seat. The children clambered off the tailgate and began an impromptu game of tag.

Hank cast an eye to the west. A few white puffy clouds gathered on the horizon. He hoped rain wouldn't ruin their outing. "I'll be back to pick you up around three."

"Thank you, Hank." Her hazel eyes fixed him in place. "It was kind of you."

Why did he get the distinct feeling she wasn't talking about driving them to their picnic?

Chapter 10

Hank pushed the plane along the edge of a cedar plank, producing thin curls that reminded him of the tendrils of hair that fell around Amelia's ears. He closed his eyes and invited her image to grace his musings. Her soft voice echoed in his memory.

Perhaps this afternoon—what would he say to her? How should he broach the subject? Certainly he owed her an apology for the tactless way he'd spluttered out his proposal.

He couldn't fault Amelia's statement. A real marriage needed a foundation much stronger than good intentions. Giving the children a home was a fine thing, but he should have told her first how much he loved her. He reckoned most women wanted to be courted and romanced. There just wasn't time. He prayed God would prepare Amelia's heart to hear what he wanted to tell her.

"God, if You'll give me another chance to say it right, and if Amelia says yes, I'll romance her for the rest of my life. Order my words, Lord, so she'll know she's loved."

A rumble of thunder interrupted his prayer. Muted, murky light replaced the earlier sunlight. He poked his head out the door. What happened to the bluebonnet sky and cottony clouds? Angry greenish-gray mounds churned across the sky where the sun should have been. Ominous swirls billowed in from the northwest.

Alarm clenched his stomach and a chill sliced through him. He grabbed his jacket and jogged to the backyard where the horses stamped and snorted in nervous agitation. His fingers flew through the task of hitching the animals to the wagon. The team tossed their heads and whinnied as Hank leapt into the wagon seat. He released the brake and blew a piercing whistle through his teeth, slapping the reins down hard. The horses lurched forward.

"Lord, please protect Amelia and the children until I can get there."

He turned onto the street and met Emil Lange, the father of one of Amelia's students, coming the opposite direction.

"Emil, follow me! I'm going out to get the children. This storm is coming up mighty fast."

The man nodded his head. "Lead the way."

Before Hank reached the edge of town, he heard a sickening shout.

"*Twister!*"

Hank rose up from the seat and hollered at the horses. "Giddyap. Go!" He slung the ends of the reins down across the animals. He didn't know if Emil still followed behind him. He focused solely on Amelia and the children.

The sky unleashed driving rain and crashing thunder. "Oh God, please hedge them about with Your mighty hands." He urged the team on and shouted above the tempest. "Lord Jesus, You spoke peace and the storm stilled. You walked on the water. Overpower this storm with Your might. Protect them, Lord."

He struggled against the buffeting wind to remain in the wagon and the horses slowed to a nervous, high-stepping trot, shying in their traces. Hank forced them forward. "Go! Go!"

Lightning slashed across the sky accompanied by immediate explosions of thunder, shaking the very ground over which he traveled. Air pressure nearly burst his eardrums. Bits of hail now pelted his face, and the wind and rain so hampered his visibility, all he could do was pray he was headed in the right direction.

"Guide me, Lord. Cover Amelia and the children with Your hand and lead me to them." His voice broke as he cried out his gut-wrenching plea. "Oh God, please protect them."

The wind slowed and the rain diminished enough for him to see and he pushed the team to pick up their pace. Thunder rolled through the hills in the wake of the storm.

Broken limbs and uprooted trees littered the landscape. Hank's heart hammered and his lungs heaved in their effort to draw breath. Water dripped from his hair and saturated clothing.

A child's bonnet swung from the ripped branches of a scrub pine. A lunch pail sat upside down in the dirt. One of the quilts Amelia had stacked in the back of the wagon wrapped around the twisted trunk of a mesquite.

His heart in his throat, Hank hauled on the reins and pulled the team to a stop. He jammed the brake lever forward and leapt from the wagon, running through the now-soft rain, shouting Amelia's name.

"Amelia! Where are you?"

Small heads poked upright from a gulley along the base of the hillside.

Elsie and Joy screamed in unison. "Uncle Hank!"

Hank charged in the direction of the children. Others now raised their heads, some crying, some simply staring wide-eyed. A few of the older students comforted the younger ones. Micah scrambled to his feet and launched himself into Hank's arms, sobbing.

"Uncle Hank, I was scared. The wind roared real loud and it almost blowed us away." He looked down at himself and his cries intensified. "The shirt Miss Bachman gived me is all wet and dirty."

"It's all right, buddy. That was a bad storm, but it's gone now." Hank squeezed Micah, but his glance bounced wildly about. "Where is Miss Bachman?"

Elsie's panicked voice reached him. "Uncle Hank, Miss Bachman won't wake up."

He lowered Micah to the ground and ran down the slope where Elsie and Joy sat on either side of Amelia. A violent shudder rattled through him when he caught sight of her motionless form. Bits of leaves and grass clung to her and the stains on her dress testified that she'd crawled through the mud, presumably trying to protect the children.

Hank knelt and brushed tangled hair and debris from her face. "Amelia. Amelia, open your eyes. It's Hank. The storm is over."

The children crowded around their teacher, begging Hank to make her wake up. Behind him, Hank heard the other wagon pull up, and some of the children ran to meet Paeter Lange's father, but Hank remained in place patting Amelia's face. He slid his fingers around the back of her neck, searching for injury. Inch by inch, his hand traveled upward until he located a large lump on the back of her head. Ever so gently, he parted her hair and found matted blood.

"Der kinder seem to be all right." Emil jogged down the slope, his belly heaving with exertion. "Miss Bachman, she is—"

"She's unconscious." Hank's throat was so tight he could barely push the words out. He indicated the back of her head, and Emil bent to look.

"Ja, she got pretty bad goose egg."

Hank rose. "Let's put her in the back of my wagon. Elsie, see if you can find one of the quilts from the picnic." The little girl ran to do as Hank bid her and Hank turned to Emil.

"Can you take the children back to town?"

Emil bobbed his head. "Ja, I make sure they all get home safe." He paused a moment. "My Paeter, he say Miss Bachman told all der kinner to lay flat, and she keep them down." His voice turned husky. "She save their lives, ja?"

Indeed, when Hank came up on the scene, all the children were in the safest possible place in the gulley at the base of the hill. "I believe so."

"Uncle Hank." Elsie called to him. "I found a quilt, but it's wet and dirty."

"That's all right." He instructed her to spread it in the back of the wagon.

While Emil gathered the rest of the children and directed them to his wagon, Hank slid his arms beneath Amelia's shoulders and knees, lifting her as if she were made of fragile porcelain. She didn't stir. He carried her to the wagon and laid her gently on the soggy quilt.

He let his fingertips stroke her cheekbone momentarily before securing the tailgate.

God, please let her be all right.

"Uncle Hank, is Miss Bachman gonna die like my mama?"

Hank jerked his startled gaze around to see Elsie, Joy, and Micah standing behind him. He knelt and gathered the children close.

"She just has a bump on her head. We're going to pray and ask God to make her better."

Tears filled Elsie's eyes. "But I prayed for Mama and Papa to get better and they didn't."

Elsie's statement slammed into Hank with a force so intense, he lost his breath for a moment, and his heart ripped in two. How could he make promises to these children he wasn't sure he could keep? They'd already endured much more pain than children ought.

"You three go with Mr. Lange. I'm going to take Miss Bachman to Dr. Keidel."

He hugged each one and nudged them toward Emil's wagon. "Go on, now."

With his heart bleeding for the youngsters and fearful for Amelia, Hank climbed up and whistled to the team, steering them back around toward town.

He held the horses to a less reckless pace, not wanting to jar Amelia any more than necessary. He glanced at her over his shoulder every few minutes, longing to see her eyes flutter open, but they didn't.

Hank lifted his voice to heaven's throne. "Please, God, let her be all right." He repeated the prayer until he pulled up at the doctor's office in town. A small crowd gathered as he gently lifted Amelia into his arms and carried her inside.

Quiet voices pierced through the dull ache in Amelia's head. Fragments of memory slowly came together: the children, the swirling storm clouds, the wind... She forced her eyes open despite the pain and she struggled to sit up. Her vision swam and blurred.

"Whoa there, where do you think you're going, young lady?"

"The children—"

"Are safe, thanks to you."

The voice was familiar but the cobwebs in her head prevented recognition. She lay back down and rubbed her eyes. Gradually the face in front of her came into focus.

"Uncle Will?"

Her favorite uncle grinned at her. "It's me. Thought I'd surprise you by coming a couple of weeks early, and you surprised me by being my first patient."

Confusion still spun in her brain. "But when—"

"I arrived on the stage this morning just ahead of the storm. The man at the depot told me the schoolmarm and students were on a picnic today." He leaned closer. "Amelia honey, don't you know you're supposed to pick a sunny day for a picnic?"

The regular town doctor leaned over Uncle Will's shoulder. "Miss Bachman, I'm Dr. Keidel. You gave us a bit of a scare. You have a concussion, but you're going to be all right."

She looked from one to the other. "You're sure the children are all right?"

"They're just fine," Dr. Keidel said. "But you have a very impatient visitor waiting to see you."

Uncle Will winked at her. "I'll bring him in." He shook his finger at her. "But you have to promise to lie still." He followed Dr. Keidel out of the room.

A moment later Hank slipped in. The sight of him set her pulse to dancing. He closed the distance between them in four long strides. The lines across his brow softened as he reached her side. He picked up her hand and held it between both of his own.

"Amelia." His breathless whisper was bathed in relief. "Praise God you're all right."

Hank's nearness coupled with the warmth of his hands enveloping hers drew a perception of safety over her. A tiny smile tugged at the corner of her mouth. "I am now."

Air whooshed from Hank's lips in a deep-throated chuckle. He lifted her hand to his lips.

Her breath caught when he placed his gentle kiss on her fingers. An apologetic prayer formed in her heart, recanting the times she'd asked God to take away her growing feelings for this man. She understood now why God hadn't granted what she thought she wanted.

His eyes glistened. "I begged God for another chance to do this right because I bungled it the first time."

Still holding her hand, he lowered himself to one knee. "Amelia Bachman, I want to spend the rest of my life with you, not just because of the way you love the children, but because of the way I love you. Will you marry me?"

Epilogue

Amelia straightened Joy's hair ribbons and smoothed Elsie's dress, while Hank tucked in Micah's shirt. Pastor Hoffman waited patiently in the gazebo Hank had built in the middle of the field of wildflowers.

The preacher grinned. "It's not every day I get to marry an entire family."

Amelia's bouquet of bluebonnets, daisies, and white dogtooth lilies trembled slightly in anticipation. Her foolish declaration of becoming a teacher so she could remain single echoed in her ears. How silly she'd been to try to limit God. She never dreamed being a teacher would lead her to three precious children and a fine, godly husband who loved her.

Pastor Hoffman smiled as the five of them stepped into the gazebo. Elsie and Joy, the bridesmaids, stood to Amelia's left, and Micah, the best man, stood to Hank's right.

"This gazebo is Hank's wedding gift to Amelia," the pastor announced to all the assembled townsfolk. "The stone foundation is indicative of the faith we have in Jesus Christ." He gestured to the gleaming white gingerbread trim adorning the uprights. "This structure reminds us of how beautiful love is—God's love to us and our love for each other."

Hank smiled down at Amelia and her heart turned over.

Pastor Hoffman continued. "Finally the roof represents the canopy of God's faithfulness, always sheltering us from the storms of life."

Hank took both Amelia's hands in his and they repeated the ageless vows, pledging themselves to one another and to God. At the pastor's prompting, Hank bent his head toward Amelia's. He paused, an inch away from her lips.

"I love you, Amelia Zimmermann."

CONNIE STEVENS

Connie Stevens lives with her husband of forty-plus years in north Georgia, within sight of her beloved mountains. She and her husband are both active in a variety of ministries at their church. A lifelong reader, Connie began creating stories by the time she was ten. Her office manager and writing muse is a cat, but she's never more than a phone call or email away from her critique partners. She enjoys gardening and quilting, but one of her favorite pastimes is browsing antique shops where story ideas often take root in her imagination. Connie has been a member of American Christian Fiction Writers since 2000.

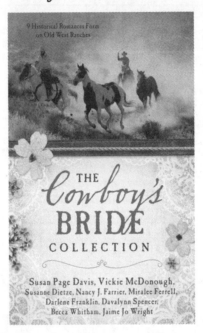